Phantacea Publications featuring

Jim McPherson's

I0674555

PHANTACEA Mythos

- ### *PHANTACEA* One to Six
  (A series of comic books with artwork by various artists)

- ### Forever & 40 Days – The Genesis of *PHANTACEA*
  (A graphic novel with artwork by Ian Fry, background material and a short story featuring the Damnation Brigade, the Death Dodgers & Signal System)

- ### Feeling Theocidal
  (Book One of *'The Thrice-Cursed Godly Glories'* Trilogy*)

- ### The War of the Apocalyptics
  (The first full entry in the *'Launch 1980'* story cycle*)

- ### The Thousand Days of Disbelief
  (Book Two of *'The Thrice Cursed Godly Glories'* Trilogy, consisting of three mini-novels: *'The Death's Head Hellion'**, *'Contagion Collectors'** and *'Janna Fangfingers'**)

- ### Goddess Gambit
  (Book Three of *'The Thrice Cursed Godly Glories'* Trilogy*)

- ### Phantacea Revisited 1: The Damnation Brigade
  (A graphic novel featuring a complete story sequence primarily excerpted from Phantacea One to Five, various artists)

- ### Nuclear Dragons
  (The second full entry in the *'Launch 1980'* story cycle*)

*E-versions also available

Somehow the entire Cosmic Express was still intact.

Dozens of pinpoints of light were approaching the vessel. The smaller ones kept coming. The largest, the brightest of all, resolved itself. To Cosmicommander Avatar Sol's fractured mind, it was at least ten times the size of the Express.

And what it was – what it appeared to be – was a single, impossibly huge and disembodied eye. Its pupil had lips and teeth and a tongue. A mouth. An eye-mouth. And it spoke!

"YOU PIG-WHUMPING, MECHANICAL LOLLIPOP, LOOK WHAT YOU'VE DONE!"

In the cosmic control capsule, Sol could think of only one thing. "Fire second stage. Let's get out of here."

"Second stage fired, sir!"

"AND AFTER ALL THAT, YOU'RE TRYING TO GET AWAY. WELL, PUKE ON YOU. A LITTLE GOD-SUCK WILL TEACH YOU SOME MANNERS!"

Pursing its lips, the eye-thing slurped the entire Express into its mass and began to chew it. To Sol, whimsically, it was akin to what clothes must experience inside a washing machine.

He felt for all the still-living oysters he'd chomped on as a child.

RRRUURP!

"BLOODY HELL! YOU OUTER EARTHLINGS TASTE AS LOUSY AS YOU DID SIX THOUSAND YEARS AGO!"

The eye-mouth spat them not just out of its craw but out of wherever they were in the first place.

"YUK!"

NUCLEAR DRAGONS

THE *LAUNCH 1980* STORY CYCLE CONTINUES

A *PHANTACEA* MYTHOS MOSAIC NOVEL

Conceived, written and produced by Jim McPherson
Front and Back Cover artwork by Ian Bateson

Phantacea Publications

(James H McPherson, Publisher)
74689 Kitsilano RPO
2768 West Broadway
Vancouver BC
V6K 4P4 Canada

Library and Archives Canada Cataloguing in Publication

McPherson, Jim, 1951-, author
    Nuclear dragons / Jim McPherson.

(Launch 1980 ; bk. 2)
ISBN 978-0-9878683-6-7 (pbk.)

    I. Title.

PS8625.P535N83 2013   C813'.6   C2013-906137-1

Nuclear Dragons - Auctorial Preamble

****

Sometimes one thing leads to all sorts of other things.
Which, in turn, begs the question: How much back story is too much back story?

========

In some respects, the book-in-hand could be considered two extended prologues, or preludes, and a mini-novel. One prelude, *'Indescribable Defiance'*, definitely leads into "Helios on the Moon", the upcoming third entry in the *Launch 1980* story cycle. That much I can tell you. As you might expect it also leads into the second prelude, *'The Strife Virus'*.

What I can't tell you is what that leads into, other than the mini-novel itself obviously, which is also "Nuclear Dragons" proper. That's because I still haven't decided where to go after HELIOS. Quite conceivably I'll carry on with the Outer Earth aspect of this here *PHANTACEA* **Mythos**.

That being the case, the second prelude will also lead into it. I might even call the post-HELIOS story sequence "Outer Earthlings". After all, titles are mutable. For example, this book was supposed to be called "Centauri Island", where virtually all of it's set. Needless to say, not just the title didn't turn out that way.

That said, what with Crystallion, Hell's Horsemen, and their titular atomic firedrakes on the way, in all probability any Outer Earth follow-up won't take place on what's left of Centauri. Unless it's set prior to 1980, that is, which actually is a possibility.

I can also tell you that the 5980 framing story of the "Janna Fangfingers" mini-novel leads to the same place, albeit the book-in-hand as a whole. Then again, FANGERS also leads into "Goddess Gambit", the third and final instalment of *'The Thrice-Cursed Godly Glories'* epic trilogy.

Of course, in its turn GAMBIT eventually picks up from where "The War of the Apocalyptics", the first entry in the *Launch 1980* story cycle, left off. Hence my opening statement. To which I could have added: *'Whereupon said other things invariably lead into many more other things'*. (So-called Shared World writing certainly does get complicated.)

Indeed, FANGERS' sixth chapter, *'Contacting the Stars'*, features two of NUKE's major characters in such a way that its readers may not even realize they're in both books until midway through *'Mind Tap'*, the first chapter of said book-in-hand. It consequently behooves the writer-at-hand to quote from a pertinent passage of FANGERS.

Should first note that Devauray is our Saturday. Should additionally note that neither Gottfried Kenton nor Jordan Tethys appear in NUKE. As for the herein referenced Mr Centauri, he more or less does. (Except that, this time, when it comes to him it's almost always a matter of more. Beyond that, well, um, I've probably said too much already.)

Kenton reached into his suit pocket – only a guy like Kenton would wear a suit on a Devauray morning – and pulled out a list of names. "Be a goose and have a gander at these goslings; I mean godlings. Bet you could do a damn fine series of portraits of this loathsome load, as Mr Centauri reckons most of them."

Tethys obliged. The list had over fifty names on it. Some weren't names real devils used – not that devils used names as such, just called each other by their attributes – but he had no trouble visualizing each and every one of them. Kenton's smile was unwavering and the scar in the middle of Tethys's forehead hadn't stopped itching since he first beheld the glad-handing bastard through the peephole upstairs.

That only ever happened when …

"What I meant was, if they're devils, they're fourth generational devils. And surely your Illuminaries have told you there's no such thing. More likely they're deviants, the offspring of regular men and women possessed by Tantal Thanatos and his sister-wife Methandra, Mithras's Virgin obviously no longer. For one thing, they were born in pairs, not triplets, and something else everyone knows is Master Devas are born in litters of three."

"Yet Illuminaries have a Constellation Thanatos don't they. As it happens, I've one of those very things, their star charts, right here in my briefcase if you want proof." Correction, only a guy like Gottfried Kenton would wear a suit and carry a briefcase on a Devauray morning.

He placed it on the table, opened it up, pulled the map of the night's sky out of it, shut it, and laid the star-chart atop it. His briefcase wasn't all he opened. [Most devils {Shining Ones} have three eyes; they also have subtle matter bodies, meaning they can hide or reveal their third one at will.] Neither was his voice his anymore.

"Now let's scrap the pleasantries, shall we."

=========

A few pages later on we have the following sequence.

The first speaker is the aforementioned Jordan Tethys, aka the legendary 30-Year Man, also 30-Beers. He's the hero of *'The Thrice-Cursed Godly Glories'* epic trilogy. If a **PHANTACEA Mythos** series can have heroes, that is. (Which, seeing as how it's *Anheroic* fantasy – meaning *'without heroes'* – it can't.)

The second speaker is not the titular Janna Fangfingers, though she was named after her. It's Janna St Peche-Montressor. She doesn't appear in Nuke either. However, her husband does and so does the devil who isn't possessing her in this passage. They're two of Alfredo Sentalli's Untouchables.

"You've always struck me as more sensible than sensitive, Janna. Tell me, you have any idea why I wrote this?" He flipped to another page. His Brainrock quill had a much better memory than he did. While he was in his Zen-state it had rewritten what he'd last used it to write, though he somehow sensed not so much in the sky as within it, if that made sense.

"*'Rendezvous here'*," she read. Carefully considered her response: "Nope. You?"

His sketchpad suddenly burst into flames. He hated it when that happened. Hated it even more when he had no idea why it happened. He dropped it with a yelp. They watched as it burnt into a cinder. Both registered the letter *'D'*, drawn at an angle of 90 degrees clockwise, linger glowingly before surrendering to ash's inevitable triumph.

"Not anymore. I like this life too much the way it is. How about APM, SPM?"

Janna looked shaken, not stirred. For a change she didn't say *'not possessed, Jordy'*; said instead: "Got a spare beer?"

She had his while he went to the infirmary.

=========

Might Kenton in the first blockquote have been possessed by the *'D'* in the second? And, if so, why was this *'D'* trying to get Tethys (who, thanks to his Brainrock quill, more so than any innate talent, is an extremely gifted artist) to draw portraits of over fifty named devils, including those in Constellation Thanatos?

To send them an invitation of course. And, given they're now stars in the night's sky, what's with the coordinates on the star map? Answer to that is obviously why he wrote: *'Rendezvous here'*. Which in turn leads us back to the book-in-hand as well as the answer to the query I posed at the outset. Which is: *It depends*.

Thanks for that you might be saying. But it does and, in the interests of brevity, if hopefully not at the cost of clarity, I've chopped bags of back stories already. As near as I can make out, short of eliminating them altogether, there are a number ways of dealing with what's left. Character companions, parentheses, footnotes and/or an addendum come to mind. I've chosen parentheses.

While the reader can skip them as he or she pleases, I'd recommend perusal. Especially when in comes to "Nuclear Dragons", I do some of my best work in parentheses.

Jim McPherson
Creator/Writer
The *PHANTACEA* Mythos

****

Nuclear Dragons - Contents

NUCLEAR DRAGONS

— November-December 1980 —

Jim McPherson

A *PHANTACEA* Mythos Print Publication
James H McPherson, Publisher

ISBN 978-0-9878683-6-7
First Published 2013

Part One: **Indescribable Defiance**

NUKE 1: **Mind Tap**

========

<u>Saturday, November 29, 1980</u>

His Enormity regarded himself. "I don't like him."

His other Enormity stroked what passed for a goatee – more like neverthe-less nicely groomed tufts of hair sticking out between rolls of facial flab – as if in thought. Finally he responded: "Hey, I'm not too chuffed about how I look either."

The third person in the room, a tall, rail-thin, oriental-looking fellow who'd apparently watched too many Fu Manchu movies, coughed. Being a chain-smok-er, he did that a lot. "Will you two please knock it off. Need I remind you, sir, you were supposed to be practising; not playing with yourself. That's a homo, not a long lost twin brother."

"Just joshing," said the other Enormity considerately, then added: "Which beats jowling, not that I have any choice in the fatter-matter."

"Correction," said his Enormity. "I don't like it."

========

At dawn, Professor Romaine Kinesis and his sixteen-years-older friend, O'Ryan James Maxwell, stood on the quiet, sandy beach in the Hawaiian archi-pelago. Kinesis outstretched his arms as if feeling an insubstantial shape in the still cool air. Was it his imagination or was there really something else there? Something that approached the ineffable if not, at the end of the day – a very long day, trailing away into the unforeseeable future – the ultimately inexplic-able?

"Don't you sense it, Max? It's vast, unearthly, unnatural, bordering on im-possibly immense. I reckon it more than a passing aberration, an aerial anomaly. It's ancient and it's structural, deliberate: a huge, impermeable dome, a massive interspatial membrane, a dimensional shield or some such. You can't see it; can't touch it; can't go through it – not any way I can figure anyhow – but it's there!"

"As if aliens on the Moon weren't bad enough, you're telling me there's a hidden world in the middle of the North Pacific? Forget it, pro. The only thing I see is the highest paid scientist in the entire world cracking up for lack of sleep. Come on, Rom. You haven't been to bed for three days. The launch is tomorrow and there's nothing more you can do. I'll give you four choices: a dart, a hypo, a pill, or my fist. Which will it be?"

"None of the above. But I take your point. Let's go back."

=========

Centauri Island was a tiny island near Molokini and not far from Maui, Hawaii. As a landform, it wasn't much; too small to even warrant dots and a name on most commercially available maps of the archipelago. A series of three, inactive volcanoes – since 1964 named Mounts Zeross, Heliopolis, and Kinesis – its pimply peaks barely stuck out of the tempestuous ocean. Originally with no running water and virtually no vegetation, it had been uninhabited until the young and energetic Alfredo Sentalli adopted it in the mid-to-late Forties.

With the dedication of a madman seeking to create his own utopia, not to mention the apparent wealth of a Croesus, he began to link its peaks together such that, today, much of its surface, and virtually all of what lay hidden deep beneath it in concrete laboratories and thoroughly reinforced rocket silos, was manmade.

Although nominally an American possession, the island functioned as an independent corporate state, the headquarters for the worldwide trading empire known as New Century Enterprises. This last, NCE as it was commonly known, was the source of Sentalli's Croesus capacity. It wasn't his brainchild, though. NCE had existed, as its name suggested, since the beginning of the century, but Sentalli had been running it since Loxus Abraham Ryne, the still-living son of NCE's long dead founder, Noah Charan Ryne, retired on the first of January 1956, his fifty-sixth birthday.

Loxus Ryne was probably the most famous, fabulously rich person on the planet. His life was a one-man history of the twentieth century. Born in Amsterdam, of Iraryan-Gypsy descent, at the stroke of midnight in the first second of the year 1900, he'd been everywhere and done just about everything there was to do in this century — or any other, albeit only figuratively speaking. Succeeding at most things he'd started or tried to resolve, yet seemingly failing at all the crucial times, he lived most of his life in the public spotlight.

By contrast, Sentalli had virtually no history at all. His birth certificate said he'd been born in Toronto, of Italian-Canadian parents, in 1927. He enlisted in the American navy, using false papers, in 1943. Lost at sea in 1945, he was not heard from again until 1946 when he bought the chunks of rock that he turned into Centauri Island.

He'd offered no cash, nor any kind of personal collateral but, since NCE had guaranteed the purchase, no questions were asked and none answered. His word was his bond. He had never let any one down, then nor yet.

While Sentalli had his quirks, primarily his prodigious appetite and insistence on using a wheelchair despite the fact that he could walk as well as any everyday ordinary, humanoid tub of lard, his work ethic was unquestioned and his effectiveness indubitable. Under his guidance, even before he became chairman of the board and chief executive officer in '56, NCE prospered to the point it became the most successful corporation in the entire world.

He was a visionary – though his vision was usually espoused by Loxus Ryne. The Fatman, as almost everyone referred to him, often to his face, hadn't left his island since the late Sixties. Nor had he been photographed in almost that long. If Loxus Ryne was the most public billionaire in the world, Alfredo Sentalli was the most private.

On Centauri Island, the United Nations flag flew above the American one. Like the United Nations in New York, NCE paid no taxes for the Hawaiian island. Quite the contrary. Also like the UN, governments paid him – rather, they paid his corporation, which amounted to much the same thing – to maintain NCE's commitment to what he, and therefore they, called Project Centauri.

Unlike – according to many – the UN, the money was well spent.

=========

Alfredo Sentalli was slightly over six feet tall and weighed much more than four hundred pounds. He was swarthy, pink-faced, and artistically goateed, though that tuft of fur was largely lost in his massive cheeks and multiple chins. Fifty-three and balding, what he'd lost up top, in terms of hair, he had gained down below, in terms of size. His head was almost as bloated as his body. Notwithstanding first impressions, it was filled with intelligence, not fat.

He disdained exercise so much so he unapologetically designed, and had built, an electronic wheelchair – one adapted from a battery-powered golf cart – specifically to his accommodate his crippling girth. Getting around took less effort that way, don't you know. He professed never to worry about his physical condition, let alone his heart; claimed his *'internal health'* freed him from such petty concerns. Beer was by far and away his favourite *elixir vitae*. He called it the incredible thinking fluid and of necessity, being the boss, he thought a lot.

Around noon, the buzzer went off in Sentalli's inner sanctum. The Fatman not-at-all-laboriously wheeled over to his desk and flipped the switch.

"Listen, Yataghan," he spat angrily, "I told you never to contact me here. This is the only place I ever get any privacy."

"Sorry, Fatman." Yataghan's strangely accented yet rich, golden baritone came over the intercom. "But we got problems."

"If they're technical, tell Samarand. If they're security, tell Maxwell or Dulles. If they're financial and Hannibal doesn't want to fork over, send me the bill. Monday. Better yet Tuesday. Understood?"

"Wish it were that simple, boss. I'm afraid you better get out here. Otherwise your whole bloody island might sink."

"What are you talking about?" Jowls jiggling, Sentalli yelled into the intercom. "Are we under attack? Sound the alarm."

"Can't! No electricity. No power. Nothing's working."

"Damnation, man, I've got power!"

"You're on a different system, Fatman. I'm on Centauri Island and you're..."

"I know exactly where I am. And stop calling me Fatman. I'm your fucking father." Sentalli flipped the switch. After a few minutes consideration, he clicked the intercom back on. "All right, Yataghan. Come and get me."

"Can't, sir," came the response, "Can't move. Nobody can."

"Look, if things are that bad, get hold of Kinesis. He can do damn near anything he wants with that Godstuff of his."

"That's just it, sir. He's the demented bastard responsible for all this."

=========

On the surface, Centauri Island appeared a semi-tropical isle, almost idyllic with its isolated location and resultant tranquillity. A reasonably fit man or woman could probably walk around it in a couple of days. Most of its inhabitants lived in a small town on the leeward side of the island. Some of them worked at the state-of-the-art airport or hospital nearby; more at a larger, though equally modern, adjacent port.

Some manned the two resort villages, one inland and the other, ten years older, on the windward side. A token work force kept the sugar and pineapple plantations in the centre of the island in production but, since no tourists nor uninvited military personnel were allowed on the island, a casual visitor would have difficulty understanding what all the people did there. He or she would also wonder why so few had tans.

These would be difficult questions to answer. Which was why there were no tourists nor military personnel – nor casual visitors, for that matter – allowed. Officially, it was a privately-held island owned by New Century Enterprises and maintained exclusively for NCE's own, highly secretive purposes. Except, they weren't all that highly secret.

Heads of State from all over the world, including those in mainland China and the Soviet Union, knew exactly what was going on here. So did dozens of upper echelon scientists, military commanders, and the chief executive officers of most of the biggest global conglomerates. So did many a man in the street; had since Humankind first walked on the moon in 1969, though his wasn't so much knowledge as hope.

Project Centauri was the construction and ultimate launch site of the first manned spaceflight to the stars — namely, the Cosmic Express.

=========

In these strange days, sputniks and other military satellites were more interested in what was happening on the moon than they were Centauri Island. That didn't keep a tiny fleet of surface ships and at least three submarines far away from the islet. Of course, every nation and most of the larger corporations were nominally cooperating with NCE on Project Centauri.

A huge fish packer flying the Japanese flag wasn't really supposed to be in the vicinity but it was heeding directions to stay away from the restricted area.

Seemed to be minding its own business, too.

=========

Below decks, the packer had been gutted. Instead of refrigerators full of frozen fish, it had been equipped to be more than just a spy ship. It was a one-boat floating armada with technology that could neither be described as alien nor futuristic, though it looked to be both. Related to some of the breakthroughs incorporated in the Cosmic Express, it was much the same gadgetry, speculated the few who knew about it, that went into the United Nations of Earth Ship Liberty.

With a crew of over a hundred and fifty men, the Liberty was currently in orbit around the moon looking for a nest of aliens permeating the earth with thought beams. Had they known of it, those aboard the packer would no doubt wish it well. They were in the same business after all — destruction!

"Do something, Milo!" demanded Salvatore Dis L'Orca.

"What? My Mind Tap seems to be working perfectly, yet what we're receiving hasn't changed for twenty minutes. Either Maxwell's gone cataleptic or something else has gone wrong. Either way, Daemonicus will be pissed."

Salvatore Dis L'Orca was a Spaniard born in Equatorial Africa in the early Forties. A vain man, he sported a black and silver-etched goatee and moustache. Thin-lipped, with jutting cheek bones and a down-turned nose that looked, in silhouette, like a shark's fin, his forehead was somehow scrunched forward. The outer edges of his bushy eyebrows arched sharply upwards. He parted his hair down the middle and his greying forelocks were deliberately combed to resemble a set of stubby horns.

As always, he wore tinted glasses. Those who'd seen his eyes without shades described them as two blood-soaked orbs with tiny, pinpoint pupils. As was his habit, he was dressed formally, like the Spanish Don he was, in a tightly-tailored, red matador's jacket, side-striped, equally red pants, a white, flowery shirt and a string tie. He walked with a bad limp, due to the fact that he had a clubbed right foot. To help him along and, equally importantly, to add to his image as a man of power, he carried an opera cane, complete with retractable blade.

His late father, Hadrian Dis L'Orca, had been a respected psychiatrist then a Spanish diplomat under Francisco Franco, the Fascist Dictator remembered, rarely fondly, as El Caudillo. Salvatore, though, made and squandered huge amounts of money privately, as a dealer in contraband. He worked for anyone who paid enough and Daemonicus certainly paid more than enough for what he had to do.

Most of his colleagues figured he was a brilliant junkie. In truth, he was addicted to heroin, the primary good he smuggled around the world. Most also figured he controlled the fearsome entity called Daemonicus. They couldn't understand how Dis L'Orca in effect managed to *broadcast* the apparition – and, as more than a few currently on-board could attest, not just in the confines of the faux fish packer. Surely such an abomination couldn't be real.

As for his – make that its – horrible eyefire, they couldn't figure out how Dis L'Orca generated it either. But, all agreed, it definitely was real.

Dis L'Orca paced nervously behind his seated colleague, not even trying to conceal his limp. "Yeah, he'll be pissed and we'll be fried." (He'd have said fired if he meant fired.)

"This is preposterous. On the day before the launching of the Cosmic Express, this happens. Without our Mind Tap in Maxwell, we'll never know the exact second of lift off. Without that, we can't release the kamikaze. Damn Daemonicus back to whatever hell he came from. I told him a missile was all I needed. But, no, we have to have a human pilot, so he insists. Bloody idiocy could well cost us our lives."

"And I told you, Maxwell wasn't the best person to implant the tap." Major Milo Mind removed his cybernetic head gear and scratched his scalp. Despite his fifty-seven years, he still had most of his hair. He'd lost his sanity instead.

"His brain patterns are the weirdest I've ever come across. Even back in the war, when I graphed the likes of Donar Lancz and his wife Freya, as well as the younger Rynes, D'Angelos and Agenor Heliopolis, for the old Baron, Tyrtod von Alptraum, I never saw anything like Maxwell's. And they were all Godlings; hardly human any more. Lord knows what Maxwell is, though I've told you my theories."

"Joli Blon's forty years ancient history and the Secret War of Supranormals, which you and my father helped wind down so comparatively bloodlessly, ended a quarter century ago. Anyway, even if he does work with an undeniable genius like Aran Ryne, Moses Callion's grandson isn't trying to restart it. Couldn't. From what I've heard he hasn't a wit on the original.

"Ask me you dwell too much in the past, major. The present is all that matters; especially how it affects our future on Easy Street."

"Forget the past and you won't have a future, youngster."

Milo Mind was a major but not in India, not like his father and grandfather before him. At the beginning of the Second World War, Mind postponed enrolling in medical school and enlisted in the British Army. During the retreat to Dunkirk, he was captured and spent the rest of the war in various POW camps.

At least that was the official version. There were those who claimed he collaborated with the Nazis in some of their most insidious experiments not so much in human nature as human physicality. He was cleared of those charges after the war and went on to become a famed neurosurgeon, the best in the world.

The late Forties and throughout the Fifties, when he worked for the Great Man, Aran's father, Loxus Abraham Ryne, as part of the Alliance of Man, were his glory days. Their invention of *'amnaesthetics'*, in 1949, did indeed provide the foundation for the eventual end to the so-called Supra War. (Then as now those relatively few who knew, let alone remembered, howsoever little of the existence of supranormals referred to them as supras.)

Amnaesthetics were an effective and humanitarian way to neutralize supras threatening to go public with their powers. Without the memory-wiping qualities of Mind's drugs, the humanitarian Sisterhood of Flowery Anthea, its more aggressive offshoot, the War Witches of Athena, who could be thought of as armed suffragettes, and the King's Own Crimefighters – themselves supras – would never have gone along with the senior Ryne's efforts to render the world safe for normal men and women.

As he knew from a tangential involvement in its denouement, that crusade culminated on Christmas Day, 1955, with the eradication of the Crimefighters themselves on a desolate hump of land in the Aleutians known as Damnation Isle. Too bad for not just Major Milo Mind, his drugs couldn't be applied more universally because, with supras barely five years gone from the scene, in 1960 an organization known as the Worldwide Order with the Right to Life and Death began to operate.

WORLD figured the time was right to establish the equivalent of a Fourth Reich, albeit without the strictly German base. Accordingly, one of its first acts was to conscript him in the proverbial manner: Join us or you're dead. Mind's task became the development of the ultimate non-apocalyptic weapon: namely, total mind control.

How far he might have come towards that goal remained anyone's guess. Captured in 1965, the full extent of his wartime crimes two decades earlier were finally revealed. Whatever his accomplishments might have been, his methods were variously described as monstrous, inhuman, diabolical and, ultimately, homicidal.

When, ostensibly, Daemonicus forced Dis L'Orca to start this dubious venture in September 1977, Mind was languishing in an asylum for the criminal insane. His escape early the next year caused barely a ripple in intelligence circles. How could indications of WORLD's resurgence compete with aliens on the moon?

"Damnation, Milo!" Dis L'Orca slammed his walking stick against the control console for effect. "Maxwell was the only big wig from Sentalli's island we could get; the only one we knew would be on the launch pad who ever left the island at any rate. Hell, it was pure chance that Alorstro Sian and I came across him in San Francisco a year and a half ago. Just because his brainwaves are a trifle out of whack, doesn't mean we can't use him."

"Trifle? More like triffid, he's that far out there." Mind's control console buzzed audibly. Something had to be happening on Centauri Island.

"Wait a minute!" The moment he snapped back on his cybernetic helmet the screen in front of him lit up. "Someone just moved into Maxwell's sight line. It's Kinesis. Should have realized he was behind all this crap. Gypsium is nut-so stuff and he's been known to as good as bathe in it."

He also might have been one of the three masked men most responsible for Hadrian Dis L'Orca's death by ordeal and his own long term incarceration fifteen years ago.

========

Power was restored to the underside of the island as soon as Sentalli rolled out of his private suite into the open office-cum-reception area on the top floor of the island's perhaps incongruously luxurious hotel. He pressed a button on his arm control. Elevator doors automatically opened him.

No need, not yet.

========

Simultaneously, poltergeist-like, the balcony doors on the opposite side of the seating area slammed open entirely unbidden by him. Wheel chair and all, he was unceremoniously whisked into the air as if by an unseen hand; one that he realized could belong, no matter how detached, to only one man.

He was flying – more like blipping, sooth said, in bitty blinks of time. In a few horrifying moments he went from the hotel's scary heights to near ground level, along thankfully deserted street blocks and around corners until he arrived, wheels still not touching anything but air, at what might have passed, in a big city, for the upside-down, concrete U of a subway entrance.

More doors opened as if on their own. This time he did enter an elevator. Down, down, it descended. (The man behind the unseen hand obviously didn't know, despite all his years on the island that, given the right commands, Sentalli's private elevator could reach the island's lower levels directly.)

Once this elevator reached its destination, the grossly overweight Peter Pan in a chair, albeit with no visible Tinkerbell, recommenced his journey. Into and across the subsurface tarmac he rocketed. Technicians, rubbing feeling back into their limbs and wondering how come they hadn't been able to move for the past half hour, couldn't help but notice the Fatman in his airborne wheelchair.

Didn't faze them, though. Professor Kinesis was a common sight, hovering around the Express without any visible means of certain support. Somehow or other, that ridiculous-looking, non-exhausting, but obviously functional canister strapped to his back kept him up. It, with its seemingly prehensile tubes, ending in delicate rods, running along each of his arms, also allowed him to get about while aloft.

If he could fly, why couldn't the boss?

========

Sentalli, the inexpressible shock of such unheard of movement having taken his breath away, thus far had only a speculative notion as to what was happening to him. He screeched to a stop inside one of the many boardrooms within the concrete bowels of the island and found himself in his usual position, at the head of the table. Son and chief bodyguard Yataghan moved into position standing behind him whereas, at the far end of the long table, Professor Romaine Kinesis glowered at him.

Confirmation of responsibility thus attained Sentalli frantically began trying to click in the code to disable the destruct mechanism he'd triggered shortly after Yataghan contacted him so far away, yet so short a time earlier. Kinesis, already on his feet, chuckled amusedly as he uncharacteristically cursed his plump, sweat-streaked fingers for their inability to hit the precise, too tiny keys on the controls built into his chair.

"Oh, I wouldn't worry about that, Fatman." Reputedly the highest paid scientist in the world addressed Sentalli irreverently but without any trace of maliciousness. "I learned how to circumvent your failsafes weeks ago. I'm the only one who can blow this little island sky high and, believe me, I will, if you don't start listening to reason."

One thing Kinesis wasn't was hunchbacked. Before anyone could respond, say anything, even boo, he bombarded the room with motive-retarding Gypsium particles via little hoses presumably attached underneath his lab coat to his hump. Once again, unless he willed the Gypsium to let others do so, only he could move.

A handy knack to have, one of those others, O'Ryan James Maxwell, couldn't help thinking. Too bad he couldn't do the same in reverse. Not yet anyhow.

========

Romaine Kinesis was about five feet ten and weighed around a hundred and eighty pounds. His darkish skin and thick black beard bespoke his Mediterranean background. Few people knew he was actually of gypsy descent – the Great Man's mother Athena become Ryne was born a Kinesis, though one only distantly related to his side of the family.

(That Athena – Kinesis become Ryne, not the Greek Goddess of War and Wisdom – was the War Witches' Athena. Before her death, during the Godling Guild's so-called Summoning to the Himalayas in the Spring of 1920 she was more than just a very rich, by marriage, and hence very visible suffragette. Her insistence on carrying a gun, usually a revolver, at all times scandalized polite society of the day.

(Even today her only surviving offspring, the Xuthrodites' patriarch, Loxus Abraham Ryne, and most of his passel of grown up children, her grandchildren, rarely went anywhere unarmed. The lone exception, besides the preteen youngsters, Megan and Pauline, was Aranyani once Maxwell, always Nightingale, Big Max's ex.

(In terms of witch sisterhoods Aran, who never knew any of her grandparents, classified herself an Althean Healer. Given that she deliberately crippled TJ, their firstborn, shortly after his birth, Max reckoned calling herself a healer – pharmaceuticals were her specialty – wasn't just counterintuitive. It was an insult to the language.)

With his broad shoulders and fairly tight gut, Rom might have been mistaken for a 44-year-old athlete, one only slightly past his prime but hanging on gamely. In truth, he wasn't very fit at all. About his only exercise was riding his bike to the laboratory every day; a flat, hardly gruelling two mile distance between his surface bungalow and the hidden elevator that took him into the real heart of Centauri Island.

There, for the last fifteen years, he had spent most of his waking hours designing the Cosmic Express, the unique casing that cloaked it and its six, bus-sized shuttle crafts (called cosmicars), and, most importantly, coaxing – for that was the correct word – Gypsium to act as their primary propellant once the Express escaped Earth's atmosphere.

Although he looked directly at Sentalli, with Yataghan – his big but somewhat dim-witted and vaguely greenish-skinned (make that chlorophyllous) son and bodyguard – standing behind his father, he was very much aware of the other ten people sitting along the table, five on each side.

'*Big Max*' Maxwell, the island's chief of overall security, was a family friend and the only one he'd really known before joining NCE in 1960. Their parents were buddies even before the war and, though at least fifteen years his senior, Kinesis thought of Max as his only ally on the island.

Of the others, although he'd known of Adolph Dulles for over twenty years, he'd only met him a few times before he came to work on the island two years earlier, after graduating from the Houston Academy of Man. Now twenty-seven, Dolph had been raised by Jock and Bonita Maxwell, Max's foster parents – might even be Max's bastard – and was now Maxwell's right hand man.

Five of the eight others were scientists he'd handpicked, mostly by reputation, to head up the various research teams he needed to build the Express. The other three – the chain-smoking oriental with a Fu Manchu complex, Hiyati

Samarand; the Arabic *'suit'*, George Hannibal (he preferred Carthaginian to Tunisian); and the ironically tall, for the daughter of a midget, coldly beautiful Scandinavian, Connie Lindquist – were Sentalli's people; three of the Fatman's dozen or so so-called *'Untouchables'*.

Lindquist was the Fatman's personal physician and performed much the same function, as head of the medical team, for the sixty odd members of the Express's crew. Hannibal was Sentalli's lawyer and financial adviser. He controlled the purse strings, or thought he did at least. Kinesis wanted the stars, Hannibal offered him the moon, and Sentalli signed for the sun. Samarand was technically his boss.

As Project Centauri's overseer, he was the Fatman's personal *'scientocrat'* — an odd conjunction coined by Sentalli to explain Samarand's role as both supervising scientist and chief bureaucrat. Al was only interested in results; technical details he left to Kinesis and Samarand. In their years together they rarely spoke outside the worksite but, on the job, they got things done.

"As you know," Kinesis began, "Tomorrow, we plan to finally launch the Cosmic Express. Today, before it's too late, I intend to abort the mission."

He looked at the frozen faces around the boardroom. Only their dilating pupils registered their alarm. "I do not propose to debate the matter. My mind is made up. What I am offering is an option. We can move the launch site to Florida or Europe, even to the Soviet Space Centre in Central Asia. It might take a year to set ourselves up but, given the to-me-obvious alternative, we can afford to wait. Then again, I can destroy the island, and the Express with it, right now.

"Given mobility you might ask me why. More likely you'd try to stop me. You won't have a chance to do the last but, as to the first, my reasons are simple. There's something out there, something ages old and, very probably, very evil. It covers the entire North Pacific from Siberia to Canada, from Alaska to Hawaii.

"What it is I can't say because I don't know for sure. Yet I know it's there and I know its name – Shelter! How? Because I sense it and Gypsium has confirmed my senses. What's more, I think some of you know it as well. Your choices, gentlemen and lady." With little more than a shrug and an apparent thought, he somehow deactivated the motive retardation of the airborne Gypsium particles. "You first, Max."

Maxwell didn't speak; he spat. The tranquillizer dart – an old War Witch trick that; a life-loving Anthean one, too, one taught to him years ago by the likes of the White Witch, Morgianna Sarpedon, and her upper level predecessors in the Superior Sisterhood – hit Kinesis in the left cheek. He immediately collapsed. Maxwell lumbered out of his seat and struggled to his friend's prone form.

He knew a little about Rom's Gypsium canister, its hoses and its prongs. The left one emitted particles that slowed things down; the right one particles that speeded things up. The pad controls for each one were in the palms of Rom's hands. Maxwell took a quick look. Three keys on each pad, no indication of what any of them did.

Rather than try to guess which one to hit, he made it as far as the doors, flung them apart, and yelled for help.

When everyone was able to move again, Yataghan went over to Maxwell and Dulles as if to help them lift Kinesis onto the table. Instead, with surprising speed for a big man, he knocked both of them away from the professor, yanked his curve-bladed dagger out of its sheathe, and held it to Kinesis's neck.

"Thumbs up or down, boss man?"

Maxwell and Dulles both came up loaded for Yataghan bear. From his chest holster, Dulles had pulled a '44 Magnum. Maxwell had a Colt in his left hand and a dart gun in his other. He held the Colt unwaveringly pointed towards Yataghan's chest and the dart gun moving in an arc that covered everyone else in the room, including Sentalli and Dulles.

"Don't try me," warned Maxwell. "Some of you might think I'm past it but I can still send puke-puss to the promised land and drop most of the rest of you before you can so much as scream."

If Yataghan was worried, he didn't let on. "Say the word, father."

"Kill him," bellowed Samarand. "The madman's served his purpose. He's too dangerous to be allowed to live."

"Be silent, Dr Samarand," ordered Alfredo Sentalli.

The Fatman knew Maxwell's was no idle bluff. He'd seen the man in action and wasn't the only one thankful Max rarely shot anything more than darts. He may have missed the occasional coffee break in his time but he rarely missed a target. No matter how strong or fast his strange son by Emeralda born Plantagenet was, he couldn't possibly get out of the way of a bullet.

Even though he was familiar with Emeralda, her three sisters, and her lone brother, all of whom were long gone, Sentalli also knew that Max had no love for Yataghan. He'd often remarked that the boy drank too much olive oil. It wasn't that he was prejudiced against Latinos; just that he was wary of people whose skin pigmentation was distinctly greenish. (This despite, being half-Plantagenet, Yat's chlorophyllous complexion came naturally.)

Mind you, he wasn't all that fond of Samarand, Lindquist, or Hannibal either. Max had an uncanny knack to know whom he could trust.

"Put your shooter away, Mr Dulles," advised Sentalli. "Very slowly please. And you, Yataghan, while I applaud your industriousness, do back off. I have no wish to plant you beside your mother and hope you re-grow yourself. Your mother never has and she's had decades to try." Dulles hesitated until Maxwell nodded, but Yataghan dropped his dagger immediately.

"Crawl away, Martian," commanded the Security Chief sternly – he really didn't like Plantagenets, though he'd always been at least civil to Yat's mother Emeralda when she was alive. "Backwards, hands and knees, until you're up against the wall. Then I want you to get up and hug it. Leave your over-sexed corkscrew where it lies, thanks kindly."

"Mr Maxwell, there's no need to humiliate the lad," protested Sentalli, sensing anger in his son. "I've told him not to harm the professor and he won't. Don't push it."

"All right," agreed Maxwell. "Just remember overall security's my business, kid. You concentrate on protecting your old man. Leave me to do my job and we'll get along fine."

Yataghan picked up his dagger and sheathed it. Springing agilely to his feet, he gave Maxwell a glare then walked over and stood behind his father once again. Maxwell re-holstered his Colt under his right arm and stuck the dart gun back in its place on his bandoleer.

"Gentlemen," sighed Sentalli in obvious relief, "And lady. This meeting is concluded. Mr Maxwell, please remove Professor Kinesis to his quarters. Dr Lindquist, I believe you can prescribe a series of sedatives that will keep our resident genius asleep until after the launch tomorrow."

"Excuse me, sir," interrupted Maxwell, "But Dr Lindquist will have her hands full with the final physicals for the crew. My own staff doctor, Paul Creel, should be able to handle Rom."

"Very well, Mr Maxwell," granted the Fatman. "But I hold you personally responsible for the wellbeing of both Professor Kinesis and the safety of the launch."

"You're right, sir. Security is my responsibility."

========
Milo Mind removed the cybernetic helmet and turned to Dis L'Orca.
========

"Whew! Shelter, eh? Haven't heard mention of that in what? ... Fifteen years, maybe more. Back in the days before the Anthean Sisterhood ceased operating, at least out in the open, the few of us men who knew anything about any of their hush-hush rigmarole tended to think of it in the plural, as the term they used for their secret places.

"We called them Anthills, jokingly of course. But no one I ever heard suggested there was a kind of singular Super Shelter out there or that it was so vast." He paused as if to marvel the more. "What do you think, Sal? Figure Kinesis has anything or has the strain just cracked him?"

"Rom Kinesis is not a man who cracks easily," considered Dis L'Orca. "Nor is the idea that Gypsium, a seemingly inanimate substance, talks to him all that preposterous. As you well know, he's not the only one to do remarkable things with the stuff. I need not remind you of his stepbrothers, Aristotle Zeross and Kadmon Heliopolis.

"They're the ones responsible for your capture and my father's untimely death in '65, but they were just young punks in their twenties. Gypsium bears the ultimate responsibility for my father's murder. Without its gifts, the damn Cretans could never have brought down Hadrian and your fellows in that Order. Fortunately, Kinesis is the only one of them left alive. A shame the Fatman's son didn't kill him."

"As to that, we're in agreement. So, what if there is something – a shield, a dome, whatever else it could be – out there? Makes sense actually. You're too young to remember Satan St Synne's devil-ray. It turned ordinary people into supranormals and, though he first used it in Europe during the war, he always claimed it worked best in the North Pacific, particularly Japan or Sakhalin Island, where he made his base after it.

"Maybe Shelter's Hell, the place of demons. Maybe, we blow up the Cosmic Express tomorrow, and, with its Gypsium fuel, we break down whatever's keeping it away from the rest of the world. All the money Daemonicus pays us isn't going to be worth diddle if we're dead and doomed simultaneously."

"Sounds fantastical but when you consider what our benefactor calls himself, I take your point. Perhaps we should take what we've already got and run."

"And where would you hide?"

"Daemonicus!"

Appearing out of nowhere came the swirling, ectoplasmic shape they had come to fear as Daemonicus. While it couldn't rationally be there, the brimstone stench, the way it made one's skin sweat and itch, the way it made one's ears ring and hair stand on end, the way it made one's bowels tighten, made one want to kneel down and pray for forgiveness – all were unmistakeable. The hellacious, incessantly smiling wraith was there and it was terrifying.

With a flat-topped mitre that completely covered its hair and neck, it looking like a clean-shaven Greek Orthodox bishop. Its black raiment, so typical of that priesthood, reinforced the image. Facially, the creature had dramatically boned, starkly pink skin, thin, purplish lips upturned in a perpetual rictus grin, gleaming bright teeth, two hollow, white eyes, and a third one, just above the bridge of its nose, about where its eyebrows almost met.

It was slender but strong-looking, with too many fingers, all of them extraordinarily long by a knuckle or two, and nails as thick and as sharp as claws. Its robe had pockets; a glowing sash held it together by. From its neck on a golden chain dangled a pair of shrunken skulls that also glowed. When it was in a coercive mood, both men had seen it produce and play a glowing panpipe.

It wasn't in a coercive mood today. It was as furious as they were frightened.

"Nowhere in this world, nor in the other – nor in the next, be assured of that. I am a generous master. Yet I am unrelenting in the pursuit of those who have wronged me. You will do exactly as instructed. There shall be no variations. No deviations. If you fear Hell coming to Earth, look no further than me.

"Eyefire-burn, Milo Mind!"

From the phantasm's third eye came a burst of blazing fury. It engulfed Mind only briefly then dissipated. The major fell out of his chair and, smoke or vapours of some other sort still rising off him, began to weep uncontrollably.

"That was unnecessary, St Synne," Dis L'Orca bravely criticized the insubstantial whatever-it-was. "We were only talking speculatively. Besides, Milo's not a young man. And he's no more stable mentally than he is physically. Without him, we haven't got a Mind Tap; without that, we've got no way of knowing the exact second the Express lifts off and you know it."

"Do not trifle with me, Salvatore. And do not presume to call me that detestable name. I have only a casual acquaintance with Sedon, or Satan, St Synne. I have given you a name to remember me by and a small sample of my abilities. Make no further presumptions!"

"Don't come the high and mighty with me, you hundred and whatever year old spook. Daemonicus, my Spanish butt! I'm no Iberian imbecile, You can't fool me. What you may not know is that I know exactly where you are. The pseudo-prison in Palo Alto you've been stuck in for the better part of the last two decades? My people infiltrated it the moment you hired me. The life support system that keeps your body going while your mind ranges freely? They'll shut it off tomorrow unless I'm alive to order otherwise.

"When you put me in charge of this business, you guaranteed me and mine a great deal of money. Fair and fine enough. You also guaranteed us not survival as such – we're well-aware of the attendant risks – but promised that, with success, we'll be able to spend that money as we see fit. You guaranteed us freedom and, as you said yourself, your word is your bond."

"As it is, as it always has been, since time immemorial. Persist in your delusions of my identity, if you like. But look you to your Homer's Odyssey, Book Four, if you wish to know whom I truly am. 'He who makes life easiest for all men,' that's who I am, yes, but I am also 'he who can make life murder for all men'. Think on that, Salvatore.

"Not that you'll be able to remember it after I've left."

That said, Daemonicus vanished.

========

"That was foolish," said the scientocrat sometime later on Centauri Island. "You should have sent out your homo. That's what homunculi are for – to take the risks sanity says someone as important as you are to all we're doing has to avoid."

"Hey," said his Enormity. "It's not like I came out alone." A third eye opened in his forehead. The scientocrat bowed.

"Sorry, father. I didn't realize you were here. You so seldom speak to low-borns like me."

"Wasn't your father talking, Yati. Even when he's in me, I'm perfectly capable of speaking my own mind. Besides, controlling a homo long distance gives me a headache."

****

Nuke 2: **OJ Maxwell**

========

<u>Sunday, November 30, 1980</u>

Dawn. If everything went well, today would be the most important day in the world's history since the first simian jumped out of a tree and set about evolving into humanity.

========

O'Ryan James Maxwell led a patrol of twenty handpicked, hand-trained, heavily-armed men on a final go-round of Centauri Island. It wasn't necessary. If Sentalli had spent billions of dollars constructing his island and building the Cosmic Express, he'd spent multi-millions on security. Maxwell had been there since late 1968. He'd been given carte blanche to protect the island. Planes and helicopters were always in the air; armoured patrol boats, jeeps, personnel carriers, amphibious vehicles on the water, roads, highlands, and beaches.

Using bribes, political leverage, and the good offices of most of the nations on Earth, he'd acquired the very latest in weaponry: from ground to air missiles to laser cannons capable of spotting in-coming rockets and incinerating them from hundreds of miles away. NCE satellites monitored the world and, just for good measure, nearby outer space as well.

The President Elect of the United States had already made discreet inquiries about the system Maxwell had designed to protect the island. Seems he was considering using it as the basis for a continent-wide defence cordon. If so, the effort would probably bankrupt the States ... but not before the Soviet Union spent itself to oblivion trying to keep up.

One technology exclusively NCE's that the former governor and actor would never get his hands on was the retractable curtain of Gypsium particles that Kinesis had developed and that he, Samarand and Sentalli insisted be available in case they needed to umbrella the island. Maxwell hadn't much liked the idea. He feared anything to do with the wondrous Godstuff that Kinesis called Gypsium.

'*Whomsoever touches Gypsium,*' the professor often claimed, '*Touches both the unknown and the unknowable.*'

Begrudgingly Max went along with them, not that he had any choice in the matter. Still, he'd known Rom since he (Rom) was a youngster in war-torn Greece and, if there was one person on the island he trusted, it was Kinesis. Most of the others could go to Hell or, in Samarand's case, go back there – the sooner, the better.

=========

"Right, Dulles," he radioed his lieutenant, Adolph Dulles – he never called him son or Adolph; seldom ever called him Dolph either. "The island's tighter than Mother Mary's holy hymen. All a spy has to do is breathe and we'd have his ass in aspic."

"Countdown's begun as per schedule," Dulles radioed back. "You coming in, Max? The Fatm ... I mean, Mr Sentalli's just shown up and wants to see you."

"Roger that dodger, Dulles. I'll be there shortly. And remember, it's the Fatm... I mean, Mr Sentalli's day. Give him all due respect, Dolph. If this thing goes off without a hitch, we'll be so rich, we can retire and build our own island."

"A-OK, chief. Expect you momentarily."

Maxwell signed off and told his men to take up their posts. He drove alone towards the nearest monorail station. "So fucking rich," he mused, "I'll be able to take Timmy to every specialist in the world until he gets his legs fixed. Then I'll find his Satan-sainted mother and break her God-cursed neck."

OJ *'Big Max'* Maxwell not only appeared to be of indeterminate age, he was. At the minimum he figured he had to be at least sixty. After all, it was over forty years since the war began and he'd been no pimply faced brat in 1940. Still, he didn't feel sixty. Nor did he particularly look it: no grey except a fringe in his dusty blonde beard; hair that hadn't receded an inch in twenty years; no age spots, no wrinkles, no symptoms of encroaching old age. When people asked him the secret of his longevity, he'd venture: *'It sure isn't from living right!'*

His first memory was that of a small boy, probably no more than five. He wasn't OJ Maxwell in those days. His name was Viktor Richter and he was a thin, sickly waif wandering lost, alone, and crying through a bleak forest full of gnarled trees and monstrous toadstools. He recalled meeting up with an ogre, a horridly hump-backed, crush-faced old gnome.

'Mustn't run away like that,' said the ogre in Cajun-accent English and grabbed his hand. *'Ain't safe, what with you being newly born and all. Woods are full of predators, most of them human.'* He remembered being hauled home – a castle perched precariously atop an impossible-to-climb cliff overlooking the Baltic Sea in what was now part of Poland.

His next memory was seemingly over half a decade later; had to be the early Thirties. He must have been twelve or thirteen, entering puberty. He knew that because he remembered showing off his wares to his childhood playmate, Günter von Alptraum – who was about the same age as he was, maybe even to the day – when a little girl, a plump, jolly blonde of about six or seven, Joli Blon as the ogre called her, caught them.

They were in the same Prussian castle of his earlier memory; Günter was its owner's son. The bossy little bitch bawled them out so loudly that the old gnome, the man who had either adopted him or was his real father, the spine-twisted hunchback – Moses Callion was his name – limped into the room and gave both Prince Peashooter and him the whipping of their lives.

Peashooter, yeah, that's what he always called Günter von Alptraum. Because he was perpetually playing with his pee-shooter, his tiny prick.

Odd, thought Maxwell as he neared the monorail station, forty-five years ago was about the last time he knew Günter von Alptraum as his friend. Sure, they'd been sending each other Christmas cards ever since, but it'd only been about fifteen years since they'd stopped putting bombs in the envelopes. From '40 to '65, they'd spent most of their times together trying to kill each other.

Although he couldn't remember seeing Joli Blon again, he recalled others from those days. How could he forget them? Perhaps most notably, albeit in retrospect, one was that sixty-to-seventy-odd year old Frenchie, the one with the brimstone breath and sulphuric farts. In those days, he called himself, innocuously enough, Sedon St Synne.

These days, that was his name again, though the undying fossil had been on life support for almost two decades. After his mysterious reappearance in 1943 – he'd been thought dead for four years – until his supposed capture by Soviet supras allied with the Society of Saints in February of '45, he had been known as Satan St Synne.

Other faces, other names, came back to him. All were frequent visitors to the castle, none more so than Loxus Abraham Ryne. Even then, the Great Man was probably the most famous billionaire in the world. Using his vast wealth, most of which was inherited from his father, he ran the Alliance of Man, a philanthropic organization dedicated to the pursuit of excellence.

(Supposedly the Family Ryne was named after the fabulous Rheingold, upon which Richard Wagner based his operatic *'Ring of the Nibelung'*. Purportedly the source of unlimited wealth, Max knew it to be true that the Family Ryne had a Midas Touch that could be traced back centuries, both in Europe and in their ancestral homeland of Persia, which wasn't officially named Iran until the mid-Thirties.)

Abe also revived the long floundering, virtually extinct Illuminated Faith of Xuthros Hor; was in fact its patriarch. Like the Alliance, Xuthrodism was intended to propagate the notion that human beings were a collective God. Its motto was *'For the good of all and the greater glory of mankind'*. Naturally enough, established churches and governments condemned it as being Bolshevik, socialist, unionist, elitist; whatever happened to be the catchword putdown of the day, country, and religion.

Through good and bad, Loxus Ryne persevered; became a legend in his own time, albeit no more so than his father had been in his. Noah Charan Ryne founded New Century Enterprises in the late 1890s. By the end of the First World War, it was the most prosperous international company in history. Charan, though, had a greater interest than making money, which like his father before him and his before him – and so on back perhaps as far as Burgundian times in Europe – came almost too easily for him.

As a young man he became a member of the almost legendary Godling Guild. As such, he was obsessed with finding a physical link to the domain of the old, pagan gods from the epic of Gilgamesh, the Vedas, Homer, the Bible, the Eddas, and other antique manuscripts or even more ancient, verbal traditions. Among their most successful expeditions were the unearthing of Troy in Turkey, Knossos on Crete, and the controversial *'discovery'* of the remains of Noah's Ark, high atop Mt Ararat, also in Turkey, though not far from Armenia.

Less known was their dismal failure in Tibet in 1920. Charan and his wife, Athena nee Kinesis, a distant relation of Rom's branch of the family, was killed on that expedition. (Among the many others who also died were Rom's grandparents, Philip and Olympias Kinesis, Michael and Leonora D'Angelo, their eldest daughter Celestine, Louise nee Riel St Synne and her daughter, Cybele, who was only eleven years old at the time.)

Strangely, though they didn't find a gateway to Shambolic, or Shambhala, or whatever they were looking for in the Vale of the Visionaries, they did rescue another eleven year old white girl. This was Eden Nightingale. At the age of eighteen she married Loxus Ryne. In 1929 she bore him the twins, David and Saul, and, four years later, gave birth to Aranyani Nightingale Ryne. In 1961, Maxwell married Aran. It was the dumbest move of his life.

His mind lost in reverie, he paused to gaze at the rising sun. So beautiful. Yet it came from the ocean and, if Romaine Kinesis was right, the North Pacific was the site of some kind of hidden world; an Inner Earth perhaps, though from the sounds of things neither underground nor underwater, like speculatively Sunken Atlantis.

Be it hell or heaven, be Kinesis full of shite or shine, the sunrise was still as beautiful as his life had been, at the very least, busy.

========

He pulled up in front of the monorail station.

Getting out, he handed the jeep's keys to one of the attendants, who'd park it properly. While waiting for the train to arrive he checked his weapons. The revolver was primed for quick reloading, additional cylinders pre-packed with bullets in the pockets of his bandoleer. For ease of access he secured his dart guns and throwing knives there as well. His self-designed rifle could fire heavy ammo or darts, depending on which trigger he pulled. Atop it was a miniature bazooka. What it fired could stop a tank. It, too, was set to go.

Finally, almost ritualistically, he placed a suppository-like capsule containing a sleep dart between his lower gums and cheek. It was a habit he'd carried on from his days with Ryne's anti-terrorist group AMERICA – the Alliance of Man for the Extermination of Resisting International Criminal Associations. (Perhaps inspired by WORLD, Abe Ryne, who came up with the name, loved acronyms.) It wasn't as lethal as a cyanide tooth but, as he'd shown yesterday, it could be used offensively as well.

Satisfied, he sat down on a bench. In a matter of moments, the monorail would take him below. He massaged his skull forcefully. He felt one of his migraines coming on. Although he'd suffered severe headaches all his life, now just wasn't the time for it.

He stretched out and closed his eyes.

========

His real memories, the stuff he was sure about, began in 1939. A young man with his first growth of beard, he could have been fifteen, more likely twenty or perhaps even older. The ogre, Moses Callion, and Loxus Ryne came to see him at Castle Nightmare, as he now thought of the von Alptraums' coastal pile and grounds. Neither looked any older than they seemed when he was twelve or thirteen; the gnome didn't look much older than he had when he was about five.

'*We have to move quickly,*' said Callion. '*Mr Ryne's come all this way to rescue us.*'

'*Tyrtod warned us,*' explained Ryne. '*Donar Lancz and his Gestapo cronies are coming to take Moses away. They want you too, kid. Already have Günter.*'

Oddly, Max had never heard of the Gestapo before then. He'd gone with them anyhow —to London England. There that Dr Callion left them, never to be seen again; not by him, at least not that he could recall. He did meet Callion's son and grandson any number of times once the so-called Secret War of Supranormals (better or at least more simply known as the Supra Wars) got well and truly underway as, some said, a never-acknowledged sideshow to the global conflagration.

Grandson, like father – a member of WORLD who predeceased its 1970 demise – like grandfather, was a doctor named Moses. As hunch-backed as his precursors he was currently working on research projects at the Houston Academy of Man. Which of course meant he was working on behalf of Loxus Ryne, whose ample coinage kept Academies of Man going throughout the world.

For thirty years Max, too, worked for Ryne, whom he addressed as Abe rather than Loxus. Even though they ceased speaking to each other in '68 over the way the patriarch handled the Black Rose affair, he stuck with AMERICA, more on than off, until WORLD was history. But that was a long time ago. Bridges had been mended and Ryne proved a better grandfather to Timmy than Max ever was a father.

"Mr Maxwell?" Someone prodded him. He opened his eyes and recognized the East Indian Roderick Paraja, a long time crony of Dr Samarand and, at least nominally, the chief engineer during various construction phases of the Express, it hub craft and its cosmicars. "Wake up, sir. Been looking everywhere for you."

"Uhhh," yawned Maxwell. "Say what?"

Despite obvious exasperation, Rod repeated himself. "Mr Sentalli's going ape-shit bananas down there. Sent everybody not busy to find you. The crew's ready to board the Express. Come on, get up. Let's get going."

There, just for a moment – but Maxwell caught it – in Rod's forehead ... the glimmering of a third eye!

========

"*That was a narrow thing,*" said Milo Mind. "*Last thing we want is for Max to sleep through the launch.*"

"*Tell me about it, major.*" Dis L'Orca wiped his brow. "*Maybe Daemonicus has some connections on Centauri Island after all.*"

"*Then why didn't he share them with us?*"

"*Don't ask me. Got a make on that guy?*"

========

The Mind Tap worked like a miniature visual and sound recorder. Everything Max had seen or heard in the eighteen months since it had been implanted had been copied and stored on the packer's computers. That included the personnel files which Maxwell habitually reviewed. Mind signalled one his technical assistants. Paraja's face was quickly matched and the information transferred to Dis L'Orca's screen.

"Figured as much. One of Sentalli's Untouchables, his mystery folk. Starred like the other dozen or so Maxwell marked for special attention." Dis L'Orca called them up onto a multiple viewer. "Doctor, lawyer, even this one, an East Indian chief no less. Maxwell didn't like their references. Hell's Teeth, he must have known all about Connie's background but like you're always reminding me, Sentalli vouched for them, so what could he do?"

(Dis L'Orca was right about Dr Connie Lindquist. She was a known factor. Besides being the Fatman's personal physician and de facto head of the Express's medical team, she was the daughter of a couple of very dangerous players in the Supra Wars and afterwards. Her mother, codenamed Soanso was dead, but her father, Greygreave Translav, was very much still around.

(Was still a board member of WORLD as well, though that Max couldn't have known because he wouldn't know the Worldwide Order was back in business.)

"These last two are particularly interesting," Dis L'Orca added. "Dr Hiyati Samarand, no less than Project Centauri's overseer, has been there for decades but has no credentials from any university Max could find. And what's this note about Colonel Avatar Sol, the on-board mission commander? No previous – *anything*! His emphasis."

"What kind of a name's Colonel Sol anyhow?" queried Mind, who put together the bios personally – by videotaping, via his Mind Tap, and thereby copying from the originals Max was reading at the time. "Sounds like one of those old time supras. You know, like Old Man Power, Wilderwitch, Radiant Rainbow Rider, for Christ's sake! Mr Brilliant, Mr Automatic, Mr Attraction, Baron Justice."

"Major Mind," added Dis L'Orca, somewhat sarcastically.

"Beside the point now," granted Mind, whose real name was just that, Milo Mind. "Maxwell's on the rail. Ten minutes, he'll be on the pad. The Jap ready?"

"Kamikaze Kaligula is always ready to die."

========

From the moment he went to London, during the Blitz forty years ago, to the present day, OJ Maxwell had lived an action-packed life; one full of adventure, intrigue, and downright, out-and-out strangeness. Perhaps because of its apparent ordinariness, his strangest experience had been the years he'd spent married to Aranyani Nightingale, Ryne's daughter by Eden also always Nightingale.

========

Born on Good Friday, 1933, Aranyani was always an odd one. Fey was the word they used to describe her, so Ryne often told him. She disappeared in late 1939, along with her mother Eden and a number of others. Supposedly they were on a plane, somewhere over the Himalayas, that was sabotaged by Donar Lancz, a former Godling who had embraced Hitler in a big way.

(Earlier that same year, Lancz had tried to have Ryne assassinated. The rifleman – actually a riflewoman – narrowing missed Ryne, hitting his ten year son, David, instead. The boy survived, though he was never what you might call normal again. Neither was his twin Saul, although his non-physical abnormalities did not become apparent until a few years later.)

Not that he should have but Ryne never forgave Lancz for the assaults on he and his family. He was very clear that, should any of his operatives come across Lancz, they'd do well to bring him his head, detached. In 1943, on a mission in Germany to kill Günter's father, Tyrtod von Alptraum (by then the Nazi Nightmare), Maxwell ended up doing just that.

Although he missed von Alp, he nailed Lancz, who was married to von Alp's marital niece Valfreja (or Freya, nominally born Faust but always Volsung), who had a definite *'thing'* for him, albeit as Viktor Richter. Finding his way back to the relative safety of England, all the way carrying Lancz's head in a satchel and his (Lancz's) infant son, Simon, on his back, was another of the bizarre, often horrifying experiences he would never forget. Remembering it now, Maxwell had to smirk at the grim irony.

Like all Godlings, Donar Lancz was a mystic at heart. He headed a group of Nazi supranormals that he called *'Herminones'*. Also spelled *'Hermiones'* and *'Irminones'*, the word itself translated accurately, but to Max's mind altogether inappropriately, as the Harmonious Ones. Lancz named them after a possibly mythological tribe of blue-eyed, fair-haired and heroic pagan priests described by Tacitus in his *'Germania'*.

(Herminones also featured in Ario-Germanic cultism as the intellectual or priest-king heirs to the sun king. Their priesthood was called the 'Armanenschaft' — 'Armanen' being the Germanic form of Herminones. The Alliance of Man, which coordinated the activities of supras ostensibly loyal to Allied Powers, perhaps too flatteringly called them the Teutonic Templars.)

Lancz likened himself singularly as the Teutonic Templar. He was better known among his contemporaries as the Teutonic Terror, though, an appellation he didn't object to either. Officially however, Lancz's codename was *'Baphomet'*, after the legendary talking head the real Knights Templar supposedly worshipped. He even had (the 14th Century's version of) Baphomet's sigil, a Maltese Cross (the skewed superimposition of clockwise and anti-clockwise swastikas), tattooed on his forehead about where his third eye would be had he had one.

When Big Max presented Baphomet-Lancz's severed head to Loxus Ryne for approval, the patriarch snorted: *'Why aren't you talking now, Donar?'*

Upon which Jock Maxwell opened the head's jaws and out flew hordes of newly-winged midges; a duly sworn not apocryphal occurrence that famously caused him to mutter: *'Thou'rt misnamed Baphomet. Truly be ye Beelzebub, Lord of the Flies.'*

Ah, Jock, you cantankerous old Scotsman. You and Bunnie, you're the only parents I ever really knew, reflected Maxwell as he stepped off the monorail. And while you may not be the only parents my Timmy ever knew, you're the best for him as well. God bless and keep all three of you healthy.

"You seem a bit lost, Max," remarked Adolph Dulles as Maxwell climbed into the electronically-powered cart he was driving. Like Timmy, Simon Lancz and Bruce Dre'Ath, Dolph was brought up by Jock and Bunnie. He bore such a striking resemblance to Max that many people thought him his illegitimate son. The truth was a bit stranger than that but Max made no secret that Dulles was more than just his deputy.

"Not really, pal. Just reminiscing. You know, the smartest thing Auld Jock and Bunnie ever did was not getting married."

"You're thinking about the witch again, aren't you?"

"Don't you dare call Aran a witch," snapped Max, not really angry. His antipathy to his ex was not only widely known. It was widely approved. After what she did to Timmy, witch was an exceedingly mild term of reproach. "She's an Anthean. They're different, that's all. I'm the only one who can call her a witch because I'm the only one who truly knows what a fucking witch she truly is."

"Was, Max," corrected Dulles. "Seems okay to me nowadays."

"Is, mate," rejected Maxwell. "Is, was, always has been, always will be."

"Sorry, Max. You're thinking about the fucking witch again, aren't you."

"That's better."

========

Aranyani Nightingale, reportedly killed at the age of six, reappeared at her father's New York City penthouse some sixteen years later, on New Year's Eve, 1955. (Witch that she was even then, at the hardly innocent age of 22, Aran must have been thoroughly conscious of the fact that Abe's 56th birthday came precisely at midnight.) She offered often contradictory explanations as to where she'd been, how her mother had died a week earlier, and how – shades of James Hilton's 1933 novel *'Lost Horizon'* – they'd survived 1939's plane crash in the Himalayas.

(Supposedly Lost Horizon – and with it the popular notion of Shangri-La as a spiritual, harmonious land subsequently demonized as a communistic dystopia by the FDR-haters – was based in part on the Godling Guild's 1920 expedition to the mysterious Vale of the Visionaries, which was where the Godlings came across eventual Mama Eden in the first place.)

No matter, Aran was back and Daddy Abe, who was about to enter into his third marriage, couldn't have been happier. Or more indulgent, for about six years. Then, his patience exhausted after a succession of failed affairs, public scandals, and private suspicions as to her sanity, that she might even be Faceless Strife, the patriarch demanded she marry and settle down.

(Strife was one of most bordering-on-inexplicably persistent, not to mention thoroughly pernicious supranormals ever known. Worse, while many supras strove to keep their day-to-day identities secret, she was one of a very few who didn't so much succeed as (arguably) successfully got others blamed, and punished, for being her. And, yes, she literally was faceless; didn't even have bumps for ears or a nose, indentations for a mouth or eyes.

(Clearly a master illusionist – a not unusual talent among upper level witches, who consequently weren't considered supras – what she did have was a shock of red hair that was often just a top knot or ponytail on an otherwise shaved head, and a skinny, waif-like body that never seemed to change in the nearly thirty years she plagued mankind.

(Aranyani didn't have red hair; hers was black, with white bands in it just like her mother had. Furthermore, since Strife first appeared in 1943, when Aran was all of ten and, besides, thought dead for four years, it was hard to argue with the Anthean Sisterhood's assertion that she was some kind of possessive spirit.

(Spook or otherwise, a supranormal with ethereal abilities perhaps, she was unmistakably malevolent and probably still out there. The bad ones always were. Along with Steltsar, another recurring supra with ties to WORLD, albeit one with a definite identity – none other than Tyrtod von Alptraum himself, somehow transformed into the living embodiment of a Nazi Nightmare – Strife was one of the fundamental litmus tests he used when it came to finalizing island security.

(He was forever asking himself as much as the designers he worked with: *'Will it stop Strife and Steltsar?'* He figured the sum total of all his *'its'* would.)

Her biological clock no doubt ticking wildly by then, Aran acceded to her father's demands. In the summer of '61, she officially hooked up with O'Ryan James Maxwell (who if he was a Summoning Child, as many believed, would have been 40, eleven years her senior at the time). For the next three years, she and Max were the perfect public couple. They were also the perfect private couple.

The legitimacy of marriage allowed them to carry on without anyone caring, just as they always had, albeit now carefully keeping out of the spotlight. In February 1963, they came together long enough for Aran to become pregnant. At Vancouver's St Paul's Hospital, around midnight on the 31st of October, she gave birth to Timothy James Maxwell.

'Saints be praised,' cried Bunnie O'Ryan, *'The lad's born on All Saints Day.'*

'Saints preserve us,' swore Jock Maxwell, *'The lad's born on All Hallows Eve – Witch Night!'*

Aran was horrified. Antheans weren't supposed to have first-born boys. Sons were too dangerous. They never worked out. Look at what had become of her twin brothers by the patriarch and her mother, Eden Nightingale. David and Saul died monsters, supranormally gifted and hardly human at all. When it came down to dust, on Christmas Day, 1955, they destroyed each other.

In a fit of insanity she tried to kill TJ; succeeded in leg-crippling him. Big Max, agent of the devil, as she often called him, stopped her from doing any further damage. Thereafter she became both resigned to her fate and a surprisingly good mother until, in the summer of '65 and once again pregnant, she disappeared.

Last year he came across her again. They didn't talk then, still hadn't, but Max had connections everywhere. He now knew that there was a fifteen year old girl living with Aran near the Academy of Man in Houston. Father's last name: Callion; Mother's maiden name: Nightingale; daughter's first name: Firenze.

He knew who Callion was, Moe III, the grandson of the first Moses Callion, the old ogre who helped raise him at Castle von Alptraum in (presumably) the Twenties and Thirties. Since Moe III was as small and misshapen as his father and grandfather before him, whereas Aran's girl was reputedly as tall, as correspondingly gawky yet, to many eyes, as attractive as her mother, Max had no doubt this was his child, Timmy's sister.

What he still couldn't decide was whether he wanted to see her. Like grandmother like mother like daughter, he figured. Did he really want to be the father of a witch? Although he'd had blessed little to do with the Superior Sisterhood, nor any of its offshoots, in the last fifteen years, he'd seen enough of Antheans – he called them Ants – prior to that to last a lifetime.

Not to mention an afterlife, which Ants wholeheartedly believed in. Had a name for it as well: *'Big Shelter!'*

========

"We're here, Max."
"Here? What? Where?"
"There," pointed Adolph Dulles.

THE COSMIC EXPRESS!

****

NUKE 3: **Double Devastation**

========

<u>Sunday, November 30, 1980</u>

It was early 1978 that the signals were first detected. They came from somewhere out in space. At first scientists, while publicly holding their tongues, were extremely excited. Finally there was proof that humanity wasn't alone in the cosmos. Science fiction had become science fact. Experiments were begun to decode the signals and send messages back.

Then, about a month after their initial discovery, the source was pinpointed. Delight gave way to shock then to near panic.

The beams were coming from the Earth's moon!

========

There were extraterrestrials out there all right. But they were right on top of us, on *our* Moon, as Loxus Abraham Ryne emphasized, and not some far distant planet or spacecraft. Question was, if the aliens were that close why didn't they make direct contact? Why were they squatting on the Moon permeating the Earth and its people with indecipherable beams?

There seemed only one reasonable answer. They were softening us up; bombarding our brain cells until we were too weak to resist. They'd invade and it would be all over. The world would be colonized and humanity would either be wiped out or enslaved.

In an extraordinary session of the Security Council, the United Nations agreed to meet this off-worldly intrusion aggressively. Although hardly forgotten, suspicions and ideologies were put on the back burner for the nonce. Industrial and resource-rich states all over the planet agreed to pool their knowledge, wealth and manpower in order to confront this alien menace and send it packing. Earth would not be a planetary sitting duck.

The first step was to set up the Society for the Prevention of Alien Control of Earth (SPACE or the Space Council). To head this organization, the governments agreed to appoint Loxus Abraham Ryne, the very man who, with his fondness for acronyms, named it. Among the many hats he wore or had worn, the Dutch-Iraryan businessman once ran New Century Enterprises, the world's largest corporation, AMERICA – mostly for Americans – and still did the pan-humanist Alliance of Man.

Abe, as he allowed his friends – and many of his enemies, of whom he had at least as many as he had friends – call him, was also the patriarch of the non-denominational, Illuminated Faith of Xuthros Hor. (Which, perhaps shockingly in this day and age, was a brotherhood, no women allowed. Then again the Anthean Sisterhood and its offshoots didn't allow men into their ranks either. They did marry, though; usually to Xuthrodites, as it happened.)

As old as the century at seventy-eight, Ryne took to his latest and perhaps greatest challenge with a vigour and surety belying his age. He immediately clamped a total blackout on the activities of SPACE. Under no circumstances was word to leak that there were aliens on the Moon bombarding humanity with behaviour- and/or attitude-altering thought-beams as a presumed prelude to a full-scale invasion.

With cold-blooded efficiency he began to enforce his mandate. He cut through bureaucracies, technological impasses, resource, capital and supply management problems. He even demanded, and got, access from the Soviet Union to the secret papers of Jesus Mandam, a supranormal who was variously known as the Conqueror, King Conqueror or the Conquering Christ from 1943 to 1953. Thus, in a manner of speaking anyhow, he finally realized a nearly three decade dream.

(It wasn't until 1951 that Mandam even revealed himself to be this Conqueror. Before that, on the very rare occasions when someone saw the Conqueror, and lived to tell about it, he was wearing a grotesque helmet. It appeared to be a whole, head-covering boulder of ridged black, but sparkling, Caribbean brain coral.)

A highly gifted, almost futuristically ground-breaking genius, Mandam had been the patriarch's nephew, the son of his twin sister, Mary also Magdalene, and her equally late husband, Joseph Mandam. Although he proclaimed political nonalignment, and although he was virtually unknown to the general public, he spent much of his (relatively short) adult life in the Soviet Union.

A Summoning Child like so many eventual supranormals, he was killed on Christmas Day 1953, during an unannounced explosion of a hydrogen bomb on a South Sea lump of land howsoever presciently named Salvation Island by grateful, 16th Century, Portuguese missionaries to Micronesia. (This, presumably, was due to the fact that the natives never tried to eat them.) Being thus vapourized was, to be put it mildly, a hell of way to celebrate one's 33rd birthday.

The Soviets preserved his notes and many of his miniature models, a few of which were surprisingly functional. When the beams were detected, they shared them with the UN's Space Council and the Alliance of Man – the latter mostly because, through Ryne and Sentalli's NCE, it was already well on its way to finishing Project Centauri; or at least its first-step-spacecraft. Consequently it already had the wherewithal in terms of expertise and by then surplus personnel to help construct the UNES Liberty (UNES = United Nations of Earth Spacecraft).

Mostly for strategic reasons, but also in part due to its generous sharing of the Mandam-Conqueror's left-behind insights and designs, NCE ended up building the Liberty in the USSR, not on Centauri Island. The UN craft also had to make do without any Gypsium or *'Solidium'* components, this despite the massive Tunguska deposit of the former and the Conqueror's own proficiency when it came to intertwining the latter into some of his most awe-inspiring gadgetry during the Supra Wars.

Ryne via Sentalli – more like Hiyati Samarand and his *'Untouchable'* cronies – deemed NCE's acumen when it came to both of these bordering on miraculous, as yet only partially man-mastered substances too proprietary to entertain any notion of reciprocity with the Soviets.

(Even in the face of presumed aliens on the Moon, and despite the fact Centauri Island still was officially their territory, they refused to parcel out glimmerings of their accomplishments in this regard with American authorities, especially with its military. So why would they pull a Conqueror and do it with the USSR?)

Consequently conventionally fuelled, the Liberty was now in place orbiting above a specific crater on the Moon. Next question, not least for those on the Liberty, but almost as crucially for those down here waiting for word as to what'd they found up there, was where were the damn aliens?

Unless, put another way, they were moon dust.

========

The Cosmic Express looked almost minuscule atop its fifteen-storey high firing rockets.

========

In actuality it was quite large: three or four storeys in its own right. Six Cosmicars adhered to its outer shell. Each was the size of a transit bus and comfortably held a seven-member crew. The central stalk held another fifteen people, mostly relief staff, while the bud on the head of it, the control capsule, was virtually a cosmicar unto itself. Nine people would always be there or a quick hop, skip and a jump nearby in their minuscule living area. These included the overall commander, the chief engineer, the chief navigator, their first officers and alternates.

The Express was cloaked by a hardened carapace made out of another mysterious substance, this Solidium about which Dr Samarand was so protective. (In moments of distraction, Max had heard Samarand call it *'Stopstone'*; which in turn led him to recall an alternative term for Gypsium, namely Brainrock.) The theory, proven in endless simulations, not all of which took place in laboratories, was that it would burn off leaving the planet's atmosphere. Depending on the cosmicommander's orders the Express would thereafter function either whole or as independent compartments.

Sixty-six people would be on the Express. Either sixty-six reached Outer Space or a minimum of sixty-six would die that day.

========

"Ah, Mr Maxwell," Sentalli, masking his annoyance rather well, greeted his security chief. "Everything's A-OK I trust. You took quite a while getting here."

"Couldn't be better, sir."

"It doesn't have to be better, Mr Maxwell," observed Hiyati Samarand, Project Centauri's overseer. "Merely as good as it's supposed to be. Which is perfect! Correct?"

"Nothing's perfect," noted Maxwell cautiously. Was Samarand goading him? Had he noticed something? Was something wrong? "We're only human, after all."

"Um, quite," said Sentalli, wiping his brow. "The crew are aboard so I'm afraid you've missed saying good-bye to them but Commander Sol and his cosmicaptains are waiting for you."

With the Fatman leading the way in his automated wheelchair, Maxwell fell into line with Dulles, Samarand, Yataghan, Lindquist, Hannibal, and the heads of the various departments. (Tragic, thought Max, that Kinesis couldn't be there after all his work. But the sooner the Express was launched the sooner he could get Rom off the tranquilizers they'd been feeding him since yesterday afternoon.)

Maxwell had spent many hours with Avatar Sol and the six cosmicaptains, supervising their physical training and that of their crew. Of the two hundred or so trainees, the sixty-six that were finally chosen had passed rigorous muster. While mental preparedness was as important as physical fitness, one went with the other. Overall he was pleased with the results.

This was as bright, as tough and as determined a group, as he'd even seen. He wished the people who had worked under him during his years as Operations Head of AMERICA had been collectively half as good as this bunch were. Maybe then the Worldwide Order, with its phoenix-like capacity to rise out of its own ashes, wouldn't have survived as long as it did.

Of course there were always exceptions. He wouldn't have picked Dmetri Diomad to be a cosmicaptain. The Greek quisling was the same age as Dolph Dulles, not even thirty. In Maxwell's opinion, even though he had been an undercover agent for AMERICA starting in his very early teens, that made him too young for such a position.

(That wasn't all of it of course. Thanks to Dem's Dim, as Maxwell sometimes still thought of him, back in '68, Max and his men managed to trace Kadmon Heliopolis, the leader of the Black Rose of Anarchy, to Trigon, his isolated Aegean island hideaway. Without Diomad's back-stabbing, therefore, Heliopolis might have escaped to Turkey or, more likely given Grecian antipathy to Turks, to the mountains of Crete, like his WWII predecessors often did barely a quarter century past.

(As it was, Kadmon – Rom's childhood friend – was a sitting duck and even AMERICA couldn't miss. Kadmon had been good to Diomad, too. The ability to betray friends wasn't the kind of qualification Maxwell would have used to pick a Cosmicaptain but, he supposed, all that was trolls under the proverbial toll bridge.)

Then there was Colonel Avatar Sol, the primary flight commander. A more obvious alias would be hard to find. Maxwell even thought he knew who he really was: Chthlonius *'Tiger'* Tiecher given some moderately hefty plastic surgery. The half-Jewish, Israeli-trained born-Cypriot had worked with AMERICA against the Worldwide Order throughout the first half of the Sixties.

The major trouble with Max's notion in this regard, besides the fact that Lon Tiecher would be almost forty whereas Sol was thirty-three, was that he was dead: killed on Trigon at the same time as Heliopolis and the other so-called Spartae. That his intelligence sources in California indicated there was a System Seer codenamed Solar only made him more distrustful of Sol's credentials.

The bombers that were supposed to soften up Trigon before AMERICA sent in ground troops hit something on one of the island's three spiralling peaks. The resultant eruption literally blew the comparably tiny isle out of existence. It just wasn't there anymore. According to experts in such matters, Trigon's explosion should have rivalled that of Santorini, a much larger neighbouring island that, some fifteen hundred years before Christ, had blown its core, its heart, into the sky.

That volcanic cataclysm had wiped out the entire Minoan civilization. Even if had just sunk, which islands occasionally did, it should have caused a devastating whirlpool. That it simply vanished was unprecedented. Nevertheless, whatever happened to Trigon, not even Ti Tiecher could have survived.

So, who was Avatar Sol? *'Why, Avatar Sol, of course,'* said Alfredo Sentalli, *'And I want him to lead this mission.'*

That he'd only shown up on Centauri Island in 1978, that he'd replaced Mik Starrus (Maxwell's choice for commander), that he had no credentials for the task, not even birth records nor any kind of documented military background, any kind of background whatsoever, made no difference. He was the best man for the job, no question of it, insisted Sentalli. Max realized this Sol was another of the Untouchables and, as such, there was no point arguing. The Fatman had made up his mind.

Then there was Mikelangelo Starrus. Born in '43, he was an American citizen despite his Romanesque-sounding name. He'd taken his demotion from overall mission commander to captain of Cosmicar Two in stride. Cosmicars would be on the front line when it came to exploring other planets and Mik enjoyed being in the middle of things.

As a young man, already a Vietnam veteran, he'd led the squad of bombers that hit Trigon. It was one of his bombs that, according to subsequent reports, struck the top of Mt Telepassa, the island's highest spire, thereby triggering the disappearance. Understandably he had been quite shaken by the episode; talked as if it was somehow his fault for years afterwards.

It was only when he described the event to Romaine Kinesis, in Maxwell's presence, that what must have been the truth was revealed. The bomb had hit an outcropping of Gypsium, probably the original one that Rom, Heliopolis and five year old Aristotle Zeross discovered in 1948.

'Whomsoever touches Gypsium,' Rom recited in Max's mind.

'Yeah, I know,' he finished, equally to himself, *'Touches both the unknown and the unknowable.'*

The other four cosmicaptains all met with Maxwell's approval. Even though three of them were women and he was an admitted dinosaur when it came to placing women in life-threatening situations, Nehrini Purandar, Alexandra Gagarin and Elizabeth Dre'Ath – an East Indian, a Russian and a Brit – had impeccable credentials. All had a PhD, in different though equally difficult and demanding fields, and all had been in their respective country's space programs.

Maxwell was particularly proud of *'Lilabet'*, the daughter of his war-time compadre Nathan Dre'Ath – the nephew of Max's adoptive mother, Bunnie nee O'Ryan Galvin. It wasn't just that Lilabet was virtually family; she'd worked damn hard and deserved her place amongst the elite of the Cosmic Express. So did the last one, Sango Belzem, a Portuguese who'd earned his doctorate studying under Rom Kinesis.

All in all, a fine group. He told them as much as he shook their hands a last time.

========

As Sol and his cosmicaptains entered the elevators that would take them to the Cosmic Express, aboard the phony fish packer miles off the coast of Centauri Island, leaders of a revitalized WORLD readied themselves for their own launch. Nervous anticipation was the common state of affairs in both places but calm professionalism was equally the order of the day.

For an anxious hour the countdown continued.

========

"Thirteen minutes," intoned Hiyati Samarand.

Maxwell heard him and through Maxwell – through Major Mind's Mind Tap – those on the packer heard him as well. Only the improbable but irrefutable phantasm known as Daemonicus was smiling. He smiled all the broader when Samarand announced: "Twelve".

"Abort!" screamed Maxwell. "Abort! Goddamn you to Hell, Samarand! Stop the countdown!"

"Too late. Let him fry." This from Samarand.

"No!" This from Maxwell.

Suddenly, as if he had his own private Mind Tap, Daemonicus burst into a rage: ***"What madness is this? What's going on? No, don't panic! Follow Yati! Keep counting till he, and he alone, aborts!"***

========

"It's fucking Kinesis," yelled Dulles, ripping the long gun off his back. Max cuffed his adoptive father's illegitimate son to the floor then pulled off his own multi-purpose rifle.

"Up there. In the roof struts," spotted George Hannibal.

"Forget him, Maxwell," demanded Samarand.

"With what he can do, you forget it, Fu Manchu. Abort, I'm telling you. Do it! Gypsium works for Rom, not us. Stop the countdown, I say. And you, Yataghan, get your old man out of here. Now!"

"Wait!" ordered Sentalli. "He jumped."

========

Two hours earlier the ceiling above the launch pad had been opened.

========

It was a fine day, couldn't ask for a better one. Everyone on the island hunkered down in front of their television sets to begin the long wait until ignition.

There was a scuffle in one of the living quarters at the windward resort. No one had reported it because no one could move after it was over.

Romaine Kinesis, groggy from the drugs they been dosing him with, but no less determined to stop the launch, had immobilized his guards with residual Gypsium that permeated his body from years of exposure. He didn't have enough left to fly, or whatever he did in technical terms, so he commandeered a jeep and careened across the island to the now open roof above the launch site.

Clambering down one of the safety ladders unnoticed he made it into its reinforced concrete innards without incident. The same, almost predestined luck got him as far as his own laboratory, where he easily overrode the security codes meant to keep unauthorized personnel out. Wasn't difficult. He supervised the techs who wrote it so, even if he was now one of those denied approval, he had no problem remedying such a sorry situation.

His extra canisters, hoses, and hand prongs were there, as were his sky sled and Gypsium Irradiation Chamber. (Twelve years earlier, his lifelong friend and closest collaborator, Alastor Molorchus, had been disintegrated inside this last. Correction, not entirely disintegrated — his left arm had survived. And that was all that'd been buried in his grave in the cemetery at the foot of Mt Kinesis.)

No time for the Chamber. It'd take too long to prime, though he started it up just in case. The canister, hoses and prongs would have to do. Strapping them on, he burst out of his lab, whereupon his good fortune finally ran out. No matter. He quickly disabled, non-lethally, the two overly curious passersby.

One, a big Hawaiian didn't go down quite as cleanly as he should have. What was his name? Marsh? Something like that. Somehow he managed to reach a button on his belt before immobility set in. Alarms began ringing. He was for it now. Probably couldn't have blown up the island anymore anyhow. Max would have seen to that.

He'd have to stop the Express himself.

========

As soon as Samarand noted thirteen minutes to lift off, alarms began to sound. Steadfastly he ignored them and went to his computer console to find out what was going wrong. With twelve minutes to go, he realized the alarms had started in the proximity of the professor's lab. Maxwell ordered the mission aborted.

Compliance instantly proved unforthcoming.

========

"The fuck he did, Fatman. He's goddamned flying. Get back."

Max blew out the superheat-resistant glass with a blast from the mini-bazooka atop his readymade rifle. Lights went from flashing to stroboscopic, alarms from blaring to screeching. Computer voices began bleating an incessant message: *"Evacuate. All personnel, evacuate."*

"Eleven minutes to lift off," intoned Samarand, either supernally calm or reflexively lapsed into the state of an automaton.

"You'll have to kill him, Maxwell," he shouted, not quite so calmly.

"I'm working on it, for Christ's sake. Junior, get going. You others, fucking vanish!" Yataghan rolled Sentalli out of the control room. The rest of the technicians scrambled after them. Two of the security guards gathered up Adolph Dulles and dragged him along. Only Samarand, Hannibal, and Lindquist stood their ground.

"Have it your own way, fat heads." Max cracked out the rest of the safety glass, propped a leg on the ledge, and took aim.

Kinesis flitted around the Express, directing particles of motive-accelerating Gypsium at the glass shields surrounding the far perimeter of the launch pad.

Maxwell fired.

========

"*Bastard missed!*" *gasped Dis L'Orca.*

"*Maxwell doesn't miss.*"

"*He's old. Past it. They're going to have to abort now.*"

"*Ten minutes,*" *droned Samarand, nervelessly.*

"*His kind are never past it, Salvatore. Not if I'm right about him. No, he's deliberately missing, stalling for time, hoping Yati cancels. But he won't. Carry on!*"

========

"Use heavy ammo, you idiot," demanded Hannibal.

"And risk damaging the Express? Grab a brain, lawyer, and get out of here. Take Doc and Fu Manchu with you."

"Abort, Yati," implored Lindquist in a voice that didn't sound her own. "This isn't working out. Kinesis could be a Mithradite."

"You think Great Byron wouldn't have sensed it, APM? No, there's another way." Samarand bent over his computer console. "Take him out, both of you. Take them both out."

Maxwell whipped around. Too late. Something blew him out the window. The tarmac lay twenty storeys below.

========

Romaine Kinesis turned his attention to the control room just as Maxwell hurtled out of the already-shattered window. Two creatures – couldn't call them human – ran up to the ledge. They sent something at him but he was already on his way to rescue his friend. He caught Maxwell in a tractor beam of Gypsium particles and brought both of them softly to the tarmac floor.

"Ten," Samarand pronounced.

"Again?" groaned Maxwell.

"Ten seconds. Hiyati's accelerated ..."

========

"*Launch Kamikaze ... NOW!*"

========

"...THE COUNTDOWN!"

"NINE-EIGHT-SEVEN-SIX-FIVE-FOUR-THREE-TWO-ONE-ZERO! WE HAVE IGNITION! WE HAVE LIFT OFF! WE'RE ON OUR WAY!"

So was Kamikaze Kaligula!

========

Kaligula was under no illusions about her role. She was kamikaze but the 'divine wind' she rode was not that of death, but rebirth.

Daemonicus had told her to think of her mission in terms of a jailbreak. She took him as meaning 'breaking the shackles of these mortal coils'.

That was hardly what he meant at all.

========

Inside the control capsule, Commander Avatar Sol writhed under the stress of take off. It was ditto on the distress factor for cosmicaptains Mik Starrus, Dmetri Diomad, and the sixty odd others aboard the Express. On Centauri Island, though, there was only jubilation.

With the primary containment area around the perimeter of the launch site decimated because Rom Kinesis had blown out most of the protective glass, personnel had fled to secondary control rooms. It was a two minute dash but Yataghan, pushing his father, made it just in time.

"We did it. She's off."

Elation!

"Sir, we've picked up a blip on our radar. It's on an intercept course with the Express. They're going to collide!"

They did.

Dejection!

========

Kinesis used Gypsium to shield both himself and Maxwell from the exhaust of the Cosmic Express launching.

========

The heat was incredible.

Max mercifully passed out from lack of air but Kinesis, suffused as he was after years of experimentation with Gypsium, was barely affected. He left his still breathing friend on the tarmac and, apparently out of nowhere, summoned his sky sled – a flying, wheel-less chariot that needed no Pegasus, nor any angels, to draw it. Gypsium did all the work and Kinesis was intimate with that miraculous substance.

He knew he couldn't catch the Express – even Gypsium wasn't that miraculous – but he wanted to get airborne just in case something happened that he could do anything about. He breached the artificial caldera of Centauri Island in time to witness the aftermath inversion of air that resulted from the collision between the Express and whatever it was that hit it. Then Gypsium took over and, as if with a mind of its own – which Kinesis was convinced it had – whisked him north-eastward over the Pacific.

That was the thing about Gypsium. It wasn't a propellant as such. It wasn't a fuel. It was a teleportive agent.

========

Colonel Sol had seen many a strange sight in his time. A few even matched this.

========

Somehow the entire Cosmic Express was still intact. Whatever hit it managed to inject the Express into some sort of dark, grey space. Sol felt a sense of deep joy, almost of accomplishment. Dozens of pinpoints of light were approaching the vessel. Were they stars, faeries, angels?

Devils!

The smaller ones kept coming. The largest, the brightest of all, resolved itself. To Sol's fractured mind, it was at least ten times the size of the Express. And what it was – what it appeared to be – was a single, impossibly huge and disembodied eye. Its pupil had lips and teeth and a tongue. A mouth. And it spoke!

"YOU PIG-WHUMPING, MECHANICAL LOLLIPOP, LOOK WHAT YOU'VE DONE! NOT ONLY HAVE YOU RIPPED MY HOLY HALO AND PIERCED THE FORBIDDEN ZONE, YOU'VE FREED SOME OF MY JACKASS OFFSPRING AS WELL!"

In the cosmic control capsule, Avatar Sol could think of only one thing. "Fire second stage. Let's get out of here."

"Second stage fired, sir!"

"AND AFTER ALL THAT, YOU'RE TRYING TO GET AWAY. WELL, PUKE ON YOU. A LITTLE GOD-SUCK WILL TEACH YOU SOME MANNERS!"

Pursing its lips, the eye-thing slurped the entire Express into its mass and began to chew it. To Sol whimsically – his long gone, only barely remembered, father was prone to whimsical flights of fancy as well – it was akin to what clothes must experience inside a washing machine. He felt for all the still-living oysters he'd chomped on as a child.

RRRUURP!

"BLOODY HELL! YOU OUTER EARTH-LINGS TASTE AS LOUSY AS YOU DID SIX THOUSAND YEARS AGO!"

The eye-mouth spat them not just out of its craw but out of wherever they were in the first place.

"YUK!"

========

Either a sixth sense he never knew he had or, more likely, Gypsium warned Romaine Kinesis to duck as Cosmicar Four came out of nowhere.

Then something even more remarkable came out of the air itself.

========

Kinesis almost fell off his sky sled.

He'd never beheld such a being before. Its upper body and head were blue. Its lower body was obscured by a whirlwind holding him aloft. It seemed humanoid and male. Except, it had a third eye just above where its eyebrows would have met had he had them. As remarkable as anything else was a knot of hair jetting out of the top of his otherwise shaven head. It glowed not unlike Gypsium.

Mustering a bravado he didn't know he had, Kinesis challenged the being. "Stay your own hand or regret it!"

"No, human. You're the one who'll rue the day you crossed paths with the Whirling Deva."

"I defy you!"

"Then let that be your name: Defiance! And thank whatever devic gods or goddesses you hold dear that it's beneath the dignity of Shining Ones such as myself to take the lives of potential worshippers; mere mortals that you are. Should I fail, pray my decathonitized brethren still have the same compunctions."

"Don't know who you are or what you're talking about, three-eyes. Haven't the time to find out right now either. But I like Doc Defiance."

========

Kinesis pointed his right-hand prong at the whirling, blue-skinned creature. Fired it full of motive-accelerating Gypsium particles.

He wanted to get whatever it was out of sight, out of mind. Worked as well. Momentarily!

****

NUKE 4: **Their Stories … Plus**

Sunday, November 30, 1980

On Centauri Island, jubilation became deflation the moment an unidentified craft collided with the Cosmic Express. For a few long minutes, the silence of failure reigned.

Then despair gave way to renewed optimism.

========

"Sir," said a technician, "We've picked up traces of two Cosmicars and the Control Capsule. One car's reading Aleutian islands. The others are out by the Moon."

"The Moon!" Alfredo Sentalli grasped at the straws of hope as he would the last meatball or a final strand of linguini. "That's where the Liberty would be. Samarand, get me Houston. I want to speak with Loxus Ryne personally." The Fatman barely paused to catch his breath before shoving a pudgy finger at the nearest technician.

"You!" he ordered the suddenly terrified underling. "Get me a fix on where in the Aleutians the other one's gone. Yataghan, set up a troop-carrier, one of the big ones. Find Demios Sarpedon and get him aboard. About time he started earning his retainer. Hannibal, Lindquist, you'll go with them."

The lawyer and the doctor exchanged glances. Hiyati Samarand spoke for them both. "I don't think that would be wise."

"Then it isn't. Dulles, over to you. Take as many men as you want. Just make sure Sarpedon is amongst them."

"Sir," said Samarand's tech. "We've just received a report from Houston. Loxus Ryne isn't available to talk to you."

"Why not?"

"Because he's on his way here!"

========

By Christ and be gone the three-eyed bogeyman!

Newly-christened Doc Defiance blipped further and farther north and eastward. Soon he was in the chill of the truly northern North Pacific. The Godstuff he named Gypsium had brought him hither. Its affinity for the same miraculous substance on the cosmicar must have attracted it.

Attracted him – it – whatever he-it was, too!

========

"Shouldn't have sent me away, mortal." Once again, the self-pronounced Shining One formed out of the air itself. "We'd only just met."

Quelling the urge to strike anew, Defiance forced himself to look at it close-ly. Quite honestly he had never seen the like – unless, and this just occurred to him, it was related to the things he'd seen in the blown-out control room window while he raced to save Maxwell's life back on the island.

"What are you?"

"Doom, damnation, salvation! I am Devil Wind. Millennia past your erro-neously named Olmec, Carib, Mayan and suchlike external Iraches knew me as Hurican, as in hurricane. Antique Illuminaries, the very ones who once, so very long ago by your short-lived reckoning, roamed your lands seeking us out, called me Vayu Maelstrom. You may do so as well if you please.

"I am as I said, one of not just their Shining Ones; more, much more, I am one of Thrygragos Byron's Primary Nucleoids. This is my mission, Brainrock-Man, not yours. Even though your abilities are formidable for one of your lowly kind, I sense you are new to them; that they, not you, are in control. Go home. Whatever has to be taken care of below, I shall deal with it. You're hindrance, not help."

"Says you!"

Defiance directed a blast of motive-reversing Gypsium particles at the wholly unnatural being's whirlwind. Maelstrom suddenly found himself un-supported. The devil plummeted into the sea. Upon his Gypsium-powered sky sled, Kinesis slid downwards after him. Doing so, he noted with some interest that, without his whirlwind, the bluish, humanoid creature had legs and was wearing some sort of fur loincloth.

"Well, that takes care of that. Whatever that was!"

The ocean funnelled upwards. Rom was caught in its vortex. The sky-sled ripped into a thousand shards. His canister, hoses and prongs fragmented, dous-ing him with their contents. Then, with as much suddenness as it had come, the water-spout dissipated. He had just enough time to wonder how he could fly without his sky sled; not enough time to wonder how he could instantly learn how to swim.

Maelstrom broiled out of the sea, caught Defiance in a lifesaving whirlwind and held him in the air.

"Inconsequential upstart!" he bellowed, as a mightily miffed whirling devil prone to grandiosity might. Seeing the distress – no, sheer terror – etched on Defiance's face, he calmed down considerably, became almost conciliatory: "I sense there's enough Brainrock residing within you to get yourself back to wher-ever you came from. Go there and be grateful I chose not to let you fall.

"Once I have dealt with the menace below, I may search you out for a quiet chat. I believe we've much to learn from each other."

========

Maelstrom catapulted Doc Defiance southward and west. Gypsium did the rest. It propelled him – in blips and blinks, fits and starts, leaps and bounds, now you see him, now you don't, through grey spaces he'd never experienced before – all the way back to Centauri Island. There he splash-landed just short of the beach.

He still hadn't learned to swim.

=========

Someone waded out to him. A strong arm hauled him onto his feet then helped walk him out of the foam, whereupon he released him to collapse in the sand.

"Always go swimming in your clothes, pro?"

"Max, you're alive!"

"Sure I am," he said, reaching out a hand. Kinesis took it and Maxwell yanked him back up. "You saved me. Wouldn't do to just let you croak after all your effort. Come on, my jeep's over there." Unsteadily Kinesis allowed his much older friend prop him for the first few steps before he felt able to totter onwards alone.

"So, where the hell have you been, Rom? Parts of the Express made it to space. The Fatman wants you to figure out how to get them back."

"I'd rather concentrate on getting back my sanity."

"How so?"

"I'll tell you about it."

=========

OJ Maxwell was pretty sure it was more than just Romaine Kinesis that saved his life. He figured Gypsium had most to do with it. One minute he was hurtling to the tarmac just as the Cosmic Express was igniting. Rom was rocketing towards him – there wasn't any other way to shorthand it. Next time he was aware the Express was gone and he was lying on the self same tarmac unharmed. Not even his clothes were singed.

Quite likely the miraculous substance had sent him elsewhere; must have, really. Not just conceivably it was into another dimension somehow contiguous to this one – what old-time witches called between-space, to where they also set up their personal Shelters (capitalized, though not with a *'Big'* in front of it).

It only brought him back once it was safe; the immediate area cool enough to walk on. That would make the Godstuff minutely conscious. Beneficent, too: just like God was supposed to be. He shuddered at the thought. Despite the efforts of sainted Sophia D'Angelo, foster mom Bunnie's best or at least most enduring friend, God and he were hardly on speaking terms.

Staggering almost as badly as Kinesis just had out of the water and over to his land rover, Max made his way up to the now ruined control room that he'd dropped out of so suddenly, so inexplicably, mere minutes earlier. Thanks to the exhaust from the Express, it looked as scorched as the inside of a concrete incinerator.

He found Alfredo Sentalli and the rest of the launch team, including Samarand, Hannibal and Lindquist, deep within the protected interior of the subterranean edifice. (As likeable, even pretty, as she was, he should never have trusted Connie to live and work on the island, not with a father like the treacherous Little Prince.) The last three barely managed to stifle their surprise at seeing him not only in one piece but seemingly completely unaffected by what should have been a fatal ordeal.

For his part, he couldn't help remarking to himself – and, until he told his side of the story to Professor Kinesis, no one else – that the last three had changed their clothes. Presumably that meant their clothing had been more than just singed. It had been burnt off. Their skin should have been, too. Yet they looked as unharmed as he was.

He didn't bother querying Samarand and the other two on that, though he fully intended to do so in the very near future – with about two dozen of his security officers beside him, lethal weapons in hand and pointing at the no doubt truculent trio. Not that he reckoned it would make much difference.

Because their clothing hadn't survived like his had, he also reckoned Gypsium hadn't saved them; that they were aptly named Sentalli's Untouchables. Indeed, except for one thing, their state of continued existence was vaguely reminiscent of something his quarter century dead friend, Yehudi Cohen, might pull off.

Cohen was a Summoning Child the same as Rom's mother Roxanne and so many others, including (maybe) Max himself and four of his fellow King Crimefighters (Blind Sundown, Dervish Furie and the Elemental Twins, Aires and Thalassa raised D'Angelo). Remarkably, given who his father was and how he was brought up, he eventually became an honorary – as in very unofficial – founder of the Jewish nation.

Subsequently, though never a blinkered Zionist, far from it, the indisputable Israeli patriot attained worldwide celebrity status as an archaeologist who specialized in Biblical digs. As he himself put it, in one of those moments of whimsy to which he was prone, it was a far, far better thing to specialize in than digging graves.

(Unlike Günter – Prince Peashooter, not Prince Translav, Connie Lindquist's mendacious midget of a father – the old Baron, Tyrtod von Alptraum, never got around to acknowledging Yehudi as even his bastard. Mostly that was because Cohen's mother was not only a Jewess. She was the widow of a Rabbi; a very influential member of Charan Ryne's Godling Guild, in fact.

(Somewhat to his credit, von Alp the Elder did pay for his illegitimate son's upbringing, mostly in private, extremely expensive, boarding schools. Nevertheless, two decades' prior to somehow transforming into the first, and likely only, Steltsar, he simply didn't have the courage to declare a no matter how German Jew his son in any way, shape or form.

(Some of that was down to his unforgiving mother-in-law Hulga Faust's both traditionalist and populist proclivities. Most of it, though, was due to the times. Particularly after the forced humiliation of an unconditional surrender to end the First World War, even a proud Prussian nobleman, one who was also a forward-thinking industrialist of considerable means, wasn't immune to irrational prejudice.)

That one thing? A long time supranormal whose ever-so-appropriate codename was the Untouchable Diver (UD = Yehudi) or, more commonly, the Diver, his clothes wouldn't have been burnt away. Cohen would have made them just as untouchable as he made himself. Which begged a rather fundamental question, two of them actually.

What else were Hannibal, Lindquist and Samarand? And what about the rest of Sentalli's Untouchables?

========

By mutual agreement, Max and the professor put off returning to command central. As head of security, the former had a number of private offices both in the various communities and work places on the surface, as well as in the sub-surface areas where the Cosmic Express was built and eventually launched in the strictest secrecy.

In his land rover he took Kinesis to probably his most obscure hideaway, his own apartment. Which he used almost exclusively for sleeping, assuming he was in the neighbourhood when the need hit him. While Rom showered, Max cooked them both omelettes and some dubious-looking sausages. (He really must make better use of the freezer.)

Finally he brewed up some of his patented, bulletproof coffee. It may not be capable of stripping paint off a wall but, as Max himself sometimes boasted, it was so strong it could have beat the pooh out of Samson, pre Delilah giving him that buzz-cut. Heartily wolfing everything down despite the potential danger to continued good health, they compared notes.

"You're sure Lindquist called Samarand *'Yati'* and said I might be a *'Mithradite'*, whatever that is?"

"Well, whatever it is, Rom, Samarand scoffed at the notion. Said someone called Great Byron would have sensed it and called Connie *'APM'*."

"The creature I told you about, the blue-skinned supra with the third eye and a whirlwind for a lower body, also said something about a Byron: Thry … something-or-other … Byron. Probably the same one. Also said he was Devil Wind, the Whirling Deva. That strike a bell with you; the word *'Deva'*, I mean?"

"Never was much of a wordsmith, I'm afraid, but the third eye shit's familiar from a long time ago: my ancient history, if you will, not to mention that of your parents and many others. During the war, Sedon St Synne, though he called himself Satan in those days, created supranormals by bombarding until then apparently normal folks with beams from what he named the devil- or devaray. Deva, devil, not much difference between them.

"A few years later, between '46 and '49, the faceless Ant bogeywoman we knew as Strife, but always assumed was St Synne's daughter, granddaughter, daughter-granddaughter, or some permutation thereof, used what she called her *'Miracle Key'* to create similar supranormals. When her supras used their powers they often manifested a third eye. Figure there's a connection?"

"Has to be," said Kinesis.

Although deliberately kept ignorant of the true fate of his parents, his cousin Europa Heliopolis, and the identities of two or possibly three former Strifes, all of whom were still alive, Kinesis knew something of the so-called Supra Wars. He knew, for example, that it raged – though that wasn't the exact word for the almost invariably clandestine encounters between supras – from roughly '38 to '55. (Which was when the Diver and the rest of King Crimefighters were killed in the Aleutians.)

"Even you're too young to remember the Godling Guild," Professor Kinesis carried on professorially. "But your adoptive parents, young as they were at the time, and both sets of my grandparents were members of it. So was St Synne and Charan Ryne, Loxus Ryne's father. The Great Man's mother Athena was, too, but you'd know all that. You'd also know Athena Ryne and I are distantly related."

(As a direct consequence of the Summoning of 1920, all four of his grandparents had died sixteen years before he was born. However, his Heliopolis grandmother survived long enough to give birth to his mother Roxanne – whom Max would remember, in all likelihood very fondly.

(Hot Rox wasn't called that because of her love for saunas. It was for what she did in them, and damn near anywhere else, when the mood struck her.)

"The Godlings had this thing about how the old gods and goddesses, all the multifarious pantheons of mythology, actually existed. I was brought up by the Zerosses, Angelo and Megaera, who was also my father's sister. God rest their souls – not that Angie and Meg were great believers; quite the opposite in fact.

"Anyhow, while they were far too young to be full-fledged Godlings themselves, they schooled me in ancient myths. One of their primary assertions was that the Hindu Vedas were the oldest written record of the gods. Many of them had three eyes; a lot of them had blue-skin as well."

"You think this supra, this Devil Wind you encountered, was a Hindu god?"

"Well, he also said antique Illuminaries – who, from what he also told me, sound a lot like long pre-Christian Godlings – called him Vayu Maelstrom. I have a few shelves of dusty old books in my library back at the cottage. A few of them were even illustrated by my paternal grandmother Olympias.

"She died, or disappeared, around the time my mother must have been conceived, if not born per se, but wherever she went – assuming she didn't just die in the Himalayas like Ryne's parents and the rest of my grandparents did – she described a lot of those gods the Godlings thought existed. She even drew a few; must have had a knack for it because her drawings are quite good, even if I do say so myself."

"Which you just did."

"So true. And they are good, though a few of the older ones are signed by someone named Jordan Tethys, who isn't the same as Olympias Kinesis I'll also grant you. Anyhow, in the back of my mind, I recall there was one called – I don't know – Vayu or Vaya, something like that. Recollect how I described the two creatures I saw come up to the window just before I rescued you?"

"*'Couldn't call them human'* is all you said."

"And I was moving rather rapidly but, upon reflection, I'd describe one of them as a female form composed entirely of eyes."

"Big help that."

"But the other one was Babar."

"Babar?"

"A popular kid's character. Started out in France, I believe; must have been back in the Thirties, if not before, since I remember him from when I was just a kid myself. He's a bipedal, gnomish, blue-skinned elephant."

"With three eyes, I suppose."

"Two. I told you, it's a kid's character. But the one I saw had three eyes."

"Babar's a devil?"

"A Deva, capitalized. And not Babar: Ganesh or Ganesha, the elephantine Hindu God of Wealth." He had another thought. "I wonder ... Got a dictionary?"

Max dug around in a box that had probably sat unopened since he moved in, pulled one out and handed it over. Kinesis flipped through a few pages; whistled when he found what he was looking for. Max gave him a look; Kinesis obliged.

"Sanskrit, as good as the Indo-European mother tongue. It means divine: literally *'the Shining One'*. Which is something else the creature called himself. Never thought of it before but you're right: that's probably where our word devil comes from, too." Had another thought, flipped back a few pages and nodded.

"He was right about hurricane, too. It's Spanish but it does come from the Mayan via the Carib Indians, who I think were the natives Columbus met when he landed in wherever 500-odd years ago. As I recall his diseases pretty much wiped them out. Guess they didn't do for their gods, though."

"Who wouldn't have been Hindu."

"Might have been; if everyone's gods came from the same family."

"I think we better have a look at your grandma's books."

"So do I."

========

A good distance off the coast of Centauri Island, those aboard the converted Japanese fish packer that served as the floating launch pad for Kamikaze Kaligula were quietly congratulating themselves on a job well done. In the communications room on the upper deck, Major Milo Mind was continuing to use the Mind Tap implanted in OJ Maxwell to monitor events on the island, at least from Max's visual and spoken perspective.

"What do we care about this crap, Sal?"

========

Mind glared at his nominal superior; the too-often drug-addled, only son – there'd been a daughter too, Garcia, but Salvatore never spoke of her – of his actual friend and mentor, the fifteen years' gone, but still personally missed, Hadrian Dis L'Orca. "We should be packing up this packer and getting the hell away from anywhere near here while the getting's good. Our mission's accomplished. We're rich as Rockefeller's fucking rooster and I know just the henhouse in Honolulu to start spending it."

Salvatore Dis L'Orca regarded the nearly sixty year old major disinterestedly. He was tempted to say: '*Your mission is accomplished, Milo; WORLD's is just beginning.*' It was the truth but he refrained from voicing it. Mind was integral to Daemonicus's grand scheme. They'd have accomplished nothing without him, if what they did to the Express could be considered an accomplishment. Besides, he was right: WORLD's contractual part in whatever that was had been fulfilled.

Regardless of that being the case, what they had left to do had nothing to do with St Synne, if that was who Daemonicus truly was, and Mind was too old, too bent, to be trusted with WORLD's business. The major – and he was a legitimate major – might be psychotic but he was no Saul Ryne, no supra-Psycho. He couldn't read minds. Nonetheless, there was still a chance his Mind Tap into

Maxwell's physical brain, if not its immaterial immanence as such, could come into play again.

First though, Daemonicus had to pronounce himself satisfied with their performance and sign off. Then, and only then, would he and the other three directors of the Worldwide Order determine how dispensable the major was or was not. Perhaps they'd drop him off in Honolulu; more likely, they'd just drop him off – as shark feed, at a hundred fathoms and wearing a proverbial pair of cement overshoes.

"We shall withdraw in an orderly manner, as per our contract with Daemonicus, Milo. Until he has activated the transferral of funds into our accounts and we have received official notification of that fact, we are technically still on his payroll."

"Manure to your orderly manner, Sal. Me, I'm satisfied with the down payment. You haven't felt his eyefire. I have. I say we cut our losses and stay alive."

"WORLD doesn't operate that way," Dis L'Orca lectured patiently. "Didn't when my father and – I'm assuming here – your old bosom buddy, Countess Ramona Avar as Strife, founded it; didn't when Baphomet took over; didn't when a finally properly functional Steltsar-cyborg reappeared on the scene and took over from him."

"Which explains why Baphomet vanished without a trace in '65; why Ray's been a house prisoner in Hungary for the better part of a decade; why the Seventies' Steltsar went the way of all his previous rebuild jobs; and Hadrian froze to death trying to prove his innocence by ordeal all those years ago."

"My father's spirit lives on in me, major."

"So you said when you brought us together for Operation Obliteration. Not that it was advertised as such. Don't get me wrong. You handled it brilliantly. Hadrian would have been proud of you. I knew him well and he'd agree with me. Get Sian up here and call the other two. If they want to stick with it, so be it.

"But, don't forget. I'm an independent contractor myself. I'll take one of the helicopters to Oahu. Markazi and Translav aren't in the firing line, and I'll bet Sian and even you – if you'd care to speak your real mind for once and give over with this *'Hadrian's spirit'* bullshit – would agree with me. Daemonicus be damned, let's move."

"The arms of the world," pontificated Dis L'Orca, "Number more than five or six; more than the Glomen the little prince left on this packer; more even than the usurious Mafioso dons Dr Cyanide's trying to re-ingratiate himself with for fear of his life. We're no money-grubbing Octopus Corporation by any name. We work for worldwide order; we work for the world. We have no masters save ourselves.

"We are the successors to Jesus Mandam, the Conquering Christ; albeit minus his fixation on what my father, who never believed himself one, once laughingly called supranormal *'civil rights'*. We shall not defile Mandam's memory by abandoning his dream for the betterment of all. We shall abide by our contract with Daemonicus. Contracts are as sacred as our word and Daemonicus says he's genetically bound by his.

"Our greatest profit comes in the long term. I'm even prepared to bet the rest of the directors share my feelings on this. Want to take my bet, Milo? I'll wager three-quarters of your guarantee, what you've been paid already, against three-quarters of mine. And, believe me, I've been paid a lot more than you have."

"Gambling's for saps and suckers, in that order. I stick to sure things. Money in the bank, that sort of thing — same as Hadrian did. Mandam was an impossible dreamer; from what I've heard the son of his mother more so than his father. I never met either but the Magdalene, the Great Man's twin, was accounted a religious nutter.

"Be that as it may, despite his grandiose rhetoric, when it came right down to it all he really cared about was conquest. He should have called himself the Conquering Caesar."

Dismissively, as if nothing more need be said, Milo Mind returned his attention to the view screens: To what OJ Maxwell was seeing and hearing.

========

Kinesis's compact, shake-roofed cottage, with its very Hawaiian garden gone predictably wild, wasn't far from Maxwell's apartment.

========

As a precaution, Max covered his land rover and drove them there. The streets were virtually empty but the bars seemed to be doing baby boomer business. The apparent destruction of the Cosmic Express had caused mass depression. Max's people, his equivalent of MPs, would probably have their hands full tonight and over the succeeding weeks.

There'd have to be a major league inquiry about the disaster. The question of sabotage would come up, as would the stability of the Gypsium stored in the cosmicars, the central stem and command bud. Rom would be on the hot seat for his efforts to prevent the launch and Max himself for his failure to stop both Kinesis and whatever it was that hit the Express. No doubt Hiyati Samarand would be out for blood and Sentalli might be in no mood to discourage him.

However, he had a few bones to pick with Dr Samarand, not to mention George Hannibal and Connie Lindquist. Not human, Kinesis had described the two he saw at the window – the two who'd tried to kill him – an elephant man and a woman composed entirely of eyes. Sad to say neither was that farfetched.

Not human to his mind meant supras, like the somehow de-neutralized ones who'd tried to take over the island fifteen years ago. Lindquist's mother was Soanso, a face-dancing master illusionist. She could have pulled off All-Eyes; maybe her daughter could, too. (Notwithstanding Sentalli's admonitions, he'd looked into her background extensively and there was no evidence she inherited anything out of the ordinary from either of her parents. Still…)

An elephant man might be a sphinx, though both Seth Kephren and his son, Horatio, were, as Abe Ryne might put it, history. Nonetheless, a remarkably resilient confection of those involved back in '65 were still around: Corona Power, though that had never been proven; Crystal St Synne, Corona's daughter, albeit obviously not by her husband, Obadiah Melvin Power (the King Crimefighters' OMP – Old Man Power); Günter von Alptraum (the Diver's consequential half-brother); his mute, overgrown but childlike manservant, Herr Kopf; and Demios Sarpedon, who was actually on the island right now.

Although Demios refused to talk about them, likely his wife Morgianna, the early to mid 1950s Mother Superior of the Antediluvian Sisterhood of Flowery Anthea, and, possibly, the trickster, Superior Sarpedon's little mother, weren't far away. Von Alp, Kopf and Corona were: his well-paid connections in the Ukraine, for the first two, and Japan, for OMP's ex, accounted for them on a weekly basis.

Very much unfortunately, the same couldn't be said of Crystal, whose acknowledged father was the old satyr, Sedon St Synne; hence her surname. Years earlier, '65's certain Strife had simply dropped out of sight. That held for more than a few of Max's other *'usual suspects'*: Milo Mind, Salvatore Dis L'Orca, Alorstro Sian, Shaikh Ali Ars Markazi, and Lindquist's father Greygreave Translav, to name five former higher-ups in WORLD. Out of sight, though, did not mean out of mind. Not to him it didn't.

Additionally the Steltsar cyborg – or, rather, yet another *rebuilt* version of the old Baron, Tyrtod von Alptraum – might be back in action. One good thing was that the big two definitely left over from the war and immediately thereafter, Sedon St Synne and Ramona Avar Ryne, couldn't be involved. He made sure he had daily reports on them.

(In her favour – and in support of the Sisterhood's notion of Strife as a malevolent possessive spirit – Ray was arguably only bordering on for sure Strife in 1960. She was, however, without doubt Strife in 1970, because that was the year he blew off Strife's hand and guess who was thereafter handless? Ray, though, wasn't to blame for the brutalities of 1965. She was still in a Houston insane asylum under watch 24/7.)

No, when it came down to it, Max was inclined to blame Sentalli's Untouchables for what went wrong with the Express. The Fatman wouldn't let either he nor his predecessor, Doubleman Sean Smythe, properly vet any of them, hence their assignation. Of course that didn't mean that both he and Smythe hadn't done so anyhow; just that they kept the results, which were zilch, to themselves. To do otherwise would cost them their jobs and, unlike Smythe, Max had signed on for the duration.

(Possibly fortuitously, Sean Smythe was now on the Liberty in moon-orbit. The other Doubleman, Johann Schmidt, yet another close confederate of Big Max from his days with AMERICA and the Supra Wars before that, wasn't but, knowing him, he was likely employed in some capacity by Ryne's Space Council.)

That one of them, Colonel Avatar Sol, the only Untouchable who made it onto the Express, had apparently died in its destruction didn't mean the rest of them were innocent. All the more since, as now seemed irrefutable, Samarand, Hannibal and Lindquist tried to kill Rom and him. Guilt by association might not be politically correct but Max had been more concerned with correct results than how he attained them.

It also wasn't lost on him that, even though Samarand's first name was Hiyati, Yati could equally refer to Yataghan, Sentalli's oddball son by Emeralda

Plantagenet and yet another Untouchable. (The Fatman never did tell him where, let alone how, Emeralda died; only that she had. Her grave, at the foot of Mt Kinesis, might even be empty for all he knew.)

There may well be devils – properly spelt and capitalized as Devas, Max now apprehended – on the island. Samarand might indeed be one of them. He doubted it, though. He didn't think the Untouchables were members of a distinct race, let alone divine Shining Ones: the gods and goddesses of not just ancient civilizations. On the contrary, he was almost one hundred percent convinced they were devil-ray victims.

That should point to Sedon – once Satan – St Synne or Faceless Strife. Except it didn't. It couldn't. They were sorted.

Clearly someone else wasn't. But who?

========

Lots of thoughts occupied his brain as he drove Kinesis to his cottage. So many thoughts, he almost forgot about the rest of the Untouchables.

Then he spotted the apparent East Indian sitting in an electronic vehicle outside of Rom's building.

========

Kinesis, too, was lost in reverie.

Much of his life was marked by tragedy. His formative years, at least what he could recall of them, were spent in terror. It was wartime and his free-dom-fighting parents, members of the original Black Rose (as led by Agenor Heliopolis, Kadmon's father), were gone for months at a time.

They left him to be raised by Auntie Meg and her husband, the renowned, assuredly anarchist philosopher Angelo Zeross, mostly on Trigon, which the Zerosses owned. The tiny Aegean islet was also home to a number of war or-phans including Mother Roxanne's nephew and niece: Kadmon and his half-sis-ter, Europa Heliopolis.

Another of the war orphans was Thaddeus Hyperenor, a future member of the Trigon Spartae and the son of Angelo's other sister, Artemis. She and her husband, Thaddeus's father Nester, were killed on the other side of the world, on Sakhalin Island, in February 1945. In the same place, at the same time, Agenor's second wife, Europa's mother, Mnemosyne D'Angelo, was also killed.

Three other future members of the Spartae – Capnan Udaeus, Rathegar Pelorus and Echion Sangati – were also brought up on Trigon, as was the man who became his best friend, Alastor Molorchus. For a period of time, David Ryne, Loxus Ryne's son by Eden Nightingale, recuperated there. (He'd been shot in the head, by the Silver Arrow assassin known as Sagitta, in 1939. As he only found out himself, much later on, Sagitta turned out to be none other than Artemis nee Zeross Hyperenor.)

All of them – the younger Ryne and twin brother Saul, Molorchus, the Heliopolises, the Spartae, his parents Alexandros and Roxanne, the Zerosses and their three children – were dead now. With the major exception of Headmistress Virginia Mannering, virtually everyone he ever cared about was gone.

In some respects, 1948 was the best year of his life. He was twelve, Kad was eight, and Aristotle, the Zerosses' middle child, was five. They were inseparable, mostly because Harry wouldn't leave the older two alone. One day, in the Spring of that year, they climbed one of Trigon's three peaks, Mt Telepassa.

There they found a glowing boulder that either they'd never noticed or it hadn't been there before. It looked like a large, pulsating brain. Little Harry touched it and was immediately transported to Mt Cadmus, one of the island's other peaks. Kadmon followed suit and was taken to the third peak, Mt Harmonia. He touched the rock and wished them back to his side. They came as well.

Naming the miraculous substance Gypsium in honour of Rom's wandering gypsy heritage, the three of them vowed to make it their life's work.

Clambering down the peak, they couldn't wait until they told everyone then on Trigon about their discovery. Naturally some of the others, including his parents, wanted to try it out. He distinctly remembered his father, who didn't drink much in those post-war days, being the first up the peak. The rock was still there but Alex couldn't get it to function. Neither could anyone else. Even the three kids failed.

The Zerosses were born wealthy; nowhere near as wealthy as the Rynes but only War's privations could, and did, interrupt their enjoyment of it. (Those who said it was easy to be an anarchist when you were so well off, had obviously not read anything Uncle Angie wrote.) Later on that same year, 1948, Angelo and Megaera decided they should have a party to celebrate midsummer.

Yachts and float planes began arriving and, by the solstice, Trigon was brimming with mostly British, French, Canadian and American visitors. Things got a little out of hand. Rom got hammered, but alcohol wasn't the only intoxicant available. Nor the one most used.

Some of Roxanne's young female friends – Rox was only twenty-eight herself, having had him when she was barely sixteen – went feral, untamed as well as very much un-timid. Demonites, the eldest Zeross at eighteen, and his young bucks joined in wholeheartedly. People started dressing up, then dressing down. It was nymphs and satyrs all over again. There was even a Pan, an Africa-born, Jamaica-raised black man whose real name was Jervis Murray.

One thing led to another.

Caught up in a Dionysian frenzy, Rom lost his virginity, some said his virility, to Alastor Molorchus, who was cross-dressed as the Corn Goddess and even more out of it than he was. They were found the next morning sleeping together in the woods. Alex was disgusted; Hot Rox only slightly less so. (She demanded open-minded tolerance from everyone else of her free-loving ways, but did not apply it to herself when it came to her, as she put it, *'Nancy Boy'* son.)

Both Rom and Molorchus were traumatized by their reaction. No one had ever told them homosexuality was wrong. Among the over-forty crowd, the distinct minority, a great many discussions were held. Finally one of them, a woman named Dolores Rivera, the sister of the by then late Mnemosyne nee D'Angelo Heliopolis (Europa's mother), called Roxanne and some of her more spirited gal-pals into the main house.

Seven year old Europa overheard Dolores shrieking at them. She dutifully reported to Rom, whom she had a crush on, that the Sisters were going to fix him. This traumatized him even further. (Impressionable as he was, fixing meant gelding, as in rendering him a eunuch, an Aladdin without a functional lamp.)

From that day to this he quite literally shrank from the attentions of women. After a rather severe beating administered by his father three years later, at the age of fifteen, he avoided any kind of sex except masturbation, which properly speaking wasn't sex at all. Even at that young age, he became, as is said, married to his work.

One thing he didn't avoid was Gypsium. And, while he didn't bathe in it, or even shower in it, especially not regularly, not so long ago it as good as spoke to him, at least subliminally. In a voice distinctly reminiscent of twelve years dead and gone Kadmon Heliopolis, it warned him, years belatedly, that Centauri Island was not the place to launch the Cosmic Express.

Wasn't that the definition of schizophrenia? Didn't only madmen hear voices? Had Sentalli been right to have him drugged. No matter. He'd heeded it; tried to stop the launch yesterday and again today — before he saw Babar and All-Eyes; before he saved Max's life; before he came across Devil Wind far to the north and accepted the appellation of Doc Defiance from him.

He now knew he wasn't mad. He now clearly understood what Max and Ginny (Headmistress Virginia Mannering) had tried to convince him of years ago, when telling about his parents, among many, many others he knew, met and/ or, in some cases, grown up with on Aegean Trigon.

(Mom was codenamed Slipper, they said. She was Gypsium-gifted, they added. Dad was codenamed Pluman. His abilities were based on Solidium, its counterforce. Max even speculated dad had turned off the Gypsium that he, Kad and Harry – the Trigon Triumvirate as they thereafter thought of themselves – first came across on Mt Telepassa, unless it was Mt Harmonia or Mt Cadmus, in 1948.)

There were such things as supranormals. And he was one of them.

========

"Hey, that's where I live," Kinesis exclaimed, as Big Max calmly drove on.

"I know it and they do too," he responded, referring to East Indian engineer staking out Rom's cottage.

========

"I thought you were the nameless *'they'*," Kinesis joked. "You and your security team. At least that's what my associates always called you."

"They also called us the Fatman's Gestapo. You and yours are the brains; we're the brains' police." A block away from the apartment building, he pulled over and shut off the engine. "The guy sitting in the golf cart's a genuine *'they'*. Name's Roderick Paraja in case you missed him. That's as in *'pariah'*, a low-caste Hindu I've also heard called Dalit and Harijan.

"He's one of Sentalli's dozen or so Untouchables. Want to know who the others are? Hint. They're the ones the Fatman vouches for. Know what that means?"

"They're the devils."

"I don't believe in these devils. Not even the one you encountered a while ago, the guy with the hodgepodge of names and blue skin. They're supras, victims of St Synne's devil-ray passed onto Simon Lancz or, more likely, Strife's Miracle Key. Strife, by the way, is my wife, Aranyani."

"Surely to God, Max, supras, Strife — they're things of the past. Forget about them."

"WORLD is not a thing of the past. Trust me on that, Rom. I've a nose for this sort of thing. Something destroyed the Cosmic Express and that something was the Worldwide Order. They're back, boyo — and with a vengeance. Only this time they might be run by the Soviets."

"The USSR's cooperating on both Project Centauri and the Space Council."

"That precludes absolutely nothing. Think about it. A lot of AMERICA's fancy gadgets came from discoveries made by Ryne's nephew, Jesus Mandam, in the Forties and early Fifties; so did the Order's stuff. The patriarch accessed the same technology to make the UNES Liberty fly and I know damn well this Shelter was its primary designer; its System Seer, as they're known. And where do you think he lived until not so very long ago."

"Should I know this answer?"

"The Soviet Supra City, that's where, if you don't."

"You're not back to hating Günter von Alptraum again, are you?"

"Prince Peashooter is the least of our problems. Count them down, Rom, your cousins and childhood buddies: Shelter and the Liberty; Sasquatch and the Amsterdam Academy; Sharpshooter and Signal System; Styx and WORLD. And Sol here, Solar in their superstitious lingo, helping out you and Samarand with the Express, probably reworking a devil-ray on the side for Sentalli at the same time.

"Catching my drift? It's all about reclaiming Jesus Mandam's high tech shit, all of it. Only now brighter lights like you have got it working properly."

"That's five," Kinesis slowly grasped. Max wasn't just talking about System Seers. He was talking about the Trigon Spartae. "There was a sixth one there in '68."

"Something's on the Moon and it ain't aliens. Ain't Ants either, though they're undoubtedly involved somehow. Nor is it these devils your grandmother drew."

"Kadmon?"

"That a question or a statement."

"With a question mark. Got an answer?"

"Not definitely. Wouldn't surprise me in the least, though. But, mark me, our immediate enemy is WORLD. That much I can say damn near for sure. WORLD means Strife and, no matter what you say, Strife's my wife. She'll have to be dealt with this time, once and for all. Her and her boyfriend, Moses Callion the Third. And like his father twenty years ago, he's probably rebuilt Steltsar."

"Will it stop Strife and Steltsar?" Rom remembered one of Max's mantras from a number of years back.

"And supras."

"Them too, unless it's three by now."

"Mind you, if these Spartae types are Moe Two's clones, as I once speculated, there might even be a new Jesus Mandam out there somewhere. And he, not

Heliopolis Junior, might even be the Man on the Moon. Right now, though, my concern's Aran's latest batch of victims: Samarand, Lindquist, Hannibal, Paraja, Yataghan, Sarpedon, and the rest of the Fatman's Untouchables.

"I'm afraid I may have to deal with Sentalli as well. Money and impetus has got to come from somewhere and NCE's my best guess where."

"You're not making sense, Max. Say Kad or even a Jesse-clone is on the Moon. Why would Shelter design the Liberty to take him out? Say Sol was who you think, the Cypriot Ti Tiecher ..." (Once, when he was in a state of despair after Molorchus's death, Max and Headmistress told him Chthlonius Tiecher, nicknamed Tiger, was the son of two supras, the Diver and Fisherwoman.)

"He is, has to be."

"Say he is then, if it'll make you happy. Answer me this instead: Why would Styx, Capnan Udaeus, set up a new Worldwide Order in order to destroy the Express and kill him in the process? And what've Cousin Thaddeus, Sharpshooter, and Rathegar-Sasquatch got to do with anything?"

(System Seers kept their true identities secret but Max, out of frustration, had previously confided that he believed the five biggies besides Strategos Simon Lancz, who might be his own son by Valfreja Lancz, were the Trigon Spartae somehow still alive and, under their Silver helmets, not noticeably aged.)

"To meet the menace on the Moon," Max speculated, "Abe Ryne charged Bruce Dre'Ath and the Academy in Amsterdam with redeveloping a relatively standard, fast-maturing variety of supranormal beings called Manimalians – think zoomorphic Egyptian gods and goddesses akin to the Kephren Sphinxes of fifteen years ago."

"Didn't you tell me Simon Lancz and this Sharpshooter brought Signal System together in order to wipe out supranormals of any kind?"

"From what I was been able to ascertain, yes, at first. But now Abe needs supras back and he's doing whatever he can to do just that."

"Bloody ridiculous!" Rom protested. "You're telling me Kadmon and the Spartae have divided into three sets of pairs and are trying to wipe each other out like in a World Cup playoff match. What happens when there's three left? Will two of them gang up on the third, then go after each other until there's only one left? They'd have to be lunatics."

"As in lunar twits? Hah! They're anarchists, Rom; Etocretan extremists just like their parents, yours too. Maybe this is just their way of having fun." Maxwell took his hands off the wheel and reached into the back seat for his patented three-barrelled air-rifle. Also there was Rom's beaten up backpack with its tubing and nozzles.

"What are you going to do?"

"Go back there. Mr Paraja looks overworked, needs a nap. We're going to take him below and, when he wakes up, have a good old-fashioned chinwag." He seemed to dwell on Rom's gadgetry, what he'd come back with after his supposed encounter with Devil Wind up north. "You got any more of these?"

"A few earlier prototypes," admitted Kinesis. "Nothing that worked particularly well."

"Where are they?"

"In my laboratory, downside. Why?"

"Because my people are going to need weapons and the best we have against these devil-rayed supras are yours – this canister and others like it. We're going to start some clandestine mass production, you and I."

"Gypsium doesn't work like that. It's semi-sentient. It only performs for its friends."

"Next thing you're going to tell me is you have semi-sex with it."

That was enough for Kinesis. He put one hand on the cracked, but not-quite-empty, Gypsium canister then gently touched Maxwell on the shoulder. It was a risk, but theoretically harmless. He'd tried something similar the day before and it worked. He figured it was worth the effort again.

Something had to be done about these characters, devil-ray victims or not. They couldn't be handled by a bunch of gung-ho, glorified policeme armed with gizmos he'd provide but probably wouldn't work for them. Devils, for want of a more descriptive word, had power. So did he and had access to a lot more — three not exactly bubbling craters worth to be exact.

The Untouchables were about to become eminently touchable.

========

As Maxwell went rigid, Kinesis effortlessly levitated him onto the passenger side and took over the wheel.

It was time to become the Gypsium Man!

****

NUKE 5: **The Indescribable Mr No Name**

========

<u>**Sunday, November 30, 1980**</u>

The screens in WORLD's converted fish packer went blank.

========

"Damn!" cursed Milo Mind. "Bastard's done it again." He fiddled with the controls to no avail. "Only this time Maxwell's out like a light. What were they on about, Sal? Are you in league with Aranyani Nightingale and Moe Three?"

"Don't be absurd. They're Ryne's people, all the way down the line. Otherwise they wouldn't be allowed to operate."

"Then what's he on about Strife and the old Baron? Did Callion build another Steltsar?"

"After the mess you and Moe Two made of the one in the early part of the Sixties, I doubt that very much. Stay with it, Milo. I'm going down to see Sian and radio the others. Even if we've no idea why, they'll need to know what's happening. Know what I'm thinking?"

"That you're finally coming over to my way of thinking; that it's time we upped anchor and moved to Waikiki."

"You sure you're not a mind reader?"

========

Romaine Kinesis drove Maxwell, still immobile but, disturbingly, now unconscious as well, to an old garage on a backstreet in the town.

========

Since its owner happily looked after his bicycle – his normal mode of transport – it was the entrance he most commonly used to get to the lower levels of Centauri Island. He had the attendant call below such that they were met by Adolph Dulles. Knowing better than to ask questions, Dolph saw his patron, if not his father, to the safety of the infirmary and left him under the care of Paul Creel, a former field surgeon in AMERICA and NCE's chief, non-Untouchable physician on the island.

Dulles then led Kinesis to Control Central where Alfredo Sentalli was waiting impatiently. With the Fatman were a group of his Untouchables: the lawyer George Hannibal; the Express's on-ground medical officer, Connie Lindquist;

Yataghan, Sentalli's thirty-something son by the long gone Emeralda nee Plantagenet; and Hiyati Samarand, technically Rom's superior.

Hannibal, Lindquist and Samarand had been in the original operations room when Maxwell was sent hurtling out of the window a few hours ago. Kinesis consequently regarded them warily. He noted no third eyes. As well, as near as he could make out anyhow, there wasn't a Babar or a woman composed entirely of eyes amongst them. Nevertheless, he stayed close to Dulles and his men, the ones Max said he could trust.

"About time, professor," Sentalli snarled. "Where've you been?"

"Nowhere in particular," answered Kinesis equivocally. "Let's just say I'm back and leave it at that."

"Leave it? Hell's teeth, man! We lost the Express. Boom! Just like that. Then one of the cosmicars appears in the Aleutians and we detect another near the Moon a few minutes later. Minutes, mind you – and the Moon, for Christ's sake. This is your Gypsium's doing."

"Seems so," agreed Kinesis, not wishing to overstate the obvious. "Though I don't quite see how it managed to blow up the Express. Gypsium generally doesn't come equipped with missiles."

"It wasn't a missile," argued Hiyati Samarand. "It was another aircraft, probably at least partially fuelled with Gypsium. We'll find out where it came from eventually," he assured them.

"Let's worry about explanations after we retrieve the cars we've located," suggested the Fatman. "Assuming the Yanks or Russians don't beat us to it, we can handle the Alaskan one. It's the one in space we can't do anything about. Unless of course you've got any better suggestions, that's your job, professor – yours and your Gypsium's."

"You've had no contact with Sol or any of the cosmicaptains?"

Sentalli shook his head sadly. "We had some indications the hub was up there too, at least initially. Isn't anymore, if it ever was. Ergo no more Colonel Sol either."

"All right," Kinesis considered, evidently undaunted by the notion he and his Gypsium could do something useful in outer space. "I know the UNES Liberty is up there; something to do with Martians, I understand. Sounds like serendipity to me. All the more so since our old friend Sean Smythe is on it."

"What if these Martians, or whatever's up there, had something to do with it?" wondered Samarand, thinking out loud. He wasn't the only one to have similar thoughts; just the first the professor knew not named Maxwell. "The Moon's a hot spot for Gypsium. Maybe the stuff homes in on itself."

"In which case you better stake a claim on the Aleutians," recommended Kinesis only half-sarcastically. "At the very least the Liberty could rescue those aboard the car, assuming they're still alive. Open communications with Houston. Have the patriarch patch you through to Smythe or Aremar."

"Wouldn't do any good," said Samarand. "They won't help. Some of us don't have your security clearance and Mr Smythe in particular won't overlook something like that." Kinesis mentally chalked one up for Sean. When Head of

Security on the island, throughout the Sixties, he had no use for Samarand and his ilk either. Big Max merely carried on Smythe's tradition.

"Besides, Ryne's not there anyhow," said the Fatman in exasperation. "As it happens, he's on his way here. I expect him sometime tomorrow. He'll be wanting to see you I'm sure." Kinesis caught the subtle threat. Talk about supras, the Great Man was so notoriously convincing there were those who said the effectiveness of his voice made him somehow unnatural.

"Then I better get some rest. I'll be in my laboratory if you need me." Kinesis turned to leave. Yataghan blocked his exit. Kinesis glanced at Dulles.

"We'll take care of things, sir," the acting Head of Security promised the Fatman.

"You better, young fella." Sentalli probably didn't mean to sound disdainful but no matter how unintentionally, by not calling him Mr Dulles, he did. "All right Yataghan, let them go. I trust you'll be doing more than diddling around, professor. I expect some concrete solutions very soon. Oh, one more thing."

"Yes?"

"No more heroics, okay. And no disappearing acts either. If we've detected two Cosmicars, chances are we'll locate the rest of it. Hell, maybe even the hub will turn up again, complete with Colonel Sol. If any of the cosmicompanions are still alive, I want them back here safely. I need you. That understood?"

"Right. No more disappearing acts." Surrounded by security, Kinesis left Control Central. Dulles stayed behind.

"What is it, Mr Dulles?" he asked, correcting his earlier condescension.

"I think I better stay, sir. Emotions are running low right now but things could get lunatic, pun intended, later on tonight. With Max out of commission, you'll need me. The mission to the Aleutians can be handled by my subordinates. Demios Sarpedon is already ordering people around like he was God's gift to potentates. All things considered, I'm willing to give him full responsibility."

"Mr Sarpedon's an able leader," agreed Sentalli, who always seemed to know vastly more than he ever let on.

"Very well. Keep me posted on Mr Maxwell's condition and, above all, I want the professor kept under constant surveillance. He's holding back. I'm not suggesting he sabotaged the Express but he certainly tried to prevent its launching. You may go. I'm as whacked out as Dr Kinesis, so I'm off to nap land. Dr Samarand will remain available. If you want to contact me, I'll be in my quarters in the hotel."

Yataghan and the Fatman left, along with Lindquist, Hannibal, and the others. Once Dulles and Samarand were alone, third eyes manifested in their foreheads just above where their eyebrows would have met. They communicated silently, Samarand taking the lead.

"What is it, Headstrong?" Even though they were immediate siblings – brood brothers, two of three – their joint father left Yati in charge out here.

"It's this shell, Dragon. Despite what some of my cousins might call me, I'm not the Headcase. It's this shell. I want another one. Dulles doesn't possess easily."

"You have done well with the raw material given you. An ideal shell is like mine, a homunculus manufactured specifically to house my spirit. Failing that, the sentient should be properly bred and prepared such that his free will does not interfere with ours. These outsiders have a highly sophisticated immune system that rallies against us.

"They are very difficult to occupy, let alone retain control over. Both Maxwell and Kinesis proved entirely impossible – the latter because he's infused with Brainrock; the former, well, who knows? And even Great Byron has not been able to maintain control over Sentalli for more than a few days at a time. But Dulles? You shouldn't need to prove your possessive superiority with the likes of him."

"Nevertheless ..."

"Fagh! No matter. Do as you please. What else?"

"Demios Sarpedon, he's the genuine article. So is his eye-stave – though for some reason its orbs don't activate automatically like they should beyond a protectorate."

"I know all about Sarpedon, Hektoris, and so should you. The Fatman sent him out to take care of rogues, not the likes of us. His is no ordinary eye-stave, recall, and he needs its prison pods for a lot more than nailing us. Besides, he starts showing off in front of Maxwell and all his trigger-happy Hawaiian cronies, well, even its eyeorbs can't stop every bullet."

"Whatever the case, I think he should be dealt with prejudicially."

"For one seemingly snake-bitten all his life, Mr Sarpedon is remarkably resilient. That I'll grant you. Sooner or later his luck will run out but right now he's not out enemy. Let's leave him be. That changes, you'll be the first one I call on. In the meantime go persuade Mr Dulles to have a rest. When he wakes up, best you're not inside him if he's so difficult. It's you I want readily available, not him. Have you chosen a new shell?"

"I think I'm going to body-bounce until I find someone more conducive to our needs. I'll let you know who I am at regular intervals."

"See to it then."

"One last thing. What went wrong? Who's behind this disaster? Mithradites? Lazaremists? Horrites? The Sedon-cursed Celestials? Any idea?"

"Dozens, ranging from any of the above to demon-loving Hellions and Antheans gone bad, again, to whatever's on the Moon, to this Signal System seemingly set up stateside by Judge Warlock, Wiccan's children, or the ones Mr Maxwell calls the Trigon Spartae. We may never discover the truth but I can tell you one thing ...

"What may be a disaster for some, a frustrating but comparatively minor setback for us, must make someone very happy. I just wish I knew who."

========

Dulles awoke with a start. Alarms were sounding everywhere.

Tad was standing over him, shouting something. Dulles shook the cobwebs out of his skull and yelled at the man to repeat himself.

========

A native Hawaiian with a name too long and with too many vowels to fit on a chest tag, the officer was called *'Tadpole'* in deference to his bulk. Once a lineman in the NFL, then a professional wrestler, he and his tag-team buddy *'Marsh'*, who was almost as large as Tad, had worked on Centauri Island for over fifteen years.

If Maxwell believed in seniority, they would have been many levels of command above Dulles. As it was, Tadpole and Marsh were just more meat, hired muscle, who reported to Maxwell and Maxwell alone. Dulles didn't like the arrangement but none of his subordinates seemed to mind, probably because they believed implicitly in Big Max's innate integrity.

The officer repeated himself then, frowning, said it again even more loudly: "Maxwell's vanished."

Dulles finally seemed to understand. "Bloody wonderful. The Fatman's going to love this. Where were the men? The doctors? The nurses? Don't tell me he just walked away."

"In the infirmary. Max was in a private room with his bed behind curtains. Someone went to check on him and he wasn't there any more. I've had the room sealed and personnel evacuated to the ends of the hall. Six of our best were with him. I've had them sealed inside the room."

"It's fucking Gypsium," swore Dulles. "I'll stake my life on it. Where's Kinesis?"

"Tinkering in his lab. Don't worry. We've never lost sight of him. Wouldn't even let him sleep without our people in the room with him. Dumb, in a way. The pro's exhausted but he can't sleep with us around. Those were your orders, though. Constant eye contact, correct?"

"You're not questioning my orders?"

"Certainly not, sir. I just wish we'd had the same orders for Mr Maxwell. He's my boss, but he's my friend as well."

"Yeah, well, now I'm your boss and you know how I operate. No beer halls with the boys, not me. All right, let's go. Time to earn our keep. Has Dr Samarand been notified?"

"And Mr Sentalli as well. He's waiting for us in the infirmary."

Dulles unlocked a drawer. He pulled out a heavy automatic and dumped his regulation dart gun. This was no time to take chances. He noted Tad was similarly armed. The kid gloves were off. Up until this morning only he and Max were allowed to openly carry lethal weapons, and then only their multi-purpose long guns, so Sentalli must be truly miffed to allow lesser officers of his private police to pack bullet-firing pistols. According to local folklore that hadn't happened since '65.

He found the Fatman outside the sealed door to the infirmary room where Maxwell was last seen. Yataghan, as always, was behind Sentalli's wheelchair, but the rest of what Maxwell had called his Untouchables weren't around, not even Hiyati Samarand. Security men were up and down the corridor, all armed with killing guns.

Marsh loomed large. As the ranking officer, he'd taken charge in Dulles's absence. After a quick exchange with Marsh, Dulles went over to the Fatman.

"I'm sorry, sir. I can't explain what happened to Max."

"Too many of today's events can't be explained, Mr Dulles," growled Sentalli. "Open the damn door."

"Is that wise, sir? I mean, shouldn't you be somewhere else? It might not be safe. We don't know what happened in there."

"Yataghan, bust it open." Sentalli's vaguely greenish-skinned son made a move but Dulles raised his hand warningly. "As you wish," deferred the Fatman. "Stand aside, son."

Dulles nodded to Tadpole and Marsh. Every security guard in the corridor unholstered their guns. Three of them moved between Sentalli and the door. Tad rapped it three times. From inside, three more raps were heard. Marsh unlocked it from the outside, someone else unlocked it from the inside. The door opened and a half dozen more guards leapt inside.

The other six were fine. (Mugwump, their equivalent of a sergeant and another oversized Hawaiian with a name too long to fit on a name tag, was yet another very capable veteran of Centauri Island's Security Team. Like Marsh and Tad, he'd served under Sean Smythe prior to Big Max.)

Dulles entered next, quickly confirmed it was secure and motioned for Yataghan to wheel in Sentalli: "Nothing here, sir. Allow me to speculate ..."

"Later." The Fatman indicated Yataghan should have a look round first. As he did so, Dulles thought he saw the etchings of a third eye on Yataghan's forehead. A momentary hallucination only. The man went through the place as if with a fine tooth comb. What was he looking for? Whatever it was, he came up empty.

"Speculate freely, Mr Dulles," said Sentalli, after Yataghan admitted that, other than he'd found nothing unusual, which was highly suspicious in and of itself, there was nothing there.

"Gypsium, sir. Mr Maxwell has been teleported elsewhere."

No one laughed. Even the security guards knew Gypsium had teleportive qualities. It wasn't science fiction to them. They had all seen Romaine Kinesis fly on his Gypsium beams. It was science fact; inexplicable perhaps, even the professor admitted that, but it was a reality: the reality upon which the Cosmic Express was designed and constructed.

"Indeed," Sentalli was remarkably calm. Not even his jowls jiggled. "Mr Marsh, Mr Tadpole, please find and escort Professor Kinesis to my suite. Yataghan, take me to the hotel. Mr Dulles, see to it that Dr Samarand joins us there."

Suddenly Mugwump pointed to something under Maxwell's bed. "Christ, what's that?"

What it was a puddle of protoplasm, forming as if out of nowhere. Unless it had dripped down from the underside of the mattress. It expanded. Some kind of blob.

Then it began to pulsate. Dulles had his gun out. "Fire after me!"

"Wait," ordered Sentalli, then screamed in his best B-movie skreigh: "It's alive!"

In the space of a heartbeat, the blob grew into a human-like shape; picked up the bed underneath which it had formed and hurled it at Sentalli. The security officers took the brunt of the assault. Dulles had his gun out and fired point-blank into the creature. Six shots, none missed. None apparently hurt nor even slowed down the thing.

"Yataghan," shouted Dulles, "Get Sentalli out of here. Shoot, you assholes. Shoot!"

Yataghan wheeled his father around and shoved him into the hall. The creature buckled under the gunfire of the security guards. Buckled and went to its knees.

"Cease fire!" commanded Dulles.

There was no blood coming from the creature. The bullets had pierced its skin, gone into it, and stayed there. If anything it became bigger. It was as if it was absorbing the bullets.

"Fall down, doughboy," Dulles told the thing, as if it would listen – all the more so since it had no visible ears. "You took two dozen slugs. Fall over and die!"

Doughboy was an apt description for the creature. It looked like nothing less than a large mass of uncooked flour and water given a bulbous, vaguely humanoid shape. It had arms and legs, plump fingers on even more lumpish hands; a head, a couple of pinpoint eyes, and the semblance of a nose. Besides no ears, as yet it had no mouth. It was in pain and dug its fingers into its stomach and chest.

The guards watched in amazement as it felt around its torso, found the bullets lodged therein, and began to push them upward. Now it had a mouth. It spat. Dulles ducked. The bullets shot into the wall beyond him. The creature adjusted its forearms. Made them akin to a shovel and smacked Dulles on the head. He went down hard; went down to stay from the looks of still thankfully bloodless things.

With the acting security chief out of action, it turned towards the other guards. Some fired wildly, two were hit by stray bullets, the rest backed towards the door. Altering his arms once again, they became fat, flat, fly-swatters. The thing slapped them unconscious. Yataghan ducked out of the room and slammed the door behind him.

The creature didn't bother smashing it open. Instead, it changed itself into a narrow spatula of basic substance and slipped underneath the door frame. Filling itself up again in the corridor, it focused on Sentalli's son. Yataghan was at the end of the hall, standing in front of another door. He unsheathed his pretzel-curved, suddenly glowing blade.

"Who the fuck are you?"

The creature's first words, in response to Yataghan's demand, were: "I have no name. Let that be my name."

"What are you?"

"Isn't it obvious? I'm indescribable."

========

"The screens are working again, Sal." Milo Mind activated Dis L'Orca's.

"There's some kind of fight and Max seems in the middle of it. Looks like the Plantagenet's going to skewer him."

"Spread the transmissions throughout the ship, Milo," demanded Salvatore Dis L'Orca. He'd met briefly with Alorstro Sian and radioed the other directors of WORLD. Much to his delight, theirs was a wait-and-see attitude. Safe for the time being, and without Daemonicus signing over the rest of their money, they had decided to keep their options open.

"I want everyone to see what's going on. One of them might be able to figure it out. You haven't won your bet yet, major."

========

Yataghan was waiting for an opening. The nameless thing shambled towards him, seemingly unafraid.

"Stand aside, puke puss," it cautioned in a voice that was unmistakably that of OJ Maxwell. "It's the Fatman I want."

When Yataghan didn't budge, the creature stretched out its forearms, its hands becoming akin to the jaws of a fork-lift. With speed, Yataghan ducked and sliced his curve-bladed dagger upwards, cutting off the blob's arms at what passed for its elbows. Mr No Name stared dumbly at its fallen appendages. Then its grotesque maw yawned wide in something akin to a grin.

With first one foot then the other, the thing touched its arms. They were immediately reabsorbed, whereupon it formed new ones.

Yataghan stumbled backward in shock. No Name turned its left arm into a tuning fork and drove it at Yataghan, pinning him to the wall behind. He sheathed the curved blade inside its other arm and began to contract it. The two foes glared at each other. Now it was Yataghan's turn to smile. As he did so, a third eye opened in his forehead and his greenish skin colour became almost aureate.

He snarled at No Name: "Truth will out, creature. I don't know what you are but I've an idea — a fucking faerie's my guess, though I rarely feel the need to guess anything. Maybe one of the made-to-order fay fuckers manufactured by Utopian biomages up in Sedon-sanctioned Cabalarkon or over on Witch Isle, though that would be speculative.

"You didn't know what I was either; probably still don't. Name's Damon Goldenrod, according to some; the Golden or Gleaming Deva, according to most. In Peru I was kin to Cain, the First Inca; to Europeans I was Byron's Apollo. But, regardless of what either of us are, I'm your better."

From the right arm into its shoulder, the 3-eyed, doughy thing began to glow a rich, poisonous yellow. Yataghan's blade was composed almost exclusively of Gypsium, it must have realized. With that realization came a new strategy. Somehow it knew how to alter its bodily components. Even without knowing the chemical configuration of the stuff, it turned its right arm into Solidium, the one substance that could contain Gypsium.

The arm became hard. With a snap of its shoulder, No Name flung away the dagger with its arm still encasing it. It landed down the corridor. No Name immediately started to re-grow its arm. Yataghan's third eye faded, his original skin colour returned. It was as if No Name expunged whatever was possessing Sentalli's son the moment it removed him from contact with the twisted blade.

No Name poised its newly-reformed arm, its fist shaped like a hammer, above Yataghan's head. "You and I are going to have a quick blab. Or I'll crack your skull like an eggshell and see what spills out. My bet is it'll be your brains." Yataghan swooned and fainted. No Name withdrew the tuning fork pinning his neck to the wall and let Yataghan slump onto the floor. "Have it your own way, snot-face. It's the Fatman I wanted anyhow."

"Lose something?"

Someone chucked its Solidium arm down the corridor. No Name – unless it was Big Max Maxwell again, or Viktor Richter or perhaps even Baron Justice, Richter-Maxwell's codename during the Second World War – calmly reabsorbed it, kicked the dagger to the other end of the hall, and only then looked toward the one who spoke.

"That you, pro?"

The newcomer stepped out of the shadows. If it was Kinesis, he was much better developed, with muscles rippling where Rom barely had skin. The sparse hair and greying goatee had become thicker and darker. He was wearing a white, sleeveless cotton tunic open to the navel – the better to show off his thick, trunk-like arms and the mat of fur that covered his chest – a pair of dark, skin-tight trousers, and black boots that went up to mid-calf.

Attached to each forearm was a long rod that came out of a rectangular – more like an oblong, as opposed to cylindrical – cartridge-like canister strapped on just below each elbow. The canisters glowed, so did the rods, so did the entire man. This wasn't Rom-Kinesis, this was Rom-Hercules, the embodiment of the Golden-Brown Warrior of so many ancient myths and legends all over the globe.

"Romaine Kinesis is on hold, muffin man. I am Doc Defiance ... the Gypsium Man!"

========

While he appeared to be tinkering, he was priming his Gypsium Irradiation Chamber. He'd designed it on the sly using some scribbled blueprints he'd copped from Avatar Sol; scribbles Sol didn't seem to understand but he did. The alarms distracted the security men in the laboratory long enough for him to dash across the lab and get into it.

When he stepped out of it, he dispatched the guards as humanely and non-fatally as he could then went in search of Alfredo Sentalli and Big Max Maxwell.

What he found instead was the Indescribable Mr No Name.

========

No Name wasn't impressed.

It turned its whole being into a ramrod and piledrived down the corridor. An apparently irresistible force, it met an immovable object. Defiance had formed a force shield of Gypsium around himself. Becoming semi-anthropomorphic again, No Name probed the shield for a gap. Finding nothing, it spun itself web-like around the entirety of the shield, willing itself once again into Solidium, then contracting.

The shield held together. From within it Defiance began sending out Gypsium rays. They ripped into No Name, bombarded its being, distorting and contorting it with pain. No Name sought for and found more substance seemingly out of nowhere. It redoubled its efforts to crack the Gypsium shield.

Protected by it, Defiance shouted in defiance: "Freak! What do you think that'll accomplish? My Gypsium beams will tear you apart. Give it up ...

"O'Ryan ... JAMES ... MAXWELL!"

"Maxwell?" No Name gave it up and collapsed. Incredibly he changed into his real self then literally vanished.

"Did you do that?" asked Paul Creel. NCE's staff doctor had been watching the action unfold from behind a door halfway down the corridor.

"Not me," said the transformed professor dubiously. "Gypsium must have. Always said it had a mind of its own."

Warily, Doc Defiance relaxed his repulsion shield. Yataghan was stirring and he helped him to his feet. He immediately scrambled for his dagger. Defiance lifted him off the floor with a thought; with another, he lifted up the curved blade, taking care to keep them both separated.

"Get this straight, Yat. I more like met than knew your mother and some of her siblings but I've never particularly liked you. After yesterday's shenanigans, I doubt I'll ever be able to trust you again. A bit of a conundrum, I think you'll agree, since we have to work together. Have any solution to the problem we're having?"

"My word is my bond," he pleaded.

"And what word are we striving to attain here, pal? I'll give you a hint. It begins with the letter 'Y' and it's not your name, though an 'I' in front of it would be welcome."

"I yield. I promise never to try and harm you, nor anyone else, so long as they don't threaten Alfredo Sentalli."

"Not much of a yield but I'm not one to deprive you of your job, let alone your father. All right." Defiance let Yataghan down. He quickly grabbed and sheathed his dagger. Looked much better, all of sudden. "Now where's the Fatman? We need to talk, him and I."

"I can't tell you," insisted Yataghan, as defiantly as Defiance had been a few minutes earlier. "You heard my vow. Respect it."

"No matter. He's in there. Behind that door." Defiance stepped towards it. Yataghan reached for his blade. "Uh, uh, pal. We have an accord."

Glowering dangerously, young Sentalli nevertheless withdrew his hand from the hilt of his dagger. (Were all the Untouchables left-handed, Defiance asked himself almost absently. Oh probably. It was the sinister affliction after all.) The door wouldn't open; didn't seem locked, the handle turned easily enough, but nothing budged.

Walls shouldn't be a problem for Gypsium. Only yesterday he'd used the Godstuff to get Sentalli, wheelchair and all, from outside his inner sanctum on the top floor of the hotel all the way to the downside boardroom unhindered. Now though, it wasn't responding the same way. Having tremendous abilities that in effect only functioned when they, not him, wanted was extremely frustrating — to put it mildly.

With nothing else for it, Defiance took a deep breath; sucked in on himself. Professor Romaine Kinesis, slender, pot-bellied, weak-limbed, with greying, thinning hair, looked absurd in the smock, boots, and (no longer tight) pants of Doc Defiance. The rods and cartridges were still visible so Yataghan had no doubt the Gypsium Man could be back in a flash.

He hunched onto his haunches while Kinesis leaned against the wall. "Patience isn't always a virtue," the professor said. "Sometimes it's a necessity."

Yataghan reposted with a simple but confirmatory grunt. They'd wait together.

By the time twenty minutes elapsed, Yataghan and Kinesis were joined in the corridor by Adolph Dulles, looking entirely the worse for wear, two dozen security officials, a half dozen members of the professor's handpicked research and development team, and, other than Yataghan, not a single one of the Fatman's Untouchables.

Just as discussion turned to forcing the door, one of them, Demios Sarpedon, walked up the corridor.

When told that Mr Sentalli was unavailable at present, the man whose skin was as black as midnight on a starless, moonless night simply announced: "We'll be off then." He shot Yataghan a final, intentionally challenging glance: "Hope you're feeling better by the time I return." Yataghan paled visibly. Sarpedon smiled brilliantly but said no more.

Ten minutes later they heard a click. Yataghan stood up and opened the door. It led to another corridor ending in an elevator.

"Mr Sentalli," he smugly announced, "Is well and truly unavailable by now. I suspect he'll meet you at, say, ten, for a nightcap in the hotel. Do be on time."

Yataghan entered the elevator, pressed a button, and the door shut. Significantly, the others heard it go down, not up.

"How far down does this place go?" wondered Creel.

"Don't ask me," said Kinesis. "I've only worked here for nearly twenty years."

========

Topside, the one-time Ace of Spades readied himself to board the huge flying fortress. His ultimate destination, though he knew it not, was Damnation Island.
****

NUKE 6: **Trouble by any Name**

========

Precisely at 10 pm Yataghan wheeled Alfredo Sentalli into the VIP Lounge in the island's modernized, but nevertheless oldest hotel.

With father and son were Hiyati Samarand, George Hannibal, Connie Lindquist and two others. One of them, whom both Rom Kinesis and Dolph Dulles were relieved to see, was OJ Maxwell. More remarkably to Rom's mind was the other one. She was the little girl he'd last seen in the company of Harry Zeross not much more than two months ago — the trickster!

"Ah, gentlemen," pronounced the Fatman. "Sorry to keep you waiting. Even on this day, the most important in most of our lives, family comes first. Allow me to introduce my niece, Dorothy Dodgson, though she prefers her nickname Hush. She flew in from Honolulu this evening."

"Hello, daddies," she enthused, holding out her hand friendlily.

========

Over the years both Max and Headmistress Virginia (*'Ginny'*) Mannering, whom he'd known since even before WWII (when she, along with so many others, lived with the Family Zeross on Aegean Trigon), took turns trying to convince him of the existence of supranormals.

Even if his parents were supposedly a couple of the most enduring, in that they lasted until 1960 with not just their abilities but their awareness of them intact, Rom pooh-pooped the whole notion of super-powered human beings. Supras were fantastical, Rom believed, said at first mention and repeated whenever it came up for years afterwards.

Since there weren't any active, as in fully functional, supras left to dissuade him, Max in particular was reduced to regaling him with stories of the so-called Secret War of Supranormals. As much as he trusted Max in almost every other respect, suchlike improbable derring-do was simply too comic book for him to accept.

(Then again, when Kinesis finally got around to seeing Star Wars, barely a year ago now, he claimed it was awfully tepid compared to what he, and they, were already capable of doing thanks to Project Centauri. He did, however, know Darth Vader was based on Dr Doom, but this was due almost exclusively to the fact that those under him sometimes called Hiyati Samarand either/or.)

Last summer, though, once his work on the Cosmic Express and its Gypsium propellant was, except for some mandatory final tests, essentially done and the Express was all but ready to go, a number of things happened that gave Kinesis second thoughts. For one, Demios Sarpedon began flying onto Centauri Island on an almost weekly basis.

Although, according to Max, Sarpedon wasn't one himself, back in the early Fifties he was associated with various bands of supranormals. He even had a codename, two of them in fact: *'Blackguard'* and, the one he preferred, *'The Ace of Spades'*. Somehow him showing up on Centauri regularly caused Max to unburden himself of what little he could remember of the self-pronounced Antediluvian Sisterhood of Flowery Anthea.

(Ants not only believed in the Great Flood of Genesis they insisted theirs was the Superior Sisterhood because it had been around before the Deluge. By the same token, albeit on the staff, not the distaff side, so did adherents of the Illuminated Faith of Xuthros Hor. The Xuthrodite Brotherhood, in fact, claimed their namesake was none other than the Biblical Noah. And, yes, thanks to the Golden Apples of Idunn, not Eden, he was 600 years old when he, not Almighty God, caused it.)

Demios, both Max and Ginny (when she was visiting the island) told Rom, was married to Morgianna nee Nauroz Somata, the Antheans' Mother Superior from roughly '52 until '65. Again, strictly speaking, not a supra, she was as day-white as her unusually tall, broad-shouldered, very strong-looking husband was midnight-black.

Superior Sarpedon may not have had a codename as such but her skin colouration, coupled with an approaching expressionless face, was why she came to be known as the White Witch in the very early Fifties. This was sometime after her and Demios returned to prominence, as it were, after hiding out for most of the war years.

Ginny, more so than Max, knew them fairly well prior to the war. However, they were both much more familiar with Demios's supposed twin sister, Melina. So was Kinesis, albeit not until much later on. Stunningly to not just Max and Ginny – Rom was just as flabbergasted when he heard about it – Mel, as they knew to call her, married Harry Zeross, who was almost 25 years her junior, in a private ceremony sometime in late April, early May 1964.

(In spite of seemingly endless protestations as to the irreproachability of their personal honesty, virtually no one believed Mel and Demios were even related, hence the supposed qualifier. She wasn't an albino, not in any detectable sense. Nonetheless, she was whiter-skinned and even more facially impassive than Morgianna. So how could she be Demios twin? Howsoever controversially, that the Sarpedon Summoning Children were freaks of nature answered that.

(That she was a highly skilled, perhaps even supranormally-gifted healer in her prime wasn't at all contentious. It was altogether undeniable. She was so talented she earned her own codename: Illuminatus. Indeed, without going into too many details both Ginny and Max strongly implied they were hardly the only ones who owed their continued existence to her.)

Like Ginny, Morgianna was always close to Loxus Abraham Ryne. Nonetheless, back then – and until relatively recently – Alfredo Sentalli couldn't stand her. Since he was his nominal boss after '68, the fellow supposedly running NCE since the Great Man retired (in late '55 or very early '56), and who was left in complete charge of Project Centauri, some of that animosity didn't so much rub off on Max as confirmed his long-serving distrust of the White Witch and, by association, the Ace of Spades.

Indeed, though neither Max nor Ginny said they never found out why, the Fatman barred her from *'his'* island for years upon years. Sooth said, even though Demios was a regular visitor nowadays, the professor couldn't remember ever seeing Morg, as Max sometimes referred her when the Fatman wasn't around, on Centauri Island. So maybe she remained persona non grata hereabouts.

Max also told Rom about Strife and a gaggle of female supras he knew by more than just their codenames. As it turned out, Rom did, too — a few of them anyhow, albeit without being aware they even had codenames. Or, as Max was prone to putting back to him, again referencing amnaesthetics (the forget-me-now drugs supposedly invented by Milo Mind and Hadrian Dis L'Orca in the late Forties), without Rom being able to remember that he was once aware they had codenames.

These included: Solace Sunrise (Sorciere, whose putative mother, Louise nee Riel, once married Sedon St Synne), the flat-out gorgeous Laodice Atreides long now Hent (Electrocretan, later on aka both Solenoid and Electra Snap-Zap, a Summoning Child who, like his mother Roxanne and Kad's mother Argiope, was born or at least brought up on Aegean Trigon) and Scylla Nereid (the slightly older Fisherwoman, another Trigon regular Kinesis recalled from his childhood, whom Max claimed was Colonel Sol's mother, always assuming that Avatar Sol was Tiger Tiecher).

However, Max seemed most in awe of someone he claimed was a perpetual seven year old. He knew she preferred to be called Hush but, instead, almost invariably referred to her as the Trickster, not necessarily capitalized. Kinesis still wasn't buying into any of it until he was experimenting with Gypsium one day in the early autumn; not long past the equinox, as it happened.

Inspired by Max's stories of Kid Ringo, he was learning how to point his Gyps-Beam at various locales and thereupon use it to look through the dark grey universal substance of Samsara, into wherever he was pointing it. Outside the island's main hotel, the lone building that still stood from the start of linking the island together in the pivotal late Forties, he focused in on Sentalli's big, as in wide open, office-cum-reception area on the hotel's top floor.

As usual the Fatman was accompanied by his son Yataghan, but there were three others with them. He couldn't hear them; hadn't perfected audio – still hadn't – but he recognized Demios Sarpedon and one of the others immediately. It was Aristotle Zeross, whom both Max and Ginny said was first codenamed Kid Ringo, but by now was going by Ringleader, the same as father Angelo reputedly did during the Supra Wars.

Although, from Max, he'd heard rumours that Harry was still around, he'd thought his cousin dead since shortly after his marriage to Melina Sarpedon in '64. (Supposedly Gypsium was responsible for the cancer that killed Rings' sister, Oriani, Loxus Ryne's fourth wife and the mother of his last set of twins, Pauline and Megan, a couple of years earlier. Being a scientist Kinesis never gave credence to suchlike speculative assertions that either Gyps or Harry were killers; contradiction in terms weren't they.)

The third person caught his particular attention. She was a little girl, no more than seven – undoubtedly this Hush, the trickster Max often talked about with so much admiration mingled with both fear and amazement. So here he had Ringleader and the trickster, masters of Gypsium both, in one place along with his boss, the Fatman's son, and the Ace of Spades, a known associate of supranormals from the Fifties who seemed to come and go as he pleased.

Demios made no bones about being the husband of Morgianna hence Sarpedon – once the Sisterhood's Mother Superior, conceivably the mistress of Big Shelter – and Max sometimes oddly referred to Hush as her *'little mother'*. She had a real first and last name, too, this trickster. It was Pandora Mannering, the same as Ginny's (Headmistress Mannering), the very woman who'd helped bring him back from the brink of abysmal despair after Alastor Molorchus's death in October 1968.

And here she was in the flesh!

========

Dulles obligingly shook her hand.

Even though it stayed attached to his wrist, Kinesis hesitated. He'd heard enough about the tiny trickster from Big Max to be extremely cautious.

"Aren't you up a bit late, little girl?" he said instead, heavy on the sarcasm.

========

"Be that way," Hush huffed. She'd noticed something about the professor; brightened accordingly. "You've still got your ring. Want one, Daddy Dolph?" Before either man could respond, like the prestidigitator she was, the little girl materialized a ring and slipped it onto Dulles's left ring finger. "That's better."

"Why thank you, miss," said Max's lieutenant. "It's very nice."

Kinesis looked at his. To the best of his hazy recollection, in 1948, his mother Roxanne chipped a stone out of the rock of Gypsium they found on Trigon and mounted it in a Zeross family heirloom. Usually he kept it in a Solidium case but, for some reason, he put it on after showering, for the second time today, earlier in the evening.

For some reason was now abundantly clear. His recollection was getting that way as well. Hush used it to control him. He tried to take it off but it wouldn't budge.

"Glad we understand each other, Daddy Professorial Deniance."

As if to gainsay her verbal profligacy, first impressions had Hush every bit the cute little kitten she purported to be despite the late hour. She was certainly dressed age-appropriately, albeit expensively, in a colourful dress. Plus, with her blonde hair braided so very precisely, she looked a lot like Tenniel's drawings of the Alice who went to Wonderland, through a looking glass. Kinesis, though, no longer trusted first impressions.

While she may very well be from some such place, it was most likely a Brimstone Wonderland. He realized immediately there was nothing of the young innocent about her.

"Good to see you rested up so quickly, Dr Kinesis." Sentalli endeavoured to seem like he didn't know either what had just transpired or what went on earlier that evening.

"Like the rest of us, you are of course very familiar with Hush's – let me get this straight – great-grand-aunt, Virginia Mannering. Headmistress, as we all refer to Ms Mannering, is very much still around. Tragically, though, Hush's parents were killed in a car accident in Carolina, must be five years ago."

All this struck Kinesis as an extremely odd thing to say. The Fatman, as much as anyone who'd been on the island a decade ago, would have known Headmistress, together with Hiliarti Schroff Zeross and Raphael D'Angelo, was the main reason he was able to start working again after the traumas of 1968. Whether that meant this somehow wasn't the real Sentalli, there was no point speculating.

After a day like today, reality had either gone topsy-turvy or there was more to the cosmos than even he'd thought possible. Wisely he held his silence.

"I had hoped to show her the launch of the Cosmic Express," continued the Fatman. "Well, you know what happened there. Gush of water under the troll bridge I'm afraid. Go ahead, Mr Maxwell. My island's yours to police again."

Max winked at Kinesis. (Was it significant neither he nor any of the others, not even Connie, wore rings?). He then had a few quiet, reassuring words with Dulles before they left the lounge together. Yataghan immediately moved to take his place behind Sentalli's wheelchair but Samarand took him by the arm, whispered something in his ear, then signalled Hannibal and Lindquist. The four of them followed Max and Dolph elsewhere.

"My son," acknowledged Sentalli, "Will be otherwise occupied for a time. As will the others. They've been neglecting their duties too long, especially Dr Samarand. There are still a stem, bud, and four cosmicars to be found and the two we have located still have to be retrieved. I trust I'll need no bodyguard with you around, professor."

"I'm not sure what you mean," said Kinesis as a waitress came up and took their order. Rom recognized her as another one of the Fatman's Untouchables – Persephone Urartu, he somehow recollected. Seems the (very, very) big boss was never entirely without bodyguards.

Sentalli waited until she was out of earshot. "I propose to be brutally frank with you, sir. It's like this. Dorothy Dodgson isn't her real name. It actually is Hush and she's a Mannering, just like Headmistress. It's a bastard name among her kind. It doesn't mean they're related, as I understand things; though they do pass their surnames down matrilineally, I'm further told. It just acknowledges that they had parents, one of whom was a man, even if no one's absolutely certain who either of them was."

"She's a witch."

Sentalli didn't seem particularly surprised at the professor's awareness of suchlike obscure esoterica. He and Hush had already spoken with Big Max at some length.

"An Anthean witch, yes," he granted. "Though she's as much bewitched as bewitching. You see, young Hush isn't so young after all."

"In fact, she's been a seven year old for something like seventy years."

========
Salvatore Dis L'Orca stepped out of his private cabin.
========

"Well, major," he said to Milo Mind jubilantly, "It seems we are about to become even richer than today's business has already made us. Daemonicus has just released all our monies – plus a substantial bonus for destroying the Cosmic Express with, as he put it, such happy results. What's more, he has agreed to a new contract.

"He's consumed with curiosity about the transitory creature Mr Maxwell apparently turned into back there and requires as much information as we can gather on the cutesy little girl, Professor Kinesis, and what he can now become, this Gypsium Man. He was particularly effusive about your Mind Tap and the fact that you hear what Maxwell hears as well as see what Maxwell does when he's this doughboy. Apparently even he doesn't have that faculty."

"I don't like it, Sal. At the risk of repeating myself ad infinitum, our mandate was up the moment the Express went down — or wherever it went. I was looking forward to a few wild weeks in Waikiki before I retire to India."

"That retirement's been temporarily postponed."

"Why? What more can we do? Besides, we keep losing Max. Where was he between the time the doc took him down and he reappeared with the Fatman and this Hush creature?"

Having invented them, amnaesthetics didn't work on him. Consequently, unlike Dis L'Orca, Milo Mind was very familiar with the perpetual child. He wasn't prepared to admit how familiar he was with her – not even for a million bucks – but he'd known her under an imaginative variety of cover names for over forty years. When he did think of her, howsoever rarely, he usually did so as simply the trickster.

"I believe this should satisfy your concerns."

Dis L'Orca handed Mind a slip of paper. It was a series computer printouts from a number of Milo Mind's hidden bank accounts.

Then again, Mind whistled to himself, for two million dollars ...

"It seems Daemonicus has put you on a personal retainer," grinned the Spaniard as if waiting for his fifteen percent agent's fee. "Remember what I said about me making a lot more money than you? Seems I've been proven wrong. Forget your wild weeks in Waikiki, why don't you just buy a few of its condos and have yourself a wild lifetime."

Mind took another look at the numbers and, Dis L'Orca worried, flushed so much so it seemed he was about to have a heart attack. Instead, he broke into a big grin. Greed it seemed was the cure to cowardice, at least in the major's case.

"Tell Daemonicus I accept. Also tell him I have a down payment to offer on my side of the bargain."

"Which is?"

"Tell you what, cut yourself a bit of the pie, Sal. Send Sian or some of Translav's Glomen to the Houston Academy of Man. Have them find out as much as they can about what Aran and Moe Three are up to nowadays."

"Why?"

"Let's put it this way: you know what a clone is?"

Dis L'Orca played dumb. His own was probably already out of its development tank and being subliminally wired in Houston as they spoke. "A copy of some sort?"

"An elementary answer, my dear boy. A clone's a synthetic, which is to say a manmade and deliberately developed lifeform. I think you'll discover that Moses the Third is a clone of Moses the First. Furthermore, cross-reference, if you can get into the Alliance's annals of supranormals, Callion Clones.

"Cross reference as well the various Steltsars, the Slimy Man – you'll find a few of those too, men and women, I guarantee you – the Emperor Mammalian and his Manimalians, both Sphinxes, the Headsman, or Baphomet if you prefer, Prince Peashooter, a certain Viktor Richter aka Baron Justice, and a little girl called Joli Blon, among many other things, not all of them cute or even polite."

"Save me the trouble. What'll we find?"

"A lot of references to Anthean witches for one thing. Also Althean Healers, Korant Corn Queens, Lovely Lady Afrites, Hellion Horrors and Athenan War Witches. Names like D'Angelo, Schroff, Tedesco, Dvina, Heliopolis, Mannering, Nightingale, Avar, Maenad, Morgan, Somata, and Nauroz will keep popping up. You might even find an O'Ryan James Maxwell."

"You're saying that nameless thing, Big Max, Mr No Name, was an artificially-created being?"

"I'm saying more than that. Unless I'm very much mistaken, Callion Three and Aran Nightingale are at it again. They're making a new generation of supranormals — out of cryogenically-preserved cells of the last generation!"

"And Loxus Ryne knows about it?"

"He's paying for it. The Great Man's pulling out all the stops to combat whatever's on the Moon."

"Well, at least we don't have to worry about that right now." He looked at his watch. "Come on, Daemonicus promised us a surprise outside."

Mind joined Dis L'Orca and his right hand man, Alorstro Sian (a supposedly *'neutralized'*, Summoning Child contemporary of Hadrian born in Sicily) on the lower deck. Excepting Daemonicus and Strife, whomever they currently were, the three of them, along with an Arab, Shaikh Ali Ars Markazi, and the midget, Greygreave Translav, the self-proclaimed heir to the Czardom of Russia, formed the brain trust of WORLD.

The latter two were off-ship – probably already spending their *'lake of lucre'*, as Salvatore often described the impressive sums Daemonicus paid them. (Where did it all come from anyhow? And was it really all gold bullion converted to cash for purposes of banking their eventual payments?) Like Mind and

Cyanide, as Sian was codenamed during the Secret Wars, but unlike the twenty years younger Spaniard, they were veterans of Hadrian's pre '65 Order.

According to Sal, they were there to greet two more *'specialists'* hired by Daemonicus and Strife.

What came instead was only the first of a rapid-fire series of shocks to them all.

=========

"You're right and you're wrong on that, pops," corrected the apparent little girl more than just somewhat disrespectfully. *"I've been a seven year old for only about sixty years. Before that I was seven just once – when I really was seven – but that was around seventy years ago."*

"I sit corrected," joked Alfredo Sentalli.

=========

"I haven't the vaguest idea what you two are talking about," admitted Kinesis, dreading the truth; dreading not being able to remember it even more.

Max told him about amnaesthetics. Had even expressed his doubts that the likes of Milo Mind and Hadrian Dis L'Orca, as bright as they were corrupt, had the mental wherewithal to come up with such literally mind-blowing pharmaceuticals. As far as Max was concerned they must have stolen the recipe, if drugs had recipes, from – most likely – the Conquering Christ or, just perhaps, someone like the tiny trickster herself.

Kinesis, though, doubted the little witch needed them to edit his memory. His ring was undoubtedly more than enough.

"It's a matter of supranormals," Sentalli said. "I gather you and Mr Maxwell have already discussed the issue."

Kinesis felt compelled to keep the conversation going. "As it happens I became one today."

"Seems you aren't the only one," granted Sentalli. "Turns out Mr Maxwell's one himself. As you guessed, he was the nameless creature you and your Gypsium handled so expertly. As my glamorized colleague seems ready to accept, the Whole Earth's ripe for supras – what she considers deviants – again."

"Better ripe for than rife with, one supposes."

"Just so, professor. However, as one who lived through the last outbreak of deviancy, I'm obliged to inform you that supras can't just go crazy. They're much too dangerous to be given that kind of freedom. Fact of the matter is they have to be trained. Hush is the best qualified person I know of to train you and Max. In many respects, at least in this century, she was the first supranormal."

Kinesis regarded the non-child with even more interest. He told her how he recalled her from Trigon in '48. Did much more that actually. Now that he had on her ring – and it was her, not his mother, who gave it to him way back then – he recalled a number of her other aliases.

Surprised her particularly with his vague recollection of the events of '65, when the latter day Olympians of cousin Kadmon and his Trigon Spartae saved her, then masquerading as Lori Tedesco, and everyone else on Centauri Island from that year's version of the Order.

He even admitted he'd spotted her with Ringleader (Aristotle Zeross's codename, when it wasn't Rings or Kid Ringo) a couple of months ago. She was legend, especially to OJ Maxwell. As he'd once confided to Rom in a momentary burst of howsoever whiskey-fuelled exuberance, he regarded her as the mother of all supras.

"Not the mother," demurred Hush, presumably not realizing that, in Maxwell's vernacular, mother meant greatest. "More like the cause of them. When I flopped by having Saladin born Nauroz instead of Morgianna now Sarpedon first, my Sisterhood issued the Summoning of 5920 – sorry, 1920. Back then I was a normal woman: at least as normal as any other Ant.

"Yes, I am a witch; a major league witch, even if I do say so myself, though I hardly started out as one. I was bred by the Superior Sisterhood to become the Mother Mary of a new Saviour, three of them, all of whom were supposed to be reincarnations of the triple goddess, the Trigregos Sisters. What I ended up was the mother of yet another sedon, small case."

"You mean Sedon St Synne."

"Not half," giggled the little girl. "In fact there are those who say St Synne, Judge Warlock, was my father."

"Then who?" wondered Kinesis. Not waiting for a reply – not really expecting one, truth told, at least not an honest one – he made a quick calculation. "Jesus Mandam, the one who became the King Conqueror? He would have been born in late '20, early '21. Was he your son by another name?"

For some reason talking to a seven year old who, by her own admission, was much nearer to eighty came naturally to Kinesis. It was as if they were old friends.

"Missed my point, doc daddy," Hush said. "By about a year," she added, somewhat snootily. Forbearance seemed as foreign to her as shyness.

"My Sal's no Supra Summoning Child; no Conquering Christ, either," she further conceded, with no hint of regret, though perhaps with a modicum of recrimination "He's a vain, egocentric master more of weirdos than of weirdness. Hates witches, too; mostly for good reason, I have to say. My Morgianna's no Immaculate Mary herself. Sad to say she's even more troublesome than my son, but she is my Summoning Child."

"You're the one who vanished Max after he reverted from No Name, aren't you?"

"I'm quite good with Brainrock, what I suggested you name Gypsium thirty odd years ago," she admitted, again without a trace of humility. "Not that you listened. I'm also at home between-space. Daddy Enormity lied a little. I've been here all day. He was concerned about your behaviour yesterday and wanted me to check you out.

"You see, I go way back with your family. Your parents … well, now's not the time to get into that. He's right about another thing, though. I'm like Headmistress, a teacher; more, an Illuminary. I shall dutifully instruct you and Max in the best usage of your newfound abilities and I shall begin with the assertion that Strife, your nemesis since the late Forties – though there's no way you'd know that – is a possessive spirit, a Master Deva by the Illuminary-given name of Marut Kanin, unless it's Fitna Marutia, unless it's a bursting bagful of others, depends on the era."

"Never heard of either."

"Ah, but you have, singular. The ancient Greeks had her as Kore-Eris, she of the Golden Apples of Discord. Thus, our lessons begin."

=========

"What the fuck's that?" demanded Alorstro Sian, Dr Cyanide.

=========

As if out of a bank of fog came a moderately-sized freighter. It looked like a ghost ship, something that had been hoisted off the bottom of the sea and patched up. It probably was just that — there was no fog that night. Something flew off it; something nightmarish. Not Nazi Nightmarish. That was below.

Much larger than any bird they'd seen, what came at them was glowing not unlike a nuclear inferno given a pterodactyl's bordering on legendary shape. As it came closer, Dis L'Orca swore out loud: "Mother of God! Is that a dragon?" Suddenly Sian was shooting, not shouting.

A seven foot tall, armoured, ambulatory and anthropomorphic shark-creature completely impervious to his gunfire pulled itself onto the deck. Even though it spoke in German, both Mind and Sian recognized the voice. That was the one thing that hadn't changed in nearly forty years.

<<"Put that peashooter away, Herr Doktor Cyanide. Before I make you eat it — or I have to eat you!">>

=========

An hour later, Milo Mind staggered into his cabin. He slumped into a chair and started to disrobe. Just as he was pulling on his pyjamas, a female voice chimed from his bed.

"Don't bother with those, lover."

"Countess Ramona? Ray!"

=========

About the same time, overnighting at her home in Big Sur California, where she was "tutoring" – actually, in the absence of dead mother Oriani, raising – Megan and Pauline Zeross Ryne, their 80-year-old father said to Virginia Mannering, almost 60: "It's all starting again, isn't it, Headmistress?"

"Doubt it ever stopped, Abe."

****

Part Two: *The Strife Virus*

NUKE 7: **Dead Live; Living Die**

========

The 25th day of December 1955; called Xmas by Xuthrodites

Saul Ryne, the Magnificent Psycho, levitated into the twilight sky above Damnation Isle.

========

Skullcap and fake hair already doffed, brain broiling and sparking beneath his transparent cranium, he was ready for them; ready even for the cowardly child, the teleporter who had brought his twin brother and the other nine, laughingly called King's Own Crimefighters, to this snow-dusted speck of land in the Western Aleutians.

That one, the twelve year old, Harry Zeross, howsoever unofficially codenamed Kid Ringo, had taken himself away in his Gypsium rings almost immediately. When the punk returned he'd find them either dead or under his complete control. Then he'd seize the boy's will and, as needs be, cause him to take them to Mother Russia.

There, in an already partially constructed super city hidden in the Soviet Ukraine, they would continue the quintessential work his martyred cousin, Jesus Mandam, the two years' dead King Conqueror, left for him to complete — facilitating the hegemony of 'ubermensch', the over-man. If he didn't succeed where Mandam failed, the inferior, rutting rabble that made up humanity would inevitably lay to ruin the entire world with their endless wars, despoliation of nature and hideous weapons of mass destruction.

"Join me!" he shouted into their skulls "Join our cause! It is the normal, not the supranormal, who must be subjugated."

By way of an answer, the blind American Indian, John Sundown by birth, fired his solar spear. And missed! Deliberately? Must have. Two years ago to the day, Blind Sundown, the lone Crimefighter he actually feared, killed his cousin, a man Psycho revered as next to God.

Together with his hybrid mount Raven's Head, by name as well as (supposedly) by breed, he had killed many another as well, most of them deservedly.

Notwithstanding suchlike twaddle, Sundown was no soldier, no state-appointed executioner, not even an out-of-uniform policeman or, come to that, an official member of KOC. He was a mass murderer, plain and simple. (And they called him *Psycho!*)

Gloriella D'Angelo Dark, Glory of the Angels, the Radiant Rider, other than the lethal Cheyenne the most powerful of the ten, raised herself on iridescent hair. When they were both teenagers, she four years younger, he was madly in love with her. Her seemingly reciprocal feelings may have been puppyish but his were genuine. If there was one of them he'd like to save, it was her.

She extended her arms. Out of her being radiated spectacular rainbows. But spectacular was all they were. At least for the time being, there was no substance to them. Lightning zapped past him. That would be Aires, Airealist, Gloriel's brother by adoption. Were they taking turns not really attacking him?

The island, he suddenly realized, was being enveloped in a curtain of oceanic spray. Thalassa, Sea Goddess was masking Damnation in mist such that no one would see what was going on. And no one didn't just include the 12-year-old Ringleader, if he was still somewhere nearby. No, it included the Soviet submarine that, whether he had KOC under control or not, was already overdue to pick him up.

Most importantly, it hid the tiny island from the American planes he'd heard flying overhead a few minutes ago. Was that why the Russians were late?

A voice came into his mind. It was that of his twin, David aka Cerebrus. He was a lesser mentat than Saul but his abilities had been steadily improving during the last five years. Soon he might be able to challenge him. Soon, but not yet. "You're not going over to the Soviets, Saul," he imparted, as he would, cerebrally. "Neither are we. This ends now."

Psycho reached out mentally for the others. Jervis Murray wasn't even Dervish Furie yet. Wilderwitch was up to something with her ungodly agates. No Anthean was better at them, but that wasn't what made her so special. By her own admission, as confirmed by Codename: Fisherwoman, her sister in more than just Flowery Anthea, she was a natural born witch; hence her supranormality.

Fish, Sorciere, Superior Sarpedon, every other proper witch he'd met – as opposed to pretend witches like Dolores Rivera, Gilda Dre'Ath and Bunnie never-Maxwell – claimed to have worked for years, even decades, to attain anywhere near her abilities. Back in 1939, his own mother, Eden Nightingale Ryne, whom Fish insisted was yet another of her blood sisters, died trying to reach the fabled Anthean sanctuary in the Himalayan Vale of the Visionaries.

(Mother Eden hoped to conclude her training there. She must have also hoped to start daughter Aranyani, who died beside her, on her journey to full sisterhood. Hope, though, was all that was left in Pandora's Box when she let every other vice loose in the world. Hope didn't stay behind because it was a virtue; far from it. Hope was a chimera, as quick to dash you down as raise you up. It wiped out all that was good about Saul's life; replacing it, howsoever late on, with the unmitigated misery of Psycho's.)

Wilderwitch's mind was blocked to him, as was the Untouchable Diver's. That would have been her doing, too, via her astonishing agates. There was nothing witchy about UD/Yehudi; nothing warlocky either, if that was a word. Just then, from the forever-unsettled, more often flighty than merely muddled, thought processes of OMP, Obadiah Power, the ancient-looking, virtually invulnerable and phenomenally strong near-giant, he caught a brief image.

It was of an incredible landform; the stuff of impossibility, not legend. Massive, perhaps continental in size, it was shaped somewhat like a human, make that demonic, head. *'Shelter!'* – from the witch; *'Big Shelter!'* – from Power. They were planning to take him out quickly, and with as much force as necessary, then escape there.

Psycho channelled out, concentrated on the Witch and OMP. Cerebrus came at him thoughtfully. Thunder exploded. The solar spear blasted him. Sundown still wasn't operating at anywhere near peak potency but he felt it through his mind screen. He could deaden their heads but he was suddenly intrigued. He wanted to go with them.

He was starting to sweat blood out of his skin; air was becoming precious. This last was no doubt due to the Elemental Twins acting in unison, letting him know what they could do. "Go down, Saul," demanded Cerebrus, bordering on brotherly. "Johnny's holding back. We all are. Go Down Now!"

Gloriel formed a secondary glove around his telekinetic force shield, leaching energy out of it. He got the sense of Murray getting exciting – amping up, as the Aussies might put it; switching into Dervish mode. The Diver was preparing to leap. Dark's Angel let him read her surface thoughts. She didn't love him, never had ... not really; was terrified of his mind-over-mind abilities; his, to her mind, utter insanity.

They didn't want him. She didn't ... had a baby now. Remembered Barbara. He wanted ... with them. Could dead ... heads. Too crazy! Too psychotic! Too true!

Psycho's brain reached critical mass and blew.

========

That was 1955.
This was 1980.

========

Monday, December 1, 1980

After an overnight on Midway Island, the amphibious troop carrier had gone on to the Aleutians Monday morning.

Right now, as it did another three-sixty spin above the humped, beehive-like dot of land below them, Demios Sarpedon was staring out the window. There wasn't much in the way of daylight – wouldn't be this far north three weeks before the Winter Solstice – so he couldn't make out anything distinctive except that the seas were calm enough for a landing.

Besides the pilot, who was of Slavic origin, he was with two other men in the cockpit. One was Deke *'Panting Panther'* Jones, a black American who'd had his tongue cut out in Vietnam less than a decade earlier. The other was a Tex-

Mex asshole by the name of Miguel Hernandez, perhaps the foulest-mouthed man Sarpedon had ever come across in his nearly sixty years of life.

Although OJ Maxwell and, before him, Sean Smythe considered Demios one of the Fatman's Untouchables, he and his wife, Morgianna nee Nauroz (by birth) Somata (by fosterage), were actually quite well known to both of them. At least they were until 1965, when they vanished from Centauri Island under the all-too-usual, for the manifestly no longer moribund Supra Wars, highly mysterious circumstances.

Although they'd been on the scene, as it were, since the late Thirties, their coming out, also as it were, occurred in 1951 when they infiltrated the Supranormal Defense League, an organization set up and run by Jesus Mandam, also called the Conquering Christ and, as the Sarpedons knew, but not many others out here did, Wiccan Warlock.

In the SDL, white-as-light Morgianna was tagged the White Witch whereas black-as-midnight he, as her husband, constant companion, and bodyguard, quickly regained the even less complimentary codename of Blackguard. (Personally, he'd always liked the Ace of Spades; this despite there being an entirely unrelated Queen of Spades, dead since '46, whose actual name was Mnemosyne D'Angelo Heliopolis.)

Unlike Memory of the Angels, who was a Lovely Lady Afrite like her much younger sister-in-law, the Summoning Child Roxanne Heliopolis become Kinesis, Morgianna was a thoroughly well-trained member of the Antediluvian Sisterhood of Flowery Anthea. (An otherwise obscure Greek goddess of Springtime renewal, of life itself, the flirtatious Flower Goddess was pictured, albeit with only two eyes, in a famous painting by Sandro Botticelli, circa 1480, entitled *'Primavera'*.)

Although barely into her thirties and still (apparently) childless, there was little doubt Morg, as he called her despite her preference for Morgianna, would eventually become the Sisterhood's Mother Superior. In '51, Memory's older and last surviving sister, Dolores nee D'Angelo Rivera held that honour; had at least nominally for the second time, the first being in the late 1930s.

However, notwithstanding the fact she was the natal sister of Celestine D'Angelo, the Celestial Superior (Dolores and Memory's oldest sister, Morgianna's grandmother, and, arguably, the greatest Superior the Anthean Sisterhood ever had), Sister Sorrow was regarded as a bit of a lame duck. She was far too meek and mild for such an important position in those trying times. A too young, but nevertheless ambitious and impatient woman, Morgianna was already plotting to hasten her succession.

In early '52, a malevolent spirit peculiar to Antheans returned after an absence of three years. Her name – more like designation – was Strife. When Superior Sorrow couldn't handle her, she resigned and let the White Witch succeed her. To take care of the spiteful spook, Morgianna reorganized an offshoot branch of the Sisterhood named after Olympian Athena, the Greek goddess of both wisdom and war.

Athenans carried heavy, killing weapons; guns and knives to go along with the dart guns and irritant sprays most witches carried to defend themselves; were also fitter, faster, and much more skilled when it came to self-defense. Far more aggressive than Sorrow's Antheans (who were mostly a sorority of Althean healers anyway), they usually got the result they wanted, no mater the cost.

Regardless of whether it was Morg and her Athenans' doing, Strife once again went into forced retirement; presumably, though hardly for the first time, irrevocably. Perhaps because of her loss, that September Jesus Mandam called for a colloquy of supras to be held in Vancouver Canada on the upcoming Equinox.

(Demios found it curious how often the quarter and cross-quarter days of the eight-armed Sun Cross – symbolic of the Wheel of the Year pagan calendar – became significant dates in the 17-year, not-to-him Secret War of the Supranormals. A lot of that probably had to do with the pagan gods, though that was something else neither he nor Morg bruited about out here.)

The Sarpedons attended what Mandam intended to be a supra coming-out-party. (It wasn't, in the end; nowhere near.) And what a party it was! Like almost everyone else there they were caught up in the ensuing Dionysian frenzy. Just after the summer solstice nine months later, their only child, Andaemyn, was born, also in Vancouver. Well before then, though, the SDL fell into irretrievable disrepute.

That Xmas – as the Illuminated Brotherhood of Xuthros Hor had called Christmas reputedly since long before there was a God-made-man named Jesus Christ – Mandam was eradicated on Salvation Isle. He didn't go down alone; took with him The Rache, a group of unrepentant Axis supras who were the real force behind the League.

The Conqueror's conquerors? A renegade American aboriginal, Blind Sundown, and Raven's Head, his absolutely inhuman *'Beauty'*, commonly called Raven.

She was a bird-headed, black-feathered, horse-shaped creature; had talarial wings like a Hermes or a Mercury, on both sides of all four of her hooves. Had, as well, a self-generating, obscuring or, more precisely, obnubilating nimbus, and could fly at speeds at times superior to airplanes.

She could also protect herself and her Johnny with their so-called cosmic aura and communicate comprehensively, perhaps even telepathically. Sundown wasn't the only one who could understand her either. Morg, for one, said she could, too. Demios, though, never picked up the knack.

All in all, though otherwise not much in terms of ability, Raven was decidedly the most impressive-looking supranormal he'd ever come across.

They didn't make them like that anymore, that was for sure.

========

The next two years saw supranormals turn against supranormals in unprecedented numbers. Morgianna's Athenans joined Loxus Ryne's Alliance of Man and the all-male Illuminated Faith, old-time allies of Sorrow's Antheans, to begin systematically neutralizing supras. Their most effective agents were, ironically, the regrouped King's Own Crimefighters (often shortened to King Crimefighters), perhaps the most powerful group of supranormals ever known.

Among them were Cerebrus, Old Man Power, Dervish Furie and three D'Angelos – two of whom, the Sarpedons suspected, were Dolores's unacknow-ledged offspring while the third, who looked as well as acted like an angel, was the daughter of Dolores and Celestine's brother, Raphael. Blind Sundown, Raven, Wilderwitch, and the Diver were ancillary members, only called upon in extreme situations.

Too bad for them, what goes around comes around.

Christmas Day 1955 was exactly two years after the death of Jesus Man-dam and, as they later learned, the same day Eden Nightingale actually died.

(Eden, with Aranyani in tow, had made it to the Sisterhood's Shelter in the Vale of the Visionaries back in 1939 after all. Over the intervening years she had also become Sorrow's *hidden* predecessor as Superior; hidden as in unknown to the rest of the Sisterhood at large. She was also, by Loxus Abraham Ryne, the mother of Saul, David, and Aranyani; Aran being the Great Man's lone, non-twin.)

On that selfsame fateful day, the King Crimefighters were wiped out on the very Aleutian atoll they were flying over right this minute. (It was, Demios knew, hardly the first time Damnation Isle figured in the Supra Wars but it was, until now, the last. The Japanese actually targeted it for takeover during the War, whereas Sundown and Raven supposedly rescued none other than a teenage Wil-derwitch from them there in 1943.)

Ah, but were they wiped out? No bodies were ever found.

========

Although they never became particularly welcome visitors to Centauri Is-land, in the early Sixties Morg's tightness with the Great Man, the main money-bags behind New Century Enterprises even after retirement, assured them the opportunity to figuratively bury the hatchet with Project Centauri's visionary spearhead, Alfredo Sentalli. As it turned out that was as big a mistake on Sental-li's part as their own.

A tragic series of ill-advised moves that, it had to be said, they themselves initiated, coupled with completely unforeseen circumstances, culminated there in June 1965 with the total humiliation of the Sarpedons. Anthean elders, who had to be over 50 and were collectively known as Nightingales, forced his wife to not just resign her position as their leader but to accept banishment from their Superior Sisterhood forevermore.

The leader of the coup against her? None other than Morgianna's bewitched, perpetually seven year old little mother.

While his reputation wasn't so badly tarnished – he'd taken out the entity known as Daemonicus, with one of his eyeorbs, and would have handled Strife if Ringleader hadn't beaten him to the proverbial punch – it wasn't until early '78 that Demios dared return to the largely manmade Hawaiian island.

Dared wasn't the right word. He was as good as summoned ... by the self-same Hush Mannering and her favourite daddy, Alfredo Sentalli.

========

"Take it down!"

========

The Fatman had just acquired a new adviser, one Avatar Sol by name. The little witch was highly suspicious of the newcomer, and not just because of his comparative youth. Apparently not yet thirty, Colonel Sol had an incredible knowledge of the, to some, earthshaking discoveries of Jesus Mandam

The self-proclaimed Conquering Christ, a man also once known as both the King Conqueror and simply the Conqueror, died years before Sol could have become a teenager. Furthermore, they were so totally dissimilar to behold there seemed little chance they were even related.

Sol was a big, muscular tiger of a man whereas Jesse was awkward, wimpy even, some might say effeminate. Indeed, he bore a superficial resemblance to the celebrated pharaoh Akhenaton: the world's first recorded, presumably non-Jewish monotheist; the husband, maybe even husband-brother, of the equally renowned (for her great beauty) Nefertiti; and, only arguably, King Tut's dad.

Despite their altogether unalike looks, Hush told him she thought he might be a Callion Clone of Mandam; either that or a victim of a reconstructed devaray. The Fatman went beyond that. He wondered if Sol was a shape-shifting devil, a Master Deva, a Shining One, one of the pagan gods and goddesses neither he nor Morg dared mention lest those not in the know reckoned them stone cold bonkers.

Which was why he'd been summoned back to the island in the first place. Not just Demios fancied himself a devil-slayer.

========

"We're down!"

========

"Someone's been here," said Hernandez, interpreting Panting Panther's sign language for Sarpedon's benefit less than a half hour later. "Earlier today he says. Two tents, big one and a little one, were right here. Easy to spot. Land's dry where they'd been set up. Rest of the island's covered in a thin sheen of ice.

"Huge storm here yesterday or the day before. Tidal wave too. Some of the others found fish on high ground. Recently dead. No birds around, no seals either. Must be staying away. Fucking weird. Local weather pattern? Yeah, I never heard of such a thing either, Panther. Got any bright ideas, Juju Jack?"

Sarpedon didn't rise to the bait. Hernandez was an annoying man, probably a mercenary by trade. Sentalli's OJ Maxwell, an occasional nemesis of his and his wife's in the Fifties and Sixties, had a reputation for taking on *'projects'* and straightening them out. They didn't cost much in terms of salary and tended to look upon Max as something akin to a god. Of course, he also trained them damn well. There was no doubt Miguel was good at what he did; it was just his personality that was abhorrent.

"I want pictures and film, Hernandez," Demios ordered. "Designate a couple of radio men to keep in contact with the plane and make sure that everything is relayed to Centauri Island as it happens. We've got a satellite up there tuned directly to us and it says the cosmicar's around here somewhere."

"Fella, you're taking down to me. Communication's my fucking speciality."

Ten men had come from the troop plane in three dinghies. All were wearing heavy-weather, Arctic combat outfits. Their weapons, automatic shotguns, were wrapped in swaddling to prevent freezing. Sarpedon had one of the guns strapped over his shoulder but he had no intention of using it. That was what the others were for.

Instead he opened a height-length black box that he always carried with him. In it were a long, blunt-ended, staff or pole made out of some kind of metal and a number of apparently skin-covered pods or ovules that looked akin to good-sized eggs. Not that he needed to, at least not urgently, he stuck three of the pods into his jacket pockets. Then, even though it didn't seem to have a socket, attached one to the top of the shaft.

The pod immediately began to glow like a light bulb whereupon, shockingly, it layered open. A comparatively large single eye poked out of it. Hernandez involuntarily crossed himself while Jones gurgled in tongueless amazement. Sarpedon trembled as the eye stretched out of the pod on elongating tendrils and examined the two men.

"You're clean," Sarpedon pronounced nervously, moments later, after the eyeball had mostly, but not quite completely, retracted into the egg.

"What the screaming hell's that thing?"

"This is an eye-stave; the ovule's called an eyeorb, for reasons obvious. You should know its eyeball generally comes out only when I require it and I didn't require it to come out just now. That means, in case you doubt me, it did so of its own volition. And that has never happened before. Not to me it hasn't, not for sure anyhow."

(Demios had, sort of, inherited his eye-stave from Ubris Nauroz, Morg's paternal grandfather, a member of Charan Ryne's Godling Guild. While he recalled most of what he'd been told about it, he only suspected he hadn't uttered the precise truth. Even all these years later, the events of '65 were scrambled up in a runny omelette of confused recollections, Anthean memory-redaction, and recurrent nightmares.)

"That can also mean only one thing. There are or, up until just recently, were devils on this little island."

"A what?

"You heard me: a little god, a Shining One, spawn of the Devil, capitalized."

"Fucking wonderful, isn't it, Panther? Twenty years from now's the Twenty-First Century and the Fatman sends us up here with a refugee from the Dark Ages. And I mean dark. This bugger's so black he makes you look like a white trash drug dealer from the bestial burbs. And he's spouting off about goddamned devils! No wonder I call him Juju Jack.

"Know what I think? I think you're the only fucking devil here. Take a look at Panther. That ain't no regulation shotgun he's got. It's a goddamned baby-bazooka. Frag a tank, it would. Calls it his gook-zook. This here's Aunt Jemima." He patted the barrel of his gun and pointed it at Sarpedon's mid-section. "I call it that on account of it'll make a hole in your stomach about the size of a raspberry pancake."

"Might!" Sarpedon smiled brazenly, even tauntingly, as if he feared a shotgun blast about as much as Hernandez plainly feared civility. "If it got through to me. And don't ask me what that's supposed to mean. I'm tired of your idiotic posturing. You're an ignoramus, Miguel. Go ahead and fire if it'll make you feel any better. I said shoot!"

"All right, Juju," backed off Hernandez, no doubt wishing he could take Sarpedon up on his offer. "Your word's your beastly bond. Let's get on with it. This place is creepy enough without you adding to it. Thing gave me the jitters, that's all." As a peace gesture his laid Aunt Jemima against his shoulder, like a soldier did his rifle while on parade.

"This *'thing'* is probably all any of us have that'll work against devils."

Seemingly led by the still slightly open eye-egg at the end of his shaft, Sarpedon walked ahead of the pack. (Pack wasn't a bad collective noun for this load of louts, he reflected. Maybe the disembodied eyeball still staring out of his prison pod was its solo snout.) Off a rock sticking out into the ocean he paused and looked down into the sea.

"Radio Centauri Island," he shouted back. "Tell Sentalli we've found his precious cosmicar. Only it's under about ten metres of the Pacific and all bashed up. Wait!"

The discorporate eye contracted visibly. (That's what it was – what else it was, rather – an externalized extension of his own senses; his sensational tellies, as his sister sometimes put it unhelpfully, referring to what pretentious paranormal investigators also called psionics.) "Say there's no bodies in it. No sign of the crew. Request instructions."

He turned to his men, just in case they hadn't heard him. All nine of them were pointing their weapons at him.

"This ain't our idea," grinned Hernandez malignantly. "Blast him!"

They blew him into the sea then, in a final fit of horde madness, turned on each other. When the smoke cleared, only Jones and Hernandez were left standing. Offshore, the suddenly panicky pilot was revving up the troop plane. Too late. Jones levelled his bazooka at the cockpit and blew it apart as well.

The two men looked at each other in satisfaction and, without saying – or signing – another word, began to dump the bodies of their fellows into the water. When they'd removed all evidence of their presence, they went to the beach, loaded two of the dinghies with stones and shoved them into the sea. They got into the third one and rowed it away from the island.

Sinking the other two, they shot a hole in the bottom of theirs, embraced like the old friends they were, swallowed the business ends of their still smoking guns, winked in solidarity then pulled the triggers. To their fractured minds, shotgun sandwiches never tasted so good. No need to hold the ketchup, either.

They weren't worried about their physiques any longer.

========

Even though, strictly speaking, Demios Sarpedon was no more a deviant than Ringleader or most witches, his staff and eyeorbs bequeathed him many supranormal-level abilities. The pods themselves operated much like Anthean agates; were, in fact, very similar to them.

Except, they automatically charged on naturally-produced psychic eman-ations. They therefore worked best around higher functioning sentient beings. And, somewhat remarkably to Sarpedon's way of thinking, even someone like Hernandez qualified as a sentient being.

When attached to eye-staves, the orbs gave him tremendous advantages over normal men and women (Norman and Norma Normalcy, to use a supra term). They granted him far-sight, what would have been called television in centuries gone by but was now taken by an appliance. They allowed him not so much the ability to read peoples' minds as deduce what they were thinking with a fair degree of confidence.

He could coerce others to a limited degree; albeit never into doing some-thing they wouldn't ordinarily do, such as kill themselves. While they couldn't alter his appearance per se, they could be used to affect how people perceived him both outwardly and inwardly, as in physically and psychologically. If he was projecting or, more accurately, wearing what was known as a glamour, pictures taken of him would show just that, not how he really looked.

When he was alive, Jesus Mandam sometimes called them *'Speaking Sticks'*. In sub-Saharan Africa – where Sarpedon wasn't from – tribesmen, and women, passed around something they called the same thing, Speaking Sticks. They did so to indicate whose turn it was to speak, without fear of interruption, in council sessions.

(Most African speaking sticks had a knob at one end but it wasn't detach-able. The person could use it to bonk anyone who dared interrupt him without fear of reprisal.)

Besides being both detachable and ejectable with a thought when full, Sar-pedon's, and ones like his, were different. Among many other things that New Agers might call tellies (telepathy, telekinesis, telecasting, etc.) or, less familiar-ly, psi (psionic) faculties, they could actually force folks to talk true.

The pods acted as brainwave foci (not focuses); thought talismans, as some described them; psyche amplifiers, as others did. Demios was hardly the only one who could use them; just one of the most accomplished. Levitation, exclu-sion-shields and psychokinetic extrusions – invisible thought-beams that pound-ed tangibly, like hammers on heads – were three other supra-level abilities he could generate.

If Sarpedon was at all beyond extraordinary for one with his background and training, it was because of his superior survival instincts. Even in the com-parative vacuum of Damnation Island, with only a few others around, his eye-stave had no trouble projecting a protective force-field that absorbed the brunt of the murderous assault.

He was knocked into the freezing ocean but, again, his orb was able to en-case him in an insulated ball long enough for him to rise out of the sea and effect-ively float back to land as if in a soap bubble. (Wits familiar with comic books and newspaper cartoons dubbed them, not overly facetiously, thought balloons.)

By then the others had killed themselves, Jones had taken out the plane cockpit, pilot with it, and he and Hernandez were rowing out to sea; whereupon with three booms to sink the other zodiacs and blow a hole in theirs, followed by two more for themselves, they committed suicide. Gratefully alive and relatively unharmed, he nevertheless despaired for his chances of continuing that happy state of affairs for much longer.

The only thing he could think of was finding a way to activate the Brain-rock in the sunken cosmicar. But that was about as probable as hitchhiking a ride from a passing sperm whale, assuming such things weren't extinct out here. Still, sticking a thumb out on the shore couldn't hurt.

It'd certainly give him something cold to suck on before he froze to death.

========

Suddenly the eye-egg again activated against his will.

========

He became warmer and drier in an instant. Was there intelligence on the island? Had to be. Once again he let it guide him. Camel-humped as it was, albeit only dromedary so, Damnation Island was actually quite small. In a crevice not far up its solitary hill – what made it reminiscent of a beehive or manmade tholos – he quickly found what was charging his orb.

"What are you?"

"Not a devil."

"That I can see," responded Sarpedon, too shocked at what he beheld to be disturbed that it could read his mind. "Answer me!"

"As you can plainly tell, Blackguard, I'm a brain with neither head nor body. Seemed to have lost both of those somewhat crucial appendages in the course of nearly a quarter century in what I learned to call Limbo. Can still see and hear and talk and, yes, I can even smell you.

"As for who I am, you'll have already guessed that from all of the above. Howsoever briefly, once upon a time, forty odd years ago, we even attended the same school: the Amsterdam Academy of Man. Age made you a senior; a very rich father made me your better."

"Saul Ryne — the Magnificent Psycho!"

"When I had the usual accoutrements of a human being, yes indeed. And, ditto that deed, from the Forties until the mid-Fifties I was the supranormal known by that unflattering codename. Magnificent I may have been but, until just now, I was no Psycho, capitalized or not, as in psychopath; also not to be confused with cycle path, of which there are none here. Desperation has driven me to extremes."

"Where I come from your type are referred to as deviants. You compelled my men to try and kill me. Then to kill each other."

"A purely defensive reaction, I assure you. When dealing with a mob of terrified killers, trained or otherwise, especially ones armed for polar bear, you'd best strike first. Can you imagine what your Messieurs Jones or Hernandez would have done had they come across an oversized, discorporate, yet still functioning human brain? Besides, compulsion's a family trait."

Sarpedon would have agreed with that – unlike his wife, he was never a fan of the Rynes – but he was still attempting to comprehend how a brain, especially one without a body, could survive a quarter century and remain operable. Hypo-thermia made you dopey, yet hallucinations rarely conversed so coherently, let alone with some small sense of humour. And if he was dead or dreaming, why did he see his breath?

"I'll admit to being a bit boggled by all this," carried on what was left of Psycho in, it seemed to Sarpedon, the understatement of this or any other century. "Don't take offense but I only vaguely recall you. Seems to me you weren't a supra; at least, you weren't deemed one by my esteemed father and his Alliance of anti-abnormal, judge-jury-and-executioners. How did you survive?"

"How do you know about devils?"

"I've recently seen at least seven of them in action."

"Seen?"

"With my mind's eye. Your turn."

"Call it extrasensory perception," Sarpedon felt obligated to answer, "Except it's not really me who has it. You see, once Trinondevs plug in an eyeorb, we project an invisible shield about ourselves. My eye-stave automatically hardens it impenetrably around me if it perceives danger; which it obviously did.

"Their gun blasts rocked me into the ocean but didn't hurt me. Unfortunately, I was dazed. I recovered too late to stop them from massacring each other." He paused. Brain working properly again he mulled over not just his own situation. "Not that I'm complaining overly much," he carried on, "But I don't see what you gained by causing them to kill themselves.

"I mean, with your compulsive abilities, you could have required any one of them to hide you underneath his clothes or in his gun bag until we were safely away from here. After that, you could have had the pilot fly us anywhere you wanted to go. So why didn't you? Or have finally gone like you say, seriously psychotic?"

"Not a bad analysis. And I did consider doing just what you said. Except I don't want to go anywhere, not with you and especially not your mercs. Besides, I doubt you'd have been allowed to leave. You see, there's at least one still around. I need protection from him."

"I knew it! Which one?"

"Calls himself Vayu Maelstrom, Devil Wind."

"One of Great Byron's Primary Nucleoids," said Sarpedon without volunteering how, let alone how much, he knew about devils.

"Two, three, maybe even four millennia ago, Byronics got most of their worshippers in what eventually became known as the Americas, North, South and a whole bunch of Central. Some of Vayu's devotees, the Caribbean and Gulf Coast natives, called him *'Hurican'* when he was out here on a regular basis way back then." He had another brain wave.

"Hold on. You read minds. Why didn't you compel me to act in your defence?"

"Except superficially, on an emotional level, you are opaque to me. I might be able to propel you but I can no more compel you than I could a rock. Besides, you are not of my kind. Two of them are on their way back here as we speak. Plus, I'm working on contacting yet another: my sister Aranyani, if you have to know.

"As you can appreciate, I lack the legs to move. Nor do I have any idea either how I survived, especially like this, or what I need to stay alive. Aran's a resourceful lass; has to be, as I thought her as dead as I should be. She'll sort everything out. The other two will protect me until she gets here."

"I am a devil-slayer."

"Pardon me but, from what I saw of Devil Wind, there's no such thing. By your boasting I doubt you'd know a devil if one tweaked you on the nose and blinked its third eye. You're all bluff and bluster, Blackguard. It wouldn't surprise me if Vayu was your forbearer. He was so full of hot air it's a wonderment the Diver didn't start calling him Brimstone Breath."

"Wait a minute! *'The Diver'* ... *'two others'* ... *'not my kind'* — you're saying the King Crimefighters were here as well? Twenty-five years after their deaths?"

"You *'head'* me – that's a word-combination of *'heard'* and *'hear'*, by the way. And they've their bodies."

"Unbelievable!"

The disembodied brain went silent a few seconds. After reflecting on what he/it had become, it/he let out an audible thought-chuckle. "Hardly a relevant exclamation. Are the dead coming alive again, especially in the midst of those who were just living dying, more believable than me? Yet here I am."

"So I see!"

"Precisely my point. Seeing is believing." Again the pulsating mass of grey matter paused briefly before continuing. "The Damnation Brigade – that's what they call themselves now – took Maelstrom apart like an insensate frog in a high school biology class. Yet he's still around. I can sense him. And as soon as he pulls himself together again, he'll be back with a vengeance. All he has to do is blow away your eye-stave and pods, mighty devil-slayer, and you're dust in his windbag. You are no use to me."

"I would like to reacquaint myself with these almighty friends of yours."

"They're hardly friends but here comes your chance."

=========

Blind Sundown and Raven's Head, entirely inhuman as she was, lightened the twilight as they blazed out of the Grey.

Psycho couldn't compel them to kill the man he derisively called Black-guard. He could, however, strongly suggest, mind to minds, that they dispose of him someplace immediately irretrievably. After skimming 'the top' of Sarpedon's mind, its unshielded "mental epidermis" as it were, he could telepathically suggest the perfect drop-off spot for the would-be devil-slayer.

Should they choose to heed him, it went without saying. Which they did.

=========

Blind Sundown fired his Solar Spear. It immolated the prison-pod atop Sarpedon's staff. Raven swooped low.

Sundown, who could see through her eyes, gathered Sarpedon, not even close to being a small man, up in his strong arms. They flitted through the dark grey universal substance of Samsara – which they'd only just discovered, or more likely rediscovered, they could do – and dumped him off near a fish packer far to the south.

Blinking back through between-space, they returned to Damnation Island …

"Well done, old friends, older enemies," imparted the disembodied brain. "Soon you will be freed of the onerous – make that honourless – duties I've thrust upon you. Once I contact her, my sister will find her way here on one of Wilderwitch's carelessly discarded Anthean agates and cart me to safety.

"When that happens, you may of course go your own way. But, in the meantime, I have forged a mind-link with my twin, your Cerebrus. Through him I shall long-distance-ensure that our return to the world is thoroughly shrouded. You and the rest of your Brigade will be able to forge new lives. That I guarantee you."

"Twenty-five years too late," muttered Sundown. Raven's Head flashed him a thought. "I suppose you're right, Beauty," he responded, with a twinkle in his voice; not, being eyeless, in his eye. "There is a silver lining in our nimbus. When it comes down to it, Psycho is the devil we know."

And Vayu Maelstrom was the devil in the deep blue sea. Did he stir?

========

The now nominally Sharkczar-cyborg pulled Demios Sarpedon out of the nearby drink. "My, my, what have we here, Crystallion?"

"The Ace of Spades?"

"Inexplicably enough, I think you're right. For our purposes though, he's a joker. The Wild Card we've been looking for to rid ourselves of Daemonicus and Strife."

Sarpedon opened his eyes. Even though he hadn't seen the thing in years, even though it had changed radically in that time, there was no denying whom, what, it was.

"Steltsar!"

****

NUKE 8: **The Strife Sorority**

========

Mid-November 1980

Countess Ramona Avar Ryne woke early.

========

Absolutely inexplicably – and only after a thorough, still predawn search of the Budapest mansion where she'd been held under house-arrest for most of a decade – she finally satisfied herself she was alone. No keepers, no guards, no soldiers patrolling the grounds of the hilly estate within sight of Buda's famous castle. What was going on?

(Buda, roughly the western third of the Hungarian capital, took its name from the historic Attila the Hun's brother. Her long gone mother's notorious half-brother, Etzel born Sangati, claimed direct descent from Attila. Indeed, even though he generally went by Bleda – Bleda being but a Hunnish variant of Buda – Uncle Etzel's father had the same given name.)

Dressing carefully, though awkwardly – she had never been fitted for a hook to replace her lost forearm – she glanced into the mirror. Despite turning 50 three years before, she thought of herself as still quite handsome. The grey could go, so could about twenty pounds, but overall she felt and looked damn good, things considered.

She heard a car pull up and panicked momentarily. It was only a mail van. The driver left a decent-sized parcel on the stoop then drove away. A few minutes later, still perplexed as to how the van got through the estate's usually locked gate, she tentatively opened the door, grabbed the package, and hastily slipped back inside. The box contained a stump protector with a series of attachments wrapped in brown paper. She tried it on; found it fitted perfectly.

Excited despite a taciturn nature developed by such a lengthy and, to her mind, entirely unwarranted detainment, she checked out the attachments. One was a light-weight, otherwise standard hook; another packet held a heftier meat cleaver. Both looked made-to-order. She screwed in the cleaver first.

"Thought you'd go for that," came a female voice out of the air. "Always figured you for the Lady Guillotine type. No fey Captain Hook you, eh, latest mother."

A tiny stone glowed on the floor. Off of it stepped a scrawny woman wearing a black body-stocking under a tattered red mini-skirt and pink blouse. She wore no shoes, had a spiked Mohawk died purple and green, and no face. Put better, what face her head had was blank, totally featureless, not a nose-knob nor any shadowy dips for eyes or mouth visible.

"You're Strife."

"Got that in one, mom."

"Anhita?"

"Balkis."

"I have no daughter named Balkis. I've a girl named Anhita, and her twin, a son named Erech. Their father's Loxus Abraham Ryne, the big cheese of the patriarchal Xuthrodites."

"You also have a daughter named Balkis and a son, my twin brother, named Solomon. Our father was Ryne's nephew, the son of his twin sister, Mary Magdalene."

"Oh my God!" Memories, long suppressed by either amnaesthetics or the enchantments of witch covens, flooded back. Many weren't particularly pleasant. Worse, the farther they took her back the clearer it became that memories of those Ramona thought of as her parents were somehow implanted. "Jesus Mandam, Wiccan Warlock, the Conquering Christ! I was Strife."

"When you were a lot younger than I am now, yes. But you weren't the first nor the last. I am only the latest. And, unlike most of them, I've taken her on voluntarily. Your father was Sedon St Synne, not Zygion Avar, the alchemical supra once codenamed Count Viper. Your mother was Sed-son's adopted daughter Cybele, not one of the incestuous bastard's many other daughters, the lovely but drugs- and drink-damaged Mata become Avar but always Ararat.

"Cybele was the first Strife of the modern era. Our father was St Synne's son, not Old Joe's. Would you like to know who the other Strifes were?"

"Does it matter? All I want is revenge."

"That you shall have in spades, latest mother!"

Another horror appeared out of the air, off the stepping stone. This one was a mass of darkness in human form with a pink face and hands, these last with too many knuckles on too many digits. He also had a third eye. She had never seen him before; not that she could remember anyhow. And surely she'd remember someone with three eyes.

He was smiling. She sensed he never stopped smiling.

"You may address me as Daemonicus."

========

Her life had not been an easy one.

Great swathes of it were missing — as if someone else had led it for her. That someone was Strife. But exactly what Strife was hadn't been clear to her until that Budapest morning.

========

Interminable imprisonment followed her capture by AMERICA in 1970. She had no idea how she got there, the Worldwide Order's then headquarters in Hong Kong. Nor could she explain how it came to pass her left forearm had been blown off during a firefight between her, the cyborg-thing Steltsar, WORLD's home guard, and the agents of AMERICA.

OJ Maxwell, the aging leader of AMERICA's strike-force, had more than his share of witnesses to back up his explanation, however. She had become Strife, again, and the only reason she wasn't dead was that Steltsar had shielded her with his body in the final minutes of AMERICA's offensive. It had been a damn good body, this then latest Steltsar's, but it hadn't been indestructible and Maxwell had pictures to prove it.

The Strife this Steltsar died protecting had been taken into custody. When the illusion of blank face and geyser of red hair wore off, there was Ramona Avar, minus her forearm just as Strife had been deprived of hers in the explosion. Of course she protested her innocence. She'd done a ditto a decade earlier when she, as Strife, had been nailed fleeing the funeral of Belificent D'Angelo briefly Zeross.

It was a cruel game. Whoever the real Strife was – and she had no doubt it was the then fifteen years dead supra by the name of Wilderwitch – she just kept on using her as a fall guy.

The whole thing was sheer madness.

'Yes,' Max agreed. *'Yours.'*

Neither Big Max nor her ex-husband, Loxus Ryne, were persuaded she was the only Strife. Regardless of their convictions to the contrary, she was nonetheless sent to her (evidently only thought) native Hungary, where she was held in near total isolation for virtually all of the Seventies. Only a select few were allowed to visit her and they, if they chose to stay in the same, howsoever luxurious house, had to endure the indignity of being kept under twenty-four hour guard the same as she.

While not specifically banned, Erech and Anhita chose to stay away. Her twins by the Great Man didn't even write to her. Which explained why her love for them soured to bitterness bordering on hatred. She'd become so disconsolate that, when old friend and occasional lover Günter von Alptraum brought news that Oriani Ryne, Abe's fourth wife, had died, she took a perverse pleasure learning that Oriani's final illness was caused by her brother, Dr Aristotle Zeross, the same Harry Zeross whose bride Strife – supposedly her – killed in 1960.

As she sunk deeper into depression, she gave into the insanity that she supposed was her Strife persona. Except, she remembered every bit of it. She began fantasizing ways to get even with her oppressors. Towards the end of the Seventies, she often lapsed into nightmare. Many times Steltsar appeared in them.

Claiming he was actually Günter's father, the old Baron Tyrtod von Alptraum, he promised her revenge. More! He promised they'd both be there to exact it.

Now it seemed that promise was about to be realized — by the very person responsible for ruining her life in the first place.

========

One of the first things Strife and the demonic phantasm explained was that her guards hadn't simply left her. They were still within the Budapest mansion that had been her surrogate parents' house until Zygion and Mata Avar were killed halfway through the war. They'd placed her in a kind of fairyland between space, yet still within the mansion. They called it Little Shelter, a word she'd hear more of, and promised it was only for a few days; just long enough to make certain that the woman they'd arranged to take her place settled in and started dying convincingly.

Daemonicus – who apparently possessed Solomon Mandam – having business elsewhere, Strife-Balkis stayed with Ramona between-space for the next two weeks. During their time together, her thankfully not always faceless, supposed daughter refreshed her memory even further. For example, while she had been born in 1927, Ray hadn't been born in Budapest. On the contrary, she'd been in a place Antheans call Big Shelter but was actually better known as something else.

Ray's given name wasn't even Ramona. It was Meroudys. Her surname was Maenad, the same as that which Cybele adopted once she decided to stay in Big Shelter back in '20. Her hometown was called Corona City. Reputedly the oldest metropolis in the entire world, it was both big and bizarre; many of its inhabitants weren't even human; weren't aliens either, Strife-Balkis insisted. It lay on Apple Isle – Ap Isle, as Balkis frequently called it – and, you know what? The rest of the world lay east of it.

Which made it, she claimed, at least conceivably, the Biblical Garden of Eden. Almost for sure, she further put to her, it was also the Garden of the Hesperides, home of the Norse Goddess Idunn, keeper of the Golden Apples of Eternal Youth. That Eden and Idunn were near homonyms pretty much cemented that notion as far as Balkis was concerned.

After having a child – also named Meroudys and a quarter century dead now – in '42, Ray was brought outside by her father-grandfather, Sedon St Synne (aka Judge Warlock on the Inner Earth of Big Shelter). Cybele was with them, as was Ramona's lover, Jesus-Wiccan. Although she was only sixteen and he was apparently the father of her first child, whom they'd left in the care of the Nightingale clan, Jess or Jesse hadn't been her first lover.

That dubious honour fell to a twenty year old boy named Osiraq. He died in '41, an unfortunate victim of the ages-old rivalry between Nightingales and Maenads, Antheans and Korants respectively. Cybele's primary motivation for coming out was to pursue another sixteen year old, the Anthean deviant whom even Balkis-Strife called Wilderwitch.

Cybele (aka Miracle Maenad) blamed the Witch, often capitalized, a member of the Nightingale clan supposedly gone rogue, for the death of Osiraq, her chosen son-in-law. Even though Ramona, then Meroudys, was content with Mandam, Miracle's enmity transferred to her daughter as if by osmosis.

When Wilderwitch returned to Big Shelter in '46, Miracle-Cybele went after her. Ramona stayed behind and assumed her mother's Strife persona once removed. (Someone else had Strife between early 1938, when Cybele lost her, and 1943, when she got her back. Evidently, Balkis confided, getting pregnant was the one sure way to get rid of Strife.)

In '49, Wilderwitch was back on the scene. After a series of confrontations that lasted most of that year, the Witch finally got the better of Strife-Ramona. She dismantled her Miracle Key and thereby, so she put it, abolished Strife. She never revealed her identity, though, and even allowed the Conqueror to take care of her, provided he kept her out of trouble.

Such was the situation until '52 when Aranyani Nightingale – not quite 20 and then only recently returned from Big Shelter – became infected with the

Strife virus and passed her back to Ramona. That summer she became pregnant by Jesus Mandam – the Conqueror, King Conqueror or Conquering Christ having unmasked himself the previous winter. Strife, who for reasons unspecified could not abide occupying a pregnant woman, was thus abolished a second time.

When Ramona asked why she couldn't remember her two legitimate times as Strife, Balkis said that Strife didn't leave memories behind. As for why she couldn't recall her years in Big Shelter, that was her mother's doing. Cybele-Miracle didn't think it would do any good if she knew about Big Shelter or, more importantly, that she was the result of an incestuous union between her mother and her father, both their fathers.

Nor did it seem particularly relevant that she'd had a first child named Meroudys, that she died as a result of yet another vendetta between Maenads and Nightingales, Korants and Antheans, in late '55, or that she had a set of twins before she had Anhita and Erech. But for her lost forearm, appeased Strife, playing to Ray's mostly justifiable vanity, after five children and the same amount of decades she looked miraculously well held together.

Ramona was equally curious about the two later times she apparently became Strife: in '60, when she was caught fleeing Bel's funeral (Bel = Belificent born D'Angelo become Zeross, briefly), and '70, when she ended up with the lower half of her left arm blown off. Balkis said there was no Strife in '60. What happened then was some other sister's doing.

Yes, conceivably Wilderwitch's. But that was highly unlikely. That particular witch was well and truly dead. In fact, Balkis added, from '52 to '65 there was no Strife at all; just bad girls and the occasional bad boy making it seem like there was one when it suited their needs. As for '70, well, though self-preservation wasn't a problem for her, Strife's hosts were skilled at covering their butts.

"Who was '70's actual Strife?"

"I thought you weren't interested."

"I told you, I require revenge."

"That may not be wise," advised Balkis. Ramona had finally become used to the way Strife and Balkis traded personas. Even though their look wavered between Balkis – a twenty-eight year old, fit, and slightly less-Slavic, short-haired version of Lady Guillotine, as Ramona had begun to think of herself – and the very distinctive Strife, the voice never changed.

"In the first place, she won't remember her time as Strife. In the second, you may need either her help or that of her friends."

"So, if I can't avenge myself on you; if Wilderwitch – who, as I always knew deep down inside, was responsible for my misfortunes – is dead; and you won't tell me who did me in either in '60 or '70; then who can I avenge myself on?"

"Loxus Ryne," suggested Balkis-Strife. "Your children by him, the ones who have ignored you for most of two decades? How about Alfredo Sentalli? If he'd paid Bel's ransom in '60, she might be alive to this day, Ringleader might never have remembered about his rings, and you might still be happily, if ignorantly, married to the patriarch."

"Couldn't I just pull the plug on St Synne? Without him, none of this would have happened."

"If you're that desperate for revenge, you might just as well kill yourself. It'd be a real waste, though. You were my favourite shell. Could be again."

It was Balkis who smiled beguilingly but Ramona knew it was Strife doing the talking.

"Where do I start then?"

"Anhita's an easy target. So is Centauri Island. If we can lure Ryne there, hey, if that isn't a start, I don't know what is."

"And after that?"

"Erech's the patriarch's heir apparent." Ramona was pretty sure it was Balkis expressing herself, but it was getting increasingly difficult to tell.

"You're his mom. Oriani's dead and her kids are barely twelve. Aranyani's illegitimate — your blood sister, in fact, and a paternity test will prove that if she contests it. The Tempest Twins disavowed any claim on his fortune years ago. Virginia Mannering's a Summoning Child. She's getting on and, anyway, she's not a part of his will in any substantive way.

"We show you're rehabilitated; Erech accepts you; NCE, the Alliance of Man, the Illuminated Faith of Xuthros Hor, follow suit ... well, let's just say Bob's your uncle even if Sed's your father and he didn't have any brothers. Neither did Sed's Red, Cybele; not paternally and let's not even start with maternally because no one really knows how that went down. What better revenge than taking over everything?"

"The world?"

"Why not? Ryne owns a disproportionate amount of it already. By rights all that should be yours anyway."

"I see. Then, of course, I come up with the story that you and Sol are my kids by Saul Ryne ..."

"A known affair," Balkis hastened to observe. "Made the press, as I recall reading in our family history. Wouldn't do to say we're Jesus Mandam's of course. He was a villain to many and, besides, he kept out of the limelight. Saul, though, was a public figure and Solomon shortens to Sol, as in Saul. Genetically speaking, Psycho and the Conqueror not only were first cousins but Mary Magdalene and Loxus Abraham were twins. The elder Ryne only married you out of guilt, don't you know."

"Erech dies a natural death ..."

"We witches are good with nature," agreed Balkis.

"You two take over and the world, not just WORLD's your oyster," finished Ramona, grasping every straw of the plot. "I end my days rich, secure in the knowledge that I've hurt everyone I can who hurt me first."

"You see, sister. I told you she'd understand everything!"

"I wish you'd stop doing that," Ramona chastised Daemonicus.

========

Sunday, November 30, 1980

Milo Mind staggered into his cabin late Sunday night. He slumped into a chair and started to disrobe. Just as he was putting on his pyjamas, a siren sang to him from his own bed.

"Don't bother with those, lover."

========

He didn't — but he did flip on the light.

Had the shock of seeing the phantom freighter and what came out of it killed him? Was he in heaven? He sure as hell hoped not; sure as heaven reckoned he wasn't in that other place either. Wasn't often a man could relive his wicked youth. Lying in his bunk, minus her left forearm and all her clothes, was the late Countess Ramona Avar Ryne.

Did he care that Strife, via her Korant kernels (as Corn Queens called their witch-stones), had just brought Ramona to WORLD's converted fish packer? Did he care that she'd been pronounced dead only a few hours earlier, in bloody Budapest no less, according to a newsfeed he'd received on board the fish packer? Nope, not in the slightest.

As for making love to a one-armed woman, that was just another first in a day as full of them as his bank accounts now were of the glittery stuff that really mattered.

========

Monday, December 1, 1980

"My, my, what have we here, Crystallion?" wondered the still largely anthropoid, cybernetic organism after it – unless it was a he – hauled Demios Sarpedon out of the drink.

"The Ace of Spades?"

Sarpedon opened his eyes. He'd never seen her as she was now. He hadn't seen the toothily selachian thing either; certainly not as it was presently configured. Nonetheless, as radically as it had changed since the last time he'd come across it, from the accent alone there was no denying whom, what, it was.

"Steltsar."

========

Crystal St Synne was now Crystallion. The Old Baron, Tyrtod von Alptraum, was not so much Steltsar as Sharkczar. Neither of them had much left of their humanity. She now referred to herself as a *'technopomp'*, a name she adapted from *'psychopomp'* since she was more technological horror than psychical one. She was also more a maker than a carrier of the dead — though her nuclear firedrakes did carry Hell's Horsemen (who, in not just her parlance, also fell into the category of technopomps).

He was a *'trinary'* (also ternary; albeit as a noun, not an adjective), a tripartite being: part machine, part replica, part man; cyborg more so than android, one with the still-functioning brain of the Nazi Nightmare and an artificially-grown body reinforced by robotics. Although she hadn't been born until 1946, by which time he had already been killed and made anew, their actual acquaintanceship dated back almost to Crystal's first step.

She wasn't quite two years old when, in 1948, Steltsar, then thought to be a Soviet supra, kidnapped her from her mother, Corona Power, a Japanese deviant codenamed Crimson Corona. That caused a vicious confrontation between the King's Own Crimefighters and the Soviet Supra Supreme, as run by the Collective Will (with ample assistance from the Conqueror and, though they didn't know it at the time, Sedon St Synne, Crystal's father).

Their battles, mostly confined to the Gypsium-replete, but sparsely-inhabited Tunguska region of Siberia became quite bloody; even threatened to flare into the public's eye. Which would never do. And didn't. Not even years later when, in June of 1965, Steltsar was wiped out for at least the third time and yet another Strife was captured.

Almost twenty years after her birth, this time she proved to be Crystal St Synne.

Crystal was *exorcised* – an oddly ecclesiastical word but one deemed appropriately applied to describe ridding the world, not capitalized, of such a then-thought only figurative devil. Nonetheless, within a year Strife and a fourth Steltsar, much improved on the early Sixties' version, were back in action.

This was the heyday of the Worldwide Order and it was generally acknowledged that Strife was Crystal St Synne again. And perhaps she was —for part of the time. In 1970's final confrontation between WORLD and AMERICA, Big Max blasted Steltsar out of existence, yet again, and recaptured Strife.

Whereupon, also yet again, she proved to be Ramona Avar.

========

Now Ramona, Steltsar, Milo Mind, Crystal, Hadrian's son Salvatore and Demios Sarpedon, the husband of Strife's most relentless enemy Morgianna, were on WORLD's packer.

Funny how stuff happens. Not that there was anything funny about the Worldwide Order.

========

Sharkczar (once Steltsar) had tailor-made his own body to suit his new nomenclature. It was based on – *duh!* – a shark's: with a head shaped like a claw-hammer, an oversized mouth and three layers of sharp teeth. Nearly seven feet from tip to toe, he stood on legs like a man but his feet were webbed and disproportionately long.

His arms doubled as ventral fins. His hands had long, spindly fingers that ended in talons. He had a pronounced dorsal-like fin that stuck out of his spine from just below his neck to his tailbone. His skin was dun-coloured; inlaid with a grey, metallic mesh that took the place of clothing. It was a body built for battle; there wasn't much it couldn't withstand and not much that could withstand it. He could breathe underwater as well as in the air but was best adapted, and hence most comfortable, in the ocean.

The craftsmen who put him together this last time had known their business. They'd also done a job on Crystallion. A striking-looking child, Crystal had grown into an attractive teenager. Her mixed blood – her mother was Japanese whereas her St Synne of a father was half-French, half-Ainu – looked to give her great beauty as an adult. Unfortunately, shortly after she was exorcised of Strife in '65, at the age of nineteen, her life literally started to fall apart.

She began to lose weight at an alarming rate. Her skin jaundiced and she became palsied. Her mother, Corona Power, had been in Hiroshima when the Americans dropped the A-Bomb and, though she didn't become pregnant until the next year, atomic radiation undoubtedly had something to do with Crystal's condition.

Corona had herself contracted cancer during the early Fifties and, though it had gone into a kind of protracted stasis, she had much of the same symptoms her daughter developed years later. Corona's way of dealing with her affliction had been to withdraw from society. Since 1955, she had refused to leave her Hiroshima apartment. (Still hadn't after a quarter century, though someone who looked very much like her had been behind the events of '65 and, probably, been the one who actually killed Belificent in '60.)

Corona's life had been a mystery ever since she and Obadiah Melvin Power, the fay-saying, Xuthrodite supranormal more commonly known as OMP or Old Man Power, emerged from the Hiroshima blast. Because of her talisman, she acquired the supra-codename Crimson Corona. She infiltrated St Synne's stronghold on Sakhalin on behalf of Maxius Skullian and, while there, the then not-so-old satyr seduced and impregnated her with Crystal.

Reconciled with OMP, they lived relatively happily from '49 to '53. Then, on the Summer Solstice, she gave birth to a baby girl in Vancouver General Hospital. Another result of the Dionysian frenzy of the previous year's supra-summit, they named her Tsukyomi. Sadly for her parents more so than Tsukyomi, the infant died in hospital within a matter of days. Consequently dangerously unstable and realizing it, Corona allowed Obadiah to take Crystal to the Houston Academy of Man while she retreated to Hiroshima.

Thereafter, due to OMP's public activities on behalf of the Illuminated Faith of Xuthros Hor, his clandestine ones as part of the King Crimefighters, and his death in late December 1955, Crystal was raised almost exclusively by Virginia Mannering. Headmistress, the unmarried, childless, Anthean teacher whom Loxus Ryne trusted more than any other woman, looked after her until the events of '65. Whereupon Crystal began to deteriorate even more rapidly.

As Headmistress, ex-Superior Sorrow (Dolores Rivera) and Hiliarti Schroff-Zeross, then still an up-and-coming Ant, were forced to admit, the young woman was beyond the help of even Sisterhood healers. (They called themselves Altheans, a word that just meant healing. Contrary to some beliefs, it didn't come from the goat whose milk supposedly kept the infant Zeus goo-goo-gurgling on Ancient Crete. Her name was Amalthea.)

The Steltsar of the late Sixties found out about her plight and recognized a kindred spirit. In a bizarre case of déjà vu, he kidnapped her, just as an earlier Steltsar had seventeen years earlier. From then on, in a variation of what psychologists often referred to as the Stockholm Syndrome nowadays, they were practically inseparable.

He couldn't cure her but did somehow manage to find a way to turn her into Strife again. That kept her going until 1970, when AMERICA finally crushed WORLD for the last time until this time. Although Ramona was once again made to take the fall, Crystal immediately reverted to her deteriorating state.

Those who kept reconstructing Steltsar could, and did, save her, but at the cost of what little humanity she had left. She became somewhat akin to him, Steltsar: something, as much as someone, that could now be rebuilt. Renaming herself Crystallion, she became an altered, almost Jungian animus who lived in a radiation-containment suit.

Her helmet looked like a Japanese demon's mask. In medieval mythologies, psychopomps were supernatural beings who conducted souls safely to the afterlife. In her personal mythology, a technopomp was someone like her: more made than born; more artificial than natural; more supranormal than supernatural; more death than life.

Psychopomps were often also described as mystical horses that shamans rode to the underworld to commune with spirits or retrieve the souls of the sick. Technopomps had horses too, but they weren't mystical: they were nuclear dragons. Technopomps didn't ride them to the underworld; they used them to send others there.

As soon as Daemonicus gave the word, she would lead Hell's Horsemen to Centauri Island and destroy it.

========

Ramona Avar, Lady Guillotine, lazed on the deck of WORLD's converted fish packer.

Here, well off the coast of Centauri Island, she had never felt such contentment.

========

The most recent Steltsar reconstruction and one of her fellow former Strifes, Crystal St Synne now Crystallion, dragged Sarpedon before her. He was semi-conscious, dressed in a soaked grey robe like a black Buddhist monk, and held a long, pole-like, blunt-ended shaft as if his very life depended on it.

Stupid man! Tyrtod – Steltsar, she reminded herself, make that Sharkczar – would probably use it like a toothpick. As for what Crystallion would do with it, well, she deliberately limited the scope of her imagination. (Mata Avar, whom Ray-Meroudys now accepted was not her mother, was a Lovely Lady Afrite. It was best not to think of an Afrite's appetite but it was not unlike that of a satyr.)

They'd only met that morning. Nevertheless, though they were both terrifying-looking specimens, ones who were clearly not normal (she'd never come across a talking shark nor anyone who rode a nuclear dragon before), she believed them cloaked with illusions, like Strife and Daemonicus had been between-space in Budapest. To her mind, that made them completely human, as in mortal, albeit – only perhaps – supranormal.

She addressed them as such. To do otherwise would shake her fragile grip on what currently passed for sanity.

"What have we here, the Ace of Spades?"

"Funny, sister," Crystallion grinned beneath her demon-mask. "That's exactly what I said."

"Not funny," growled Steltsar. "Uncanny."

Ramona improvised an explanation. "We onetime Strifes have an affinity for each other's thoughts." The previous two weeks she had learned so much about her life, and those of Sedon St Synne's various daughters, granddaughters and great-granddaughters, it made as much sense as anything else.

Learned? No, told. Ah, but was she told true? There was no way to be sure. However, after a night and most of the day talking, and not just talking, with Milo Mind, whom she regarded as the voice of reason, she was pretty certain what was going on — and who was responsible for all these horrors. The witch and her lover might be good but she and Major Mind would prevail.

"There's something familiar about him. I knew his father or uncle, I think. What's your name?" Sarpedon groaned and finally passed out.

"We're not going to get much out of him for a couple of days," said the selachian three-thing. "Your instincts are right except for one thing. He's same one you knew in the Fifties. I knew him then too, and long before that, when he and his oppositely coloured sister and just as snow white, eventual wife were still in their late teens. Mind you, it hasn't been nearly that long since we've had the displeasure of each other's company."

Sharkczar (Steltsar) laid Sarpedon on a lounge chair and picked up his eye-stave. "This is quite the weapon. If we were inside, in the right place, I wouldn't want to be Crystallion. Mind you, Demios Sarpedon's quite the guy. Search back in what's left of your memory, Meroudys Maenad. Compute, if you can: Black-guard, Morrigan, Superior, Corn Queens, Theopolis Hill, Tholoi, Beehive Ghost Houses, make that Guest Houses of the Gods, Ap Isle, Apple of your mother's eye. Want some dates to go with it?"

"He doesn't look much more than twenty-five or thirty," remarked Ramona, who'd already decided to stick with Ramona or Ray; unless she started answering to Lady Guillotine, which was beginning to appeal. She made a further mental note that Strife had cleverly sucked in Tyrtod – that's what she'd call him, forget dumb supra-codenames – just as she'd tried to do to her in Budapest.

"He's almost sixty, a Summoning Child like so many others from the Supra Wars and a Utopian, a naturally-born Trinondev of Weir. No clone this one, there's nothing artificial about him. Not like me. He doesn't age like you do, either. Utopians never do. Although, like all of us except apparently Daemonicus, he's entirely mortal. Something about their genetic makeup retards the aging process.

"He and his wife should be our allies. Actually, they once were, years ago now and, um, not altogether hereabouts, though you'd probably be surprised how close it is. Our alliance didn't last and he and his have caused me and my Lemurian and Tellurian associates, as well as some of our onetime mutual, bio- and technomage confederates, a ton of trouble ever since.

"He and his immediate family are sort of related to these last in that they have Utopian blood. You can't really call them countrymen, not after having been separated by centuries, but they are supposed to share the same anti-devic reason for being. And his wife is the mother of one of our main movers; albeit from all reports by a fucking faerie: a *daemon* with an '*Æ*', not just an '*E*', after the '*D*'.

"Trinondevs style themselves devaslayers," he concluded, sounding more dismissive than merely sceptical, as if there was no such a thing. Or, if there was, Demios wasn't one. "So he reckons himself superior to folks like us and the mages who helped make us what we are. And, again apparently, Daemonicus is a Master Deva."

 More whaledreck, Ramona cautioned herself, piled atop the vast tons of codswallop Strife and Daemonicus had already tried to load into the tabula rasa of her sorely scrambled, more so than even close to empty, memory cells. Deva, she somehow knew, was just a Hindu – or was it Zoroastrian? – term for Shining One: a divinity, a god; all right, a devil, a little god.

(Errant, make that aberrant, thought that. Where did it come from? Was she somehow channelling Meroudys Maenad? Tyrtod hadn't said how many years ago he and the Sarpedons were supposedly allies, had he. They were all so old and variously experienced it may well have been in the late Forties or early Fifties.)

Supras, she also knew, liked to pretend they were somehow supernatural. They weren't; weren't even witches and warlocks, except in their own delusions of grandeur. They did have knowledge, though; something she and Mind were only just gaining; unless (there it is again) it really was more a matter of regaining remembrances that had been redacted, wiped out, replaced and/or rewritten.

How far could she trust Tyrtod with their insights? Was he a potential ally? Would he stand in her way once she figured out how to make Crystal pay for '60 and '70? Did she have to pay? Was she just another victim? Perhaps at first, but was she still? Like a game of five card stud, she kept the ace of her awareness hidden and dealt her next one – a metaphoric king, as she fancied – face up.

"Daemonicus purports to be my son by Jesus Mandam, the Conquering Christ. Says his real name is Solomon; that his twin sister is Balkis, like the Queen of Sheba. All very Biblical of them, I'm sure, but it gibes with I recall hearing the prick Abe complain about his nut ball twin, Jesse's mom. Makes lots of other claims as well. How does this guy slay devils?"

"Willpower – and this. Watch!"

Steltsar reached into Sarpedon's pouch and removed an egg-like orb not much bigger than the size of a billiard ball. This he attached to the top of the staff; adhered, more like, since he didn't screw it into place. Whatever it was in actuality, it cracked open immediately. An otherwise incorporeal, solitary eyeball poked out; regarded the four of them. Satisfied, it withdrew back into its casing.

Ramona took a few moments to catch her breath. Sarpedon was either yet another supra, she realized, or he could cast illusions unconsciously. She looked to Crystallion. Time for test two; didn't need to show a card for this one. She tried to think the devil out of her and into the pod. It didn't work.

"If you're supposed to be possessed by a devil, how come that thing has no effect on you?"

"I'm mostly a mandroid," recited the demon-headed, transformed technop-omp almost by rote. "We're something sometimes also called a mantel or man-nish tellurian. I'm not possessed as much as constructed – by the Utopian bio-mages Sharky here was just speaking about howsoever, um, non-circumspectly.

"So long as we're not keeping secrets from each other, I may as well tell you that I was made to contain one specific Master Deva; one chosen by All of Incain and Amphitrite of Lemuria to further their goals: namely, the eradication of devazurkind. If I have a devil inside me, it merely energizes me, gives me my power and acts as my motor. Like those brought down by either the devaray or the Miracle Key over three decades ago, its will is subject entirely to me. So I'm told anyhow."

"Do keep the motor away from your mouth," advised Ramona nastily. She put a negative 'X', rather than a question mark, against Crystallion's name; crossing her off her mental checklist of potential allies. Not much hope for this one. Victim or not, she's too far gone. "Let's try out this gadget, Tyrtod."

"On?"

Good sign that. Accepts his normal name and, if her re-developing Korant sensibilities were any indication – as dear Milo insisted that morning in bed – seems open at least to the notion of retaliation, of vindication. She knew full well who had to be punished for her lifelong misery and probably that of the old Baron's as well.

Step by slow step, Mind had instructed her, as if reciting a mantra. Patience isn't a virtue; it's a necessity. He'd told her much the same thing twenty odd years ago when he was one of the more unorthodox therapists Abe Ryne hired around the same time she got nailed as the Strife that wasn't in May 1960. At her age, in her present extremis, plodding along in slow mode wasn't the best advice he could give her.

Acceleration was what she required as much as revenge. It'd be nice to be rich and running more than just her own future.

It'd be better if she ran the WORLD.

========

Time for another prod, another symbolic card as she'd trained herself to think. It was the queen of the same suit as her imaginary king and ace in the hole — the Death Card.

"Who else? Strife!"

****

NUKE 9: **The Houston Academy of Man**

========

Wednesday, December 3, 1980 AD

Aboard the SPACE jet, O'Ryan James Maxwell and Professor Romaine Kinesis left Centauri Island towards dawn Tuesday morning. They went to Honolulu for the balance of the morning then flew across the Pacific to Los Angeles Tuesday afternoon. After spending the night there, they'd gone on to Houston.

An ocean and half a continent away from Ryne and his voice, it didn't take Max much in the way of persuasion to convince the pilot to disregard his boss's orders. Of course, when your travelling companion was a Gypsium Man, matters were made all the easier. A quick demonstration – Rom levitating a fire extinguisher in the cockpit simply by pointing at it – was enough.

The pilot kindly gave them a four-hour window of opportunity to visit the Houston Academy of Man.

========

1980 currently, Houston was the fifth largest city in the USA. With a population of one and a half million, it was the railroad, freeway and airport hub of the south and southwestern states. Like the Academy of Man situated there, the city offered more than its share of arts, humanitarian and cultural components.

Loxus Ryne's name was attached to its symphony orchestra, ballet and opera companies. (Astonishing to some, since he was so stridently anti-Axis once the war began, the Great Man loved Richard Wagner's Ring Cycle. In point of fact, their mutual love of Wagner came into play when he famously convinced Adolph Hitler to shave off his moustache the time they met, face-to-face, all those years ago now.)

A true city father, the patriarch of the stridently secular Illuminated Faith of Xuthros Hor also helped fund a number of museums and theatre groups. There was even talk of him eventually opening up for public consumption his private collection of priceless artifacts gleaned from explorations conducted and/or funded by the Alliance of Man and, before it, his father's Godling Guild.

Perhaps because its full name reminded many of the probably fabulous – as in apocryphal or non-existent – Illuminati, some suspected the Faith was a seditious secret society along the lines of the Freemasons. Its beginnings were deliberately obscured. And not just by the passage of time. The Great Man's father, Charan Ryne, dead since 1920, was listed as a funding, but certainly not founding, member when its charter was made public in the 1890s.

That it or versions of it had probably been in existence for hundreds, more likely thousands, of years before then was, today, almost as much lost in history as the Godling Guild had been fascinated with Ancient History. Xuthrodism, after all, held that Xuthros Hor (the tenth patriarch of Golden Age Humankind and, therefore, the Biblical Noah), and not God, capitalized, caused the Great Flood of Genesis (which they consequently referred to as the Genesea).

The original Academy of Man was established in Amsterdam in the early 1920s. Well before the Nazis invaded Holland, Ryne relocated the Amsterdam Academy, at least the majority of its staff and most of its students, to Edinburgh. A few years later, in the late Forties, he reopened the college to complement both the one in Scotland and one he'd subsequently set up in Houston. During the following three decades, Academies were established all over the world. The one in Houston, where the patriarch lived, was by far the largest, however.

Associated with such state-supported educational facilities as the University of Houston and Texas Southern, the Academy was nevertheless privately-funded, the same as Rice, St Thomas and the Baptist University, all of which were in the vicinity. Specialized branches of it worked hand-in-glove with the Texas Medical Centre, the Lyndon B. Johnson Space Centre, and various research and developmentally-oriented industrial parks.

(Long before the JFK assassination seventeen years earlier, Ryne learned never to trust LBJ and his cronies, who'd pretty much ran Texas the way they wanted to for decades. The Great Man, though, rarely let personal feelings get in the way of either political or financial expediency. He'd dealt with Hitler, after all, as well as many another equally or almost as unsavoury character mano-a-mano many times. As he put it, he'd do business with the Devil Himself so long as he had his hearing aid turned on.)

Academy graduates found employment in all sorts diverse manufacturing fields. Around here you wouldn't have to dig too deeply into ones dedicated to petrochemicals, synthetics, insecticides, fertilizers, electronics and agriculture – particularly rice, the dominant crop of the area – before you unearthed a Houston graduate. That was true of every Academy of Man throughout the world; albeit, naturally, their specialties differed area-to-area.

Academies of Man provided a disproportionate number of Agents of AMERICA during the Sixties and up until the early Seventies, when it was disbanded. Graduates also worked for Ryne's SPACE, Simon Lancz's Signal System and, again probably, whomever's WORLD. (Chances were the Worldwide Order, with its Daemonicus-access to an apparently bottomless pit of gold bullion, paid better than any of them.)

Something like one-in-four of the men and women employed on Centauri Island did their bachelor and/or post-graduate degrees in Academies or affiliates thereof. An even greater percentage were cosmicompanions. Thinking about it on the way over, Professor Kinesis and Big Max Maxwell agreed that wasn't as much surprising as scary.

A large number of those who either went to Academies or had their education at least partially funded by the Alliance of Man – the philanthropic organization that ran the Academies and presented the official face of the Illuminated Faith – had similar backgrounds. That, though, Max insisted, was only as it should be.

The majority were direct descendants of members of the Godling Guild, either that or ones whom Xuthrodite research judged likely to have been *'summoned'* in 1920. (Back in the mid-Twenties Abe Ryne and his closest colleagues, notably Angus Dre'Ath, determined there were a number of Simultaneous Summonings issued circa Imbolc, Ground Hog or Candlemas Day 1920.) Some were relatives of known supranormals active during the remarkably still largely secret Supra Wars, the roughly eighteen years between early '38 and late '55.

As for the rest, Maxwell shuddered as he told Kinesis, they may well be modern era supras — trained then suppressed by amnaesthetics or, just as likely, techniques employed by almost as secretive Anthean sisters, whom many a Xuthrodite brother married. If so, either the Alliance didn't expect them to return or aliens, should they encounter any, beware.

The Academy was near the Astrodome, where the NFL's Oilers and baseball's Astros played. It wasn't so much a campus as a series of high-rises. Most of the faculty lived in outlying regions of the city and commuted to the Academy by car. (Typically of most of the southern states, public transport was not one of Houston's claims to fame.)

After landing at the William P. Hobby Airport, they hailed a cab and went to the Academy. So much to do. So many people to see — though, Max promised Rom, not to kill.

Could yet prove not the first time he broke a promise.

=========

For confirmatory purposes that only became relevant – even vital – to him after their Sunday night meeting with the little trickster (Hush Mannering), Max wanted to talk with Moses Callion. That he'd likely come across his ex-wife, Aranyani always Nightingale, was unavoidable. She was Moe Three's partner; possibly in more than just work if, adopted or otherwise, the birth records for one Firenze Nightingale Callion were in any way legitimate.

If she was Strife, and he could prove it, he'd kill her. Even if she wasn't, he still might.

=========

Security in most of the buildings was fairly lax but the research centre where Dr Nightingale had her expansive (meaning expensive), subterranean laboratory was thoroughly guarded, physically and electronically. Howsoever significantly, as well as opportunely, the Academy was sponsored by the Alliance of Man and New Century Enterprises, which technically employed Maxwell and Kinesis, was the cash-cow behind the Alliance.

Additionally both men were longtime lecturers at various Academies – Centauri Island being a favourite site for academic field trips. Not just for its climate either. Although Max had been in Houston within the last year, neither he nor Rom had visited the Academy's campus in many moons. Nonetheless, both retained top security clearance.

Much less than four hours now and counting …

"Hello, Aran. Long time, no see."

Nightingale, in her lab, was given no warning they were coming to visit her. Unquestionably shocked by their sudden appearance (not that – their new alter egos being hidden at the moment – they physically looked much different than they usually did, just a few years older than last time), she managed to keep her composure.

"Hello, Max. Ditto!"

If time's passage had marred the two men, it had barely affected Aranyani. Still tall and gawky, with too big a nose and a body more pear-shaped than bar-belle, her two most prominent features – her deep-set eyes and two-toned hair, white slabs against jet black tresses – were as outstanding as ever. As always her complexion was sallow: too many hours spent inside, under fluorescent lighting. She nonetheless seemed healthy and stress-free.

Although some old-time Antheans, be they also Althean Witch Healers or Athenan War Witches – the likes of the Morrigan, Wilderwitch, Sorciere, Electrocretan, Fisherwoman and Soanso – often appeared as young as they wanted, Aran clearly disdained illusions. She actually looked her real age, an albeit impressively fit forty-seven. Her outfit matched her hair: black pants, blouse, and boots over a starched-white lab coat. Whatever she was working on, it agreed with her.

"Been awhile," she acknowledged.

"Too long."

"How's Timmy?"

"Safe. No thanks to you."

Distressed by his response, she regarded her ex-husband's companion "And how've you been doing, Rom? You look tremendous."

If Mother Eden's Superior Sisterhood – though more traditional Korants might dispute it, all the other Sisterhoods were merely branches of the Anthean Tree of Life – had had its way, Romaine Kinesis would have been her first and only mate. That, observably, he'd gone gay on them pretty much put the kibosh on the Sisterhood's mating strategy for her. (Observable at the same big summertime bash on Aegean Trigon in 1948 wherein she, barely 15 and wearing a very fetching glamour, was supposed to seduce him; gay as in homosexual – the word had a different, as in proper, meaning in 1948.)

"We're not here to trade pleasantries," Rom provided unpleasantly. "You know bloody well how I've been doing."

"Who are you talking to, Nightingale?" A fourth voice interrupted.

A gnomish hunchback, slightly less than that five feet tall, completely bald, with an over-large head spotted with ugly warts and wearing a smudged lab coat, walked into the room. He took one look at Maxwell and Kinesis, panicked, sought to run away. Rom started to glow, bodily filled out. His loose-fitting clothes were suddenly straining at the seams, on the cusp of bursting. Neither

Nightingale nor Callion had ever seen anyone like Doc Defiance before. Or, if they had, they couldn't recall it.

The transforming professor pointed a finger at Callion, held him in step. "You'd be Moses Callion the Third," he noted nonchalantly.

"The fuck with this *'Third'* shit," exclaimed Max. "He's a clone of *'First'*. Not my father ... my creator!"

========

Since No Name had come into – or out of – his life on Sunday, Max had been doing a great deal of thinking.

========

After seeing the little trickster again, for the first time that he could recall since the events of '65 on Centauri Island, he became convinced she was Joli Blon, his mother-creator. That she'd admitted as much at their meeting, with Rom in attendance, only further persuaded him that he and Günter von Alptraum (Tyrtod, the Nazi Nightmare's son) were veritable twins, albeit not in the usual sense womb-wise.

Identical, in this respect, to The Rache's Baphomet Headsman, whose genetic *'threads'* came from Donar Lancz, the Teutonic Terror, they were Callion Clones. Likely so were the various Slimy Men and Slimy Women that had been active from the war years up until the early Fifties. (Conceivably – pun intended – the Conqueror's mandroid monstrosities, amongst them the Russian Steltsar of the late Forties, had a different, though presumably related, origin.)

Callion Three, he was equally certain, was no different. Like father, like grandfather and, possibly, if perhaps not as yet positively, like grandfather before that, they were all clones. It should have been obvious to him years ago, even when he was Herr Richter or Baron Justice. Probably had been, any number of times in fact.

But Major Milo Mind and Hadrian Dis L'Orca (aka the Hypnosis King, once also the Herminones' Torquemada, their Grand Inquisitor), they with their amnaesthetics; Loxus Abraham Ryne, he with his *'voice'*; or any number of witches, with their agates or Afrite bulbs or whatever witch from whichever Sisterhood called her stepping stones on a given day, month or year, had always been there before.

Now they weren't. He was with Doc Defiance. A new age of supranormals had begun.

========

"Ye Gods!" exclaimed Aranyani Nightingale, gasping at the physical change in Romaine Kinesis. "What's happened to you?"

========

"What's happened to him is nothing compared to what's happened to me. Would you like to see?"

Max had been practicing in the mirror; had it down pretty damn good. His face suddenly lost all colour. Next went its distinctive features. It ballooned into a doughy wad with two little raisins for eyes, a slight protuberance for a nose and a gash, like one made by a breadknife, for a mouth: this in complete contrast to his trademark turtleneck sweater, casual jacket, and jeans.

He maintained the effect only long enough for it to register then reverted to his normal look. "Happy now?"

"An illusion," attested Callion, nervously looking to his partner for confirmation.

Dr Nightingale Ryne-Maxwell staggered backwards, fingered a nearby stool, and plopped down upon it. For a moment she lost some of her self-control and appeared a fully middle-aged woman: still handsome but with more grey in her hair and more lines in her face than she commonly allowed others to see. She motioned for Defiance to allow Callion III, who appeared on the verge of fainting, to sit on a similar stool.

The Gypsium Man had already spotted the Anthean Agates underneath both stools and knew them for what they were: Gypsium pellets, witch stepping stones. A ray shot out of his fingers, vapourized or, just as likely, absorbed the pellets, then levitated Callion and placed him none-too-gently on another stool.

He glanced at Maxwell, who nodded. Defiance relaxed, retracting his bodily glow and concomitant girth. Professor Romaine Kinesis and O'Ryan James Maxwell, fortyish scientist and sixtyish security officer, pulled up two other stools and sat opposite healer-Ant and cloned Frankenstein. "I trust we have your attention?"

"You have that, professor," agreed Callion, throwing back a glass of water. Nightingale was as back to normal as the other two but was clearly stunned and lost in thought.

"What are you two doing here, Aran?" Maxwell demanded of his long-estranged wife.

She looked at him blankly at first then smiled. He remembered that smile. It could melt ice; at least melt his cold, hard heart. A little more than a decade and a half ago, when he found out what she'd done to their son, he was going to kill her. That smile, probably that smile alone, was what saved her life. It was doing much the same today.

(When Jock and Bunnie demanded an explanation for what she's done to TJ, Timmy to his dad, she flatly stated that Ants like her shouldn't have boy babies, especially not as their first born. As proof she mentioned, among others, what happened to Solace Sunrise's sons by John Sundown. Each of them died on or about their seventh birthdays.

(They were whole-bodies, though, she protested. Now that he was a cripple, she further insisted, the same fate no longer awaited Timmy. Which of course was both true and irrelevant. So was the fact that Aran was still amongst the missing when Sorry – Solace's nickname, after her supra codename Sorciere – died, along with the last of her offspring, in mid-June 1953. She was clearly murdered, however, either just after or while she was giving birth to a stillborn male, whereas each of her three boys died mysteriously, of sudden but different illnesses.)

"Turn it off, witch. I'm in no mood for your glamours. Answer me!"

She frowned beatifically and sought to deflect him by turning her attention to Kinesis. "That wasn't necessary, Rom," she chastised him in a perhaps forced or faux-offended manner. "We weren't going anywhere; have nowhere else to go. I never thought you would develop into a supra, especially at your age.

"On the other hand, at least from what my father told me, Max had his modestly metamorphic moments in the sun as Baron Justice. But that was over so long ago I expected he was permanently neutralized." Avoidance wasn't doing any good so, turning back to her ex, she answered the question. "What are we doing, Max? Making more supras, if you haven't figured that out already. Making, as now seems obvious, more like you."

"Want to see?" chirped the gnome.

========

"We've problems," Sharpshooter, in Vancouver Canada, radioed to Shelter, in Houston Texas. "Mammalian's apparent control over Barry and Lapin are the least of them."

========

The System Seer and current field-leader of a squad of six other Silver Signallers – Sapphire, Spartan, Subitor, Shadowswirl, Stiletto and Stupendo, S-names all and always – proceeded to relate how they, judged the best of the field-ready bunch, had just had a close encounter with three apparent supras.

Horrifyingly, to him if not to Shelter, who revelled in horrors, whoever they were in reality displayed the mentat abilities of either Cerebrus or Psycho (David or Saul Ryne) and the Elemental Twins (Airealist and Sea Goddess, the codenames for Aires and Thalassa D'Angelo, whose adoptive parents still lived in Vancouver).

After exchanging, and discarding, a number of options Shelter was left with only one, inescapable conclusion: "I can't explain it but your training and skillsets are unrivalled so, if they've given you that kind of trouble, you may well have the real thing on your hands. Other than Old Man Power, they wouldn't be all that old.

"Air, Sea, the Diver, Dervish Furie and Blind Sundown were Summoning Children. That means they would be just turning sixty. Cerebrus and Psycho would be barely fifty. Wilderwitch was an Ant – you know what they're like. Raven's Head was some kind of mutate and the various D'Angelo supranormals reputedly didn't age beyond twenty or so."

"All right. What about you? Could do with all the help I can get. Despite us clearing all six for action, Spartan and Swirl are the only ones I'd really trust in a dust up."

"And Sapphire's just a kid."

"Strategos's kid to boot — and not just up the ass." (Strategos was Simon Lancz, a technological wizard, the chief designer or System Seer and nominal head of Signal System. Sapphire Lancz was his daughter by none other than Tereza nee D'Angelo, one of the Elemental Twins' three (of thirteen) surviving siblings.

"I better not. And I don't mean kicking Saffy; I mean coming through. Abe Ryne's on Centauri Island. He's been in contact with Doc Dark, Rainbow's ex-husband, but he won't tell me what it was about, which isn't like him." (Dr Immanuel Dark was another Summoning Child. He was once fused with the supra known as Mr Brilliant. Since their forced separation in 1953, Doc Dark, who was individually brilliant science-wise, had been confined to a wheelchair.)

"Something's going on," Shelter continued after a brief pause. "Something very big. It has to have something to do with what's on the Moon, the destruction of the Express and Solar's untimely demise. Tell you what, forget about Styx and Sasq. They're going to have to sort themselves out. These potential Crimefighters have to be your priority.

"I'll send you Spherus and Selene, along with the rest of the semi sort of roadworthy Signallers whose Silver's ready for use even if they aren't.

"Oh, and just to be on the safe side, I'll go have a word with Moe and Aranyani."

========

Nightingale and Callion led them deep into the bowels of their complex. As they walked, the hunchback told them this particular building was constructed at the same time as the nearby Astrodome. In fact, insisted Callion, the Astrodome was built largely to mask what this building was ultimately intended to house.

"Here," Callion claimed once they reached their apparent destination, "Is immortality."

========

"Looks more like mason jars," observed Maxwell.

"I doubt they're making jam, Max," said Kinesis.

"Quite right, professor. In these rooms are the genetic strands of virtually every supranormal who has existed since my grandfather – yes, my original template, the first Moses Callion – joined up with Magister Mandam, Athena and Charan Ryne, Leonora and Michael D'Angelo, Gilda and Angus Dre'Ath, Louise and Sedon St Synne, Belus and Aerobe Heliopolis, and the rest of the Godling Guild in the early decades of this century."

"Not to forget Philip and Olympias Kinesis," Rom interrupted, not wanting Callion to leave out his grandparents, who were paid up Godlings in their own right. As for Max, he didn't follow suit primarily because he now realized he didn't have parents, let alone any grandparents, as such.

(Rom's father Alexandros and his aunt, Alex's sister Megaera, were also on the Godlings' ill-fated trek to the Himalayan Vale of the Visionaries in February 1920. Despite their presence they were too young to be considered proper Godlings. As for his mother Roxanne, she was born as a result of the Summoning. Tragically – also suspiciously like a few other Godling women who emerged from it pregnant – Rox's mother Aerobe died in childbirth having her.)

"You would have heard about Walt Disney, how he had his body frozen in the hopes that one day, maybe centuries from now, technology would be such that he could be defrosted and continue his life. Even way back then, Charan Ryne had a different vision. He didn't think an individual's life could be preserved indefinitely but he felt an individual could be re-grown; duplicated, if you will.

"We are not talking about eugenics nor euthenics: the one, controlled selection of parents; the other, equally controlled selection of environmental factors. Those methods produce approximations only and, to my knowledge, are barren science." Consciously or unconsciously, he was lying, Max knew but didn't interrupt.

(Three's *'father'*, Moe Two, largely under the influence of Loxus Ryne and, behind the scenes, Sedon St Synne, was very big on euthenics. What was barren were the results: Despite their regimented upbringing, not one of Two's latter day clones had developed into a supranormal.)

"What we are talking about is not so much reproducing an individual, nor just his or her abilities or knacks. We are talking about re-investing them with their own uniqueness, the fullness of their being. That is why we concentrate on supra-strands. Supras had demonstrable attributes. Those attributes can be duplicated; have been, in fact.

"Witness the success of St Synne's devil-ray during the war. Or Strife's Miracle Key in the late Forties. Nita D'Angelo, for example, became Madame Midnight; her aunt, Mnemosyne Heliopolis, became the Queen of Spades. Their supra-talents were virtually identical but the way they individually used them were much different.

"Uniqueness is found in DNA; not that DNA, as such, was isolated when my grandfather and his helpers were doing their formative work in the Twenties and Thirties. What he had were tissue samples. What he tried to do was develop a bath wherein those tissues could multiply and, in time, become the living replicates of their initial templates; not so much copies of individuals but the individuals themselves.

"Things didn't work out at first. He couldn't just scientifically reincarnate individuals. It wasn't until '34, or so, that he could even grow individuals. That was when the freakishly forever-young Ant he called Joli Blon came into his life. Together they grew – rather, re-grew – the first true clone: Anjou Plantagenet. A bit later they grew you and Günter von Alptraum."

"The truth, at last," recognized Max. Even though Callion was only confirming what Hush had told him, it was good hearing it from another source.

"Maybe, maybe not," cautioned Aranyani. "You see, you were born normal, at least normal to their minds. You and Prince Peashooter – as not just you came to call your tank-twin Günter – were unique, yes, but unique to yourselves. To be blunt, you both were deadly dull. You could twist your shape, alter your bodies, but only marginally. Clowns in a side-show could do much like you two could.

"What made you so special was that you aged so fast, five years in the space of one. You were pubescent before you should have been off your mother's nipple. Fortunately, though equally inexplicably, by the time you were five you looked more like twenty — and semi-sort-of-stayed there, aging properly thereafter."

Max had never been too sure of Callion's family history. According to Jock Maxwell, the man who became as close to a real father as he would have, Moe One died not long after moving back to the States; this in turn was shortly after Abe Ryne took both of them to London in 1939.

Moe One claimed he was initially from Louisiana. Supposedly Moe Two, One's son, was born there a number of years prior to One moving to Germany. Therefore not so much abandoned as left behind when One went away, Two grew up normally; raised in bayou country by a cousin or aunt after his mother – conveniently, as was now apparent – died under the usual mysterious circumstances.

Reputedly Two was kidnapped and taken to Germany by Donar Lancz shortly before Britain and France officially declared war on Germany in September of that same portentous year, 1939. Be that as it may, Two became the Monster Maker a few years later, in the early Forties. As such he was blamed for, among others, the Baphomet Headsman (much later on discovered to be Donar Lancz's clone) and Steltsar (the old Baron von Alptraum's whatever-he-was in actuality).

Two was, also speculatively, responsible for the Headsman that came into existence in the early Fifties (and was still around, living in the Soviet Supra City with the not-so-young-anymore Baron, Günter van Alptraum). Even less certainly, many believed him the man (gnome?) behind the first Steltsar, the one that may have lasted as long as 1965, whereupon he was wiped out on Centauri Island along with, less arguably, the Strife of the day.

Because Caliban Kopf, to give the second Headsman his Christian name, turned out so disastrously – he had the body of a near-giant and almost supranormal strength, but his brain never progressed much beyond that of an infant's – Moe Two abandoned his father's methods of producing rapidly aging proto-humans, as he called clones way back then. Instead, those he in effect made-to-order were brought up as if regular children.

Max now figured Moe Three was one of those and, after recounting what he knew of the Callion family tree, primarily for Rom's benefit, asked him.

"Your facts are a little off," the artificially manufactured hunchback corrected him. "My immediate progenitor was engendered a couple of years after you and von Alp looked to be becoming such successes. He was accelerated, dramatically so compared to you and von Alp the Younger, yes, but it wasn't in Louisiana. Jock and his handlers must have made that up well after the war, when the Great Man and his Alliance sought to rehabilitate Moe Two.

"The truth of the matter was the Nazi Nightmare, Tyrtod von Alptraum, the Teutonic Terror, Donar Lancz, and the latter's wife, the former's golden-haired sister-in-law, Valfreja always Volsung, *'birthed'* Two, by bringing him out of his development tank, at the same place, in back of the von Alptraums' family estate on the Prussian Baltic Sea coast, that you two were.

"His upbringing was supervised by them and a few of the other Herminones, the anything but Harmonious One Lancz called his own even before the SS or Gestapo got hold of them. I know some of their names I but I bet you, as Victor Richter or Baron Justice, not only knew most of them personally, you probably killed a few of them later on, either during the war or within a few years after it.

"They didn't birth him, if you'll allow me to use that word as a verb, until after Abe Ryne and Angus Dre'Ath spirited you and Moe One off the von Alptraum estate in whichever it was, '38 or '39. Until then he was just another tub baby gestating in the same rudimentary cave-lab you, as Viktor, and von Alp the Younger called womb more so than home.

"You're mistaken about Moe One too. He was a real man, natural born and, as you might remember, quite elderly by the time he left the estate. It is true that, at his own request, he relocated to Louisiana before the war began but he died not long afterwards. Myself, I believe he was killed, probably by some Nazi sympathizers who were trying to drag him back to Germany, but I can't say for sure.

"I don't know how Moe Two managed to mature so rapidly either. He did, though, compared to you and Günter. He was a fully grown man by the time the first surviving picture I've seen of him was taken in 1941. I've long suspected witch work. Joli Blon wasn't around anymore – I don't think she was anyhow – but there were and are plenty of other Ants in whomever's pants. Plenty of witch sisterhoods, dot-ditto.

"Korants like Valfreja's mother Hulga Faust, yet also always Volsung, come to mind. Any suggestions, Max?"

"It's your story, Callion, though Hulga Faust was dead and buried by early '38."

(Despite her brilliant, golden hair and sunny disposition – at least as far as an admittedly extremely biased, young Max-Viktor recalled – Hulga referred to Valfreja, a Summoning Child, as her *'grey baby'*. She did so entirely due to the fact that she was around forty by the time she had her.

(After the death of her husband, Baldwin Faust, she and Freya lived almost exclusively at Castle von Alptraum, the old Baron's ancestral seat. She died, most of twenty years after Baldwin's passing, under the usual extremely un-usual, as in outright oddball, circumstances.

(Berchta, Hulga's much older middle child, was von Alp Senior's wife and, as was now apparent, only Günter's foster mother, not his actual birthmother as he and Max, as Victor Richter, had been brought up to believe. Rather, put better, as he and Prince Peashooter thought they had been brought up to believe.

(That, unlike Freya and Günter's supposed twin sister Brunhilde, Burn-ing Hell by supra codename, they weren't Summoning Children no longer disappointed Max; if it ever did. As for von Alp the Younger, whether he was as yet aware of his proto-humanity, that was not Max's principal concern right this second.

(It might become that, though, once they'd dealt with the Menace on the Moon. Wouldn't do for there to be two Mr No Names running around loose.)

"Was she really? Hmm. What about you, Aran?"

"You know who I blame, Moe: Six letters, begins with an 'S', ends with an *'e'*."

"Impossible," Maxwell snapped. "No one heard of Strife until '43, when she somehow murdered Freya Volsung."

(Max hated referring to Valfreja as Lancz. Donar had married her, however, in late January or early February 1938. As Max also knew, even though it was now apparent he wasn't there except, maybe, as a rapidly aging child, their wed-ding took place at Castle Nightmare within a few days of Hulga's death.)

"No one with a cock, maybe. We witches are a different matter."

"Tell me about it," said her ex, seemingly begging for a fight.

"Finish your story, Callion," Kinesis urged calmingly. He was more interested in Callion Present than Callion Past. Who, potentially, were in those mason jars anyhow?

"That I shall, professor. It wasn't until Germany started losing that the second generation of Callion Clones came into being. They're why Moe Two was justifiably called the Monster Maker in the particularly bad old days when the World and Supra War raged simultaneously.

"His clones were just that, monstrosities; thankfully short-lived ones. Sloppy science, the loathsome load of them, done in a hurry and artificially bumped to adulthood even more rapidly than he was. You're also right when you suggested I qualify as a third generation clone. Like dozens of others ..."

"Dozens!?!" gasped Maxwell. His exclamation struck Kinesis – if not the other two (who, for good reason, clearly distrusted Max) – as one of genuine surprise.

"Oh, yes, dozens, maybe even hundreds, though I couldn't name you more than a couple, one of whom is me and the other of whom is Herr Kopf, von Alp Junior's simpleton. Caliban, as some bright light familiar with Shakespeare's Tempest named him, both predated me and wasn't brought up slowly. In fact, as I believe you alluded to already, he was the last of the accelerated proto-humans."

"Get on with it, Callion."

"Then stop interrupting me." If looks could kill, thought Kinesis, Max and Moe Three would be already. They weren't, self-evidently. And Max did shut up, quietly.

"I was brought up slowly, by what witches like my dearest Aranyani here call *'development teams'*. In other words, as I like to say, I aged the same as fine wine. Parenthetically, I'm not even thirty. Moe Two was part of the Worldwide Order and, as you know, was killed over a decade ago. I have no intention of sharing his fate."

The gnome paused to collect his thoughts. "Along with Günter von Alptraum, you constitute the last progeny of the man I shall always refer to as my grandfather, Max. As such, as what might be considered a first generational proto-human, your existence, what you can do, may shine some light on what our current projects may yet become."

"Failures," Nightingale stated flatly.

"Different," the gnome countered. "We use the same techniques my grandfather and Joli Blon did to make the first generation. We then accelerate them like my father did, after it was done to him. But they're not turning out to be monsters, not even supranormals, not as near as we can make out.

"They do age quickly, though; faster than Moe Two did, if you must know. Nevertheless, as frangible as the situation may yet prove to be, so far they seem as normal as you and Günter did once you turned twenty-one. Even if you didn't, not really," he stumble-mouthed. "Outwardly, in appearance, I mean. Yet, and this is the poser you've presented us, von Alp is still a Norman Normalcy whereas you're ..."

"A nameless thing," contributed Max.

"Ah, but, to judge from a brief glimpse, one not only with tremendous potential but one completely under your control. If we can find out what triggered you into becoming that thing, as you put it, we might be able to duplicate the process. How would you like to have a half dozen brothers and sisters?"

"I'd rather have one less of me than six more. Besides, I have no idea what set me off."

"It's not sheer orneriness," the professor said, still trying to lighten the mood. "Because you've always been that."

"Thanks," Max said. Wisely Dr Nightingale said nothing.

Ignorant as he was of the Mind Tap Milo Mind planted in his head while on a trip to San Francisco in mid '78, Max had narrowed it down to two possible reasons. One was Kinesis hitting him up with Gyps: first on Saturday, then again on Sunday. The other, far more likely to his way of thinking, was being struck from behind by whatever blew him out of the control room just before the Cosmic Express was launched.

He wished Hush hadn't forbidden him checking out Yataghan Sentalli, Hiyati Samarand, George Hannibal, Connie Lindquist and the rest of the Fatman's Untouchables until they knew more about Mr No Name. More to the peripatetic point, he wished he'd ignored her.

Although he didn't have a ring like Dolph Dulles now did – and Kinesis already had, apparently for decades – Max reckoned she could nevertheless exert at least a modicum of control over his better instincts. She probably had been able to do so since she was Joli Blon and he was still stuck in his *'development'* tank (and therefore *'unbirthed'*, if that was any more of a verb than birthed).

Despite his formidable *voice*, neither he nor the professor volunteered anything to Ryne about three-eyed devils during their interview-cum-consultation Monday night. They could arguably be proud of that. But the Great Man, who wasn't allowed to go about armed on Centauri Island, already had plenty of witnesses to attest to their becoming No Name and Doc Defiance.

They therefore couldn't keep their transformations from him and didn't bother trying. That contemplated, never said aloud, no one other than he, as No Name (when it came to Yataghan-Goldenrod), and Kinesis (with respect Babar-Hannibal and Connie All-Eyes) had seen any of these devils.

Max wasn't about to change that for the benefit of an admitted clone and an Anthean witch; especially not for Abe Ryne's daughter. Even though there had been intimations in the past that he wasn't her father – that it might, in fact, be that insatiable old satyr, Sedon St Synne – the patriarch doted on her and she reciprocated. They were exceedingly close.

"So you have six projects already out and about," prodded Kinesis. "Where are they?"

"I'm afraid that's classified information," said Moe Three, patently regretting his earlier enthusiasm and resultant lack of restraint. "I'd have to have prior authorization from Mr Ryne before I could answer that."

"How would you like to crawl around on the ceiling for a few hours, Callion?"

"Might be an interesting experience, professor, but I'd still need prior authorization before I could tell you. I gather you don't know Mr Ryne very well."

"Leave it be, pro," recommended Max. "Moe won't tell you anything because he can't. Even Doc Defiance couldn't force it out of him. Take my word for it."

Kinesis reflected on that. Thinking back to Monday's dinner-plus with Ryne Senior he could understand their perspective. It wasn't as if he or Max really wanted to go to the Moon; it was more that Ryne wanted them to go. What Ryne wants, Ryne gets. He'd heard much the same thing about God.

"Pardon me, Max, but he's already told us quite a lot of what I would consider classified information. I mean, if everything's so hush-hush, what's with the tour?"

"It hasn't been expressly forbidden," said Aranyani. Was it the professor's imagination or did she perk up when he said hush-hush. He decided he wouldn't probe her further, though he couldn't help wondering if the ring he was now openly wearing would preclude him from even asking her if she knew Hush Mannering.

"You and Max have top level clearance," she rather hastily explained. "Brother Erech might freak but he's in Budapest and I doubt the old man would gripe. My guess is he prizes you two above almost anyone except himself right now. Ever since whatever's on the Moon was detected, he's been hell-bent on finding ways to bring supras back into action only to have you two old-timers, if not exactly old friends, virtually fall into his lap. Let's keep it short, though. I know you've a plane to catch and we've work to do."

Unsaid but understood by Callion and, probably, Maxwell was her failure to grasp why her father hadn't unleashed all the presumed supras trained, then closeted, by various Academies of Man over the years. She supposed he was keeping them in reserve. Then something else occurred to her. A lot of them were killed when the Cosmic Express was destroyed. Were any left?

"By all means," agreed Kinesis. "Lead on, Macs." Both Max and Aran gave him icy glares. "Shakespeare, you know," he felt obliged to explain. "Lead on, Mac Duff. Well, I thought it was funny." It was pointless. Too many years in laboratories had robbed him of his delivery, if not altogether his sense of humour.

About the only man who could make a crack like that work was Avatar Sol. Or, as Max would have it, Lon Tiecher.

Callion and Aranyani took them through some impenetrable-looking, trebly-locked vault doors and down to the lowest level of the complex. In a tub within an immaculately – pun intended, said Aranyani, whose own sense of humour was as twisted as some of her deeds – sterilized lab, what looked to be a human foetus was developing.

Consequently womb-free, it was floating in something akin to amniotic fluid, supposed Kinesis. If he was any judge of such things, which he wasn't, it – a he to be, he didn't need to judge – looked a couple of months shy of fully formed.

"Talking about strands, Aran," Max chanced, "Where did this one's come from?"

She checked the chart and did one of her grins. "One of my other brothers. Saul, as it happens."

The Indescribable Mr No Name came out of Big Max Maxwell without leaving anything else behind, least of all Max himself. Perversely still clothed, it overturned the tub – fluid, foetus and whatever else it contained in the way of nutrients and/or accelerants – onto the floor. With its made-big, floppy feet oozing out of Max's shoes, the doughy grotesquery squashed said substances into the drain. Only then did No Name revert to Maxwell again.

"Was that tit-for-imagined-tat, Max?" seethed Aranyani.

She was clearly referring to what she'd done to young Timmy when he was but a babe in swaddling. Nonetheless, she spoke as maliciously as Kinesis had ever heard anyone. It sent a chill down his spine. Witches weren't supras but that might not mean they couldn't curse or put a spell on you.

(It wouldn't be magic either, they'd say. It'd be witchcraft: emphasis on craft, as if witchery was akin to knitting or carpentry. Yet only they could do pull it off.)

"You just cost us five years of research," shrieked Callion.

His voice was so shrill, so high-pitched, Kinesis was momentarily reminded of a spoilt brat. For the first time, the professor wondered if Moe Three, whom he'd never heard of before a few years ago, wasn't one of those accelerated clones Nightingale had spoken of so disdainfully a few minutes earlier.

"Wrong!" said Maxwell, almost as angrily. "I just gave you the opportunity for another five more years of life, maybe more. Make of it what you will."

He turned to leave but Kinesis, none-too-gently, grabbed him by the arm. "Why'd you do that, Max? It wasn't as if they were remaking the Magnificent Psycho."

"You heard them, pro. That's exactly what they were doing. I know you met Saul in your youth but chances are you'd have only heard about what he could do, not experienced it firsthand. Ask me there's no more insidious knack than mind-control. Sacks of supras had it, to one degree or another, but he was one of the worst. Made his old man look like a piker."

"Trying to do," protested Aranyani. Already three-quarters recovered, she was using a bit of her own form of the Ryne *'voice'* in order to calm herself as much as the other three down. She couldn't quite quell her tears, however. "That was our fourth go with Saul. Looked liked our first success as well, you bastard. We dumped the others down the toilet, sure. But only after we'd put them to sleep gently. We didn't stomp them through a goddamned metal grate!"

"But you didn't shuck the other six," said Kinesis, far more cruelly than was usual for him. He believed in abortion for all the wrong reasons: population control. The world was entirely too overcrowded as far as he was concerned. Still, he had even less regard for an unformed clone than an unborn foetus. "Who were their templates?"

"Does it matter now?" snapped the disheartened witch. "I've had two children. But I just had them, the same as your mother Roxanne, whom I met and liked a bunch of times, had you. Nature took care of the rest. I made the others virtually from scratch, just like Joli Blon made Max. Can't you appreciate the distinction?"

"You Rynes always were ones for playing God," snarled Max, rounding on the gnome. "How'd your so-called grandfather make me, Callion?"

"I told you!" The hunchback sounded too terrified to lie. "The same way my father made me: tissue samples, basic nutrient bath. He called it Cathonic Fluid but it wasn't just that. Added a decent dollop of Ant-essence for good measure. Temperature control. Usual stuff. Development tanks are pretty elementary."

"You're not telling me everything."

"Like I said," braved Moe Three, "If you want precise details, you'll have ask Mr Ryne. He'll probably be happy to release them to you. I can tell you this much: It won't work without an Anthean who has had children of her own. Don't ask me why. Call it magic if you want. But that's the way of things."

"How can he tell you everything," interrupted Aranyani, protective of her partner, "When he doesn't know everything? Like his father, he works from notes made by the Conqueror — my genius cousin, Jesus Mandam, though he must have been in his early twenties when Moe Two became the Monster Maker. Moe One and this Joli Blon, whoever she was, took the full process with them to their graves. Now go away."

"How much difference does the raw material make?" inquired Kinesis, ignoring her protestations. (Although he was wearing his mother's ring, the one Hush claimed to have ensorcelled in 1948, it was by now clear to him that Aran couldn't manipulate him like the little trickster could.) "You said yourself you came from Callion One. What about the others? I mean, does it matter whose DNA-strands you use?"

"As near as I figure it," obliged the gnome, "And I've been at this, grandfather, father, and son, for a very long time, not really. Günter came from his father, the Baron Tyrtod von Alptraum, who was alive when they were taken. Moe Two came from Moe One, who was also alive at the time he was made.

"The same was true of both the Baphomet Headsman and his imbecilic successor, Caliban Kopf. They were grown out of the tissues of the Teutonic Terror, Donar Lancz, prior to you doing your own headsman bit." (As obviously Moe Three was aware, Maxwell, by then codenamed Baron Justice, had cut off Lancz's head in order to save space in his rucksack for the relatively newly born Simon Lancz.)

"I say it makes no demonstrable difference mostly because of you, Max. Your donor was long dead when cellular samples were taken from him."

"Who was he?" Maxwell demanded.

"Do you really want to know?"

"Might as well."

"Charan Ryne."

"Does Abe know that?"

"He did, forty-five years ago," admitted Callion. "His memory might not be what it once was but I imagine that's one thing even he could never forget. My grandfather wasn't charged to create supras like we are; his task was to find a way to bring back Charan and Athena Ryne.

"Their bodies were found frozen in the denouement of 1920's Godling Guild Summoning; frozen, I say, but otherwise undamaged from everything I've heard. Need a guess who funded all his research? The same person who's funding ours. Your Abe, Loxus Ryne."

"The old prick," snarled Max. "Why didn't he tell me?"

"As to that, I don't know. But I will tell you why. It wasn't that he wanted his father back, per se. What he wanted was his father's memories. Ryne wanted to find out what really happened in the Himalayas in 1920. He still hasn't learned the answer but he may have supposed it by now."

"You know?"

"Not in detail. Ask your ex."

Both Max and Kinesis looked expectantly to Aranyani. Once again she was semi-lost in space, having hardly heard the conversation. When she spoke, it wasn't entirely with her own voice. "You've business on the Moon, gentlemen. I suggest you attend to that first. When you come back, I'll tell you all about my life."

"Time is getting short," agreed Kinesis. "Maybe we better get back to the plane."

"You're probably right, pro. Okay, Aran. We'll take a rain check but we'll be back. Mark me on that."

=========

After the gnome escorted them out of the underground laboratory, OJ Maxwell and Professor Romaine Kinesis returned to the aircraft. To their credit the pilot and crew were still there – presumably the threat of more than just levitating fire extinguishers overruled their better instincts to flee. Either that or they really liked their salaries.

Two hours in the air later, the first said to the other: "I could have cracked her, Rom. She knows so much. She'd have told us everything."

"Isn't it better this way, Max? If you know all there is to know, what else is there to learn or experience? Where's the challenge? Myself, I've never been to the Moon."

Endgame them!

****

NUKE 10: **The Tentacular Seven**

========

Wednesday, December 3, 1980

After escorting Kinesis and Maxwell out of the complex, Callion returned to their shared facility deep underground.

========

"Congratulations, Ryne maiden," he applauded his much taller colleague in collusion, if not necessarily crime as such, after breaking off their (familial, more so than lovers') embrace. "Brilliantly handled, Nightingale. You've your mother's natural-born Ant-abilities but you seem to have inherited your father's compulsive knacks as well."

"Not inherited, Moses. Loxus Ryne wasn't my father. Sedon St Synne was."

The gnome was used to indulging her fantasies. "Then how did you get them to leave?"

"I didn't. It was my brother Saul, very much long-distance and twenty-five years dead no longer. He's been trying to get in touch with me since Sunday night. He's finally figured out where he is and that it's safe for me to bring him here. You better start a new tank lickety-split. He's going to be pissed, not having a body."

"What do you mean by that? What's left of him?"

"His brain, Moe. It's probably all he needs, but try telling him that."

========

"Try telling who what?" demanded the newcomer.
"Shelter!"

========

The System Seer was dressed in personally modified silver armour.

Like all of Signal System's operatives, Shelter sported distinctive headgear. Since he was the only one who kept himself entirely anonymous, neither of them had seen him bare-faced, let alone bare-headed. Nonetheless, they knew from his helmet that he was not just eccentric but, in all likelihood, an exceptional engineer gone entirely insane. Then again, that's probably precisely what he wanted them to think.

House-Head's house-like head-covering was today more a mansion with three hundred and sixty degree windows on the second floor, handle-bar moustache-like pillars around his mouth-hole on the ground floor and, off the roof, horn-like chimneys that actually emitted smoke. (No doubt this last was his way of showing them he was royally steamed.)

He wore an ordinary leather butcher's apron, complete with various knives and silver cleavers. If only to top off the impression of madness he clearly liked to project, he sported false breasts with stiletto-sharp nipples sticking out of them. Did all of that make him a cross-dressing, wannabe hausfrau with a penchant for do-it-yourself butchery? Oh probably.

"I see you've had some visitors," he noted, in the neutral, sexless tones that all Signallers mechanically transmitted. "Unless your drain has inexplicably backed up foetal as opposed to faecal matter."

"Where's your speaking stick?" adlibbed Aranyani, trying not to indulge him overly much. Since speaking sticks supposedly forced folks to talk truthfully, it was her way of saying her lips were sealed, though he was welcome to try to open them.

"I doubt it'd work on an Ant," he acknowledged. "Or her partner," he added, in deference to Moe Three. "I'm sure you've secreted an agate on him somewhere." Crazy he may be but dummy he definitely wasn't. Shelter must have known Anthean agates were superior to speaking sticks when it came to guaranteeing silence.

"Hadn't you better make that brother, brother?" Having just dealt with a Gypsium Man and a No Name thing, Callion had no problem toughing it out against one of his father's proto-humans.

"Fancy playing with me, do you, Doc?" Shelter gave as good as he took. "Very well. I won't disillusion you quite yet. Watch your backside. I'm keeping a special eye on both of you from now on. A house isn't necessarily a home and Shelter can be the storm."

"Don't worry," Aran assured the trembling gnome after the venomous, King Snake of a Signaller left them alone. "Whether or not House-Head's a Moe Two clone or the real Echion Sangati, once Saul comes home he'll quickly come to apprehend there's no supra quite like the Magnificent Psycho."

"I can hardly wait. Now, if you can spare me, I've got an escape to make."

"You're joking."

"Were you?"

"No."

"Just so."

========

"Let's test this gadget, Tyrtod," said Ramona Avar-Ryne a couple of days ago.

"On?"

"Who else? Strife!"

========

Crystallion's firedrake – apparently a living thing and not a machine, as the Countess and Major Mind had initially speculated to themselves – returned for her Monday night. (It might be a mandroid, a manmade half-life related to the Sphinxes' Egyptian-inspired whatever they were, Milo speculated.)

She went back to the phantom freighter and neither her nor it had been seen since. However, the continuing presence of Steltsar, who had been reconstructed yet again, but somehow still retained the mindset of Baron Tyrtod von Alptraum, the Nazi Nightmare, was reminder aplenty that it, her, and they, Hell's Horsemen, were still out there somewhere.

Sharkczar, as the cyborg had more appropriately renamed himself, or Crystal may have suspected Ramona had marked her for vengeance. If so, they weren't going to give her a chance. Milo Mind was glad of that. With their non-existent access to weaponry – even if they had them, they wouldn't know what to do with them – and their almost complete inexperience when it came to taking revenge on anyone, if they did, say, try to shoot her, the best they could hope was that Crystallion died laughing.

Besides, provided they missed themselves and put a bullet through her containment suit, they'd probably die of radiation poisoning anyway.

Sharkczar, as Mind preferred to either Steltsar or Tyrtod, stayed on the converted packer. Wasn't there right now, though, having recently gone fishing, as he put it. (Which meant he'd gone for a long swim, presumably in search of a Great White to wrestle, mutilate, mangle and munch.)

Well after dark Wednesday, Shaikh Ali Ars Markazi and the little prince, Greygreave Translav, arrived by helicopter from a yacht berthed in Kihei, on the island of Maui. Milo and Salvatore Dis L'Orca were in the control room off the bridge, with their underlings and monitors as well as, just possibly, Strife, Daemonicus, or both. It was left to Ramona, Lady Guillotine cleaver screwed in and polished shiny, to greet them.

Shaikh Markazi was quite slender; dressed like the Iranian, rather than Arabic, potentate he was: in white robes and headdress. With a greying goatee and moustache, he cultivated a regal bearing. His curved sword was sheathed to his side. Mind, who'd been told they were coming, had warned her that only his ornamental scabbard was ceremonial; that, when he drew the blade, he not only knew how to use it but was about to do just that. (Hence in part her ensuring Lady Guillotine cleaver was screwed solidly into her arm sheathe.)

The midget, Greygreave Translav, as Mind unnecessarily reminded her, maintained he was the son of Anastasia Romanov and therefore the rightful Czar of Russia. He had gone native and was dressed in kid's shorts, a monogrammed *'Elvis Lives'* tee-shirt and open-toed sandals. The little backpack he carried looked soft and probably only held sweats and a raincoat. No weapons for this man-child: he let his Glomen do his dirty work.

Both men were Summoning Children, born in late 1920, early 1921; were therefore nearing sixty years of age. Translav, though, if he shaved his face and applied some heavy makeup, could still pass for a boy of seven or eight. Like Avar-Ryne and Major Mind, both were implicated in the activities of WORLD throughout the Sixties. Unlike either of them, Ray and Milo, neither had ever been incarcerated for their perceived misdeeds.

"Well, well, if it isn't two-thirds of the terrible trio," she smirked as they came aboard. "Where's Dr Cyanide?"

"Sian's not here?" The Romanov wannabe reacted with a detectable tinge of concern.

Neither man had been surprised to see her on the boat but Translav sounded more than a little put out by Alorstro's absence. For some reason no one had bothered to inform him that Alorstro Sian, yet another Summoning Child and WORLD's lethal but ever effective Number Two, had left the packer, also by helicopter, on Monday morning.

"Would I have asked if he was?" Ramona responded condescendingly. The little prince and the sheik exchanged nervous glances. Something was definitely up.

"Is Daemonicus aboard yet, countess?" wondered Markazi deferentially.

No doubt he was privy to WORLD's scheme to replace Loxus Ryne with her at the head of the Alliance of Man and New Century Enterprises, among other places. (Notably the bank or penthouse office wherein he signed really, really large cheques.) The deference in his voice suggested he was also privy to experiencing Daemonicus's fearsome eyefire.

"You mean Solomon Mandam, my self-proclaimed son?"

"As you wish," Markazi allowed, as if unclear as to the reference.

"Surely you mean Solomon Ryne," Translav twittered, "Your son by Saul Ryne."

"Just testing, prince," she said, seizing on the reprieve. She really would have to force herself to start calling Sol Saul's if their ambitions to displace Abe Ryne and take over NCE had any hope at all of succeeding. "Could be. When it comes to the dastardly D-dude, who can say for sure. So, what brings you here, Shaikh? Must be money problems. Haven't been paid?"

Like the Family Ryne, Markazi claimed an Iraryan heritage; his, though, he'd tell anyone within earshot, was unadulterated. He also preferred Iranian to either the nowadays' (thanks to the Nazis) somewhat controversial Iraryan or the basically Greek term Persian.

Appropriately enough, while the word 'markazi' just meant 'central' in Farsi, his surname derived from the name generally applied to the Central Bank of Iran under the recently deposed Shah, Muhammad Reza Pahlavi. A supremely well-connected, doubly and trebly insulated, financier by trade, his control of WORLD's purse strings didn't mean he was adverse to lending them out, as he might put it, as garrotes.

"Quite the contrary, countess. We are continuing to be paid. I am here to discover what we are being paid for doing exactly."

"What he means is we've been summoned," offered Translav. "Let's hope it's only to receive our severance pay, not our severance." He giggled in that same little boy way Ramona remembered, with a certainty, if no particular fondness, from two decades earlier.

"Not funny, Translav," disapproved Markazi. "We go, he goes with us."

Ramona shuddered at the thought. She knew most of the onboard technicians and crewmembers were Glomen. Glows blow, Mind had also reminded her unnecessarily. She hadn't been in her right mind at Bel's funeral in April 1960 – Strife had been in it for her – but she vividly recalled them exploding themselves rather than be captured.

"Which is why you said *'yet'*? Daemonicus is the one who summoned you, isn't he? Well, to be honest, I have no idea. He tends to come and go as he pleases. Much like his supposed sister, Balkis, Strife." Markazi would definitely be aware of Strife. "Mind telling me what's going on?"

"Regretfully," Markazi half-apologized, "If you do not know the answer to that, I have already said too much."

"Which is uncharacteristically careless of you," said Dis L'Orca, who had just walked onto the promenade deck. "Your performance better improve in short order. Please come. You also, countess. Seems we have all been summoned." He stressed this last meaningfully. Even though everyone there at least in part owed their existence, if not their persistence, to the Simultaneous Summonings of 1920, the significance of his emphasis looked lost on them.

As always, Dis L'Orca was formally dressed – today in ship-board whites, and carrying his trademark straight-black opera cane with its hidden stiletto. He escorted the three of them through the bridge, past the monitor room and into the captain's galley. Already there were blank-faced, flare-haired Strife and Major Milo Mind.

"Grab a pew," suggested Mind, with false frivolity. "In your case," he told the little prince, "Just be careful which one you choose. It might be wired."

Fifteen years earlier, Translav had whacked Mind over the head with a standard, everyday stool and left him to freeze to death in a Sherpa hut high up on Mt Everest. Rescued by the three bronze-masked, otherwise anonymous, *'Judges of Olympus'*, Mind ended up confessing to numerous war crimes.

(Moderately significantly for scholars of the post Supra War era, which perforce Milo Mind became, the three traditional judges were named Minos, Rhadamanthys and Aeacus. The first two were mythological sons, by Zeus, of the Phoenician princess Europa Agenorid. She actually had triplets; the third, as Ramona knew as well as Mind did, was Sarpedon.)

Even though he pleaded to having no choice in the matter – *'it was my life or theirs'* was but one of his litany of excuses – he was justly locked up for well over a decade. Understandably, therefore, he and the would-be-Czar of All the Russians had barely been on speaking terms ever since. After all, both being members of the Order's upper echelon did not require speaking, just not shooting each other.

Greygreave Translav took the nearest chair available. "Then again, they all might be wired, mightn't they, major?"

"As it happens," insisted Dis L'Orca, "None of them are. Be my guest."

He offered Translav his seat – significantly not at the head nor the foot of the long table – but the prince kept the one he'd chosen.

Ramona took her place then did some mental arithmetic. "Who else are we waiting for?"

"Why do you say that?" queried Faceless Strife, even though she had no mouth with which to speak.

While Balkis – unless Strife had chosen someone else in the last few days – was thoroughly obscured by, Ray assumed, witch-worked glamour, her voice wasn't muffled. It came through loud and clear. Ramona, who still hadn't managed to convince anyone to address her as Lady Guillotine, made certain her voice was just as authoritative sounding.

"Until Strife brought me here via witch-stones, I was given to understand the high command of the new Worldwide Order was you, Salvatore; you, Milo; plus Markazi, Finances; Translav, Global Menace; Alorstro Sian, Mafia; Daemonicus and Strife. I was to be the eighth. It naturally made me think today's WORLD was a kind of Octopus Corporation, albeit with eight legs but only one head, that being Daemonicus."

"I trust you're joking," said Strife, the humanoid antithesis of joking.

She had been. Ramona nevertheless shook her head sternly. Strife took that as an invitation to carry on.

"Very well, since you seem to need humouring, as of Sunday evening WORLD disbanded and simultaneously reformed, primarily for your benefit. Daemonicus brought in Sharkczar – affiliate him with the old-time Rache – and Crystallion, Hell's Horsemen. Consider them private contractors. They are here in order to attend to matters which, strictly speaking, should have nothing to do with the Order anymore."

"We now know what that is," provided Dis L'Orca. "Unfortunately, it has left our new WORLD in a somewhat awkward position. Quite conceivably, Daemonicus and the rest of us have found ourselves at cross-purposes. Conflict of interest would be an entirely inadequate understatement."

"It wouldn't have been if you'd been forthright," snarled Strife, be she Strife-Balkis or Strife-someone-else. "Rehabilitating our latest mother had nothing to do with Sentalli's island."

"On the contrary, New Century Enterprises isn't worth the effort we're putting into acquiring it without Centauri Island." In the few days since she'd reacquainted herself with him – and the decade and more she'd known him before that – Ramona had never heard Dis L'Orca sound so flustered. No, make that scared.

"Mind acting as an interpreter, Milo," she requested her lover of the last three nights.

"Bit of ancient history comes into play here," he obliged her. "I don't want to get into it, particularly whose idea it initially was, but the WORLD of the early Sixties was obsessed with rediscovering the discoveries of Jesus Mandam. Hadrian Dis L'Orca, Sal's father, made taking over Centauri Island a cornerstone of the Order's efforts back then. He died, of course, but WORLD continued trying to do just that.

"It came very close in June of '65, as Strife could verify. She, as Crystal St Synne, and another version of Steltsar were involved back then, right up to their proverbial armpits. Sixty-five, though, turned out to be a royal fuckup. Now it seems Crystal, as Crystallion, and Steltsar, as Sharkczar, have been contracted by Daemonicus, who also appears to have had other incarnations and may have been around fifteen years ago, too, to sink Centauri."

"Don't be so mealy-mouthed, major," condemned Strife, almost sarcastic-ally. "They're going to give the island the old Atlantean heave-ho. Even if it doesn't sink, it'll be uninhabitable for human generations."

"Another Mission: Mass Murder," grasped Ramona. "Like Project: Pro-jectile the Cosmic Express." What Mind had described to her dispassionately as Project: Cosmic Express (aka Project: Centauri, in corporate and political backrooms around the world), she'd taken the liberty to characterize for what it turned out to be.

"Daemonicus has given us what he calls a window of opportunity," said Dis L'Orca as if he'd negotiated it. "He's agreed to hold off Crystallion and Hell's Horsemen until the beginning of next week at the latest. There's no chance of extending it any further, he tells me, so we've got to make do with what we've been provided. Question is, can we do it?"

"My Glomen are in place," said Translav. "They're every bit as good as the technicians I recruited for this tub."

Glomen was short for Global Menace so Ramona figured recruit was a euphemism for conscript, on threat of either their lives or those of their loved ones. Markazi, whose brain for details was almost as precise as the invariably accurate mental abacus he had for financial matters, wasn't as enthusiastic and said as much.

"Our systems are such they can download Sentalli's computers to our data bases in South Africa and Argentina via satellite very reliably – with failsafe cop-ies sent to the mainland via cable, and thence to California via methods we've previously discussed. And paid for," he quickly added.

"Can it be done?" demanded Dis L'Orca one more time. Ramona could all but hear Markazi's mental abacus clicking away.

"However," he was calculating, "If we have to confine ourselves to a very limited time frame – less than a week, you're telling me – we'll have to be very, very selective as to what's most important. Professor Kinesis's Gypsium research would take priority over, say, Dr Samarand and his folks' hull design for the individual cosmicars.

"As to the latter, speaking entirely pragmatically of course, NASA would pay grandly for the secret of the Solidium sheathe. But, as to the former, teleport-ation made practical, the mind – not the major, sorry Milo – boggles. What could be more valuable? Nothing answers that."

(The Solidium sheathe was the coating designed to protect the cone and individual cosmicars as they left Earth atmosphere. That the cosmicars could purportedly teleport, even if it was only in outer space, might not be common knowledge but the Worldwide Order wasn't made up of common criminals. The mind didn't boggle at what they would do with teleportation technology. It ran and hid.)

"So yes," he concluded. "It's definitely manageable. But arranging for an exodus of Sentalli's starred scientists or Translav's Glomen – especially without rousing undue suspicion – well, I can't speak to that. Dr Cyanide handles field operations. I merely raise the requisite backing."

"And Sian's not here," Mind was quick to point out.

Dis L'Orca was nowhere near satisfied. "So, should we risk the time and manpower necessary to salvage what we can of the island or should we abandon it to the fates – or waves, if you prefer – and concentrate on the countess's ascension? Surely, once we have NCE, we'll have all Centauri has to offer."

"Don't I have any say in the matter?" Major Mind butted in again. He wanted nothing to do with supra-doings.

"Only as mother's lover," said Strife.

"Then, with all due respects, lady, ladies," bowed Mind. "Let's piss off!"

"Exactly my recommendation," agreed Markazi. Translav nodded his approval vigorously.

"Seems such a waste," remarked Ramona.

"Give over, mom," smirked Strife, albeit only verbally; she didn't have requisite mouth to do so visually. "Those on Centauri Island should have even less interest to you than those on the Cosmic Express. Your Anhita was aboard it. What do you care about Al Sentalli, the patriarch, and a bunch of brain boys?"

"The Express was before my time," Ramona pointed out. She had never even heard of the Cosmic Express prior to it being too late to do anything about it. "If I'm reading this correctly," she further noted, "What's been developed on Centauri Island isn't just Mandam's work put into practise. It would significantly add to our accumulating trove of knowledge and, not to put too fine a point on it, our treasury."

She paused then, just in case she sounded indecisive, made her recommendation. "You're saying NCE would have computer records anyway, but you can't know how complete it would be. I'm saying you'd be well-advised to concentrate on getting the scientists, if not everything they've built, off island. What they've already accomplished might be nothing compared to what they will accomplish."

"The infrastructure built into the island over the last two decades is unmatched in the world," expounded Markazi. "That's why we wanted the whole kit and caboodle. A hurried operation, such as Mr Dis L'Orca proposes, makes no sense. Nonetheless, if we – make that you, since the demon seems to regard you as his mother. If you could convince him to call off Hell's Horsemen altogether, then I see no reason why our initial operation cannot be put into action."

"That is not an option," restated Strife emphatically. "One does not trifle with Daemonicus. His mind is set. Not only are his reasons beyond reproach but they are not for your ears. Suffice to say Centauri Island is an abomination and must be abolished. Take what you can and forget the rest."

"See to it, Markazi, Translav," Dis L'Orca instructed the Arab and the Russian. "Expect no help from Sian. Strife, I don't believe your mother should be on this boat. I strongly suggest you use your stepping stones to take her elsewhere. As for Milo and myself, at Daemonicus' request, we shall remain here. I believe that concludes this meeting."

"Not quite," disagreed Strife. "You were not summoned to discuss WORLD's various plots and schemes, at least those not yet realized. As it happens, the real reason you were brought her has been lurking in the Grey for some time." Strife did some sleight-of-hand and produced a tiny, glowing stone about the size of a fingernail. She placed it on the chair at the foot of the table then returned to her own. Two seconds later, Aranyani Nightingale Ryne materialized.

"Congratulations, witch," Aran said to Strife. Ramona's heart skipped a beat but Mind gave her a stern look. "I had forgotten you could sense someone hiding in Shadowland."

"Except for these last few months," Strife confessed, speaking now with no hint of Balkis, or whomever she was currently possessing, "I've lived in it for most of a decade. It's you who must be congratulated. You are the first sister I've detected travelling through between-space in all that time. I use the word sister both generically and specifically, by the way. Might I ask how you discovered I was out again?"

Ramona knew from Strife-Balkis that the vast majority of members from the various Sisterhoods hadn't used their stepping stones for teleportation purposes since the Fifties in order to avoid becoming infected with Strife. The few that did were usually desperate enough to assume they weren't daughters of a small-case-sedon. It was crazy, Balkis confided to her in Budapest. How could they be absolutely certain their father wasn't a sedon.

Strife's question was valid; Aranyani's answer was elusive to the extreme. "I have my sources."

"Still only makes seven," mumbled Ramona before directing her attention to yet another former Strife. "You don't seem surprised to see me, step-daughter." In terms of age, Nightingale was more like Ramona's younger sister but, having married the Great Man (Aran's father, Loxus Abraham Ryne) in the mid-Fifties, the countess was correct to address her as step-daughter.

"Why should I be, countess?" There never had been any love lost between Ramona and Aranyani; can't lose love if you never had it to start with. "Moses and I made the surrogate woman who took your place. I didn't think they were after a fifty year old sexpot." Aran looked at her wrist. "Damn! Forgot my watch."

"Not funny, Nightingale." Strife certainly didn't sound amused. "If you're trying to say time's running out on the Ramona-clone, we know that already. Now, state your business."

"Alorstro Sian is in Houston. If I hadn't been in a super-sensitive state, I would never have detected him. Who sent him?"

"I did," acknowledged Dis L'Orca. "We wanted to find out what you and Moe Three were up to."

"Up to? You know bloody well what we're up to, Salvatore!" Aran was about to spill some giant-sized bean, minus both Jack and the stalk, but couldn't resist sticking it to Dis L'Orca while she felt she safely could. "Making short-lived copycats of you – not to mention on contract to you – just in case your pet demon decides you've outlived your usefulness now that you've destroyed the Cosmic Express."

(Being a mother of two teenagers, one of whom she was raising herself, she hated drug dealers. Feeling safe, though, had nothing to do with motherly bravura.)

Dis L'Orca was severely shaken by her revelations. "How the hell did you learn about Daemonicus?"

"Punning now, Sal?" Aran smirked – not that characterizing Daemonicus as a creature from hell made for much of a pun. It was more a statement of fact than anything else. "Why not ask how come I'm using agates to get around again? Why not ask how I knew there was a new Strife around or that WORLD did in the Express? Things came together when I spotted your Dr Cyanide. Wasn't that Sian's codename, Milo?"

The major granted that it was. "Earned it honestly. His mother was Lucrezia Borgia." Despite striving to follow Aran's lead, this was not the time for humour.

"As for Daemonicus," she carried on, "I saw him in 1965 on Sentalli's island; saw him slaughter – yes, that's the word for it – three innocent, four year old girls. I'd never seen anything so wanton, so cruel. Then I heard about what happened to the Cosmic Express. My daughter, Fire, Firenze, looked up to Anhita, your own daughter, you godless madwoman."

Ramona was about to protest she had nothing to do with WORLD until Sunday but Aranyani didn't give her a chance. "If my Fire had been a few years older, she'd have been on the Express. Ask yourself, short of Hitler or Truman, who could be so calculating as to wipe out sixty odd people, almost all of whom had supranormal parents or relatives? Had to be Daemonicus."

"Pretty wild assumptions all the same," noted Translav. "Unless, of course, you'd some dealings with the demon recently," he added cannily. "I thought Markazi approached you with the contract to make a clone of the countess."

"On the thing's behalf," acknowledged the sheik, who spelled the word the Iranian way, not the Arabic way, as '*Shaikh*'. "Were you in a super-sensitive state that day as well, doctor? I know I didn't tell you anything about either him or Strife."

"She was me," imparted Strife, somewhat disconcertingly to most of those around the table. Dis L'Orca and Milo Mind, who knew more about Strife than the rest, still had difficulty with the concept that the Order's co-leader was some kind of sentient infection. "Unwittingly perhaps, and only long enough to give me back to Ramona in '51, but she was as much me as I was her for that time. As my mother remarked a couple of days ago, we've an affinity for each other. We're sisters, after all."

If Strife was trying either to throw her off-stride, or wriggle out the truth of this '*super-sensitivity*' of hers, Aran wasn't biting. She'd long ago resigned herself to the fact that that notorious sensualist Sedon St Synne, not Abe Ryne, was her father. As for the truth of her uncommon (for her, not Strife) perspicacity, they'd learn that all too soon.

"Except I can read you better than you can me," she continued brazenly. "After I had Firenze, I spent nearly a dozen years becoming a thoroughly trained Anthean. I don't know much about you, countess, but you and your mother – be she Mata Avar or, as I've also heard, Cybele St Synne – are Korants, members of a distinctly inferior Sisterhood.

"As for the various female D'Angelos, including Tereza's brat Sapphire Lancz, and Crystal, thanks to Headmistress and Superior Sorrow, they've no training whatsoever. Moses Callion and I have been aboveboard with WORLD.

You haven't been anywhere near as honest with us. Why did you send Sian to Houston? The truth, Sal."

"You think we sent him to assassinate you?" asked Mind.

"When you're already dealing with mass murderers," confirmed Aran, "What's one more killing? Especially among friends."

"It was Milo's idea," responded Dis L'Orca, finding himself somehow compelled to speak honestly. "Not to kill you, don't mistake me. To find out what you're concocting for SPACE. He says the clones you're making for Ryne are based on old-time supras; are potential supras themselves. Just like OJ Maxwell — but I suppose you don't know what your ex-husband has become."

"He showed me."

"What! You mean he's in Houston also?"

"Was. Max and Romaine Kinesis had a brief stopover there earlier today. Right now, they're on their way to Cape Canaveral I believe."

"Why didn't you inform me, Milo?"

Major Mind scratched the stubble under his turban-strap nervously. "How was I to know? He's been out of range of my monitors since he left LA this morning. Truth told I haven't had a very good fix on him since he left Hawaii yesterday. I've been trying to tune the signals from his Mind Tap through our satellite system but he's been moving so fast I can't keep up with him."

"Put bluntly," realized Dis L'Orca in horror, "We've lost contact with him. That Mind Tap was our meal ticket. If Daemonicus finds out, we'll be no use to him."

"You maybe, but I have a way of ingratiating myself with my superiors. I reckon I'm still invaluable or at least fully deserving of my expensive account."

Aranyani rose to her feet and spat verbal venom at Mind and Dis L'Orca. "I told you not to lie. You ordered Sian to assassinate Moses and I! I know. I got into his mind."

"You what!" Dis L'Orca felt the world, not to mention WORLD, eroding beneath his feet. "I gave no such orders," he reiterated.

"And I'm just a freelance operator," protested Milo Mind with a faint grin. "Where would I get that kind of authority?"

"I did!"

========

As Daemonicus manifested himself at the head of the table, Ramona muttered loud enough for all the hear: "Knew there had to be an eighth."

****

Nuke 11: **Daemonicus Demystified**

========

Wednesday, December 3, 1980

Alorstro Sian arrived at Houston International Airport earlier that day.

========

He found his way to the Academy of Man only to discover that OJ Maxwell and Professor Romaine Kinesis had preceded him. Biding his time until he saw them leave, he entered the underground complex and located Moses Callion the Third easily enough. The gnome was surprised to see him.

"What's the matter, Alorstro? I told you Dis L'Orca's and your clones would take a little longer to develop than Markazi and Translav's. Normal men and women are always easier to replicate than supranormals. Ramona's is doing fine. The other two can't have malfunctioned already."

Sian didn't even know they'd been delivered. "Where's Dr Nightingale?"

"Elsewhere, probably elsewheres by now. Why?"

"That's for me to know and her to learn. I'll wait."

"Fine with me. Just wait somewhere else. I'm cooking up a date with Gloriel D'Angelo."

========

The darkness-shrouded, pink-faced and three-eyed phantasm called Dae-monicus fully appeared in the galley. He was not alone either.

========

With fingers too long to be natural he was holding onto Demios Sarpedon by his neck. As uncomfortable as that must have been for the dazed and beat up Untouchable-no-longer – not on the Order's converted fish packer – it confirmed something Mind had never been too sure about before.

As Ramona insisted, even though the demon had always seemed entirely insubstantial previously, the thing had to be solid. Not only that, it had to be supranormally strong. How else could he (it?) manhandle someone that big, that well-built, so seemingly effortlessly. If that was her son, Mind wanted to slip back into her womb whole-bodily and come out of it again a reborn superman.

He had never heard of an apparition who could put someone through a ten-minute trip to Hell and leave him stripped naked, scourged and burnt blacker that he already was. The torture foisted on him by Daemonicus's eyefire had been psychological. Sarpedon had been physically brutalized.

The thing tossed Sarpedon onto the captain's table and began to rant. *"Untrustworthy mortals, you sought to hide this creature from me. But that was only the latest example of your audacity. It was Major Mind's idea to create a proto-human for the countess – an inspired notion I thought at the time – but the rest of you went further than that.*

"You conspired with Callion and this Ryne-witch to manufacture living, breathing imitations of yourselves; ones that you no doubt control through two-way transmitters, artificial agates or brain-bonds of some sort, like the Gynosphinx did hers fifteen years ago. Why? To hide from my vengeance should you fail me.

"That very act has failed you! You, Markazi! You, Translav! You are not truly here! Eye-fire burn, duplicates!"

The thing opened its third eye: immolating Markazi and Translav where they sat, in their chairs. With their chairs. Further proof, as if Milo Mind needed any, that Daemonicus was more fantastic than phantasmal; more he than it — though there was still a lot of an it about him.

"Make no move, you others. Leave them melt in the hellfire of their own rightly-judged perdition. I only pray their real selves are suffering the same fate as those abominations are. You too, Nightingale, are also not fully here. You are not a duplicate, a Callion Clone, like those two were, though. You are an illusion, a talking soul self.

"Even if you are mentally attached to this mind-projection, it is doubtful I can make you hurt so far away from where you really are. No matter! I have already dispatched Sian to slay you and your misshapen accomplice, Moses Callion. Likely by now you have no body, no life, to return to — as is only just, given your perfidious nature.

"What possessed you to betray me, witch?"

"How could I betray someone I didn't even know existed until today. Your phony Ramona is functioning as we guaranteed Markazi. So what if Moses and I contracted with SPACE to make more supras or, at least, creatures similar to Steltsar? So what if we also contracted privately to make short-lived copies of Sian, Dis L'Orca, Shaikh Markazi, and Prince Translav?

"One contract does not preclude the other. We work for WORLD, we work for its individual members, we work for the United Nations. Work is what we do; work – provided we're paid – motivates us. We are scientists, Callion and I. The overriding ethos of science is to learn, to gain knowledge. What others make of that knowledge is not our concern.

"Clearly you did not understand that. Clearly we no longer work for you, whatever you are. Clearly we have become enemies. Stay away from us, demon. You have been warned."

Her likeness blipped into the dark grey matter of Samsara and was gone.

Daemonicus laughed out loud. *"Who is this unusually aging witch, this anti-life monster maker, to speak in such terms to me? I have been warned!*

Indeed! Hah!" The horror fixed Mind with his three eyes. *"Clones, major. Your idea!"*

"Wait a minute!" protested Mind, shooting Ramona a desperate look. She casually reached her lone hand into her pocket. "You said it yourself. I was inspired."

Daemonicus had him wriggling on his sadistic fishing line. *"Your idea also to send Sian or the Glomen to Houston to check on the good doctors. Your intuition was correct. How did you put it on Sunday: Using strands from supras from the Forties and Fifties to make a new generation of deviants for the Eighties? Or words to that effect.*

"The Ryne Witch as much as confirmed it. 'Or at least creatures similar to Steltsar' were her exact words. Be it consciously or unconsciously, they are making more Maxwells, more No Name things, more doughy blobs capable of terrifying the likes of Damon Goldenrod, Byron's Apollo. Well, there will be an end to that! I am in your debt, major."

"Thank God!"

"And my clone?" demanded Ramona, still keeping her hand in her pocket.

"Are you a supranormal, latest mother?"

"Of course not."

"Then it shall be allowed to die according to plan. As for you, Dis L'Orca, you anticipated what I would do to you once our business with Sentalli's island is completed. Though you anticipated wrongly, I cannot abide mistrust. Circumstances have therefore changed. Can you give me a single reason why we should not permanently conclude our relationship here and now?"

"I am a businessman, Daemonicus." The Spaniard trembled but soldiered on bravely. He spoke almost as if he was lecturing the apparent demon. "Businessmen make deals then deliver on them. Which is what the Order has done. Project: Cosmic Express was terminated as you specified. You even described the results as happy, as I recall."

There was no question he was on the edge of a precipice. However, while he couldn't fly, he thought he might be able talk himself down to a soft landing. "You're a superbly paying customer and we certainly don't want to turn off any financial faucets, especially ones fed by the lakes of lucre you can obviously tap.

"However, bear in mind that, though business exists to turn a profit, businessmen wouldn't be in business if they couldn't spend that profit. Markazi and Translav jumped the gun slightly — luckily for them, though not their proto-human doppelgangers, as Moses Callion would have it.

"I wish I'd been so fortunate but it's too late for that. I must now rely on your wisdom and commonsense." He was on a roll and saw no reason to stop. "True, once mine and Sian's were delivered, should you try to eliminate us, you would destroy only clones that wouldn't have survived long in any case. You would think us dead but we would be alive to spend your, make that our, money.

"The Callion Clones amounted to life insurance policies; failsafes, if you will. Do not forget you had Markazi commission the countess's double. At the time none of us had any reason to suspect OJ Maxwell was not a perfectly normal man. We meant you no harm but you scare us with your sudden appearances and fearsome looks.

"Yes, we should have trusted you, but we also had a personal obligation to cover all our angles. Is self-preservation not reason enough?"

"You stood to benefit from the plans Strife and I began with Countess Ramona's carbon copy replacement. You'll take the money but not the chances. You are not worthy of my patronage."

"I have stated my case," said Dis L'Orca defiantly. "WORLD had no intention of going out of business just because we had fulfilled our contract with you. To use a familiar expression, we have more fish to fry."

"Had," contributed Strife.

"As you know," Dis L'Orca stayed the course, continuing to address Daemonicus directly, "The Order had our eyes set on Centauri Island. It makes no sense to destroy it."

"And destroying the Express did?"

"Quite honestly," Dis L'Orca put to the evidently also physical phantasm fearlessly, "None of us believe it's destroyed. If that was your sole aim, why bother with Kaligula, her so precisely designed Kamikaze craft, something as elaborate as this packer, that freighter out there, or an organization the size of WORLD?

"Sian and I could have done it with a missile, Crystallion with one of her firedrakes or, probably, Sharkczar with his bare hands. Simpler still, given your abilities to go in and out of anywhere, you could have popped into the Express, set a bomb, and got away before it went off. Sinking Centauri or rendering it uninhabitable is something quite different."

"I have heard enough. Crystallion and Sharkczar were recruited to destroy Centauri Island. You and your organization are no further use to me. You should never have sheltered this thing from me. That I cannot forgive." Daemonicus pointed at the prone form of Demios Sarpedon.

Dis L'Orca lost his bravado and protested desperately. "You cannot hold that against me either. Sure, I knew he was on board but Sharkczar, your own ramrod, rescued him and the countess wanted to keep him. He seemed harmless enough. Besides, who am I to go against your own mother's wishes?

"No one informed me he was your enemy. I'd have slain him had I known. Mother or monster, the countess or Sharkczar, notwithstanding, a true businessman looks after the interests of his client."

"You truly have a glib tongue, Dis L'Orca. Sharkczar, as you call him, is a Mandroid Monstrosity, a recognized enemy but a necessary evil. There is much more to Centauri Island than meets the eye; all the more when you're not handicapped with merely two of them. Very well, I shall give you the momentary benefit of a doubt. Do as you and WORLD wish with the island until Monday, though I strongly urge you to do nothing."

With a dismissive wave, Daemonicus turned to Ramona. He regarded her as warmly as a pink-skinned, friendlily smiling fiend in a swirl of darkness could. *"What is the matter with you, latest mother? Have I not promised you revenge? Have I not guaranteed its delivery? You should be happy we are about to destroy Centauri Island. Are not those who have hurt you the most on it as we speak?"*

"I only said it was a waste. A properly-executed takeover, followed by a few selective executions, would gain me a measure of revenge as well as keep Centauri Island the golden egg within NCE's nest."

"It is not your concern, latest mother," Strife reiterated.

"Perhaps not," she granted. "Tell me. Why do you two keep calling me latest mother?"

"We are immanent beings," Strife imparted. "You are our shells' mother, therefore you are our latest mother."

"I see. Is that also true of Sharkczar?"

"Steltsar was a mistake. After his physical and simultaneous dream battle with the first Olympian, his human body, that of the Nazi Nightmare, Tyrtod von Alptraum, was ruined beyond reclamation. But his mind or spirit fought on. Had it not, his brain would have died within a few minutes. The Conqueror should have let it."

"Admit it, demon, or Solomon, whomever or whatever you purport to be," vented Ramona, at least as careless of the consequences as Dis L'Orca had been when he stood up to the inhuman revenant. "You're the one who should have let it — you and your mad mate, the witch who has always been Strife. Were it not for you, there would be no Steltsar. Without you, von Alp Senior would have stayed dead back in the war.

"So, who else knows your secret? Clearly not Dis L'Orca. He would have been too young to know you during your last go-round. Major Mind? Yes. That's why you're being so solicitous to him. Mind may be a poor excuse for a neurologist, even less as a psychiatrist, but one thing he is good at is cybernetics. I'll wager he's adept with computers as well.

"What'd he do to win your favour? Blackmail, knowing him. A secret code in some system like the Alliance's that he has to renew regularly or you stand revealed for what you truly are? Latest mother, am I? Your former mother wouldn't have been Mary Magdalene born Ryne, would it?"

"You are trying my patience, countess. How can you be rehabilitated if you continue to spout lunacy? I am not my father. He killed himself on Salvation Island trying to slay the Devil Himself."

"Did he, indeed? And countess, is it now? Well, perhaps I am, though only by adoption, if that. Otherwise, the Countess Ramona Avar is a fiction dreamed up by my father – also your father, Sedon St Synne – to cover what you claim is my true identity but which these others seem absolutely ignorant.

"To answer your question: Vengeance is not enough reward for being made a fool of time after time, year after year. Revenge is more personal than that. And motherhood is the most personal of personal we women have." She pulled out a half dozen eye-eggs, pods she'd taken from Demios Sarpedon on Monday. Two of them opened.

Before either the demon or Strife could react, a third eye to match Daemonicus's appeared in the centre of Strife's forehead. Then both inexorably extruded and shot out of their respective skulls — sucked into and by the orbs. The two pods immediately closed, immanent spirit beings secured within them. Instead of Strife and Daemonicus, the Budapest Balkis and an effeminate-looking man who could have almost, but in the absence of female breasts, not quite, passed for her twin sister lost consciousness and collapsed.

Ray hadn't really expected him to turn out to be Jesus Mandam somehow still alive but their resemblance to both him and Virginia Mannering – Jesse's likeliest twin since he and Barsine Mandam didn't look at all alike – was unmistakable. And, yes, they did remind her of images and statuary she'd seen of the rogue pharaoh Akhenaton and his wife Nefertiti; the former beautiful, the latter not so much so.

Truly Lady Guillotine now, albeit not human-lethally, she leapt to her feet in appreciable triumph. She was entitled to it. Neither witches nor warlocks could cast glamours if they were unconscious. Gone with their threatening looks were whatever threat they actually posed.

They couldn't hear, either. Not that it stopped her from talking down to them in terms that approached the Biblical: "Thus I exorcise you of your demons. Be you proper children of mine or not, motherhood is served. Free again, free as you probably never have been before, your lives are yours to live as you please."

"Magnificently done, countess," applauded Milo Mind. Dis L'Orca glared at him.

"You knew what she was planning all along?"

"We do more than sleep together, dear boy," beamed Mind. "Put better, when we're not hot we plot."

"Sarpedon falling out of the sky was a godsend," said Ramona. "Or maybe a shark-send," she added, allowing herself a relieved laugh. She couldn't disguise how shocked she was that they weren't who she figured they were and admitted as much. "Though I'm more than a little surprised these two turned out to be who they apparently are after all."

"Who did you think they were, St Synne and one of Sophia's grandchildren — Star Dark, maybe, or Natasha Dre'Ath?"

"Hardly," admitted Milo Mind. "We were thinking more in terms of the King and Queen Conqueror."

"Jesus Mandam," said Ray. "He and his life's mate, Wilderwitch."

"Come again?"

"I did not believe anything Strife told me of my past," said Ramona. "To say the least it was preposterous. I suspected Wilderwitch and Milo felt – didn't know, I feigned that bit – that Daemonicus was the Conqueror, somehow either still alive or reincarnated. A Callion Clone was what he actually thought."

"You don't need to be a supra to recognize personality traits," elaborated Milo Mind. "I was just a kid living in India with my parents when I first met Sedon St Synne and Jesus Mandam in the mid-Thirties. I might have been a couple of years younger than Jess but we chummed around together. Shared an interest in oriental faiths.

"I was curious about what made the religious believe. Mandam skipped that bit entirely. He wanted to know what made religion real. I was interested in the mind; he the ineffable, the soul itself. I was a normal who became a licensed psychiatrist a half decade after the war. He was a supranormal who, to stretch for a comparison, became a psychic.

"The root word *'psyche'* is the same." (He pronounced it *'see-shay'*.) "It means the soul, the breath of life. He knew instinctively reincarnation existed; I wanted proof. Trying to reconcile the now with the then in order to improve the future was my fixation. What was then was still now, according to him. Except, he wasn't talking like I was, in philosophical terms. He was talking existentially.

"Progress, the future, we agreed, was ongoing. My logical mind said it would continue without me. Jess, though, enjoyed flying in the face of everything you and I'd consider commonsensical. His numinous reasoning said he would too — in a physical, not a metaphysical sense. It remains to be seen, probably always will in his case, which of us was right."

"Can the commentary and cut to the chase," Dis L'Orca encouraged. He knew it was futile. Mind was given to extemporizing in the extreme. "You're telling me this Conqueror character thought he, not just his soul, was immortal."

"Supras are a cord in the thread of actuality," Mind continued to ramble. "A shoelace in the spider web of Fate. You thought Daemonicus was St Synne, Sal, because you knew St Synne – as ancient and decrepit as he is – was still alive. I was prepared to entertain the possibility that Daemonicus was Jesus Mandam because I knew Mandam was a supra; the first one ever born, according to his own skewed mythology. And maybe he was, albeit only by a matter of a few seconds.

"Was Daemonicus the Conquering Christ risen from the dead twenty-seven years late? By my reasoning, Crystallion was the proof. I knew the Conqueror as good as created the first Steltsar. Ramona can verify that, she was there. I also knew there was a good chance he'd been Emperor Energy during the war. The way I figured it Crystallion was nothing more than Emp En revitalized by Aranyani and Moses Callion with the Conqueror's help."

"Then again, major," pointed out Dis L'Orca, "You are certified as insane."

"There is that," agreed Mind quirkily. "Nurture, my life's experience – not nature, what I was born to be – has seen to that. It also seems I was wrong.

"Unless they're under a spell of some sort, these two aren't the Witch and Jess. However, they bear enough of a resemblance to both Ramona and Jesus Mandam that they're probably the genuine article; their children, just as they claimed. Unfortunately that lends credibility to the rest of their gobbledygook: Big Shelter, a hidden continent, devils."

"Missed some shots, have you, Milo?" wondered Dis L'Orca.

"No, but you missed the boat, Sal. You shouldn't have blamed me for Hadrian's demise. You should have told me about your clones."

"What for? I thought our business was concluded when the Express went up in smoke. When Daemonicus said he wanted to keep you on the payroll, I cut myself in on the pie."

"Like I suggested you do."

"Before that actually. I acted as your agent. When you came up with the suggestion to send Glomen to Houston, I thought – why not? Cut Translav in on a slice as well. I didn't know then that Sian had agreed to kill Nightingale and Callion. Still can't figure that. What's so worrisome about Callion Clones if the likes of Daemonicus and Strife, assuming there are more of their ilk, can be put out of the way with a couple of skin-covered eggs? Think they'd work on Crystallion and Sharkczar?"

"They didn't seem to." Ramona recalled her introduction to the pods on Monday. "Daemonicus said he and what's become of Tyrtod were enemies. Presumably theirs was an partnership of convenience. The former, and I'm reluctantly coming to believe that he and Strife were supernatural beings, was more concerned about doing in the Express. Tyrtod – hell, call him Sharkczar – is intent upon destroying Centauri Island.

"I bet Daemonicus had some kind of hold over Sharkczar, a power of some description. Either that or, for his own reasons, Sharkczar wanted the same thing. Clearly neither the demon inside Solomon or Shark have any further use for the island. That goes for Strife as well. Crystallion and her firedrakes are Sharkczar's equivalent of the Order: instruments only."

"Which suggests we were, too." Mind suddenly started to fret. "Daemonicus and Strife served their purpose. Shark used us to get rid of them so that he could get on with his business without any more delays. Chances are he'll get rid of us, too. We better get on that copter and hope the yacht is still out there waiting for Translav and Markazi."

The same thought had crossed Ramona's mind but she was awaiting further instructions. "Tell you what I'm not going to do." She expertly juggled the two orbs in her hand. "And that's see if I've enough willpower left to release Daemonicus, stick him back into Solomon and try to get some real answers."

"So what are you going to do now, countess?" She'd begged the question. Dis L'Orca congenially obliged her.

Seemingly slipping back into coldly calculating Lady Guillotine mode, Ray regarded the galley contemplatively. The two chairs, where the clones of Greygreave Translav and Shaikh Ali Ars Markazi had sat, smoldered. It was almost remarkable the noise hadn't brought reams of WORLD's security men – Glomen all, she recalled – bursting into the room. Almost but not quite, she smirked to herself.

Her putative children from Big Shelter were slumped on the floor, still breathing and still not conscious. So too seemed Demios Sarpedon, lying naked on the table. (Daemonicus had really done a number on him.) Milo and Salvatore remained riveted in their seats, glaring at her expectantly. Even without Strife inside her, her innate leadership ability was coming to the fore.

"I was promised revenge," she snarled.

"Revenge is a mean and generally unrewarding business, countess," Dis L'Orca counselled, playing her along so expertly she wondered which side of her was buttered. "It does, however, have its uses. You've a formidable will. Your single-minded determination must have made those orbs trigger. One wonders if they could do more."

"Such as?"

Holding the other end of his cane, he test-fingered the release mechanism for his blade. It was working. He could also spring a derringer out of either sleeve, his '44 out of its shoulder harness, or bend down to tie his shoelaces and, he felt certain, pull his '38 before either of them could move.

"How about forcing Crystallion to sink her freighter then turn on Sharkczar for example? With them out of the way, we could go back to our original plan and take over the island."

"An interesting notion. One I'll certainly discuss with Milo and Demios before deciding."

"Deciding?"

"Isn't it obvious, Sal? I'm in charge of WORLD now."

As impressed with the eye-eggs, and what Ramona had done to Strife and Daemonicus with them, as he had been, Dis L'Orca had no doubt that, should the occasion warrant it, he was more than a match for two over-fifty, out-of-shape lunatics who probably couldn't out-fence a fencepost even in their prime.

He snapped his blade, sprang a derringer; was on the ground before he realized Sarpedon was off the table. As battered and humiliated as he was, even at barely a month shy of his sixtieth birthday Demios was easily Dis L'Orca's better in almost every respect, especially when it came to fighting.

Solomon and Balkis began to stir. It was a good thing Demios only slew devils. Slaying devic shells was something entirely different.

It was murder.

========

The three of them stood on the top deck and watched as the helicopter took off. "Can I trust him to look after Mandam's children?" Ramona asked Milo Mind.

"Sal has his instructions, countess."

========

"I gave him a couple of empty prison pods," noted Demios Sarpedon. "Just in case he runs into any more like Strife and Daemonicus. Of course, especially in my hands eyeorbs have all sorts of uses. I can fairly safely guarantee that, as long as he has them on his person, he will have little choice but to do as you required him."

"I should have gone with him," complained Mind pointlessly. "Just to make sure he carries them out."

"Sorry, major," Ramona apologized half-heartedly. "As I explained, you are too valuable at my side. The receivers for your Mind Tap aren't exactly portable and I want to know the moment Maxwell and Kinesis come back. Besides, in terms of security, I'm confident the packer is still the best place for us. What about the others?"

"I can't speak for Sian, Markazi and Translav – assuming they're still alive – but they'd be crazy to abandon the Order especially now that Strife and Daemonicus are no longer an issue. I believe your ascension is assured, countess."

"See it remains so, Milo."

"I captured Daemonicus once before," cautioned Sarpedon. "And Harry Zeross caught Strife in one of his ringots. Which were designed literally centuries long gone by to do just that, capture devils and keep them that way. That was fifteen years ago, granted, but, unless there are more than one of each, they obviously escaped. It is imperative I get back to Centauri Island ASAP to ensure they don't do so again."

"And what else will you do there?" wondered Ramona.

"Even if you had Korant Kernels and knew how to use them, you could neither compel me to answer nor read my mind. All I ask is you get me close enough to the island and give me a runabout. I will not volunteer anything about any of you, that I promise. However, I would be derelict in my duty if I did not warn Alfredo about the mandroid dragons and the phantom freighter."

"Mandroids?"

"Artificial men and women, countess. They aren't flesh and blood, so they're not clones, but they are extremely dangerous."

Mind shook his head in disbelief. "It's almost as if the war never ended. As if Seth Kephren hadn't died or Moe Two hadn't opted for slow-brewing his clones."

"Be thankful you don't know much more than that, Major Mind," warned the onetime Ace of Spades.

"Maybe we should ask him."

Mind pointed into the sea at a shark's fin. Sharkczar showed no signs of slowing down. Then suddenly he went under the boat. Rushing to the other side, they spotted the fin again. And, far to the west, in the aureole of the setting sun, there it was — the phantom freighter.

"Knew that was a risk," sweated Ramona.

"Staying on this tub is the risk," panicked Mind – a condition not uncommon to a certifiable coward such as him. "Not only could the real Translav detonate the Glomen below from afar, without Daemonicus around to at least partially control him, Shark would think nothing of torpedoing us."

"Good thing he doesn't know you took care of the demon then," said Strife, striding onto the deck as if out of nowhere. Beside her was Daemonicus.

Sarpedon instantly activated his eyeorb. Nothing happened; other than the ever-smiling fiend actually laughing out loud, that is. "We meet again, Blackguard. Seems I was only partially right about you. I still say you wouldn't know a devil if it winked its third eye. Can't say the same thing about your orbs. Most impressive devices those."

"That's not his voice," said Mind. Even though he should have realized that so much of what had happened these last couple of days could only be explained by a supra equally gifted with far-sight and the ability to control minds, the truth was still not even close to dawning on him.

"Not Strife's either," pointed out Ramona. Ever since Demios Sarpedon as good as dropped in her lap on Monday afternoon, she'd known things were far more not what they seemed than what they did seem. There was more than just a phantom freighter out there. There was a phantom puppeteer.

"At least not Balkis-Strife's. Drop the illusions, step-daughter. I did exactly as you told me from between-space."

Sarpedon gave a complimentary nod to both of them but spoke specifically, though none-too-friendlily, to the apparent Strife.

"Seems young Nightingales have teeth after all," he complimented the female of the two. "Not that I'm overly surprised. Nightingale is ordinarily an honorific amongst higher end Ants but yours is a formidable clan, deserving of its arrogation. Still, your birthmother in her heyday, and her blood sisters in theirs, couldn't do what he can. Plus, what was left of him on Damnation Isle did tell me he was trying to contact you."

Aranyani cast off the illusion of being Strife. As she did so, Daemonicus stood revealed as a young man in his mid-twenties. He was expensively accoutered in whites and wore a Panama Hat. This he doffed. His cranium was transparent. The oh-oh-moment next to instantly thereby became an oh-no-moment.

With very few exceptions, his own father once acknowledged, no supranormal was more worthy of a retroactive abortion.

========

"You remember my brother Saul, don't you, Maenad? You were lovers a lot more than once."

"Psycho!"

****

NUKE 12: **Moon Angel**

========

Sharkczar went straight through the ghost ship's hull.
It opened rather than he opened it – which is what he had every intention of
doing to the fish packer until he detected Daemonicus still on the ship.

========

This particular model of Steltsar was akin to a bounty hunter adapted for survival against all odds. As such he wasn't equipped for particularly innovative thinking. He was, however, provided with superb, make that extraordinary, predatory instincts. With them came an animal awareness of what was good and bad, for him, that was so wide-ranging it verged on the supranormal in its scope.

That the Daemonicus he'd detected wasn't the demon he first knew as Judge Warlock; that it was actually a projection broadcast by the Magnificent Psycho (whom the old Baron, Tyrtod von Alptraum, Sharky's template, first met when he was just a prepubescent Saul Ryne) therefore never occurred to him.

Even sharks strove not to bite the hand that fed them, all the more so when the hand in question was pink, had too many joints on too many fingers and quite conceivably belonged to a benighted body-bouncer with brimstone breath. Provided of course that he or she or it bothered to breathe.

He had his task, a time frame and the backup necessary to accomplish it. None of that had changed. However, an exiled Trinondev – especially one of Demios Sarpedon's unquestioned calibre – falling out of the sky had been too much of a temptation to resist. He frankly didn't expect the Smiling Fiend to still be around; expected Sarpedon would have taken care of both Daemonicus and Strife by now.

Tough tiddlywinks that he hadn't. Sinking would have to wait for another day.

(Sarpedon reputedly held the oldest eye-stave in existence. It was so old that, given enough Brainrock, it could manufacture its own eyeorbs. Many within Sharkczar's acquaintance considered the fact that Ubris Nauroz, the Celestial Superior's *'Nubian'*, passed it on to him instead of his grandson, the current Master of Weir, proof that he, Sarpedon, and not Saladin Devason, his brother-in-law, should be Cabalarkon's Master.

(Demios agreed with their assessment. That he wasn't already had a great deal to do with wife Morgianna. She wanted the Mastery too, albeit for herself.)

Likely, being on the other side as they were, his benefactors would never find out he'd tried to jump the gun by torpedoing WORLD's fish packer. Hopefully neither would Daemonicus. Bizarre how the likes of All of Incain and Amphitrite of Lemuria would even work with an obvious, not to mention invidious, devil.

Then again, for countless human generations, until 5950, All was as good as Pyrame Silverstar's servant – and she was a Master Deva. She was much more than that, Sharky knew. That, circa what was thought of as 4000 BC out here, she was the first third generational Shining One given a name was perhaps the least of her accomplishments.

That Saladin, her treacherous half-son, the current Master of Weir, was privately – never publicly – referred to as Devason and not Nauroz was indicative of her major claim to fame. She was the devic half-mother of all the small-case-sedons. (Upper-Case-Sedon was of course their devic half-father.)

As the mighty Moloch usually in the sky above his Headworld determined shortly after raising the hence called Sedon Sphere, without mortal sedons living on both sides the Dome was too weak to stand without Mother Earth's tacit, as in mystical, support. Should it collapse, then as now such a disastrous turn of events would mark the onset of the second Great Flood. Or, at the very least, the start of surf season atop what was now the Rockies or the Andes or the Urals or …

That Sal was one of only two sedons left was bad news. That the old corpse, Sedon St Synne, was the other was much worse news.

He was already over a hundred.

=========

The freighter was only partially beyond Shadowland.

How it came to be between space at all, how it was able to traverse the Cathonic Dome – something even devils couldn't do except via the Wandering SAG Gap (after Sodom and Gomorrah) and, from 5945 onward, the always Stationary Nag Gap (after Nagasaki) – was beyond Sharkczar's capacity to fathom.

It might have something to do with All's male equivalent, the Egyptian Sphinx. More likely, it had to do with its currently much depleted cargo, what Sharky was by now conditioned to call Brainrock but was usually referred to as Gypsium out here, beyond the Dome; the same reason he could pass through the freighter's hull intangibly.

(Sometimes, Head-side of Cathonia, the SAG Gap didn't wander. More often than not, it stayed in one place. For fully embodied devils, that place was unreachable. In no small measure that was due to a severe, for them, overabundance of the usual suspect, Brainrock-Gypsium. In molten form it not only destroyed their debrained daemonic bodies, it melted their power foci irretrievably. Just ask Strife about that last.)

All had a fortuitous knack for employing small amounts of the Godstuff. This was somewhat remarkable since she – and she was, at least in what passed as her own mind, a she, definitely not an it – was mostly Stopstone-Solidium. Indeed, too much Brainrock-Gypsium would probably either destroy or else render All as moribund as her equally millennia old boyfriend.

(Reputedly, Sharky had heard from his bio- and technomage makers, most of whom had howsoever corrupted, Illuminary training, that All's creators initially had her as Ginny the Gynosphinx. By the same token, they originally named her boyfriend Andy the Androsphinx. Although shape and size shifters, their usual, altogether anthropomorphic heads were of said makers: the Male and Female Entities.

(She, Ginny, commonly had wings; he, Andy, never did. The latter also had been sitting, massive but immobile, on the Giza Plateau not far from Heliopolis, a modern day suburb of Cairo, Ancient An, the Biblical On, since centuries prior to the Genesea. And Heliopolis – Agenor Heliopolis, to be precise – was the last name of the supranormal, the first codenamed Olympian, who'd killed him, Tyrtod von Alptraum, in 1944.)

As he stomped through the hold, past dormant firedrakes, their radiation-suited hostlers, and a helmetless few of Hell's Horsemen, he glimpsed the answer. Crystallion was arguing with another woman – one who looked vaguely familiar. Couldn't be. She was dead and gone. Whoever it really was spotted him, smiled enigmatically, then both her and Crystal vanished.

"Wilderwitch?" wondered Sharkczar dimly.

========

"Welcome to the Moon!"

"The Moon be damned, witch," snorted Crystallion. *"We're still in Shadow-land. This is your Shelter."*

"All right. Welcome to my Shelter on the Moon!"

========

Even Crystal, barely nine when she last had the dubious pleasure of seeing the Witch, capitalized, recognized her immediately.

After twenty-five years she was remarkably unchanged. Seemingly with a life of its own, her dark hair twisted in, on, and around itself, like snakes in a group grope. She was dressed in a buckskin-laced leather top, fur skirt, and moccasins; had glowing rings on her fingers, barbed bracelets and anklets, a pouched bandoleer across her chest, cut-anything hunting knife sheathed on one hip and bottomless bag strapped to the other.

No, there was no denying whom she looked like. Question was, who was she in reality?

"Strife!" spat Ramona Avar, who was in the same nebulous space. She both looked and sounded dazed. "You're the source of all my troubles."

"Troubles? Joys, delights, fun, all of the above yet none of the above."

"Mocking cunt," cursed the countess, who'd come – or been brought – up here minus her Lady Guillotine appendage. Which was undoubtedly a good thing, probably a deliberate thing as well, given her long-festering, hate-filled attitude to all things supranormal in general and Family Ryne in particular.

"Auntie?" queried Aranyani Nightingale. "Guess I shouldn't be so shocked. If Saul's back, why not you? Where's David?"

"I didn't know the Witch was your aunt, Nightingale," admitted Ray, recovering her equilibrium slightly. "Mind you, when it comes to Ants, very little surprises me. They're arch-deceivers, though; so good with glamours this could be anyone. So what's all this crap about your brothers, Psycho and Cerebrus? Has this witch convinced you the King Crimefighters are all still around?"

She knew Aranyani quite well, knew Wilderwitch too, if not better, and would have known Crystallion, albeit as Crystal St Synne. Would have still, were she not so horribly transformed and wearing a goggle-eyed, demon-headed, tip-to-toe radiation suit that might have doubled for a burqa were it black not (mostly) white.

What she could have added, but didn't, was that if the Witch was a Ryne, what did that make her? Her stepmother and another of Aran's aunts simultaneously? The Balkis-Strife had, after all, mentioned the possibility that she (Meroudys Maenad), Wilderwitch and the real Ramona Avar were triplets. She'd also mentioned that the real Witch believed Fisherwoman and Aran's undoubted mother, Eden Nightingale, were her older sisters; meaning they'd be Ray's as well.

"Does this help?" the fourth one obliged, sensing the total bewilderment, even incipient despair, of her increasingly reluctant guests, who were related both maternally and paternally. A third eye materialized in her forehead, about where her eyebrows would meet if they met.

"Devil!" realized Crystallion, who had some dealings with the unholy but godly extraterrestrials during her makeover and subsequent training.

Crystal hadn't heard much about witches or even supras. What she had came secondhand from Steltsar – who must have been reconstructed a good half dozen times since he could have had any contact with the real Witch – and his most recent makers, Shenon's bio- and technomages. Rather, the witches who engaged them.

"Shining One!" agreed Avar, channelling her Meroudys Maenad persona.

Mama Miracle (Cybele St Synne; perhaps disputably, also Crystal's paternal sister) worshipped devils, one specifically: Divine Coueranna, Kore-Concord. Miracle Maenad was in fact an honorific reserved for that Kore's High Priestess. She addressed her goddess as, among things, *"Oh Great Shining One."* So did Meroudys-Ramona, when they'd met in the, for her, distant – as well as perhaps imaginary – past.

"How about this?" The being, who must be a mind-reader as well as a master illusionist, made her face blank, straightened her rat's nest hair, turned it blood red, and cascaded it as if a geyser out of the top of her suddenly otherwise bald head. She kept her third eye, though not the other two.

"Strife's a devil," Ray realized, then she had it. She wasn't just any devil; she was Kore-Discord. Had she known that before? Must have. Aran certainly had.

Aranyani hadn't spent the years between 1939 and 1955 in a Himalayan Shangri-La; hadn't returned to that non-existent place between '65 and '77. She had been to Sedon's Head. The last time there, while Firenze was being looked after – call it for what it is/was, *indoctrinated* – by elder sisters, Aran rose painstakingly, level by even-more-demanding level, to higher and higher planes in the Superior Sisterhood of Flowery Anthea.

She couldn't officially become a Nightingale, in title as well as arrogated surname, until she reached the traditional age of fifty. That didn't mean she couldn't have qualified for it solely on the grounds of acquired knowledge. As part of her studies, she had gained a hefty degree of expertise when it came to a highly specialized and, especially by Outer Earth standards, exceptionally esoteric type of demonology.

She was therefore very familiar with the history of the devazur race. Indeed, as best any Anthean could understand it anyhow, she could detail the background of many of its seemingly innumerable individuals. Nevertheless, no devil she'd ever heard about, female or otherwise, commonly appeared with a blank face, red hair, and a single eye. Correction, no devil on record assumed that look.

Devils, though, could look like anything and anyone. So there was no guarantee they'd been absconded by the second wife of Thrygragos Varuna Mithras, his Ewe for Aries (as opposed to her brood sister, his Boss Cow for Taurus, Divine Coueranna). No guarantee they were in the presence of the devic half-mother of Chrysaor Attis (by way of her and Mithras possessing the Dual Entities when he was conceived circa 2000 YD), thereafter renowned as the endlessly recurring Universal Soldier.

Still and all, her Inner Earth teachers clearly believed that Strife, the malevolent Mistress of Mayhem, howsoever else you characterized her; had adopted that look after she fled to Outer Earth circa 4000 YD (the Outer Earth's Year 0 Anno Domini). They further claimed she did so in order to escape Sedonic retribution for the unconscionable killings she'd committed as part in Phantast Thanatos's Crimson Conspiracy.

Unless – and Aran was stunned that this had never occurred to her before – that's what happened to every extremely highborn devil who attempted to swim across a lava lake full of molten Brainrock in order to reach the (then not wandering) SAG Gap. They wouldn't just lose their power foci (in her case, the Golden Apple of Discord) in an effort to escape to the Outer Earth. They'd also lose his or her face, eyes with it.

Of course even her mother sometimes complained how pixilated, as in fairy-touched fanciful, Aran could get.

"Marut Kanin," she provided, showing off slightly.

"And Fitna Marutia and Kore-Eris and Kore-Discord and so many more names even I have lost count," said the currently cyclopean face-dancer. "I'm myrionymous. But I'm also not her. I'm a three-thing. You got one, Althean; I can be part devil. I'll give you number two. I'm part mandroid, which is to say part artificial and part computer as well, sort of like Steltsar and you, Crystal."

(Althean Healers weren't necessarily Antheans but most were. Furthermore, Ants trained on the Outer Earth were almost always Alts: doctors, nurses, attendants, midwives, chemists, pharmacists, herbalists and so forth. They couldn't use agates, like Aran now could, for anything other than what anyone could, which was nothing special. Nor did they know anything about the Hidden Continent of Sedon's Head or its exotic denizens. In nearly every case they didn't refer to themselves as witches either.)

"But I was also a human being. And not that long ago in terms of what's commonly conceived as the linear passage of time. As a human, I was known as Mnemosyne D'Angelo Heliopolis. To devils, I am known as the Memory Entity. To All of Incain, I am her prototype, her progenitor; in effect her mother."

All three of Memory's *'guests'* knew something of the first Mnemosyne, Memory of the Angels, one of the most famed supras in the secret annals of her day. For her part Ramona drew a blank when it came to the Memory Entity. For their parts, neither Crystallion nor Aranyani had ever connected a once-living human being with the not-so-legendary Female Entity of the Head and earlier – a being Antheans and Lemurians spoke of with unmitigated awe.

In the late Forties, when she was still a teenager, Aranyani even met a female who purported to be the Entity. With her then, besides her mother and a few others, had been the real Wilderwitch. And it was her who claimed to be not just the Witch's mother (in 5927) but Fish's (in 5918) and that of those she referred to as the Trigon Triplets, one of whom was Eden herself (in 5909).

They tried to speak at once but Memory raised her hand. When she lowered it, she was a two-eyed woman in her mid-thirties dressed in a black blouse and pants, with a pastel scarf tied around her head and forehead that covered her dark, short-cut hair. Her skin was creamy and her face slightly oval. It wasn't much of a stretch to see the D'Angelo family in her.

Aran thought immediately of Nita (Anita), a Summoning Child and, therefore, the eldest of Raphael and Sophia nee St Synne D'Angelo's eleven, non-adopted children. (As Aran found out long after the fact, Nita Nyx, or Night, was the first of them to die as a result of being exposed to their maternal grandfather's devil-ray – the first but hardly the last.)

She had finer features than that Memory's other still living sibling Dolores (Superior Sorrow). Dolores, Aran knew, must be nearing eighty; Raphael was even older and that Memory would have been nearing or just past seventy, were she still alive. This one, though, well … You didn't have to be a man to think of her as a knockout, a stunner, which that Memory certainly had been right up until her death not long before World War Two ended.

It wasn't hard to see a lot of Wilderwitch in her, either. If the Witch was maternally a Nightingale, she must have had a D'Angelo father. It certainly couldn't have been Raphael, who was born in 1897 and would have been all of twelve when Eden and her fellow birth date triplets, that Memory and Mama Sofa's sister, none other than Cybele St Synne (Miracle Maenad), were born.

Nor could it have been Papa Rafe and Mnemosyne's father, Michael, who died in 1920, seven years before the Witch was born. Unless Michael hadn't died during the Summoning, which was vaguely possible. (The only one who claimed to remember all there was to remember of the Godling Guild's Summoning was – with a name like hers no surprise – Mnemosyne D'Angelo, who was all of ten, turning eleven, at the time.)

"My joint spirit is wild," declared this Memory, before Aran could ruminate much more on the sadly tragic Family D'Angelo. (Eleven natural children for

Papa Rafe and Mama Sofa, two adopted, only three left alive: Tereza now Lancz, Anna Maria now Dre'Ath and Father John Paul, a Catholic priest whose usual posting, as a papal delegate no less, was Centauri Island.)

"Wild throughout time and space," she continued to extemporize. "Sometimes, oft times, it is out of control. I am perpetually in torment – which is why I have been called Discord or Strife, though never Strife as you know her. If I have a devic forbearer I pray it is Datong Harmonia, the Unity of Balance, also of Panharmonium. Even if Unholy Abaddon effectively murdered her five hundred years ago, thus setting off the 1000 Days of Disbelief, she I admire to this day.

"But I only resemble her physically. I am in no way her equal. Balance, stability, harmony, these I strive for within myself as much as for others. Sadly, though, I am a scattered being, have been for a hundred lifetimes, some shorter than my first one, some longer than even that of very long-lived Utopians on both Old and New Weir.

"I'm back now; have been since '75. Back to the century I was born and have so far died in twice. I'm not going to endure any more of this bullshit, to use a term dating back at least to the Age of Taurus. I have a man on the Moon who has endured much the same torment as I have. Together, we're going to make everything right. You can be help or hindrance. What say you?"

The older two, Ramona and Aran wanted to hear more. Crystal, though, was thoroughly locked in by her own madness – and her own suspicions.

"A few minutes ago," she exclaimed, "You came to me as Wilderwitch, whom I only vaguely recall from my childhood, and claimed you were All's mistress, no less than her mother. You tried to countermand her instructions and that of Queen Amphitrite; tried to order me not to destroy Centauri Island."

"Because devils," Memory countered, rehashing her argument mostly for the sake of the two who weren't on the phantom freighter, "Other than the Byronics already on the island, got loose beyond the Dome. The Express was redirected correctly by Kamikaze Kaligula but the bastard Sedon, whom I helped whelp, either deliberately or accidentally fractured it into its constituent vessels and sent them helter-skelter all over the place.

"He can't help himself. It's his nature to fuck everything up. Whenever he becomes involved in anything, everything goes sour. I told you earlier and will repeat it now: There is no point closing the Nag Gap until all the devils are brought or bring themselves to the Head and are trapped there, inside All on Incain, as they should have been already.

"We only have six of sixty-six here … actually more than seventy escaped the Sedon Sphere ... and don't know where any of the others have got to as yet. By any standards of reckoning, that is entirely inadequate." (Had Memory read Aran's mind like she had Crystal's, which she clearly hadn't, she'd have learned what Saul told her about a number of others.)

"And your thought beams," Crystallion continued to challenge her, "The ones that were supposed to render Outer Earthlings immune to devic possession?"

"Are taking longer than anticipated to grab hold," Memory allowed sullenly.

(Crystallion had been superficially briefed on the Panharmonium Project, as hatched by Aortic Amphitrite and her mostly female allies to isolate devils on the Head. There All the Invincible, who could move around, as well as travel between-space, could and would eat them. Thus inhumed they would be stuck, once and forevermore, in her and, through her interspatial digestive tract, the Giza Sphinx.)

"So, well over sixty Master Devas could be beyond the Dome, beyond All's grasp. If they made it to the Outer Earth they'd have billions of possible shells to re-enliven themselves. Worse, they're occupying cosmicompanions in teleportive ships, so many of them might be even farther away by now."

"The entire cosmos is their oyster," Aranyani grasped.

"This is beyond me," Ray admitted.

"Beyond God the Mother here too, it seems," Crystal put to Memory.

"Some certainly did escape the planet," she acknowledged. "Otherwise how could we have nabbed the six we did way out here? It could take months to locate the rest; perhaps all eternity if, as I suspect, some – including their overall commander Avatar Sol, one of the most dangerous men alive – got thrown into the time stream."

Machine-Memory paused, let out a very human sigh of what might be construed as resignation more so than determination. "One just never knows with Gypsium. And I should know one never knows when it come to Gypsium. We wouldn't exist as we exist without it. Yet, that we do makes no sense to anyone, including us."

"Bah! We are being asked to join forces with a Mad Mother of a mendacious machine and a Man on the Moon who is probably just as insane." Crystallion turned to the two other former Strifes, Ray and Aran. "You can stay here if you want. I go my own way, to hell and back if necessary. Or do you intend to decommission me, Memory?"

"You call us insane!" The Mnemosyne 3-Thing sounded outraged. How dare Crystallion spurn her offer of assistance? "We could cure you. We could do so much more, for the betterment of everyone, once devils are out of the way. We need to keep all our options open – and one of them needs be keeping the Nag Gap just that."

"Last chance. Return me whence I came or I start blasting my way out of here and into wherever, even if it is the fucking moon."

"Oh, it is, cousin. But neither Helios nor I kill sentient beings; not anymore we don't. By the time it came for you to act, we would have evacuated Centauri Island. As it is, there is no point. We need the Nag Gap functioning, not destroyed. Strike if you please but don't be surprised if Thrygragos Byron and his offspring find a way to thwart you.

"Don't be surprised if I do, too. Be gone!"

========

The demon-helmeted technopomp found herself back on the phantom freighter. Sharkczar was waiting for her.

========

"Where did you go? Was that who I thought it was?"

"I'm not sure what it was," Crystallion admitted. "She went through a bunch of transfigurations until she ended up claiming she was Mnemosyne D'Angelo. Looked like pictures I've seen of her too, except with shorter hair. Then she tried to convince me she was really the Female Entity; the one All called her very own Mothering Machine whilst we were being primed for this business.

"Ask me it's more likely she *was* Machine-Memory than Wilderwitch. But what do I know or even care? Regardless of whomever she is, she knows all about Strife; all about what she hired us to do and says it's too early to destroy the Nag. Says the Great God will stop us. Says she might as well."

"Then why hasn't she?"

"She says she's part computer. Plus, she mentioned someone named Helios, calls him her Man on the Moon. You and I both remember a Helios. The most dangerous man alive my father once called him. And she also said Cosmicommander Sol was one of the most dangerous men alive. So I'm guessing her Helios has to program her – or at least instruct her – to stop us before she can act."

"Helios, eh?" considered Sharkczar. "There's been a few of them: father, son, sister of the father, sister of the son, father of the father during von Alp's Summoning, brother of the father before and for years afterwards, right through the war years from what I recall, not that von Alp lasted that long. Even Mnemosyne D'Angelo was a Helios once; hence the son's sister. But they're all dead so I wouldn't worry about that lot.

"Master Devas are a different matter but we're ready for them. Shining Ones want nothing to do with nuclear energy; even their grandfather, the Mighty Moloch Sedon Himself, is terrified of the stuff. The Byronics will flee in panic back to the Head once you and your Horsemen start the assault. And I'll be waiting in the Gap like a spider for a dozen or so flies."

"And if she is the Mnemosyne Machine? If her and her Man on the Moon are the Dual Entities?"

"Then let them do their worst. We'll withstand them as best we can. If we fail, we'll get ourselves remade and make it personal."

"On the moon?"

"Wherever and whenever. I was redesigned, at my insistence, for ensnaring devils. It's an opportunity I won't waste."

"Then why must we continue to delay?"

"You know the answer to that. As ironic as it seems, All is powered by the very devils she imprisons. Two of her primary fuel rods, for want of a better description, were the so-called Idiot Twins, Tammuz and Osiraq. The latter, unless it's the former, charges you now; acts as your motor, as it were; and you in turn use him to energize your horsemen's firedrakes."

"How about fuel gods?" she injected, non-lethally.

"Very witty, Crystal."

"Couldn't resist."

"Point being, All relies on Tammuz, if it isn't Osiraq, and the others incarcerated within her to maintain her sufficiency. Without them, she'd inactivate just as her brother Sphinx did long before the Genesea. Consequently, in order to keep the freighter not just between-space but roving betwixt and between the Inner and Outer Earth, she needs power from other devils, primarily the Thanatoids of Lathakra. Naturally they demanded recompense: namely, the return of their lost children to the Head."

"And they may have ended up beyond the Dome."

"Yes, except that's hardly the extent of it. For devils there are only two ways back to the Head and one of them is the Wandering SAG Gap. But, if it isn't wandering on this side as well, it opens in what's called the Totem Pool. And it lies in an underground cave that can only be reached by diving beneath the Brainrock Lake within the caldera of Sedon's Peak.

"Assuming they can find where its entrance is on the Outer Earth – and, from what I understand from my makers, it always wanders – they try to come back that way, their Tvasitar Talismans will melt. So will their debrained daemonic bodies. No more talismans, no more bodies: they discorporate; become lowly, next-to-useless azuras again.

"And, if they try to come back through the link All has forged with her moribund mate, they'll be automatically imprisoned. That's what Sphinxes do. That's why All's involved – to nail as many devils as she can. As for the one we use, the re-floated freighter Amphitrite and her witch allies somehow rigged up using the Brainrock found in its cargo hold, that won't last forever.

"It may not last long enough to get us back again if Memory, who's obviously the brains behind the bitches' crew of Panharmonium pipe-dreamers, follows through on her threat to terminate our operation. So, again assuming they even want to return, the only safe way for the decathonitized devils to get back inside is through the Nag Gap.

"Mind you, if the Express had brought all the devils to the Head like it was supposed to do ...."

"I know. Machine-Memory, I guess it was her, told me all that. So where does that leave me? My firedrakes won't stay charged much longer, another few days at the most. They dry up, Osiraq dries up with them. We'll have to go over to Incain and convince All to give up Tammuz. Or vice versa."

"Which All won't do; not unless she's got hold of Novadev, the last of the Atomic Triplets, by then. He's out of the Sedon Sphere but we don't know if he's on the Head or beyond it. My personal inclination is to proceed as planned. Catch as many Byron Spawn as I can while you seal the Gap or at least turn Centauri Island into a mini-Ghostlands. Bide your time. I'm going to approach All and hope Amphitrite's there as well."

Sharkczar went to the other side of the freighter and dove into Psychron, the Head's eastern ocean, and swam towards the Prison Beach of Incain.

=========

In her Shelter on the Moon, the Memory Entity frowned as she sent Crystallion back to the phantom freighter. "Hindrance, that one. What about you two?"

=========

"I must have met your real life counterpart, Mnemosyne D'Angelo, many times when I was just a kid," considered Aranyani. "But I can't say she made much of an impression; nothing that you might call, um, memorable anyhow.

However, I met someone who claimed to be the Memory Entity in early '49 and she did."

"Over thirty-one years ago for you," agreed Memory. "That's four years after my first death but nearly ninety lifetimes later for me now. I would have been possessing the demon-devil most know as Pyrame Silverstar at that time. On and off, for something like forty years, the Pauper Priestess and I had a very productive relationship – and I say productive advisedly."

"As I recall," said Aranyani, not wanting to confuse matters by asking her what she meant by that, "You wanted nothing more than to destroy Dark Sedon. The real devic All-Father – not Sedon St Synne, who called himself Judge Warlock in there, whom you also told me was the Moloch's half-son."

"And a foundling, in aftermath of the Battle of Little Big Horn no less. Yes. And I believe the exact terminology I would have used was to bring him down to Earth. To get him under control, not destroy him per se. By the time you came across me, we were preparing to move on the Weirdom of Cabalarkon. Once we had the Big Bad's generative father in our hands, we figured he'd do as we wanted.

"Unfortunately Pyrame and I parted ways the next year. She was cathonitized and, shortly thereafter, my Man in the Moon was killed, by himself if you have to know. Even if I don't die myself – and I rarely do – when he does, he takes me with him into the time stream. We have a much more sophisticated plan this time, as I've already hinted."

Ramona was content to let Aran prod further. "Mind elaborating on that a mite?" obliged Dr Nightingale, who had never used Maxwell, her married name. "I gather you wanted to darken the Cathonic Dome. And you did, by extracting the Shining Ones acting as its stars and getting them into the Cosmic Express's occupants, its cosmicompanions."

"One of whom was my Anhita," Ray did contribute.

Nightingale ignored her, although not before she silently reminded herself that, had it been a few years later, one of them might have been her precious Firenze. Probably not her Timmy, though. Not unless NCE and the rest of those behind Project Centauri had changed their recruitment criteria to include cripples by then.

(Nightingales taught her that small-case-sedons had to have two devic half-parents: Large-Case-Sedon and Pyrame Silverstar, aka the Pauper Priestess. It seems their half-mother stuck to possessing Antheans and only boys, preferably firstborns, qualified as Sedon's mortal surrogates on both sides of the Dome.

(It further seems that the Master Devas' selfsame grandfather proved some six millennia earlier that imperfect Sed-sons were useless as mystical bulwarks when it came to maintaining the Sedon Sphere. All of that combined was why she crippled TJ. He'd have become a Sed-son had she not done so. But how could she explain any of that to either TJ or his father?

(She *couldn't* answered that; didn't even try. Neither did anyone else; not on her behalf; not on anyone's behalf. It wouldn't have lessened the condemnation she received subsequently; better to have killed the lad than crippled him, many said anyhow. That's what the Conqueror did to Solace Sunrise's boys, one after the other, on or about their seventh birthdays.

(Besides, when it came right down to it, who could explain any of that to anyone? Who was left? In the then absence of Morgianna Sarpedon and her little mother, Hush Mannering, she was the only full witch left out here – below here? – who could recollect the Hidden Continent of Sedon's Head.

(Plus, as her superiors in the Superior Sisterhood stressed prior to letting her come back outside after her mother's death in the midwinter of 59/1955, the Hidden Headworld must remain just that, a veritable Inner Earth, one for the most part inaccessible as well as unknown to outsiders. To blow its cover, as it were, well, a second Great Flood would never make the papers or even the nightly news if everything was underwater again.)

"I realize," Aran soldiered on, "Things didn't quite work out that way but, had the devils been brought to the Head, what was next on the agenda?"

"Put in capsule form: Seal all egress from the Head, make sure Outer Earthlings were self-confident enough to guarantee devils could no longer possess them, then get the Moloch Sedon to collapse the Dome – slowly, so as not to swamp the continental coasts on either side of the Pacific, even if most of the islands would go the way of Atlantis."

"In other words what we sisters call Panharmonium."

========

And so they carried on, Strife's former shells the three of them – tellingly, the 3-Thing, Miracle Memory, foremost amongst them by about four thousand years.

Finally she concluded: "Panharmonium shall unite all men with all women. For the Good of Humanity and the Greater Glory of Sentient Beings everywhere."

Except, she intentionally left unsaid, those on the Phantom Freighter.

****

NUKE 13: **Redundancy Click**

========

<u>**Wednesday, December 3, 1980**</u>

"Wrong, dear countess," proclaimed the young man, a few hours earlier. "You may now address me as Magnifico!"

========

"Don't be so pompous, Ryne," challenged Ramona Avar-Ryne. "Magnifico, my royal Hungarian ass. It'll be Saul or Psycho. Which do you prefer?"

He simply smiled. Lady Guillotine screamed, fell to her knees in shock and promptly passed out. "That's for your insufferable egotism, Ramona. If you didn't have the willpower to pull a devil out of Crystal on Monday, how did you pull two out of Daemonicus and Strife tonight? You didn't. I did.

"Just as I sent Blackguard to this tub in the first place. Just as I knew Strife was occupying Balkis Mandam and that it was therefore safe for Aranyani to travel through between-space on her agates. It's all down to me and me alone." He turned his attention to Milo Mind. "Long time no see, major. Still pushing your drugs to the Alliance and them to what's left of my supras?"

Mind didn't need a psychic-shove to slump onto the deck beside the countess. His was more feint than faint, though. He deliberately touched Avar-Ryne's pocket, the one within which she had the eyeorbs containing the spirits of whatever had been possessing the Mandam Twins.

With a name like Mind, one would expect he'd possess considerable willpower. And he did. Suddenly it was Psycho's turn to scream. He began to shake visibly. His shape changed. He became a mass of darkness with a pinkish face and a third eye. Daemonicus grinned triumphantly – then his form began to change back. With a flash, a bolt of energy shot out of him and into the orb at the end of Sarpedon's eye-staff. Even when one eye-egg cracked another could and would redo the job.

"As I said, Blackguard, most impressive gadgets those." Magnifico turned to Mind. "Nice try, major. Didn't take, though." He mentally raised Mind to his feet. "There are any number of things I could do to you for that and dozens of other slights you have foisted upon me in the long gone past. I admit to curiosity, however. Let's chat." He then addressed his sister.

"Aran, Strife seems confined so it's still safe for you to traverse this Grey you Ants love so much. Kindly take Countess Ramona somewhere else. I'd say the bottom of the sea, with rocks in her socks to match the ones in her head. Or maybe into the concrete foundation of an a-building high-rise over in Honolulu or somewhere close by. But I'm no Dr Cyanide and you're no Silver Arrow assassin. Back to her home in Budapest would suffice. We have no further need of her."

Aran shouldn't need coercing so he didn't compel her to obey him. Sarpedon, though, was a different matter. "Blackguard, you look out of sorts. Go to your cabin. Have a proper lay down. After I shrive Mind of his memories, if not his sins, we'll talk and, though you're opaque to me, come to some arrangement. Truth be known, I can hardly wait. For some reason I sense what you have to say will be much more interesting than what I take from Milo's mind."

"The countess promised me a ride to Centauri Island."

"The countess does not speak for me. Remember Damnation Isle, my friend. Best stay that way. Best also to remember these are Glomen, not a bunch of homicidal mercs like the ones you took up north with you. This is a ship and, even thirty years ago, Glows blow. You'll find my patience is limited."

Getting the message, Sarpedon started to walk to his cabin. Aran held him up. "The staff and the rest of your orbs please, Demios."

Sarpedon thought to protest but didn't bother. Even though he had respected her mother, he knew Aranyani well enough to know she wasn't much of an Ant wunderkind. Was more of an Althean Healer, sooth said, like Dolores Rivera, Superior Sorrow, and the not so young anymore new kid on the sisterhood block, Hiliarti Schroff-Zeross, their less laudable, more laughable, current Superior.

Since Psycho, Magnifico, wouldn't put her in danger, his weapons were better off in her hands than his. It was, he knew, a questionable strategy. Without his staff and orbs he was just a regular Utopian, albeit one with all his smarts left. Still, Psycho wouldn't be able to read him and he'd never suspect his sister could be turned against him with a little concentration.

"Just remember," he advised her, "These things are far more than overgrown agates. You do know what happens if you play with fire, don't you, Althean?" (He deliberately didn't call her an Ant, even though she was probably one of them by now, too. She purported her true loyalties lay with the therapeutic sciences anyways.)

"Hey, there are female Trinondevs," she countered, pleasantly enough. "At least there were, pre-Sal." Demios had forgotten how much in the way of memories she'd somehow managed to retain of the Head. Mind you, he reminded himself, it wasn't as if either he or his wife spent any time cultivating her friendship. It was her father's, the Great Man's, they needed and wanted to retain out here.

"None as dark as you." After years in laboratories, Nightingale had a fluorescent tan. She knew what he meant, though: Utopian women were white as light. "At least not quite yet." She knew what that meant, too: Demios had designs on the Mastery of Weir, replacing his brother-in-law, the aforementioned

Sal (Saladin born Nauroz). Then again, his wife (Morgianna also born Nauroz but become Somata) did ditto.

Sarpedon handed them over and took his leave, dutifully trudging off as required.

"What was that all about, Aran?" asked Magnifico-Psycho.

"Want to shrive me too?"

"Indubitably. Later. Come along, old man."

Mind had no choice in the matter. Magnifico telekinetically levitated him off the deck. Whereupon he floated him into the cabin below the bridge area that served as his and Salvatore Dis L'Orca's monitor room. (It was where, off one of her agates, in what was therefore her personal Shelter, Aran hid his brain. In a nice touch she'd first placed it in an ornate jewel box that had once belong to their mother Eden.)

He left Nightingale to attend to Lady Guillotine, Ramona Avar. She bent to place agates on Ray's shoulders in order to lighten her load.

As soon as they touched, both disappeared.

========

Magnifico interrogated Milo Mind for much of the night.

========

At first they went over their mutual past: notably the war years when, early on, both became prisoners of Donar Lancz (the Teutonic Terror, also Baphomet). After Codename: Baron Justice (Viktor Richter) assassinated Lancz (by decapitation) in 1943, they both became the *'custodial wards'* of the Great Man's former friend and colleague in both the Alliance of Man and the Xuthrodite Brotherhood, Tyrtod von Alptraum (the Nazi Nightmare, post-mortally Steltsar then Sharkczar), who was an actual baron.

Mind admitted that, by the time the old Baron – finally a card-carrying Nazi after years of disparaging Adolph Hitler as that uppity little corporal – got hold of him, he was less a prisoner than a collaborator. He nevertheless stuck to his personal mythology that he did what he did only to save his life, if not his sanity.

They moved onto the immediate postwar period, when both were *'rehabilitated'* by the Alliance. Even touched on events that led to Milo, along with the late Hadrian Dis L'Orca, inventing amnaesthetics in '49 – primarily as a way to humanely neutralize Strife's Sinister Sisterhood, if not Strife herself. (There was nothing humane nor, as they now knew, even human about Strife.)

That was when Magnifico discovered a – to him especially – very interesting tidbit at the back of Mind's mind. It seems, not that either of them would have been able to recall it at the front of their minds, that Dis L'Orca and Mind were *'assisted'* in this regard by a cute little witch Milo mentally identified as one Joli Blon (*'Pretty Blonde'*).

Her and a 16-year-old genuine kid thought dead for a decade, one with two-tone hair and different coloured eyes: none other than Aranyani Nightingale Ryne.

========

These reversible drugs allowed supranormals to forget their abilities; indeed, their past lives. They also helped the Alliance create new lives, new pasts, for former members of various supranormal groups. In this way it in effect created a bank of unaware supras. Not only that but, if they married (or were married) and produced (or already had) children of their own, the Alliance would find a way to insinuate itself into their lives.

These children – and there were joyful and not so joyful bundles of them – would be rigorously tested. If they turned out to have supra skills, either latent or patent, they would be given therapy such that they wouldn't know about their powers and could continue to lead a normal life. This had been happening in the early Fifties (when Magnifico was around, albeit not under that name) and, to Mind's just as certain knowledge, continued to this day.

In his opinion, if you had a list of those who graduated from the various Academies of Man throughout the previous thirty years, you would have a who's who of closet supras. He further claimed that a great many, if not all, of those on the Cosmic Express were just that. Perhaps that was why WORLD destroyed it.

Also of interest, Styx (no known other name), the Master of the WORLD before Daemonicus and Strife came along, was connected to Signal System; the S-name gave that away. (Gave it a sway?) At least ostensibly that organization wanted to eliminate supras altogether. Either that or, more likely to the major's mercantile sway of thinking, bring them under System's umbrella instead of the Alliance's.

Magnifico found all of this fascinating. However, when Mind talked about the Worldwide Order and AMERICA, he frankly doubted these were struggles between two non-supra groups. Mind assured him otherwise. If you excluded robots, clones, Anthean witches and the occasional mad scientist, neither organization had anything to do with supranormals. In the Sixties and Seventies, supras were pretty much a non-issue.

No longer, Magnifico assured him. Once they secured Centauri Island, he would reactivate the Supranormal Defence League. Supras would flock to the island and, if Mind was interested in staying alive, it would be his job to reverse the effect of the amnaesthetics; to make supras supranormals again. Of course they'd first have to find a way to get rid of Sharkczar, Crystallion, and the threat posed to the island from Hell's Horsemen and their nuclear firedrakes.

Odd, Mind mused. He had helped Ray dispose of one set of masters, Daemonicus-Solomon and Strife-Balkis, not to mention Salvatore Dis L'Orca. He reckoned he had established himself, howsoever reluctantly, to run WORLD alongside the countess. Then, within a few short hours, they were serving Saul Ryne, a disembodied brain now calling himself Magnifico.

Undoubtedly, as well as unwittingly, they had been since – as Psycho boasted, without fear of contradiction – he arranged for Blind Sundown and Raven's Head, a couple of supposedly dead supras, to as good as drop Demios Sarpedon into their laps. He thereupon long distance coerced Avar to turn his orbs against the two immanent whatever-they-were: Norma & Norman Normalcy, closet perverts, who could say? Who could say their real names were even Balkis and Solomon Mandam.

And who was Magnifico? Another dead supra – one even more psychopathic than Sundown – whose body was becoming increasingly transparent but whose brain, all that was apparently left of him, had somehow survived twenty-five years in the Shadowland of a grey Limbo. It was now hidden safely away somewhere, presumably by Aranyani in this Big Shelter he was getting sick of hearing about. All in all, matters were becoming almost too much for a sane man to handle.

Correction — too much for even an insane man.

========

Thursday, December 4, 1980

Early the next morning, Demios Sarpedon was still locked in a cabin below decks when he was roused from his stupor by a voice he rarely heard anymore.
"How's it hanging, Daddy Son-in-law? Low and slow, I hope."

========

Too low to be heard by anyone eavesdropping in the hallway, or be picked up by any bugs that might be planted in his cabin on WORLD's converted fish packer, it was coming from the Anthean Agate grafted into his shoulder — the reason he would remain opaque to both Psycho and Aranyani despite giving up his stave and orbs.

Nevertheless, he cuddled into his pillow and whispered very quietly. "Can't talk, trickster. Not safe. Need help."

"All right. Are you alone?"

"For now."

"Stay put. No lights."

There was a slight change in the air. Suddenly a little girl was sitting on his pillow. She gave him an endearing smile and a quick buss on the forehead then, motioning him silent, rolled off the bed. Scampering over to the cabin door, she slipped something tiny underneath it and promptly vanished again. A few minutes later, the door opened and one of the Glomen guards came in with Milo Mind.

"You sure it's okay, sir? What with so many things happening around here last night, I don't know who's in charge any more."

"Perfectly understandable, chappy. I'm a little confused myself. Fact is this boy's needed upstairs. He may be a bit groggy still, so I might need you to help lift him." The guard flipped on the light. Sarpedon was relieved to see it wasn't Milo Mind at all. Wearing his illusionary likeness was Young Life, generally known out here as Hush Mannering.

In Mind's voice, the enchanted, perpetually seven year old faerie fright, his wife's little mother (Pandora Mannering by birth, by whomever), if she was to be believed – which, being what she was, she wasn't – told him to get up if he could and follow them. He did. Shockingly, the guard crawled into bed and took on his features. He promptly went to sleep. Sarpedon now wore the guard's face and clothes.

"Where's your staff and eye-eggs?" asked Mind-Life.

"I'll be able to sense them. Three cabins down, I think. Any way you can find out who's in there or do you want me just to burst in and bash heads off walls?"

"Let's be subtle-buckle." Mind-Life produced another agate. He knew she wasn't there any more, though she left twin illusions behind. A half second later she was back. "Empty. Spotted some agates. They've the taint of a Corn Queen about them, though. Not proper agates, but hey, nay probs with the jobs. In a pinch or a punch, I can still make them work. Any other women aboard?"

"The captain and some of the technos, I guess. Aranyani Nightingale was here. She's the one I gave my staff to. I think she took the countess back to Budapest."

"Countess? Budapest? Ramona Avar was here? I thought she was dying."

"Everyone dies, Hush. Except maybe you."

"Oh, I'll die. And when I do, I'll stay dead too."

"Stop with the fay-saying will you."

"Don't be so sensitive, daddy Dem."

(His wife, Hush's daughter if you believed her, had a child when she was only fourteen. Not only was she stolen by faeries as one of their own, Morg didn't even recall she had her until some years later. That child, whose father was a faerie-type known as Tammuz Rhymer, was now Tsishah Twilight, the soon-to-retire Aortic of the non-Lemuria Aorta – properly speaking, more like an Atrium – on the heart-shaped island of Shenon.)

"I'm not. But it was her all right, born Meroudys Maenad, though she fancies herself Lady Guillotine nowadays. For good reason too, as near as I could gather."

"That doesn't explain the Korant Kernels. Ray's no idea Sed's Red switched her for the real Ramona in an effort to avoid Kore's Curse all those years ago. And don't ask me how I know any of that. We haven't got time for scholarly dissertations." (Sed's Red was Cybele St Synne, among the many who disappeared during the Godling Guild's Summoning of 1920. The Kore of the curse was, as one might expect, Kore-Discord, aka you know who.)

"And Strife. But Ramona took care of her. She's in one of my pods."

"Strife, eh? Thought I felt her presence but, after all these years, it's damned difficult to be sure. Her host must have been one of Sed's brood."

"Grandchild, name of Balkis."

"Ah, her. She's trouble even without Strife occupying her. How'd she get out here?"

"Not through the Nag Gap, that's a given. Korants are mostly Mithradites and the Nag belongs to Byronics and their shells. Maybe the SAG's wandering again. Methandra Thanatos controls it, doesn't she?"

"Hot Stuff's got no love for Korants either, but All might."

"Daemonicus, too."

That took Hush aback.

In the late Forties, under one of her many aliases, she'd made up the character of Daemonicus as a kind of fantasy male-equivalent of Strife – an inter-space bogeyman – in order to dissuade the likes of the then prepubescent Harry Zeross, aka Ringleader, and the King Conqueror, Balkis's father, better known as Jesus Mandam, from be-bopping through the dark-grey Universal Substance of Samsara, as between-space was sometimes inaccurately known out here. In '65, that fantasy very nearly killed her.

"Curiouser and curiouser cried Alice," said Hush, who, as a pretty blonde, bore a deliberate resemblance to Sir John Tenniel's versions of Alice in Wonderland. "Things just keep going from bad to worse then even more so. Know what'd be worst of all? If Daddy Ryne is right, Psycho and the King Crimefighters are alive and well."

Demios held his tongue for the time being. One never knew how far to trust a trickster.

"Look, here're the keys, big boy," she said. "Your stuff's inside. I trust you can find a way to get us both back to the island once you've your Weir-staff back."

He nodded; asked where on Centauri they should head. She told him hers was the room next door to Alfredo Sentalli's suite in the island's lone hotel. She reckoned that might expose them overly much, so it'd be better to make for the nude beach. What with everything going on there, going wrong there, chances are it would be deserted. After that they'd play it by ear.

"It'll be risky," she further advised. "The island's on full alert and, with Strife and this Daemonicus around, I can't chance taking you – or myself, as far as that goes – anywhere via my agates. Whatever else, don't lose your marbles, Daddy Dem. Once we're safe I want a look at what's inside them."

By that, (he hoped) he knew, she meant two his full-up eyeorbs and the cracked, now useless one Milo Mind got Daemonicus out of – and into Magnifico – howsoever impressively but, thankfully, briefly. "Despite what I've always publicly maintained, Strife and Daemonicus aren't illusions thrown by Ants gone rogue. She's real and, somehow or other, he must be too."

"They're not the only ones, I'm afraid."

"Care to enlarge on that?"

"Not right now. Mystery loves company."

"Maybe so, but it make me miserable."

"You'll survive. You always do."

========

Ramona Avar crept into Milo Mind's cabin. It took a while to wake him.

"What is it?" he groaned groggily.

"Love me."

"I always have."

"Love me better!"

========

Dawn Thursday Aranyani Nightingale went into the monitor room on WORLD's converted fish packer. Magnifico had allowed Milo Mind to return to his private cabin to get some well-deserved sleep. He was alone, lost in thought, his illusionary body see-through.

"I didn't take Ray to Budapest, Saul. Seemed pointless. Her clone's already on its way to Houston. Last chance saloon and all that. Sol's doing. Her Sol – not you – before she took Daemonicus out of him yesterday afternoon. That where he was, though he's shunted all the credit onto Erech. He's the brother you've never met, bit of a stinker actually."

"Aren't we all? Comes with the chromosome."

"I'm going to save her, in case you haven't figured that out yet. Rather, I'm going to snuff it and pronounce Ray cured. We'll catch up with it there."

"Where were you then?" the disembodied brain telepathically imparted from its hiding place in Aran's private Shelter. "After you made such a big deal about them, you left Blackguard's eye-stave and orbs on the deck. I had one of the Glows lock them in the cabin you wanted. Figured you'd come back there on your agates."

"I didn't," she admitted. "Not quite. I already checked by the way. They're gone. So is Demios. Ray's in a rage. You wouldn't know where he went by chance?"

"The islands obviously, Sentalli's probably. I heard a skiff pull away a while ago. Never thought much of it. We're so far out I didn't think a boat that size would go far."

The voice she was hearing him transmit was flat, lacking in confidence if not interest. Was despondency setting in?

"Trinondev prison pods are powered by the thoughts of others," she pointed out. "That's why they operate best in populated centres. I don't know how much of a charge they hold, or if he'd have picked up enough from just those on this boat, but it wouldn't compare to, say, a decent-sized town.

"I've seen Trinondevs levitate," she continued. "They can virtually fly. Not that Demios would do that out here. He doesn't project a nimbus like Sundown and Raven's Head did; can't hide in a rainbow like Radiant Rider. But, if he's desperate enough, which he must be to make a run for it, he gets close enough to Centauri or wherever, he'd chance it. No question."

"Knew I'd underestimated him."

"This makes things very awkward," Aran acknowledged. "I don't know if Strife and Daemonicus can free themselves from Sarpedon's orbs, not by themselves, but they might be able to if he has to concentrate on flying. If he's lost her and I travel through Samsara, Strife might attach to me again."

"What do you mean again? In my time, Strife was active with Satan's Syndicate and her own Sinister Sisterhood from roughly '43 to '49. You were just a kid then and I wasn't much older. A couple years later, and then only briefly, she led the Queen Conquerors – as the Queen Conqueror. No one was ever certain who she was in reality but I made love to her and Ramona Avar at different times.

"I remember the first time, the first time literally for me. Back in '43, that fanatical Gestapo bastard, Donar Lancz, put Ray and I through some pagan ceremony straight out of a Germanic grimoire from the days of the Druids or whatever they were called in Teutonic times. It included a mock wedding. I got into the sack and there was Strife. Sometime later I got to know her, Ray, face-to-face, if you get my meaning. Shall we say they had similar interests?"

"So long as you're talking creativity and not procreativity, then I'd probably agree with you."

"You're telling me I screwed my own sister?"

"At the age of ten, I sure as hell hope not." Aranyani was certain he hadn't thereafter either but, as she'd heard a few times, Strife didn't leave memories behind. "There've been a history of Strifes," she told him, trying to convince herself as much as him. "Ray may have been one – in the Forties, Fifties and Sixties – but she wasn't the only one.

"Crystal, Sed-son's daughter by Corona Power, was WORLD's Strife in '65 and again, probably, in the late Sixties as well. I gather I was a Strife myself in '51 or '52; might even have been the initial Queen Conqueror. I'm still not clear on much of anything except Strife is a possessive spirit, a Master Deva. Do you know what that is?"

"Some kind of god in Ancient India?"

"Gods to Hindus; devils or demons to Persians. All sorts of other words derived from it. Divine and devil are a couple. But the word itself means Shining One or Ones, pluralized. And believe you me they are extremely real. My Flowery Anthea, Botticelli's Primavera, the Mistress of Life, is one. They live on the Hidden Continent of Sedon's Head, Big Shelter, where they're collectively called devazurs.

"If you've read my mind already, you know that's where I was throughout the Forties and much of the first half of the Fifties; where I was again from '65 to '77. But until today, I thought the only way left to get there was through a secret passageway located at the Sisterhood's Shelter in the Himalayan Mountains of Tibet.

"Now I have my doubts. I think there's another way, maybe two, three or even more. One I'm not so sure about might have been on Damnation Isle, which is how your brain ended up back there – albeit, howsoever inexplicably, without your body – but another's definitely on Centauri Island."

"Now why doesn't that surprise me?"

"Because you're magnificent."

"Besides that. Quit beating around the bush, Aran. Where did you and Ray get to? And don't tell Big Shelter because then I'd be seriously miffed."

"Um," she considered. "About that ..."

========

One thing about being 80, almost 81, is that you're always glad to wake up again.

For Loxus Abraham Ryne, a new day was an added bonus to a life already replete with wonders. His immediate problem was figuring out which day it was.

========

"Thursday, sir," said Adolph Dulles. "It's already afternoon in Houston. Centauri Island's a few hundred miles east of the International Date Line."

"Thank God for that." Ryne hauled himself to the edge of his bed and let Dulles place a dressing gown around his shoulders. "You just never know these days."

"It is a bit confusing," granted the acting Chief of Island Security, trying not to sound too indulgent. Although still a great man as well as the Great Man, capitalized, Ryne had many of an old man's infirmities; encroaching senility being just the most obvious. "Sorry to wake you so early but we've had another transmission from Moon Orbit."

"Max and Kinesis made it to the Liberty?"

"That'd be Saturday, sir; two days from now if all goes well. The Liberty sets its watch by Houston time, though it probably works on Greenwich Mean as well."

"So, in Tokyo, it's what? Already Friday?"

"It's coded, sir. For your eyes only."

"What? Friday?"

"No, sir. The message."

"Quit with the ignoramus bullshit, Dolph. Big Max and I go back forty years, to when he wasn't very big nor even a Max as such. There isn't a code he hasn't broken or had broken. Even if he didn't sire you, he trained you. I'm betting half of Sentalli's people already know what it says. Read it to me."

"Cosmicaptain Mikelangelo Starrus is on the Liberty. James Aremar's wondering what to do with him."

"There's more?"

"You know it. Seems he has a third eye."

"Strife."

"Sir?"

"Where are they? All of them? You've an hour."

"An hour to track down all the Strifes?"

"No. An hour before you wake me up again!"

"One thing, sir. About that."

"What?" yawned Ryne. "Resent being a human alarm clock?"

"Erech, that'd be your youngest son, has authorized the transferral of your third wife, Ramona Avar, the only Strife I know about, to the Houston Academy. She's dying of an unknown disease. An affliction peculiar to Strifes, so I've been told. Seems it's similar to what hit Crystal St Synne in '65 and, a dozen years before that, her mother Corona Power, either immediately before or after she lost that baby in Vancouver."

"Thought she'd died already."

"Which one?"

"The one I married, damn you."

"Erech again, I'm afraid. Put out a false report. Media gobbled it up, like he knew they would. Misdirection. Wanted to fool Max as well as her jailers, I understand."

"That doesn't sound like Erech. Too bright."

"No, it sounds like me," Dolph put to him, trying to inject some levity. "At least it better sound like me." Ryne glared at him. "At any rate it's a done deal. Apparently Dr Nightingale, one of your daughters," he added, perhaps necessarily — though Ryne was already drifting off into his own world, "May have a cure. But, if she doesn't, or it doesn't work, who's the wiser? Thought you'd like to know, that's all."

"An hour!"

========

Unwilling to use her agates despite the fact that Strife was presumably stuck within one of Sarpedon's eye-eggs, Hush joined Demios in the skiff. Neither of them were particularly accustomed to machinery so they were pleasantly surprised when it brought them to within sight of Centauri Island's distinctive three pimply peaks.

Not needing to use his eye-stave for anything besides a prop, Sarpedon beached the boat somewhat less than expertly. So far so good, he grinned, figuring that Big Max would thank him for evidence of the Worldwide Order's re-emergence if nothing else. Hush, too, was delighted.

However, as they climbed the hill to the dirt road that would eventually take them to town, she became increasingly antsy, as she'd put it herself.

"Hate to say this, Daddy Dem, but how many orbs have you got?"

"Six, counting the ones holding Strife and Daemonicus: three vacant and one cracked. But I can repair it or generate more as needed. I do have the oldest eye-stave in the world, you might recall. So long as it's loaded with Brainrock, it generates its own eyeorbs. Why?"

"Doubt even they'll be enough."

========

Adolph Dulles worried the patriarch was becoming decidedly doddery, seriously senile; wondered if Ryne should still be in charge of the Space Council and responsible for trying to eliminate whatever was on the Moon. SPACE's Number Two, Immanuel Dark, might be a fuckhead but he'd probably do a better job.

Now wasn't the time to doubt the Great Man, though; nor the United Nations. No more than usual anyhow. He had his own set of responsibilities. He went down the hall to rouse Ryne's personal physician, a Brit named Angus Skullian whose antecedents, his father amongst them, had supranormal history.

Skullian, though, was already out for his daily constitutional. There didn't seem much point calling Paul Creel – he was a military field doctor and no gerontologist. Or looking for Dr Lindquist, as far as that went. Like all of Alfredo Sentalli's so-called Untouchables, Connie had been out of sight since Sunday.

When he asked about that, the Fatman said he'd sent them to Oahu for a week's break from the stress and fallout – read recriminations – of failure. Dulles didn't question him. With Loxus Ryne on the island and, given Maxwell's suspicions that they were devil-rayed victims of Strife, the move made sense.

As for Sentalli himself, another of Big Max's suspects in regard to Strife, he had been given over to Tadpole, Marsh, or any one of another half dozen handpicked security officers. They never let him out of their sight during the day, stayed outside his suite at night, and reported directly to Dulles. The whole island was on red alert and, for once, the Fatman didn't object to Dolph's men going about fully armed.

Feeling his immediate duty done, his day just beginning, Dulles went underground and reviewed everything his specialists had exhumed on Strife: all the known and potential Strifes. He'd barely dug into the data when Mugwump – yet another native Hawaiian with a volume of vowels in his virtually unpronounceable surname – and a couple of others he couldn't place rushed in to tell him there was something he had to see on the tarmac.

It turned out to be a mid-Sixties-era transport plane, an airborne troop carrier nearly the size of the one lost up north on Damnation Isle. It was empty.

"Who was on it?" said Dulles, a bit dully. "More importantly, where are they now?"

"Just the pilot," said one of the men he hadn't recognized. "The rest of us were already here. My name's Cromwell Necator, by the way." Dulles immediately realized he was dealing with a hardened professional. Trifle with this one and you'd get a one-way ticket to the foot of Mt Kinesis, the island's cemetery.

The gun now at his temple had something to with that epiphany.

"You're a Gloman!"

"Not exactly. We're protectors. I am *the* Protector! To be polite about it, Centauri's Island is now under our protection. You are hereby declared redundant."

Having already figured out he was out of his depth against someone somehow *'already here'*, Dulles braced himself for the obligatory click that inevitably accompanied such a statement in the noir movies all the Maxes loved. When it didn't come – not that this Cromwell fellow wavered in the gun-at-temple department – he opened his eyes and glared at the devil he knew.

"What the fuck's going on, Mug?" he demanded.

Before the Hawaiian could answer, they heard gunfire coming from the town. Young and dumb, Dulles went for his pistol.

========

When he was next conscious – and the booming in his ears had sufficiently subsided such that he could remember his name and where he was– he found himself with the patriarch in an underside suite, one of the island's virtually never used, Max-dubbed 'celebrity cells'.

"That was a lot longer than an hour, Dolph. What the fuck's going on?"

****

NUKE 14: **Magnifico Munched**

========

Thursday, December 4, 1980

The woman was composed entirely of eyes. Sarpedon's six pods opened of their own volition. More would be on the way momentarily.

The woman was still composed entirely of eyes, just not as many as before.

========

Dr Angus Skullian, Ryne's personal physician, had flown in with the patriarch on Monday. He had third eye.

So did one of Samarand's statisticians, Patrick Monk, who now actually looked liked an oversized monkey in an Hawaiian business suit – no tie, short sleeves, pressed pants, shoes and even socks. Hush had never seen George Hannibal with a trunk before. She did recognize Ganesh-Babar, though. It was him she addressed.

"You pimple-brained pachyderm, you just released Strife – Discord, Marut Kanin, Kore-Eris, Fitna Marutia, whatever the fuck you want to call her – Mithras's bitch, his Ewe for Aries."

"Such language," boomed the elephantine devil. "And from one so young, too."

That was more than enough for Young Life, as devils would best remember the probable faerie. She dropped an agate, grabbed Sarpedon by the arm. He was holding his eye-stave in both hands, like an ungrounded military mortar, but she didn't give him time to generate, let alone activate, any more eyeorbs.

With barely a half-step forward she whisked them both into the Grey and was gone. It was left to Vach-Hathor, who usually occupied Rowena Raymond, one of Paul Creel's nurses, to concoct a new aphorism. "Small is beautiful. Tiny is elusive to the extreme."

Pretty Parsis, she who was used to acting as the barmaid, Persephone Urartu, had to laugh. "I knew you were afraid of mice, great panjandrum of merchants — but Ants?"

(The enchantress was sitting cross-legged, East Indian style, on her hovering replacement carpet. Miss Myth, Methandra Thanatos, she once of Mythland, the Jewel in Sedon's Crown, had her original Brainrock power focus. Hot

Stuff, as devils tended to call the invariably masked Mithradite firstborn when she wasn't around, had a knack for stealing, then using other devils' stuff, their Tvasitar Talismans.)

"They crawl up my legs," justified Ganesh, as Hindus might have had him.

"Your craw, more like," criticized heroic Hektoris, better known among his brothers and sisters as Headcase, for his power focus helmet, not his mental state. After abandoning Adolph Dulles earlier in the week – for being too hard to handle – he'd eventually settled on Dr Skullian as his latest shell.

"Enough already," snorted the devic occupant of George Hannibal. "As long as we preserve the Nag Gap, maintain father's way back with Wind and his immediate siblings I care nothing for your snootiness. I'm just glad All-Eyes was here to neutralize the Trinondev's eye-stave. It isn't any fun being stuck inside one of those things."

"Wouldn't know, would I?" twinkled APM, Aphropsyche Morningstar, the highborn Byronic who usually occupied Connie Lindquist on this side of the Dome.

When you're seemingly composed of nothing but eyeballs in a (very shapely) female's form, you twinkled. You didn't smile.

========

Dulles raced for the door. It was locked.

========

Bars clamped in place over the windows. A monitor built into the wall crackled on. A picture formed.

Alfredo Sentalli was flanked by son Yataghan and Hiyati Samarand. "Nice try, Loxus, but you should have known better than to try the same stunt twice. I thought you'd have learned your lesson. Even if it was fifteen years ago, I'll never forget how you tried to replace me and mine with Günter von Alptraum and his explosive buddies.

"I twigged as soon as you sent Max and the prof away. Without them – without what they can become – to hold the fort, I've had to rely on internal expertise in order to protect my island from you and WORLD." The screen abruptly went blank. Either the Fatman had said his peace or something else had happened.

Having already had the pleasure of meeting some of that internal expertise in the form of the Protector and one of his fellow, *'already here'* protectors, Dulles reckoned the former. He also had a glimmering of what the Fatman was talking about from briefings Maxwell gave him when he brought him in from Vancouver, at Auld Jock's insistence, in order to become his Number Two.

"Don't know how, but Sentalli must think we have Glomen on the island."

"Have you?"

"Don't worry about it, sir," Dulles assured the old man. "It's only a possibility and Max knows his stuff. And not just from working directly for you for so long. Everyone who works here has to have immunization shots. Nurses and staff doctors administer them but Paul Creel mixes all the batches."

"You're saying you've the antidote for Glomen?"

"We don't want to advertise it but, yeah. Have had for years apparently. Maybe for that selfsame fifteen the Fatman was just talking about; long before

I got here anyhow. What the little prince, Greygreave Translav, can make, NCE can, too, with the right test subjects. It wouldn't do to take chances with something like the Cosmic Express." Big Max hadn't, but the Express was hit nonetheless.

"And you didn't tell Sentalli?"

"No point going into that." Dulles wasn't sure how much Big Max might have told Ryne about the devil-ray or Miracle Key. Chances were very good he wouldn't have said he suspected Sentalli was a victim of one or the other; all the more so after aliens were discovered on the Moon and Ryne took it upon himself to in effect reinvent supras as a countermeasure. "Are you working with WORLD?"

"After spending five years, up until 1970, wiping it out? Don't insult me." (He hadn't. WORLD was an acronym and the Great Man delighted in making up clever acronyms. Witness AMERICA. Witness SPACE.) "It may not be the Order on the Moon, but they've something to do with it. Mark me on that ... But only after you do some talking about what else is going on here."

Thus obliged by the Great Man's voice, Dulles told him about Cromwell Necator and his claim to have been hired by Sentalli to protect the island. Told him further about the dummy aircraft and made the rather blatant observation that there was another way onto the island besides conventional transport.

"Necator? Name's somehow familiar. What's he look like?"

Dulles described him as fair-haired, pink-skinned, tall, strong-looking, around thirty or thereabouts. Probably Scandinavian. Could be a German. His buddy, the other one he didn't recognize with Mugwump, was an albino: "Smelled a bit funny too. Not one for washing his socks, let alone himself," he added, attempting to lighten the mood.

"Smelled dead?"

"To be honest, sir, I've never smelled a dead man."

"I'd have thought Big Max or Auld Jock would have taken you to a morgue the first day you expressed an interest in following in their footsteps. Dead folks go with the territory in your line of work, young man."

"Jock did. Never said I hadn't seen a body before, but morgues don't stink of death so much as chemicals. Buried a dead cat once, only to have my dog dig it up again. That sort of smell."

"So Al Sentalli thinks I'm trying the same stunt as '65," he began summing up, seemingly speaking more to himself than Dolph Dulles. "Brings in a fellow named Necator, one too young to have been anything but a kid fifteen years ago. Could have a father or uncle. Has an albino buddy who reeks of ripe corpse. Secret ways onto and presumably off Centauri. Sentalli reckons he's into a déjà vu situation."

Dulles listened attentively, making mental notes. To derail the Great Man's train-of-thought just would not do.

"So should I," Ryne muttered, again mostly for his own benefit. Max did that sort of thing too, using Dulles as a wall off of which to bounce ideas. "Except, in my case, what's already been seen hasn't been remembered. Amnaesthetics? Witch-work? Bit of both probably. Protectors. Miracle Key or devil-ray: still equals Strife to my mind."

"At least they didn't have three eyes, sir."

"Not that you could see," the patriarch assumed. "Not yet anyhow. Do me a favour, Dolph. In my wardrobe there's an ornate box made out of Solidium; not that you'd recognize it as such, I suppose. Consider it akin to lead and what's in it akin to Kryptonite. Bring it to me."

(The ordinarily pistol-packing Great Man had always been a fan of cowboys and comic books. It was in his file. He'd even financed and published a bundle of the latter during the War for propaganda purposes. A lot of them were about cowboys in uniforms. Hired first class writers, artists, letterers and a decent editor or two, even credited them, which wasn't the norm of the day.

(*'Baron Justice'* was a top seller for its day, rivalled Stupid Man, as Dolph still thought of Superman. A series entitled *'Airealist'* did pretty well for itself as well. Collectors' items now of course. Dolph had a trunk full of not just Ryne published material back home at the Maxwells' place in Vancouver.

(So did the brat, TJ, Big Max's crippled son by the consequential bitch, Aranyani always Nightingale Ryne. In truth, Dolph kept his trunk locked, the key with him on Centauri Island, for fear of Timmy raiding his collection to supplement his own. Foster children, even ones separated by a decade or more, were as prone to sibling rivalry as regular kids.

(Dolph had felt much the same about Simon Lancz, another of the Maxwell brood, when he was growing up, albeit mostly in Ottawa rather than Vancouver.)

"Hope it's not Pandora's," he joked.

"Actually that's exactly what it is. I'm afraid things have deteriorated to the point where I need the ring inside it."

"The Fatman said something about that on Monday," recalled Dulles. "Is it one of Harry Zeross's whatchamacallits – his ringots?"

"More like Aladdin's lamp, only the genie's not named Jeanie. Ever heard of the little trickster?"

Dulles had completely forgotten he was wearing something likely just like what Ryne wanted him to fetch.

========

The Protector may not have been a roundhead but there was nothing cavalier about him when it came to establishing control of an island — Sentalli's, not Britain.

========

Within a couple of hours of Dulles's enforced redundancy, the patriarch's SPACE personnel were disarmed and ensconced within the subterranean complex that had served as Control Central for the Cosmic Express. Abe Ryne himself issued the order for them to offer no resistance. He had to, if only to avoid further bloodshed. Necator's protectors didn't believe in anaesthetic darts.

The majority of Dulles's men were also confined to the subsurface zone. So were technicians still involved in the by now seemingly futile task of tracing remnants of the Express. Martial law was declared on the island and it was left to Sentalli's private army to implement, though there was increasing concern it wasn't the Fatman's army at all.

Non-essential personnel, the mostly Hawaiian workforce who tended to general upkeep and the so-called Joe-jobs at the island's plantation, seaport, airport, resorts and convenience facilities – the places that didn't require a PhD or a gun license to handle – were allowed to go about their business on the surface. Which they did, warily, and only under the constant watch of Necator's newcomers, many of whom were foul-smelling albinos akin to the one Dolph described to the patriarch.

Dulles and a few of the Hawaiians he relied upon most – Marsh, Tadpole, Mugwump and some of their more respected underlings – were allowed restricted movement up top. The locals in particular found their mere presence, more so than their now broadly believed past-tense-authority, soothing if perhaps not overly reassuring.

They hadn't given up their weapons – hadn't even been asked to – but their security clearance was surreptitiously withdrawn. They understood their task implicitly; had simply to maintain a superficial semblance of continuity for the benefit of the Norman and Norma Normalmen and Normalwomen on the largely manmade island. The nuts and bolts of their regular duties were diverted to Necator and his fellow protectors.

All of which was fine with Marsh and Tadpole. They had been on Centauri in '65. Despite their inability to remember much of anything that happened then, they were pretty certain they knew what, more so than who, they were dealing with today. Both were convinced that there was no point shooting it out with men and women who had transcended death already.

Valhallans would just get up and shoot back.

========

Carrying an attaché case, Dulles returned from a late afternoon meeting with Alfredo Sentalli, son Yataghan, Dr Hiyati Samarand and Cromwell Necator, who admitted friendlily enough that he was indeed named after that Oliver Cromwell, the so-called 'Parliamentarian' so demonized in today's United Kingdom of Great Britain and Northern Ireland.

He wasn't pleased with the turn of events but was onside, at least for now.

========

"So, what's all this about, Dolph?" asked the harried eighty-year-old. For the first time since he arrived on the island, the patriarch actually looked his age.

"Sounds like you're the one who should be answering that, sir. Mr Sentalli's convinced you've gone loopy."

"Did you tell him about the Glomen?"

"I asked what he meant by explosive buddies. He said that's how WORLD operates — gets hold of trusted employees or their families, then injects them with a potentially fatal, but reversible, potion. He even told me that Prince Translav came up with it in the Forties thanks to his Slavic bonding with Zygion Avar, Count Viper, who would have become your father-in-law had he survived the War."

"Which he didn't."

"Anyhow, once they're injected, the Global Menace sends them back to work; albeit now, as Mr Sentalli puts it, as the perfect espionage agents. He further assured me that Glomen – short for, you got it, Global Menace – are undetectable, do as they're told, and when their job's done are given the antidote. No fuss, no mess. Unless they blow, of course. Which they wouldn't without triggering."

"Almost all of which is true, too. Did you tell him he had nothing to worry about?"

"There wasn't much point. We can't do anything about Glows off island, or those coming in, and ours are already neutralized."

"Do they know that?"

"You mean did we put a notice on the bulletin board? *'Glows, you don't blow but you'll be sucking on the wrong end of a shotgun if you keep spying for the WORLD!'* Hardly. Remember, we didn't know there was a WORLD around. Still don't, when it comes right down to it. We aren't even sure there are undetected Glows on Centauri Island, though we do know who Connie Lindquist's father is. Or was."

"Likely is, Dolph. The Little Prince is kin to the common cold. He goes away only to come back when you're least expecting it."

Dulles paused indulgently, as if to give Ryne's characterization of the Romanov pretender, Greygreave Translav, due consideration before not so much dismissing it out of hand as deeming it not worth a comment. Whereupon he carried on as if the Great Man hadn't said diddlysquat.

"The other thing is, sir, most of these folks – the research scientists, technicians, even Max's men – have family off island. So do Max and I, for that matter. Though, in my case, his is about all the family I have besides mom's so-called brothers. Who are nothing of the sort, to judge by their last names."

"Seems to me I've heard differently, Dolph," smiled Ryne. "My Number Two in SPACE does have a beautiful red-haired daughter."

He was referring to Dr Immanuel Dark; rather, he was referring to Doc Dark's daughter Estrella. But for the ginger hair, Star, as everyone called her, could have passed for her long-gone, normally silver-haired mother, the luminous Gloriella nee D'Angelo – the Radiant Rainbow Rider. (Unless it was plain old Radiant Rider, which it couldn't be since their was nothing plain about Glory of the Angels. Nor Star Dark, for that matter.)

"Guess that's not much of a secret," said Dulles, unable to avoid blushing. "Star and I grew up within a few blocks of each other in Vancouver. We had our seasons in the sun, to quote that sickeningly schmaltzy   song by Terry Jacques that was all the rage a few years ago. But that's past tense. I suffer no such distractions these days. Had to break it off or Max wouldn't have brought me in, don't you know."

(Ryne didn't but he did know that, like Necator, Star Dark was aptly named. She was as wildly outgoing as Gloriel had been repressed religiously then matrimonially.)

"Translav could have got to any of them," Dolph elaborated, still talking about family and relationships. "So, while Max had Creel administer preventative medicine to everyone here, we did what any super-secret governmental agency or corporate R & D installation would do. We secured it. Locked it up tighter than Mother Mary's holy hymen, as Max used to say."

His adoptive father Jock did too, the Great Man couldn't help but think; still does. Max was something of a cipher when it came to the Colonel.

"So what's Sentalli on about then?"

"Ask my opinion," speculated Dulles, "He's setting us up for some serious action up top and doesn't want witnesses."

"Action of the supranormal variety?"

Dulles resisted the temptation to answer in the affirmative. As far as he was concerned – as far as he was supposed to know – the seventeen-year, so-called War of the Supranormals had never happened. "Look, he wasn't very pleased with you sending Max and the professor away, especially without asking him. He was there when you told me to contact the Academy of Man and knows what you said to Dr Dark.

"I heard his reaction, too. Star's Dr Dad wasn't very good at hiding his shock. So it didn't take a genius to figure you've called for backup of some sort. Then you did the same thing with Strategos Simon Lancz at Signal System. Wouldn't be a backup for your backup, would it? Or, put a little nastier, back-stabbers for your backbone?"

"I'd expect something like that out of Max or Auld Jock, not you, Dolph," criticized Ryne. "Don't apologize for whatever Sentalli said to you. By some sort of bafflegab-choked, backdoor alleyway, you're intimating it's me who's employing supras, not him." The patriarch had forced it out of him.

"And Silver Signallers," emphasized Dulles, in a voice verging on disgust. "More of Shelter's bent, silver slime-buckets; the ones you'd hire to put supras back in the Alliance's proverbial pockets after they've exhausted their uses, possibly even their lives, for your greater good. Yeah!"

"Al told you this?"

"You ignored the Fatman's suggestion to open Pandora's box and call upon Aladdin's ring until this morning. How come?"

"Put bluntly, I wasn't that desperate until today." Dulles regarded the old man sceptically. "All right," Ryne acquiesced. "I owe you this much. I did not contact Doc Dark to release bagels of closet supras, brother-in-law Ringleader in particular, hence the bagels. All I indicated was a Crimefighter Alert, a protocol that goes back a quarter century, to the end of the Supra Wars.

"It means treble the security around their surviving friends and immediate relatives, including Estrella Dark, your erstwhile beloved, and her D'Angelo cousins. That means Simon and Tereza Lancz's Sapphire, Bruce and Anna Maria Dre'Ath's brood, and their grandparents, Jock and Bunnie's best buddies Raphael and Sophia. It means dig into the archives and dust off all the gear and gadgets we thought would be effective against them.

"That's why I wouldn't talk to Shelter or Shooter. Other than burn victims – and sometimes not even them, if you know anything about Yehudi Cohen, the Untouchable Diver – folks who wear masks nowhere near Halloween are not always crooks. Nor jokers, who fancy themselves comic book superheroes. Or villains, for that matter.

"Signallers have something to hide, my lad. And that's because they, or their parents, are the inspiration behind a lot of old-time comic books. Wouldn't be old-time comic books if it weren't for SOS, initially, and KOC later on. Hell, the Signaller called Sasquatch is big enough to be Old Man Power whilst Avatar Sol had the Diver's sense of humour, such as it was. Or is, if I'm right."

"You never believed they died, did you?"

Rather than providing an obvious answer, Ryne chose to rearrange the subject matter: "What I've done amounts to a precautionary measure only. What with everything happening the way it's happening, I see it as a prudent step. Better make that a mandatory one. Even though he was only involved on the periphery of supra-doings, I can't understand why Sentalli would object."

"Unless he is the one employing them, not you."

The Great Man nodded. "Next time you're doing your homework, Dolph, check out the Sisterhood of Anthea, their teleportive agates and Shelter — the big and the little personal places, not the man Headmistress calls House-Head. Read up on Panharmonium. James Aremar, whom I'd trust as much or more than I trusted his father back before Diomedes was killed, thinks Big Shelter is on the Moon and witches are using it as their base for broadcasting subliminal Panharmonium Propaganda."

"Cue Pink Floyd." Ryne gave him one of those looks. Dulles zipped his lips.

"Ringleader, Aristotle Zeross – the second Zeross so named, I might add, though his father was more usually called Ringkeeper in the very early years of the Secret War – bops back and forth to somewhere we can't locate. His just-as-elusive wife is an Ant – a Summoning Child over twenty years older than him, in case you didn't know. Her codename was Illuminatus back in the day. And their kids are all girls.

"Blackguard, the Ace of Spades, Demios Sarpedon, is blacker than midnight but he's Mel's twin brother, also in case you didn't know, and she's white as light. He was working here, right here, on this island; his only child's a girl and her mother, his wife Morgianna, who could be dead or alive for all I know, is a former Ant Superior.

"Al Sentalli knows all that. Emeralda born Plantagenet, Yataghan's mom, long gone now, not that I ever saw her corpse, was one of them — albeit a Green Witch, or Sylvan, as she preferred. Which is why I always reckoned her and her siblings weren't descended from English royalty in the Middle Ages so much as actual plants."

Dulles resisted the temptation to point out that Emeralda Sentalli's only known child was a boy or say that the patriarch's second wife Barbara was Emeralda's sister. That his first one, Eden Nightingale, was openly an Ant or Ant wannabe. That Ramona, his third, was Strife. Or that, between them, they had four boys to go along with three girls, all Rynes.

He didn't even bother noting that the sister-in-law of Oriani Zeross, his late fourth wife, was Hiliarti Schroff-Zeross, who just happened to be the acknowledged Mother Superior of the current Sisterhood. Rants, as this time Jock often said in that whiskied-up brogue of his, are more likely to deafen the ranter than the rantee.

"There are bushels more men than women up top," he did observe, unsealing his lips. Very diplomatically, he silently congratulated himself.

"And you've spent more time with Bunnie than Auld Jock."

"She's a lot nicer," allowed Dulles.

"If you're leaning towards Bonita's matriarchal disinformation, Dolph, here's a few facts for you." Like a preacher the patriarch was more than just deaf to differing positions. He was also just warming to the task. "In 1968, an entire island disappears in the Aegean Sea, not far from Crete. No earthquake, no volcanic eruption, no tidal wave, no anything natural to mark its passage.

"Three years earlier, things went on here that no one has ever been able to explain to my satisfaction. Hell, I was one of the ones here and, at best, I've only the occasional bad dream of what happened. Undeniably, though, there was an old whalers' chapel upstairs, down the road from where the church is now, that local contractors didn't demolish. It blew up then burned down. Why? How? Like Trigon, no one knows.

"Five years before that someone, supposedly Strife, kidnaps Belificent D'Angelo-Zeross in Toronto. Both Maxwells – Jock, who wasn't far past his prime then, if at all, ran the RCMP, and Max, who'd the best of an embryonic AMERICA at his command – had over a week to track down Strife's whereabouts before Bel's murder. Yet even with the help of Superiors Sorrow and Sarpedon, of Headmistress Mannering and her teacher, your precious Bunnie, they couldn't find hide nor hair of her. Getting the picture, Dolph?"

"She could have been in her personal Shelter," grasped Dulles, then finished the painting. "And five years before that the King Crimefighters, including your eldest children, David and Saul, vanish without a trace on Damnation Isle. Teleportation, Shelter, Anthean witches, Gypsium. Can't be coincidental." He'd done a lot of homework since Monday.

"The Cosmic Express," picked up Ryne. "Crewed by graduates of various Academies and, yes, closet supras the majority of them. The Express, which NCE – read me – funded, a spaceship full of Gypsium, gets blown away. Not up, please note. Away, as in elsewhere! A remnant ends up near the Moon, vanishes a couple of days later. Another part of it turns up on not just any isle in the Aleutians."

The old man paused to collect his breath more so than his thoughts. "As we've now confirmed, a bilious bouquet of hardened soldiers of fortune, some of them ex-Agents of AMERICA, decide to play shooting gallery on each other there. Max and Kinesis becoming supras at their age. Mik Starrus showing up on the Liberty with a third eye. Of course it isn't coincidental. Somehow or other a new war of supranormals has begun."

"So you call in Signal System."

"Because Signallers are armed and trained specifically to handle supras."

"Sentalli takes offense and brings in his bravos."

"Even supras need foot soldiers."

"To supplant us — literally! Lock us up down here, where the sun don't shine. Christ! They'll slaughter the Signallers the moment they arrive."

"One wonders if they even care about System," Ryne, as was his wont, ruminated aloud. "But you're right in another way. The real King's Own Crime-fighters, even a comparative minor leaguer like Wilderwitch, would probably chew Silvers up then spit them out, like dislodged tooth-fillings, quicker than they'd brush and gargle after a meal."

"A lot quicker," remarked Dolph, who'd read that witches, Wilderwitch in particular, liked their baths bloody.

"Here's the way I figure it," speculated the Xuthrodites' patriarch, no doubt more absently than accurately. "You've got to have two sides to fight any war. The same holds true for supranormals. Sentalli is working with the Superior Sisterhood and a supra-elite, conceivably orchestrated by Kadmon Heliopolis, that's based on the Moon.

"Another batch of supras are part of WORLD or some such alternative crowd. It amounts to Panharmonium versus Pandemonium." The octogenarian launched into a mockery of a song: "*'Anarchists to the left of us, fascists to the right, and here I am, stuck in the middle with you.'* We're the meat between two slices of different varieties of bread. One's rye, the other's Ryne — as in my son, Psycho-Saul!"

"One's crap and the other's a crapshoot." joked Dulles, who had no taste for either of them. "So, if Sentalli is on the same side as the *lunartics*," he additionally joked, parroting his Big Max of a boss, who most likely wasn't his father, "Why is he prepared to let you keep in touch with the Liberty?"

"Come again?"

Dulles opened his valise and pulled out a sheet of paper. "I scribbled everything down and had the Fatman approve it before coming here."

Ryne put on glasses, took the paper, and began to read. "*'You will be allowed to maintain contact with the UNES Liberty and Groundbase Houston. You are advised that all transmissions will be vetted through a secondary control tower currently being established and staffed by Mr Necator's men.*

"*'Dr Samarand or one of those you like to characterize as my Untouchables will be on the spot twenty-four hours a day. Be assured, they will know if you are sending unusual or hidden-meaning messages to either place. Should you make an effort to alert anyone of your current distress, Dr Samarand or the others will immediately terminate your privileges.*

"*'This is a temporary situation only. In a few days, matters will be back to normal. At which time, Mr Sentalli will debrief you thoroughly.'* He's a lot of fucking nerve addressing me like that. When I first met him, what?, damn near thirty-five, maybe even forty years ago now, he was a beefy braggart with nowhere to go but weight-watchers. If it wasn't for Papa Rafe ..."

"Correction, sir," Dulles once again sought to mollify the patriarch before Ryne got too carried away. "What he has is a band of certified and probably certifiable butchers backing his play. And if Max was right, he has a devil-ray, or Miracle Key, that he uses on his Untouchables, if not this Necator and his protectors.

"Additionally, if you're right," Dolph placated the more, "The Fatman may also be in cahoots with a nest of viperous witches, this rogue Ringleader and, just possibly, the King Crimefighters. Please read on."

"*'Just concentrate on your business on the Moon'*," obliged the octogenarian, "*'And you will not be further put out. He asks only for your cooperation and added that you will understand why he did not tell you this personally.'*"

"There's more, sir."

"*'Words from you'* – you being you, Dolph – *'Are preferable to me'* – Sentalli – *'hearing your voice'* – that is, mine. *'Remember '65!'* "

"How could I?" wondered Dulles. "I was only twelve."

"That's what you wrote."

"The hell I did!" Dulles took the paper back. "What's this bit at the end, *'No – I did, Daddy Dolph'*? What the flying fuck?"

"Um, Dolph?"

"Yes, sir?"

"You know Pandora's box, the one with Aladdin's ring in it? Forget it. She's already here."

"Plus, you should have said *'what the flying fairy fuck'*," came a disembodied voice less in their heads than as if out of nowhere, "Cuz that's what I yam."

"In addition to Pandora," Dulles put to the little girl who had just stepped out of nowhere.

It was the best he could do. He was too young and fit to have a heart attack.

========

"Quit quaking, major," Magnifico instructed Milo Mind. "You're shaking so hard you're rocking the boat."

By that he didn't mean the fish packer. They'd left it behind less than a half-hour earlier. He meant what they'd left behind it on.

========

"I scanned all the ones on the packer who were pilots," he added, as much brainily as authoritatively. His illusionary self-projection seemed altogether more substantial now that he was in closer proximity to his sister. It was so much so that his every command was, if possible, even more irresistible. Mind, though, shook, rattled and rolled on nonverbally.

"This guy's no Gloman," Magnifico psychically reinforced what, to his mind, albeit evidently not to Milo's mind, should have been unnecessarily. "And there's the yacht, bang on the button. We'll be safely on our way to Houston in no time."

The Order's luxurious, fallback vessel was still not much more than a speck below and to the east of the fish packer's helicopter, but it was there. Terrified of using their stepping stones – in Ray's case the ones Balkis called Korant Kernels and which she (largely unsuccessfully) tried to teach her how to use in Budapest, if only to kill time – because Strife might be lurking in the interspatial vicinity yet again, Aranyani Nightingale and Ramona Avar were naturally elated.

Major Mind was anything but, naturally or unnaturally. In the previous two seconds, he'd gone from a similar feeling of inflation to one lower than deflation.

Emotionally he'd become flatter than a pancake forgotten in a waffle iron that no one had bothered to turn off.

Of course, unlike the countess or the real and the illusionary Ryne twosome, as well as the pilot of reference, whose life had suddenly become as immediately terminal as theirs just had, he wasn't looking either downwards or straight ahead. He was looking more like to the left side and upwards.

"Glomen aren't what'll kill me," he barely got out in time.

Milo Mind was not being prescient.

========

Crystallion rode down the copter. Her nuclear dragon opened its maw, spat flames and, as the helicopter exploded, she congratulated herself.

Her firedrakes did feed on destruction!

****

Part Three: *Supra Survival*

NUKE 15: **Amoebamen**

========

<u>Thursday, December 4, 1980</u>

"Hello, daddy homunculus!"
"Hello, baby button-nose. Hello, Mr Sarpedon. We thought you were dead."

========

"We were right about you all along, Centauri," Demios Sarpedon as good as condemned the Fatman – the we being his wife Morgianna born Nauroz then Somata, his twin sister Melina now Zeross, and their fellow Utopians of Weir, its current Master Saladin Devason, Morg's year older brother, included.

"Those were Byron Spawn. You are in league with devils!"

"No time for that, son," said the little girl. "She's got me! Mind if we use your closet, daddy." She didn't wait for an answer. Sarpedon picked her up, ran into the Fatman's bedroom then his roll-in clothes closet. They didn't come out again – though something else manifested herself briefly.

"Don't like it on the Head, do you, Strife?"

"The twisted little trickster will be back, flesh bag. She's never far from where the action is and I'm usually at its centre. Besides, even if she smartens up and stays away for a change, Judge Warlock has plenty of other female offspring and so do they. Sooner or later, one of them will get hold of some stepping stones out here and travel through the Weird again. And that's where I'll be, waiting for them. I'm a patient spook." That said, more like spat, Strife returned to her own sort of Limbo between-space.

Technically speaking it wasn't a private Shelter – what witches conjured off their individual witch-stones – because her Shadowland was damn near ubiquitous, not personally specific. As Moon's Angel might have explained to Aranyani Nightingale and Ramona Avar after she sent Crystallion back to the phantom freighter, once in it there was only one way out of it.

She had to possess a small-case-sedon's daughter or the direct, female descendant of one. Strife nevertheless not only had the ability to take herself far away from the environs of Centauri Island, she did. Even the malevolent mistress of malice wanted nothing to do with nuclear firedrakes.

Unless … she suddenly had a delicious thought.

It was always fun to take over a former shell. Besides, when it all came down to dust, she wasn't particulate like Byron's usual mouthpiece Smoky Sedona. She wasn't faeriedust, wasn't radioactive dust either. Not yet. She was a ghost. And, thanks to the Idiot Twins, what else lived in the Hidden Headworld's radiation-poisoned Ghostlands except Death's Angels? More immediately relevantly, what powered Crystallion and her firedrakes except an Idiot Twin?

Having a touch that kills might come in handy for a destructive spirit like her.

=========

Amos Annulis was a medical doctor in his late Thirties.

=========

With a dark, Mediterranean complexion, to some he looked more Greek or Turkish than Armenian, which is what he purported to be. (Then again, modern day Greeks and Turks were so interbred, as were Armenians, there wasn't much difference between any of them anymore.) Seemingly around 5'9", well-proportioned and in the best condition of his life, he had curly black hair and a thick moustache.

Having taken indefinite leave from his practise five years earlier, he toured the Western World promoting the ideal of an Independent Armenian State. He hadn't received much in the way of international attention during that time but President-Elect Ronald Reagan, interested in destabilizing neighbouring Iran and the Soviet Union, looked and sounded intent upon changing that.

Annulis had it on good report the unscrupulous former actor and Red-Hater, as well as Red-Baiter, had already managed to *'encourage'* the Iranian authorities to delay releasing the American hostages their lackeys held until after his election was secured. He therefore figured that he already had all the attention he'd need to further his goal. Too bad about the Armenians, though.

(Annulis assumed Reagan and his cronies used the same intermediary he had – WORLD's Shaikh Ali Ars Markazi, who would happily bribe anyone, for a percentage.)

Tonight he was in the Mohave Desert's Death Valley, on the border between California and Nevada, with his own private cargo plane fuelled and running. Men in warehouseman overalls were loading the contents of two dozen camouflaged US Army vehicles into the plane. He undoubtedly reckoned very few of them were actual civilians. If he did, he'd reckoned wrongly.

When they were finished he walked up to their spokesperson, an elderly man designated *'Jockey'*, and his adjunct, a sixtyish character currently styling himself *'Doppel'*. In what amounted to another life, he was familiar with both of them. They though, glamourized as he was, apparently had no idea whom he was in reality.

After exchanging a few pleasantries, they parted company. The vehicles withdrew to the perimeter of the air field. Jockey and Doppel got into a jeep while Annulis entered the plane. The cargo doors closed and it rumbled onto the runway then took off. Climbing into the sky, it headed eastward on a flight plan that would take it to Florida, where it would refuel before taking off again. Its ultimate destination was eastern Turkey, in the area where that country intersected with the Soviet Union and Iran.

The Turks were already *'officially entered'* in the good books of Reagan and his backroom boys within the US military and intelligence elite; this for their somewhat suspect aid in acting as a go-between in the continuing negotiations to release the Teheran hostages. Nevertheless, helping Annulis strike an inflammatory blow, no matter how insignificant, on the Soviets would earn them even more brownie points from the incoming administration.

Although they had problems aplenty with their own Armenians, not to mention their Kurds; although Annulis had an almost inbred hatred for them; he genuinely hoped the Turks did not end up with too much egg on their faces when the plane never got close to their country. Egg was too good for the heathen occupiers of his homeland, the now-again Greek island of Crete, for far too many centuries.

Still and all, if they did threaten he and his cargo, he'd have no qualms about providing them with splattered eggs of the far beyond ego variety.

========

"Think he fell for it, Jock?" Doppel, sixtyish but fit, passed his much more elderly, long retired friend and mentor Jock Maxwell, Jockey, a flask of whiskey.

"You mean Amos Annulis or Aristotle Zeross?"

"Oh, that's Ringleader all right, Colonel," Doubleman Johann Schmidt, to give Doppel his actual name and sadly current designation, assured the remarkably hardy Scotsman. "Ask me the real Annulis hasn't been active for months, if not years. Might not even be alive anymore."

"Can't see it myself," admitted the eighty-four year old, well-preserved and relatively still with-it veteran of just about every war fought this century — including the supposedly secret one of supranormals. "The lad's certainly changed in twenty odd years. Oh, the build's about right, he's filled in nicely, and the hair's curly enough, but the face is all wrong. How can you be so sure it's young Harry?"

"Although I've only come across him a few times in all that time, I've spent much of those same twenty years on his tail. It's him all right, no doubt masked by Anthean splendours or that of some other sisterhood. Old-timers like Morgianna Sarpedon can do that sort of thing and even if we don't know for sure what's become her we know her husband's still around."

"That'd explain his appearance, sure enough, but it brings up another problem. Wee Bunnie's one of their teachers – was forty odd years ago anyhow – and Harry's wife, whom we both remember as Codename Illuminatus, is an Althean, a Sisterhood of witch-healers connected to the Ants."

"Melina." Schmidt had no problem remembering her name. Probably Jock didn't either but, despite the passage of so many decades, young Mel's involvement with the fairy-cursed Dre'Ath clan obviously still troubled him. "It was before even my time but she cared for Maxius Skullian once he got crippled big time, in what? '38, '39."

"1938, laddie. And it wasn't before your time. Just Doubleman's."

"Who wasn't Doubleman then," Smythe agreed. "Wasn't even a Septuple-man then," he added needlessly. "But there were witches; real ones, too. Not like your Bunnie. And Mel's a Sarpedon. Her sister-in-law's Morgianna, Superior Sorrow's replacement back in the early Fifties. His sister-in-law, Hiliarti, dead Demonites' wife, is the Sisterhood's current superior."

"Well acquainted with them all," Jock acknowledged, "Morgianna's Demios as well. We used to call him Blackguard. They're supposed to be twins. Except – talk about witch-work – he's the pot the kettle called black and Mel's no kettle. She's as fine a white porcelain cup as any in our cupboard back home."

"Then as you no doubt also know, since you and your wee Bunnie were very much around in those days, Melina's even older than me. Which means she's a third again as old as Harry. Doesn't look anywhere near it and, from what I've been able to find out about her, she still doesn't. I reckon she's aged about one year in two or three since she first attended the Amsterdam Academy way back in '39. Even Demios hasn't aged much."

"Some supras didn't age much. In fact, some of them didn't age much beyond their twentieth birthdays." Jock was thinking specifically of the Terrible Twins, Aires and Thalassa D'Angelo, whom Schmidt would have shared bathrooms with in Roma (Rome), most of a decade pre-Septupleman. "Then again, none of Morg's crew are supras in any other way."

"Wish I could say the same thing, especially when it comes to aging. But my point was what would a bunch of Ants and their boyfriends want with a plane load of heavy armaments? Other than dart guns, which aren't particularly life-threatening, I never heard of Ants, let alone Alts, using modern day weaponry."

"Wee Bunnie would be up in arms if she heard of them using weaponry, period." (In many respects Jock and Bunnie, who never married, were polar opposites. Which might explain how they'd managed to stay together for so long. Opposites attract and all that.)

"The CIA did most of the groundwork negotiations through intermediaries like Shaikh Markazi, whom no one ever seems capable of properly busting down for all the scurrilous deals he's made over the decades. One of their bright lights got suspicious when he saw the list of weapons Annulis requested."

"How so?"

"Put it this way. You'd think a mob of hit and run freedom fighters would be interested in conventional guns and rifles, mortars and such like, stuff that would cause maximum damage from a distance. Instead, Annulis wanted relatively close range antipersonnel shit – what we call splatter packages."

Old Max nodded, understanding the somewhat colourful reference. "What doesn't explode, flames. He doesn't want to kill people so much as obliterate them.

"Thinking WORLD," Schmidt carried on, "The CIA called up Abe Ryne and the patriarch lent them James Aremar. First thing he did was demand to meet Annulis face to face. Which was quickly arranged. Man had definitely done his homework on Armenia, that much can be said. More than Aremar had at least."

"Not surprisingly. Jimmy always did most of his reading in the morning. Off the back of cereal boxes and in a foreign language."

"There was no doubt Annulis had extensive medical training as well. However, almost from the onset, Aremar realized he spoke the language more like a Turk than a native in its traditional territory, either side of the border. Had virtually no Russian, only a smattering of Kurd, and could speak English nearly as well as Turkish."

"Give him credit. Like I just said, Jim-Boy has an uncanny knack for languages. Some might even call it a supranormal gift."

"Also, just by chance, Aremar noticed the guy was wearing too many rings and, inspirationally for him, started talking in Greek. Annulis clearly understood him, even if he caught himself before he responded. That was the real kicker, hence Aremar's conclusion."

"That he wasn't dealing with the real thing."

"That this Amos was a native Greek largely brought up in the States or Canada. Which the real Annulis wasn't; not as far as we knew anyhow."

"But we both know a certain well-educated doctor with a passion for rings who was, don't we?"

"Maybe it wasn't much, colonel. But it was enough for me to get involved."

"*'Not much'* is an overstatement. I gather the Greek bit's what twigged Jimmy he might be a phony. Nothing to say the real Annulis didn't know Greek. Fact is, if memory serves – and dear old Buns makes me take my vitamins – he must have. I knew his father, didn't I?"

"More likely his grandfather, Jock."

Schmidt tried not to sound indulgent. He didn't say that Maxwell needed more than just vitamins, for example, though he had to wonder what possessed the powers-that-be – read the Great Man, Loxus Abraham Ryne – when they activated Auld Jock again. Had to wonder hardly for the first time, as well.

Then again Abe Ryne was getting up there himself. Few, if any, of the men and women he'd grown to trust over such a long and eventful lifetime were young and sprightly; let alone, Schmidt included, even middle aged anymore.

"Jason Annulis," recalled the octogenarian with some difficulty. "Corinthian, wasn't he? Knew his father too. Peleas."

"Aeson actually," Schmidt corrected him without referring to any notes. "Peleas Annulis was Doc Jay's uncle. Like you they were both Godlings. Unlike you they both died in the Himalayas during the Guild's famously ill-fated sojourn to the Vale of the Visionaries and the Sisterhood Shelter there in early 1920."

"Same as Harry's granddad and a couple of his uncles. Yeah, I've got him now. Grandfather you say. That'd make the father ..."

"Apsyrtus. Spot on, sir."

"You're a little old to call me sir, Doubleman."

"Old habits die harder than old men, Jock."

"Certainly old guys like me and the patriarch. You were saying – about the Annulises?"

"Way back in the Greco-Turkish War of the early Twenties, a young Doc Jay helped coordinate the Armenian Republic's losing effort against the Turks. While there he hooked up with another Armenian woman – though she might have been born in Georgia or somewhere nearby, in what amounted to ancient Scythia.

"Ironically enough, given his mythological namesake, Amos's Jason married a Medea – Medea Aeetes, to be absolutely accurate. Doubly ironically, she was an Anthean witch."

"A Hellion, Johann. There's a world of difference. A killing difference, and I mean that literally. Besides, her I don't need any vitamins to recall. Medea of the Ararats was as venomous a viper as I ever came across. Worse than her brother-in-law and he called himself Count Viper. About her only saving grace was she was a stunner."

"So was her brother-in-law," said Schmidt, who did not need vitamins to recall Zygion Avar. "They didn't call him the Chemical Cobra because he mixed placebos for fun. For some reason the Great Man liked him, even married his daughter, though that didn't stick. Except in his craw, I suppose.

"Their son, Doc Jay and Mama Medea's Apsyrtus I mean, Amos's father, seems to have got lost in the shuffle."

"Didn't they all?"

To a one the Summoning Children, by far the largest group of supras ever known, were born on or within less than a month after the Winter Solstice of 1920. They were also the reason that the first Academy of Man was built in Amsterdam. Many were as mercurial as Wills of the Wisp: here today, gone tomorrow, and back the day after it; tomorrow, that is.

For the life of him, Auld Jock couldn't recall what had become of Medea's scatterbrained son. Clearly, even though he was (nominally) almost as much of a Summoning Child as Apsyrtus, neither could Johann Schmidt. Couldn't find out, more like. Or so it seemed. For reasons Maxwell was one of the few who knew, Schmidt's memories didn't extend as far back as the Amsterdam Academy of September 1939.

"Lost in the files then. Other than it might have been one of his half-sisters," Johann continued, "We're not sure whom he hooked up with, though he apparently did with someone, somewhere. All we've got on him is based on some scratchings made by the real Doc Jay just before he died."

"Killed himself, don't you mean? Didn't Medea drive him mad?"

"That's the story anyway."

"So Apsyrtus could still be alive."

"We've nothing to indicate otherwise."

"I see. And by half-sisters you're not referring to the old bugaboo that Medea was the Morrigan's mother, are you?" The Morrigan was Morgianna nee Somata Sarpedon, a disgraced former Mother Superior of the Anthean Sisterhood. (Some said Somata, like Mannering and Nightingale, was a generic cognomen used by females-first Ants instead of fatherly surnames.) "That being the case then she'd have had to be Apsyrtus's twin."

"While there's little doubt Mama Medea was as fecund as she was virulent, what I'm not suggesting is that the Morrigan was Amos's mother. We just don't know, do we? Whoever it was, though, it was in time for her to have Amos sometime in late '43 as near as we can tell."

"The same year Harry was born – to Meg, Medea's niece, and hubby Angelo, the first Ringleader."

"My records indicate he was codenamed Ringkeeper."

"Your records came from the Alliance, correct?"

"I get your gist. Things were pretty messy back then." And so they were. So much so that Schmidt's records of himself did not match his own memory of himself. As Colonel Jock might have put it – had in fact put it, to his face, too – Alliance of Man records weren't so much made to be broken as rewritten.

"My pencil gist, don't you mean?" Had he been a quicker wit Johann might have said the same thing. After all, old Max had done most of the rewriting during the last war.

"Same day, too," he said instead. "From what we understand," he qualified in much the same spirit. "Getting the picture?"

"Spooky."

"Oh, it's gets spookier than that." Johann took a sip from the flask. "Know anything about Xuthrodism?"

"Me and Abe Ryne being best buds for the better part of sixty years and you ask me that?" Schmidt was well aware of their relationship; was obviously just looking for a segue so he could prattle off some of his more obscure discoveries. The man was an inveterate researcher.

"In ancient times, say around 1500 BC, Armenians were known as Urartu or Ararat, the same as the mountain where Noah's Ark supposedly ended up after the Great Flood. Their great goddess was Arubani, the Spring Maiden. Same as girlish Kore or Persephone, Aphrodite, and the original flower child herself Anthea: Botticelli's Primavera."

"Ants don't consider their Ant a goddess, laddie," Jock noted. "Neither do Xuthrodites," he added just to demonstrate his knowledge of their esoterica.

"You're right of course," agreed Schmidt. "They identified Xuthros Hor with the Biblical Noah and believed Anthea was the never-written-down name of Noah's wife – the mother of Ham, Japheth, Shem, and at least an equal number of equally never-named daughters."

"At least. Unless they were the lads' cousins, Methuselah's get."

"Whatever. Point being that, by Alexander's time, Arubani was worshipped under that very name."

"Anthea? Really?"

"Really. Want more? The Armenians also had a lot of Zoroastrian influence. Their Zeus was Ahura Mazda, which means Great Lord. Aka the Assyrians' Asher or Asura. Aka also the Hindu Mithra, Varuna Mithras, Mitravaruna, the Lion Lord of the Sun, Sol Invictus and none other than Helios. His Hera – rather, his Aphrodite – was Anahita."

"Abe Ryne's daughter, the one who just died on Alfredo Sentalli's private spaceship, was named Anhita," contributed Jock, not wanting to fall asleep through lack of input. "The D'Angelos had a daughter by the same name, Anita or Nita. She was their Summoning Child. Died around '43."

"Too true, unfortunately," said Schmidt, who had more than just a passing connection to the Family D'Angelo. "But, beg pardon, sir, too irrelevant also. Almost as irrelevant as the fact that in some traditions Anahita was Mithras's mother, not his wife. At any rate, Annulis's movement is called Meherr. It's supposed to mean Lion – as in, maybe, Lion Lord of the Sun – but how about me-her? Maybe men-her?"

"Menhir," offered Maxwell sarcastically. "Like in Stonehenge."

"Afrites, Korants, Antheans, Athenans, even Hellions for that matter – after Hela or Hel, the Norse Goddess – they're all named after one incarnation or another of the Great Goddess, Mother Earth herself. I mean, Hera and Rhea are anagrams of just that, minus the '*t*', and Erda isn't far off either."

"I knew a Herta once, earthly sort of gal. Liked to get down and dirty."

"Very clever, Jock," Schmidt allowed. "Whichever way you look at it, we're talking matriarchal Goddess Culture misandry."

"Misandry?"

"Also misandria, in contrast to misogyny and not to be confused with misanthropy, which means hatred of mankind, as in humanity. Emasculators. Female supremacists."

"Ah, them. Tell me about it. I've been living with a girls-on-top gal for something like forty years. This leading anywhere, boyo?"

"Indulge me, colonel. Abe Ryne says many plants and animals originated in the Transcaucasia and Armenian regions. Exactly where you'd think they would if the Ark landed there. He's archaeological evidence to back it up."

"And I've the scars."

Wisely, Johann chose to ignore the cantankerous Scotsman's constant jesting — more like jovial jousting. It struck him as trivializing what he thought very serious stuff. "The Book of Byblos says Noah's first action after the Flood was to plant a vineyard in the lower slopes of Ararat."

"A man after my own heart."

Auld Jock took another swig out of the flask then filled it from a mickey he pulled out of his inner coat pocket. Almost as if it was the bad old days again, when he and Abe Ryne along with the likes of Ted Mayhew, Diomedes Aremar and Angus Dre'Ath spent constant hours yakking at each other well into the early morning, he was getting into the spirit of things. Drinking it, too.

Clearly so was Johann, who wasn't as dour and always down-to-business as he liked to pretend. Fancied himself something of a polymath when it came to matters syncretic, as opposed to Laodicean. In this respect he was very much a latter day Godling Guildsman.

(Syncretism = reconciliation or fusion of differing systems of belief, as in philosophy or religion, especially when success is partial or the result is heterogeneous. Laodiceanism = the quality of being indifferent in politics or religion. Laodice Atreides was the name of a drop-dead-gorgeous, Etocretan Summoning Child born as well as brought up on Aegean Trigon, the Zeross Family's ancestral home.)

"Fact is, Armenia was the first place the vine was cultivated. Wouldn't it be something to find an old cave and a jar of Château Noah in it. It'd give well-aged an entirely new meaning."

"And I here thought I was." Schmidt laughed at that. Which secretly delighted the, as far as he was concerned, overly old man. "Okay," Auld Jock bit. "So Abe's filled your head with all sorts of Xuthrodite quasi-religious pseudo-history. Connected Noah with Anthea, albeit somewhat thinly, to boot."

"Great Mothers are always fat," Johann said, as if accepting a challenge to carry on pontificating. "As in pregnant. Go to Malta and you can see one of the first ones ever found. Goes back something five thousand years, I heard. Damn near to the Great Flood if you're to believe that Usher fellow."

"More of Abe's crap by the sounds of things."

"Might be crap but it's also fact." Jock scowled. Johann chalked one up for himself before re-gathering the wool of his argument. "Where was I? Right, we've traced the real Amos Annulis to the Superior Sisterhood, via his grandmother; maybe even his grandmother on both sides of the bed; as well as maybe his sister on at least one-half the bed. That probably indicates Mt Ararat's the witches' Big Shelter or some such offshoot coven's convent."

"Big Shelter's a myth."

"So you say. Me, I wouldn't dare."

"You still haven't convinced me that was Harry Zeross or come up with any sensible reason why he wants all those frags and incendiaries."

"After studying the guy for years, I immediately picked up in Annulis some of pal Harry's mannerisms – the way he carries himself, kind of awkwardly; stutters a tad, that sort of thing. Other than a few not so much farfetched as far-out theories I've developed of late, I have no idea what he's up to, but that's Harry. No question of it."

"Annulis' organization – this Menhir's legitimate?"

"A hundred percent. That's why we, the Alliance, gave the guy a clean bill of health. Did more than that. Notwithstanding the involvement of WORLD's fundraiser, Shaikh Markazi, we convinced the CIA and the US military to cooperate fully with him. Hell's Teeth, Jock, maybe he is taking it to Armenia."

"And maybe Ararat is the mother mountain of all Anthills."

"Say it is, if only for argument's sake. For all I know maybe the Superior Sisterhood is tangling with a bunch of – I don't know, demons or some such on another astral plane. Things that have to be blown apart because killing doesn't stop them."

"Sure this whiskey isn't Rye – as in ergot?"

"Ergo, LSD," understood Schmidt. "Say what you like, we've got that prick now."

"Why didn't you take him then?" Johann gave Jock one of those looks young – make that younger – characters did when he, in either his cups, his doddery dotage or, as was the case currently, both, opened mouth and inserted foot. "Oh, I get it. Daft old fart that I am, it just takes me a while longer than it used to. You've tracers in those boxes, don't you?"

Schmidt smiled but neither confirmed no denied it. Jock did not need a response; he was already onto the why. "Abe's as obsessed as ever with finding Big Shelter isn't he. He still thinks Ants are responsible for the Summoning and supranormals. Blames them for the death of his supra-sons. Blames Harry for Oriani's cancer."

The sons were his long dead, firstborn set of twins by his equally late – sixteen years even longer late, by contemporaneous accounts – first wife, Eden Nightingale. An old-time Ant if there ever was one, her sons names were David and Saul. Perhaps not inadvertently, Oriani's older brother, the real Aristotle Zeross (Kid Ringo, the second Ringleader), helped get rid of them a quarter century ago this coming Xmas.

Most folks suspected Ryne had put him up to it. Very few ever ventured that opinion to his face. Auld Max was one of them. And the Great Man hadn't denied it. They – respectively codenamed Cerebrus or Mr Mental and the Magnificent Psycho – had mind-over-mind talents. Which made them extremely dangerous to everyone; Abe Ryne perhaps more so than most.

In December 1955 the Secret War was all but over. The only way to dispose of the *'all but'* bit was to dispose of his sons and their remaining supranormal buddies, the rest of Cerebrus's otherwise triumphant King's Own Crimefighters: Ryne's Own Aces, as they were referred to just as commonly. The patriarch didn't like loose ends and Saul in particular was looser than just about anyone else, including Montezuma.

Oriani was the Great Man's fourth wife, the mother of his youngest set of twins, Megan and Pauline, who were now ten or eleven. Harry's younger sister was also the third child of Megaera born Kinesis and Angelo Zeross. Jock knew that her cancer, which claimed her life three years ago, just before her thirtieth birthday, was actually a form of Gypsium sickness.

That she developed it was almost a hundred percent down to Rings. Of course, that Meg, Angie and their first born, Demonites, were no longer in the land of the living was very nearly a hundred percent down to Abe Ryne. Tit for tat and all that fate-for-Jake stuff; all that counting Dmetri Diomad, Johann Schmidt, Mikelangelo Starrus, James Aremar, and even himself.

"Give over, sir. Admit it. You're as curious as the rest of us about Ants and their Shangri-La. Otherwise you wouldn't be here."

"All the same, I prefer my fantasies straight. They turn out to be real, that spoils them. Besides, I liked the kid." (Because he was only five when he first acquired his Gypsium rings on Aegean Trigon, and only twelve when he last used them – prior to Bel's 1960 murder, that is – Zeross was commonly called Kid Ringo or vice versa.)

"Not to worry, colonel. I've no intention of harming him. Not yet anyhow. The patriarch just wants to know where he gets to."

========

The patriarch was hardly the only one.
****

Nuke 16: **Homo Sapient**

========

Thursday, December 4, 1980

"The Fatman," said the Fatman, "Says you were out of line, Dr Samarand. Says having your rogue biomages grow a remotely controlled homunculus – he means me – specifically to house Thrygragos Byron and stand in for me, him, when the need arises, is one thing. Usurping control of the island is quite another."

========

"Let's skip the he-me dichotomy shall we," interjected Rod Paraja, who wasn't really Paraja, especially not with a third eye beaming out of the centre of his lower forehead, between his eyebrows. (Him not being who he purported to be wasn't overly surprising, Sentalli knew, given that Paraja didn't exist as an individual human being.)

"I know enough about homos to realize you're in immediate contact with your real self. So how about you say '*I*', even if you're not him?"

"Perfectly all right with him – I mean me," said this Enormity.

Roderick Paraja was an individual. That much could be said about him. He just wasn't really much of anything else, let alone qualified to masquerade as an engineer. He was nothing, nor anything, less than another homunculus, this one built for and possessed by Djerrid Ruin, Byron's Bowman.

A Zodiacal (Sagittarius), from one of the Great God's double-digit litters of three, he reported more to Yati, a fourth-born, than to Byron's occasional shell and Paraja's nominal boss, Alfredo Sentalli (more commonly Alpha Centauri on the other side of the Nag Gap).

Hiyati Samarand, who also wasn't human, used him to keep a finger to the pulse of the island. With their father and two of the second-born threesome outside since last night – they were now somewhere up north looking for Vayu Maelstrom (Devil Wind), the third of the Second – he had no qualms about speaking to Centauri's made-to-order sit-in (more so than stand-in) as the non-threatening inferior he was.

"That's another thing that fries my socks," the faux Fatman digressed, as was the actual Enormity's wont. "Can you please explain the differences between an homunculus, a Callion Clone, a Sphinx like the ones that plagued us in '65, a replica from Temporis, the Sleepers of Cabalarkon, and these amoebas our little Ant-friend has been nattering at me about recently? Surely they're all just variations of mandroids and therefore potentially very dangerous to your kind."

"Homunculi are quite common in my land," said the just-as-three-eyed scientocrat unapologetically. (Yati knew pretty much all there was to know about homos, as devils referred to homunculi. Of course he did. The decadent biomages who made them worshipped him, Byron's Dragon, back home in what was alternatively named Samarand, hence his adopted surname.)

"Samarand is not on the Outer Earth," this Enormity reminded him unnecessarily. "And that is not what I asked."

"Very well," began the oriental-looking project overseer, who was no more oriental than he was a scientocrat. (Byronics tended to assume the likenesses of their worshippers and Yati's were for the most part Asiatic in appearance.) "My homeland was Sedon's Tongue before Grandfather Moloch took it into what's left of his head to semi sort of switch Twilight with my domain. Only, in one of those quirks he's notorious for, he rendered it his Outer Nose rather than a replacement tongue."

Twilight was once Daybreak, a Lazaremist land on the far eastern, occipital side of the Head's upper mainland. (If you could see it from space, which you couldn't, the therefore Hidden Continent looked to be a nowadays-hornless demon's head from the perspective of its left side.)

By contrast, it being originally a Byronic territory, which is to say one located in the vicinity of the Head's mouth, lips, lower jaw and goatee, Sedon's Tongue wasn't so much Yati's domain, let alone his protectorate, as where he hung his hat (when he wore one, which he rarely did, and deigned to take it off). In other words, he made it his home when he was on the Hidden Headworld, which of late was even less rarely than he wore a hat.

(In a vagary of commonplace Headworld practice amongst the three Great Gods, Bodiless Byron didn't divvy up his traditional lands amongst his devic children. Rather, he doled out provincial pockets wherein they could collect worship most assiduously. What the Unmoving One gave he could also take back and whatever worship they did receive had to be subsidiary to that devoted to him and the Moloch Sedon, the top gods' Top God.)

"Yes, yes, I know all that. It was a way to break up the spheres of influence on the Head. Twilight's now a buffer zone between the tribes of Byron and those of Mithras. Samarand is now on the East Coast, in Lazareme's upper lands, and Lathakra's in the Libertine's southern realms across from The Argent and the Strait of Clouds in the Cattail Peninsula. Get on with it."

"I was trying to." Samarand lit one of his omnipresent Marlboros. He clearly hadn't noticed there were still two burning in his ashtray. (His failure to notice them may have been due to the fact that there was nothing clear about the air in his immediate vicinity.)

"Though, to be frank, it was more punishment than anything else. Simplistically put Grandfather thought highborns like the Lazaremist Mariamne Dawn-star and the Mithradite Thanatoids of Lathakra were getting too big for their proverbial britches. Seems I got roped into it as a warning to Father Byron."

"Who doesn't wear britches on account of he has no legs."

"True enough. But you get my point."

Sentalli-Centauri did. "In other words they were syphoning off too much of his worship for themselves."

"Just so. Anyhow, in long lost Old Weir, before there was such a thing as Shining Ones, let alone devazurs or even a Devil, capitalized, Utopians fashioned homunculi to house the spirits of departed loved ones. At some point in time, Old Weir's Mother Machine found a way to make these previous inanimate objects animate.

"They were the first mandroids but only in a manner of speaking. Yes, they're both produced artificially but mandroids don't live and breathe like homos do. They more like click and whir. Homos weren't clones either, not exactly, and certainly not yet. Clones came about centuries later."

Project Centauri's overseer provided a quick history of how Master Devas, their parents and lone grandfather came into being. He went on to note more so than describe in any detail how they – with only a couple of exceptions, then only insubstantial Spirit Beings – declared war on the Mother Machine, her mandroids, if not the Utopians native to Old Weir itself, and won.

Their victory made devils Public Enemy Number One in the initial Weir System. It would since ancient Utopians relied upon their planetary Mother Machine and its substations throughout its millennia colonized solar system to provide for their day-to-day comforts. Still did, in some respects, within the Whole Earth's last remaining Weirdom, that of Cabalarkon.

"As you know, the Male Entity, Heliosophos as he styles himself, time-tumbles. A number of lifetimes after he helped create the first of us out of the biogeneticist Grandfather keeps at least passably alive to this day up north, in his devic Eyc-Land, he returned to old Weir's solar system."

(When he was altogether alive, the scientocrat Dark Sedon regarded as his father specialized in biogenetics. That he still *'slept'* in the Weirdom named after him was one of Sedon's strangest quirks. Why leave the howsoever tightly sealed tub of life-preserving Cathonic Fluid containing your precious father-creator in the hands of your greatest enemies? For fun, Sedon answered enigmatically.)

"The Entity soon realized just how successfully we'd proliferated in the multiple human, even Utopian, generations he'd been away. In one of his all too frequent bouts of mass murderous madness, he had his constant companion, the unimaginatively designated Female Entity, ignite Old Weir's sun.

"It went supernova. Astronomers in my homeland even predict we'll be able observe evidence of that out here near the end of the decade. It exploding wiped out vast numbers of we, even then Shining Ones, plus most of the ages-old Utopian civilization whose body parts helped make our parents. Not all of it, though; nor all of us, either.

"Sedon managed to save a few thousand of us, most of whom we've subsequently lost. But, in anticipation of what he was about to do, the Male Entity and his wrench of a wench – who started off as a somehow humanized version of the Utopians' Mother Machine, hence the alliteration – had already set up New Weirworld for a select million or two of Old Weir's survivors.

"However, the starburst left them at least temporarily infertile. Rendered Sedon and the six Great Gods, our parents, a ditto to that dot, as your little pet trickster likes to phrase it. To their credit, New Weir's scientocrats, Cabalarkon amongst them, remained both unfazed and steadfast in their by now racial hatred of we devils.

"No doubt with the assistance of Heliosophos and/or his Machine-Memory, they used much the same technology the now destroyed Mother Machine devised to animate homunculi. They thereby managed to preserve their race. These new breed of homos did not house the spirits of departed Utopians, though. They developed an intelligence of their own. These then are the first clones."

"The present day Trinondevs of Weir, something like sixty percent of them anyhow, are made the same way." Both Enormities, the one here and the one there, were with him thus far. The story was familiar, though Utopians like the Sarpedons gave their renditions of it a much more anti-devic skew.

"Sixty percent no longer," puffed Samarand. "But now is not the time to go into the improvements Aristotle Zeross, who fluked onto, into, Cabalarkon the place when he was still a teenager in 5960, has brought to modern day Utopian fertility rates." (At the urging of his wife, Demios's white-as-light twin sister, he could have added but didn't.)

"The Sleepers of Cabalarkon are only partially clones. The vast majority of them were born naturally, of sexual unions between men and women. Like regular long-lived Utopians, they aged normally, as in very, very slowly by human standards. However, when they came close to dying they were preserved, body and mind, in a constituent variant of what's called Cathonic Fluid, Distilled Brainrock.

"They can be awakened, these Sleepers. So can Cabalarkon the man, even if he is a long pre-Earth Utopian. But, the more they are, the closer they come to actually dying irretrievably. Utopians therefore draw a distinction between Imminent Death, which is when they're preserved, and True Death, when their bodies completely expire."

"They still have old-fashioned homunculi to preserve their spirits, though."

"Actually, no. Grandfather Sedon, who maintains a kind of veto over what goes on up there, forbade that practice something like forty-five hundred years ago, for reasons I'll get to momentarily. The homunculi of Samarand, what's now in the easternmost region of the Head's occipital mainland, are fashioned somewhat biblically. They are shaped to the desired form then breathed into life."

"I had to kiss mine," recalled Sentalli-Centauri through the thing he'd kissed.

"As did we all," concurred Samarand. "The sapience homunculi acquire is not that of a departed spirit. Nor is it self-developed like the clones of Cabalarkon. In fact sapience might even be overstating their intellect. What (let's call it) intelligence they do have comes from a psychic bond with, in your case, you; in my case, me. Human or devil, it doesn't matter; sentience is what counts.

"If either of us withdraws from that bond, no matter how temporarily, the homunculi carries on as we would. However, if either of us dies – not that I can – the homunculi will pine away, following suit, fairly rapidly. It's not so much a case of giving up his ghost as his ghost, his spirit, his inspiration as it were, has given up on him."

He paused for another puff or five. For a change he didn't immediately light up another cancer stick after stubbing it out. "The opposite does not hold true. Like a doppelganger for an important head of state, should the double be assassinated, the king, president or whatever, will simply carry on."

"I understand that."

"Samarandin homunculi are therefore safe. So, too, are the replicated Mantels of Temporis. Dand Tariqartha, a Lazaremist highborn, initially crafts them only to exist for specific periods. That's why he's called an Earth Magician. During these times they only do what their templates did beyond the Dome. Which is also why he's called both the Chronocollector and the Time-Space Displacer."

"But he uses the same tellurian stuff used to make mandroids."

"Different programming. And that's the point. Imagine watching the same movie over and over again. Reps don't watch, they live it. Turn off the film, rewind it as much as you like, there's always a beginning and an end that never changes. As such they too are safe." He could wait no longer. It was already past time for another cigarette.

"You asked me about amoebas, specifically about these body-builders the Antheans' enchanted emissary talks about. In 1943 out here, Leandro D'Angelo was hit by a devil-ray. He thereby acquired the powers of a cathonitized devil. It doesn't matter which one right now. His amoebas are individually intelligent. He dies, which he did in 1946, body, soul and spiritually – read consciously; mentally, if you prefer – they don't necessarily. They're not clones either."

"Which means they're safe, too," the great big man, as opposed the Great Man (Abe Ryne) or Great Byron (his Enormity's occasional occupant), put forward. "But mandroids aren't. Need I remind you we fought a war against them in Godbad, you and I, more than twenty years ago? Me with my fellow men and women, you with your brother and sister Byronics."

"Quite true. Mandroids are dangerous. Are, in fact, best thought of in the same terms as devil-eating, earthborn demons; tellurian ooze subject to Lemurian matriarchs and the likes of All of Incain and her moribund male equivalent, the Egyptian Sphinx. They're barely semi-sentient and can only act on the prompting of others – the believed supranormal Gynosphinx, in the case of '65."

"The one Max claimed was a dead ringer of a young Corona Power, not All of Incain itself. Apparently she used a replicated Crimson Corona, whatever that is."

"One of the Trigregos Talismans," enlarged Samarand. "They're the power foci the highborn Lazaremist, Tvasitar Smithmonger – whom we call Anvil the Artificer, or variations thereof – crafted in absentia for our mothers, the Trigregos Sisters, somewhat more than four thousand years ago."

"The Great Goddesses who simultaneously bore you Master Devas in litters of three," Sentalli-Centauri further recalled.

"The very ones, not that any of us know which one of them had which one of us; not that it matters either. We exist thanks in no small measure to them but we're here, and they're not, thanks to Grandfather Sedon. He abandoned them on New Weirworld once he determined they'd become as impotent as the rest of us had after the starburst I just mentioned."

"They must have been terrible scolds."

"They certainly weren't ones to kowtow, which he didn't appreciate."

"They came to hate him."

"Irreducibly. And again, not just him. It, the unwavering animosity they bore their father-creator, encompassed their Great Gods brothers long before Sedon took us away from New Weir on the Sedonshem. We, their third generational children, be they male or female, weren't immune to it either. How could we not be? Sedon made us incapable of disobeying our fathers, not our mothers, so they came to despise us too."

"Straight out of the Bible that."

"Except it said *'Honour thy father and thy mother'* didn't it."

"Not the version I was taught."

"No wonder Great Byron finds you such an agreeable host. Anyhow, their sheer loathing of Sedon, their disgust with their brothers, their revulsion of those they were forced to have, somehow transferred cross-cosmos to their talismans. As weapons they're as effective against we devils as they are ordinary mortals.

"More, in some respects, since they don't even need to be turned against us to be effectual. Simple contact with even one them will drive any of us absolutely insane; even kill us, as Unholy Abaddon proved when he did in his sister unity, the incomparable Harmony, at the inception of the Thousand Days of Disbelief five hundred years ago.

"That was the Susasword, correct?"

"Might just as well have been the Amateramirror or the tiara cum garrote. And there's the rub, you see. Corona was born Takeda Mikoto. Like her father, Kronokronos Mikoto, she's therefore the offspring of Temporis replicates. Go back to our film analogy. In the Thousand Caverns of Tariqartha, if the characters didn't have children in the movie they shouldn't have children in Temporis.

"However, being a Lazaremist and therefore prone to irrational spontaneity, and with an exuberant – you might even call it hyperactive – life-force to go with it, Dand Tariqartha occasionally lets his caverns diverge from their programming. In other words, they're not rewound and replayed endlessly."

"They come alive."

Samarand nodded, stamping out his cigarette and lighting yet another. "Takeda Mikoto got out here in August of 1945, when the Hiroshima A-Bomb went off. She thereafter assumed the manufactured identity of Corona Power. Her husband, Obadiah Melvin Power, was a ditto to that dot."

"Old Man Power wasn't a supra."

"Not really, though we don't believe he was ever a Mantel either. We do reckon the Gynosphinx was Corona's replicate, however; the replica of a replica given life instead of just a loop. In other words she was somewhat similar to what happened when Tyrtod von Alptraum, the Nazi Nightmare, was dying back in '44."

His Enormity knew this, albeit from Hush Mannering, who figured it out subsequent to disposing of the thought-supranormal Gynosphinx. "Except, back then, the King Conqueror, Wiccan Warlock, went to Temporis and snatched away his replica, which he proceeded to rehabilitate, in a manner of speaking. Wiccan Warlock was Jesus Mandam. He's dead."

"But Judge Warlock isn't and wasn't. This Conqueror or some biomages in his employ – maybe the same howsoever illuminated traitors who gave him access to their technology in the first place – shunted the real von Alptraum's mind into his replicate's body. After a few trial and error makeovers, he or they, doubling as technomages, came up with Steltsar, the mandroid monstrosity that led the rebellion in Godbad during the Fifties."

"No reason Steltsar couldn't have done the same," proposed APM-Connie. "Dand Tariqartha could have made any number of replicas of the same person, even one of his come-alive, got-away copycats if they made it beyond the Dome. And Corona Power did that. Hell, there might be a few copies of her lying around in one cavern or another.

"You, too. And not just you, I'm sorry to say, if he's replicating us right this minute or did at some other time in the last few decades."

Alpha Centauri was well known for his cast-iron digestive system but even he, his Alfredo Sentalli homunculus, was having trouble swallowing the barrage of information Samarand and the rest were tossing at him. A few dozen questions kept welling up but he only asked the one that struck him as most immediately pertinent.

"You're telling me the King Conqueror – Jesus Mandam – duplicated the process you alluded to earlier, the one forbidden by the Demon Sedon?"

"That was for homos, like fatso here, fatso there," interrupted Hala Sadrapa as rudely as Paraja had earlier. "Sedon's not precognitive; none of us are. What Yati's leading up to is a different kind of artificial being, one that no one could have predicted. We're talking about a Utopian-style clone gone wildly wrong, one catalyzed, as near as we can make out, entirely by accident rather than forethought or design."

"Catalyzed, not produced?"

"Certainly not deliberately, not if we've conjectured correctly." Another of Byron's Zodiacals (Scorpio), the one who, but for a third eye, appeared to be Mavis Chester (a black psychologist and computer wizard on the Express's ground crew) proceeded to drop her trump. "The catalyzing agent's our very own eyefire."

"O'Ryan James Maxwell was a Utopian clone?"

"Made with a Utopian recipe anyhow. And became a Multivoid when APM and Elephantine blasted him on Sunday, yes."

"Became a what?"

"You heard me. Believe it or not, suchlike abominations – to the likes of us anyway – feature in Buddhism as the too-good-to-be-true Bodhisattvas."

"Your eyefire resulted in an artificial Boddhi?"

"A Multivoid, yes again."

"They were pre-Earth enemies of devakind," provided Angus Skullian, the now three-eyed host of Headcase, also Headstrong, heroic Hektoris, Yati's brood brother. "We eventually learned how to handle them too, so don't think we've just given you a formula for devic destruction." If Sentalli-Centauri was thinking Angus-Hek was protesting too much he wasn't saying so.

"Multivoids were extraordinary beings – star creatures, according to some – but they weren't artificially manufactured. They occur naturally; at least we think they do. Maxwell, though, was a cosmic fluke, plain and simple. Which isn't to say it, he, couldn't happen again; just that we, and only we, have to make sure it doesn't."

"Wouldn't dare. I still can't believe the No Name thing actually has a name."

"His type do," Samarand inserted. "And let me assure you they were threats we took very seriously on our journey here all those thousands of years ago. The proverbial jury's still out on the accidental one you – the real you, I'm assuming – encountered on Sunday. But it very nearly put our elder brother here into the universal substance on a permanent basis."

He was referring to Damon Goldenrod, the third-born who generally possessed the real Centauri's son by Emeralda Plantagenet. "Do you still say I'm out of line?"

His Enormity, the one who wasn't here, had to think about that. As he did so – not so very far away as the crow flies (not that an everyday ordinary crow could fly to where he was) – the one who was here managed to avoid answering: "I still don't understand why you've taken over my island."

"It was expedient and necessary, sir," argued Benoit Dugas, more in his own voice than that of Petrogod, the devic overlord of Iraxas Province in north-eastern Godbad. "We cannot let Loxus Ryne and his latter day Xuthrodites find out about Sedon's Head; about our dual lives, here and there."

"More immediately," mollified Scorpio-Chester, "As of today, we have to protect the Nag Gap. So long as he's out here, Father Byron requires it of us. He loses access to the Head, the air out here will debilitate him as much as it already has us, with or without the piss-poor shells these homos make."

"We've no choice in the matter," Paraja-Ruin reiterated. "We must maintain the Nag. Protect it with our very existence if it comes to that."

"You've gone beyond that," railed the Fatman. "For over thirty-five years I've worked with Great Byron. It's been mutually beneficial, granted. I couldn't eat and drink to my heart's content without him around to keep it ticking. But our main goal has been to find you a safe haven beyond the planet.

"Much of that time I've dealt as much with Hush Mannering and her life-loving Ants as I have with your father. This morning, coming up from the locals' favourite nude beach, you had the nerve to terrorize her. Worse, you exposed your presence here, and my involvement with you, to Demios Sarpedon.

"I shouldn't have to remind you he's a Trinondev. They're born and bred to be your mortal enemies. You have put my relationship with him and his wife, the Hellions' Morrigan and Athenan War Witches' Emeritus Superior, at risk. Need

I remind you of our efforts, partially on your tribe's behalf, to free Hadd? Need I remind you that, as impossible as it seems, Hush is Morgianna's mother."

"It is the Mannerings' Pandora," argued Dr Samarand defensively, "Who bears ultimate responsibility for our admittedly otherwise precipitous action."

"Meaning?"

"Your ancient peoples often turned our history into their mythology. Inevitably, they corrupted it. For example, not that we had names in those bygone millennia but our equivalent of the Hellenic Greek's Prometheus was Tvasitar Smithmonger. I mentioned him a few minutes ago: the one we address as Anvil the Artificer; making things being his attribute. Instead of bringing us fire, he brought us the ability to become substantial, as opposed to the simple spirit beings that our azuras remain today.

"The Hellene's Pandora was another name for the Biblical Eve. Supposedly this Pandora brought evil into world. Supposedly Eve cost Golden Age Mankind its immortality by discovering sex and having the first human child, the Biblical Cain, whom we recall as Anti-Patriarch Cain and know for a fact was the son of Demon Queen Lilith. Had Abel then – whom Cain, who obviously wasn't altogether human, did kill – and a clutch of others, including your Adam's successor, Pseth Ra, and his sisters.

"Philosophers may argue that reproduction was a form of immortalization. What Eve's gift effectively did, though, was bring death into the world. Our Pandora was Marut Kanin, the second-born Mithradite who produced Chrysaor Attis, the first solid offspring solely of Master Devas. Fortunately, it seems the Attis or Theattis, fabled as your Universal Soldier, was another accident; a stroke of good or bad luck like your Maxwell becoming a Multivoid. We Master Devas could never repeat her feat."

Sentalli-Centauri had often discussed such matters with his drinking buddy, Jordan Tethys, the legendary Thirty Year Man. "Patriarchal societies," he contributed, "Tend to blame women for most of what ails them." In saying this, he was merely echoing his earlier comment about being brought up with the Fourth Commandment lacking a reference to *'mother'*.

"They fantasize a Golden Age of Mankind," he elaborated, "Wherein, literally, there were no women and every man could live forever. It wouldn't surprise me if Eve is the root word for *'evil'*. But, by slamming her as that kind of Pandora, you're suggesting my Hush, your father's staunchest Ant ally, the one who calls me daddy and I call baby button-nose, is a traitor to devazurkind. It's – what's the word? – calumnious."

"Isn't that a cloud," cracked Paraja-Ruin.

"Is it?" Samarand countered, ignoring the tasteless snickering of his disrespectful fellows, particularly Damon-Yataghan and the younger ones. "She is obsessed with the discredited Anthean notion of Panharmonium. And by that I don't mean the Lazaremist version of it, which had nothing to do with bringing back our mothers either in person, if they're still around, or somehow reincarnated, if they're not.

"That Panharmonium lasted nearly 500 years, from roughly the turn of the last millennium to its mid-point circa 5500 YD, but it wasn't the retrospective, renewed Golden Age non-devils speak of so fondly beyond Godbad. It was a hegemony of lawless license masquerading as freedom to do whatever you could get away with.

"At any rate, hers is an understandable, even – dare I say it – expectant obsession. She was, after all, deliberately bred to bear the Trigregos Sisters Reborn. Thanks to the Moloch Sedon and Pyrame Silverstar that didn't happen in 5919, when she had Saladin Devason instead of three great goddesses to come.

"Thanks to their daughter – if she is that, as many believe, the demon more so than devil child Tralalorn – who devolved her a year later, after she came so very close to realizing a third of it by having Morgianna, it can't happen now. But it was her, your Hush, the Mannerings' Pandora, as Joli Blon, who brought Trinondev technology to the Outer Earth in the early Thirties.

"Either that or, if Moses Callion already had it, she got it to work. Whichever the case, out of the cryogenically preserved genes of Charan Ryne she sought to re-grow the Horrite himself. The result, forty-five years later, was the No Name thing your Maxwell became. Be assured, that will not happen again."

"Necator, more precisely, his father's Valhallans have been coming out here for years," said Paraja-Ruin, whose abundance of worshippers on the Inner Earth gave him credence above and beyond his relatively lowborn status. "It was your idea and, on your instructions, they've been busy infiltrating top secret labs all over the world. They're kind of like Glomen, except they don't blow. When they seemingly die, their buddies just exhume then send them, with their accumulated secrets, back here."

"Whereupon," finished his Enormity, "They're waxed and polished, or sewn back up, those that can be, and sent to infiltrate somewhere else." The Fatman approved of industrial espionage so long as it benefited NCE, the Liberty's largest contractor, and not its competitors.

"I understand your desire to preserve this island, especially now that your father is outside. However, I still see no reason for you to bring Necator and even more of his hot shots out here. If, despite your well-beyond-supranormal abilities, you devils are not satisfied with my security arrangements; if you reckon you need Valhallan bully boys, you should have brought the ones already out there back here.

"Instead you've imported dozens of my own Godbadian elite from inside. That's going to take some powerful explaining."

"Perhaps the others didn't express themselves very well," acknowledged the oriental-looking overseer as he opened another pack of fags.

(Headworld dragons did indeed breathe fire. Some of them did, rather – there being a few different varieties. Since that wouldn't do in the comparatively polite society of Centauri Island, he inhaled and exhaled vast amounts of smoke. It was almost as if his brothers and sisters in Byron expected it of him.)

"There are two issues here. One is protecting this island and the Nag Gap until Father Byron returns. That is what the Protector and his men are doing here. As for explaining them, there is no need. They won't talk even if they are captured. They'll blow instead."

"You've turned them into Glomen?"

"They voluntarily accepted the drugs, yes. Sometimes the kick of living beyond death wears off without the edge, as opposed to the eve, of destruction."

"How? What's your connection to Greygreave Translav?"

"It hardly matters, does it?" ventured the obvious answer (Dr Lindquist), although it was APM, Aphropsyche Morningstar, doing the talking. "We're taking care of that aspect of things."

(Connie All-Eyes, Gorgeous George Hannibal and Yataghan nominally Sentalli out here, Montressor in there, were the only Untouchables not homunculi. As third-born, APM and Yataghan's usual occupant, Damon Goldenrod, were Yati's superiors. Heroic Hektoris, sometimes Headcase, other times Headcase, occasionally both, tended to defer to Yati even though they were fourth-born brood brothers.)

Sentalli-Centauri wasn't satisfied; just didn't have much choice in the matter. Plausible deniability, however, was second nature to him. Had to be when he was the most visible face of anyone anywhere out here who knew the most explosive secret the Whole Earth kept: namely, that there were two sides to it.

"I suppose, if it comes down to it, we could always reveal the existence of the subterranean submarine pens."

"If it gets that far, I suppose we could," admitted Samarand.

"You said there were two issues. The second one better not be assassinating Hush Mannering."

"Master Devas, at least ones still obedient to their fathers, which all of us are, do not kill lesser beings," Samarand reminded the Fatman. "Our servants do not have such deep-seated restrictions. However, in the case of Young Life, that shouldn't be necessary. Still and all, unfortunately for her the howsoever remote possibility that more potential No Name things could be produced cannot be sneezed at; make that glared at."

"I thought you just said a devil wouldn't do that?" Devic eyefire, his Enormity didn't doubt, could be as lethal as it usually was psychologically debilitating.

"Strife might."

"Ah …"

"What I'm saying is that Mr Maxwell No Name is anything except Mr Inconsequential Nobody. Nor is he necessarily Mr Lonely, as in the one and only. Your Hush is not the only full blown Ant we know of out here. There is at least one more. That's why we did not recall the Valhallans already out here to defend this island. That's equally why I have deployed them elsewhere."

"And didn't inform me?"

Sentalli-Centauri was disgusted with Samarand's presumptuousness; worse, his complete disregard for his authority – an authority delegated to him by Great Byron himself. Perhaps worst of all, Samarand had no appreciation of the inviolability, the sanctity even, of the Outer Earth.

Shining Ones – and not just because they openly referred to themselves as devils (little gods) – were not allowed out here, at least not off island. Since it opened thirty-five years ago, the Great God their father had dedicated immeasurable, worship-gleaned energy keeping the Nag Gap for his and his use alone. Things must be truly desperate for Bodiless Byron to void his own precepts.

(Byron was all head. He'd lost his body in what couldn't be considered pre-Biblical times just because the event wasn't recorded in the Book of Byblos. He lost it in a confrontation with the eventual tenth patriarch of Golden Age Humanity, Xuthros Hor, the Biblical Noah, who was then not much more than 240 years old.

(The same confrontation cost Number Five, Mahurus Zir, the Biblical Mahalel, his life at the tender age of 895. Daily Golden Apples really did keep the doctor away.)

"I took it upon myself to look after our better interests."

"You took it upon yourself to ignore me, Dr Samarand."

"I did what had to be done."

"You do not support me. You support Thrygragos Byron."

"I see no distinction."

"Then you are blinkered, sir. Yataghan, please escort Dr Samarand back to the Head. We have no further need for his services."

"I can't do that, father."

"Then you are not my son."

"That depends on your perspective," said Damon-Yataghan. "I am Unmoving Byron's son – as are the rest of us; those who aren't his daughters, that is – but I possess your son by blood. Since you usually speak with Byron's approval, if not always with his voice, such as it is, ordinarily I would do as you request. It's just that he Great God's needs strike me as paramount right now."

"Not just his, Goldenrod," Hala-Chester emphasized. "The Whole Earth's do too." His Enormity didn't know what her sting could do, but doubted it'd be pleasant.

Hiyati Samarand took up their theme. "Our father is now on the Outer Earth, together with his Primary Nucleoids. The Nag Gap must be preserved at least until he returns. For that reason, and that alone, we have brought in Cromwell Necator and your Aka-Godbadian security forces to add to your Outer Earth numbers, as competent as they usually are.

"We dare not trust Dulles, not with Maxwell and Kinesis off-island and especially not with the Horrite, Loxus Ryne, on-island. We dare not trust the Nag Gap to outsiders."

"Are you suggesting I am your prisoner, just as Loxus Ryne is as good as mine?"

"You made your arrangements," concluded Samarand, nowhere near as dismissively as Paraja-Ruin or Damon-Yataghan had been when addressing the Fatman, either of them. "We made ours. Were you a more any day accommodating host for the Thrygragos, you would not question our decisions. We do only what is necessary."

"And these other Valhallans. Where did you deploy them?"

"Houston, Texas."

========

On the other side of the Nag Gap, in here's enormous reality of Alpha Centauri briefly broke contact with out there's substitute enormity of Alfredo Sentalli.

========

"What do you think, baby?" he asked the little trickster sitting on his lap.

Hush, whose birth name was indeed Pandora, was holding his hand – the hand with his rings, one of which she gave him. With it she was listening in on his cross-dimensional discussion with the Byronics out there. "Pandora's box held more than just human woes," she ventured. "Which ancient Antheans and their Xuthrodite menfolk ascribed to devils in any case. It had Hope, capitalized. It seems this latter day Pandora has delivered on that.

"I don't know, except in the vaguest terms what happened 4500 years ago and Samarand still hasn't got back to it. But it obviously had something to do with rebellious replicates, if there was such a thing back then, and Utopian homos almost nailing the Moloch Sedon."

"I'll ask Jordy, next time I see him. He'd know."

"Or if he didn't he'd make something up."

Jordan Tethys was a storyteller. Hush had known him all her life. He recurred, for a maximum of thirty years, hence the legendary 30-Year Man. One of his incarnations married Tsukyomi Mikoto, Takeda-Corona's paternal aunt. Another had been a nun, Sister Jordan, who lived right here in Aka Godbad City during the Godbadian Civil War. The current one began life as George Taurson, Miracle Maenad's son by her Taurus of the day, an Outer Earthling by the name of Jason Annulis.

"Me, I just wish I'd known I had a recipe for eliminating all that troubles us forty-five years ago. It would have saved me a lot of strife since." Despite her recent threat on her independence, if not her life as such, she thought that was funny. Centauri wasn't laughing. There was nothing funny about Strife. Neither should she. "Trouble, I mean."

"You didn't know you held the secret to destroying devils?"

"Not until now I didn't. But clearly someone did. I thought I was just helping Moe One clone Charan Ryne, the Great Man's father, after he so badly botched bringing back his mother Athena. All very interesting, I'm sure. Next time I see a certain Female Entity, we're going to have to have ourselves an extended chinwag." She gave her daddy a playful tug on his goatee.

"What should I do?"

"It's too late to do anything about Houston," she told him. "I'm not taking a chance of getting nailed by Strife again by bopping there on my agates. If I have to take her on, it'll be just outside, a quick jump away from the Nag Gap. And you won't be allowed to make a phone call. Besides, their target's Aranyani Nightingale and Demios told me she's not there.

"Take my advice, keep Daddy Ryne underground and get ready to evacuate the island on a minute's notice. Everyone who belongs inside better start getting back, even Hannibal and Connie. If they know what's good for them, which they don't seem to, the devils better, too.

"I mean the spleen, look what happened to Granddaddy Sed – the mighty, lord-on-high muck-a-muck, not my Granddaddy Sed – and that was just one lowly H-Bomb, not a fleet, or whatever you'd call them, of nuclear fucking dragons." (She was referring to events on Salvation Island, Christmas Day 1953.) "I'll take care of the rest."

"How?"

"Trust me! They don't call me the trickster for nothing."

"That's what I'm afraid of."

========

Mama Sofa was Sophia D'Angelo, daughter of Hush's Granddaddy Sed (Sedon St Synne, later Judge Warlock) by Louise nee Riel. Sophia was the mother of a number of boys and girls by Raphael D'Angelo (Papa Rafe). Once you included the adopted twins, Aires and Thalassa, there were thirteen in all. Leandro was one of her natural-born sons. He was dead.

Along with first daughter Nita (Anita), a Summoning Child like the Terrible Twins and so many other eventual supras, the three of them and the rest of her natural-born children, her own father effectively killed him in 1943. He did so – doomed him, put better – in Vichy France when he, by then calling himself Satan St Synne, exposed them to his devil-ray, what he also called his devaray.

Sort of dead, rather. A couple of Leandro's aspects were still alive. Sed-son was too. Sort of!

****

Nuke 17: **Doubleman Times Three**

========

Thursday, December 4, 1980

"Me, I hope it isn't Harry. Hope Big Shelter is a myth and Rings isn't going there. Otherwise Abe might be crazy enough to do something absolutely insane like try to invade it."

The hope Jock Maxwell was referring to had nothing to do with Pandora Mannering. It had everything to do with Dr Aristotle 'Harry' Zeross, Ringleader.

========

"Let me tell you," Johan Schmidt offered the old colonel, "If he's anywhere on this earth, even somehow or other beyond it, we'll track him. Like I said, though, I doubt it even exists. My guess is Harry's heading for Africa; probably South Africa, like he did before. Still and all, even with his amazing rings, how he keeps eluding us I can't figure."

Jock took the reference. The last proven headquarters for the Worldwide Order with the Right to Life and Death, as the Strife-led, unregenerate Nazi-riddled, terrorist organization styled themselves in the Sixties, was in the outlaw state of South Africa. "You still think he's in league with WORLD? Not that I'm acknowledging there is a new Worldwide Order, you understand."

"I think he runs the Order, along with Crystal St Synne or some other Strife, possibly this wife of his, Illuminatus, Melina Sarpedon. No one denies that Strife's a trained Ant but I doubt she's a rogue witch. Not like your Bunnie, the Great Man's Ginny, and the rest of those witch-apologists always insist she is."

"I thought they thought she's some kind of infectious spirit."

"The only infectious spirit I've ever heard about is alcohol. Assuming alcoholism's infectious."

"You're such a prig."

"At least I'm not a superstitious prig. All this crap about ghosts, haunts, and revenants is, well, a load of Ant-shit. Even supras stay dead."

"Never come across the Black Death I guess."

"Actually, as you're no doubt well aware, I have. Ants weren't the only ones who could cast illusions or get about between-space. Even if we never could figure how they pulled it off, let alone how to duplicate the feat, it's clear the likes of the Moirnoir midget or the Conquering Christ did."

"I heard Moirnoir was a fairy, like OMP."

Schmidt seemed take that seriously; momentarily, anyhow. "Obadiah Power was a genuine supra. He was also genuinely nuts, what with the way he fay-said everything. Auguste Moirnoir wasn't anywhere near that bad but, yeah, he was certainly a trickster, I'll give him that. Nor do I think Strife's akin to a university program, like learning how to become a lawyer; something Ants can aspire to becoming."

"Or, regardless of aspirations, inadvertently become once they lose their mind. Bunnie always says that a crazy Ant's worse than a crazy man; even a crazy man with a gun. Fortunately, given what especially old-timers like Old Man Power could accomplish, she also claims that crazy Ants usually just drop dead; that it's part of their training to do so. Which suggests Strife skipped classes."

"You're not going to start claiming Strife's an individual again, are you? That was discredited decades ago. Sure, they all look the same – bodily young and skinny, with a blank face and flaming red hair – but the first Strife was seen in the early Forties and the last one less than a decade ago. Blank face or no blank face, thirty odd years is an awful long time to stay young and skinny."

"You're the one who mentioned illusions."

"All the same, sane or not, it can't be the same person."

"Why not? If she's a supra, one who escaped the net we cast all those years ago, then who's to say what she can and cannot either do or be."

"Now you and I are finally getting to the same page."

"How so?"

"Go back twenty years to Joan's murder," Schmidt continued – Joan being Joan Smith, Trebleman, one of what were once seven so-called Psychic Siblings. (The others were Sean Smythe, Bill White, Mary Schwarz, Ann Bianco, and Barb Black.) "What was all that money Abe was forced to fork over for except to get supras back in action?"

"And here I thought it was to ransom Belificent Zeross."

"You know what I mean. It was to reactivate still-living supranormals, the ones who didn't remember they were supras anymore, and bring them into WORLD's camp instead of the Alliance's. Strife was the Queen Conqueror, recall?"

"And the King Conqueror, the Conquering Christ as he preferred, was Ryne's oddball-looking nephew. What of it? You saying Strife, then and now, only now with Harry Zeross as her King instead of Jesse, is lonely for more of their kind?"

"Are you saying they're not?"

"For one thing, Harry wasn't a supra. He just had these amazing rings. For another I'm saying any of today's supras would have Simon Lancz's Signal System to worry about."

"Personally," Schmidt in effect pet-peeved, "I think WORLD is behind Signal System as well. Lancz's father was Baphomet, the blazing bastard really running the old King and Queen Conquerors in the early Fifties, and Simon's the one keeping the old corpse, Sedon St Synne, on life support."

"I was wondering when we'd get to Sed-son." For reasons that remained somewhat obscure, almost everyone called St Synne Sed-son back in the old days.

What wasn't so obscure was that St Synne was the one primarily responsible for killing Nita D'Angelo, his own granddaughter, back in the Vichy of 1943. At the same time, his devil-ray was the main reason the seven Psychic Siblings, of whom Johann was one of only two survivors, came to exist in the first place.

"Next thing you're going to tell me is he's not as good as dead; that they've got some doppelganger on life support and that he's the brains behind WORLD."

The *'they'* besides Lancz, and the hypothetical Order in general, was Tereza, Simon's wife. Tereza was yet another D'Angelo, though there were those who claimed she was more of the devils than of the angels. Perhaps not by coincidence Jock would be attending a gathering of D'Angelos this weekend in Vancouver.

"I wouldn't go quite that far but I wouldn't go too far the other way either. Your Sed-son's still ticking at well over a hundred; the first Strife was considered his plaything for good reason; he reported to Donar Lancz, codename Baphomet, during the war; was a prime mover behind the Supranormal Defense League, which spawned the Conquerors, after it; and has been the suspected, pardon me, ringleader of all the various incarnations of WORLD."

Even though, depending on the day, Ringleader, St Synne, the Superior Sisterhood and Strife were close seconds, the Worldwide Order was clearly Johann's Number One bogeyman. For him, the something wicked this way comes pricking his thumbs wasn't Rummy Ronny Reagan's red menace. It was WORLD.

"All this coming to a head now's all about supras?"

"Looks that way to me. You've heard about the Cosmic Express?"

"I may be out of the loop for the most part but I'm not that much out of it. I knew a lot of the, what did they call themselves … cosmicompanions?"

"Knew them or their parents?"

"Both; grandparents, too, in some cases." A dawning of not so much awareness as dread suddenly came upon the old man. "Old buggery!"

"Took the words right out of my mouth. Naturally it goes without saying the Order's on the Moon and that Harry's rings are the only realistic way they got there. Therefore …"

"Strife, illusions, on the Earth or even beyond it – you think the Express didn't explode; that Rings transported them to Big Shelter and that it's the Moon!"

"I did say I was full of theories. We'll know soon enough."

"If it isn't the Moon?"

"Look, whenever, wherever, that plane comes to ground, be it down here or up there, we'll be on it quicker than you can remember what AMERICA stood for."

AMERICA, as Jock Maxwell was well aware, was short for the Alliance of Man for the Extermination of Resisting International Criminal Agencies. Unless it was Associations. Seemed to him it had changed a few times over the years. Needless to say Loxus Abraham Ryne came up with the name.

The patriarch loved doing that sort of thing – witness, most recently, SPACE: the Society for the Prevention of Alien Control of Earth. He didn't rise to Schmidt's bait this time, though; had more important matters on his mind. "And what'll you do then? I may have been retired for over fifteen years but I keep up my reading. It doesn't take a genius to realize that if you've built tracers into that shipment you can also build triggers."

"You're right of course. We can blow Harry and them sky high – or sky low, if that's what's required – at any time. But we'll give him a chance to come onside first. You've the Alliance's word on that."

"Murder's thirsty business." Auld Jock took another swig.

"The Worldwide Order murdered people on an almost daily basis throughout the Sixties. We believe they're well and truly started up again and that Rings is right in the thick of things as usual. As Ryne must have explained when he recruited you to help us out, Harry trusts you more than anyone short of Big Max or Rom Kinesis."

"Twenty to thirty years ago, maybe."

"For a guy who's hardly been seen in twenty years, that's about the best *maybe* we have. Even if Joanie died trying to protect him and Bel in '60, he's not sure about me. Mind you, he may not know of our link. But the pertinent point remains: If anyone can get him into the fold and expose the Order, wherever they are and whatever they're up to, it'll be you."

"I still can't believe WORLD's on the Moon bombarding the Earth with thought-altering beams," protested the octogenarian.

"Thought beams aren't science fiction fantasy, sir. Madison Avenue ads in books, radio and television are proof of that."

"True enough," Maxwell acknowledged. "And if any organization's capable of the technology to transmit thought beams selectively, in hundreds of languages, to people all over the world, I suppose it'd be WORLD."

"Got that in a nutshell. You can't deny they wanted supras back in 1960."

"Can if I want to." Colonel Jock was nothing if not obstreperous. "Fact remains that in their heyday, certainly from '65 onward, they were more focused on understanding the King Conqueror's discoveries of the Forties and early Fifties. Were getting pretty good at it, too, by the time AMERICA took them apart."

"Not as good as Al Sentalli and his techno-wizards, Professor Kinesis predominantly, are these days. Don't forget, Rom and Harry Zeross are first cousins."

"And, like we've already talked about, the Conqueror was Jesus Mandam, grandson of yet another Kinesis, aye. So is the patriarch for that matter – the son of a Kinesis, I mean."

"Which, Mary Magdalene Ryne being his mother, is what made Jess his nephew. But, don't you see, familial relationships aren't what ties it all together."

"Still – the Moon!"

"You'd prefer extraterrestrials? That's what just about every government in the UN thinks is up there. Nope. It's got to be the Order and it's got to be Ringleader. There's no other sensible explanation. The one because of Mandam's technology; the other because even it's no good until you get there."

"Not if it's Big Shelter, Doubleman."

"No? Then why haven't the Ants done it centuries ago? Think technology some more; think of the incredible machinery they have to have in order to do what they're doing up there. There's no friendly moving company to the Moon; not yet, there isn't. The only way to get that much hardware there is through Harry's rings."

"The frags?"

"To defend their stronghold against whatever we send against it, maybe. Wouldn't be the first time countries like the US and the Soviet Union have sold weapons that are ultimately used against either/or would it."

"Probably not. Madison Avenue's a good thought. Except it sells products. Not megalomania. Besides, if it is Harry, why wouldn't he use those self same rings of his to steal the armaments instead of bargaining for them?"

"To live outside the law you must be honest. Bob Dylan said that, though he probably wasn't the first one. Guy's a notorious plagiarist. You do know who Bob Dylan is, don't you?"

"I probably read the same file. Ask yourself this, instead: Why would he need armaments anyhow? WORLD had labs and factories all over the globe. They need weapons, they'd build them themselves."

"I just said it makes sense."

"Years ago – as you'd know better than most, laddie, since you lot were one of them – we used to say that when dealing with supras, there's no such thing as a sensible explanation."

"Watch it with *'the one of them'*, Jock. I might have missed a bug."

"And I might have missed my afternoon tea."

"Did you?"

"Of course not. Which's exactly what I was saying. This whole business doesn't even come close making sense. I mean, Ringleader and the Order? Your turn to give over, boyo. The first WORLD killed his wife."

"Still and all, ask me it beats the purple petunia pants off any other theory. Aliens especially."

"Bah! Abe should've brought me in earlier. I'd have sorted things out."

"Might yet get the chance, Jock. Harry will listen to you, be assured of that. We are."

"We?"

"Our profilers, then. Pretty obvious. You and Bunnie gave him a home away from Trigon after his parents moved to Canada but were busy almost everywhere else except Ottawa. If he doesn't trust you, he doesn't trust anyone; any one of us anyhow."

"What about my trust in him? If he did go over to WORLD ..."

"Then it's you who's been betrayed. That proves to be the case, I'll hand you the button myself. Rest assured, we pin him down, you'll be on the first flight to wherever."

"Glad to hear an old cack like me still has his uses, even if it is as an assassin. So long as it isn't to the Moon, I suppose I'm up for it."

"Never doubted that for a minute, either. Speaking of flights, that'd be your plane for Vegas I hear revving up. You'll be in Vancouver and in bed by dawn. Come party time Saturday you'll be fit as a fiddle." Johann was referring the D'Angelos' get-together scheduled for the night of the Sixth.

"Give Schmidt's best regards to Papa Rafe and Mama Sofa when you see them. Drink a toast to Leandro, too. He'll be missing the family's five year reunion for the eighth straight time."

"That you will, Doubleman. Keep in touch."

"Tomorrow soon enough?" He handed old Max the flask.

"Aye, tomorrow. I'll ask Mama Sofa to pray for you."

"No need to ask. If it wasn't for her, I doubt either Sean or I would still be around."

========

In terms of being alive, the best that could be said of Sedon St Synne was that he wasn't altogether dead. In terms of being psychic, however, the best that could be said about the two remaining Psychic Siblings was that they could still communicate with each other telepathically. On occasion anyhow.

Sed-son was certainly one up on the other five Septuplets. For much the same reason too. He wasn't altogether dead. Was just as telepathic, though. Likely much more so. Just was not too interested in either of them was all. True Xuthrodite that he was, he'd always been more interested in the females of his extended family. Which also meant that he had a great deal of similarities with Xuthros Hor, the Biblical Noah.

When it came right down to it what else could he, Noah, have done? How else could you repopulate the Whole Earth after a Genesea except by porking your own gals?

Ditto supras!

========

Jock Maxwell made his way to the plane the Alliance sent to take him back to Las Vegas and thence to Vancouver. When it took off Doubleman, half of the last two remaining sevenths of Septupleman, walked towards the mobile unit full of communication equipment. A young smart, a graduate of the Virginia Academy of Man, rushed to intercept him.

"This just came in from the Moon via Houston, sir. It's a bit grainy."

"I can see that." Schmidt could also see that the picture was of a building with a dome and three triangular towers. "From the Moon, you say?"

"That's where it came from," said the smart. "Supposedly," he added quickly.

"You're telling me there's a structure on the Moon?"

"I agree with you, sir. Can't be."

"Then find out what can be," he demanded. "I'll be in my motor home. Don't bother me until you know for sure."

"Your plane for Houston is waiting to go."

"And it will continue to wait, mister. Any news so far? About the shipment, I mean?"

"Nothing yet. You'll be the first to know."

"See that I am."

Once alone in his travelling bus, Johann Schmidt closed his eyes.

"What's up, Sean?"

For a long time there was no contact. Schmidt was starting to become concerned when, finally, from the Liberty, and using their unique mental link, Sean Smythe told him about Starrus and his third eye. Told him a few other things as well. Primarily that neither the Liberty nor Groundbase Houston had been able to contact Centauri Island all day.

"Do tell. A devil, you say, and the first Olympian's boy back from the grave? Not suffering from a touch of lunar lunacy, are you?"

The answer was negative, though not with the certainty Johann might have hoped. "If Auld Jock thought Rings, Ants and WORLD on the Moon make no sense, wait until he hears this latest. Don't like this bit about Ryne going offline, though. Not now and not there. Alfredo Sentalli's always meant bad luck for us. Come again?"

Schmidt concentrated all the more. "I see. Yes, I appreciate what has to be done, but that's a little farfetched even for us, isn't it? I mean we've got kids, so did most of the others but ..." Doubleman Sean Smythe laughed in his head. "Yeah, I know it's not as lunatic as what you're going through." Understatement. "I know who his father was – he just left me – and who else he was raised by." Non sequitur. "So what if ants domesticate aphids? Supranormals aren't aphids. Besides, Antheans are vegetarians." Commentary. "Granted, they probably do use supras for their own purposes but that doesn't mean ..." Joke.

"Thick as a brick I might accept. How do you know I don't have diarrhoea?" Verbal abuse suggesting he had a complete void in the imagination department. "Sauerkraut is cabbage too, Sean. Sure, it isn't necessarily boiled but to say it doesn't have wit slurs the Plantagenets and their kin. It's actually quite sharp."

Recrimination. "Not funny. Guess not. Sure I'll try it. Might even be able to pull it off but chances are it'll waste me. Might be better if I skipped Houston and went straight to Al's island?" A few moments pass before he receives a response.

"All right. I'll go to Houston. With Ryne in Hawaii and knowing what Doc Dark once was, it'd be good to have someone else on site at Groundbase. You sure you're okay?" Affirmative. "Even if he doesn't prove receptive, we'll have to rely on Barb's little Hitler to look after the old man until we can get there."

'Devils or demons, what's the difference?' Schmidt was thinking as he headed towards his plane. Just before boarding it, he turned to the young smart from the CIA.

"Got any more of those splatter packs?"

"Tons of them."

"Good. Have a few crates sent to Pearl Harbour. This time we strike first."

"You're a German, sir. You were the Japs' allies."

"Who said anything about Japanese? We're all human beings."

"If you put it that way, then why ..."

"And they're not!"

=========

"You know – Pandora's box, the one with Aladdin's ring in it? Forget it. She's already here!"

"You must be Pandora," Adolph Dulles said to the little girl.

"Call me Hush, though right now I'm in a huff!"

=========

"That's an old joke, trickster," said Loxus Ryne without any affection. He'd known the perpetual seven year old for the better part of three human generations and was no more happy to see her than she was to see him.

"Sorry, daddy do-dick. Right now I feel more humus than humorous. Seems we skipped worse and went straight to worst, as in worst possible scenario. Not that I'm denying worse altogether. The way things are going, worst will soon be bad then a synonym for best. Real worse is yet to come and that's no liverwurst."

Until he decked him, Dulles had seen Mr No Name in action on Sunday. He'd heard from Paul Creel afterwards that a transformed Professor Kinesis caused him to disappear just after he'd reverted to Big Max Maxwell. However, this was the first time he'd seen someone appear as if out of nowhere. It was an unsettling experience and it took him a few seconds to find his tongue.

"I gather this is an everyday occurrence for you, sir. Me, I'm afraid I'm going to need an explanation for how she got here. I'm afraid, period."

"Don't worry about it, Daddy Dolph," said the little girl familiarly. "Call it witch-work and leave it at that. Actually it's you I'm here to see. Let me tell you a bedtime story."

"Usually it's the other way around. Adult to kid I mean."

"And I'm afraid, compared to us, you're the kid here, Mr Dulles," said Ryne. "And before you ask, no, I won't explain that. Just listen."

"Thanks again, doddery daddy," said the little trickster, then turned to Barb nee Black's lone son. "Remember what I asked you to do when I gave you that ring you're wearing?" Dolph said he didn't. Hush said: "No, but you did it." Ryne told her to get on with it. She did: "See, once upon a time, there were seven folks who could communicate with each other mentally. Some had children but none of them inherited the same abilities. Except, I hope, for one."

"Me?"

"You!"

=========

Loxus Ryne was sleeping by the time the UNES Liberty finally got through to SPACE's contingent on Centauri Island, so Dulles stood – or, rather, sat – in for the octogenarian. It wasn't Aremar he spoke to. It was Sean Smythe. When he woke the Great Man, he was still in a state of stunned stupefaction.

"Smythe says it's Heliopolis all right, except he called him Helios. Seems to have incredible technology at his beck and call. Something else. Claims Mik Starrus is on the Liberty. Or was. Has powers. Used the word supra but said

Starrus was something else – a big, three-eyed East Indian wielding a lightning bolt. I swear that's what he said. Got to be a supra, right?"

Hush, who materialized the moment Dulles and Ryne were alone, knew better but decided to keep up the charade as long as possible. Like not just her Daddy Alfredo, like all the devils she was still mad at for freeing Strife from Sarpedon's eyeorb – free her to possess her, again, howsoever briefly – she didn't want the patriarch or Dolph, nor anyone who might be listening in to their conversation, via bugs no one had found yet, to learn the truth of Big Shelter.

"Incredible technology must mean Heliopolis mastered the Conqueror's discoveries," she said. "Just like his Spartae apparently have as well," she added, without further elaboration. "All three supranormal Olympians – Agenor Heliopolis, Megaera nee Kinesis, and Meg's eldest son, Demonites Zeross – could conjure lightning bolts."

"So could Airealist," considered the Great Man, more dreadfully than thoughtfully. "Aires, an adopted D'Angelo, one of the King Crimefighters," he provided for Dulles' benefit, probably unnecessarily. "The first Olympian, Heliopolis's father, also had a lightning sword. Starrus must have been hit with a devil-ray."

Dolph pointed out the obvious: "Mik Starrus isn't East Indian."

"And Peter – Pietro – D'Angelo wasn't made out of stone," countered Hush. "But he sure as buggery-be-Jesus looked like he was after he became Demon Land in 1943." She paused not so much to frame her thoughts but to stifle her incredulity. "No, that's who we're dealing with all right. Got to be.

"In October of 1968, El Draco, Kadmon Heliopolis, and the other five junior Dragon's Teeth – Sangati, Hyperenor, Udaeus, Tiecher and Pelorus – must have been spirited away, along with the entire island of Trigon, to that mysterious part of Big Shelter where Sed-son and Jesse were throughout most of 1939 right up until 1943."

"The same place Demios and Morgianna stumbled upon in the early Sixties," twigged Ryne, remembering the series of events that led them to hook up with 1965's Strife and Günter von Alptraum. Together he and the Sarpedons had tried to boot Alfredo Sentalli off his own island. Just as the Fatman thought he was doing to him again today.

"If you say so, daddy diddlehead."

"Oh, I say so all right. And you're right in the thick of things as usual, aren't you? You and your Superior Sisterhood. Out with it, trickster!"

"We have been cooperating with saucy Daddy Cheese Sauce on the Cosmic Express, yes," she freely admitted, albeit substituting fay-saying for silliness. (Alfredo, as in Sentalli, was a sort of cheese-based spaghetti sauce.) "A lot of women on it had a degree of advanced Anthean training in addition to whatever education they got at the Academies. Your Anhita was one of them, true as well. But we had nothing to do with its destruction, nor any mad man on the Moon.

"There are other branches, though. My Ice Queen darling dearest of a Morrigan is a closet Hellion and her Athenans are war witches — the same as your mother's gun-toting suffragettes were going almost as far back as the last century. They're no more adverse to killing than Silver Signallers are and, like Signal System, they're anti-supra to boot. Or shoot, put better.

"Since most of those on the Express had supranormal forebears or near relatives, they might be behind blowing it away. If so, that probably means it isn't a new WORLD. Especially not if Strife's involved – and she is, believe you me. Or not, on account of I'm a trickster. She's a Korant Corn Queen. They're very much pro-supra.

"As for Helios, he could be in league with Afrites. His aunt and stepmother were Lovely Lady Fuck Monsters and, if his sister's still alive, she'd likely be one too by now. Then again, given who a number of his other, mostly older female relatives were, we could be talking more Hellions or even Ophirants. There's just no way to be sure in the blur."

"Even about you," snarled the Great Man. "Don't suppose you'd care to start making sense to us illiterate layabouts?"

"How about this, then? My faction's all in favour of stopping the Man on the Moon."

"So you say, little one. But not to the point of letting us above ground, right?"

"Look, daddy dopey, other Daddy Alfredo is convinced WORLD destroyed the Express and that you're in a king-size bed with them – like you were when you created it in 1960."

"I just needed an excuse to funnel a bundle of bucks into a supra revival. Belificent D'Angelo was not supposed to be killed. No one was. Ask your darling dearest about that." (If Dulles was shocked about Ryne's admission of culpability, he didn't show it. WORLD was an anagram and Ryne loved anagrams.)

(He also supposedly loved Zerosses and D'Angelos going back to his father's time and earlier. That, too, was in his file. Yet look what happened to a bunch of them in 1960 and later on, in 1968. Plus, the Great Man blamed Harry Zeross for 4th wife Oriani's death three years ago.)

"Morg's a morgue to me," Hush admitted with more than just a perceptible tinge of motherly disappointment. "Hellions and Ants should never mix, never worry."

"Which means?"

"No more beans. Not for Daddy Nearest Star, either." (Ryne knew Alfredo Sentalli as just that, not as Alpha Centauri, so he missed the reference.) "When he sent Yataghan and the rest of his so-called Untouchables away on Sunday, it wasn't for any holiday. It was for bacon-saving purposes, As soon as they left, he got on the phone to Cromwell Necator and organized a pre-emptive takeover by his own people.

"Once you contacted Immanuel Dark and Simon Lancz after you decided Saul, David, and the rest of the Crimefighters were back in action, that only cemented his suspicions. Maybe losing the Express has unhinged him, but he figures they won't attack if they think you're his prisoner instead of in his protective custody.

"However, thanks mostly to me, he wants to remain in the United Nations', read the States', good books." There was no telling if she was making this up as she went but it didn't matter, not really. "So you just look after your business, keep in contact with the Liberty and, if you really want to earn his trust, call off the Signallers."

"I'll do no such thing. Assure the fat fabulist I have nothing to do with any new Order or what happened to the Express. I also had no intention of kicking him off this island — though, after this, I undoubtedly will fire his obscene ass and maybe move here myself. You might also tell him that Saul and David probably are back, at least back in action, and, chances are, they don't like him any more than I do right now."

"I don't see how ..."

"Neither do I but, if anyone has designs on his precious island, it's them, the supras. The Signallers are as much for his defence as mine. And, if Al really wants to earn my trust, tell him to shut off his damn devil-ray." Dulles reckoned Ryne knew Hush well enough to also know his voice-work would have no effect on her. Kudos for trying, though, he further figured.

Hush heaved a sigh of frustration but maintained her comparative cool. "I could compel you, I suppose. But the elders, read me, don't approve of that sort of thing anymore. Take some advice, don't try to escape and stay well below ground. And by well, I mean bottom of it, the well. Whoever, whatever, took out the Express is still out there and probably preparing to hit us.

"Things are going to get terminally nasty if I don't come up with something creative very soon. Just wish I knew what I was going to come up with." As if to prod her inventiveness, she turned to Dulles. "Who else was there?"

"Some of Necator's albinos, Yataghan, the Fatman, and his physician, Connie Lindquist. I saw the lawyer fellow, Hannibal, and that cocky Hindu, Roderick Paraja, lurking in the background."

"I want a list of the Fatman's other Untouchables, the ones Max thought might be devil-ray victims. Chances are one or another of them will be with you and Abe whenever you go for a walk. Any new faces, memorize what they look like and try to get their names."

"All of the albinos and the rest of Necator's men are new to me," Dolph protested.

Hush waved her hand imperiously; told him to forget about the ones who reeked of death. What she wanted to find out, what she said she wanted to find out at any rate, was whether Sentalli had trained his devil-ray on anyone else. "These will be the ones he trusts to stick with you," she put to him.

"You know how to neutralize supras?"

"Not supras. Not like the Crimefighters, if they're back and come against us; both of which I can't accept. But I can put victims of the devil-ray out of their misery — and not by killing them, either. So, did you try it? Thought-transference, I mean."

"I kept thinking: *'Sean, Sean, I know about Leandro.'* But I don't know if he got it. The Liberty's orbiting the moon after all. Even if he is sort of my uncle, as you say, and he had a mental link with my mother, that's a long, long way."

"He's the one who contacted us. Not Jimmy Aremar. Since you've been wanting that all afternoon, it suggests he's receptive. Good! Things proceed apace in this space." She reached out her hand and tapped the ring she'd given him. It looked identical to the one Ryne had in Pandora's box. "Don't take that off. If things get sticky in the wickets I can get through to you on it. Either mentally or physically if necessary."

Clearly not wise when it came to witch-work, Dulles looked nervously at the patriarch. "Up to you, Dolph," said the old man. "I haven't been wearing mine. Never have, hence the box. But, given the circumstances, I might start. Just don't put it in your pocket. Even Hush is a little large to come through in your pants."

The little trickster smiled for the first time in quite a while. While she didn't laugh – no one laughed at his jokes – the sight heartened the old man.

"Glad you said *'through'*, otherwise you'd be a real dirty daddy." She turned to Dulles, unable to stop grinning naughtily. (Faerie tricksters were considered chthonic creatures, meaning earthborn. They certainly were earthy.) "I want you to concentrate on the other Doubleman, Johann Schmidt. Same thing: *'Johann, Johann, I know about Leandro'*."

"This Leandro wouldn't have been another D'Angelo, would he?"

"Just so you don't think I'm a liar, Dolph, yeah. Got that in one. Unfortunately, a long time ago now, he was put out of his misery the other way."

She left them again. Vanished, albeit omitting the traditional *'Poof'*. Left him wondering where that left him. If his mother was a body built by this Amoebaman supranormal, did that make him a D'Angelo like his erstwhile sweetheart, Star Dark, Glory of the Angels' daughter Estrella. More to the point, if his mother was actually once a man, how did she-he get pregnant? Was he born or did he just pop out of the void like Hush and Mr No Name?

"You know, Dolph," speculated Ryne. "If you can communicate with Doublemen – or is it Doublemans – Smythe and Schmidt, I wonder if you've picked up a few of their other knacks. You're a bit older than they were when they lost them but, before their abilities atrophied, they were extremely formidable supras."

"In what way?"

"First things first, young man. Got to crawl to be tall."

"So long as I don't have to kiss anyone's ass."

"Missed my point, Dulles. To do that, they'd have to be sitting on the floor."

========

Once there was indeed a supranormal known as Amoebaman. His given name was Leandro D'Angelo and he could split himself into semi-separate, semi-sentient individuals. Leandro died. Not all of his semi-separate, semi-sentient individual selves did likewise.

Seven survived. These were Septupleman, the Psychic Siblings. They were separate and fully sentient. Today only two were left. These were Doubleman Sean Smythe and Doubleman Johann Schmidt. Most of the Septuplemen (not Septuplemans) had children. Most, four out of seven, were also female.

One, Barb Black Dulles, had a child she named Adolph. He was currently on Centauri Island while one of his 'uncles' was just arriving in Houston Texas.

His other uncle, the other Doubleman, was elsewhere — in the United Nations of Earth Ship Liberty.

    Orbiting the Moon!

****

Nuke 18: **Doubleman Singular**

========

<u>**Friday, December 5, 1980**</u>

As his plane circled the runway awaiting permission to land, Johann Schmidt was lost in thought. "Leandro, eh. So we do have a link. What else did he say?"

"'Imperative. Ryne wants Signallers cancelled'," came back Sean Smythe. "Only thing is Dulles isn't very good at it. I got the sense he was being compelled to say that."

"Not by the patriarch, though."

"No. The impression of a little girl kept filtering through his thoughts." Schmidt knew who that was immediately. Smythe wasn't finished. *"The other strange thing was the mental signature of the voice he used. It's weak – make that nascent or just an echo – but I swear it was Prime."*

"Leandro's dead."

"That doesn't mean he hasn't been reborn, bro."

========

Arriving in Houston shortly after midnight, Schmidt didn't bother going home. Instead he took a cab to his office at the Academy of Man and called his wife. She gave him an earful on the topic of their eldest son going to the Oilers football game on Sunday then getting so drunk that he'd stayed in bed Monday morning rather than attend classes — him with his mid-terms coming up next week, too.

And their daughter, the punk: she'd burned her brassiere at some kind of sickening ceremony last night and was now wandering around with a safety pin through her left nostril like some sort of bone-through-the-nose cannibal. Next thing you knew she'd be filing her teeth and looping hoops around her neck until it stretched without a noose.

He said he'd talk to them when he got the chance but couldn't guarantee he'd be home until next week. "Might have to go to Hawaii. Business reasons."

They had already booked tickets for the whole family to visit her sister and his best friend, her twin's husband, Sean Smythe, at Christmas. What with the kids acting up the way they were, she was more than willing to leave a couple of weeks earlier than they'd scheduled. He said he'd phone her in the morning and hung up.

Stripping off, he lay on his office cot. Sleep didn't come easily, much too much to think about, but he did manage to doze fitfully until after dawn. He sensed the newcomer in his room and concentrated on keeping calm. He felt the jiggling on his bed and opened his eyes. It was the gnomish hunchback, Moses Callion, the third by that name and the second he'd known. All were misshapen, more dwarves than midgets, equally gifted and probably the same person – cloned once, now twice.

The first Callion had been associated with the Godling Guild, of which the real Schmidt's father had been a member. That one, quite elderly by then, died early in the war. The second Callion, the Monster Maker, the truly dangerous one, was intimately involved with the Supranormal Defense League of the Fifties. In a perverse way that was highly ironic.

Moe Two was as much an orthodox Jew as Moe One and the SDL proved a front for The Rache, a gaggle of unrepentant Nazis intent upon revenge for Hitler's defeat and still holding to *der Fuhrer's* faith in *'ubermensch'*, the superiority of the Aryan race, white supremacy, and concomitant antisemitism.

That Callion survived Ryne's supranormal version of a pogrom and, in the Sixties, became a member of the Worldwide Order. He'd been killed in 1970 when AMERICA, Schmidt included, overran WORLD's operational headquarters in Hong Kong. This latest Callion showed up five years later and had been working for the Alliance of Man, primarily at the Houston Academy, ever since.

A couple of years later he was joined by none other than Aranyani Nightingale, Loxus Ryne's now forty-seven year old daughter, the one-time wife of Jock's adopted son, OJ Maxwell. She quickly became Moe's closest friend, co-worker, and, some said, lover. Involuntarily Schmidt cringed at the notion. Aran might not be beautiful in any classical sense but she was well held together whereas Moe Three was damn near a walking gargoyle.

Even though they were based in the same building, Johann and Three rarely spoke – for very good reasons. If he was just another version of Two, they went back a long, terribly dirty way. Too long and too dirty for words, though terrible worked to an inadequate degree. At least polite ones; those of common conversation.

"Thank God you're here, Schmidt," whispered Callion. "Thank God someone's here. The Academy's being taken over. They're destroying all my experiments. All my work."

Doubleman raised himself onto his elbows. "Who? When?"

"Right now. Stinking albinos!"

"Glomen? WORLD?"

"How the hell should I know? I arrived about an hour ago and let myself in. I was down in my lab when I saw them coming on the monitor. After all that's been going on, I wasn't about to wait to see what they were up to. Lit out the back exit and came up here. Your office was the only one open. Where's your phone? I'm calling the cops."

Within fifteen minutes the entire complex was not only surrounded, there was a police helicopter overhead. Cops were everywhere but there wasn't an albino to be found. Callion was right about one thing, though. The laboratory he shared with Dr Nightingale had been ransacked. It was Schmidt who spotted the bomb. Evacuation was immediate.

Turned out there was not one bomb but many. When the explosions finally subsided and firemen were mopping up the ruins, it was clear the damage was very deliberately confined to the basement workrooms of Moses Callion III and Aranyani Nightingale. Whatever they were working on, it was back to Square One.

Actually, considering what they were working on – cloning supranormals out of cells Moe Two acquired a minimum of a quarter century earlier – there was no square one to go back to anymore. Predominantly that was because there no more supras; not that Moe Three was aware of anyhow.

Which wasn't saying much, Schmidt reflected, given what was going on upstairs, way upstairs, on the Moon.

========

Shortly after dawn Saturday, Tokyo Time, street rioting began throughout Japan. Word leaking out of China indicated the riots were spreading westward. With the rising sun, aka the heliosphere.

========

It was past noon, still Friday in Houston. After the disaster at the Academy, Doubleman stayed with Moe Three throughout the tedious questioning by police and fire investigators. To his credit, Callion stuck to his story; the one he gave Schmidt, which suggested to not just Doubleman that he was fudging the truth only minimally.

He had come to work early to catch up on some pressing research, spotted the albinos, a half dozen or so, on the TV screen and skedaddled out the back way. He found Schmidt sleeping in his office upstairs and thereupon called the police. No, generally the Academy didn't employ internal night security. The electronic gadgets throughout the building were always sufficient in the past.

No, he had no idea how they breached the state of the art security system. Possibly they had keys, like he and Schmidt did; possibly the janitors just forgot to turn it on when they locked up for the night. No, he had no idea why a clandestine demolition squad targeted his lab. The Academy's board of governors authorized everything he did. Pretty much had to didn't they; they paid for it. But, no again, sorry, he couldn't be more specific about his projects; not without the Academy's approval.

Maybe they were terrorists. He was a Jew and Loxus Ryne, the Academy's main moneybags, had acquired colostomy bags of enemies over his eighty years; at least sixty of which were spent in the public spotlight. And no yet another time, he didn't know where Dr Nightingale was. She'd left suddenly, Wednesday afternoon, and he hadn't heard from her since.

The police were no more satisfied than Doubleman but they allowed Callion to go with him to the nearby Space Centre, where security wasn't just electronic.

Once alone with the hunch-backed gnome, Schmidt tried to get hold of Ryne on Centauri Island. Got through as well; so much for the island being unreachable.

He was told the patriarch was busy at present but if it was important Adolph Dulles, Barb born Black's little Hitler, as he and Sean called the comparatively young man, was available to pass on a message. This was too good an opportunity to miss. Put him, said Schmidt, and they did.

He went over the bombing of the lab, whereupon Dolph dropped a bomb of his own. Countess Ramona Avar, Count Viper's daughter and the odds-on favourite for being Strife, wasn't dead after all. It was faked. Worse, also thanks mostly to Erech Ryne, her son by the Great Man, Ray was on her way there, to Houston, for a cure. And guess who was going to cure her, albeit obviously not in her destroyed lab anymore?

As they spoke, Schmidt did more than absorb the disturbing news of, possibly, Strife's return. He tried to forge a mental link with his *'psychic nephew'*. There was an awkward silence on both ends of the line. Doubleman caught a seemingly errant series of thoughts: *'Supras ... Devil-ray ... Crimefighters Alive ... Little Girl ... Trickster ... Ryne Still Wants Signallers.'* Finally came a chilling thought: *'Albinos Here Too!'*

Then Dulles, sounding a bit bewildered, said aloud: "Bad nudes, but I can't disturb the old man. He's up to his ear-holes with space debris. And I mean that in small case as well as capital letters. The Express was destroyed. I've placed the island under the equivalent of martial law and from what I understand things are very dicey up in the UNES Liberty.

"Best advice is to double security at Groundbase Houston. And, just to be on the safe side, have someone check on the rest of Mr Ryne's family. Their itineraries will be somewhere nearby. Like I said, Erech's in Budapest, or on his way back by now, but who knows about the Tempest Twins or the others. Get back to us when you have something definite. Sorry I can't be of more help. We're relying on you, Doubleman."

"I'll do my best." Johann broke off the connection and went into a private conference with Immanuel Dark.

The Great Man's not quite sixty year old, wheelchair-bound Number Two at SPACE had once been intimately connected to the supranormal codenamed Mr Brilliant. He, in turn, had been more traditionally intimate with one of most powerful supras ever to live, Radiant Rider, aka Gloriella D'Angelo. Intimate, at least at first, if rape counts as intimacy, that is. In the absence of confirmation to the contrary, intimate like married couples thereafter, it presumably went without saying.

Codename Brilliant – Brill Brit was his nickname – and Rainbow, as Gloriel was also known, had a daughter, Estrella Dark. Star had once been close to Dolph Dulles, who was almost exactly the same age as her — she having been conceived on or about the Autumnal Equinox of 1952; he a season later. Which compounded the weirdness since that meant, albeit only after a fashion, they were cousins.

To compound it even further, secret annals of the time asserted that Mr Brilliant was not Doc Dark's evil alter ego. On the contrary, one displaced the other.

In other words, they were two separate entities. Furthermore, at least as far as he, Doubleman, understood it anyhow, Brilliant was neither a supranormal nor, technically speaking, even a human being.

What that made him, Johann had never quite figured out. His rational mind rebelled at the notion that Brilliant was an incarnation of Lucifer primarily because Brilliant had been around for maybe as long as five years before Dark was exposed to St Synne's devil-ray in 1943. Nevertheless, even though Immanuel had been Brilliant-free since '53, Doubleman was still more than just a mite wary of him.

He could not ignore him, though. For one thing, Ryne relied on him. For good reason. Dark was a brilliant man in ways beyond his one-time affinity for Mr Brilliant, whatever he was. He had an incisive mind. Was full of intriguing perspectives. Would make leaps of logic that would never occur to others. Might well have insights Doubleman didn't and he had to have had as many and more pieces than Schmidt did, or could find, in order to put together the puzzle.

"A Crimefighter alert after all these years?" Schmidt had trouble believing his ears but it made as much sense as anything. He'd been thinking of issuing one himself.

"Oh, they've always been out there," Immanuel shrugged as if it was self-evident. Like Ryne was with Big Shelter, he was as fixated as ever on the King Crimefighters. "My wife's probably been shacked up with Obadiah Power for years and the Witch is undoubtedly running the show by now – along with her boyfriend, Saul Ryne, the Magnificent Psycho."

Glory of the Angels was the one who, in early 1953, eliminated his Brilliant persona, if you could call it that, and left him a cripple; this after his alter ego howsoever accidentally killed her last remaining (not adopted) supra-brother Gabriel (codename Klarion). How the first led to the second was another of those mysteries Schmidt had never quite figured out, but the fact remained that Rainbow took pity on Dark and married him.

That she was already pregnant with Estrella likely had something to do with her decision but, romantic that he was, he still hoped that love and not just Gloriel's Roman Catholicism eventually entered into the equation, at least on her part. It may or may not have in Doc Dark's case; probably the latter.

Always an insecure and jealous man, the British-born theoretical physicist retrospectively hated her almost as much as he professed to love their wild child – and, as Dolph Dulles would no doubt attest, Star Dark was altogether untamed. Yet, to the best of Schmidt's knowledge, Gloriel had never been unfaithful to her husband. She was only a friend of OMP, Old Man Power, who was himself a married man. Albeit unhappily.

Takeda *'Corona'* Power was very much still around; had never gone away, truth told, despite what was diagnosed as incurable cancer a year or two before the King Crimefighters did go away. Of course, without her Crimson Corona, what she sometime called her power focus, the miserable Mrs Power – whose daughter was Crystal St Synne, a long-missing, possible Strife – was no more a supra than Doc Dark was now.

Or Schmidt was either, for that matter. But for his mind link to Smythe, that is. Then again – and here was a thought he couldn't recall having before – that, over two and a half decades later, Corona still had incurable cancer may indicate she yet retained certain, not entirely unheard of, supranormal attributes. An inability to die for example.

As for Wilderwitch and Saul, Dark was hardly the only one who thought her Strife and blamed Psycho for corrupting him such that Brilliant joined the relatively quickly disgraced Supranormal Defense League. Strife, whoever she was, and Psycho likely were onetime lovers, but that was the only grain of feasibility in his embittered, otherwise fanciful rant.

"I've spoken to that disturbing nut-ball the patriarch seems to think is worth cultivating," Immanuel said after confirming that Ryne had requested Strategos, Simon Lancz, send his Signallers to Centauri Island but that System had been unable to oblige him. "You know: Shelter, the fellow, if he is a fellow, Headmistress calls House-Head."

Headmistress was Virginia Mannering. Even though there was an otherwise never identified supra who went by that name in the closing years of the war, at least supposedly it wasn't her. In fact, Ginny was one of the very few Summoning Children who had never manifested any supranormal attributes. Any recorded ones anyhow.

Ms Mannering earned the name two ways. Firstly, because she was the overall head teacher at the various Academies of Man and, secondly, because she was the chief mistress of the Academies' head for as long as there were Academies of Man. Since before there were Academies, according to some old-timers.

Through four marriages, all of them ending tragically, Loxus Ryne never stopped loving her; loving her in all senses of the word. That they never married might have been because Ginny was reputedly infertile. More than likely, though, it was due to the fact that she was a Lovely Lady Afrite, a love-loving witch sisterhood that scandalized even witches from most of the other sisterhoods, Korants especially.

The Great Man was therefore hardly her only man; given his cold-hearted, no-nonsense reputation, was probably not even her greatest man. That he would have had to share her would not have disturbed him overly much; that he would have been called a cuckold because of it would have. Much better to be her headmaster and she his headmistress.

As for Shelter and why Ginny called him House-Head, that was self-evident. All Signallers, when wearing their Silver, were supposed to have on their headpieces. Some, like Strategos, Simon Lancz, didn't always bother. Which, besides the fact that he liked being famous, was why his identity was known.

A few others weren't as careful as they should be. Which was why they weren't as anonymous as they should be, either. Not to nosey parkers like Johann Schmidt. Shelter, though, seemed never to be out of his Silver; was never seen without his helmet on; was therefore a complete mystery man. Make that complete mystery being.

Needless to say, his helmet was shaped like a house: with windows for eye sockets, a doorway for a mouth, a balcony for a nose, a porch for a beard and so on. Hence also his codename, which did not sound too macho. In fact, there were some who claimed that, under his silver, Shelter was a woman.

A very mysterious being then but, be that as it may – all Signallers could have been either sex and, when wearing their headpieces, always spoke with a synthetic, neutral voice – you didn't need to be a psychiatrist to agree with Dark's assessment of his or her sanity. Everything about the Signaller bespoke the notion that she or he was, to say the least, an eccentric.

"Shelter doesn't say much," Dark told Schmidt. "But he's tight with that other forever-helmeted mystery man, Sharpshooter, who's supposed to be one of Signal System's chief designers but I reckon is their chief assassin. Anyhow, Shelter hinted that System has its hands full in Vancouver."

"Hinted?"

"It was enough for me."

"So you issued a Crimefighter alert. Before or after you talked to the patriarch?"

"What do you want me to say? In the Great Man's absence I have complete authority when it comes to SPACE; indeed when it comes to Alliance affairs."

"Name's Johann, doc. Not yoyo, as in imbecile. Not *'you're only young once'* either, as Abe Ryne might have it."

"Very well. My daughter's there right now, so is Lancz's Sapphire, and so are a lot more Silvers than just Shooter and a couple of his compadres."

"Just as their names always begin with an *'S'* or an S-sound," perceived Doubleman. "Silvers always travel in S-numbers — six, seven, sixteen and so on. How many more?"

"Like I said ..."

"Signallers being in Vancouver was enough for you."

"I'm flying there tomorrow morning myself."

"Ah!"

"You know where you can insert that *'Ah!'*, Schmidt. A Crimefighters alert is standard procedure in such cases is all. Been that way since you also bloody know when; the day Trebleman became Doubleman."

"The D'Angelos' five year reunion."

"If they're going to come back ..."

"When else?"

"Just so."

"So maybe I am Yoyo Johann after all. I was with Jock Maxwell last night. Just never made the connection."

"Papa Rafe and Mama Sofa notwithstanding, yoyo; them calling themselves the Society of Saints during the war equally so; *'of the angels'*, even if D'Angelo more like means *'of an angel'*, singular, can also mean of the fallen angels."

"Touché, doc. I guess. Mama Sofa's father did call himself Satan instead of Sedon during the Second World War; hence the devil-ray, I suppose. Wonder how many heart attacks it'd cause if – if you're right about the Crimefighters being back in action – Rainbow, Air or Sea suddenly popped in for a visit after twenty-five years?"

"Oh, I'm right all right but, whatever else she is, Gloriel would never be that callous. Aires and Thalassa are a different matter, not to mention Psycho or the Witch."

"Or Leandro, after thirty-five years."

"Come again?"

"Never mind."

========

Not having time for a long conversation, Doubleman Johann Schmidt relayed sort-of-nephew Adolph Dulles' spoken words, though not his thoughts, and issued Immanuel Dark some instructions – recommendations, make that – of his own. They included a warning about what Erech Ryne was up to in Budapest. Curiously, at least so it seemed to Schmidt, Dark already knew about the phony death story and deliberate misdirection regarding Ramona.

Even though Johann did not have any authority at Groundbase Houston specifically, nor with the SPACE Council even more specifically, he was a trusted figure in general; one known to be close to Headmaster Ryne. Which was really all that mattered to Dark. His recommendations would be heeded.

Besides, Immanuel thought they made sense. No question Ryne's other children might be in danger. Equally so, there was no question that the youngest two were currently in the care of Headmistress Mannering. Ginny may or nor be a D'Angelo, fallen or otherwise, but, even if she never was a supra either, she was a practising witch. Now there was someone worth taking to, said Dark as they were also saying their goodbyes.

Doubleman refrained from stating the obvious: that, even at the age of sixty, Ginny was worth a visit for lot more than just talking.

Lovely Ladies always were!

========

Taking his leave, Schmidt made some phone calls then returned to Moe III.

========

"What in God's name were you and Nightingale up to that WORLD and the Global Menace, assuming it was them, felt obligated to obliterate?"

"I told you. I came to work early."

"I know what you told the police and admire your restraint, particularly when it comes to the Little Prince's human bombs. If they knew there were a bunch of potential fall-down, go-boom guys wandering around Houston this minute, we'd never have got away from them. Now answer my question!"

"I don't think I should, but I'll tell you one thing. I don't think they were Glomen."

"Why not? They were albinos. Too much of that shit Glomen swallow when they go on assignment drains pigment out of the skin and colour out of the hair. That makes them albinos. Known fact, that. If they don't get the antidote in time, they blow. That makes them double-dog-dangerous. Spill it, Moe, or I'll find some of Ryne's pros around here to extract the information."

"All right. We, that is Dr Nightingale and I, had a commission. For WORLD, if you must know."

"You work for the Order? After what happened to your so-called father ten years ago?"

"That has nothing to do with it. Aran and I are independent contractors. Specialists. They wanted us to clone and rapidly accelerate four of their higher-ups. Don't ask me why. They paid big bucks and our research is too costly for even the Alliance to afford all by itself. It seemed a harmless enough assignment."

"Nothing's harmless when it comes to WORLD."

"But it wasn't WORLD. Can't be. Alorstro Sian came to see me Wednesday afternoon."

"Wait a minute. Sian's in Houston? Dr Cyanide, the old Worldwide Order's Mafia connection?"

"The same. Though I imagine the money would have come from Shaikh Markazi, not the Mafia. The Shaikh doesn't grease palms, he oils them. But Sian's our contact with the Order. He wanted to see Aran but she'd just left. Said he'd wait. Seemed to be under a lot of stress." So did Callion but he didn't show it so much as Schmidt felt it.

"He hung around until after six then went away for a while. Then, about an hour later, he came back, his usual charming self again."

"Just as there are snake charmers, there are charming snakes."

"Just so," Callion agreed. "He must have received further instructions and gave me another commission."

"Do tell."

"As it happened – purely by coincidence, I think – Aran and I'd been working on an identical project. Just that day we'd had a major league setback. I thought we could still salvage some of it, though."

"Why doesn't that surprise me?"

"He helped me set things up again but without Aran around there wasn't much more we could do. He took me out to supper then home. I kept working on it yesterday and the rest you know."

"You still haven't told me what your project was. Just who were you trying to clone?"

"What does it matter? It's destroyed now. Our whole DNA bank's up in smoke."

"I'm no expert but can't you go back to the donor and get more. Even if he's dead and buried, you can still clip enough material to make a clone, can't you?"

"Not if the person didn't bother leaving his body around to be exhumed."

"I don't like the sounds of that but I'm willing to give you the benefit of the doubt. So maybe it wasn't WORLD. Albinos still mean Global Menace to me. Maybe the Little Prince, Greygreave Translav, has taken his services elsewhere. Maybe it's the Soviets; though, given Translav's claim to be the rightful Czar, that isn't too likely."

"I don't believe it was Translav either. You see, the clones we made for WORLD included one of the Little Prince."

"Christ!"

"Not yet," chortled Callion in that ghastly, Quasimodo-like way of his.

"Very funny. What else?"

"From what I saw on the monitor they were big guys. Didn't look sickly let alone radioactive. I doubt there was a death wish among them. Not unless it was on the giving end, not the receiving end, if you get my drift. You saw the disaster they made of my lab but the upper floors were barely damaged."

"Yeah, I wondered about that."

"You did? Amazing. Didn't think you had an original notion in your head."

"One of the cops mentioned it, if you must know."

"That explains that then," Callion chuckled again in that annoying, gap-toothed way he had when he was right and you were stupid.

"It smacks of trained professionals is what I'm saying; guys who work out when they aren't working out how to kill you. Glomen are amateurs, generally speaking; terminally ill amateurs. They act as spies and even assassins in order to guarantee their wives and children better lives after they're gone."

"Matches what I know about them but that doesn't mean Translav hasn't changed his policies in the last ten years. Or decided one clone of himself was enough. Besides, he's getting on. We all are. Not many of us left from the war years or the Fifties' aftermath anymore."

"Present company excluded," grinned the gnome.

"The point is, the Little Prince could be losing it. Then again, someone else might have got hold of the formula. It wasn't his to begin with and we both know there's still one Avar left; one who's apparently on her way here to be cured by, well, I'm looking at him, aren't I."

"What if I told you Aran and I were trying to make copies of supranormals? Heavy duty ones like the King and Queen Conquerors, the Crimefighters, even Mnemosyne D'Angelo and Agenor Heliopolis?" Trying not to inadvertently give away what Smythe had told him, Johann whistled softly. "And what if I told you Loxus Ryne knew all about this and, through SPACE, funded our work?"

"Why would Ryne fund your work? He went out of his way to eliminate the last of the supras twenty-five years ago." He could have added that among the eleven killed on Damnation Island were two of Abe Ryne's own children, his former bodyguard, three D'Angelos, and, in Obadiah Melvin Power, his sometimes exceedingly eccentric front man for propagation of the Illuminated Faith of Xuthros Hor.

"That'd be a rhetorical question."

"Would, indeed. The answer's simple. He'd do anything to get a force together capable of challenging whatever's on the Moon."

"But what if there's more to it?" Moe Three proposed equally rhetorically. He might not have been around during the Supra Wars but, with a mind as devious as his, he'd have fit right in. "How about if I told you that someone else found out what we're doing and that someone already had his own supras?"

"Or doesn't need them because they're supras themselves."

"Either way Ryne doesn't have supras yet. I mean, we've only been at this for three years, Aran and I; our work's quite literally still in its infancy. What does this other guy do? Pre-emptive strike, of course. There goes Ryne's last shot at resurrecting supranormals any time soon."

"You're saying this other guy wants supras exclusively for himself. Blows up the Express because he knows it's full of potential meta-functional men and women then takes out your lab."

"Meta-functional?"

"It's the current double-speak, Callion."

"Is it really? Guess a Doubleman would know."

"Guess he would. So, it might be whatever's upstairs; might just as easily be someone who doesn't want supras around at all. Why couldn't it be Signal System?"

"Don't complicate things more than they already are," criticized the hunchback. "Look, I've thought this out carefully. First of all, let me tell you where I think the albinos came from. They're mercenaries from Centauri Island." From what he'd retrieved from Dulles, Schmidt already knew there were albinos there. Had been before as well. In '65, his research as well as, to a much lesser degree, his memory indicated. But he wasn't about to tell Callion that.

"You think the Fatman's behind this attack?"

"I'm not saying Alfredo Sentalli sent them, though I doubt anything goes on there without him knowing. What I'm saying is that there's no question in my mind the albinos came from there. You see, two of Sentalli's supras came here yesterday, just before Aran left and Sian showed up."

"Now we're getting somewhere. Who were they? Recognize them?"

"Claimed they were Romaine Kinesis and OJ Maxwell. Except, they could do things the professor and Big Max never could before. Not even in their wildest dreams."

"What?"

"Wrecked one of my projects, the same one I tried to salvage for Sian. Probably realized it was salvageable as well but, by then, they had more pressing business in Florida. Did you know NASA's Space Shuttle project is a go already?" Schmidt did. Its acceleration was one of the tradeoffs rather than by-products of NCE being allowed to build the Liberty in the USSR. He didn't see the relevance of the question, though.

"I'll try that again. Not what did they do. What could they do that made them supras?"

Callion told him, whereupon he finished his initial train of thought. "So they sent their albino cohorts to do in the rest of my place. Succeeded as well, it seems."

"And you told me not to complicate things further."

Doubleman's stock and trade was espionage, intelligence-gathering, recruitment and training. He was too old to be in the field, hadn't owned a gun since AMERICA put paid to 1970's WORLD, and was already planning his retirement. Fat chance of that; fat as in the Fatman chance of that.

First Ringleader, then Helios on the Moon, and now Kinesis – the Gypsium Triumvirate Ryne was always so afraid of – coming together. Add to that talk of Ray dying then not dying; the Crimefighters, the female trickster, Psycho and Strife back in action; Maxwell going supra; and a second generation Amoebaman who might be a new Prime thrown in for good measure.

This wasn't just a recipe for Armageddon. All the ingredients not only were in it, but the pot was already well and truly boiling. Schmidt despaired of anyone being able to keep the lid on it. And by far and way the worse thing about Callion's assertions was that he was probably right about Centauri Island.

Even though he knew it only second-hand from Maxwell and Smythe, that was where he had been the only other time he was apparently around a large number of big, fit, professional soldiers, ones who were mostly foul-smelling albinos and liked to blow things up.

(1965 and in the thrall of a Crimson Corona – not Corona Power but a Gynosphinx facsimile of her – had not been the proudest moment of his life. If it hadn't been for Big Max, however, it would have been a particularly inglorious death. All of which meant he viewed the island worthy of his attention.)

"This is getting real crazy," he said aloud, not caring if Callion or anyone else heard him. Both Cerebrus and Psycho were mind-readers.

"Crazy is as crazies do," offered the gnome.

"Profound as hell, Three. But you're right. The Cosmic Express fragments but leaves no wreckage, Erech Ryne flies off to Budapest because his mother, a known Strife is dying, only she isn't, not immediately, a new WORLD, your made-to-order clones, Max and Kinesis suddenly supras."

"Aran vanishing," contributed Moe.

"Centauri Island goes offline for twenty-four hours; no explanation offered," Doubleman carried on. "Aremar and Starrus, who might be the twin sons of Emperor Energy and the supra Headmistress, two of the mightiest supras ever seen in action, hook up on the Liberty; a huge structure that no one noticed before shows up on the Moon; riots in the Far East. I don't see how but somehow it all has to fit together."

"Better than World War Three, I suppose."

"Know what's even more terrifying, Callion? Maybe none of them are crazies."

"Crazy or sane, that's the truly terrifying thing."

"Huh?"

"The plural."

========

It had to fit even tighter a half hour later. In an undamaged section of what was left of the Houston Academy, another of SPACE's seemingly ubiquitous, too smart for his taste, young technicians brought Schmidt the results he'd been waiting for since he left Death Valley the night before.

That proved that, then. Amos Annulis was Aristotle Zeross. Unless, that is, Harry had taken to lending out his rings.

========

Location tracers secreted in the shipment of Splatter Packs he and Jockey had signed over showed that the plane had refuelled in Florida. He asked where. The tech told him that, too: Same airport as the supra-versions of Kinesis and Maxwell would have touched down before they were transferred to Cape Canaveral.

Coincidence, sir? Maybe. He'd have to look into the timeframe more close-ly. After that the plane flew over the Atlantic. Whereupon it disappeared over, where else – *'wait for it, sir'* – the Bermuda Triangle. Johann groaned, as if on cue. It was all so apropos. "But," added the smart, "And this seems impossible, we picked up the tracers hours ago."

"Hours? I should have been notified instantly!"

"Sorry, sir. But we figured our instruments had to be faulty. Still do, to tell you the truth, but that's why I tracked you down. Don't ask me to explain it but the plane seems to have reappeared somewhere in the mid-Pacific. Coordinates are more than a little askew but the closest landform we could place it near is ..."

"Oh, no!"

"Centauri Island!"

========

"What the flying fuck!" swore Mugwump, hours ago.

*A huge transport plane careered out of the sky. No, a glowing hole in the sky! It nosedived. There was nothing he nor anyone else could do except stand still, gawk and very probably die. The hotel was history, maybe so was the is-land. Then it vanished. Into a glowing hole either in the ground or just above it. Was that his patrol partner Marsh exhaling or did it just go ...**Poof!**?!*

****

NUKE 19: **Heading for Trouble**

========

Thursday, December 4, 1980

Cromwell Necator barged in on the Fatman, Hiyati Samarand and some of the other Untouchables in the oriental overseer's downside workroom.

All had only two eyes showing.

========

"Everything's set in Houston. We'll take out Nightingale's lab in the morning. I'll have men in Big Sur within a couple of hours but I can't see much hope of getting to the Tempest Twins at the foot of the Baja or tracking down Erech Ryne. We just don't have the bodies. Why do you want the old man's family followed anyhow?"

(Jade Tempest, male and female, were the stage names for Jane and James Plantagenet-Ryne, the Great Man's twins by Barbara *'Thorns'* nee Plantagenet. Daredevils by both trade and inclination – as well as lifelong bedmates by incestuous deviance – they were born in late 1950.

(The Conquering Christ revealed he was Jesus Mandam at their christening. About to give birth in June of 1953, their mother killed herself. Many believed Saul Ryne, her undercover lover – ha, ha – and coincidental step-son, long distance coerced her into it. And maybe he did, albeit on instructions from the selfsame Conqueror, whom Saul damn near worshipped.)

"To ensure Mr Ryne's continued cooperation, Mr Necator," said his Enormity. (Homo or otherwise, Necator knew him best as Alpha Centauri, not Alfredo Sentalli.) "I know he somehow squeezed a message out to Immanuel Dark on Monday. Probably to activate some of the Academy's closet supras and send them here. Same thing with Signal System.

"I want those instructions rescinded. For the next few days, we can't afford to draw any more attention to ourselves than we already have. Back in WWII, Donar Lancz got hold of a young Saul Ryne in order to keep Ryne out of the war effort on the Allies side. Worked too, from what I heard. And what works once …" He let his sentence trail off. Necator caught the drift.

"I suppose we could hire someone to fly to La Paz."

(Jane and James *'Jade Tempest'* Ryne lived near Cabo San Lucas, where the Pacific Ocean roared into the Cortes Sea, aka the Gulf of California. Megan and Pauline, Ryne's twelve year old twins by the late Oriani nee Zeross, more like stayed than lived with Headmistress Virginia Mannering at her ranch, which lay in almost a direct line far to Cabo's north, in Big Sur, California.)

"We'd rather keep this strictly Headworld business, protector," said Samarand. "Your men must not be detected."

"My men were handpicked by my father. They're the best he could spare in New Valhalla. We've been training for months and not one of them shirked at becoming a Gloman. Like I told you before, or told someone before, you lose your edge when you can just get up again after being shot down."

"And fear of being blown to smithereens keeps you on your toes," confirmed Connie Lindquist, whose natural father once reckoned he held the patent on Gloman technology. And he did, until she stole it for Necator's father, whose name was Godfrey. (That was the name on his tombstone, too. Not that there was anyone, least of all Godfrey Necator, in the grave.) "We got that message."

"That may be true for your men here," George Hannibal said. "But the ones you're using stateside aren't."

"And Mexico's a foreign country," added Roderick Paraja. "We don't need any further complications."

Centauri concurred. "The business in Houston will be on the newsreels. We'll make sure Ryne sees it. Get us some pictures of the two Zeross girls, preferably with Headmistress. What can be shot with a camera can be shot just as easily with a gun. If he doesn't realize it already, it will serve notice that I am deadly serious about maintaining control of my island.

"Ryne's a tough and resourceful old bastard, though. He'll probably continue to connive away – which is why I believe we should take charge of his babies."

"Why don't we just kill him?"

"This is one of the most important men on the Outer Earth, Cromwell," objected Samarand. "Whole nations, including ones with atomics, are beholding to him. Through the UN's Space Council, he is attempting to deal with the menace on the Moon; a menace which was probably responsible for what happened to the Express and therefore threatens the Inner Earth as well as everywhere else."

"You were brought out here for two reasons, sir," said his Enormity. "Number one is to prevent Ryne's people from running roughshod over us and perhaps discovering the Nag Gap. Number two is to add muscle and experience in order to defend us against the external threat to our sovereignty, if I dare use such a term in what technically is still the United States. Independence might be better.

"Demios told me some interesting things about this new Order, for that's what it is. They wanted this island fifteen years ago and undoubtedly still covet it. He also saw Saul Ryne, the Magnificent Psycho, which means supras, and thinks he saw Steltsar, which means mandroids. You are outfitted to handle the latter if not the former, though you should be able to handle most of them as well. This island is a fortress. Do your duty. Hold it!"

"I haven't the numbers or weaponry to do that, Mr Centauri. Not for long. If we are hit with a full scale invasion, be it of the conventional variety, by deviants, mandroids, or a combination thereof, we either retreat to the Head and seal the portal or we'll have to bring out the Godbadian Army."

"Neither is an option," discounted Samarand. "The Nag must remain open and no more non-Glomen are going to come out here. With my concurrence, Mr Centauri has already directed all my insiders back to the Head. Other than your men and the twelve of us, no one can be captured who can reveal anything about a hidden continent.

"Your men will blow and we will die before we're taken. That's the long and the short of it; one size, as they say, fits all. There are other matters at hand which are of no interest to you. I firmly believe this is a very short term situation. I shall inform you when you can withdraw."

When Necator left them, the Untouchables relaxed, let their true forms stand revealed. Even the Fatman had three eyes – whereas Connie Lindquist was all eyes.

"I have been in contact with Father Byron, albeit through Spellbinder, his usual conduit," said Damon Goldenrod. Along with APM (Aphropsyche Morningstar), the devil seemingly composed entirely of eyes, he was the eldest there. "He and the other two found Wind this morning. He's in very bad shape. I urged father to bring him back here at once but he has other priorities."

(The other two were Chimaera Glimmenmare, Byron's ever-changing Stallion, and the afore-referred-to Spellbinder, Smoky Sedona. Together with Devil Wind, whom Illuminaries named Vayu Maelstrom instead of *'Hurican'* for their own perverse reasons, they made up the entirety of Byron's second-born threesome. They were also the Great God's Primary Nucleoids; in other words, his chief enforcement officers.)

"To my mind astonishingly, he has been in contact with the deviant known as Cyborg Cerebrus, the son of none other than our reluctant guest, the Horrites' patriarch, and the twin of this Psycho the Trinondev spoke about to the Fatman. Apparently father is considering an offer of an alliance from the younger Ryne and his fellow supranormals in something they've ludicrously deemed the Damnation Brigade.

"From Wind he has determined they are extremely powerful. They humiliated the Whirling One last Sedonda on Damnation Isle then proceeded to vanquish the Primary Apocalyptics and a couple of their cronies. Rather too easily, father feels. Yesterday two of them, Blind Sundown and Raven's Head – a mutated ravendoe, as you might gather from her name – returned to the island and thoroughly humiliated Maelstrom yet again.

"As if that wasn't bad enough, another member of this D-Brig of theirs showed up about the same time. She answers to Wilderwitch. An unnatural Anthean if there was one, some of you might recall her from the Forties as Queen Scylla's younger sister via the Dual Entities. Demonstrating knowledge no mortal should have, the Witch promptly chopped off his head and buried it a thousand miles away from Damnation, where she left his body."

(Queen Scylla was Fisherwoman. Her given name was Scylla Nereid. After she and her husband, ex-King Achigan Auranja, were deposed, she became Lady Achigan.)

"An alliance?" gasped Pretty Parsis. "With outsiders who can stop Wind, take out the Apocalyptics, and know how to kill devils?"

It was question that needed asking but even Yati (Byron's Dragon) and the brood-older third-born there, Byron's Apollo and APM All-Eyes, weren't much help when it came to answering it. Much discussion ensued. Talk eventually drifted to who in there they reckoned most responsible not so much for the destruction of the Cosmic Express as its insertion into the Sedon Sphere and the jailbreak that resulted.

"Neither would Divine Coueranna," Elephantine Ganesh was saying. "She's the real ruler of Apple Isle, even if it's from her volcano. If it wasn't for the fact that Lord Yajur and some other Lazareme Spawn are loose, as are some of our naughtier siblings, I'd say it was the Thanatoids. As it stands, I don't know who to blame."

Pretty Parsis wasn't so blasé. "Don't be so trunk-tied, Merchant. You may be the Lord of Obstacles but it shouldn't prevent you from thinking. Sarpedon seeing Steltsar's all the clue I need. Mandroids mean Lemurians. Lemurians mean Queen Amphitrite and her sometimes lookalike buddy, Lady Achigan, this reborn Witch's older sister in the Entities.

"I don't believe there's any way through the Dome for devils besides the Nag – unless the SAG Gap is wandering again, which it shouldn't be this early in the decade. But Steltsar was connected to All of Incain and big brotherly Beast, Rudra Silvercloud, saw the Thanatoids on the Prison Beach a couple of days ago."

(The Silverclouds were Byron's surviving firstborn. Their immediate sister, Serathrone Hallow, never made it to the Whole Earth. Rufous Rudra was called the Beast of Byron. He was also called Savage Storm. His brood sister, Umashakti, was Byron's Moon, his mistress of Gravity. Like Tau Hanuman, who occupied the Patrick Monk homunculus, both were named after Hindu gods – the bygone Illuminaries of Weir who gave them names, instead of going by their attributes, were nothing if not inconsistent.)

"Master Devas and Lemurians are an unholy alliance," Yati granted, "But it's not without precedent. King Cold and the Scarlet Sorceress are Mithradite firstborn. They're so powerful they almost took over the entire Headworld, save our Godbad, twelve hundred years ago. Plus, they're desperate to get their children back. They could care less what horrors they unleash on the rest of us so long as that happens. Got to be them."

"We'll get to bottom of it eventually," supposed Headcase Hektoris. He reverted to Sentalli-Centauri and let his Enormity speak in his own, how so much so *borrowed* voice.

"For now we keep the portal open. Professor Kinesis did leave us with the Gypsium Curtain, recall. It can be raised as required; though what'll happen then, who knows? If it means having to reveal yourselves in order to fight off whatever comes at us, so be it. OJ Maxwell thought I had a devil-ray and, even if it'll be a complete fabrication, it's beginning to look like I'll have to own up.

"Cromwell Necator was right about one thing. He can't hold the fort for long."

"We may have to get our hands dirty," agreed Samarand. "But if it comes to that, remember Grandfather Sedon's dictates against killing lesser beings."

"Sage words, Yati," said APM. "But mentioning Lord Lazy's Lord Order reminded me just how effective the Moloch's dictates are. Zilch!"

(Lord Lazy was their uncle, Thrygragos Lazareme, the Hidden Headworld's only other surviving Great God. Lord Order was a firstborn, one of his three Unities, Thunder and Lightning Lord Yajur. They now knew that Yajur had been decathonitized the previous Sunday.)

"Whoever proves to be behind all this is no lesser being, Morningstar." With those words, Goldenrod reverted to his human form. So did the others. Just in time.

They'd sensed a technician in the corridor. He was part of that rare breed of island veterans who wasn't an Untouchable but who'd nevertheless turned out to be one of Necator's men. Was, in other words, a deep-cover fifth columnist; one, embarrassingly unbeknownst to his boss, attached to Samarand's staff for many years.

He knocked then entered when bade do so. Like all of the Protector's protectors, he was strictly a no-nonsense sort. In a testament to his long-service embedding out here, he didn't smell particularly off either. "Sir," he addressed Sentalli directly. "It's the Liberty. The number two guy, Big Max's predecessor Sean Smythe. He's insistent he talk to Mr Ryne straightaway. Shall I patch them through? The Protector says we need one of you around before he can allow that."

His Enormity (Hektoris-Headcase) mentally spoke with Dr Samarand, who shook his head. "Tell him Mr Ryne's indisposed. Ask him if he wants to talk with Mr Dulles," said the devil within the Fatman, careful to speak in Sentalli-Centauri's measured tones. The techno dutifully went away. Keeping his third eye repressed, the boss who wasn't the boss, not in most respects, turned to the underling who was actually the overseer.

"I don't get it, Yati. We've got to let Ryne talk to the Liberty. Otherwise they'll get suspicious and we'll end up with even more unwanted visitors."

"I don't trust the Sedon-cursed Horrite. He's some kind of low-grade deviant. The real Centauri often warned me about this voice of his. Until Necator's men secure his babies, I want to keep him offline as much as possible. You possessed Dulles, Headcase. Dull sort but hard to control, you told me once, but a normal. I want pseudo Centauri there to monitor what he says. You should know if he's trying any tricks.

"Goldenrod, APM, go with him. Bowman, Merchant, stay with the techno. Double-failsafes. No mix-ups, understood?"

As Hannibal and Paraja called for the technician to wait up, Damon Goldenrod (as Yataghan) glared at Samarand. "I am always with Centauri when father occupies him. For appearances sake I will continue guarding the homunculus. But you should remember who is the eldest here, Dragon Lord."

"And you should remember that father put me in charge of Project Centauri more than twenty years ago."

"Come along, Yat," said APM (as Connie Lindquist), slapping him on the back familiarly.

(Not to mention conjugally. On the Inner Earth of Sedon's Head, APM's usual host was Janna St Peche-Montressor, Yataghan's wife and the mother of his only child, the Fatman's lone grandchild, a girl Centauri always called Gudrun even though her given name was actually Chlororain, after her grandmother Emeralda Plantagenet.)

"The golden warrior can put off battling the infernal wyvern of Nether-Neverland for a few more days."

Clearly APM All-Eyes regarded her immediate brother in Byron – both her immediate brothers in Byron, Nevair Neverknight being the other one – in much the same way OJ Maxwell regarded Yataghan Sentalli: as a dimwitted simpleton too full of testosterone to be taken seriously. Except, in part because she was Byron's Venus, and then only when Goldenrod wasn't possessing Yataghan, in bed.

Lovely Lady Afrites were choosy. So was their goddess.

========

Friday, December 5, 1980

Hush came out of not-quite-nowhere to join Loxus Ryne and Adolph Dulles for an early supper Friday evening. She was a little perturbed and said as much. "Hello, daddies. What's up, Dolph? Why did you call me?"

========

Dulles deferred to the patriarch.

"It didn't work, trickster," gloated Ryne, referring to Hush's efforts to have Dulles, on Ryne's behalf, call off Signal System. "Signallers could be here as early as tomorrow afternoon. Even if they aren't, it's all over for you, your sisterhood, Al Sentalli, your devil-ray and his private supras – all over at least down here.

"Heliopolis, who's undoubtedly responsible for the riots crippling big cities everywhere from Australia to Russia, may last a little longer. But Max and the professor will be on the Liberty shortly, if they aren't already. They can't resolve this peacefully, Aremar's going to blast holy hell out of your Man on the Moon's crater."

"Good," said the little girl circumspectly.

She'd had plenty of dealings with Kadmon Heliopolis (whom Headmistress Virginia Mannering nicknamed *'El Draco'*, the Dragon, when he was growing up) and his Spartae (*'Dragon's Teeth'*) prior to Aegean Trigon going the way of Atlantis in 1968. She didn't like any of them much; didn't particularly like Kad's father either.

(She quite liked his tragic mother, Argiope (*'Bright Face'*) born Zeross, who died having him, his consequential half-sister Europa, her children and their grandmother, Europa's mom, Mnemosyne born D'Angelo. She also knew the Male and Female Entities; wasn't too found of them either, though.)

"What do you mean at least down here?"

Dulles took over. "Doubleman Johann Schmidt's been in touch with me. He says Ringleader didn't make it. His plane crashed in the Pacific somewhere just west of us. He and his phony Armenian freedom fighters will be shark feed by now. Schmidt didn't take any chances and blew its cargo anyway. Called in the US military, too. Come tomorrow, or Sunday at the latest, this little island's going to be a Marine version of Club Mediterranean – only they won't be on furlough.

"He told me not even to think about evacuating Centauri. The navy's on patrol, the Air Force is overhead, and the militia's already in place on Maui and all the nearby islands. Anyone comes from here, they'll be interred. They've got a big supply of amnaesthetics and what he called *'splatter packs'*. Said you'd know all about that since you and your sisterhood are in cahoots with Zeross's WORLD."

Hush glared recriminatory needles at Ryne. "Next time you have Dolph summon me, daddy doofus, make sure it's not for a bedtime story."

Dulles winced at her rudeness but Ryne merely smiled. "You hide your emotions well, little one," he put to her, evidently having no idea what *'doofus'* meant. "But you're the one fussing. I know why you wanted us kept down here now. Ringleader was bringing your supras and albino foot soldiers a plane load of heavy-duty ordnance. What were you up to? Use this island as an arms distribution depot, yes, but for what?"

"Never thought you of all people would go buggier than Bugs Bunny. Guess I was mistaken. You're as ditsy as Alois Alzheimer's Aunt Maybe!"

"Reduced to insults now, trickster?"

"When haven't I? A doofus is a twit, not a fuss bucket. And here I thought you were tit for tatting me. You're who's doing the real insulting. Ants wanting splatter packs, whatever they are – grab a brain!" Even Psycho's, she thought but didn't say. "You've obviously lost yours." She didn't give the old man a chance to respond.

"Look, mine was a simple enough request but, in honour of your sad-sack senility, I'll repeat it. Keep to your business and I'll keep to mine – keep the others to theirs, too. One more day was all I really wanted anyhow. You better hope the marines surf over here on tomorrow morning's tide, great patriarch. If they decide to go for a moon-tan on Centauri Island, they're going to get baked blistering badly."

She could have said more and, just before she took herself away, did: "As for you, dull-as-dishwater Dolph, you're lucky I don't deafen you on the spot. Daddy Ryne's an impressive voice, often makes semi-convincing sense, but he's about as aware of what's really going on as an oyster who doesn't clam up at low tide – apologies to Fisherwoman, wherever she is.

"He's about as with it as the rest of his know-it-all, manly know-nothings. Fancies himself an Illuminated Xuthrodite, does our big bad bully boy. Let me tell you, Dolph, if our Anthea's numb-nuts Noah was around today he'd drown himself in the nearest toilet. Out of sheer mortification at having such a whale-dreck pod of poop-heads named after him!"

"Had your piece yet?" snarled Ryne, rising to her bait (also as Hush's just referenced Fish might fishify). "Aren't you going to sign off with your usual codswallop: *'Can't trick a trickster'*? Or are you just going to go home and cry into your teddy beer? Have another soggy night of once was, if only, or what should have been?" (Fishifying, like fay-saying, was contagious.)

"Why don't you go cry in yours, daddy dipstick?" (Hush would have known Ryne wasn't much of a beer drinker but, when trading insults, relevance was irrelevant.) "When I tell Daddy Ring-Blings you think he's all crashed and burned, he'll either shake his head and touch his bobbin noggin in that wavy way of his, or laugh out loud in fright-free delight.

"Not that you'll remember I told you that."

"See, Dulles," said the patriarch after she'd left them. "I told you tricksters are inveterate liars as well as piss poor losers."

The old man hadn't even realized he'd put on Aladdin's ring.

========

The place was Vancouver International Airport, late Friday evening.

"Let's have a cup of tea first." Cyborg Cerebrus (David Ryne), well disguised, pleaded with his bed mate – immediately before Limbo and, after a quarter century as minds separated from their bodies, again the last couple of nights – as she made her way to Customs and Immigration.

Codename: Sea Goddess (Thalassa D'Angelo), wasn't interested. "No point," she refused. "My mind's made up."

========

She waved her first class boarding pass for the late night flight to Los Angeles. "Seeing some of my adoptive family was too much. I've got to get away. Be by myself for awhile. Don't worry, lover. I'll be in touch." Sea-she gave Cerebrus a big hug then turned to her twin brother, Aires (*'Aerialist'*).

"Come with me, Air. I checked. There's an empty seat right beside me. Just for a few days. We've got a lot to talk about. There are some things I want to share with you."

"I don't think so, 'Lassa. I like it right here. Besides, I couldn't live in your underwater palace. I'm no Diver and I hate swimming. Don't worry about me. We're always in touch. If you need me, cry out. I'll come as quickly as I can."

"Better come now."

"Maybe in a few days."

Thalassa gave Cerebrus a nasty glare. *'If you're keeping him away from me, David,'* she thought, knowing full well her boyfriend could never resist reading her, *'I'll never forgive you.'*

'I'm no Saul,' Ryne thought back at her, deliberately denoting disappointment that she could think such a terrible thing of him. *'I was, I'd never forgive myself.'*

========

Thalassa was wrong. The seat next to her wasn't empty.

========

A young man in his early twenties sat beside her. Until the plane took off he chattered inanely, too nervously for her taste; probably a lousy flyer.

She wasn't much better. Just as Air hated swimming, she hated flying, especially on something this size. (The comparatively dinky floatplane the Witch procured for them last Sunday in the Aleutians, and which Aires flew on Monday to Anchorage, was the first time she'd been in the air – in a machine, not riding Raven's Head – in years minus a quarter century.)

She barely paid attention to him. After twenty-five years, there was no possibility they'd met before. Nonetheless something about him was oddly familiar.

Once the plane left the ground, he calmed down; became serious, bordering on alarmingly so given what she now knew OMP (Crimson Corona's estranged husband, Obadiah Melvin *'Old Man'* Power) had been doing in terms of dream-casting, one of his supranormal knacks, since their return. He'd been preparing their surviving loved ones for the reality that they were back, and altogether unaged, after so long.

"Forgive my forwardness," the man finally braved, after studying her closely – far too closely for Sea's sensibilities. (She knew she was drop-pants-gorgeous, as the Diver put it. Even pedestal perfect, except when compared to her adoptive sister, Gloriel, Radiant Rider, that is. But most of the Summoning Children were and right now she was in no mood for admiration, any which way.)

"I had a dream about someone who looked just like you the other night. Any chance you know my parents? My name's Erech Avar-Ryne."

========

An hour or so later, the Byronhead took the eight remaining members of the Damnation Brigade into its mass. It thereupon vanished between-space, quite literally, as well as invisibly, heading west over the Pacific Ocean before turning well south.

The last thing they saw of their newly bought and paid for, but already blazing, homestead was a helicopter landing on the snow-covered barbecue patio.

It was silver.

========

Saturday, December 6, 1980

Vancouver constabulary had the area cordoned off.

========

Given full access behind police lines, sixteen Signallers in body armour and individually distinctive helmets were sifting through the still-smoldering rubble of a large, ranch style house. It was near a private golf course on the west side of Vancouver, in its high-priced but remarkably rural Southlands neighbourhood.

The Fraser River rolled by at the foot of the property as calmly and undisturbed as ever. Yet the main domicile had gone up in flames for no decipherable reason. Even stranger, it looked like something gigantic had smashed in its roof from the outside. Where was the crane, where was the wrecking ball, where was the meteor, where was the horse that, to judge by its leavings, must have been in the barn, and where were the casualties?

No bodies, no witnesses, no clues whatsoever. They'd been at it since midnight and had only come up with more questions.

"Got anything, Spherus?" asked the group leader.

His real name was Gus Soldakis but, when in the Silver, he answered to Space-Age Spartan. His identifying helmet was akin to that of a Greek God or Goddess — Athena perhaps, as she once stood in the Athenian Parthenon or Poseidon, as he did to this day in its National Museum. He was not in a good mood.

"Not much, Spartan." This Signaller's helmet was a silver globe. "Tracings of a lot of Gypsium usage but that would probably be consistent with what we know about the Crimefighters – which is next to zilch. Do you really think it could be them? I know Sapphire claims she saw three of them this evening at the airport. But where have they been for the last quarter century? And how come they haven't aged?"

(Said Sapphire – Saffy or Sappy, as her parents or near-relatives, dependent his or her mood, sometimes called her – had an *'S-name'*. Unusually for a Signaller, even a temporary one, hers was her given name. She had been at YVR, the Vancouver International Airport, across the Fraser River from the city proper, at the time to which Spherus was referring.

(Along with uncle John Paul, a Roman Catholic priest, aunt Anna Maria, and Anna Maria's three children by Bruce Dre'Ath, her cousins Michael, Raphael Jr and Natasha, she was waiting for her now forty-one year old mother Tereza, Strategos Simon Lancz's wife, to fly in from California for the Family D'Angelo's 5-year reunion.

(While they were in the coffee shop, they were approached by an odd individual Sapphire now believed had to have been David *'Cerebrus'* Ryne. He left accompanied by two stunningly gorgeous had-to-be-twins. The woman's hair could have been described as white-capped and the man's cloud-white.

(And it had been, forty odd years ago, at Mama Tereza's christening, the last time they'd had their picture taken with their adoptive parents and siblings.)

"System thinks the Alliance has been keeping them in stasis, possibly in cryonics chambers. As to why they haven't aged, that was a known quality of the Elemental Twins, who *"officially"* – in quotes – disappeared during the War. For the rest, it might have something to do with the fifteen years inactive Anthean Sisterhood. Wilderwitch was a very high level, natural born adept; hence why everyone accounted her a supranormal."

"Nothing at all concrete?"

"Only what fell out of the roof. Hell of a mess. Looks likes a tornado been through here. Neighbours complained about the noise, sounds of a fight or some such. But they're a long way away and the hedges are high. Don't know what collapsed the roof and the fire wasn't anything like a gas line going.

"Tell you what, I'm glad none of us were in there; even in the Silver. Must have been quite something. Think they went at each other?"

"Don't know what to think do I. Gypsium, you say. Any chance it could have been Ringleader?"

"He hasn't been spotted in over three years; not by anyone reputable. But, hey, when it comes to supras, who can say?"

Sapphire came up to them. Because of her age – she'd just turned fifteen – she was only an honorary member of Signal System. However, she had already demonstrated an extraordinary affinity for the artificial agates produced by her supposed father, Strategos Simon Lancz, at his Stanford laboratory. Accordingly, her helmet was a stylized jewel.

"Found an agate."

"Get anything out of it?"

"Na, it was over by the stable. Nothing happened there as near as we can make out."

"Put it back. Wilderwitch teleports on those things. She might decide to pop back for a visit. Mind rigging up one of your bubbles, Spherus?"

"My pleasure. Oh, by the way, Spartan, I wouldn't be certain it's the real Crimefighters. Even back in the Fifties, there were doppelgangers, sphinxes, mandroids and the like. More to the point there were such things as Callion Clones. They'd be grown up by now."

"How would you know?"

"How about I tell you when, and if, we nail one of them?"

"Oh, we'll nail them all right," the voice of Sharpshooter came through their helmets.

Although his was shaped like a shell casing for a high-powered rifle, and therefore should have earned him saucy sobriquets such as *'Bullet-Brain'* or *'Ballistic Balls'*, another Signaller, Nick Stiletto (to give him his S-name), called him *'Shadow-Shooter'*. He did so due to his penchant for staying in the background; not because he was an assassin, though he might have been that, too.

Shoot was a System Seer, one of the dozen or so chief designers behind Signal System. He'd accompanied the other sixteen when they were only six and first arrived in Vancouver, not just to see them through their first mission. He actually enjoyed being in the field. His putative parents did, too, some said. And they, if they were his, in which case they'd been dead since the mid-Forties, were assassins – the Silver Arrow Assassins.

"System knows where they've gone. Hope you brought your suntan lotion because Hawaii's where we're heading; a dinky islet ambitiously called Centauri Island."

========

Even though it was past her bedtime, Hush was on the Head with her Daddy Alpha Star System and the Byronics usually found on said tri-peaked dinkiness.

========

The Great God, his Primary Nucleoids – Vayu Maelstrom, Chimaera Glimmenmare and Sedona Spellbinder – and the Damnation Brigade detectably traversed the Nag Gap shortly after midnight Hawaii time. They didn't stop once they came out the other side. Instead, they carried on north, towards Sedon's Cranium and the subterranean realm of Temporis that lay beneath the top of the Head.

"Godspeed," muttered the island's namesake, who nevertheless wasn't called Alpha Centauri beyond the Dome.

"God has nothing to do with any of this," proclaimed the Golden Warrior, Damon Goldenrod, one of the Great God's two third-born there atop the Fatman's dwelling in Aka Godbad City. "At least not Celestial God. Our duty hasn't changed. We still have to preserve the portal from outsiders and other insiders until he gets back."

"Who cares anymore?" wondered Young Life, whom Byron's Dragon once called the Mannerings' Pandora. "I mean, if you're so damn worried, Damon, seal it!"

For a change APM sided with her brood brother. "Not our decision to make, fairy fart. The Gap is still our only reliable way to the Outer Earth. Father will need it to take the Brigade back out here. Assuming, that is, they manage to drive the Apocalyptics out of the Thousand Caverns and the Nucleus cathonitizes Mother Murder and those she carries again."

APM All-Eyes was no fan of faeries, especially fairy tricksters like Young Life and Young Death. Their daughter Morgianna, then as now the Hellions' Morrigan, wore a pantsuit demon. While it didn't eat her, once, during the latter stages of the Godbadian Civil War, APM possessed Morg, who promptly sneezed, reflexively blew her nose and thereby trapped APM in her handkerchief, which was a Ghast *'Hankering Hankie'*.

For a matter of months thereafter APM was pocketed between-space inside Morg's denim-demon.

========

The riots that started in Tokyo just after dawn on what amounted to yesterday and followed the rising sun around the world had reached New York and were by then breaking out in Los Angeles. By the time Schmidt's plane, with its two hundred man Intervention Team, landed in Pearl Harbour it was already besieged.

By its own men!

****

Nuke 20: **Trigger-Fingers**

========

Saturday, December 6, 1980

They called themselves the Damnation Brigade, the eight supranormals the Byronic Nucleus took up north, to the top of the Hidden Headworld, to Sedon's Bald Spot and they thence below it. Shining Ones might call themselves devils, but were they self-determinedly damned like these supras, who originally numbered 10?

While that may be a matter of debate there wasn't much doubt they didn't dwell in any Christian, Jewish or Muslim Hell; not by that or any other name. Indeed, with riots spreading throughout the external globe, the Hidden Continent of Sedon's Head, what some also called Big Shelter, looked damn good; an earthly paradise even. Centauri Island wasn't doing too badly, either.

In most respects, that is, and some said, knock wooden head. Until some of those there remembered what lurked nearby — Hell's Horsemen.

========

Mindful of what was happening off-island, Angus Skullian joined Hiyati Samarand and some of the others for breakfast at the hotel Saturday morning. All agreed that with Thrygragos Byron and his baggage safely on the Head they could recall Cromwell Necator and his Valhallans.

More contentious was how important it was for them to stay out here. Friday had been a comparatively uneventful day but, as word of the tumult gripping much of the world reached Centauri, there were signs the natives were getting just as restless – which only made them more nervous, the ever-perceptive Dr Hiyati Samarand in particular.

"As you know," he was saying, "One of my most valuable sources for the technology we refined for the Express's carapace in particular was the Lazaremist, Biblio Drek, known to most of us as Librarian. Throughout much of our Age, Drek has been acting as Lazareme's ambassador to Godbad.

"When I mentioned these thought beams coming from the moon, he said they reminded him of the Dual Entities. Some four thousand years ago, on one of their previous sojourns to the Whole Earth, they strongly influenced the so-called Goddess Culture of the Outer Earth's Middle Sea basin.

"According to Librarian, their theory was to discourage the worship of male gods. That made it very difficult for our paternalistically-oriented azuras to possess them. This was during the time when Divine Coueranna, Kore-Concord, was contesting for supremacy with her ex from the Age of Taurus, Thrygragos Varuna Mithras, who was then currently besotted with another Kore, Kore-Discord, his Ewe for Aries.

"Thanks largely to the recurring Attis – Discord's half-son in there, who was first born at the outset of the Goddess Culture's five hundred year dominance out here – and his all-male Aryan armies, that Kore, Kore-Concord, was thwarted at every turn. But they could be trying something similar now. We've known they've been back for five years."

Like cow-faced Vach-Hathor and the seductress, Pretty Parsis, Connie Lindquist – rather, her occupier APM All-Eyes (Aphropsyche Morningstar) – was one of many female Master Devas, from all three tribes, who benefited from not just Myrionymous Kore's long ago efforts to balance azura-loyalty. She shared Samarand's concern.

"Two other things we know. The Memory Entity was based on old Weir's Mother Machine and, as such, built All of Incain on behalf of her staff half, his Maleness. The other is that, as is usually the case when they pop by for a visit, they secreted Trans-Time Trigon in Absudyl, the Subterranean Land of the Mandroids. Regardless of whether they're still there or have somehow transferred Trigon to the Moon, there's nothing we can do about them from here."

Devils stayed away from Absudyl (which was sometimes, though not very often these days, also known as Minius, after the Death's Head Hellion's Chaos co-opted nemesis, Magnus Minus; he of twelve hundred years earlier or thereabouts). Like demons, mandroids could harden them immobile. They were also tenacious. What they got hold of they had no need to let go. Demons, even those spelled with an '*a*', were nowhere near so utterly continent.

Yataghan Sentalli raised Montressor, Damon Goldenrod's shell, sounded another note of dread more so than caution. "If Librarian was right, then those exposed to these thought beams might be primed for rejecting not only authority, which seems to be the point of all these riots, but possession. In other words, should it be the Entities upstairs, they're intent upon denying both we devils and our azuras access to shells."

"And," grasped Djerrid Ruin, still inside Roderick Paraja, "Without shells our azuras are little more than spiritual fluff — insubstantial dust in the wind; any wind, not just Devil Wind blowing off steam after his humiliation up north. If they can't survive in any meaningful way then we'll have no hope of holding onto our adherents, especially out here."

"Where," noted Samarand dispassionately, "Thanks to the prevalence of monotheism, most of us don't have any anyhow."

"True enough," APM agreed. "But I don't necessarily buy into your perennial pessimism, archer. Even never-possessed, sentient beings will worship us if we prove worthy. What is true is that we won't be able to hide inside of humans anymore. We'll have to stand and fight on our own; out in the open, as it were."

"Fine with me," said Djerrid-Paraja. "The Entities are dead simple to deal with. Kill History and Her-Story goes with him, as does Trans-Time Trigon."

Along with the likes of Rudra Silvercloud, the Primary Nucleoids, heroic Hektoris Headcase, Nevair Neverknight and the Golden Warrior, Byron's Bowman enjoyed nothing more than inspiring his followers to go on a bloody rampage – something which had always disturbed their father, who was conciliatory by nature.

It remained to be seen how good he – or any of the other hard-wired, mostly male, machismo sorts amongst them – was at fighting someone mano-a-mano (as in hand-to-hand, though man-to-man howsoever incorrectly worked just as well). Devils weren't allowed to kill lesser beings so it was rare they could even be bothered to fight them themselves. Where was the sport in thrashing weaklings?

Vach-Hathor (Rowena Raymond) being essentially bovine understandably enjoyed bathing in milk and its byproducts much more than blood and related bodily fluids; the kind that spilled forth once proper skin was badly breached. "We may not be able to get to them directly but we've a bilious old goat here who is as anxious as we are to cream them."

"My thoughts exactly, Cow Queen." Samarand turned to Skullian. "You were inside him, Headstrong. What did the Fatman, through his homunculus, mean by '*he'll probably continue to connive away*'; he being the Horrite, Loxus Ryne?" (Devils tended to use Horrite rather than Xuthrodite. They thought it a putdown, along the lines of '*son of a whore*'.)

"Against us and his confinement, I assumed," Hektoris responded. "The patriarch, like Maxwell and Dulles before him, thinks we're victims of Pyrame Silverstar's devaray, though they still think it was a invention of this Satan St Synne of theirs. He also has some notion that his eldest sons and their comrades, whom we now know to call the Damnation Brigade, are intent upon either invading the island or are already here and working in cahoots with Centauri, the Anthean Sisterhood, and the Man on the Moon.

"Ryne's hopelessly ignorant – but I'll say one thing for him. He's dedicated to SPACE. He'll do anything to wipe out the menace upstairs."

"No doubt he would, and more power to him. It'd be nice to help him out. But how?"

"Find a way to befriend him, Yati," suggested the cow-faced devil within Rowena Raymond.

"And reveal what you are?" gagged George Hannibal (Elephantine Ganesh), who wasn't a homo. "What we all are underneath? Not funny, bovine."

Samarand sounded far less outraged. "There are ways to do that without admitting the Head exists. First we have to figure out how he could harm us. Is there anything we've forgotten?"

"Can't think of anything offhand" admitted Skullian, though everyone knew it was Hektoris speaking. "Centauri was right, though. I was in to see Ryne twice yesterday and came away with the same feeling. He's full of piss and vinegar, which no doubt means he's up to something. Could he be in contact with his son, Saul? He wasn't part of the Brigade, according to what we heard from Spellbinder."

"I doubt it," said APM-Lindquist. "Everyone I've been inside of over the years – anyone who knows anything about the Supra Wars, that is – believes Psycho drove Thorns Plantagenet into such a sorry state she committed suicide. Ryne Sr loved his Barbed Rose, though; would never have forgiven sickening Saul for what he did to her. And this regardless of him being equally aware that beloved Barbara had been having it off with psycho-son, possibly for years by then."

(What they didn't suspect – though APM could have enlightened them, had she been so inclined at the time – was that Saul Ryne was acting on cousin Conquering Christ's command. Saul's hero, Jesus Mandam, believed horny as much as thorny Barb was about to give birth to a small-case-sedon and, given what else he was planning, on Salvation Island later on that year, that couldn't be allowed.)

Samarand's chief statistician, Tau Hanuman, he of Bazooka Banana fame (on Centauri Island inside Patrick Monk), had another suggestion. "OJ Maxwell had a list of those with older deviant relatives or forbearers. The ones on the Express were almost all that way but, discarding them for the moment, Dolph Dulles was one of the only other ones. He could be a latent come latter-day patent."

"So," conceived the one-time Dragon Lord of Samarand, "If he is – and Ryne's co-opted him somehow – he could be a fifth-former in your otherwise four column analyses. Just what do we know about him, other than Headcase here found him too headstrong to possess without giving himself a headache?"

Elephantine Ganesh, in Hannibal's form and persona, pulled out his notebook. "Touch and go, that one. Links to Big Max. Considers him his father. Could be, though the real father's unacknowledged; most likely Auld Jock, who sort of adopted Maxwell when he was still Viktor Richter. Born in '53. Worrisome date that, though September, not June. Which would really sound the alarms."

Connie All-Eyes caught the reference. One of her favourite shells on the Inner Earth was Janna St Peche-Montressor, Yataghan's wife and the mother of their only child, a daughter Yat named Chlororain in honour of his mother Emeralda Plantagenet. Janna, though, tended to call her Gudrun. She – Janna, not Gudrun – was born in there on or around the Summer Solstice of 1953 out here; conceivably on same day that Barbara Ryne committed suicide.

"You can't rely on Alliance records; they forged documents all over the world once they started hiding supras back in the late Forties after the advent of amnaesthetics."

"So I gather," The Elephant Man Rom Kinesis once mistook for Babar had done that already, gathered. Not wool, though, and he didn't bristle at the interruption. One didn't bristle at APM. She wasn't always all eyes. Sometimes she made a wonderfully randy elephant – female of course.

"Mother, Barbara nee Black, gave him her married name," Hannibal continued, still referring to his notebook. "Questions about that as well. Her husband was apparently a supranormal. Real name Andrew Dulles, codename Mr Automatic; perhaps significantly, though, he was nicknamed Android."

"More mandroids," grasped Damon-Sentalli (Damon-Centauri, or Montressor, if they were on the inside).

"Except he was killed in 1948," discounted Ganesh-Hannibal. "Five years before Dulles was born. And by Mandasoma Plantagenet, one of your aunts, Yataghan." He closed his pad. "With no evidence to the contrary, we have to consider him a legitimate normal. Tried to read his mind but he's blank to me. So are most of Max's people and some of SPACE's personnel."

"This one isn't any easier to possess than Dulles was," said Hektoris-Skullian. "The patriarch's impossible. I already tried."

"Horrites," reaffirmed Samarand, "Unless the thought beam's already got to him. Think Ryne's figured us out?"

"Only as devaray targets," repeated APM. "Which is why Centauri said we might have to pass for just that, devil-rayed victims of whomever's device, push comes to shoving back. Beyond that, well, father never kept anything from the Fatman. At the risk of criticizing dear old Bodiless Daddy, that exhibits a deplorable lack of reticence.

"It's certainly put Centauri at risk of becoming a bean-spiller. And I don't mean from overeating. Still, he strikes me as genuine when he says no one but us and the rest of our insiders know of the Head. As for why the patriarch's opaque to us – and both Dulles and Skullian are so hard to hold onto – I'd suggest witches. And not just Pandora of the Mannerings, either."

"Sounds plausible," considered Samarand, not overly concerned by the correction. He knew Great Byron sent APM, in a variety of shells, out here more regularly than any of his other siblings. Had done for decades. Not surprisingly — she had a special knack for getting along with people. "The Faithful of Xuthros Hor acknowledge the existence of gods and devils, of demons and monsters, so they're not entirely ignorant."

"Centauri once told me that Ryne believed the heroes of Ancient Mythologies, the ones who fought off the various manifestations of Cruel Plathon and some of the rest of us, were supranormals. That, in fact, supras existed as a counter-force to such infernal deviates – his word, funnily enough. In other words, us."

"We call supras deviants," the monkey-devil in Patrick Monk (Tau Hanuman) picked on that right away. "And Xuthrodites consider us deviates. All apologies to Dante Alighieri but it seems to me this whole farce should be called the Deviation Comedy. Unless you'd prefer the Deviancies Comedy Troupe."

"Maybe you should start one up."

"Maybe you should, APM. I specialize in slapstick."

"Loxus Ryne is an impressive individual," considered Samarand, finishing his tea. "Then again so are most Horrites and both Entities. Not as impressive as us, though."

"See that isn't your epitaph, Yati," cautioned Yataghan.

"It won't be, Goldenrod. Got any more useful suggestions?"

"Only the obvious one. Those of us whose shells aren't homunculi better do some body bouncing while we still can. Even if we can't get into the Head

Horrite, we can fence him in. What we can't learn by external probing, we might be able to glean internally. We should start with this Dulles character again."

Skullian scratched his forehead contemplatively. "I was in him, Goldenrod. He was difficult to control but, like APM says, that's probably because that little horror, Young Life, Hush of the Mannerings, got to him long before the beams did. Don't see what we'd learn by going into him again."

"Let's take a walk, doctor. I'm more worried about Ryne and Dulles than I am about protecting the Fatman's homunculus. Care to join me, sister?"

APM nodded her head. "Connie Lindquist shares Dr Skullian's concerns for the Great Man's health. Have fun as Yataghan, Headcase, and, if you're still in him when you next crossover, do take advantage of it. His wife, Janna St Peche nowadays Montressor, is one of my most accomplished pupils."

"Give her heck, Hek," chortled Hanuman-Monk. Headcase's Illuminary-given name was Hektoris, so Hek worked alliteratively if not overly humourously.

"You're right, Monk. You'd make a lousy comedian. Best stick to slipping on banana peels."

========

"Hear me, rulers. My all-pervasive thought beams are permeating the Whole Earth. Changing the coherence of sentient beings everywhere. Converting your serfs to my way – the way! The way of totally self-determined freedom. Hear me, fascists. Helios is on the Moon. Destroying you!"

After that broadcast, heard and seen worldwide, no one dared doubt the identity of the Man on the Moon. One question remained unanswerable, even ineffable.

'Who the fuck was Helios — really?'

========

The riots that began in Japan the day before finally reached Hawaii at dawn Saturday its time. With its always volatile mix of indigenous aboriginals, too many of whom were poor and consequently felt disenfranchised on their own islands; Asian immigrants and migrants, often imported and subsequently employed as cheap labour; military personnel, tourists and touristic predators; Honolulu quickly became not only one of the last big metropolises hit on the entire planet. It became one of the worst.

Johann Schmidt and the Alliance's personally handpicked Intervention Team, many of whom had been with Auld Jock Maxwell (Codename: Jockey) and Schmidt himself (Codename: Doppel) in Death Valley, landed as per schedule at Pearl Harbour. They were only supposed to stay long enough to refuel and take delivery of a supply of anti-personnel splatter packs – guns that fired exploding, fragmentation-style bullets, grenades, flame-throwers and such like – before going on to Centauri Island. It didn't work out that way.

Before they'd finished loading up, the base was overrun, the airfield blocked by trucks and cars, heavy duty machinery and just about anything else the insurgents could get their hands on. Since most of them wore US uniforms and carried weapons, overrun wasn't quite the right word. Run over might have been putting it better.

Schmidt found himself in an untenable position. They dare not shoot first; might not risk shooting back either, for fear of being overwhelmed and butchered. Quite clearly they weren't going any farther. Not today, at least. The best he could do was hunker down and hope his people stayed loyal to the Alliance.

If they remained unified; kept manning the cargo barricades they hastily threw up around their own airplane, they'd still have it to board for Centauri Island tomorrow. Or whenever they got the chance. WORLD and their albinos, Schmidt felt sure, they could handle. The military gone mad was, to quote an English movie he'd enjoyed maybe a decade ago, maybe less, something completely different.

All the more so when its personnel were in the process of setting their own barracks on fire, perhaps out of sheer perversion.

=========

Centauri Island wasn't quite as bad as the rest of the world. A good percentage of that was due not so much to devils per se as brain-boggling littler devils. For that's what all of APM's eyes amounted to – detachable deviates.

=========

As the early morning progressed Damon Goldenrod switched shells like other people switched socks. He moved from Yataghan to Dr Angus Skullian then to Adolph Dulles and back to Skullian again. His breed sister, APM All-Eyes, who never left Connie Lindquist, was similarly out and about using her impressive abilities – all those eyes of hers – to help maintain the calm.

He was inside Dolph Dulles when they got together outside the *'celebrity cell'* housing the Great Man, Loxus Abraham Ryne. Given who they were beneath the skin, it didn't take much of a (third) eye-opening experience to convince the albino protectors on Ryne-watch to grant them entry to the underground suite where Angus Skullian, Ryne's personal physician, was already attending the patriarch.

Dulles came back out not long thereafter, leaving Lindquist alone with Skullian and the Great Man. He told the guards on duty he'd forgotten something in his office but when he returned, a few minutes later, he was with three of his big Hawaiians. The protectors, rightly warily, would only let him enter the cell. He was infuriated when he saw Ryne lying pale and panting on his bed, being tended by both doctors.

"He's only just fainted," said Lindquist. She had a third eye in her forehead.

"What the fuck ..." swore Dulles, stupidly going for his holster with his right gun-hand. It was latched. He was too slow anyhow. Eyefire-blasted into the wall, he hit it hard, slumped down it like a cracked egg, winded and dazed. If he knew what hit him at first, he didn't for long.

"Guess he did, too," said Skullian. The eyefire had come out of his forehead.

"I could have eyeballed him, Damon," Connie-APM complained.

"And I told you how he was hard to possess. You and I both know why, too. You said it yourself when you got back into Connie. That fucking faerie's been here as well. I'm sure of it. Besides, I didn't really roast him. He might have a headache when he gets back on his feet but he'll be fine. I'm more concerned about Ryne. I told you revealing ourselves was a dumb idea. He's an old man."

"And I told you he was tough old prick," said APM-Connie. "Anyway, what I do I can usually undo. Not so sure about concussions and head trauma you cause." Leaving Goldenrod-Skullian to keep patting the Great Man's hand in an effort to bring him around, she got up to check on Dulles. Then she spotted what the guards outside hadn't — mostly because Dulles had kept his left hand in his pocket.

"What the fuck is that?" This time it was Connie's turn to curse. "Has he always had a sixth finger?"

The ornate box on Ryne's chest of drawers opening from the inside as if of its accord, that had nothing – or next to inanimate nothing – to do with whether he did, or didn't have, a sixth finger before.

=========

Elsewhere in the island's undersides, protector-technicians finally patched Lindquist's actual father through to Dr Hiyati Samarand, as Yati called himself on this side of the Dome, by radio. Under the watchful eye(s), and ears, of the Protector (capitalized), some of the Fatman's redoubtable Untouchables, and his Enormity himself, the Romanov pretender began by making a deliberately provocative statement.

"The Worldwide Order with the Right to Life and Death invites you to join us, off-island. Because, one way or another, where you are right now is going under. Never to rise again!"

As pronouncements went, it was almost on a par with Helios's from the Moon.

=========

A Summoning Child, his claim to be the rightful heir to the Czardom of Russia was probably as fallacious as his elevator shoes.

If it wasn't, why use Translav instead of Romanov as his surname?

(As Hush had discovered some years ago, Greygreave's wife, Connie's mother, was a long dead Athenan War Witch whose maiden name was Uli Sturluson. Also a Summoning Child, Sturluson was the face-dancing supra once codenamed Soanso. She died a Miracle-Keyed member of Strife's Sinister Sisterhood before she turned thirty.)

The Little Prince – called such in part because, shoes not withstanding, he was a midget – had known Hiyati for more than two decades. In his (just revealed) capacity as the latest WORLD's spokesperson, he said he didn't know what the *'independents'* Daemonicus hired had up their sleeves but it wouldn't be just a little surprise. It'd be big and bad and go boom big-time, probably many times over.

He consequently offered to help evacuate Samarand and his people from Centauri Island. Albeit exclusively for the new Worldwide Order, they could in return continue their research projects at an unspecified, but far more secure, retreat the Order had already set up for scientists of their calibre. Could do so as well, or better, paid than they were now to boot.

Realizing even talk of raising their salaries was getting him exactly no-where with Samarand and assemblage, he decided to up the ante. "Laugh to your heathen heart's content, Hiyati. Just don't put too much stock in Big Max's treatment for *'Glomanitis'*, as I believe he calls the long late, but never missed, Count Viper's affliction and my cure. Even if it has already been applied to my Glomen, I doubt very much it has to the island's newcomers."

All eyes flashed to the Protector. Knowing that those with Samarand and the Fatman were well aware of his albinos' voluntary acceptance of the *'afflic-tion'*, Necator mouthed the words: *'So what?'* Samarand shook his head; instead he said into the radio microphone. "Are you telling me you have spies on the island, Greygreave?"

"I'm telling you a lot more than that, old friend. I'm telling you I have not only been in touch with them since the newcomers arrived but I can detonate your Glows as easily as I could my own before Max got to them."

"Impossible," this time Necator didn't just mouth the words.

"Ah," said Translav, unable to avoid showing off even though he was just a voice coming out of a radio. "That must be their leader. What kind of a name is Cromwell Necator anyhow?"

Extensive extemporization more so than negotiations ensued. This was at Necator's insistence. He needed the delay in order to gain time for his men – as well as some of Max's conscripted specialists – to discover where Translav was transmitting from, if he was indeed somewhere on the island.

Before they could come close to pinpointing him, a whacking great bang rocked the underside firmament.

========

The blast had nothing to do with Dulles's sixth finger. It instead had every-thing to with why Mugwump, one of Dolph's big Hawaiians, had had his hands in his pocket.

========

As Necator ran off to ascertain the cause of the explosion, Translav made an obvious, as well as ominous, final crack: "I hate to say I told you so, Hiyati. But ..."

He cut radio contact without finishing his statement. Flustered, Samarand turned to the others. "That couldn't be what I think it was," he said.

His Enormity, Alfredo Sentalli, shrugged his shoulders. It wasn't so much a Gallic shrug as one made in fatalistic resignation. "What can I tell you, Dr Samarand? Glows blow, but it's usually because they don't keep up their inocu-lation schedule. Max's medicine eliminated the need. So ours can't blow. As for Necator's men, most of them are beyond suicidal and none would be that sloppy. Unfortunately, if anyone can set them off long distance, it'd be Greygreave Translav."

"And the rest of what he claimed?"

His Enormity was the first to respond to that as well, albeit in all likelihood with what was, and was not, simultaneously, his own voice: "The Little Prince has always had a lot of nerve. It's a bluff of course. There's no such thing as monsters out here. Not anymore, if ever. And, if it's not WORLD that wants to destroy us, who can it be?

"Who'd have technology we can't defend against? Big Max accounted for everything short of a preemptive nuclear strike and, even then, we have lasers, particle beams and ground-to-air missiles. Not much would get through that. Finally, as a last resort, we can raise the Gypsium Curtain – though no one really knows what that would accomplish."

Some of the others wanted to throw in their two or three-eyed cents' worth but, in the continued absence of the third-born, Damon and APM, Yati and heroic Hektoris (as often called Headstrong as he was Headcase by his siblings) were the eldest. As Yataghan, the Hero of Byron glared at them. Yati and his Enormity were therefore allowed to carry on their discourse as an uninterrupted twosome.

"Translav mentioned Daemonicus," observed Samarand. "It's a Latin term used in magical rites to call upon earthborn demons in ancient times. It's also, as some of you might recall, the name of the world's first Daemon or Demon King, the one Grandfather reckoned he'd melted out of existence thousands of years ago at the tail-end of Ragnarok."

"Whereupon," Hektoris, who liked to pretend he knew stuff, broke in, "He took over his title as well as Sedon's Temple, what's now, as it was then, the daemons' homeland."

"Under a different name," his Enormity understood.

"Hell on Earth," provided Roderick Paraja, Djerrid Ruin's shell. Byron's Bowman could never resist shocking religious sorts like the real Sentalli-Centauri. "Don't know if they accept homos, though," he added, more mischievously than maliciously. "So you might be stuck going to homo heaven. God the Blob accepts anyone, even devils." (The reference was to Serathrone Hallow, the firstborn Byronic who stayed behind in the Celestial Sphere all those multiple thousands of years ago.)

"The only other time I've come across it," Samarand carried on, "Is as the name Anthean witches use to describe a male Strife. As you'll have heard ad infinitum tiresomely, Strife is Marut Kanin, a second-born Mithradite. She was myrionymous, granted, but she was also, by whatever name you'd care to use, killed by the Harmony Unity two thousand years ago. Could Daemonicus somehow be associated with her ram for Aries, Thrygragos Varuna Mithras?"

"A horrifying thought," said his Enormity. "Surely your father would know if he wasn't dead."

The others mumbled their agreement, though a couple couldn't conceal their dread. Unlike both Byron and Lazareme, the former in the so-called New World of the Americas, the latter mostly in East Asia and China, Mithras once had a massive following out here, one that overlapped Lazaremist territories as well as Europe, Arabia and Africa.

Indeed there were some who claimed he still did, albeit under a different name. That name? Christianity, wherein he was also remembered as St Michael or St George.

"No," said the Fatman, after a long pause while his real self on the other side of the Dome considered the matter. Possibly, Samarand figured, someone like Centauri's Inner Earth drinking buddy, the Legendarian Jordan Tethys, was with him and acting as a consultant.

(Which he might be. Yati didn't keep up to date with what was going on re the Godbadian effort to retake Hadd, old Iraxas, from the vast majority of its occupants, ambulatory Dead Things akin, if not identical, to Necator's Valhallans. He did know Tethys had gone there at Centauri's request less than a week ago – to the Sraddhite Monastery, on Lake Sedona – but when you could do what the recurring deviant did with Rumour's Brainrock quill, he could have got back to Aka Godbad City at anytime.)

"Much more likely, if this Daemonicus fellow actually exists," Sentalli-Centauri was saying, "He'd be the same as Strife. Which means he hangs out in Samsara, the Grey, the Weird or whatever you weirdos call between-space. Don't know how he'd get into anyone from in there. I mean, men don't traverse the universal substance as readily as women but maybe he's better than her.

"Say, for the sake of argument, he can traverse Cathonia at will. That means he's no devil, not unless he's your Grandfather Sedon's alter ego out for a lark. Which he isn't; couldn't be, I should imagine, not without the Dome coming down. Or unless there's another way through it. Which there is, but not for devils."

"Mandroids again," grasped Samarand, feeling absolutely no urgency to correct the Fatman's erroneous assertion that Dark Sedon couldn't be two places at once. For most any other devil, bilocation wasn't an option. But the All-Father of Devazurkind wasn't any other devil. He was the Devil Himself, capitalized.

"All of Incain. Amphitrite of Lemuria. Via the Egyptian Sphinx. That would explain the monsters your Translav was babbling on about, I suppose, but not what they could do to us. Mandroids die the same as anyone. Can be killed, rather, as in blown apart, if you have enough oomph. Even if she, All, can send someone or something from the Dome straight onto the island without going through the Nag Gap, there's only one thing that can harm us."

"Trinondev eyeorbs can take devils out of action," reflected Sentalli-Centauri.

"Not with APM around," Samarand reminded him. "And eyeorbs are no real danger to human beings; not in the same way anyhow. Can't take out their pineal gland, minds with it, and shrink their subtle matter bodies into amorphous mush then imprison them forever if the Trinondev or whoever's opened and closed it so desires.

"No, the only thing both our races are afraid of is Atomics and that technology only exists on the Outer Earth. As, shall we say, disinterested as Grandfather may be in all this; after being almost wiped out by a Hydrogen Bomb on Salvation Island in 1953; after being in effect comatose for a quarter century as a result; surely he'd prevent any renegade devils, or otherwise sentient beings, from developing them inside the Dome.

"Besides, the only place nuclear devices could be built would be Godbad and Centauri Enterprises wouldn't do that. Would it."

"Bite your tongue, Yati," snarled Sentalli-Centauri. "To even hint I might sanction such an abomination appals me. I won't even allow experimentation in nuclear reactors and it's not just because of what happened to me in 1945, when I first had the pleasure of encountering your formidable father."

(Who saved his life, his Enormity could have added. Just as he, in some respects, saved Unmoving Byron's. That he didn't was due to the fact that everyone there knew the story. That none of them mentioned either Utopians on Earth or the Dual Enemies – both of whom may or may not already have access to atomics, or could certainly master the technology required to produce it – that was more a matter of wishfully whistling past the proverbial graveyard. They didn't want to go there.)

"But that doesn't rule out Atomics coming from the Outer Earth. If Daemonicus can hire WORLD, he can hire anyone he pleases."

Even though Necator hadn't reported back, Samarand was still troubled by Translav's threat that he could detonate albino Glomen from afar. "Say they, Daemonicus and the Lemurians through All, have acquired nuclear weapons. Say they send out mandroid monstrosities to deliver them, I still can't see how they could get through our defenses.

"But say they could? I mean, think about it, that being the case why bother with monsters? Or any other sort of delivery system, as far as that goes? Send the bombs directly through the Weird, underneath our defenses, then detonate them either from a distance or with a suicidal volunteer. It's a logistical nightmare, sure, but what could we do about that?"

"Nothing before it's too late," agreed his Enormity. "And why are they waiting? The Express has done its job; albeit not the job we built it for. More than seventy of your kin have disappeared from the Sedon Sphere. According to Translav, Daemonicus wants my island destroyed – and, though the midget can't know about it, presumably the Nag Gap with it."

"What are you getting at?"

"Who'd be that crazy? An atomic explosion adjacent to the portal could kill the Moloch Sedon. Is that what's it all about? He was so weakened the last time he came out here, his star has only just returned to the night's sky. It happens again, so soon after the last time, that would bring down the whole Dome for sure this time."

"The Male Entity?" finally contributed Vach-Rowena. "He has a history as a Mad God. Who else but a Mad God would have detonated Old Weir's Star."

"Detonated or had detonated?" objected the Scorpion Goddess, Hala Sadrapa, through Mavis Chester. "His Story couldn't have done it without Her Story."

"Regardless," muttered Hathor-Raymond, regretting she'd opened her mouth. Youngsters like the Zodiacals could be so rude.

"Collapsing the Dome," his Enormity reconsidered, "Would only release more of you lot out here; not to mention reverse the effects of the Genesea with a payback Great Flood. Sedon's Head suddenly materializing in the middle of the North Pacific would cause it to overflow its banks; the continental shelves, no less. Millions, probably billions, would die.

"I grant it would be somehow poetic but, if that is Heliosophos up there, and if that really is what he wants, why bother with all this mind-beam crap coming from the Moon? No, I'm sure we're on the right track with Amphitrite et al. But what's with the monsters? Was Godzilla real? Do they want to get into his next movie?"

"I thought Godzilla was female," said APM-Connie. "Wasn't she trying to protect her eggs?"

"That was the sequel," said Elephantine-Hannibal. Probably neither of them had ever seen a Godzilla movie, though their shells might have.

"They're visible?" proposed Samarand uncertainly. "Maybe whoever's really responsible wants to show everyone on both sides of the Dome what they can do."

"Unless," snapped the Fatman pudgily (he did everything pudgily), ruminating out loud, "The Gypsium Field, our capacity to raise and lower it with a flip of a switch, somehow nullifies All's capacity to send anything either directly from the Head to the island or, assuming they're already outside, from near here."

"Only if we've raised it already," Samarand countered. "Which we haven't."

"Rom Kinesis insists Gypsium's semi-sentient. Maybe it'd raise itself and All, or Helios on the Moon, or whomever, knows it."

"If only Father Byron was around," despaired Samarand. "He could move the portal if nothing else. He's done it before."

"Modestly," said Sentalli-Centauri, recalling events of fifteen years ago. "But not far, certainly not off-island. Its three peaks somehow act as a containment field and all of them once bubbled with molten Gypsium. We'll have to rely on the Godstuff, I'm afraid. It wants the Gap open, then it'll have to do its part to keep it open."

"That's absurd. Why rely on anything – what's the word? – ineffable?"

"I'm prepared to order both sides bricked up. That can be done fairly fast. What I'm not prepared to do is give up without a fight. Do as you please, darling dears. Get back here or stay out there and take your chances. I want Necator and his Valhallans recalled immediately – not hidden in the depths of my island, all the more so if WORLD can set them off just like that. I've better uses for them inside; faraway from Translav, though not his buddies."

"You're going to attack Incain."

"I'm going to play the cards as I see fit, Dr Samarand. So should you."

"As you see fit."

"Just so."

"And if All's not responsible and you somehow destroy it? Do you have any idea what you might release? Ever heard of Abdullah Ziderite, the high-born Mithradite? Forty-five hundred years ago he conspired with Lemurians, their tellurian constructs, and thereby virtually recreated mandroids on the Head in the first place.

"How about Rapacious Ravana, famous from your Outer Earth's Ramayana?" Hanuman-Monk let out an involuntary yelp. "Or the Idiot Twins. Talk about Atomics, you know what happened to the first Valhalla? Not Sedon's Inner

Nose, what's now the Ghostlands, Sedon's Forehead, though they're not just that. And, worst of all, the Unnameable!"

"Unlike immortals," lectured the Fatman, "Which in your heart of hearts – not your homos' whatever – you mostly are, we human beings are used to taking chances; to tackling the Game of Life full-bore. Don't bother telling Necator to get his ass back inside, I'll do it myself. Coming, Yataghan?"

"Headcase and I have to talk," insisted Samarand.

"Yataghan?"

"In a minute, double dad."

Consequently, unusually for him, (physically) unaccompanied, his Enormity wheeled himself out of the laboratory electronically. In the corridor he passed Adolph Dulles. Big Max's youngish Number Two was flanked by a few of Max's longest serving men, including the to-his-mind – contradiction that that may be – oversized Hawaiians, Marsh, Tadpole, and Mugwump, whom he'd heard hadn't been seen since Thursday.

He asked them if they'd come across Cromwell Necator in their travels. Dulles said he'd passed him just after the explosion *'back there, near Ryne's celebrity cell'*. That shook the Fatman. Had Translav triggered the Protector's Glomen guarding the Great Man in an effort to assassinate Abe Ryne? Would he be their next target?

His Enormity gave up on finding Cromwell; instead made a beeline for the elevator that would take him to the surface and thence to the hotel.

Even homunculi were conditioned to protect their big butt-ends.

========

Stuff happens. There's no doubt of that. Of course, when it comes to stuff, sometimes it's yet to happen for the first time.

That was about to change above Sisert, the Silent Sands of Cathune, aka Sedon's Cranium.

****

Part Four: *Sinking and Swimming*

NUKE 21: Psychic Siblings

========

Saturday, December 6, 1980

Alone, Adolph Dulles – ornate box in five-fingered hand – walked in on the gathering of Centauri's Untouchables.

"What's up, Goldenrod?" demanded Kunta-Kintu Mawulisa via her shell.

========

On her devil's behalf, Kintu Matambwe, the Central-Africa-born particle physicist who'd helped Samarand develop the Cosmic Express's Solidium (or Stopstone) sheathe, was full of questions. "Is Dulles a deviant? Is that why he's so hard to hold onto? What's Loxus Ryne up to? Have they really got some sort of remote control unit that sets off Glomen?"

"Can't say for sure," proffered Dulles. "There is this. Found it in the old man's posh prison suite." He opened Pandora's Box. Inside it was the circlet Ryne called Aladdin's Ring.

"There's an Anthean Agate in its setting," eagle-eye-spotted the Vietnamese munitions expert, Bonn *'Bomber'* Kim. Somewhat ironically, since he was possessed of the All-Merciful Kannon, one of Bodiless Byron's relatively pacifistic offspring, Kim had designed some of the more unconventional weaponry carried by the Express's cosmicompanions.

Hiyati Samarand looked up from his monitor in time to see Young Life come out of the ring, but too late to do anything about it. She opened her belly bag. Fifteen solitary eyes poked out of their leathern pods. Third eyes sucked out of the skulls of everyone in the room but Dulles, Hush, and, surprisingly to her, Dr Samarand.

Dulles and Hush stepped out of the way. Marsh, Tadpole, and Mugwump burst into the room. Their handguns were drawn but they pointed their other hands' extra index-fingers at the collapsing untouchables. Not one of them blew up.

"Careless of you, Yati," the apparent little girl criticized Project Centauri's authoritarian overseer. "Should have made your homos glow, as in Glomen."

"Why? Strife isn't the only one who doesn't leave memories behind!"

"And you?"

"Who says homunculi have to be possessed to be functional?"

=========

Hours later, in Aka Godbad City, on the other side of the Dome, Hush was still in fine fettle. Catching a coterie of devils unprepared was an answer to a sixty year old dream. Finally she reckoned she had bargaining chips she could use against Tra-la-bloody-lorn.

And maybe she did. Did even if Trala wasn't a Mithradite; did even if she was instead a chthonic creature; an earthborn demon and not a skyborn devil who chose to stay a child forever.

Then again, maybe she didn't.

=========

It being the Age of Byron, she'd trade the captured Byronics to their father in return for him forcing the Perpetual Presence, child, female, also the White Dwarf, to lift her curse. Trala, as Hush called Tralalorn, her doom-dispensing nemesis, would hem and haw – maybe even go '*bah*' if she was riding her Chimera, which was a multi-headed, fire-breathing goat – but she'd do it or die, if she could.

Which, since the most purely evil of demon-devils wouldn't want to test her potential transience, meant Trala would do whatever Byron demanded to leave her alone.

(Almost from its Year One, the Head held three Perpetual Presences, capitalized, and at least one transient, as in eminently terminal, presence. This last, a small-case-sedon, had to have at least one brother beyond the Cathonic Dome or Zone. Were it not for the three immortals and two mortals, so concluded Sedon himself, irrefutably, damn near six thousand years ago, the then only relatively recently risen Sedon Sphere, Cathonia, would dissipate.

(Sedon was of course the Perpetual Presence, adult, male. As for the Perpetual Presence, adult, female, that had been Pyrame Silverstar until she was cathonitized in 5950. Rather, it was thought to have been her until she was turned into an actual star shining above the Hidden Headworld close to thirty years ago. More likely it was – and had been all along – Mother Earth, Chthonia to Sedon's Cathonia.

(That noted, the highborn Lazaremist Librarian and longtime ambassador to Godbad, Biblio Drek, was hardly a solitary voice crying out in the proverbial wilderness of ignorance when he attested it was Primeval Lilith, the Demon Queen of the Night. He further insisted that Daemonicus's luscious Lily was the real reason the Pauper Priestess became a solid individual two thousand years before most every other Master Deva did.

(Another who held this view was even higher-born Metisophia, Titanic Metis. And she wasn't called Wisdom of Lazareme because she'd chosen to remain a Spirit Being since the expansion of the Empire of Lathakra in the 48th Century of the Dome. Pyrame herself, however, never acknowledged she'd acquired Lilith either while she was stuck inside of Ginny the Gynosphinx or when Sedon released her, from what was now All of Incain, soon after raising the Dome out of his own essence.

(Devils couldn't lie but they could avoid answering the question.

(Regardless of the reality, possibly (for a change) not Illuminaries of yore; possibly her own mother (not her brood sister in Mithras's Ninth), the selfsame Pyrame Silverstar, had named the child devil – child demon, just as likely – Tralalorn. In Tantalar 5920, just after Pandora Mannering had given birth to to-day's Morrigan (Morgianna born Nauroz, become Somata then Sarpedon), Trala and Pyrame appeared in the (old) Master's Palace, not quite the most ancient, still standing structure in the Weirdom of Cabalarkon.

(At Pyrame's imperious command, Trala turned the White Dwarf, her Tva-sitar talisman (if that, not her meteoric afterbirth, was indeed what it was), on Hush and her year younger hubby, Augustus Nauroz. She thereby *'devolved'* them, to use the true little horror's own term. The tormented tricksters often known as Young Life and Young Death, albeit only in there, thereby came into being. Hush was 16; Gus was 15. Neither ever saw 8 again.)

All in all, she couldn't ask for a better dividend. Now all she had to do was find a way to save Centauri's Island.

"Except," the real Fatman disillusioned the illusionist. "I haven't heard from the Great God since he came through the portal early this morning. For all I know he could be dead." The multiplely self-named Anthean elder stuck in a young girl's form took that in stride.

Cursed with unending childhood after nearly seventeen years of being nor-mal – even more disappointingly, the result of howsoever many centuries worth of selective breeding in hopes of making her the motherly vessel of Panharmo-nium to come – what was one more frustration?

"Congratulate me anyhow, Daddy Quintillion Chins. You've as gooey good as got your island back."

"Congratulations, button-nose. You deserve it." Hush actually blushed when he tweaked her on said button-nose. "In a way that was a brilliant move, blowing up a couple of Valhallans in order to stun Aphropsyche Morningstar, she in her shell. Still, I wouldn't have thought a devil as potent as APM could have been taken out with a prison pod. Wasn't she the one who plugged up Sarpedon's last Thursday? His orbs only took out some of her eyes – and she's All-Eyes."

"Wasn't just one, or two, or even three," admitted the Mannering's Pandora. "It took a whole buggery bundle of the buggers. Fortunately Daddy Demios's eye-stave is the oldest in the known world. So long as it's got enough Gypsium – and your unsighted island's peaks are chockablock with Godstuff – it manu-factures its own eyeorbs.

"And it wasn't as if I had Daddy Dolph and his pachyderm pals trigger their fingers to knock out Connie. I already had All-Eyes, or most of them, by that time. Had big bad brood bro too, out of Angus Skullian. Connie and Dolph were just coming out of the cell when Mugwump jumped the gun, as it were. He had, quite literally, an itchy trigger finger."

"Even so ..."

"Oh, I agree. As much as I no more like devils than they like me, I will say this much about APM. She's mega-bags more impressive than Damon Gold-en-Dick."

"So it seems," granted the Fatman, ignoring what he took to be her misandrous attitude, if that really was the male version of misogynous. He was used to it by now.

"So, what did you do with the orbs?"

"Hid them in a Shelter on the other side. My agates don't work in Godbad unless APM lets them, which she can't right now, and I'm not very good with Afrite Bulbs."

"So long as they're safe. Thrygragos Byron wouldn't take it kindly if you managed to cathonitize a dozen or so of his children. Next thing we have to do is get rid of Loxus Ryne."

Blush became flush. "I've nothing against blowing up Valhallans. A man dies, fabulous fighter or no, Sangazur spirit beings should have the common decency to let him rot. But I'm not participating in any wilful murders – especially one that would let a low-watt like Erech Avar Ryne become the patriarch."

"Then we better find a way to preserve our secret and the old man at the same time."

"That wouldn't be a problem if was just a matter of keeping the existence of the Gap and the Head secret from Daddy Ryne Bread. But I told you what Sarpedon saw on the fish packer."

"Can't you co-opt Psycho the same as you did Connie? He might be able to control this Sharkczar long enough for us to do something about this charming surprise he's apparently cooked up for us."

"Twenty-seven years ago, just after he killed his maybe not one-night lover and step-mother Barbara Plantagenet – forced her to kill herself, rather – because she was probably giving birth to a new small-case-sedon, Superior Sarpedon, who along with his Cousin Jess put him up to it in the first place, tried to give him amnaesthetics.

"They didn't take. In fact, they only ameliorated his already considerable mentat might. I mean, his cranium was transparent. You could see his little grey cells burbling away underneath it once you took off his lid and Mr Macho hairpiece. That kind of thing does not a normal man bespeak. It had to indicate serious deviancy right from day one, though his latent psi-talents didn't come manifest until he hit puberty.

"At any rate, Morg came to me in desperation. Where else would she go? I am her little mother after all. I did what I could to keep him quelled but I could never co-opt him as such. He always did pretty much what he wanted. Even on Damnation Island in '55, when he was hell-bent on suicide himself and wanted to take his twin brother and the Crimefighters with him."

"And your Daddy Ryne was more than willing to provide him with the opportunity."

"He's a very dangerous daddy," granted Hush. "If only I knew what Sharkczar was up to. I got to Connie in order to get to her old man – and, again, thanks for bringing APM inside overnight a couple of days ago, by the way. But neither of them seemed to know how Sharky got involved in this time-out's WORLD. They thought it was all down to Strife and Daemonicus, not Sharky and Crystal."

"Nuclear firedrakes do seem a tad farfetched."

A couple of days earlier, Thursday beyond the Dome, Sapienda on the Head, the Unmoving One, along with two of his Nucleoids (Sedona Spellbinder and Chimaera Glimmenmare), went outside to search for their brood brother Vayu Maelstrom (Devil Wind). Fearing for his personal security, the real Centauri called APM inside to keep him company. (APM, inside Janna St Peche-Montressor, often acted as his bodyguard when he was beneath the Dome, but Yataghan was beyond it, and Byron was elsewhere.)

In APM's absence, Hush seized on the opportunity to work her witchy wiles on Connie Lindquist, All-Eyes' usual host when she was on Centauri Island. Hush was good with agates. Being a trickster she wasn't above using them coercively either. So she had no trouble compelling Connie's cooperation.

As APM must have known since she spent so much time inside her, the good doctor (from a pair of pretty bad seeds) already had a stash of trigger-fingers. That the devil hadn't shared this information with Sentalli-Centauri could probably be put down to an oversight. Who'd have thought the Fatman would risk sending his own Glomen out here anyhow?

For Hush this was a perhaps not altogether unexpected stroke of luck. It meant she didn't have to risk contracting the Strife Virus by going off-island between-space in order to buttonhole Connie's father, Greygreave Translav. As she'd told Quintillion Chins, she'd never willingly do that again, not after his devils released the faceless fiend and her ever-smiling accomplice on the nude beach Demios Sarpedon and her landed on after escaping the Order's phony fish packer.

She figured Connie had to have a way to contact the Little Prince on the qt; possibly through what War Witches sometimes, semi-facetiously, called their bullet-pellet witch-stones. (She'd reasoned rightly as well. Had Big Max come to the same conclusion? Had he chosen not to do anything about it earlier, in case it'd be to his perceived advantage to do something about it later? She'd have to ask him. Once he came back from the Moon.)

Her original theory had been, if necessary, to bribe the Little Prince to detonate Necator's albino Glomen. That circumstances obviated the need for that didn't prevent her contacting him anyhow, via Connie. It was he who told Hush about Crystallion (Crystal St Synne) and her seemingly nuclear-powered dragons. He hadn't seen them but Salvatore Dis L'Orca and the (recently liberated) Mandam Twins had.

Their description of them was enough for Translav's longtime partner in crime and dirty deeds, the usually unflappable Shaikh Markazi, to leave Hawaii with Dis L'Orca and his charges. The Little Prince, though, was made of sterner stuff. He also loved his cunning Connie dearly; wouldn't want to leave her to either Sharkczar or Crystallion's tender mercies.

As for how they communicated clandestinely, without Max and his security team, or even APM, finding out, (if they hadn't, which wasn't very likely), Hush found that out, too. And in the same way, via her agates. As Pandora Mannering, she'd given birth to most of the reason for it. The Morrigan's Hellions called their bullet-pellets hellstones but, if you were good with either/or, when it came right down to zip there wasn't much difference between the two.

Still, Translav being a man, he shouldn't have been able to use which-ever. Artificial agates were a different matter, though. And guess whose darling daughter had supplied guess who – and his darling daughter – with guess what? As for who had invented artificial agates, well, his only known children, twins, were now keeping Sally Junkie and Ali Ars Asshole company somewhere that wasn't an Hawaiian island.

"Dragons are common enough in Samarand and the Crystal Mountains," acknowledged Hush. "But these aren't Dr Samarand's pets and Crystal has noth-ing to do with the mountain range that borders on Yati's protectorate, if Sam-arand the Land can be called that. At least I don't think she does."

(Byronics didn't have protectorates; Great Byron held their domains in common; as in personally, by and for himself. That way he could hoard most of the worship directed at his offspring. He did, however, delegate governorships. He did also reserve the right to reassign his offspring at whim. And, yes as well, he was never loathe to do as much.

(Amazingly to many, his methods worked better than how Mithradites – who no longer had a father, but did have protectorates – disciplined themselves. Which was hardly at all, hence the turbulent, often warring ways of the Upper Head particularly after Thrygragon. As for Lazaremists, they were anarchists like their father. They didn't rule anywhere or anyone, not as such. Which was probably why they were so popular in their individual spheres of influence.)

"Mind you, as far as I know Yati hasn't been to that Samarand in years. Could there be a new strain of genetically altered dragons, ones with nuclear capacity?"

"Put that way it sounds preposterous," doubted Centauri. "I suppose you could ask Dr Samarand himself. You said he wasn't one of those you trapped in Demios's eye-eggs."

"But that isn't Yati. It might not even need Yati playing puppeteer in order to function Norman-normally. Metaphorically speaking, Byron's Dragon exter-nalized his soul. He's operating his homunculus from a distance, like you do, but whether from in here or out there, I have no idea and presumably neither do you.

"Guess you're right. I'll have to face Daddy Dangerfield myself. Want to join me?" (Rodney Dangerfield was the name of an Outer Earth comedian whose limited shtick the Fatman, howsoever inexplicably to her, actually found funny. Hush knew this but her reference was to her *'very dangerous daddy'*, Loxus Abraham Ryne.)

"Sorry, baby. I'm an unmitigated coward."

"Going to seal the Nagasaki Gap after I leave?"

"You told Necator that's what you wanted."

"So why didn't you?"

"First of all, I don't think anyone can close it, not for good. Second of all, only Great Byron can move it. Thirdly, as I only found out last Saturday, Profes-sor Kinesis disabled my failsafes quite a while ago. In other words, though he didn't realize it, he cut off my ability to blow up the island from in here. Finally, I'm relying on you to pull something out of the hat. You always do and it's rarely a rabbit, with or without his foot. My trust in you is unbounded."

"As in a bounding bunny," said Hush, without laughing. (Ryne and Centauri had a number of things in common, one of which was no ever laughed at their jokes.) "But you can seal up this side?"

"That I can, but there's a couple of problems there as well. The Gap forms a tunnel through the Cathonic Dome; a tunnel through Samsara as well, has to. However, as you'd know, Samsara doesn't exactly have walls. Enter the Gap from the other side and, even if this exit is shut, you might be able to slip sideways through Cathonia – to somewhere other than here."

"No, the Gap has to be sealed on both sides. Until that's done, there's no point closing just this side."

"So have your homunculus brick up the other side."

"Like template, like homo, I'm afraid. It doesn't want to be trapped out there any more than I do. In fact it's giving Yataghan quite a struggle even as we speak."

"So thought-rays work on homunculi, too. Guess they're more alive than even I figured."

Centauri, being a humane person, wasn't too happy to hear that. He decided to get the conversation back on track. "No, Yataghan will have to do it – and he will, but only at the last second. See, dutiful father that I am, I don't want to chance losing my only son unless there's no other way."

"Chance?"

"The other side can be collapsed manually. You just have to supply the dynamite, which won't be a problem since Yat has the keys, set the timer for whenever you want, scamper through the Gap, seal this side and hope it blows before anyone gets into it. Of course, with your agates, you wouldn't have to run that kind of risk."

"I get the picture, daddy. All right. See you soon."

========

It was actually Paul Creel, Maxwell's staff doctor, who released Abe Ryne. He'd been called hither by none other than Cromwell Necator (now vanished, along with all his men) to tend to Connie Lindquist. (She'd been injured when two of Necator's protectors blew up howsoever inexplicably after she left the Great Man mulling over what she and Angus Skullian had just revealed to him.)

It was a good thing they were both doctors. Octogenarians did not handle shock well.

========

Much later on, after dark in fact, Ryne was still in his comfortable, underground celebrity cell. The patriarch was feeling much better, thank you. He was also doing what he did best: asserting his authority. With his SPACE-men close enough to attend to his own safekeeping; with Dulles's men having regained their authority to complement their positions; the Great Man had taken official charge of the island's welfare.

His first act was insist someone give him a proper gun, not a dart-gun. Once Dulles did – thus demonstrating he was in charge of the island and not namby-pamby Alfredo Pasta Sauce, who detested guns of any description (but did tolerate dart-guns if only because of their promised non-lethality) – his second act was to call an emergency session of those still in an executive position on Centauri Island.

Al Sentalli, probably out of pique, refused to attend. So did Hush, which was altogether appropriate given most of those summoned thought her a legitimate little girl; the Fatman's grand niece or some such. People came and went but, eventually, only Hiyati Samarand, Dolph Dulles and Paul Creel were left. After Samarand told them about Translav's threats and vague warning about independents hired by whomever, Creel went through his scribbles.

"Connie Lindquist's wounds looked a lot worse than they actually were, Mr Ryne. She'd be up and about already if I hadn't given her a mild sedative. Of the others on Mr Maxwell's list of suspects, other than, sorry, you, Dr Samarand," referring to his notebook, he ran down their names, "Mr Hannibal is with Dr Lindquist, Yataghan is with his father in the hotel, while Paraja, Nurse Raymond, Urartu, Monk, Kim, Chester, Dugas, and Matambwe remain unconscious but otherwise inexplicably fine.

"As you suggested – and since they seem in no immediate danger – I've had them taken to the hotel ballroom and hooked into intravenous tubes. Mr Marsh and some of his security personnel are guarding it and a few of them have paramedic training. Angus Skullian, myself, and most of my staff will remain down here to deal with serious casualties from the, um, unrest up top. Is there anything else?"

Ryne checked off the twelve names and pronounced himself satisfied. "Thank you, doctor. I know you have reservations about working with Dr Skullian. It's true he's recently been seen in the company of Dr Samarand and some of those you named – as well as the now missing albinos – but I'm confident he's smartened up; learned the error of his ways. Angus is a good man. You can rely on him."

"He better be. We're in a crunch and, besides me and Dr Lindquist, he's the only surgeon on the island. Some of the casualties coming in look like they've been through a combat zone. They should be flown off island for proper treatment."

"Unfortunately, things are much worse on Maui and the rest of the islands than they are here. We'll be lucky to hold our own." The old man dismissed Creel and turned to Dulles. "Anything good to say, Dolph?"

"Not much. I know your SPACE-men were handpicked and seem remarkably resistant to the vindictive paranoia that's sweeping the rest of the world, but there aren't very many of them and virtually all are technically oriented. Not much good for security assignments. Besides, you need them to maintain communications with the Liberty.

"Which brings me to my men and women. I think we got to them in time. Those who had killing weapons turned them in and are back to carrying dartguns. These are good things. However, I quite frankly can't trust more than a handful."

"You assessed your priorities as I instructed?"

"Very quickly. Marsh will take care of the surface. Put better, he'll try to maintain a modicum of order in the town and offer as much haven in the hotel as he can. Tadpole has secured the armouries, the airport, and as much of our strategic defence systems as he can. The rest of the big shit has been shut down.

"Mugwump's folks are down here. They've got the trigger-fingers to counter albinos should they emerge from the depths and attack us, but we haven't the numbers to pursue them into the bowels of the island. It's a real honeycomb. We've sealed what we can but we don't even have schematics of what Sentalli built down there."

"And you won't get them from me," interrupted Samarand.

"You and your men, the ones Max trusted at least, are here to continue the search for remnants of the Express," snapped Ryne. "That assured, doctor, your privacy is forfeit. You will henceforth be accompanied twenty-four hours a day by assigned by my young but reliable friend here. Carry on, Dolph."

"So," he capsulated, "Marsh is in the hotel, Tad's attending to our defence, to the best of his ability, and Mug's down here. SPACE is doing its thing as is Samarand and the regulars on the Express team. We can forget about Schmidt, the American military, and any other outside help. Dr Samarand's told you about WORLD and this not so little surprise that's supposedly coming our way.

"If it does come, we'll just have to fight it off. Looks bleak, sir."

"Or we could take Translav up on his offer," Ryne reminded Dulles. "Give WORLD what it wants and get ourselves off island. That means we abandon Centauri but so be it. I can deal with the Order. Money, power, and influence are all it's ever been interested in and I can provide that singlehandedly."

"You're not serious?" gasped Dulles.

"At the risk of restating the bleeding obvious," claimed Ryne, "This is an impossible place to defend. Get upstairs, Dolph. Have Marsh rig up speaker vans and send them out. Open the port, encourage all non-essential personnel to get away, but hold onto the airport as long as you can. Nothing in, nothing out.

"The albinos' troop flyer is up there and it can sardine in a couple hundred of Sentalli's folk if they choose to leave — and have faith it isn't booby-trapped. Which you'll have to ascertain. My plane's there as well. Came back from Florida via LA early this morning. It can take all my people from SPACE as well as another dozen or so in a pinch. Let WORLD have the rest."

Not wanting to cave in, to relinquish the responsibility Max had entrusted him with, to give up his post without a decent fight, Dulles tried a more emphatic approach.

"From what I hear, there's nowhere safer than here right now, sir. Who's to say those responsible for delivering the surprise this Daemonicus has apparently cooked up for us haven't been affected by the thought beams? I mean, when it comes down to it, we've only got Translav's word – make that Dr Samarand's word – that there even is a surprise. Surely, if there was, it would be here by now. It's been almost a week since the Express exploded."

"I'm not known for panicking, Dolph," said the patriarch, annoyed with the much younger man's tone. "And your essential point is valid. Why indeed?"

Samarand, perhaps too self-servingly, echoed Dulles' sentiment. "Yataghan and George were there as well. As was Mr Sentalli. They'll verify what the Little Prince said. I only repeated it, as close to verbatim as I could. There is no empirical evidence that it does exist. As far as I know, even Translav doesn't know what it is. Only what it's supposed to do – and, other than it would go boom, a few times, he didn't say what that was either."

"All right," decided Ryne, not really having any choice in the matter. "We'll risk another night here. Assess the external situation come morning. The way I'm leaning right now, though, is we're out of here tomorrow afternoon. After all, rioters burn out. They need food and sleep like the rest of us. And the authorities aren't complete incompetents.

"Do as I say, my boy! Chop, chop. Get things organized. You and Alfredo can stay if you please, Dr Samarand, but we'll take our chances away from here."

Dulles left but Ryne held onto Samarand. "You're one of these devils Goldenrod and Morningstar told me about, aren't you?"

"I know of them," admitted the oriental overseer. "Shintoists call them kamis. Arabs, I believe, call them jinn, Zoroastrians azuras, but Hindus have them as Devas, Shining Ones."

"Even I know that much," asserted the octogenarian. "But you know much more than that. You know they're real. You're also brighter than most of the others. Otherwise the one I know as Hush Mannering, but Connie's whatever she was – occupant?, personal poltergeist? – called Young Life, would have nailed you. And don't give me any crap about this Moon. Big Shelter's right here, isn't it?"

"Not here, but I'm pretty sure I can get to it from here."

"Al's more than pretty, isn't he?"

"I wouldn't want to say."

"Let's go see him then."

"This island has to be defended to the last."

"Then, one way or the other, you and I will be the last to leave."

The statement was deliberately obscure but Samarand knew what his priorities were. Besides, despite his better instincts, he kind of liked the resourceful old man.

"I believe you're sincere. Very well. Have your man Dulles bring Dr Lindquist and George Hannibal to the hotel. We'll sort things out there."

"You can take us there through Samsara, can't you?"

"Don't be absurd. I told you the truth. I'm no devil. We'll have to walk. At least we'll have a reward for our troubles. There's better food there."

Chain-smokers had to eat, too. Some of them could even taste what they ate.

========

After first gathering up a still groggy Connie Lindquist and George Hannibal from the downside infirmary, Loxus Abraham Ryne, Hiyati Samarand and Adolph Dulles made their way topside. For security reasons Dolph thereupon drove them, by car, to the Island's luxury hotel. Taking the elevator to Sentalli's floor, they heard the sounds of a ruckus the moment they stepped out into the oversized outer office-cum-reception area.

It was coming from Sentalli's private quarters.

========

Dart-gun drawn, Dulles burst into the extended suite and through to the master bedroom. Yataghan was wrestling with his father on the bed like a seal with a walrus; unless it was like a walrus with a whale. Obviously the Fatman was having some kind of fit. Nearby was his niece, Dorothy Dodgson, jokingly called Pandora, Hush Mannering by any name. She had a hypodermic needle in hand.

"Take her out, Dulles," shouted Samarand behind him. He didn't hesitate. Without thinking, he shot her with a dart. She collapsed on the spot.

"You had no right to do that," fumed Ryne, his definitely lethal gun at the ready.

Samarand was having none of that. "The trickster's no more your friend than ours." Suddenly Hush went into convulsions.

"Christ!" cried Connie, rushing to her aid. "She's having a toxic seizure. What was in that thing?"

"Enough wallop to tranquillize a grown man for a few hours."

"But she's a little girl, you idiot!"

"I'll get a doctor."

"I am a goddamned doctor. Help me hold her down."

========

Dulles screamed, fell to his knees, mouth gaping.

*The words that gurgled out, foamy sputum with them, were in a voice immediately recognizable to some of those there. It wasn't his own: "**Johann Schmidt! Johann, This Is Sean, Sean Smythe. Amoebaman's Alive! He's A Three-Eyed Devil. No, A Six, Nine, Twelve-Eyed Bloody Hydra! He's Got Four Fucking Heads On Four Fucking Necks!**"*

It was time for sedatives all around.

****

NUKE 22: **Dragon Days**

========

Sunday, December 7, 1980

By Saturday midnight, after failing to raise the Liberty for what seemed like hours, Ryne was ready for a shot himself. Instead, thoughts of solving the mystery of Big Shelter put on hold for the nonce, the patriarch settled for a whisky; two shots. He thereupon reacquired his old suite in the classy hotel and went to sleep.

Sunday had to be a better day.

========

It certainly began well enough.

Angus Skullian woke him according to schedule. As also prearranged, they then went to breakfast together. Pry as he subtlety might, the Great Man couldn't get confirmation out of his personal physician that he, Skullian, had been hit by a devil-ray. Nor any recognition that he'd been possessed of a devil on and off since they arrived last Monday. And this from a man whose memory went beyond the merely photographic almost to the point of being supranormal.

The doctor did have some good news, however. Sentalli had recovered from whatever had afflicted him last night. Thanks mostly to Dr Lindquist's quickness, young Dorothy was also out of danger. Sentalli's niece was still sleeping in the Fatman's oversized bed upstairs – attended by the diligent and probable Althean-Anthean-Athenan up-and-comer, Connie herself – but she too would be up and about by nightfall.

Adolph Dulles's version of a seizure had been equally short-lived. He was already back on duty. Skullian had seen him that morning – they did much the same daybreak exercise circuit – and was happy to relay to the patriarch Dolph's news that things were calming down throughout the world. Schmidt might be able to get out of Pearl sometime today; probably the same was true for the Signallers, who hadn't been able to leave Vancouver Saturday because of the riots there.

What Ryne was happiest to hear was that everybody was still in place. Not one of the Untouchables, not even the lawyer or Dr Samarand, nor Alfredo or his vaguely greenish-skinned son, had gone the way of Cromwell Necator and his fellow so-called protectors.

Perhaps that meant, as Hiyati had said yesterday night, they were serious about defending the island and its secrets to the last man, woman, whatever of them. Much more likely, however, they were just dispossessed of whatever it was inside them that would do the defending.

(Satan St Synne's devaray worked one way only. It could not, as it were, recall the devil thus imparted at St Synne's whim. You got one it stayed with until you died or the ray's effect wore off. That was why there were multiple Demon Lands but only one Peter D'Angelo Demon Land. Whether Sentalli's equivalent was an improvement on St Synne's original, well, Ryne was reserving judgement on that for the time being.)

The trickster had done as she promised. Even though he didn't share his sentiments with his doctor, the Great Man was secretly pleased as Punchinello she was still around. What he wasn't so happy about was that, if he was right, he'd lost whatever punch devils like the two he'd met yesterday, Goldenrod and Morningstar, might provide.

Whatever it actually was, Translav's surprise – assuming, as Dulles questioned, it was even real and not bunk WORLD dreamed up in order to get Sentalli's people, scientific geniuses that many of them were, into its clutches – was still out there. Dare he stay on until help arrived? The morning's good news had him leaning that way.

"Okay, Angus. Sounds like things, at least in the outside world and here on the island, are improving. Wish I could say the same about whatever's going on in the Liberty and on the Moon. I'm going to ask you to stay downstairs, keep your eyes open, and your fabled memory in recording mode.

"Schmidt, Smythe, and James Aremar trained you well. I'm confident you can look after yourself. Your forbearers always did, so don't disappoint. Something's down there and I don't mean a bunch of exploding albinos, if that's where they got to. I want to know what it is. You get anything to report, contact me upstairs in Sentalli's suite."

Skullian, whose supranormal father was deaf, twisted an imaginary button at the side of his head. That could indicate he'd dutifully turned on his in-brain tape recorder.

Or it might indicate he reckoned Ryne screwy.

========

Other than the occasional cigar over brandy after a particularly hearty meal, Loxus Abraham Ryne hadn't smoked in a quarter century. Hiyati Samarand seldom stopped smoking. The oriental overseer was among those with the patriarch to hear a report from one of Dulles's security officers on the Untouchables.

From that point on the day went south, as in pear-shaped, as in to hell in a dogcart pulled by Cerberus, Hades' three-headed hellhound.

========

The octogenarian was seriously thinking of asking for one of the Asian-looking scientocrat's Marlboros; better yet a whole pack. After all, everyone around him seemed to be dying. Why should he be left out? If he ever got home and had a chance to write in his diary again, he'd be entitling this section *'The Fatal Symphony'*.

If only because no one except Mistress Fate (Dame Fortune, Lady Luck) – who presumably wasn't a 3-eyed devil – could have any idea what was really going on.

(Actually she was; rather, someone whose power focus was a Triskelion, a three-spoke Wheel of Fortune minus the rim, had her attributes. Also called Wintry Moira, the devic version of Fata Fortuna was a Lazaremist. Many of the stories regarding her were told by Jordan Tethys, the recurring deviant who boasted she used to stalk him. She may be doing so again soon if hers was one the stars that escaped the Sedon Sphere on Sedonda-Sunday.

(There was also a devil who rode around in a dogcart. Her hell, Kore's Hell, was a logically impossible, verdant paradise growing in the heart of a still venting volcano on Apple Isle, Sedon's Human Eye-Land. Known in Outer Earth legends as the Blessed Isle of the Hesperides, many thought it was the original Garden of Eden; others the home of Idunn, a fabulous figment of Norse mythology.

(Reputedly, Apple Isle's namesakes, its golden apples granted devils immortality and humans extremely long lives and eternal youth to go with it, so long as it lasted. While devils – the Moloch Sedon, Great Gods, Master Devas and lesser devils, their azuras – apparently didn't need anything except stellar energy to survive, there was some truth to the second part of that belief. The Golden Age Patriarchs and their relations did attain extremely long and very healthy lives by eating golden apples.

(Divine Coueranna, aka Kore-Concord and many another name – hence also myrionymous Kore – was a second-born Mithradite. Kore-Discord (Fitna Marutia, Marut Kanin, Strife) and Kore-Concupiscence (Lady Lust) were her brood sisters. Outer Earth legend turned them into the three nymphs eponymously known as the Hesperides. That, though, was nonsense. Lady Lust was the only real nymph among them, hence nymphomania.

(Thrygragos Varuna Mithras's Boss Cow for Taurus, rejected when the Great God chose Marutia to become his Ewe for Aries, found her way to the Outer Earth. There she became better known as the Great Goddess Cybele, Methandra Thanatos's main rival for top-dog top goddess in the Mediterranean Goddess Culture of circa 2000 to 2500 Years of the Dome beneath the Dome. The dogs who pulled her dogcart when she left her Hell were Keres Hellhounds.

(Some of them, like the fabled Cerberus, did indeed have three heads. The lava flow that streamed through her hell was called the River Styx. Since it contained loads of molten Brainrock, others called it the Stynx, for reasons olfactory. Hush's hated enemy, the perpetual child Tralalorn, aka the White Dwarf, rode a hellhound she'd transformed into a goat. Her Chimera not only had three heads, it breathed fired.

(Trala, as likely a demon child as a devil child, loved her Chimera. She also loved her living dolls. She played rough. Korant Kore Queens to this day ran hospices for Trala's broken dolls. Most of the Kore Queens who did so had been her howsoever luckier dolls. Hush was once one of them. She got away. Trala tracked her down, made sure she never got to grow up, whereupon she got away again.

(Better never to grow up, Hush supposed, than to risk being broken. Some of Trala's dolls never got as far as hospices.)

"Run that by me again. Mister ...?"

"Marsh, sir. Like I said, as near as I can make out they're dying."

The big Hawaiian wasn't sure whom he should address. In Max's absence Dulles was technically his superior, but he and Tadpole were at the airport going through the albinos' plane looking for booby traps. Alfredo Sentalli was his boss, but he was in the other room with the little girl he knew as Dorothy Dodgson and thought was the Fatman's grand niece or some such. Besides, Yataghan was blocking the doorway.

Despite his size and experience, Marsh had seen him in action against Mr No Name and knew better than to tangle with him. While he admired his fearlessness, Marsh further realized there was something of the berserker about Sentalli's son. Although no shrinking violet when it came to violence himself, retirement was still a few years off and he still hoped to get close enough to it to at least start savouring its imminent arrival.

Ordinarily Dr Samarand would take the Fatman's place, but the technician in overall charge of Project Centauri – read the Cosmic Express – was obviously deferring to Ryne right this minute. Marsh consequently felt he should do the same. Regardless of his advanced age, the Great Man was NCE's largest shareholder, still had a formidable presence, an even more impressive voice, and had doubtless earned the deference.

"What!?! All, however many of them there are, at the same time?"

"Only eight, sir. I think, sir," stumble-mouthed Marsh, taken aback by what he took to be the old man's unwarranted umbrage. It wasn't as if he, Marsh, had poisoned them. "Not the ones in this room. And yes, sir. Dying. That's why I came up here. I knew Dr Lindquist was with you and, well, Max always said they were friends of hers."

"I'll go," offered Connie. In all likelihood she was still suffering the after-effects of her head wound, subsequent sedation, and a probable concussion. Additionally, after spending the night and all of the morning attending to Hush, the Fatman and Dulles, she looked about ready to collapse again herself.

"You'll do no such thing, Ms Morningstar."

"Lindquist."

Even though he recognized futility when it kicked him in the kisser – so much for solving Shelter, at least for today – the patriarch gave Samarand an enquiring glance.

"Lindquist," confirmed the overseer querulously. "Who's Morningstar?"

"Goldenrod? Devils? Big Shelter?" shot back the old man.

"I'm sorry, Mr Ryne," apologized Samarand, putting on a concerned face. "Look, if you're tired, perhaps you should get some rest as well. We do have a number of issues that require immediate attention and, as Mr Sentalli seems to be having his own difficulties lately, it's left to me to attend to them."

"You're not leaving my sight. None of you are. Mr Marsh, call downstairs. Have Dr Creel, make that Dr Skullian, come up here and examine them: the ones downstairs, not this lot."

Someone, possibly Hush, possibly Superior Sarpedon, wherever she'd got to these past few years, but more likely his long-time mistress, Headmistress Virginia Mannering, once told him that, in Anthean lore, Strife never left memories behind. Could that be true of these devils? And if so, did that mean Strife was a devil?

He decided he better start writing things down. Better yet, recording things. Which gave him another thought.

"Tell me, um, Marsh, is all that monitor equipment in the next room working?"

"As far as I know, sir. Mr Sentalli liked to keep his finger on the pulse of the island, as he put it. So long as he didn't have to go too far, I suppose it goes without saying too loudly. Should I send someone up to check it out? He usually relied on Roderick Paraja for that sort of thing but he's ..."

"Yeah, yeah. He's dying. You told me. Have Skullian bring a couple of my SPACE-Men. He knows them better than I do. Tell him what I want and let him pick which ones." Marsh hesitated. Ryne hated hesitation. "Well? Move it, man!"

"Just one thing, sir."

"What?"

"That's just it. What is it you want?"

========

Greygreave Translav was infuriated.

========

From his sea-base on WORLD's yacht, he tried to radio his covert chief of operations on Centauri Island. As had happened yesterday, he was told Dr Lindquist wasn't available. Neither was her Number Two, Mavis Chester. The person who did respond, a man he knew best as Mugwump, informed him for the first time that he'd been given the antidote years earlier.

He was no longer a Gloman. None of the Glows the Little Prince had insinuated onto Centauri were either – hadn't been for a couple of years – and weren't interested in becoming ones again. Big Max, O'Ryan James Maxwell, had co-opted WORLD's agents in the best way possible. He'd made them his own.

Not by bribery or the threat of blowing up, either. By respecting them; by forgiving them their past with the WORLD of, in many cases, the Sixties and very early Seventies; by allowing them the opportunity to do what they did best — fool folks. Fool the whole fucking world. Not to mention, most importantly, the Global Menace itself.

Even if it was, there was nothing to fix because no one realized it wasn't broken.

========

The term Global Menace, though apt, was not one Translav came up with or preferred to use. A Gloman was so-called simply because he or she would glow just before they exploded. Ordinarily they were terminally ill people who, in return for a large amount of money for their dependents, would spy or perform a suicide mission, often an assassination.

Even though it was a departure from form, circumstances were such that, for Project Centauri, Prince Translav couldn't just recruit sick people to be his Glomen fifth column on the island. Everyone had to have verifiable, not to mention lofty, credentials in order to get work there in the first place.

With their permission, so he claimed, the Little Prince had varied the procedure, deliberately infecting his recruits, most of whom were able-bodied, with the drugs that turned them into Glows. They would function normally but if they didn't receive timely injections they would blow. He made it worth their while with higher than usual remuneration.

Big Max, though, had somehow subverted the process. For one thing, he'd employed Anthean witches on the island under the guise of Paul Creel's nurses and interned doctors. These were good witches, what used to be called White Witches, though white skin was hardly a prerequisite for membership.

White Witches were more correctly known as Altheans or Alts. Their namesake, Althea, was an obscure Greek Goddess; an eponym of their word for *'healer'*. Either that or it was an alternate name for Epione (*'Soothe'*). She in turn was the mother of, among others, Hygeia (*'Health'*) and Panacea (*'Medicine'*).

Her husband, their father, was the physician god Asclepius, famous for his Snake Staff (not to be confused with Hermes the Messenger's winged caduceus). The equally famous *'asclepieions'* of ancient and early modern times in Kos, Pergamum, Epidaurus and so on Solon, as the old nonsense rhyme went, were named after Asclepius. If they could be called that, its physicians controversially practised dream-cures.

Alts were pure healers. They were also the only kind of Ant their Superior, Hiliarti Schroff-Zeross, and her aged but still perceptive mentor, Dolores D'Angelo Rivera (who was only a couple of years younger than Abe Ryne), would train nowadays. Were the only one they ever could train, truth told, because they weren't proper witches like Fisherwoman, Sorciere, Wilderwitch, Superior Sarpedon or Hush herself.

For those terminally ill Glows who did secure a position on Centauri Island, no cures were promised. Nevertheless, with the Alt-Ants' palliative, homoeopathic medicines; holistic, nature-based approach to dealing with disease; and their almost supranormal ability to improve the functioning of the body's own immune system; there was always some degree of hope.

Additionally, Sentalli often flew employees' families to the island. So, if they did die, it would be both in comfort and in the company of their loved ones. With the help of Big Max and the Superior Sisterhood – in the spirit of Panharmonium – Sentalli promised to turn his island into a technocratic Utopia once the Express was successfully launched. And those already on the island would be allowed to stay if they so desired.

Then, and most shockingly, it was now obvious that Max and his Ant-Alts had come up with a way to neutralize his agents; a veritable cure for *'Glomanitis'*, or whatever the condition his drugs imparted was called this month. If this became what passed for public knowledge amongst the kind of person, criminal or corporate entity he normally did business with, he may well be out of work.

Even worse news for the self-advertised Romanov prince, at least in terms of the immediate, was the total disappearance of Necator's band of Glomen. Although they were infected with a different strain of Glow-Drugs, without them, without any Glows on the island, he had no bargaining chips. This fact Loxus Ryne made certain to emphasize when he spoke directly to Translav after Mugwump got hold of him.

Feigning ignorance of the trigger-fingers Lindquist had secreted somewhere on the island until a day or two ago, the patriarch pointed out that, if Translav did detonate the albinos from afar, the damage wouldn't be done to Centauri Island or its people. How could it? Necator had already left. And the Glows wouldn't necessarily blow in isolation either. Some might be on boats or airplanes heading home. It would be mass murder. In those cases Ryne would hold the Russian Summoning Child personally responsible.

Did he have to remind Translav that the United Nations wholeheartedly backed his efforts to eliminate the globe-threatening Menace on the Moon?

Every nation on the planet had either lent their expertise or contributed to SPACE financially and materially. That meant every ruler, no matter how fanatical, including those in the renegade state of South Africa, Translav's haven before the Worldwide Order lured him back into the fold, were beholding to Ryne and the UN's Space Council. If he wanted, he could have the Little Prince's head in a hatbox on his desk within the week.

Ryne did hold out an olive branch. If Translav was to aid in the evacuation, the patriarch might whitewash his involvement in the destruction of the Cosmic Express. Conceivably, again if the midget cooperated and informed on those in the Order directly responsible for it, well, they could work something out in the way of leniency and protection.

Translav readily agreed but, later that afternoon, he was on a speedboat heading towards Maui. Why not? He was rich and didn't need the aggravation. Let Daemonicus and Strife, if they were still around, Steltsar and Crystallion, if they weren't, have WORLD.

Up against the formidable old man and the tricky little witch – who'd clearly gone over to Ryne now that the albinos and his Glows were no longer a threat to her belly-bursting Daddy Alfredo Sauce – they'd likely get themselves killed. More's the pity. Or, as Hush might say, morals are shitty.

Still, it remained within his capacity to make supplementary hay. He ordered the yacht and WORLD's converted fish packer to continue towards Centauri Island. Their instructions were the same. Get the scientists, etcetera, on the Order's list off Centauri and assist with the evacuation as best they could.

Unfortunately, he said to fish packer's captain by radio, just before he left her in charge of the operation, he had been unavoidably called to the mainland. That meant, if only to avoid shame and blame both, he couldn't be there to direct them. Naturally without telling them he was buggering off, he implicitly entrusted the Great Man and the trickster to take care of his darling daughter; take care as in look after, not kill, her.

The converted packer's captain had seen Greygreave Translav and Shaikh Ali Ars Markazi arrive on Wednesday night. She hadn't seen them leave, though of course she knew they had to have because she'd just received instructions from the Little Prince to proceed to Centauri Island and help evacuate it. Since when, not mention why, did Centauri Island need evacuation?

Early the next morning she had seen Salvatore Dis L'Orca leave on the boat's onboard helicopter along with two others she hadn't seen arrive. Those two looked enough alike they could be twins. So how did they get there? Or where were they hiding? For that matter, how did the cleaver-armed countess, Lady Guillotine as she thought of her, get there a couple of days earlier?

Equally perplexingly, why had she left, once the helicopter returned later on that same day, last Thursday, with Milo Mind and yet another mystery guest, a woman with two-toned black and white hair and carrying a fancy jewel box of some sort. More to the point, why hadn't the copter come back? And why hadn't they bothered to let her know it wasn't coming back? Had something happened to it?

The ship wasn't sinking. Truth told, she didn't feel much like a rat either. But the Little Prince had left her in charge and she reckoned it past time to charge home. So she waited until the yacht's skipper reported Translav was out of sight then steered the packer south, towards the Big Island of Hawaii. She advised the yacht to do the same. It was everyone for his or her self from now on.

Their bank accounts were fat enough to do without any additional bonuses.

========

Late in the afternoon Adolph Dulles returned from the airport.

Even though Sean Smythe's cry of despair hadn't been repeated, he looked much older than his twenty-seven years. Without being invited, he slumped onto an easy chair in the den of the Fatman's private, multi-roomed suite and opened a large envelope he was carrying in his hand.

"We've got serious problems."

========

Hush Mannering was still snoozing quietly in Sentalli's bedroom, now under the care of one of the current Superior's young, life-sustaining Althean nurses, one selected primarily for her deafness. On the opposite end of the extended suite, three of Ryne's SPACE-men were tending to the monitor systems behind closed doors.

Last night's bordering on psychotic outburst at least temporarily under control – thanks mostly to the drugs Hush injected him with before she was taken down by Dulles' sleep dart – Alfredo Sentalli, in his wheelchair as always, was behind his desk in the den between the communications room and his much larger living room. The usually silent Yataghan stood behind his unhealthily obese father.

Also in the den were Hiyati Samarand, Connie Lindquist, George Hannibal – both of whom entirely human now that Hush had dispossessed them – and Loxus Abraham Ryne. Lindquist and Hannibal sat together on a couch like the lovers they were and had been for years. Along with Yataghan and Hiyati Samarand, they were all that was left conscious of Sentalli's Untouchables.

As was his wont, Dr Samarand was on his feet by the open window, smoking cigarette after cigarette. Ever the businessman, Ryne sat in a hard-backed chair to one side of the Fatman's desk. For once Yataghan hadn't made sure the Great Man was unarmed. Possibly in return, the Great Man hadn't insisted Yat remove his wickedly curved blade in his presence. Much to Sentalli's horror, Dulles and most of his upper echelon officers were armed as well.

(Like his father and, yes, his mother before him, Ryne almost always packed iron, as he liked to put it. He believed it was the right – nay, the responsibility – of every free man to carry a gun. Except, that is, when he didn't want them to, it went without saying. To do otherwise would be to accede to traditional authority figures. They corrupted too easily, he'd add, master corrupter that he was, then have a good laugh.)

"Let's play twenty questions, shall we?" suggested the old man, trying to be droll. It was a defence mechanism; was also a mostly futile effort at bravado. Like almost everyone else there, he was showing far more strain than usual. Should have joined the exodus, he must have been thinking. "Kadmon Heliosophos, whom Al here renamed one of the peaks right behind us after, is not only back from the dead. He's on the Moon and causing riots throughout the Earth. Is that the serious problem?"

"Funnily enough," said Samarand, from his window perch, "The latest reports we've received indicate things are calming down considerably. I say funnily because it doesn't seem to be the usual suspects – cops, militias army personnel – taking charge. People are forcing order out of chaos themselves. They're tossing guns and every other kind of weapons into the nearest stream, burying them, or destroying them altogether."

"Correction," smirked Ryne. "The Man on the Moon's turning everyone into simpering liberals. How about this then? The Houston Academy of Man comes under attack from a bunch of albinos whom Prince Translav swears aren't his Glomen but Al here claims aren't his either. Ours, to use the term generously, have now done a bunk. Wonder where they went?"

"Are we counting the questions?" wondered Hannibal distractedly. "I make it three, maybe four, now."

"Staying with Houston," Ryne flicked a middle finger. "I've got a daughter missing from there since Wednesday."

"More than a daughter," Sentalli reminded him. After waking up, the Fatman had told the octogenarian deliberate distortions of what Hush had learned, via Dr Lindquist, from Greygreave Translav and, without mentioning his name, Demios Sarpedon.

"Fair enough. So, if one's to believe an unconscious trickster ... Sorry, your niece. What's her name this time, Al?"

"Dorothy Dodgson. Hush is only a nickname. Same as it's always been. She's seven," he added for the others, not sure what they remembered.

"Correction again, if one's to believe a seven year old, I've a forty-seven year old daughter and a son, who should be fifty but looks like he's still twenty-six, missing. The one, whom I once thought dead for something like seventeen years back in the Forties and early Fifties, is the target of these non-Gloman Glomen's attack in Houston.

"The other's also back from the dead; him after fully a quarter century. Back along with his twin brother and nine others, according to Signal System – which is at least partially run by a plus-centenarian who should also be well and truly dead. Who knows where they've gone to and God knows what they're up to?"

"Was that one or two questions?" queried Hannibal.

"Presumably the answer to the first," offered Lindquist, "Is contained in the whole statement. Thankfully I'm an atheist."

"An atheist!" The lawyer sounded shocked. "I thought witches worshipped the devil, with or without a capital '*D*'."

"Shut up!" demanded Samarand, sick of their dissembling.

"For once we're in accordance, doctor," said Ryne. "I've two hundred of my best men, together with your sort of Uncle Johann, Dolph – whom I've just heard has gone into some kind of somatic shock similar to the bunch down in the ballroom – stuck in Pearl Harbour with an airport going up in flames around them."

"It's been put out," provided Samarand.

"I've a spaceship orbiting the Moon," said Ryne, continuing to enumerate the serious problems he perceived. "With two men, a Maxwell, like aforementioned daughter, albeit by marriage, and a Kinesis, like my mother no less, that I've known for the better part of forty years supranormals since Sunday. Assuming they made it of course, which we don't know since we've lost contact with the Liberty.

"I'm in a room mostly full of seemingly regular folks like me who were devil-possessed up until a day ago, but now pretend they don't remember any of it. There are a number of other folks dying downstairs, presumably because they aren't devil-possessed anymore either. Dying, mind you, as opposed to sitting here chain-smoking and making useless cracks.

"There's an Anthean trickster sleeping in the other room. She never kills but mercilessly helped blow up a couple of albinos who smelled like they were already dead, maybe two or three times by now."

"Tell me about it," said Dr Lindquist. "I'm still suffering from the ramifications."

"Thought I already was – telling you about it. Though, if it's any consolation, apparently you were only ancillary damage."

"It isn't. And it's my head, not my ancillary, that's damaged."

"Coincidentally manage to knock you out, then, as well as onto your keister. This would be the same little witch who's responsible for the ones dying in the ballroom."

"Responsible for them dying!" Lindquist sounded shocked. Devils, even if they were only the ex-shells of devils – unless they were victims of a perhaps non-existent devaray or Miracle Key – evidently couldn't resist playing the devil's advocates. "How the hell did she manage that when she was damn near dead herself? More to the paediatric point, if it's true, we better wake her before they do die."

Ryne still wasn't finished. "Al also tells me there's a fish packer out there with my ex-wife – whom I believed was dying in Budapest and may well be dead in Houston by now – and one of my most valued former colleagues on it. That'd be the Major Mind, who isn't a major mind, small case, but did help invent the amnaesthetics that have kept supras normal for what? Most of thirty years by now. Unless Al here has managed to undo them; hence his supras."

"I haven't. Haven't got any supras either."

"So you say," Ryne had given up on counting twenty questions; was just listing off potentially serious problems. "Also just recently there, besides everyone else who shouldn't have been there, were a pair of twins only a year or so older than you, Dolph, if that. Seems these twins are either the children of my nephew and my ex-wife or they're my grandchildren by my quarter-century dead son – who isn't dead anymore – and that selfsame ex-wife.

"Who also isn't dead, nor in Budapest or Houston for that matter. Or did I mention that already? Unless of course they're Daemonicus and Strife. Or, wait, maybe they were, are, Saul and my other dead ex-wife, your aunt Yataghan, which would also make her my ex-dead ex-wife. Got everything straight so far, Al?"

"Eminently so," the Fatman congratulated him. "Never occurred to me that Barbed Barbara was Strife, though. Mightn't that make Daemonicus be Dead Jesse?"

"Don't you get going too." Ryne caught his breath. In a moment of inspiration, he started to untie his shoelaces.

"You've made your point, Mr Ryne," understood the cynical lawyer. "No need to count your toes."

"I'll count-coup with your ears soon," said the patriarch menacingly. "And I won't stop there." When his shoes and socks were off, he carried on.

"I've got another daughter either dead or lost in space. A son, Erech, Anhita's twin, who finally decides this afternoon to phone in order to let me know he thinks he spent part of Friday night on a plane from Vancouver to Los Angeles sitting beside Thalassa D'Angelo, one of the no-longer-dead Crimefighters.

"This'd be the same son who's now in Houston with his mother, who's dying and needs a cure only Aranyani can provide. Except, to risk repeating myself, Ramona was declared dead earlier this week and Aran was supposedly last seen on this fish packer with Erech's mother – the one that's simultaneously dying in Houston – but is now believed missing, perhaps even dead yet again. This time for real.

"What else? Oh yes, a pair of twelve year old daughters in hiding somewhere as unknown as Aran's whereabouts. These twelve year olds just happen to be the nieces of the current Mother Superior of the Anthean Sisterhood and Ringleader, who probably provided the way for Helios to get to the Moon in the first place.

"Twelve year olds, mark you, in hiding with Headmistress – who isn't the supra Headmistress that gave birth to two other twins now up in the Liberty, assuming they're still there. At least I don't think she is." This drew a complete blank from those there. "Not that any of you would realize that James Aremar and Mik Starrus are the twin sons of Emperor Energy and the supra Headmistress."

"You're right about that, Abe," said his Enormity, who wasn't as up on supra history as he sometimes liked to pretend. "Guess I should have read Mik's file before I displaced him in favour of Colonel Sol as overall Cosmicommander. Maybe he could have got together with Aremar and taken out the Man on the Moon."

"It wasn't in it; the file, I mean. And don't get me going about Avatar Sol. If Heliopolis isn't history then his five sharp-toothed Spartae probably aren't either."

"Hadn't intended to; get you going, I mean. Sorry."

"Then there's the Tempest Twins, Yataghan's twenty-nine year old maternal cousins by me and my second wife, the aforementioned barbed Barbara, the bitch who betrayed me with my own psycho-son. Hopefully they're not involved in any of this but, if they find out Saul's still alive, they'll be out for blood soon enough. He killed their thorny mother after all. No dispute there.

"Finally, again according to Al, via the same trickster sawing logs ever so sweetly in the other room, there's a phantom freighter nearby he's been trying to convince me houses a bunch of atomic-powered dragons. Anything I've forgotten? Oh yes, a plane load of Signallers, who work for some of my most persistent enemies – or their children – are due in tonight or tomorrow on a direct flight from Vancouver.

"Serious problems, you say? True! Which particular one did you have in mind, Dolph?"

"Give the boy some space, Mr Ryne," prescribed Sentalli. "Can't you see he's sickly? What is it, Mr Dulles?"

"First of all the good news, the protectors' plane is clean. I suppose that means you'll be leaving us now."

"I'm sorely tempted," admitted the patriarch. "But I still haven't made up my mind And don't tell me that's because of my age. What's in that envelope?"

"Pictures, sir. Fact is, the riots never hit us anywhere near as hard as the rest of the world. Tad's had surveillance planes up most of the day. But, like Mr Sentalli suggested, they're not the only things up there. Got our first inkling when one of the pilots spotted a speedboat on fire. Of course we alerted the civilian authorities but you know what's happening off island.

"Authority's become a dirty word. Even though, thankfully, no one's killing anyone anymore; no one's doing much of anything else either. Anyhow, the pilot took some snaps and I had them run through the computers. One positive identification: Greygreave Translav. He's wearing a life jacket but looks dead. Could be unconscious."

Ryne and Sentalli exchanged glances. "Who isn't?" groaned the Fatman.

"What else?" demanded the old man, convinced he hadn't heard the worst; if there was such a thing as worst.

"More pictures: of a couple of other boats on fire. They're quite a distance apart. One's a fancy yacht but the other's a huge, Japanese-style fish packer. We've got the registration, if you need it, but it's probably legit – or was. Both boats have been absolutely totalled. Bomb, bombs, of some sort, possibly even nuclear, they're the closest thing to vapourized you can get but one's so much like the other we reckon they're related.

"There are no survivors that we can see; no bodies either, as far as that goes. One of the stranger things about it is the packer's been converted. See for yourselves."

He handed the photographs around. "Intelligence – read that as Tad – says it's been stripped down, got a helicopter pad, what looks like a kind of high-tech catapult, and enough umbrella dishes to tune into damn near anywhere. Even the Moon. Best guess is that's where the craft that destroyed the Cosmic Express came from last Sunday."

"Max has had planes up for weeks now," noted Samarand. "How did it escape detection?"

"Don't know, sir," admitted Dulles. "Mighty impressive feat to avoid it; I wouldn't have thought it possible. The packer must have been expertly camouflaged."

"Or masked by witch glamours," decided the patriarch. "Possibly by Strife, though I doubt it. My nephew mastered a lot of Anthean techniques and Helios, if I have to call him that, seems to have taken the Conqueror's discoveries to their logical extreme. He did hide an entire citadel on the Moon from the Liberty."

"Be that as it may," muttered Sentalli matter-of-factly, "I'd say so long to Major Milo Mind, the phony Countess Ramona, and either Mandam's or Psycho's twins. Can't say I'll be mourning any of them, though if your Aranyani was onboard any of them, then I'm sorry for your loss, Abe. Her I liked."

"A lot less than I did my dad," said Lindquist, dabbing her eyes.

"Yes, well," said the Fatman uncertainly. "I suppose the coast guard might get to him before the sharks do. Any proof these flaming boats are related, Dolph?"

"Self-evident, isn't it, Al?" snapped Ryne. "The various factions of WORLD are wiping each other out. Any sign of this oddball freighter his *'niece'* told Alfredo about?"

"That's the most galling part, sir," declared Dulles. "It's out there. Our planes have seen signs of it, tailings of gas, indications of radio transmissions. Thought we had it pinpointed around noon. Has to be there. Only thing is, we can't get any visuals. It's like we really are dealing with a ghost ship. It's there but it isn't. Kind of like Cromwell Necator and his albinos."

"All right, Mr Dulles," appreciated Ryne. "If there's nothing else, you better go get something to eat."

"What an excellent notion," drooled Sentalli.

"Supper it is," agreed the octogenarian, finally having decided what to do. "Then we're out of here."

=========

Tadpole interrupted desert.

"We've just lost three of our six planes," he told them grimly. "I've ordered the others back to base and cancelled your flight out."

"On whose authority?" demanded Ryne angrily.

Tadpole didn't need thought beams coming from the moon to shrug off the old man's outburst. He never had much use for authority. "Have a look at these, then tell me I was wrong." He pointedly handed an envelope of photographs to Dulles instead of Ryne, however. "One of the pilots sent them to us just before we lost contact with him."

Dolph whistled gravely. "If this shit is real, we can't deal with it."

Sentalli took one look at the picture then swore: "They are fucking dragons!"

Ryne had to grin. "And my name's St George!"

****

Nᴜᴋᴇ 23: **Seventeen Signallers**

========

Monday, December 8, 1980

With no news from the Liberty, Signal System or Johann Schmidt's Interven-
tion Team – and no further sightings of Atomic Firedrakes – the worst thing hap-
pening on Centauri Island was waiting for something worse to happen. Then, not
much more than a week after disaster in the form of Kamikaze Kaligula struck
the Cosmic Express, Roderick Paraja died.

He was only the first of the unconscious Untouchables to do so.

========

Paraja expired just before midnight Sunday The other seven expired, one by
one, as night became day and the day progressed to night again. Oddly enough,
it wasn't until word reached the island that some celebrity-seeking peabrain with
one of those freedom-ensuring gun-things that Al Sentalli hated so much had
killed John Lennon, the former Beatle, in New York City, that Hiyati Samarand
had his heart attack in Sentalli's suite.

While Dr Connie Lindquist, who'd lost her father the day before, began to
administer CPR to him, Dolph Dulles heard a helpless Fatman (Alfredo Sentalli) remark to an equally helpless patriarch (Loxus Abraham Ryne): "At least it
wasn't either of us." Then the door to his bedroom slammed open.

"Hello, daddies! What's up?"

"Hope you didn't speak too soon, Al."

========

Tuesday, December 9, 1980

With the riots become love-ins become a return to relative normality on
Oahu, the two hundred strong Intervention Team from the Alliance of Man finally
made it to Sentalli's island shortly after dawn Tuesday. Even though boats were
still leaving port, Ryne remained on shore; had, so he swore, decided to make
a stand. Consequently neither his SPACE-plane, nor that of the protectors, had
left.

Of course the real reason was that he didn't want to tangle, let alone tango,
with a bunch of radioactive dragons. He'd kept their existence a secret, how-

ever; certainly hadn't forewarned the occupants of the third big plane now on the side of the tarmac. Perhaps he'd hoped the presumably artificial beasties might want a predawn snack.

The plane that preceded the Alliance's was silver.

=========

Alfredo Sentalli was having breakfast.

With him were his son, the commonly silent Yataghan, his seven year old 'niece' Dorothy, who was pretty much the poster child for yappy kid, his personal physician Connie Lindquist – who was actually feeling better now that word had come to her that the Little Prince must have been eaten by sharks since his body hadn't been found – and his handpicked lawyer, George Hannibal. He'd just finished his second bacon, onions and cheese omelette of the morning, when seven Signallers strode into the hotel's dining room.

"Hear you've an infestation of supras," said their field leader, Gus Soldakis, the Space Age Spartan.

"Nice lids," cooed the little girl. "Got any for kids?"

=========

"And I tell you," his Enormity argued with Sharpshooter, the only one of the seventeen Silvers now on his island he would speak to, an hour later in his private suite, "There's no sign of any Crimefighters, devaray victims, Callion Clones, or whatever you think there are here. Signal System must have been mistaken."

"Do you deny," demanded bullet-headed 'Shooter, in the garbled tones that all Signallers generated when speaking through their helmets, "That you sent a group of albinos, elite members of the Global Menace, to blow up the laboratory of Moses Callion and Aranyani Nightingale at the Academy of Man in Houston?"

"Do you deny you're Thaddeus Hyperenor, son of the Silver Arrow Assassins and thought dead, like your pal on the Moon, for twelve years now?"

"System's affairs are not your business, Mr Sentalli."

As his name implied, he was more the shoot first and ask questions later sort. Except, of course, those he shot usually didn't answer questions later. Then again, usually wasn't quite the right word. Usually those he shot wouldn't be able to answer questions unless he wanted them alive to do just that. (He found it very hard to altogether miss anything.) Thus, for the time being, he kept his armaments subsumed within his Silver.

"And island affairs are none of yours, sir."

"Touché. And you're right. But only up to a point. Supranormals are, wherever they are."

Visionaries, especially those with the conviction, determination, and wherewithal to realize their dreams, were some of his favourite folks. No innovator himself, this despite the fact that he was considered a designer within System, Sharpshooter consequently admired Sentalli almost as much as he did the patriarch. However, he couldn't help but wish Shelter, Styx, Sasquatch or even Solar were here instead of him. Didactics weren't his proverbial cup of gunpowder.

"Moe Three admitted to Shelter he was trying to re-grow them: clones of some of the original Crimefighters and their buddies, that is. Claims you or one of your associates hired the Menace to destroy his work. As evidence he points to O'Ryan James Maxwell and Romaine Kinesis. They visited his labs on Wednesday. Both men work for you; have done for many years. They've clearly become supras. Where are they?"

"As to that, best speak with the person who summoned you. Mr Hannibal, please escort this gentleman, if that's what you truly are, over to Mr Ryne. I believe he and Mr Dulles are at what we now jokingly refer to as Last Stand Central. When you report to your Strategos, Simon Lancz, kindly remind him that he is beholden to Mr Maxwell."

"I'll tell him you said so. I trust you have no objections if we stay on the island for a while." Shooter didn't give the Fatman time to reply.

"Thought not. See you around."

========

Adolph Dulles was among those who greeted the new arrivals from the Alliance.

========

He accompanied the team to their operational headquarters in the same building near the airport as the SPACE contingent were once again ensconced. He and Mugwump then took Johann Schmidt and his chief lieutenants upstairs to see Loxus Ryne. For Dulles, seeing the man whom his foster parents, Auld Jock and Bountiful Bunnie (Jock Maxwell and Bonita, once Galvin, but born O'Ryan), openly called his Uncle Joe in such dire straits, wrenched his heartstrings.

Doubleman could barely walk. Ever since Dulles screamed in Sean Smythe's voice Saturday night, speculation had been rampant that Smythe had died. Even though there had yet to be any confirmation from the Liberty, one look at Schmidt all but confirmed he was now a Singleman; albeit, apparently, not for long. Self-preservative as his foster parents and Mentor Max taught him to be, Dulles prayed he wasn't heading the same direction.

"I want you to hang on, Johann," voiced Ryne, moments after they shook hands and sat down. "It is very important. There's a good chance you could be the key to turning the tide against whatever's up there on the Moon. Dolph will stay with you. He came through Sean's passing all right. Maybe he can give you strength." The way Ryne spoke he wasn't giving either man a choice in the matter.

"The extra weapons, sir," Dulles reminded the octogenarian.

"We've splatter packs," noted one of Schmidt's lieutenants, a Galvin distantly related to Bunnie's first (and only) husband James, who died in 1939. "Picked them up specially in Pearl."

"Trade them," offered Mugwump.

On Thursday a certain little witch told the one-time Gloman that fragmentation weapons worked best against Dead Things Walking. Since he and his company were still patrolling the depths expecting the return of Cromwell Necator and his protectors, he reckoned they might come in handy. That they were doing so ignorantly, as in futilely, made no never mind. How were they to know that?

"For what?" wondered Schmidt.

"Zip guns," said Ryne.

"That's zap, sir," corrected Dulles. "As in tasers."

=========

Paul Creel couldn't resist the 'Speaking Stick' that Seer Savant, one of the seventeen Signallers who arrived on Centauri Island that morning, used to compel him. Perhaps not freely, but almost certainly truthfully, he told Savant, the Space Age Spartan and the other four Silvers visiting his underside infirmary everything he'd witnessed on the island over the course of the last ten days.

Spartan sent the information to Sharpshooter via his helmet. It wasn't the directives that came back to him that shocked him so much as who transmitted them.

He had no idea Shelter was on the island.

=========

"Didn't realize you could teleport."

That's how Loxus Abraham Ryne greeted the maybe-man, maybe woman, seemingly both unsurprised and friendlily enough. Totally unannounced, the silver-armoured and forever-helmeted System Seer known only by his codename had just walked into what had become the Alliance's defence headquarters near the island's airport.

(Ryne appropriated the building housing it for SPACE upon his arrival late the previous Monday. Not so funnily, perhaps even fatalistically, it was now referred to as Last Stand Central by those who chose to remain behind on the island despite the imminent threat of – as impossible as it was for most anyone, even Silver Signallers, to feature – Nuclear Dragons.)

House-Head, as Virginia Mannering once nicknamed the top level Silver, made the best parts of his reputation by interpreting the aspects of Jesus Mandam's technology that went into SPACE and the UNES Liberty. Even though it was, as often as not, through his nominal boss, Simon Lancz (who, except on the parade ground, and then as Strategos, did not wear armour), it was in this capacity that Ryne knew Shelter; hence the comparative friendliness.

Also one of the invariably silver armour's initial designers or System Seers, he was as eccentrically accoutered as ever. Today's helmet was a variation of what he generally called his Farm-Face model. It was a stylized country cabin complete with porch. He complimented it by wearing an expansive checked dress, one with torpedo-shaped false breasts appended to his Silver underneath it, and a white, cloth shawl over it.

"Then again, my nephew could thirty-odd years ago. So, if you understand his chicken scratchings as well as you seem to, there's no reason why you shouldn't also."

"We're not very good at it yet," admitted Shelter. "In fact, I'm the only one crazy enough to try it across particularly long distances. Which the Pacific Ocean qualifies as, I'm sure you'd agree. Fortunately there are lots of Anthean Agates, real and artificial, on Gilligan Sentalli's island already. Where is the fat fool by the way?"

"God knows."

"God or gods?"

========

"That's a sick man," insisted the doctor. "What are you doing trying to move him?"

"Would you rather he die?"

========

As always George Hannibal, Sentalli's lawyer, was resplendent in a tailor-made suit, starched shirt and splash tie. His face, though, was already betraying considerable turmoil when Max's medic, Paul Creel, spotted him and Constance Lindquist hoisting Hiyati Samarand onto an intern's cart.

"Look, Paul," improvised Dr Lindquist, embarrassed by being caught in the proverbial act. "We've had a spate of deaths these last thirty-six hours. A lot of them, make that all of them, were Dr Samarand's closest associates. It doesn't take a genius to know he's in danger down here.

"There's probably a certifiable maniac out there trying to kill him; just as he or she did in the rest of what Max called Sentalli's Untouchables — except for us, that is. Put another way, if whoever it is has taken his or her shot at us and missed, we're not planning on hanging around to give either/or another one. And neither should Hiyati. We've got to get him upstairs and then off the island."

Creel had begun to suspect much the same thing. He also didn't doubt that Hannibal and Lindquist were genuinely concerned for their colleague more so than their friend. (Samarand was too much a totalitarian to be anyone's friend, not even the Fatman's.) It couldn't be a coincidence that, other than a few casualties, none of which were fatal, resulting from the rioting, only the Untouchables had died — and them, in his considerable experience, inexplicably.

"Just so long as it's up, not down," he put to them.

"What do you mean?" asked Connie, briefly losing her accustomed composure.

"Some of those Silver Signallers were here awhile ago. I told them Mr Sentalli sealed himself behind a sliding partition at the end of the corridor just before Professor Kinesis took care of that nameless thing a week ago last Sunday. The partition's closed again. Probably Sentalli triggers it with some electronic gadget built into his wheelchair. But I know there's an elevator at the end of the next corridor.

"And a guy calling himself Spartan said his fellow Silver, name of Sapperstein, could quote *'blast snot out of a dragon's nostrils without causing it to sneeze'* unquote."

"Not the most welcome analogy these days," reposted Hannibal, then whispered something that sounded like *'downstairs is out'* to Connie.

Just then Samarand went into convulsions. There was nothing either doctor, Creel nor Lindquist, could do about it. Hiyati was dead within a minute. Then yet another doctor, Angus Skullian, Ryne's personal physician, arrived on the scene. He'd seen it all and was renowned for his photographic memory.

"Don't berate yourselves," he consoled them. "Samarand was too far gone, I'm afraid."

"The boss will be devastated," said Creel. "I never liked him overly much – no one did, I imagine – but Dr Samarand was Project Centauri's overseer. He's been Mr Sentalli's closest associate on it for over thirty years."

"Interesting word, devastated," remarked Skullian.

"We better go tell the Fatman," Hannibal said to Lindquist. Unstated but understood between them was the fact that *'Skullian'* began with the letter *'S'*.

=========

Paul Creel was of three minds.

=========

He could go with one doctor, Lindquist, back to the surface with Hannibal. He could follow the other doctor, Skullian, whom Abe Ryne had assigned to stick with System's Signallers. Or he could just stay here and look after the sick. Curiosity got the better of him. Leaving the body of Hiyati Samarand to his assistants to stick with the others in the deep freeze, he joined the Silvers down the hall.

The one called Sapperstein was as good as his reputation. It took awhile for him to set it up but, once he had, he took out the partition between corridors as easily as Creel would perform an angioplasty on a hardened artery. At the other end, where the elevator was, one of the other Signallers – this one named Sub-System – told Sapperstein to hold off. He, Sub-System, who outranked everyone except the Space Age Spartan, could figure out how to call up the elevator.

Which he did.

Spartan didn't want Creel or Angus Skullian to go down with them, but they insisted. He still balked at Creel. Just because Skullian was Ryne's man and had an S-name, Creel wasn't about to be denied an opportunity to see the underside of the island he'd worked on for years. Besides, Skullian was a quack compared to him. At least he, Creel, had combat experience.

Spartan shrugged his silver shoulders, muttered an obligatory *'your funeral'*, but relented. The six Signallers – Spartan, Sapperstein, Sub-System, Savant, Stiletto and Stupendo – plus doctors Skullian and Creel, took the elevator down level by level, stopping to explore each one before going deeper.

As they comparatively quickly ascertained, it was a veritable labyrinth. Much of it was still unfinished and most of that had recently been used as a dormitory. Perhaps thirty to forty men, presumably the albinos, may have lived down here at any given time. Significantly none of them were there now. Question wasn't where they'd gone – the obvious answer was deeper – but how many levels were left?

Since the Cosmic Express had been something like fifteen storeys high and could be covered, launch pad and all, by a retractable roof, there was no snap solution. Because they were experiencing it firsthand, the scale may not be beyond belief but it was extremely impressive, even awesome.

The amount of concrete that went into this place, the engineering it required to keep out the ocean, beggared the imagination. How it was excavated didn't beggar so much as beg another question. Was it done by Cyclopes, Polyphemus and his one-eyed fellows, or Giants, the Norse Surtur, Fafnir and friends?

Was it devil-rayed Shining Ones like the devils Abe Ryne Creel-reputedly went on and on about after dinner a couple of nights back? Whatever the reality, they were supposed to scout it, risk coming upon dozens of heavily armed albino Glomen, with just eight men, two of whom weren't even in Silver? Not a chance.

Accordingly, Spartan in-helmet-radioed for Shooter, whom he didn't mind; got Shelter, whom he did, instead. The always unpredictable, if only edging towards out-and-out psychotic System Seer reluctantly freed up three more Signallers: Solano, Sonora and Static. He further wangled permission out of Ryne and Dulles for Mugwump and his men to join them as backup.

Whoopee!

========

The day progressed …

========

Three Signallers – Sharpshooter, Shadowswirl, and Sapphire Lancz – all in full but thoroughly insulated Silver, were strolling along the beach just past the rebuilt church. They were an impressive-looking trio and not just because of their helmets; Swirl principally so. In addition to her Mayan-like, Death Mask headgear, her over-top armour from the waist up looked as if it had been neatly slit into thousands of thick to thin shreds.

What those shreds could do was elongate such that, when she went into action, she had a multitude of cephalopodan appendages. Although she could eject some of these, mostly she used them for climbing, grappling and, yes, overpowering her opponents like octopi cracking crabs.

She could have opted for Squid, maybe even Spider, but she went for her S-name only in part because she melded almost invisibly into shadows. Most Signallers, thanks to their built-in Splendour Units, could do that, though. Her uniqueness derived from her strips of Silver. They swirled ragtag about her body as she moved in for the kill. Or whatever else she was intent upon doing once she got there.

Bullet-brain, as Shoot was nicknamed, had thicker than usual armour covering his torso. A series of hollow tubes went from it to his arms. When he desired, rifle-like barrels would extend along either arm such that he could fire a wide variety of specialized projectiles, many of which he'd designed himself.

Compared to the other two, Sapphire's Silver was fairly ordinary. It could hardly be considered plain, however. It glistened colourfully from hundreds of speckles: actually artificial jewels, like the stylized, oversized one that covered her head. Because of – unless it was in spite of – her father, Strategos Simon Lancz, by far the youngest allowed to wear Silver, Sapphire was taking in the sights. She wished she could be naked, or at least wandering around in her underwear, instead of no-matter-how-sparkly head and body protection.

(Punkish Goths like her didn't own bathing suits. It didn't fit the morose, sedentary image they cultivated. Many couldn't even swim. Mostly due to her father, who was something of fitness nut, she could; quite well, as it happened. Sapphire did more than outwardly subscribe to her affected ethos, however. Taking after her now forty year old mother Tereza, she couldn't be described as anywhere near in shape, just underfed.

(Minus the armour she, facially and physically, took after her great-grand-father, the old corpse, Sedon St Synne, more so than either of her parents. In this respect she even had more pronounced oriental – as in Ainu – features than almost anyone in her family excluding grandma Sophia, St Synne's only surviving as well as acknowledged daughter. Intriguingly, this disturbed Dad Si a whole lot more than it did Ma Teri.)

By contrast, due to hypersensitive skin no fan of the sun, Swirl (born Lilith Morgan) was grateful her unadorned, but essentially identical under-armour maintained an internal environment comfortable enough for even her to function in broad daylight. Nonetheless, she had sealed her Silver, even closed her deliberately spooky-looking helmet's big, Neanderthal eyeholes, and devoutly prayed for sundown.

Shooter was preoccupied with private thoughts. Even with its three by now concrete-conjoined peaks, Centauri Island was small, more islet than island. Regardless of that, seventeen Signallers really weren't enough to secure the whole area. (Eighteen, he mentally recalculated, if he included either Shelter or the Lancz child. Which he daren't do since it wasn't an *'S-number'*.)

Nine were now below under Spartan, System's regular field leader (Gus Soldakis, a veteran of AMERICA and Kadmon Heliopolis's version of the Black Rose before that). Two others, Spherus and Selene, a pair of under-thirtyish bright lights prized by the absent Strategos, were with fellow Seer Shelter in the Last Gasp Saloon, or whatever the local smartasses were calling Ryne's Defence Central this specific minute.

Taking the township for the three of them, he sent the last unassigned Silvers – Subitor, Sebastion and Sheriff – out to patrol, aboard Subitor's mutable air-car, what passed for the countryside. True, in terms of total security forces, he could have added in the Alliance's imported, two hundred strong Intervention Team and Dolph Dulles' in-house – as in regularly on-island – officers and underlings. But they only brought the total up another couple of hundred.

Plus, they were otherwise occupied covering the airport, the port, what beaches and highlands they could, manning Sentalli's impressive defence system – what would be the envy of any scruples-deficient banana republic – and scouring the improbably huge downside edifice around the Express's launch site.

Scouring for what? Mouldy protectors armed to the dentures? Glomen? WORLD? The King Crimefighters? Was this whole operation a wild goose chase? Why was System so convinced the Crimefighters, be they Callion Clones, as Spherus suggested, or the real things, had come to this place? And how? If it was Ringleader, as he suspected, then they could be, and likely were, long gone by now.

And what was all this about albinos that smelled like death warmed over in howsoever holey, but unholy, socks? Or recently dug up, more like, sepulchral shrouds and all? They'd left their plane on the tarmac, which had to mean they were still on the island. But hadn't Dulles said they'd surprised him and that, consequently, he suspected they had been on Centauri all along?

Were they glamour-casters, warlocks as opposed to witches? Warlocks with machine guns? Or did they have Splendour Units similar to System's? If either/ or, they could be damn near anywhere amongst them; hiding in plain sight, as the saying went. Wasn't Wilderwitch supposed to be a sensory illusionist; someone so good she could fool cameras as well as people? Could she, or someone who'd come close to reacquiring her supranormally high level of expertise, have masked their cemetery stench?

The more he thought about it, the more convinced he became that he should go below. Like Swirl, Subitor and himself, Spartan, Stupendo and Stiletto were well-trained. But they'd only been in the field for a couple of weeks. The others were even fresher off the rack. In fact, even he and Shelter were rank amateurs once it came to going into action wearing the Silver.

There simply hadn't been any need for it until Sasquatch, fresh in from Bruce Dre'Ath's Amsterdam Academy of Man, reported a Mammalian type in the vicinity of British Columbia's Lower Mainland a few weeks ago. (Said report got an instantaneous response from Styx, who flew in to join his long time friend and comrade in what quickly proved a nightmarish investigation; one that resulted in their unmasking and subsequent incarceration.)

To make matters worse, Sapphire, whom both Strategos and Shelter insisted he bring with them after the D'Angelos' 5-year family reunion wound down in Vancouver, was barely out of diapers. Perhaps, as he had recommended to the powers-that-be, especially as they'd been delayed there for so long, they should have stayed in Van.

The newly re-grown, self-proclaimed Emperor Mammalian had somehow got hold of Styx and Sasquatch after breaking them out Oakalla, the Lower Mainland's principal prison. Had been holding them incognito ever since. And when he joined Spartan's Signallers, in an effort to track them down, in a blinding snowstorm no less, they made first contact with what turned to be, well, he still couldn't believe the King Crimefighters were back in action, unaged after a quarter century.

Distressing, all of that. Nonetheless, howsoever else unnatural they were, the latest phony emperor and his similarly somehow re-engendered Manimalians were still flesh and blood. (The original Mammalian, Wolfgang Shekmet, was inspired to name himself thusly by the antics of Archduke Maximilian, who was the short term, Austrian-born, French-proclaimed, Emperor of Mexico from 1864 to 1867.)

They shouldn't present much trouble for a half-dozen proper Signallers; let alone those two by themselves. Like he himself, Shelter or the already lost Solar, Shooter was pretty sure Styx and Sasquatch should have been able to handle suchlike rejects from HG Wells' Island of Doctor Moreau singlehandedly. (Double-handily?)

Besides, tangling with Mammalian and his re-jigged bugbears – unless they were transformative were-creatures like Shekmet's band of latter day Godlings became after they stumbled upon the Totem Pool while looking for Alexander the Great's Fountain of Youth – would have been good practice for the newcomers especially.

Once they'd earned their (silver and black) jailbird stripes; once they'd rescued his two old comrades; System could have gone after WORLD or whomever, whatever, consigned tauntingly-named Avatar Sol to oblivion over a week ago now. It would certainly be much more satisfying than chasing wild geese, let alone herding tame ones.

(Back home, the latter was one of the childhood tasks his parents made him perform in order to encourage humility. Which didn't come readily to someone like him.)

"Look," indicated Sapphire observantly. "That jeep over there's covered in dust and dirt. Where's it been? I thought we were the only ones allowed out and about."

The jeep that caught her eye was parked outside a café on the other side of the boardwalk. A big Hawaiian was sitting in the driver's seat. Everything about him said bodyguard. Through the cafe's window, they could see two people having coffee. Everything about them said bodies guarded. Except …

"Odd," said Swirl, who had the advantage of having her visor down. Among other things it granted her a form of far-sight. "I thought I saw those two go into the hotel awhile ago."

"What of it?" glanced Shooter, having no need to access his in-helmet identification screen. System had stacks of intelligence on Centauri Island and its personnel. Not all of it came from Solar (Avatar Sol) either. "They're Sentalli's lawyer and physician. The guy driving them goes by the name of Marsh. He's been here for years."

"I said awhile, lover. Not hours. Check out the jeep. Sappy's right. They've been out and about. Hang on, our haunt's going in to see them."

Shadowswirl was referring to Yataghan, Sentalli's son, who'd been unsubtly following them all morning. He had a walkie-talkie and was running across the street. Marsh, who'd been dutifully waiting in the jeep, leapt out of it and glared at the three Signallers across the boardwalk. Noticeably he unclasped his shoulder holster's flap.

"Holy mincing mackerel, Shoot. Have a gander, through these." Sapphire held two of her filed-transparent, artificial agates in front of Shooter's eyeholes.

"Shit!" he realized, sealing his silver and switching on his own vision-filters. "They're wearing illusions. The man's a little girl. The woman's fucking Sea Goddess."

"I knew they were goddamned back," cursed Swirl, mentally (cybernetically) adjusting her filters so she could see – or see through – the illusions the other two could.

When she was a little girl herself, one about the same age, or a tad younger, than the one in the café who wasn't a man (or an adult woman, as far as that went), she had actually met, under very trying conditions, some of the King Crimefighters. Among them were their whitecap-haired, nominal goddess.

Yataghan was inside the café yelling at Hannibal — the child of the two, Shooter perceived. Marsh was between him and the café window, blocking a snap shot that never came. (Unlike Will Tombstone, the long dead American supra codenamed variously, but initially as Kid Cemetery, Shooter couldn't bend bullets to his will. Consequently he didn't bother to fire.)

"Let's get them," insisted Sapphire, who would have bristled at Swirl calling her Sappy if she wasn't so excited about engaging a legendary supra back from the dead as well as unaged.

"Wait," countermanded Shooter. "They might all be here; Callion Clones of them, I mean. The illusionist could be Wilderwitch, double-casting her glamours." He knew it had to be the tiny trickster but saw no need to illuminate his fellow Silvers. "The other has to be a copycat Thalassa, though. Couldn't be anyone else, not with hair like hers. Better not tip our hand. We want all ten."

"You're right, Shoot," granted Sapphire, sounding much older than her fifteen years. "Try to take them down one at a time, the others will twig. Go their own way and probably escape. If we could get them all together, here and now, we'd have a shot at eliminating the whole, unnatural crew."

"Might even be more than ten," Swirl warned. "Spherus was talking about them on the flight from Vancouver. He's still studying at the Houston Academy of Man and, while there, wormed his way into Callion and Nightingale's confidence. He reckons they were cloning more than just the ten who died on Damnation Isle."

"Eleven," said Sapphire, once again correcting her superiors. "Counting the Magnificent Psycho."

"I was counting him," said Shooter. "I wasn't counting Raven's Head, the flying figment of folklore Blind Sundown rode. I still don't see how she could actually exist."

"Yet she did," Swirl reminded him before finishing her thought. "According to Bubble Boy, they were trying to replicate Jesus Mandam, the Conquering Christ himself, as well as a few dozen other supras, probably including my parents." (Swirl was hardly the only one who called Spherus Bubble Boy. When your helmet looks like an inflated globe, the appellation attaches automatically.)

Her father's name was Josef (Joseph) Morgan. Half-Carpathian, half-British by birth, he was a lifelong socialist. Some Brits of the era – ones knowledgeable of the Supra Wars – went so far as to consider him a traitor because of his undisguised leanings. Her mother Theope's maiden name was Dvina, after the Russian river.

That Joseph went over to the Soviet Union during the war was due to love, though, not treachery. Both were supranormals. After the war, both attached themselves to the Soviet Supra Supreme and later joined the Supranormal Defence League or 'SDL'. Their deaths hadn't been pretty.

"Can you get a soul-take of them?" Shooter demanded of the Lancz girl. "Either one will do?"

It being too late to apply what she should have learned by studying why the Crimefighters and Psycho were taken out up in the Aleutians in 1955, she happily did as bade. Sooth said, with a composure belying her youth Sapphire was one step ahead of him; had focused her agates on the pair underneath the illusions already.

(No matter what she claimed, her artificial agates were not long distance soul-sinks any more than they were scientific instruments anyone could use. What they did was take aural impressions she could then use to track her subsequent quarry. That she could do just that was the main reason she was with them.

(No one else had as yet acquired the knack. Which of course suggested she was somehow supranormal, like many of her aunts and uncles on the D'Angelo side of her family had been decades ago. That didn't make her a target, not yet, but it probably would, eventually. For now, it made her a valuable member of the team. Despite her innate rebelliousness, she liked that.)

"Got the little witch," she chirped enthusiastically. "Sea Goddess is hopeless. Can't fix her any more now than I could a week ago in Vancouver."

"Then let's hope the one you got sticks with this Thalassa or meets some of the others." Shooter, who reckoned he'd likely be the one assigned to take Sapphire out when the time came, sounded all business. "Go around back, Swirl. I'll notify Subitor. Can't do much about the nine downstairs but five minutes is all he'll need to get here with Sebastion and Sheriff."

"What about Shelter, Spherus or Selene?" Shadowswirl queried. "They've the prototype Silver. They'd be here even quicker."

"Just do as I say." Shooter wasn't usually as sharp with her as he was with most of the others. They were lovers after all.

However, there were things he wasn't ready to share, even with her. For one, Shelter was nuts, out for blood; otherwise he wouldn't be here. For another, he was pretty sure Spherus and Selene were clones fashioned by Moe Two in the early Fifties. What was more, he had a damn good idea who their initial templates were — the King and Queen Conqueror: Jesus Mandam and Faceless Strife.

What he wasn't too sure about was which Strife had been cloned.

========

Outside the cafe, Marsh heard a whirring sound but saw nothing untoward. Until ...

========

On the beach, one of the three Signallers Yataghan had yelled at him to watch out for rose into the sky. The whirring intensified, the other two vanished, something hit the ground with a thump. That something ratcheted down whatever device he'd been using to cloak himself. He thus came fully into view immediately in front of him.

It was a man, perhaps a woman, wearing System body plating and a silver, star-shaped helmet. (Obviously it was supposed to remind kids watching the silver circus clowns of a wild west sheriff's tin star.) In each hand he or she held an old-style six-shooter. One gun was pointing at his head, the other through the window at Yataghan and George Hannibal.

Marsh wasn't stupid enough to go for his own gun. Even though he was getting on in age, he was in fine shape physically; considered suicide premature.

========

Having wasted precious hours going from one empty level to another, Spartan decided to switch tactics.

Thinking inside the box, he took the elevator down as far as it would go.

=========

His plan was for them to start at the bottom and work their way back up. In that way, hopefully, they'd squeeze the albinos betwixt and between their fellow Silvers – they in their virtually impervious armour and with ultra-sophisticated armaments – and Mugwump's much more numerous and now Splatter Pack equipped men on the no doubt multiple upper levels they'd skipped.

When they emerged at the bottom, it was in a bleak, dimly lit, almost cave-like hollow. A half dozen miniature, four- or five-man submersibles told him what it was, a submarine pen, but where were the guards, the albinos? Just then, a long vice-like wrench shot out of the wall and clasped Sub-System by the neckpiece. Which, eccentrically, had screw-in-style rails that complimented his ideal – as in lightbulb-like – headgear.

(Like Spherus and Selene, Joe Hartwig was considered something of a bright light. Unlike them, his headgear reflected it.)

"Where is it?" came a voice as if from the wall itself, a voice with a German accent. "Tell me or I kill him."

"Where's what?" challenged Spartan.

The last thing Joe Hartwig – Sub-System – ever heard was the same guttural, Teutonic-sounding voice saying: "The Nagasaki Gap!"

=========

Sebastion cannon-balled through the roof. Simultaneously the back and front doors burst open. Yet no one came through them.

Hannibal-Hush grabbed Yataghan. Together, her taking the lead, as in the first step between-space, they did their own disappearing act. Sharpshooter cybernetically disengaged the Splendour Unit that could disguise the Signallers appearance as well as render them invisible. Beside him Sapphire did a ditto.

Shadowswirl, fully visible again, came out of the bathroom holding the tee-shirt, shorts, sandals, and the cap Thalassa-Lindquist had been wearing.

"I think she flushed herself down the toilet."

****

Nuke 24: **Sea Goddess**

========

She'd been at it since Saturday.

Not that she minded. An impossible-to-anyone-else swim like this was exactly what she needed to clear out the cobwebs of a bit less than twenty-five years in Limbo and by now a bit more than week of what was, in some respects, even worse. Her brother's spirit was still leading her, though he hadn't spoken in a long, long while.

Not that that mattered either. She'd already figured out where he was heading.

Centauri Island!

========

Earlier today Sharpshooter said to his Enormity "I trust you have no objections if we stay on the island for a while. Thought not. See you around."

When the Signaller, followed by George Hannibal, the former host of Elephantine Ganesh, left them that morning in his private suite at the hotel, Sentalli-Centauri turned to Yataghan Sentalli (out here), Connie Lindquist and the tiny trickster, Hush Mannering. "Insufferable. Masked and armoured vigilantes on my island. Any chance of Dr Samarand recovering, doctor?"

"Either he or his devil are very impressive," Connie told them. In her case, as well as Hannibal's, Sentalli-Centauri's and the little trickster's, devils did leave memories behind. "All the other homos have died and he never went unconscious. Whatever happened to the devils' father Saturday afternoon or evening affected them severely. I'd say there's hope but probably not out here."

"You've still Mr Sarpedon's prison pods containing the real devils in your shelter, baby?" asked the homunculus — though, as was the case more often than not of late, it was the real Fatman speaking through his consequential mouthpiece from the other side. Dorothy Dodgson, as Hush was currently calling herself, nodded.

"Then give them to Yataghan to take back to the Head," his Enormity instructed her. "Their father seems to have fallen by the wayside, unless he's risen to the night's sky, so I don't know if there's any point in you keeping them anymore. And if I'm to become their keeper until he turns up again, I'd rather them beneath the Dome than beyond it.

"You better go too, Dr Lindquist. Unless you prefer to take your chances out here." If he had his way, Centauri's homunculus would have been back on the Head already. However, thanks in part to Hush's injections Saturday and again last night after she finally awoke, he, it, was now completely subservient to his template's wishes.

Lindquist wasn't happy with the Fatman's recommendation. "No. Not yet. And certainly not without George."

She was born on the Outer Earth but had been taken to Big Shelter shortly after attaining puberty. Her benefactor was Superior Sarpedon. Morg, Hush's acknowledged Summoning Child, must have seen a lot of potential to risk what amounted to abducting the daughter of such a well-connected neo-terrorist like her father, Greygreave Translav.

Hannibal was another outsider Morg brought beneath the Dome at a young age, one who'd subsequently lived most of his life inside. Over the years he had become Connie's lover. Other than the fact that they probably should have had children, but never did, Centauri often wondered what made them so special to the Sisterhood. Now wasn't the time to ask, though.

"I'll give the orbs to Yataghan," promised Hush.

Regardless of the reason why, somehow or other Great Byron was no longer around. That meant Quintillion Chins, both of them, was right. They'd be useless as bargaining chips against her personal nemesis Tralalorn, the demon child who'd devolved her into a perpetual seven year old all those years ago.

"If Dolph Dulles hadn't put me to sleep, if I hadn't been so out of it, I wouldn't have let the homunculi die. I didn't realize how alive they were – you too, Daddy Gigantic Ocean Liner. Catch up with George, sister, and just to be on the safe side take charge of Samarand as well. Invent some excuse to get him out of Creel's infirmary and up to Double Daddy Alfalfa Sprout's suite."

"Too risky," said Sentalli-Centauri coldheartedly. "Dr Samarand brought Loxus Ryne up here Saturday night and the patriarch's been sniffing around ever since. I agree we can't leave the overseer out here, though. If Samarand does recover, there's no telling what he'll remember. Find some way to get him into the depths.

"And, if that's too difficult, well, as much as it hurts me personally to say it, you know why we employ homunculi in the first place." Hush supposed the *'hurts me'* bit was homo-humour but no more laughed at it than she would have had the real Centauri said it. "Dr Samarand may not have as strong a constitution as you thought. Correct, doctor?"

Connie Lindquist didn't like that, either. What professionally trained healer would? She nevertheless took his meaning as she would a foul-tasting cough syrup, without making a face let alone any comment. "You're the boss. Even if you aren't, not really."

"So much for homo solidarity, eh, daddy?" muttered Hush, who had long ago learned to take her principles with a large sprinkle of ruthlessness.

"Fair enough, I suppose. Yataghan, I want you to take George's place. Stick with the Signallers, particularly this Shooter fellow, as long as you can. If you chance to see him without his helmet, I want to know what he looks like. As soon as the firedrakes attack, assuming they do, I'll meet you at the gateway downside."

Once Yataghan and Lindquist were gone, Centauri's proxy-man asked the little witch what she made of System's Signallers. "Their armour's state-of-the-art," she confirmed after a minute's consideration. "Which makes it a grade or two up from what the King and Queen Conqueror wore all those years ago. So some of System's Seers must be worth their grains of salt and pepper sauce.

"It does remind me somewhat of the uniforms-cum-survival-suits your cosmicompanions paraded about in when they got on the Express back when all this shit began. That suggests they're derived from the same source, Stopstone or Solidium. And you know who came up with that process. At least most recently."

"You think Samarand's a traitor to devazurkind?"

"Truth told, which sometimes even tricksters do, I don't know what to think anymore. He brought Ryne up here after his release and he's the one who had Dulles put me to sleep. That could be construed as trying to get hold of me long enough to force me to release his devic siblings. But it could also have been an effort to put me away permanently.

"And, without me, his sibs would stay trapped in those orbs for Lord Humping the Magdalene knows how long. Pardon the blasphemy." She knew the real Centauri was still a practicing Roman Catholic, at least when he was out here. (Which he wasn't; not strictly speaking.) She also doubted the real Jesus Christ never married. "As far as I'm concerned all this is yet another reason for us to return to the Head and seal the Gap behind us."

"Again speaking for myself, button-nose, I'd like nothing better."

========

Having already had breakfast, his Enormity decided he needed a hot bath.

He was struggling to disrobe, cursing the fact that he let Yataghan raised Montressor (during the early stages of the Godbadian Civil War) leave his side to follow Sharpshooter. Simultaneously, on the other side of the Nag Gap, Yataghan's wife Janna St Peche Montressor was scrubbing the real Fatman's back.

He had his eyes closed and was on the edge of sleep when suddenly he cried out loud. His homunculus did ditto. Something incongruous – someone, rather, hence the incongruity – came out of the steam.

"Jesus Christ, you!"

"Not Jesus Christ but you're right, it is me."

"Thalassa D'Angelo!"

"Got a bathrobe?"

========

Hush Mannering, who'd been in the living room reading a comic book when his Enormity cried out, rushed into the bathroom.

The half-dressed Fatman was still in his wheelchair, quivering like a bowlful of nerve-shot jelly. The bathroom was otherwise empty but Hush wasn't fooled. She'd heard what he screamed; knew what Sea Goddess could do as well. The difficulty was knowing how to play it. Tiny tricksters like her loved playing but some games were better off avoided.

There wasn't much else for it. Best deal with her, here and now, before Daddy Ryne River or any of the sickening Signallers found out about her.

"Bathrobe's hooked up there, Sea."

What had been a puddle on the floor became a starkly beautiful, starkly naked, white-haired, blue-skinned woman.

=========

His Enormity, whom Thalassa likely only knew – or remembered knowing – as Alfredo Sentalli, was in a panic verging on hysteria. Which probably meant Alpha Centauri, who, by that logic, Thalassa could never have remembered as anyone (because she wouldn't know anything about the Inner Earth), was too. At least so Hush reckoned. Wrongly, it suddenly occurred to her.

Showing both her age (in terms of birth, roughly sixteen or seventeen years more than Thalassa) and maturity (debatable), Pandora-Hush quickly took charge of the situation. With Thalassa's help – her Daddy Alfredo Cheese Sauce was as heavy as four men but Sea Goddess was as strong as ten – she got him dressed and calmed down.

As they sorted the Fatman out, Hush attempted to decompartmentalize everything she knew about the newcomer. As a librarian might say, there were stacks of stacks of them. None were haystacks full of needles but a great many were smokestacks. Nowhere near all of what came out of them was smoke Hush had caused. Reacquainting themselves only led her, Hush, to place Byron's Sedona Spellbinder just beneath Tralalorn as someone warranting her extreme dislike.

For Thalassa, it was an affirmation of something she had suspected for many years before Limbo. The little girl who kept showing up at the oddest moments – often accompanied by Superior Sorrow or any of a number of other upper level, Anthean witches – during the war and afterwards, the one with a dozen different looks and at least as many names, was the same person.

For Hush, who also knew that Psycho, Cerebrus, and the rest of the King Crimefighters were back, it wasn't as much a matter of keeping control as wondering how much to trust her. Once they pushed Centauri into the living room, she produced an Anthean Agate.

"Mind if I check you out?"

"So you are a witch."

Sea wasn't really surprised. Who else but a witch could change her appearance at will and stay seven for forty-plus years? However, she shied away from the agate. Wilderwitch used them to form her Shelter, to bounce around between space and to change people's appearances, but she always hinted she could do a lot more with them. Redacting folks' memories, which the Witch professed never to do, was hardly the least among them.

"What's that supposed to prove?"

"What I suspect you already know. Would you prefer I use an eyeorb?"

"You're suggesting Thalassa's a Master Deva?" realized the Fatman. Hush shot him a warning glance. Too late. Thalassa instantly picked up on his apparent faux pas.

"What do you know of devils?"

"Devas, devils," recovered Sentalli-Centauri smartly. "Call them Shining Ones if you prefer. What's the difference? What I meant was it's ridiculous." He addressed Hush directly. "I've known of her since I was nine or ten years old. My godfather, Raphael, adopted her and her twin back in – what? 1933, I think. She has powers, yes, but they were caused by Satan St Synne's devil-ray, which he called a devaray."

"Aires and I were supranormals before then," she said.

"And she managed to retain them," he was carrying on. Then it dawned on him. "What did you say?"

"We were charter members of the Society of Saints, Sentalli, and it was set up in early 1938, not 1943. By her — Jolene Callion, General *'Huff'n'Puff'* Jollity!"

Hush cringed, then regained her composure and smiled beatifically. "I still have the corncob pipe."

"You smoked?" His Enormity, who didn't (beer and especially food were his only real vices), sounded more horrified than outraged. Even if he knew everything there was to know about her, which he couldn't have, it was impossible not to feel parental around such an innocent-looking little cutie.

"Still do, and not just tobacco either. And our SOS wasn't the Society of Saints, Sea Stuff. Not the first one, recall."

That took Thalassa aback. Then she too broke into a huge grin. Like her adoptive aunts, sisters and nieces to this day, like Mnemosyne, Gloriel, Claudia and Belificent in their days, when a female D'Angelo smiles the heavens alight. "The Sorority of Sausages. I'd forgotten about them."

Then her visage darkened, as if remembering what had happened to many of them over the succeeding years. Hush braced herself for the storm. "Of course I did, didn't I?"

His Enormity caught the reference immediately. "You wiped her."

"And un-wiped her," Hush protested. "Any number of times."

"Oh, I don't doubt that," snarled Sea. No tsunami ensued, though. Instead, like a calming side eddy off a raging river, she jumped back onto her original train of thought. "Vichy France 1943, five years after the Sausages had their lone outing against Count Molech and his genie, that unmitigated old satyr Sedon St Synne, the legitimate D'Angelos' grandfather, hit almost everyone in our immediate family with his devaray. It set some of the others off on their supra careers but it only increased our abilities."

"Enough to survive twenty-five years unaged?" wondered Sentalli-Centauri.

"A lot more than that," Thalassa put to him. "Air and I never seemed to age after our twenty-first birthday. Which is the main reason we disappeared shortly after being hit with St Synne's ray. You can't stay twenty-one forever; not without folks noticing it. Not unless you're an illusionist like you obviously are, little Miss Fairy Chief."

"Hey, I'm only a button-nosed fairy child on the surface. Underneath I'm a gnarly old fairy grandmother. And there's nothing I can do about either."

Realizing they were only delaying the inevitable, Hush did a quick sleight of hand; a between-space switcheroo, more accurately. (Most decent witches were materialists, in the literal sense. They brought tangible objects into and out of their portable Shelters, which they conjured off their personally ensorcelled stepping stones.)

Instead of the agate she now held an eyeorb; one of the many she had Demios Sarpedon produce for her before he went off to rejoin his wife, her daughter, Morgianna born Nauroz, and (not that Hush was aware of it), their daughter, her granddaughter, Andaemyn, who was striped.

(Andy, as she was known, was only one of two granddaughters courtesy of Morg. The other, Tsishah Twilight, wasn't courtesy of Demios, though. Her father was Tammuz Rhymer, a fairy type better known as Tom-Tiddly Taddletale, who had her kidnapped shortly after birth. Either that or gave her over to the fays of Twilight as payback for favours rendered.)

It opened. Thalassa stood stock still as the eerie eye poked out on cellular filaments and probed her. Finding nothing of interest, it retreated into its pod, which she vanished. "What the fuck was that?" she-Sea wondered, letting herself relax. "Another show-off trickster's pointless prank?"

Hush regarded the, to her mind, justifiably named Goddess with even more curiosity. (Not just on the Hidden Headworld, Shining Ones were always at least potentially gods or goddesses.) "Funny. I wouldn't have thought you'd know how to externalize your soul. Could be a dud, I suppose. Daddy Dem churns so many eyeorbs out of that ancient eye-stave of his, they can't all be perfect."

"Happy now, baby?" all but mocked his Enormity. "Sea was one of the most celebrated supras ever, a Saint then a King Crimefighter. Hell, I wouldn't have known she survived the war if she hadn't shown up here in mid 1952, or whenever it was, when you came looking for Fisherwoman after she killed your mate, Atlantean."

"June," she recalled. "And I wasn't just looking for her, I killed her. You even took me to your three-drawer morgue to prove she was dead."

"You never believed it, though," said Hush. "You're no killer."

"Don't be too sure of that. I was spitting mad and when I'm spitting mad, it's the whole goddamned ocean I'm spitting. Still, I always had my doubts. Fish could breathe underwater, no matter how much water or how fast it comes at you. Besides, witches like her, Wilderwitch and especially Strife were forever disappearing only to pop up a few months or years later.

"The only one I ever trusted was Sorciere and, unfortunately, she's also about the only one who stayed dead. Was that Fish in the freezer?"

"What do you think?" Sentalli-Centauri asked reflexively. Then he seemed to pause, remaining as if poised to carry on but silent for a few seconds. Finally – having, to Hush obviously, received revised talking orders – he said: "Oh, hell, you might as well know. The answer's no. She used an agate to mask an old lady who died before we could get her to Maui for proper attention. Last I heard she still isn't, though there've been many times I wished she was."

"Where is she then?"

"Ask her?" he indicated Hush.

"What are you up to, daddy?"

The little girl was worried. The Fatman could have easily lied about Fish. Why was he all but admitting that devils and especially the Head existed?

"Figure it out for yourself, baby. There's no way she could have been a devil. I mean, how'd she get out here? Master Devas only exist in Big Shelter – your Sisterhood's Big Shelter – and the Nag Gap wasn't around until '45. What we have here is a supranormal, one of the best. And a D'Angelo, of the angels, to boot. That means Celestial in my books and right about now we could use some Celestial Intervention. Sea could be the answer to our prayers."

"There's another way," Hush acknowledged, deciding to force his hand. "The SAG Gap, after Sodom and Gomorrah."

"Seriously?" Thalassa had to know.

"Seriously, Sea. Seriously circa 2000 BC, dot-ditto. It's the same as the Anthean Passageway when it's in place. Theoretically, when it's wandering it can breach the Dome. I've heard, um, rumours of it happening a few times. So have you, Daddy Bellyache, if Jordan Tethys ever told you any stories about the Attis after Strongyne exploded, which he must have, or any of the chronicles of the Crimson Conspiracy from 2,000 years ago, which he may have."

Thalassa had heard vague rumours of Big Shelter and was full of questions, hardly any of which had to do with Sodom and Gomorrah. Somehow sensing where Hush was heading – hers and Aires's actual parentage – she wisely decided to wait for the apparent little girl to finish saying her piece before getting to them.

"The lead conspirator was Phantast the Dreamweaver. His immediate sister is and was Methandra Thanatos, the Scarlet Sorceress, also Lathakra's Crimson Queen. I call her Hot Stuff; hence your Sea Stuff, I suppose. She isn't the Crimson of the conspiracy, though she always dresses in various shades of red. Crimson is where Phantast made his home in Big Shelter.

"At any rate, his sister has and had an affinity for SAG. It's how he and his fellow devic conspirators passed through the barrier blocking devils coming out here. Two thousand years later, in the very late Teens and early Twenties of this century, Methandra had a number of children by her other immediate brother, Tantal, King Cold of Lathakra.

"She's his queen; hence Crimson Queen. Their children were fourth generation devils, the first and last that I know about. Until then devils could only have insubstantial spirit beings called azuras, thus the devazur race. In '33, she managed to save two of them from the Byronic Nucleus via the SAG Gap. Their names were Thalassa and Aires."

The Angelic sucked in her breath. "Was one of the ones who didn't get away named Antaeor?" Hush allowed it was.

"Is any of this true?" Centauri required of Sea Goddess, having second thoughts about opening up to her about Big Shelter too late.

"I've suspected it since a week ago Sunday," Sea admitted. "When we came out of Limbo it was because of two devils going at each other on Damnation Isle. They were the first presumably real devils I can remember seeing in my life. One of them was Demon Land. Not my adoptive brother Peter, who was a victim of the devaray. Nor any of the Earth Elementals that came about subsequently, thanks to either it or Strife's Miracle Key.

"The other one, Vayu Maelstrom, Devil Wind, kept calling himself a Nucleoid or a Byronic or combinations thereof. He called that Demon Land Antaeor and Thanatoid both. And that's my point. What bugged me – what gave me hope we weren't his siblings – was Wilderwitch not saying anything. She did say she knew how to kill devils so she must be from Big Shelter; must know the truth about them.

"I've been around her for good part of a dozen years; thirty-seven if you count the quarter century we just lost in Limbo. We never hung out together and the Witch keeps her secrets well. But, if I'm a devil and devils are the enemy, then why did she let Aires and I fight beside her all that time?"

"Because you're not devils," offered Centauri, still playing his angles. And, he hoped, his angels.

Hush couldn't hold her tongue. "Look, chinny-chin-daddy, even if I can't prove it, she's a two-eyed devil, a fourth generation one. Of that I'm certain; been certain of it since even before I began training her and her twin in 1937, though it might have been even earlier. You want to trust her, you go ahead. I thought you'd learned your lesson by now, that's all."

His Enormity paused again, as if having what must be third or fourth thoughts by now. "Cards on the table, Goddess," he told Thalassa, after yet another extended pause. "It's been my experience that devils aren't necessarily the enemy – though some of them certainly are.

"Furthermore, the word itself only means *'little god'* so they're certainly not intrinsically evil. Regardless of whether or not you are one of these Thanatoids, I'd like to have you on my side. Can you work with her, baby? Or is that no longer possible, given your reservations about Dr Samarand?"

"My sisterhood is named after the Golden Age wife of Xuthros Hor, the Noah of the Bible, but there was also a Flowery Anthea. She was a devic Goddess of Spring, of renewal, of rebirth, a daughter of Thrygragos Lazareme. Lazaremists are extremists, comes with their nature, sure enough. They're their own worst enemies; mostly because only firstborns from the other two tribes can hold a candle to them.

"You speak as one who is intimate, almost exclusively, with Thrygragos Byron and his spawn, Daddy Do Little. Generally speaking they are well-intentioned, insufferably arrogant and, sorry, dullards. Aside from the two Silverclouds and, maybe, a couple of his Nucleoids, they're virtual weaklings compared to those of Thrygragos Lazareme and Varuna Mithras's highest born. Put bluntly, Byronics are the least able of the three tribes."

Hush was on a roll and wasn't about to be shut up. "Thalassa Thanatos's grandfather was Mithras, Sol Invictus, the equivalent of the Titan Kronos, who ate his young. Mithras treated his daughters as concubines and his sons as slaves;

worse, beasts of burden. Eventually all of them stood against him on Thrygragon, but only so they could act as he did. The exceptions were his first born three-some: Phantast, known as Dream or the Dreamweaver, Tantal and Methandra Thanatos.

"The latter two, King Cold and his Crimson Queen, are either yours or your namesake's parents, Goddess. They had always rebelled from Mithras – so, perhaps, you are not as bad as the rest of the Mithradites. That does not mean I can trust you; does not mean that Daddy Lard-Ass can't trust you either. How did you come to be here?"

Thalassa didn't appreciate her tone, but there was no denying something rather fundamental wasn't right about the situation in which she found herself. And it had next to nothing to do with a forever-child approaching two decades older than her and a host so fat it was a wonderment he could get into a bathtub without a crane.

"Aires, Airealist, guided me," she said, looking about nervously, as if she half-expected him to appear as if out nowhere. Which he could do, if the no-where was air. "Not personally. His ghost or spirit or some such did. He said he needed my help. Led me to a drain and I followed him through the pipes into Sentalli's tub. But now that I'm here, where is he?"

"Not on the island," said his Enormity. "That I can guarantee. But you are and I think I know why."

"Not Celestials again," mumbled Hush, exasperated. She, like the real Cen-tauri, knew Sea's Air had gone through the Nag Gap, along with the rest of the remaining Crimefighters and the Byronic Nucleus, Friday night or shortly after midnight Saturday morning. To tell their guest that, though, would invite all sorts of complications.

"Their earthly representative then. My godmother, your adoptive mother, Sophia D'Angelo, sent you here to save my island."

"Mama Sofa! How is that possible?"

"You said it yourself. Her father's devaray increased your powers. At the same time it gave her what Papa Rafe came to call her fabulous prayer power."

"Bollocks, Daddy Wishful Thinking," Hush scoffed, almost despite herself.

She turned to address Thalassa; attempted to explain away, rather than ex-cuse, his allegations regarding Sainted Sophia, as not just Centauri thought of her. "He's desperate; doesn't have the vaguest. The devil-ray gave her no such a thing because there is no devil empowered with any such a thing. They're little gods. They get prayed to; they don't pray to anyone, unless it's to their father or grandfather, the Devil Himself."

"No?" his Enormity took up her challenge. "Devils are fallen angels. Where did devils fall from except the heavens. Her Airhead was a ghost, a manifesta-tion. That's something else Sea said. A holy ghost, and there definitely is such a thing; has to be. He said he was trapped. Where? By who? Not by me, not by Great Byron.

"It was a ploy to get her here; a means to an end – my salvation," the Fat-man put to the trickster. "Who else can stymie Nuclear Dragons?"

"Nuclear what?" gasped Thalassa.

"Pay him no heavenly heed, Sea. He's a Bad Daddy Alfalfa Pouts, bleeding blithering."

"Am I? Who else could be responsible?"

"Ordinarily I'd say almost anyone but, with all that's been going on this last week, who can say for sure?"

"Nuclear dragons?" Thalassa did it again, gasped, even as she answered herself.

"You're welcome to hang around, Goddess," said Hush, sounding resigned. "I'd ditch the blue skin and stars around your eyes if I were you. Get some shorts and a tee-shirt as well. Maybe a baseball cap to hide your hair. Not too many people have such fine white locks as you. Don't want to attract undue attention."

"Okay," said Thalassa, echoing Hush's attitude. "Nuclear dragons it is then."

"Prefer something real? Your old pal – and I do mean old – Doddering Daddy Loxus Abraham Ryne is on the island trying to run things as usual; run things into the ground, more like. Plus, there's a snaky sack of Silver Signallers around. You have any idea who they are, other than bad news in worse pews?"

"I had a couple of dealings with them in Vancouver." And – Sea thought, but didn't add – other than the worrisome one, Sapphire Lancz, whom David-Cerebrus Ryne claimed had somehow Photostatted his soul, she didn't see much about them to trouble herself. "The patriarch's no big deal, either," she said instead. "I'm not Johnny Sundown. I don't feel any need to either get mad or get even and I doubt Aires did either.

"Mind you, he can be as much of a dickhead – to use some common parlance – as he can be an Airhead, in all senses of the word. Still, I can't see him ever being so careless or so sloppy as to get captured by lowlifes like Abe Ryne's emasculated Alliance or these Signallers, no matter who runs them. Then there's the question of why he led me to you instead of him?"

"I just told you."

"So you did. It wasn't him; it was Mama Sofa somehow casting a simulacrum. I know Gloriel wanted to see her parents as soon we got back to Vancouver last week, but I think the Diver convinced her that'd be a dumb idea. That said, it's quite possible she found out we were back. What isn't possible is her holy ghosting him." It was Sea Stuff's turn to pause. Which she did but probably not to listen to any external voice-prompter.

"Tell you what, Mr Sentalli. Appearing normal's easy-peasy for me. I don't look like this unless I'm using my supra talents. Same goes for Air – which means he could be here unbeknownst to anyone except me. I'll sense him as soon as I'm close enough to sense him and maybe that's why he brought me to you – and her. Care to help me get close enough?"

"Your glamours up to taking her around the island, baby?"

Hush had finally figured out what Centauri – not his homo, the real Fatman on the other side of the Dome – wanted of her. Her task was to delay the other her, Sea Goddess. She'd been thick not to realize it right away. What was more amazing, at least to her mind, was how thick Thalassa had to be.

Mama Sofa's fabulous prayer power, Hush's button butt! How effective had it been when it came to extracting any of her children from the still secret Supra Wars and the consequences of their participation in it? Three-thirteenth, at the max; 4/14th or 5/15th if she counted Rafe and Sophia herself. How many of them had died, not just disappeared for howsoever long? Counting Marcello on one side and Belificent on the other, seven.

Answer: not very effective at all.

And Aires' ghost, or whatever it was, led her to exactly where she had to be in order to crossover without having to access either the wandering SAG Gap or All's between-space link with the Giza Sphinx. Who knows where the entrance to the former might be right now? (Unlike the SAG itself, it was never stationary.) As for the latter, if Thalassa was a (disturbingly) two-eyed devil, All might eat her.

Whatever it was? Nuts on a knucklehead. It was Methandra's manifestation, had to be. She'd brought him to his Enormity because only he could open the Nag Gap.

"I imagine so," she said, after rather cynically adding in yet another factor.

In a world, not just a Hidden Headworld, without the regulatory, comparative benignity of Unmoving Byron, what kind of damage would a wholly reunited Family Thanatos do? The answer this time, if what she'd heard about the expansion of the Empire of Lathakra starting over 1200 years ago was any example, was crystal clear.

It was too horrible to think about.

So why assist Hot Stuff with Sea Stuff, especially for nothing? The answer was just as clear; only the Crystal this time was capitalized. "All right, daddy. I guess George Hannibal and Connie Lindquist are well-known enough to be seen wandering around freely. What say, Goddess? Prefer to be a lawyer or a doctor?"

Thanks primarily to Wilderwitch, the nine years' younger sister of the still despised Fisherwoman, Thalassa was used to operating under the illusion of being someone else. "If you're anything like the Witch," she told the little girl, "I'm sure you'll speak for both of us anyhow."

"I'm not that good. Nobody was. Hopefully though, I'm good enough."

"Is," said Thalassa, herself hopefully. (She last saw the Witch with her brother and her lover from not quite a couple of years before, and no more than a short few days after, Limbo. The last two – all right, Air for sure, prick that he sometimes could be, especially when it came to lovers – she genuinely did hope were still around.)

"Is," allowed Hush.

She knew the Byronhead had brought Sea's twin, lover Cerebrus and the rest of their D-Brig inside on Friday night. She also had a pretty good idea what became of it. She didn't think supras – except for maybe Airhead – could become stars in the Sedon Sphere but she'd been to Subterranean Temporis a number of times over the years.

And she knew it was full of graveyards.

========

Sometime later, in the bottommost depths of the largely manmade island – the secret submarine nest into and out of which submersibles transported new-comers to or from the Hidden Headworld, through an elaborate system of locks – two of the most dangerous men left in the world, either side of it, went Shark-czar-hunting.

Presumably because they had no idea it even existed, it never occurred to either of them that the agate they materialized on was just in front of the Nag Gap.

****

Nuke 25: **Coming to a Head off the Head**

========

<u>Tuesday, December 9, 1980</u>

Wearing guises of Connie Lindquist and George Hannibal, while using Marsh as both chauffeur and (probably superfluous) bodyguard, Hush and Sea spent a couple of unproductive hours touring the island – unproductive in the sense that they didn't find what they were looking for.

Not unproductive in the sense that they proved to be precisely what an S-number of others were looking for: namely, supra scapegoats.

========

They'd been all over the surface but Thalassa had detected no hint of Airealist. Hush was hardly surprised.

Like her Daddy Gigantic Titanic Sinking, she was almost 100% sure he was on the Hidden Headworld; also all but definitely knew something bad had happened to Great Byron and probably his Nucleoids, the ones who'd taken Airealist and the rest of the ex-Crimefighters there in the first place. (Memory-muddling Spellbinder among them, so no loss there.)

Could something altogether unpleasant have happened to Sea's Air as well? Most likely. But the timeframe bothered her. Not only was Thalassa still seeing him this morning but Airhead initially appeared to her near Ensenada Saturday morning, relatively soon after the Byronhead brought him to the Head. Could the Thanatoids have already captured Air? Would cucumber that conundrum if they had.

She had never heard of him being able to cast an astral projection of himself. Doing so would have been a yawn in the park for someone like Miss Myth, as she'd heard Jordan Tethys refer to Mama Methandra. (Truth was, even though she'd trained them, albeit forty-plus years ago, she had no idea what the Elemental Twins' full capabilities were.) She was nevertheless certain as to why he guided his twin to the island. He, rather the glamour-caster(s), wanted to lead her through to the other side.

What was by no means clear was why, after bringing her so far, he or they suddenly abandoned her. Sea was so close. There had to be a reason and, devaray-ameliorated prayer power or not, like the Fatman Hush was beginning to wonder if it was providential. After returning from their futile tour at around 10:30, they discussed this at a beach side cafe in the town.

"*'Help me, Thalassa. I'm trapped.'* You were following him for nearly three days and that's all he said? No indication of who'd trapped him or where?"

"That's it."

"Things were fine in Vancouver?"

"Other than the Signallers and the Magnificent Fuckhead Psycho, you mean? Yeah, I suppose."

Sea didn't bother telling Hush about Murray and Aires' night on the town with Gloriel's daughter Estrella and Anna Maria's much younger Natasha. Didn't mention the airport encounter they, along with Cerebrus, had with Anna Maria herself (now Dre'Ath), John Paul (now a Roman Catholic priest, no doubt his slavishly devout parents' pride and joy), and some of the latest generation of Angels by any surname (including the worrisome Sapphire, with her peculiar prowess when it came to artificial agates). Family affairs weren't her concern.

"Yet you felt you had to leave?"

"I felt both of us, Aires and I, should leave."

She hesitated. It was exceedingly unsettling having a casual conversation with a grown man, a complete stranger until a couple of hours ago, yet knowing full well he was actually a little girl she'd known, as a little girl, for nearly fifty years. She-Hush, as he-Hannibal, mimicked size, voice and facial expressions so perfectly, even she-Sea, sitting across the table from her, as him, couldn't tell she was talking to an illusion.

She was so good she remitted reflections you'd expect to see caught in *'his'* eyes, the windows, the café's cutlery and even the napkin-holder. Could cast shadows too, indoors and outdoors, as if he, Hannibal, a big man wearing a Panama Hat, was casting them and not a little, long-haired, hat-free, cutie-pie nicknamed Hush.

Still, there was something about Hush-Hannibal that persuaded her it was fine to unburden herself to her-him.

"David Ryne and I, well, we'd been involved on and off before and, briefly, after Limbo. It wasn't working out. He'd always been a tad too domineering for me anyhow; too much like his father in that respect. And after Oannes Atlantean proved to be exactly as Fish must have more than just suspected – otherwise she wouldn't have killed him; possibly in self-defense, like she told me – I didn't want to waste even more of my life being loyal instead of smart.

"Then there's the fact Air's naturally wild. So are Wilderwitch and Murray-Furie. Lousy combination, those three together. Even the Diver, who's fairly headstrong himself, realized it. Old Man Power was withdrawn. He hardly left the room he'd appropriated for himself. Which didn't leave much space for the rest of us. Johnny and Raven wanted rid of us; nothing new about that, I suppose. They were always going off by themselves long before Limbo.

"As for the Rainbow, she simply couldn't accept twenty-five years had passed since the last time she'd been around. Her husband, Doc Dark's a jerk. Always has been, ask me. Except now he's a sixty year old jerk. Her daughter Estrella's approaching thirty. Gorgeous, for a redhead, but no real star of the firmament, from what I could gather. Unless it's of rehab clinics, that is. Turned out Star Dark's more like the Witch than Gloriel. Wild, I mean; not gorgeous.

"Papa Rafe's in his eighties and Mama Sofa's not that much younger. Despite any and all of that, Glory wouldn't let go of the notion she was still what, twenty-two, twenty-three? Didn't look a day over 21, either. There still weren't any supras active that Cerebrus – that's David's alter ego – could detect. No one we could relate to except each other and, like I said, that was an unhealthy situation. Life had carried on without us. It'd take time to adjust.

"That's about all I was thinking when I left Vancouver for LA. Then who should be sitting beside me on the plane but Erech Ryne, one of the poltroon patriarch's children from after my time. Only a few hours after I ditch him and finally get into the ocean, my twin's spirit calls me and I end up here – where he doesn't appear to be, but Loxus Ryne, the Signallers again, and you are. None of this can be coincidental."

"Sadly, I'm beginning to agree with you, You're here and you're supposed to be dead and dust a quarter century gone. That pretty much says it all, as far as I'm concerned. Look, as carpentry-contrarian as it sounds, I'm going to level with you. There are scads of scabrous shit-pontoons polluting our better nature out here. I can't even begin to flush, as opposed to flesh, most of them out in my mini mind-sack.

"Here's the biggest one. Do you remember a bright young athletic fellow by the name of Kadmon Heliopolis?"

"Harry's friend, the first Olympian's son by Argiope Bright Face? Sure. He'd be about forty now."

"Except he was killed twelve years ago. Now he's back and apparently on the Moon. Sound familiar?"

"You mean like we're back?"

Hush nodded as gravely as a little girl could; make that a lawyer could. And lawyers made a practice of being grave. "So are yet another Steltsar, Aranya ni Nightingale, who didn't die in '39 anymore than her mother or I did, a third Moses Callion, and you Crimefighters' most persistent sparring partner, Strife.

"Rom Kinesis, another of Ringleader's boyhood big brotherly buddies, and Big Max Maxwell, Aran's erstwhile hubby in case you didn't know, have become serious supranormals after all these years of being Normie Normalized. A few of your other old time playmates – if that doesn't sound too little-girlish – are still around and as much bad news as ever."

She named Corona Power, the Hungarian Countess Ramona Avar, Major Milo Mind, the young Baron Günter von Alptraum and Prince Greygreave Translav, even though she'd heard of his presumed death on Sunday. "And Sedon the Sed-son St Synne hasn't died yet. Not officially at least and he better not anytime soon.

"Thanks to the Wiccan to his Judge Warlock, he's the last small-case-sedon out here; not that you'd know why that's so significant, either. There's rat-packs more; a plenitude of mores, none of them moral. I'll fill you in when we've the time. Remember when Strife turned out to be the Queen Conqueror and disappeared in 1952?"

Thalassa nodded. "She was supposed to be pregnant by the Conquering Christ, David's cousin, Jess Mandam. Don't tell me he's back as well?"

"Thankfully, no. I don't think so anyhow. He's the Wiccan Warlock who did in all the other sedons, though. Including all of Johnny and Solace's boys, going back to the first one, John Junior, in whenever." (Hush had a long history with Blind Sundown and Solace Sunrise, both before and after their official marriage, circa 1940. She'd spent some time masquerading as their ill-fated first child, Shahiyeda, in the mid Thirties.)

"Point being, the Strife from back then was Ramona Avar. She had a pair of twins, a boy and a girl, like you and Aires. Like all the Ryne brats, too, save for Aran, which all but proves she's a Sed-daughter in my bitty brain-book." (Aranyani was hardly the only one who believed the old satyr, Sedon St Synne, was her father. Hush did, too.)

"Their names are Balkis and Solomon. All very biliously Biblical that. But, up until the middle of last week, they called themselves Strife and Daemonicus. They masterminded what happened to the Cosmic Express and, before they were taken care of by their mother, planned to destroy the very island we're sipping on."

Hush finished her last sip of coffee, no small feat when you've such small feet and the lawyer you're masquerading as hasn't; no small hands, or arms, or mouth, either. Folks who thought casting a glamour about yourself automatically changed your size and shape accordingly knew diddlysquat about tricksterism. It was hard work.

"So, what's the problem? You said they were taken care of by the countess."

Thalassa was taking all this rather well, Hush thought to herself. Mind you, given his abilities with computers, a pretty basic calculating machine back in '55, Cerebrus had probably learned most of what she'd just told Sea already; filled in her and the other members of what were now called the Damnation Brigade before they went to the Head.

"Who isn't our countess, I'm to understand. She's a Meroudys Maenad, one of the Korant Corn Queen's get. And their agents weren't. They're still out there."

"I see. Still don't see what any of that's got to do with me and Aires, though?"

Sea didn't see much of any of it, sooth seldom expressed out loud. She'd all but given up trying. Had had a brain sprain; reckoned she was suffering from some sort of stupefaction syndrome stemming from severe information overload. Cerebrus-David's efforts at enlightenment notwithstanding, she found the learning curve so steep she'd fallen off it most of a week ago.

"I'm getting to that, Wavy Gravy Drain. As folks are forever telling me, sometimes patience isn't a virtue. It's a necessity. Their agents are this latest Steltsar I mentioned, who now calls himself Sharkczar, and another mishmash creature called Crystallion. She was once Crystal, Corona's daughter by post-Satan St Synne.

"Then there's this phantom freighter of theirs ..."

========
Signal System was still in its infancy.
========

Of the two or three dozen silver suits, all that had been produced and tested thus far, Shelter's was the most advanced. Shooter and Swirl's were next whereas Spherus and Selene had some exclusive, though still highly experimental, applications incorporated into theirs: he his bubbles, she her beyond-boomerang-like lunar discs.

The rest were mostly generic, with only one or two unique features. Sebastion's, for example, was completely impregnable, had servo-motors which increased his weight-lifter's strength fivefold, but slowed him down dramatically. Sonora's had sound-oriented aspects; Solano's generated heat, and Static's electricity.

Spartan, Stiletto, Sheriff and Sapperstein were walking arsenals who used, respectively, ancient Greek-style weaponry, knives and variations thereof, pistols loaded with a large selection of projectiles, and fragmentation devices. Shooter handled most of their specifics. Suchlike deadly tools suited his temperament more so than his limitations as a designer, which weren't very notable beyond the manufacture of mayhem.

Somewhat similar to Shadowswirl's Silver, though without its ejective capacity, Stupendo's costume was akin to an ankle-length poncho with a generally malleable constituency. Responsive to cybernetic controls built into all the helmets – his looked like a bowling ball with eye-slits – it could harden dramatically while retaining an amazing degree of flexibility.

Subitor was a paraplegic, actually attached to his vehicle. It was equipped with features that System's inventive craftsmen had not yet found a way to miniaturize and incorporate into the Silver. Sub-System's was basic silver with a prototype link to System itself. Savant's was even more elementary but he was the best there was with Speaking Sticks.

Sapphire Lancz, the eighteenth on the island, the one Shooter didn't dare count as part of the obligatory S-number Signallers travelled in, was there primarily for her abilities with artificial agates. Even her father Simon Lancz – Strategos, meaning general, as he styled himself when feeling full of himself – acknowledged that she was so good with them she'd qualify as a supranormal if suchlike witchy gifts hadn't been declared perfectly normal decades earlier, at Abe Ryne's insistence.

Of course, back in the bad old days, Ryne was trying to shield the likes of Superior Sarpedon, her little mother, Sorciere, Wilderwitch and Fisherwoman from the post-war, anti-supra crowd. Another one he was trying to shield was his mistress, Headmistress Virginia Mannering. Hush sometimes called her Ginny Gemstone so Ryne reckoned she must be exceptionally good with agates. (She wasn't; there was nothing supranormal about her. Not that anyone could ever pinpoint at any rate.)

Along with Strategos, Shelter, Sharpshooter, Spherus, Selene, Subitor, Sub-System and Savant qualified as System Seers. Shelter and Shooter were also in superb shape. Even if he did say so himself, not very loudly, they were a grade above even Spartan, Stupendo, Sebastion, Swirl, Sheriff and Stiletto, all of whom were initially recruited more for their athleticism than their intellect.

To his mind, with the exception of Subitor, the rest lacked the necessary training He especially didn't approve of Seers like Savant and Sub-System in the field, reckoning them too valuable to lose. But someone had to wear their Silver if they were to increase their S-numbers, if perhaps not their strength. For his part, Shoot considered them no better than test pilots and, while he wasn't hard-hearted enough to regard them as consequently expendable, he didn't expect much from them either.

Besides himself – what with Shelter otherwise preoccupied with SPACE; with Styx, Sasquatch and Solar equally unavailable – given a choice Shoot would have only taken the original five commissioned specifically to be Signal-lers: Spartan, Swirl, Stupendo, Subitor and Stiletto. Subitor's crippling accident aside, and disregarding reservations he had about Stiletto's suitability for any-thing except a chain gang, they were still the best of the rest.

Up against the King's Own Crimefighters, unchanged as they apparently were after a quarter century wherever, that might not mean much.

Because they were the best of them all!

========

It took awhile to go through everything that Demios Sarpedon, whom Thalassa also remembered from as long ago as the pre-war Amsterdam Academy of Man, the first such, and Prince Translav, via whom Sea looked like, Translav's daughter Constance, who preferred Connie, told Hush a few days back.

"They've obviously found a way to manipulate the Weird such that they can hide in it – and not just them, the freighter itself and their dragons. They're nearby and, if Aires told you he was trapped, it might be on that freighter. I want you to put this ring on your finger and go the bathroom. Stay there until no one else is around."

Thalassa no longer even bothered to pretend to grasp much of what Hush was saying. All that flotsam and jetsam sea-trash about atomic firedrakes of un-known providence – if that wasn't a total misuse of the word – or how Aires could have gone from relative safety in Vancouver to a still floating ghost ship in the middle of the Pacific in less than the time it took her to fly to Los Angeles, then swim to Ensenada, it really was entirely beyond her ken.

Nonetheless, she did as bade. Was washing her face when Hush reflected out of the mirror. "Figured it would work. Hell, if Dumbbell Daddies Ryne River and Sententious Sentalli are receptive, it makes sense you'd be a natural. Don't know that you'd be able to use them, not even to get around, not without any training, but it's worth a shot.

"And not at that shit Shooter, either; much as I'd like to. He's a cocksucker killer; a cocksure fuck-face, dot that ditto. Supranormal sisters, even if they're not Ants, would be an absolute boon right now; in your case, a boom to boot. Think it's time you went for another swim? Maybe find this phantom freighter I was telling you about before it unleashes its cargo? Which is really to ask: Are tidal waves still a specialty of yours?"

A form of an answer came when Sebastion smashed through the café's roof on the other side of the bathroom door. The mirror she was looking at cracked.

Then it wasn't reflecting anyone either which way.

=========

"You're not seriously going to tell me she can do that?" said Shooter. "Turn herself to water and escape down the drain. Clone or the real thing, that's impossible."

"State-shifting was a known ability of the Sea Goddess," said Swirl. "Besides, you got any better explanations, lover?"

"I have." Sapphire tapped one of her agates.

=========

Shadowswirl had been reprising her earlier role as a Crimefighter expert. She was, nevertheless, as astonished as Shooter. Supras shouldn't be able to do impossible things – and, with the possible exception of the element Mercury, nothing could shift states between solid and liquid without a whacking great infusion of inferno. Sapphire, though only a matter of a few days removed from them, wasn't referring to high school chemistry lessons.

"Real witches – not Great Aunt Dolores and Hiliarti Schroff-Zeross's glorified nursemaids – pop between-space on these. I didn't think they could pop anyone else without being in direct contact with them, but who knows? Headmistress Mannering won't let anyone train me to become a proper Ant.

"She says it's because of my heritage. My mother's a D'Angelo and D'Angelos are direct descendants of Satan St Synne. Suchlike don't make very good witches, she claims. Good as in white, that is; though Morgianna Sarpedon's awfully white. And awfully awful, if you ask me. Headmistress uses Strife, Ramona Ryne and Cousin Crystal as proof of that; says they're all St Synne's get. And you can't argue with her; all the more since she probably is, too."

"Even if any of that's true, you're a couple of generations removed from the old corpse," said Swirl, who was only old enough to be her mother if she was the same age as Sappy was now when she became just that, a mother. "Unless you've got some skeletons in the closet we don't know about?"

"Don't we all? I know you and a couple of the others came out of the Tempest Twins' travelling circus of daredevils. But most Signallers know dick-fifty about each other. That's part of System's system. But you're close. And I'm closer than you think. My skeleton's not in a closet. He's lying in life support back in Palo Alto. You call him System sometimes."

"Sedon St Synne is your mom's maternal grandfather," scoffed Sharpshooter, well aware of her fantasies. "Not your dad."

Then again, he thought to himself, what if the rumours of her paternity were true? Maybe St Synne was both Sapphire's great grandfather and her father. If he was then Strategos, Simon Lancz, himself of suspect parentage, would be royally miffed quite rightly. Was that why he rarely showed any affection for the child? Worse, was that why he sent her along with them to Centauri, to get herself killed before she could thoroughly embarrass him by somehow proving it irrefutably?

"Standing around gets us precisely nowhere," said Sebastion, whose helmet was shaped like a castle keep or a rook in a chess set. Like the other two full Signallers entirely sealed within his Silver, after proper adjustment he, too, could see through illusions. "And whoever they were," he added, referring to Hannibal, Lindquist and Yataghan, "They haven't just disappeared. They had, we'd detect them. They've gone somewhere. Question isn't how, it's where?"

Sapphire must have had an in-helmet reading. She sauntered cockily out of the now-ruined café, climbed into the back of Subitor's flying speedboat alongside Sheriff and whistled for the other three's attention. "The little witch took herself to the fancy-dancy hotel with Sentalli's son. They're in his father's suite."

"Race you," challenged Sebastion

The Signaller's real name was Sebastian but he'd exchanged the *'a'* for an *'o'* – *'bastion'* – in order to better reflect his Silver-granted attributes. His armour made him so heavy he could barely walk but the anti-gravity devices built into all Silvers had been specially adapted so that he could fly almost as well as Subitor's car-cum-boat.

He levitated through the hole he'd made in the roof and streaked towards the hotel. Shadowswirl followed him the same way. So did Subitor, now with Sheriff alongside Sapphire. Only Shooter stayed behind. Through his own in-helmet contact system, he sent out a general alarm to the other twelve Signallers on the island.

"Crimefighter sighted. Sea Goddess. Thalassa D'Angelo. Likely others in pricey hotel or deep downstairs. Backup required."

It was Spherus who returned to him. "Selene's off to the hotel, Shoot. There's real trouble down below and you're the best equipped to deal with it. Activate Home-Signal-Home." That was Shelter's private designation. Responsively Shooter did exactly that, but it was still Spherus online. "Initiating Home-In-Home-Samsara sequence now. Good luck, tooth."

That again, thought Shooter. Dragon's Tooth – teeth, as in Spartae. What did Spherus know that he didn't?

========

Paul Creel took one look at the clearly less-than-ideal helmet as it bounced on the ground and, not waiting for the rest of the blood-spurting body to collapse, dove into the water. Doctors rarely being dummies, Angus Skullian was right behind him. Neither of them were aware who'd just done for Sub-System, Joe Hartwig, he altogether ex of the lightbulb headgear.

If they had they'd have remembered what sharks did endlessly.

========

Sharpshooter suddenly found himself far beneath the island. Shelter was waiting for him.

<<"What the fuck's going on?">> He demanded of House-Head in their native Greek. He could have asked something else; a whole bursting bunch of some things else. Primarily, not so much that he could teleport, but how had Spherus learned to control his Silver? Shelter might know the answer to that but he hadn't asked it; hence the answer he did receive, also in Greek.

<<"It's past time we were on the same side again, Shoot. When you were last in Stanford, I had Spherus and his techs adjust your armour. I'd have done the same to Styx and Sasquatch's, too, if Mammalian hadn't got to them first. At any rate, now you can go between stepping stones – real or artificial ones – the same as me.">>

<<"What! How dare you? I could have become Daemonicus!">> Shooter knew that Daemonicus was supposedly an interspace bogey man, the male equivalent of Strife.

<<"Not in the Silver you can't. I checked it out.">>

<<"Unless you've already become him.">>

Shelter switched to English. "Not a chance, Lance. Say Daemonicus or even Baphomet do exist, they'd just be a snack for the likes of us. This one's a full meal."

"This one?"

"WORLD's Steltsar!"

"Good. Finally someone I'm allowed to kill!"

========

The little girl was as close to freaking out as she ever came.

Popping her and Yataghan out of the Grey onto one of the agates she'd left in Sentalli's suite, Hush Mannering quickly summarized the situation for the benefit of her Daddy Alfredo Sauce and the other two in the room, the actual Connie Lindquist and the actual George Hannibal.

"Damn Signallers got gonorrhoea-gadgetry," she told them. "They can see right through my most eye-catching craftwork. Better get his Enormity out of here, yackety-yak Yat. Where's Samarand?"

"Dead," said the lawyer.

========

"Don't look at me," protested Lindquist. "I didn't do it. He just went into convulsions and that was it, endgame another mail order manikin."

"That's manling," said the Fatman.

"Perhaps it's for the best," Hush considered. "Why didn't you get away like I told you?" Hannibal told her what he'd already said to Sentalli-Centauri. The little girl shook her head in disgust. "Signallers again. Probably already at the bottom by now, not that they'd know the Nag Gap from a crack in a concrete cranberry."

"Looks like we're all stuck here," said his Enormity, in all likelihood speaking for himself. Was there a trace of triumph in his trepidation, Hush wondered.

"Don't cast your fate to the wind quite yet, Daddy Doppelganger. I wish to heavenly hell I knew more about this System. Seems they've the Conqueror's technology pretty much sussed. Which means they've the potential to mechanically accomplish stuff we witches can only do with our agates and then only after years of training. Whatever happened to taking your discoveries to the grave?"

"Potential?" came a voice in the same tones that all Signallers used when they wore the Silver. The one who materialized off the same agate Hush and Yataghan had was winged and wore a silver diadem around his or her helmet.

The helmet itself was shaped like a crescent moon. Attached to each wrist were similarly crescent-shaped disks.

"I'd say we're well beyond potential."

Sentalli's suite was in the front of the hotel. It consisted of a large bedroom with a bathroom tailor-made for a man of his girth, a living room also with a bathroom, his den, where Hush sometimes slept, and Yataghan's room, which doubled as a communication room, a mini-control centre.

The living room and Yataghan's bedroom had entrances into the hotel corridor, which was so big it might have doubled as a top floor concourse. (They sometimes used it as a reception area as well an outer office, not that Sentalli kept a secretary anymore.) Additionally all three major rooms opened onto an extended balcony overlooking the beach, boardwalk and main street of the village.

Sheriff, the Signaller with the stylized silver six-shooters and star-shaped helmet, came through the den. Shadowswirl, with her grotesque Crystal Skull helmet, her rags and ribbons twirling about her like living snakes, at least knocked before opening the door and entering the living room. On the balcony, actually levitating just off it, was Sebastion.

Just behind the massive Silver, whose helmet looked like a rook in a game of chess, hovered Subitor. His floating boat was silver; went without saying. His helmet was that of a motorcyclist's complete with face shield. With him in the back of the boat was one whose helmet was shaped like a single, corundum sapphire.

But it was the one who appeared on her agate that intrigued Hush the most. There was an authority detectable even through her electronically-altered voice.

"Let me guess," braved the apparent little girl. "Wings off your shoulders, a crown, a moon-shaped helmet. You're not Winged Victory so you have to be named after Selene, the Ancient Greek Goddess of the Moon. The female counterpart, I note with some interest, of their sun god, Helios."

"Very good," congratulated the Silver. "And you're of course not a little girl. According to System's files, you're the trickster generally known as Hush Mannering."

"Your System seems very well informed. Is he one of my daddies?"

"More than likely," granted Selene.

Hush was stalling for time. She knew the old corpse, Sedon St Synne, could well be her actual father. He was that old, that aware, at least in his prime, and that twisted to tease her, call her *'girl'*, every time they met in the now comparatively distant past. She also knew, with the same scant degree of certainty, that her mother was Celestine D'Angelo, the Celestial Superior.

(Celeste Mannering in there, her younger brother was Raphael, not just Thalassa's Papa Rafe. He was the man who found the Elemental Twins, destitute and abandoned by their parents, in Rome on the same day his Gloriel, by St Synne's daughter Sophia, and Eden Nightingale's Aranyani were being born a few blocks away. As for whether St Synne was Aran's conceptual father, well ... She called Aran sister regardless.)

What Hush actually wanted to know was who Selene really was: "Your real name wouldn't be Balkis, would it? As in the Queen of Sheba?"

That took Selene aback. But only momentarily. "Who any of us are is none of your business, little monster. Want to try me on?"

"Watch out, Selene," thundered Subitor over his hovering car-boat's loud speakers from outside the hotel. "Ants are tricky and, if she's the one you think she is, she's by far the trickiest. Watch out the rest of you, too. There's nothing special about the doctor and lawyer that I can detect but it's well-known Sentalli's son's a Plantagenet.

"His knife's a kind of kris but it might be one of those cut-anything varieties like Stiletto built into his Silver. My sensors also read the Fatman's chair contains a veritable arsenal. Seems Mandam wasn't the only one who mastered miniaturization. Sure would love to study it sometime."

"And I'd love to shoot them all," said Sheriff, his or her guns unwaveringly pointed at Hush and Yataghan, the same as they had been when they were inside the café with Sea Goddess. This time, though, they weren't set for anaesthetics darts. "Starting with Minnie Monster and Olive Oil there. Just say the word, Selene."

"Antheans and Plantagenets aren't supras, Sheriff," warned Shadowswirl.

Under her real name, Lilith Morgan, she was partially trained by Ants – her favourite teacher being the now sixty year old Headmistress Virginia Mannering. She also knew Yataghan's cousins, Jane and James Plantagenet-Ryne, intimately, from both sides of the bed. Like Estevan Hidalgo and Nick Strecchi, Stupendo and Stiletto, she was recruited from the Tempest Twins' circus of travelling daredevils.

"Then what were they doing with the D'Angelo abomination?" challenged the man or woman in Sheriff's Silver. "As far as I'm concerned supra-lovers are just as much fair game as supras themselves." It was a broad statement; one properly not shared by the other Signallers, but as yet it wasn't a broadside.

"This is intolerable," glowered the Fatman. "I made it very clear to your Shooter that there were no supras on this island. If you saw this Sea Goddess then it was because my niece made you see her. She's a prodigy, a natural-born Anthean. Even Headmistress says so."

Even though the lie might have come from Centauri, the situation wasn't just growing too testy for Sentalli. Yataghan was an inch away from going for his knife and who could predict what Hush might do. As for himself, Subitor was right. But one thing his chair didn't contain was a force shield.

"No, I'm not, daddy," interrupted Hush self-protectively. "Thanks for your efforts but natural born Ants would, by definition, be supranormals. I'm as Selene says: a faerie fucking trickster — the faerie trickster, don't you know. Sorry to pull the wool over your eyes but the real Dorothy Dodgson is still with her family back in Toronto. You're right about Sea not being here, though. I was just playing with the Silvers. Testing what they knew and could do."

She turned and addressed Selene directly. "You might as well know I'm here for the same reason you lot are. Abe Ryne called me after it became apparent that all the weirdness going on this last week or so has as much to do with this island as it does the Man on the Moon. I'm trying to figure out what its secret is and you're not helping."

Subitor was right. She was tricky. Her voice was as good or better than the patriarch's. (Thalassa calling him a poltroon earlier was a quote from the Untouchable Diver, Yehudi Cohen. UD once considered the senior Ryne his friend, not the coward he turned out to be when he set them up to be taken out by Psycho on Damnation Island.)

Selene bit: "I heard you drop something about a Nag Gap just before I came out of Samsara."

"Exactly. It leaks into Big Shelter, which you'd have heard about I assume. System certainly would have."

Selene nodded, intrigued. "That's where Jesus Mandam supposedly discovered and learned how to use all this fancy technology we've incorporated into our Silver. System never said anything about there being a way there from here. Not to me anyhow, though we'd all like to find it if it's here."

"So would I," the little girl lied impeccably. "Then I might find the sorceress who turned me into a perpetual child all those years ago. Care to help me, Sheba?" She tried again. This time it worked. Selene spurted out her real identity.

"Sheila," she admitted. "My father's name was Homer."

"You're a Skullian," realized Hush, surprised. "Homer Skullian was one of Angus Dre'Ath's four boy bastards born nine months after the Summoning of 1920. You blind too?" (Angus Dre'Ath also had three legitimate sons by Gilda nee O'Ryan, Bunnie never-Maxwell's sister, who Hush used to call Mama Goldie because of her Rapunzel-like mess of golden tresses.)

"Not in the Silver I'm not. Fact is, all my life I've been able to see things even sighted people can't appreciate."

"Then you know I'm telling the truth," tested Hush.

"I'd know if you weren't," Selene conditionally agreed. In her, the little girl recognized a fellow trickster.

Stunned by her revelations, Sentalli interrupted. "What's your relation to Ryne's physician, Angus Skullian?"

"He's my cousin. Mycroft's know-it-all son. Got a photographic memory – not that it makes him a supranormal any more that a degree of second sight makes me one," she informed Sheriff pointedly.

"Now we're getting somewhere," jumped Hush, a ray of hope suddenly shining through the Grey into her mind. Who'd have thought Signallers might actually prove useful? "Okay, let's be frankfurters. We both want the Nag Gap. I've told you it's probably on this island. Given more time, any one of us might stumble upon it. Unfortunately, like all sorts of other pooping-pants-shit, time is not on our side.

"Maybe you know this already, but there's a phantom freighter out there. In it, don't laugh, are a bunch of dragons undoubtedly from Big Shelter. God knows why, the Devil probably does too, but they seem intent upon destroying Centauri Island and this Gap before we can locate it. Might even be able to blow up big time, like the Nag's Nagasaki, in case you didn't know where the term came from.

"One thing they screwed up, besides screwing with me, is I know who's responsible for them. Her name was once Crystal St Synne, though she calls herself Crystallion now." The Signallers' body language confirmed what she'd already guessed. "Yeah, her you would have heard about."

(Crystallion, before she was transformed, was one of the last known off-spring of Sedon St Synne, the undying corpse Signal System regarded eponymously, as its living System. Her Japanese mother, Takeda pseudonymously Power, was still alive; was, not that she remembered it any longer, once the supra codenamed Crimson Corona.)

"She wouldn't have been trained as an Anthean. Wouldn't have the mind-set. But I've a feeling she is trained, either as a Korant or a Hellion. Like I've always suspected her mother was in the first case; like I know Corona was in the second. She'll have stepping stones either upon her or near her. How many of you Silvers can access them?"

"Over great distances, only Shelter," Selene told her. "But, witness the out-of-the-blueness of my arrival, it's no secret that Spherus and I can as well. At least so long as they're not too far apart," she qualified for clarity's sake. "Shelter may be as mercury-mad as your everyday-average Alice's hatter but he's ex-tremely intelligent and fitter than the world's most serious Stradivarius. So are his friends.

"It wouldn't surprise me if his buddy and, shall we say, sometimes rival Sharpshooter can, too. And, if he can, maybe you can as well, Swirl." Another thing not a secret amongst Signallers was that Shadowswirl was Shooter's lover. However, Swirl claimed she knew nothing about that aspect of her Silver and said as much.

Selene shrugged her shoulders in evident disappointment. "Maybe just the three or four of us then."

"I might be able to do something about extending your range," stated Hush, who only looked like an everyday-average Alice. "Clearly you can already fol low me through the Grey, though I'm probably more skilled at it. What say I lead you to Crystallion then let the loutish load of you indulge your bloodlust to your heart's content?"

"A couple of things," objected Selene. "First, Spherus is a thinker, not a fighter. Might as well tell you he was the first bubble boy, Cecil Mayhew, all grown up now. His immune system's as useless as ever I'm afraid. He doesn't dare leave his Silver unless he's in what he calls his *'Hughes-Home'*."

(The reference was to Howard Hughes, an American industrialist and dilet-tante movie maker who'd died three or four years earlier. An end-of-life recluse who arguably deserved a much better legacy, he was already best recalled these days for the obsessive lengths he took to avoid bacteria.)

"The other thing is, to a man, jack, seventeen of us, we're superstitious. We only fight as part of an S-number. Discarding Spherus for the moment, Shelter, Shooter, if he can teleport, and I only make three. You'd be number four. Assum-ing we can make them teleport, we'll still need at least two more."

"If I can do it for one I can do it for a few more, be assured of that. I always carry extra agates with me. Who're your best then?"

"Spartan, Stiletto, Stupendo: they're all below now. And you, of course, Swirl."

"Then the little witch would make eight," pointed out Shadowswirl.

"I'm no fighter either," insisted Hush. "But you can't go anywhere without me. So, if I have to be counted, you'll have to drop one of the others."

"You'll have to have an S-Name too."

"How about Stupid? For trusting you."

At least Selene and Swirl laughed at that. Sheriff, whom Hush had instantly decided should be fed to Crystal's dragons at the earliest opportunity, merely grunted.

"We'll have to wait for Shelter," said Selene. "Let's go see Spherus. He's with the patriarch at the SPACE-Place."

"Which is where we should be," interjected Sentalli.

"You should be," Selene corrected his Enormity cautiously. He didn't read right on her internal sensors but his wheelchair did, if right included more built-in, miniaturized weaponry than most of their Silvers contained. "Sheriff, feel free to act as executioner should the Plantagenet or these other two make a fuss. Sebastion, why don't you come in and show us what you can do."

The massive Signaller propelled himself through the glass door from the balcony. "You could have opened it first," garbled Selene in that common vocal pattern of theirs.

"I could also kill myself. With your permission, Plantagenet." He didn't wait for it. Drew Yataghan's curved kris-knife and drove it partially into his Silver. "I'm sure you would have forced it in farther, my lad, but not far enough to get to my skin. Allow me to demonstrate. This is what would have happened long before then."

Like teeth, his astonishing armour closed in upon itself and clipped off the cut-anything blade just above its hilt. The selfsame Silver spat out the rest of it. Sebastion extracted the hilt and blade bit left of the knife; handed it back to the stunned man. Was that what Signaller Silver was – mechanized No Name things?

"No need to be impressed, Sentalli-Junior. My kids never have been."

"Subitor, Sapphire, meet us downstairs." Selene turned to the Fatman. "Sorry. We'll have to walk or, in your case, roll."

"I'll push him," offered Hush.

"No, trickster," countered Selene distrustfully. "I will."

Leaving Sebastion and Sheriff in the suite with Yataghan, Lindquist and Hannibal, Selene pushed Alfredo Sentalli out into the elevator, Hush and Shadowswirl following hand in hand, took it to the lobby and went onto the main street. Subitor swept down; hovered slightly above the sidewalk. A ramp lowered from the back end of his flying vehicle. Selene shoved the Fatman and his wheelchair onto it. The other two sat beside Sapphire. Subitor took off again.

Hush was impressed. She still figured Crystallion and her Horsemen would turn them into silver Chop Suey, though.

========

"Right," Hush's 'sister' shouted at Hell's Horsemen once the phantom freighter cleared Cathonia and they'd gathered on its deck. "Listen up. This is what we'll do ..."

Their mounts needed no such pep talk, no last minute instructions either. They knew exactly what they were going to do — overcook themselves a hearty supper.

About time too. They were so hungry their riders smelled appealing.

****

N<small>UKE</small> 26: **Sharkczar Soup**

========

Tuesday, December 9, 1980

"Lotus levitate!" ordered Spartan, as Sub-System's suddenly decapitated body hit the ground.

Stiletto and Stupendo, the two most experienced there besides Spartan, responded instantaneously. Lifting off the floor they folded their legs underneath themselves and hovered in midair. Arms came out the ground and grasped for Savant. Static pointed his-her right glove, the one with the fingers shaped like little lightning bolts, at the clutching hands then zapped them.

Who said only Sentalli's security officers had tasers? And his-hers didn't need conductive wires either.

========

The hands recoiled as if from fire and withdrew back into the floor. Sonora screamed through her helmet and began to vibrate. Sound waves buffeted the others. Sapperstein, Static and Savant were knocked onto their rear ends. Something whizzed along the ground – a shark's fin. Sharkczar's head came out; bit clear through Savant's Silver and tore out his stomach.

Heat from Solano drove him back underground but it was too late for Terry Teller (Savant's real name). Too late for Solano, too, about a heartbeat later. A stalagmite with a circumference wider than a telephone pole rose out of the ground beneath Solano, caught her up and crushed her like a silver-coated tomato against the ceiling. Oussama Modise didn't have time to wish she'd never volunteered to try out the Solano Silver she'd help perfect.

The three airborne Signallers were already in motion as the concrete cavern turned into an iron maiden. Spartan gathered up Sapperstein while Stiletto picked up Static. Stupendo went for Sonora, Maria Tedesco. The pinpoint sharp stalactites and stalagmites caged her but luckily didn't pierce her Silver. Stupendo was similarly trapped but safe.

Stiletto let Static drop into the water near doctors Creel and Skullian, then went back for his friend, Estevan Hidalgo, Stupendo. He had a long box on his right forearm. From the base of it telescoped a straight, double-sided blade akin to Yataghan's cut-anything knife. This he used to slash through the protuberances pinning Stupendo.

Thus freed, the former circus performer rocketed over the water, gathered momentum, hardened his poncho-like cloak, and rocketed back. Curling himself into a ball he bowled through the stone forest then, on the rebound, snatched Sonora out of harm's way. Signallers were supposed to look after each; the better ones actually did.

"Shelter and Shooter are on their way," transmitted Spartan who, now that he was dead, took over communications from Sub-System and was in direct contact with Spherus. (The globular, as in bubble-headed, bubble boy (according to Selene) wasn't much use when it came to action but coordinating it came as second nature to him.) "We've been ordered to evacuate. Through the locks if necessary."

"What about these two?" came back Static, referring to Creel and Skullian. They weren't harmed, yet; were treading water as strenuously as they could but, really, had no escape, nowhere to go: not down, not up and in an enclosed pen, not out. "The Silver might protect us but they can't hold their breath if we have to cut our way out. Besides, the Lord only knows how deep we are."

"The elevator then," suggested Sapperstein. "I'll blast it open and we can escape through the shaft."

"Negative," Spartan ordered them. "Remember your training. We're dealing with something like the old-time supra codenamed Pluman here. It takes in Solidium and shapes it to its pleasure. Only this one seems to be able to travel in the stuff as well. Nice knack to have but it's one we have to handle here."

"Leave them," demanded Stiletto. "They knew the risks."

"The subs," snapped Stupendo.

"Didn't you hear me?" Spartan snapped right back. "Solidium, man! It accrues in things manmade, like elevators, like this whole goddamned island. And nothing's more manmade and more enclosed than those subs. He gets in the same one, we wouldn't stand a chance."

"Nothing's more manmade than our Silver, either," challenged Sonora. "That whatever it is seized control of mine briefly. That's why I knocked you ass over tea kettle. It couldn't hold on, though. Doesn't like sound."

"It didn't like Static's electricity or Solano's heat waves either," reflected Spartan. "Right, listen up. This is what we'll do ..."

========

"What's all this about?" demanded a furious Spherus, as Selene pushed Alfredo Sentalli into SPACE's compound near the island's airport. Sapphire and Shadowswirl, the latter still holding hand with Hush, were right behind them. "There's a crisis situation down below. Some kind of Solidium shark is killing Signallers in your no longer secret submarine base, Sentalli."

"Then aren't you glad your lady friend brought me along for the ride, Mr Mayhew. Take me below, Ms Skullian. We'll be safer there and, once I get into Mr Maxwell's security centre, I can access all the island's very own silvery systems through my chair."

"What for?" inquired Spherus.

=========

"That's a mandroid running amuck down there, sir," his Enormity stated calmly. "I think I can get rid of it."

He sounded as if he was glad to be of some use at last. Likely, thought Hush, he wasn't, but his puppeteer, his other Enormity, was – so long as he wasn't put at risk, it went without thinking as well as saying. Connie was bang on the button bum when she called the all-too-human homunculus a manikin instead of a manling.

She couldn't help wondering what became of made-to-order doppelgangers. Could the originals simply shut them down when not in use? Did they put them into cold storage, a tub of Cathonic Fluid like the Sleepers up in Cabalarkon, Cabalarkon included? Did that make them any less human? Did it make their templates inhumane; if not, in the Fatman's case, altogether inhuman like Yati and his fellow Byronics?

"Dulles?" Spherus turned to the acting security chief for confirmation.

"The whole underside of this place is wired. If we know what sector it's in, we can juice the walls. Drive it out. Correct, sir?" Sentalli nodded affirmatively.

"Why'd you tell them our real names, Selene?" Spherus redirected his annoyance to his wife.

"Seemed harmless enough. This little darling thinks she can get a few of us to the phantom freighter."

"What are you up to now, trickster?" grinned the patriarch.

"What can I say except trust me, Daddy Poltroonery? I think I've finally figured out a way to make these Signallers earn their supper, if not your dinnerware."

"Poltroonery?"

"Means cowardly," provided Sentalli-Centauri.

"I know what it means, Al. What does she call you, Daddy Buffoonery?"

"When I'm feeling nice," she responded before his Enormity could. "Which I'm not now. Nowhere near."

=========

Her armour blaring ear-splittingly loud, much worse than any ambulance siren, Sonora led them through the cavern. Sapperstein blew the elevator and fled up it, he carrying Creel while Static carried Skullian. Sonora followed, acting as a one person rearguard.

Their dead comrades' bodies they left below. Left Spartan, Stiletto and Stupendo, too. Did so happily, glad for the opportunity to live to not fight another day.

Some were made to wear the Silver; others were more like made to make it.

=========

"The kids are gone, whatever you are," shouted Spartan defiantly. Like the other two left behind at their own insistence, his armour was radiating tremendous heat externally while at the same time maintaining an internal comfort zone. "So no more easy pickings. Come out and play with the pros. Bet you'll make for a tremendous slurry."

From an offshoot corridor stepped Shelter and Sharpshooter. Both were slightly off the ground and their Silver almost crystalline, rendered super hard. In that state, common mobility was almost impossible, speed non-existent. If they got into a scrap, they'd be relying on projectiles that they couldn't aim so much as just fire.

"You were ordered to evacuate, Spartan," transmitted House-Head. "Do it!"

"By Spherus, and last I looked I was in charge of this monster roller derby. Besides, you don't know what you're up against. We do."

"Judging from the remains of those three," retorted Shooter. "You certainly know how to die. Get out of here and take them with you. Don't forget Sub's helmet — with his head in it. Oh, and by the way, contrary to what some folks think about me, I like to have a reason before killing anyone. That there, though, is reason enough to start."

"I'm no homicidal maniac either," volunteered House-Head, who from what little the others knew of him was much more likely to be lying than Bullet-Brain. "But, you know, once the crap starts flying I'm the last one stopping. My best advice to you is take Shoot's. You really don't want to get caught in the shit-spray."

Stiletto, whose idea of heroism consisted entirely of murdering heroin dealers in Vancouver, didn't need another prod. He swept into the cavern on shoe-rockets, not an easy thing to do, threw Sub-System's body over his shoulder and picked up his helmet, making sure the head stayed in it. Stupendo gathered the bulk of Solano while Spartan took Savant's corpse, if not all of his guts.

As the first two headed towards the elevator shaft and safety, Spartan paused. "Guess I don't need to tender my resignation as field leader. I gather I've just been fired."

"Not until we're off island and you've notified their folks they died," snarled Shooter, though it was next-to-impossible to tell he was snarling. Input whatever timbre you wanted, it came out of the Silver a garbled monotone. "And don't be in too much of a hurry to do that, Gus. The way things are going there might be a few more phone calls to make."

Once Spartan was on his way up the shaft, Shooter spoke with Shelter. "So where is this Sharkczar character?"

Before Shelter could respond, the creature itself grew out of the floor. It was an awkward looking thing – as if a ten foot long Hammerhead Shark had been grafted onto a giant's hindquarters. Its pectoral fins were powerful-looking arms and his entire body was armour-plated more like a rhinoceros than a shark.

"Ugly bastard," admired Shooter.

Sharkczar didn't think too much of the two Signallers, either. Shooter, Bullet Brain, with his fancy-looking, one-arm rifle barrel attached to his Silver by dozens of tubes or cables, and Shelter, House-Head, with his torpedo tits and granny over-dress, must have struck him as more ludicrous than ugly.

"I'll allow that crack, just as I allowed the others to get away. Your System, who's a dream-sender like I was once, but whom I know best as Judge Warlock, said you had a message for me, clone. Where is the Nagasaki Gap?"

"Clone?" wondered Shooter.

"You, of the son of the Silver Arrow assassins; him, of someone I've never heard of before."

"Echion Sangati," provided Shelter, knowing the incredible truth of his past; something Sharkczar and seemingly even Shooter didn't.

Certifiable as he may well be – may unwell be, more like – this acknowledged Sangati couldn't help but be intrigued by Shark's reference to System, to St Synne. The name Judge Warlock meant nothing to him, though. Ears open and in-brain pen scribbling away on grey cell parchment, he figured there was a painless way to find out. Of course first he'd have to learn to trust a trickster.

What precisely did System have to do with Sharkczar and all that had transpired since the destruction of the Cosmic Express? That scribed, he filed it away in the future file as another mystery he'd have to solve. Later. "And System told me you had a message for me, Sharky," he improvised. "What is it?"

"The Nag Gap!" Clearly Sharkczar wasn't biting.

"Behind us," he invented, not wishing to push his luck in order to satisfy his increasing curiosity. "Left at the next corridor. Two agates down. Your turn now. Tell me how to kill you."

<<"Forget it, shithead.">>

Sharkczar's great white head came out of the ground. Bit through Shelter's legs – and bit through thin air. Shooter came out of the hiding provided by his Splendour Unit and blew the shark's head to oblivion. Another explosive projectile took out the still-standing first version of Sharkczar. The creature hadn't realized that the Unit could cast illusions, not just cloak those who wore the Silver in different guises.

As Shelter shut off his Splendour, on the other side of the concrete cavern Shooter transmitted: "Too bad. I hear sharks make for good soup."

"Too gritty for my taste," complained House-Head. "What's that noise? Fucking Hell, let's get out of here!"

========

The walls whirred with the tell-tale sound of electricity. Barrier doors slammed into place. The locks opened. The Pacific Ocean roared into the submarine nest. Its progress was eventually blocked by more hatches remotely sealed by Alfredo Sentalli from his post in OJ Maxwell's downside operational centre.

If Sharkczar didn't like kinetic energy such as heat or sound, the Fatman reasoned he would like the Pacific pounding throughout the concrete cavern even less.

"You nail the fucker, Al?" demanded Loxus Ryne.

"You almost nailed us!" Shelter and Shooter came out of the Grey beside Sapphire. Even though Shelter's tones were evened out mechanically, there was no mistaking his rage.

"You can take it, Shelly," said Hush. "You're a big girl now."

========

A lot had happened in the short time since Sapphire (Lancz) first spotted Hush (Mannering) and what she still claimed was her teasing but illusionary casting of Sea Goddess (Thalassa D'Angelo) as George Hannibal in the café across from the beach. A lot more was bound to happened if she managed to convince System, or at least their on-island brain trust, to go along with her latest game.

Three Signallers were dead. Two, Savant (Terry Teller) and Sub-System (Joe Hartwig), were valued System Seers. The third, Solano (Oussama Modise), though little more than a fairly fit techie, one who reckoned wearing the Silver might make for a lark in the park, was for all of that no less of a loss.

On the plus side, Alfredo Sentalli had flooded his own submarine pen. Talk about overkill, that meant Sharkczar was (presumably) destroyed in at least three different ways. Not so positively, albeit just as likely terminally for their targets-to-come (if hopefully not any of them this time), the little girl now proposed they take on a bunch of manmade dragons; they in their roost within the hold of some kind of transcendent ghost ship none of them had seen.

This was the selfsame, glamour-casting freak Shelter had earmarked for an upcoming *'interview'*, with or without a Speaking Stick. Not only that, also according to Hush, their primary targets' breath wasn't just fiery. It was radio-active. Worse, should they suddenly feel suicidal – or go down hard, which they would do, one way or another – they were positively atomic.

Yet Shelter had it from Dis L'Orca that the ghost ship existed and Dulles showed them photos of the firedrakes taken on Sunday by one of NCE's doomed aircraft.

Then there was Crystal-Crystallion. With Steltsar-slash-Sharkczar out of the way, she currently topped Mammalian on his most wanted, trophy-head-on-the-wall list. Would do until he could be sure it had been the real King Crime-fighters in Vancouver and that they, despite Hush's denials, were now here.

He left the little witch, Sentalli, Ryne, Dulles, Johann Schmidt and the rest of the SPACE contingent under the watchful eyes of Spartan, in whom Shelter had lost a large degree of faith, and Sapphire, whom he never had any use for but now believed was a supra. He wasn't alone in that regard, which was another reason he left her behind under Spartan's unstated custody more so than care.

He assigned Sapperstein, Sonora and Static to temporary guard duty in the nearby underside corridors. Then, with Sebastion and Sheriff still in the ho-tel, and Subitor *'parked'* outdoors upstairs, Shelter summoned the six others – Shooter, Spherus, Shadowswirl, Selene, Stiletto and Stupendo – into a private conference room the Fatman made available to them. There he reviewed Hush's proposal then asked for opinions.

Knowing their place, Stiletto (Nick Strecchi) and Stupendo (Estevan Hi-dalgo) let the prized designers hash things out themselves. Truth was, already apprehending what they'd decide to do, all they really wanted was to catch their breath. Nearly dying wasn't the best way to spend a morning in Hawaii. Since they reckoned it all but inevitable that they were about to spend their afternoon doing the same thing, it would nice to have a few minutes of quiet contemplation first.

Selene (Sheila Skullian) was the first to offer her thoughts. "Makes sense to me, Shelter. Sink the freighter, drown the dragons as softly as possible, take Crystal if she gives us a chance, capture a few of the crew or riders, and let the others fend for themselves. Subitor could do a lot of that himself," she suggested, not trying to excuse herself from joining them.

"That said," she almost as quickly reconsidered, "It seems the tiny trickster is the only way we can find the freighter and she can't carry him through the Grey. At least I don't think she can, not with his supercar-self, and you can't have one without the other. Then again, who can say with a trickster?"

(Hush wasn't on their takedown list of rogue supranormals. Mostly that was due to her being an Anthean. Ants weren't considered supras because they had to learn their trade; weren't born already knowing everything most witches had to study hard, and practice longer, to get any good at doing. As well, despite her seemingly always being a child, which definitely wasn't normal, System considered her a victim, not a perpetrator. That may soon change, however.)

"Exactly," said Spherus, who wouldn't be going with them in any case. "And, from what little we've gathered about her, she's earned her reputation. Myself, I can't see how we can trust her. Can't put it more plainly, either. I'm still not convinced who, or even what you saw, was Thalassa D'Angelo, to be honest."

"Neither am I," injected Swirl. "Though I'm not sure what to make of the clothes left behind in the bathroom. I mean, Hush wouldn't have had time to materialize them so far away from herself, not with us coming at her from every direction." She wasn't a System Seer but her relationship with Shooter put her on an almost equal footing with the four here who were. Almost, but not quite.

"It wasn't her clone, that much is undeniable. None of Moe Two's concoctions ever exhibited any supranormal abilities that I know about and, no matter what we saw and went through in New Westminster and Vancouver last week, it's hard to credit the Crimefighters being back in action again after a quarter century.

"The little witch may well have been playing with us there as well, just like she says she was here. Ask me, though, it was more likely her cronies. Which is kind of funny when you consider witches are generally depicted as old crones." She looked around. No one had taken off their helmets and no one laughed. Just as well. Laughter broadcast through the Silver sounded had a very unpleasant, nails-on-blackboard shrill.

"Point being," Swirl resumed unbidden, "Both the elder D'Angelos and the Maxwells, even if Auld Jock and Bunnie Galvin never married, live there. The new Mammalian and crew is based there, or thereabouts. Sasquatch and Styx still are there, or were last seen there. Where troubles brew, witches accrue. Or whatever the old saying is. It wouldn't surprise me if we find Superior Sarpedon at the bottom of all this. From all reports she and the Great Man go way, way back and her husband was here last week."

"Sea Goddess aside for now," contributed Shooter, not so much ignoring Swirl's concerns as adding to them, "There's still too many uncertainties. One that leaps immediately to mind is who you actually are, Spherus? Can you remotely control everyone's Silver? Can System?" (Just because the bubble boy Cecil Mayhew was a public figure, that didn't mean Spherus was him underneath his Silver.)

"No one controls mine," Shelter assured him. Noticeably Spherus said nothing.

"Sorry," Shoot mock-apologized. "But that doesn't make me feel any more secure. Tell you what I think. Spherus here is a clone of Jesus Mandam; same with you, Selene, only of his mate, this Strife we've all heard about." It was her turn to hold her peace. Said peace did nothing to dissuade Shooter, who wasn't a peaceable man anyhow.

"Still got nothing to say, either of you? How about this then? Why did Sharkczar, like Sentalli here and Cerebrus, if that's who it was back in Vancouver, think we're connected to the Trigon Spartae? Are we clones of Echion Sangati and Thaddeus Hyperenor? Are we Sangati and Hyperenor, not dead but somehow with our minds all messed up?"

"What difference does that make, lover?" Swirl shot back. "We live, we'll figure it out eventually. We don't, who cares?"

"Try answering one of these then," Shooter continued to prod. "What exactly was Sharkczar? How much did he have to do with the Steltsar and the WORLD of the Sixties?" He spoke with the assurance of an assassin who had done his job and did not doubt for a minute that he had acquired his next bull's-eye. What made Spherus and Selene so special to System? Were they the next King and Queen Conqueror even if they weren't their clones or offspring?

"We're talking Solidium here. Have to be. So what, if anything, was his connection to Professor Kinesis's father, Pluman? Or his mother, the supra called Slipper, for that matter? To System? Was the Judge Warlock he mentioned Sedon St Synne? What's this Nagasaki Gap? And how could Sharky get into Sonora's armour; manage to kill Savant and the other two, Solano and Sub-System, so effortlessly?"

"To each and every one of those questions," Shelter interrupted, "I'll give you the same answer – who knows? I'll also echo Swirl's sentiments. In term of immediacy, who cares?" House-Head was not being fatalistic so much as realistic. "Look, Shoot. We just survived a very nasty situation down there. I was making things up as fast I could.

"I can't say if the Fatman was after Sharkczar or us. Still don't know what this Nagasaki Gap is either. But I will tell you one thing. Sharkczar's message for me was death; not necessarily as dinner either, though his teeth looked awfully sharp and he might have been feeling peckish not having a chance to wolf down his first victims."

Shelter's sense of humour was, to say the least, biting. Sharkczar's might have been just as much so; had he had one. "Fact of the matter is I'll lay you odds System wanted Sharky, and both of us, dead. In me, he picked the wrong man. I believed he picked the wrong man in you as well, Shoot. Or am I wrong?"

"I'm closer to System than you ever were, Shell," argued Shooter. "If he's playing us false, I'll be the first to unplug him. What I'm saying is I'd rather walk around naked, with my rifle on my back, than take a chance on this Silver I helped design shut me down. You say you control yours. Show me how to control mine and I'm with you."

"Don't be so paranoid," advised Spherus, finally deigning to defend himself. "No one controls your Silver but you. I indicated some commands. You initiated them, not me. That's the extent of my involvement in any of this. Hell, it was Shelter, not Strategos, me, nor even System, who wanted teleportive qualities incorporated into your armour, as well as mine and Selene's in the first place.

"As for who I am, the name really is Cecil Mayhew. And yes I am related to the patriarch's factotum in the Thirties and Forties. I'm no clone, my parents are still alive and there are such things as paternity tests these days, in case you did miss out on the last twenty or thirty years of biochemistry.

"Not that any of that matters anyhow, given the situation we're in. I told you what I think about that already. If you want to trust a trickster, you go right ahead. I'd hate to lose you but, hey, we've blueprints for your Silvers. Which I suppose would make them silver-prints. There can always be more Shelters, Shooters, and even Selenes."

"All things being equal," said Selene, doing her best to ignore her husband's unnecessarily dismissive bravado, "You with us or not, Shoot, what say?"

"Five years ago," Shelter reminded him. "There were seven of us, six men and a solitary woman. Howsoever messed up our memories might be, we agree that we lost track of her and her mate shortly thereafter. That left five – the Faceless Five, as you call us behind our backs. System gets nowhere without us; won't get much farther if we're lost, believe you me."

Even though he did not identify them, the other Signallers knew these five were himself and Shelter, Solar (the man who became Colonel Avatar Sol), and the two codenamed Styx and Sasquatch. They were the same five who may or may not have been cloned out of the original Trigon Spartae.

May or may not have been the Dragon's Teeth themselves, somehow or other not killed on Aegean Trigon in 1968 and, equally so, somehow or other, virtually unaged since then. Unaged, at any rate, since maybe '76 or '77. As for the man and woman they'd lost track of, he didn't identify them either. Could be they were on the Moon.

"Willingly or unwillingly, two of them are now with the new Mammalian and one was killed — by WORLD, when they blew up the Cosmic Express. What's left of the Order now that we've taken care of Sharkczar? Crystallion, her horsemen and their dragons answers that. So, no, we're not irreplaceable but, so also, we'd stand a much better chance of not having to be replaced if you stood with us.

"At the very least we owe it to Solar's spirit to take blood payment for his murder."

"Not one for revenge myself," Shooter finally committed himself. "Not much for doing much of anything without getting paid, either. Self-preservation's an entirely different matter and right now it looks like we can't go anywhere without getting eaten alive. Me, I've always preferred to be the devourer than the devoured.

"Besides, I've never had the chance to hunt dragons."

========

Hush had to act quickly.

========

Devils like APM All-Eyes, in the right circumstances, weren't the only ones who could neutralize Anthean Agates and their sister stones, the likes of Afrite Bulbs, Athenan Bullet Pellets, Hellstones and Korant Kernels. They weren't on the Head, though, and there was probably only one devil both out here and still active.

She was a nasty one too, about as nasty as they came; superhumanly patient as well. Akin to a between-space spider, Strife could wait around for years at a time in hopes a Sed-daughter like her came traipsing by. Said daughter, or grand-daughter presumably, ventured too near she'd ensnare them, lickety-split, in her Woeful Webs of the Weird, as Hush overdramatized as much as under-characterized them.

Caught once didn't mean she'd get caught twice. Not when you made sure you'd kept back a few more of Demios Sarpedon's empty eyeorbs. Thus armed, as good as daring Strife to try to possess her again, she stepped into the Grey. Like she'd done a million times she hesitated before taking another step. Marble bags of agates glowed in and around the island's vicinity but she knew what she was looking for – something a fair distance off it; something that wasn't at the bottom of the sea like WORLD's converted fish-packer, its yacht or Translav's getaway boat.

Found some, too; more than a few as it happened. And something else, something that shone much more brightly between-space than stepping stones. She didn't have to emerge from the Grey in order to ascertain the glowing gem-stones themselves were on the phantom freighter, but not necessarily on Crystallion, either.

Assuming they weren't all Crystal's, that could mean entire sisterhoods, not just one or two rogue witches, wanted to destroy Centauri Island after they got rid of the Cosmic Express. Either that or, if they weren't complicit, they were implicated in what the principal technopomp, her riders and their mounts were about to attempt. But she'd expected that already.

If Hush was right about her paternity then Crystal was her sister in Sedon St Synne. It followed that, if she had any proper training at all, she'd be a Korant Corn Queen. That stood to reason since their reigning Sister Superior, Miracle Maenad, was Cybele St Synne, the old satyr's "official" second born after the D'Angelos' Mama Sofa. She took a perverse, almost proprietary interest in keeping tabs on her many younger – albeit almost invariably unofficial – sisters and Crystal was even more exceptional in that she was Number Three in the official category.

As well, though it may not be particularly significant due to the fact that Cybele virtually never left Apple Isle, let alone the Hidden Headworld anymore, long before she achieved Miracle Maenad status, Cybele was an unwilling host of Strife. Indeed, as Hush could never forget, let alone forgive her for, it was Cybele who turned Strife loose beyond the Dome in early 1938. (Not five years later, in 1943, as sisters like Superior Sorrow and Headmistress Mannering, who should probably know better, commonly believed.)

Korants generally only married professional soldiers, ones known since antiquity as Mithrant Legionnaires, but there were killer witches, Athenans most notably. Not all of them were as altruistic as Sorciere (Solace Sunrise become Sunrise) or even Fisherwoman (Scylla Nereid, Lady Achigan) had been (or were, in Fish's case). Most, though not Fish, worshipped Hot-Stuff, Methandra Thanatos.

(Presumably not at all coincidentally, their consequential devic goddess was the mother of a nearly fifty years' missing, fourth generational Water Elemental whose name was Thalassa. While her protectorate was actually Mythland, to the north of the Weirdom of Cabalarkon in Sedon's Crown, hence Miss Myth, she lived on Lathakra.

(Once Sedon's Horn, it currently looked somewhat like a north-south, rather than east-west, Crete from the air. Perhaps only incidentally, during Methandra's Outer Earth heyday during its Middle Sea Goddess Culture, Crete was a thalassocracy, a sea-going trading empire. Over the centuries there have been dozens of thalassocracies.

(The Republic of Venice, the Crown of Aragon, Phoenicia-Carthage, pre-Flood Pacifica, Lemuria and old Eden, as well as the Hidden Headworld's pre-CE Pani merchant monopoly came immediately to Hush's mind. CE, Centauri Enterprises, NCE's Inner Earth equivalent, because she was in his Enormity's presence; Aragon because Jordan Tethys relatively recently told her a story about getting killed while in its service out here just before the inception of the 1000 Days of Disbelief in there.)

There were also Hellions. They dealt with earthborn demons, as well as daemons such as faeries and their as often malicious as mischievous ilk, on a near daily basis. Many of the *'dems'* without an *'a'* were omnivores; a polite way of saying thcy wcrc – or could briskly become, given an irresistible opportunity – man-eaters. (She knew who their Morrigan, their Mother Superior, was, too. She'd given her birth.)

What she hadn't expected was the still sizable lump of Brainrock-Gypsium it had in its hold. That might mean All of Incain wasn't involved after all. While that wouldn't dissuade the real Fatman going after the She-Sphinx, it did possibly implicate other near-masters of Gypsium. The Man on the Moon, if it was Kadmon Heliopolis or, equally disturbingly, Ringleader (Harry Zeross), whom she counted as a friend, might yet prove to be at least partially responsible for what went down (or up, or sideways) with the Cosmic Express and all the hellacious havoc that had transpired since then.

(Harry's much older wife Melina – a Summoning Child, Demios Sarpedon's white-as-light twin sister, as a matter of fact – was once supposed to marry her son, Morg's year older brother Saladin Devason. Perhaps because of his very much unofficial surname, Mel, whose Outer Earth codename during the Supra Wars was Illuminatus, showed just how illuminated she actually was by declining his offer of nuptials.)

Practically for certain the Godstuff in its hold explained how the ghost ship eluded detection for so long. It didn't self-generate the Shadowland in which it kept hiding. It motored to it, through the Cathonic Zone. Which of course said it could motor back there just as easily once Crystallion, et al, were done sinking Centauri. And that, more than anything else, meant time was of the essence.

Returning to Sentalli's island, she slapped one of her extra agates into the gloved palms of each of the six chosen Signallers: Shelter, Sharpshooter, Shadowswirl, Selene, Stiletto and Stupendo. One by one, in a rapid-fire procession starting with Shooter and finishing with Swirl, she brought them to the freighter. (As she had already forewarned them, she might have accepted a stupid S-name but she was no fighter. Also as she told them she would, she abandoned them. Subitor could retrieve them when the time came.)

When she came back to the island the last time, she intentionally altered her course through interspace howsoever minutely. Showing a remarkable amount of patience (for her, if nowhere near Strife-level), she waited in the Grey until nature called her own, predetermined target for midday mayhem.

Young Lancz, whose artificial agates she'd homed in on, and bided off of between-space, should never have led the Signallers to Hush and Yataghan in the hotel. Bringing them there wasn't a lucky guess. (Although, for Sappy, it was about to become very bad luck indeed.) It was confirmation of what Sea told Hush the teenage play-punk had done to Cerebrus David Ryne in Vancouver the week before.

Sure as shitting, she finally had to go to the bathroom. Spartan wouldn't let her stray too faraway from him so it was the one attached to Big Max's bunker, the underside version of topside's Last Gasp Saloon. Since Sappy could probably scream as loudly as the horrifying *"music"*, in quotation marks, she purported to love, Hush had to be careful when she came out of the Grey to confront her.

Once she'd done her business, to euphemize some – which Hush almost never did, enjoying the shock registered on folks' faces when she, at her size and concomitant cuteness, went into the smelly details – Sapphire proved precisely how unsuitable she was for the privilege of wearing System Silver. She took off her jewel-shaped, protective helmet in order to wash her studded, acne-spotted, already dull-as-dishwater, and pasty as pond scum, face.

She deserved what happened next.

========

Two and two equalling trouble down the line as far as Hush was concerned, she had to do a Cerebrus about it now. She'd teach the primping pinhead not to Photostat anyone's soul, to use returned as much as restored Thalassa's term. The silver wedgie was just for starters; the syringe that followed, proof that Major Milo Mind and Hadrian Dis L'Orca did not invent amnaesthetics. (Oh, the arrogance of men!)

She'd let the teenager remember her name, maybe even that of her favourite band, but not much else. (Hush liked Siouxsie and the Banshees too.)

For Sappy a lesson learned became a lesson forgotten in very short order.
****

NUKE 27: **Hell's Horsemen**

========

Precisely at noon, Crystallion mounted her nuclear firedrake.

On her signal the rest of Hell's Horsemen got on their technopomps, as she'd dubbed the not so much manmade as She-Sphinx-manufactured abominations. While they readied themselves to take off for Centauri Island, the All-raised and thereafter refitted phantom freighter chugged out of between-space into the North Pacific.

Time to die was nigh, though not for them. To a one, they could be rebuilt. Replicated anew, put better.

========

Thanks to a certain little witch of Crystal's acquaintance, moments after it came through on this side, Signallers began to materialize below decks.

Their Silver built with destruction in mind, they began to meticulously scuttle the ship. She resisted the temptation to join the ghost craft's mandroid crewmembers in a futile effort to fight them off. What was the point? The freighter had served its purpose. Curiosity got the better of her, though, and she waited until the last possible moment to leave.

The freighter was already tearing apart – was well on its way to sinking, again – when Shelter, his granny dress in shreds, his torpedo tits already blown off, found his way topside. The rest of the firedrakes were beyond his range but Crystallion was on her technopomp, wings fluttering furiously, just above him.

He ripped off the rest of his dress and exposed himself; albeit only in a manner of speaking. Always much more than a bite barkers, he had built into the crotch of his Silver a phallic missile. This he cybernetically launched. It exploded against the woman and her mount. Only energized her further.

"Heard you might be back, lover," she broadcast through her radiation suit's external speakers. "Thanks for the boost by the way. See you in Hell!"

Shelter didn't have time to mull over her words. As she flew off on her dragon, he spotted American planes zeroing in on the phantom freighter from above.

Now he understood what Francis Scott Key meant by *'rocket's red glare'*.

========

"That's it," shouted Adolph Dulles, looking at the transmission from SPACE's satellite. "The phantom freighter's a figment no longer, Mr Ryne."

"Finally got you bastards," exulted the Great Man, slapping the table in front of his monitor. "I knew you were out there. Had to be!"

They were in OJ Maxwell's bunker beneath Centauri Island. The patriarch had moved SPACE's operations down there as soon as the Signallers left.

========

"So what are we going to do about it?" wondered the Fatman despondently. "You said we only had three planes left after those things took out the others on Sunday."

"You might call it your island, sir," Johann Schmidt, already steadier on his feet after his little chat with Abe Ryne, pointed out. "But it's still part of the United States of non-acronymous America. And they've plenty of planes left. Let's just hope the dragons are still in the damn thing."

(Schmidt had heard of horse-whisperers but, other than the – to his mind – bogus spew uttered by so-called psychologists and their ilk, whom he regarded as charlatans, he had rarely heard of a human voice being used to talk someone back to physical health. He certainly hadn't experienced it firsthand. He had now, though.

(Even though he didn't deny the seriousness of chronic depression, the argument that, therefore, his condition had been mostly in his mind didn't gibe with how he'd felt only a few hours ago. Smythe's passing hadn't depressed him. It had debilitated him nigh unto dropping dead himself. The comparative wellness that followed Ryne's verbal tongue lashing couldn't have been coincidental.)

It remained to be seen if Schmidt's assessment of the American Air Force's prowess was warranted. He'd done his bit for it; that was for sure. Just before he left Pearl Harbour the first thing that morning, he drew Dolph's transmitted description of the firedrakes. He gave the military a copy of the drawings and the approximate coordinates of where they must have come from.

Even though things were hardly back to normal there, US pilots still knew an enemy vessel when they came across one. Now, thanks in part to corroborative evidence coming in from SPACE's satellite system, he and Ryne were making sure they came across one. Spherus, who was still in the bunker along with Spartan – the rest of their Silvers having been placed on guard outside the control room – wasn't as enthusiastic.

"Your trickster's led Selene and the others into a trap."

"Baloney," scoffed the Great Man. "If they got there in time, if they'd done their jobs properly, they'd be back here by now and we'd all be happy as wiggly pygmies in a blanket. Because they aren't, they've obviously buggered up. So, Mr Mayhew or Mr Mandam or whomever you are, bubble boy, if the American planes don't get to it before the dragons get to them, we're the ones in the trap."

"Don't like the sounds of that, sir. I'd make a lousy crab and a lousier supper."

"Not to worry. I'm not finished biting back yet."

========

As if to emphasize Ryne's grim determination for battling on, air raid sirens began to wail throughout the island. The camouflaged roof covering the vast underground launch site of the Cosmic Express closed. An even more fortified covering of battleship steel creaked into place over it.

The three fighter planes left on the island joined the helicopters already in the air. Mobile rocket launchers came out of their super-hardened concrete garages and took to the roads. Laser cannons capable of spotting in-coming rockets and incinerating them hundreds of miles away were manned and trained on the sky.

Alfredo Sentalli and Ryne's own New Century Enterprises had spent multi-millions of dollars on defence. They were about to find out if it would pay off.

Against nuclear dragons!

========

Sheriff and Sebastion were still in the hotel guarding George Hannibal, Yataghan Sentalli and Connie Lindquist when the latter screamed at them.

"Hear that, Sherry Shit-for-brains? That's no dinner bell, not unless we're planning on becoming the overdone dinner. Centauri Island's under attack. Maybe it's not too late to get out of here. The elevator in the hall goes below the lobby, to the island's private parts. Come on, I'll show you the way."

Sheriff balked. "No fucking way!"

"Aye fucking way!" cried Sebastion. "Let's get the fuck out of here!"

Sheriff's fellow Silver wasn't as thick-skulled as he was thick-skinned; make that thick-armoured. He'd heard about the dragons and was another one not about to let duty get in the way of self-preservation. Without waiting, he rocketed back through the balcony doors and fled towards the SPACE-appropriated building near the airport. Holstering his or her guns, Sheriff took off after him.

Left alone Lindquist turned to her onetime fellow Untouchables and smiled. "No time like the present."

"But my father?"

"Is on the Head," snarled Hannibal. "Which is where we're going. Let the homo fry. That's what they're for."

The elevator they took was the one built behind Sentalli's roll-in clothes closet.

========

"We're getting visuals now," shouted Dolph Dulles. "I don't believe it. They actually are dragons. Must be thirty of them. Big as biplanes. There's someone riding each of them."

"I don't care if they're Norse Gods playing Swan Maidens to the tune of Wagner's Valkyrie, Mr Dulles. Take them out."

========

Heat-seeking missiles found their targets. Some exploded on contact – amazingly, to no effect. Even more amazingly, others were swallowed whole. The firedrakes kept on coming; the ones who had been hit larger than earlier. The island's jets homed in on them. Strafing fire riveted the dragons and their riders. More rockets, more dragon food.

The jets blazed away, out into the Pacific. The helicopters also backed off. The dragon-riders ignored them entirely and whipped their unnatural beasts onwards.

"No use, sir! Don't see as we have any choice."

"All right." Sentalli flipped open his armrest and began clicking in a code only he and Dulles, of those alive and still on the island, knew.

They were flying abreast of each other – strung out across the skyline like blazing beads on a nuclear necklace – their massive wings almost touching. Then there was a flash. Six of them vanished. Fifteen of them swooped back out over the ocean. The remaining nine simply hung in the empty air: gargantuan grotesqueries caught in an invisible spider's web.

From out of Mounts Heliopolis, Zeross, and Kinesis, Alfredo Sentalli had just raised the Gypsium Curtain.

"Will it hold?" demanded the patriarch.

"Damned if I know," admitted the Fatman, who renamed the smallish, largely burnt out volcanoes after he judged the so-called Gypsium Triumvirate to have saved his island from WORLD in 1965. "You know what Professor Kinesis always said about Gypsium. Any idea how the dragons suck in everything we fire at them?"

"Look at the way they glow," said Spherus, who in his bubble while growing up had made a study of supranormals. "Back in the War there was a supra by the name of Emperor Energy. He literally fed on explosions. We never did learn much about him but Raphael D'Angelo thought he was an archangel sent by the Lord Above. Then again, he was convinced he was one, too."

"Emp En did a bunk after the second Atomic Bomb was dropped over Nagasaki," Ryne added, possibly selectively. (There were many who reckoned he knew a whole lot more about Emperor Energy and his mate, the non-Ginny Headmistress, than he ever let on.) "Was never seen again. So either it was too much for even him or he figured the war was over, his job done. Good thing you had that in reserve, Al. What does it do?"

"What Gypsium usually does, I guess. Whatever it wants, that is to say."

"Six of the dragons went poof," said Schmidt. "From what Sean told me before he died, something similar happened to one of the LAC Squads on the Moon more than a week ago."

"Fucking Hell!" swore Spherus. "It's fading."

"Didn't put enough oomph into it," reacted Sentalli.

"Got any more tricks up your sleeve, Al?" muttered Ryne disconsolately as the Gypsium Curtain vanished with the nine dragons and their riders caught in it.

"There's still fifteen firedrakes left," the Space Age Spartan noted with remarkable, almost fatalistic calmness.

"They're massing again, sir," yelled Dulles.

"Don't worry about it, Dolph." Hush Mannering appeared off one of her agates, either the one Ryne wore or the one Sentalli wore. "Got it soused!"

She giggled at her own little joke.

========

Spouts of ocean shot up. Hit the technopomps. Fire met water. Steam dissipated both.

========

Only one of the atomic dragons got through. It landed on the airport tarmac.

Crystallion leapt off it, seemed to sniff the air, dropped a hellstone at her feet and went through the Grey to confront the perpetual seven year old and the rest of those gathered in the underground bunker with her. Once there she just ignored, absorbed, all the ordinance being blasted at/into her by Dulles, Spartan, and Schmidt.

Tearing off her demonic helmet, thereby unveiling the featureless face of scarlet-haired Strife beneath the transparent radiation mask she always wore, she spat her venom. "You little monster," she screamed at Hush Mannering. "I should have killed you years ago. But I've got you now. Die!"

Crystallion shook-shoulder-shivered uncontrollably. Then her suit began to glow.

"Gloman!" someone shouted.

"Nuclear!" someone else shrieked.

"Sluts for nuts," the trickster nattered inanely – in frustration as much as horror.

========

Thalassa D'Angelo, Sea Goddess, whose water spouts had extinguished Hell's Horsemen, came out of Samsara off the same agate Hush then the other one had mere seconds earlier. She pointed her Aqua Ankh at the faceless redhead. Crystallion's radiation suit was suddenly inundated with seawater.

"Get everyone out of here, Mannering!" she shrieked, already realizing there wasn't enough time.

Sea didn't so much explode as the icy depths of the Pacific burst out of her. Thoroughly immersing her with her own aqueous substance, she took Strife-Crystallion with her.

And then it was over!

========

Sophia D'Angelo was saying grace that night at supper in Vancouver.

"Let us also pray for O'Ryan James Maxwell and Romaine Kinesis. May they succeed at whatever they're doing, wherever they are. Let us not forget the salvation of your soul, dearest Estrella, and that of our absent ones ..." Her voice trailed off. She looked upwards, as if to the heavens, and seemed to go catatonic.

She remained physically in her family's presence but her spirit essentially flew to the Moon. When she returned, she broke the chain of hands and, blaming the week's strains, took to her sewing room upstairs, across the hall from Papa Rafe and their bedroom.

After pecking at his food, John Paul, her only surviving son, chaplain of Centauri Island and confessor to Roman Catholics aboard the Cosmic Express, went to see her in what had once been his bedroom. Despite the fact that he was only thirty-six, he was already an adviser to the Pope of the same name. Nevertheless, regardless of his success in that and nearly every other endeavour he put his mind to, he had long placed last in terms of his father's affections.

Whatever resentment he retained for Raphael didn't extend to Mama Sophia, however. "Mother?"

"It's better this way, John Paul," she said. Her eyes were red but it wasn't from crying. "No one else can contain her. No one else has the fortitude."

She did more than just suspect that in his capacity as confidante to the Pope, he had much more than just some glimmering as to the reality of supranormals, of Strife in particular, and of their long ended Supra Wars; not that, obviously, they were long ended anymore. She further reckoned he knew more about what was actually going on in this world of theirs than anyone else in the house save, perhaps, for Dr Dark and, almost for sure, the elder Maxwells.

"But you're too old," he said, confirming as much.

"Then pray for me. It's always better to be prayed for than to pray for. I leave it to you to see that neither your father or I are abandoned."

"You can rely on me, mother."

========

Strife had been troubling Moon's Angel since the night before. The tripartite being that was Machine Memory wasn't satisfied with any explanation she could come up with as to how Marut Kanin, onetime mate of Thrygragos Varuna Mithras, if that was whom Strife actually was, came to possess her, no matter how briefly.

However, as she told her beloved Heliosophos, she was confident she had finally got rid of her. "I would have thought of it myself except Memory of the Grey, of the Angels, was killed before Strife became much of a factor. If you think about it, it's obvious. Fitna Marutia, under whatever name, is the devil Classical Greeks knew as Eris."

"Which almost rhymes with Ares, the Olympian God of War."

"Who's her brother, at least according to some sources, but regardless, just so. She's an affinity for females connected to Sedon St Synne. That includes me, though I – that is to say my original self – only slept with him. Generally speaking, we're an imperfect lot, impulsive, even compulsive, rather than resolute; less reflective than convective. Except for Sophia, my namesake's sister-in-law, that is.

"Wisdom of the Angels is so spiritual, so intrinsically good, I doubt even the epitome of Discord can corrupt her."

"Just what I needed, something else to celebrate."

========

Sea Goddess had already proved a natural when it came to using Anthean Agates and their cousin stepping-stones. She vanished on the agate one, Hush, then the other, Crystal, had appeared upon seconds earlier. She hauled Strife-Crystallion, too sodden to resist, with her as she did so.

Both were suddenly deep beneath the ocean, coming off yet another agate Hush had sunk for her earlier that afternoon. When Crystallion self-detonated, Strife no longer possessed her – Moon's Angel was waiting to take her on within Shadowland – and Thalassa was fully in her watery form.

Only Crystal St Synne died that moment.

=========

Or, rather, it was what Steltsar (Sharkczar), All of Incain, Quarter-Queen Amphitrite, her Lemurians and rogue scientocrats (bio- and technomages both) in the onetime Weirdom of Shenon, by exploiting her genetic heritage, had made of her that died. (When, pre-Genesea, Sedon's Head had been the Archipelago of Pacifica, Eden's Zoo, the even-then heart-shaped island of Shenon had been the Edenite zookeepers' headquarters.)

The real Crystal had probably ceased to live, at least in terms of having her own free will, the first time Strife, with the connivance of her cancer-riddled, pain-ridden and embittered mother, Corona Power (born Takeda Mikoto), took the then thirteen year old over during Witch Week 1960 (Witch Night, Walpurgis Night and/or Beltane Eve, April 30th, being its start) — in particular the day Crystal strangled Belificent by then Zeross with her riding crop!

Even changing to water, Thalassa might have shared her fate but for one thing. Using his teleportive Brainrock rings, Ringleader (Dr Aristotle *'Harry'* Zeross, long no longer masquerading as Amos Annulis) transported Methandra Thanatos (Hot Stuff, Miss Myth, the Mistress of Mythland, Sedon's Crown Jewel) from one side to the other.

With her mind-over-mind abilities as much as her sorcery, Lathakra's Crimson Queen rendered Thalassa forcibly solid again. Bodily gathering up her thought-daughter, Rings returned them through the Sedon Sphere to the Frozen Isle. Massive Tantal, Cold to his sister-wife's Heat, was waiting for them high in the Labrys mountain range atop his Glacial Palace.

Methandra handed the still stunned Thalassa to her brother-husband. She suddenly grabbed her forehead. Someone was communicating with her telepathically.

"It's Artist. Mirror's found the others. By the Triplet Goddesses, they're on the Moon!"

=========

"Bloody wonderful," muttered Harry, entirely exhausted from his exertions. "Oh well, at least I can't say it's the last place on Earth I want to go."

It was a line that would have done the Diver proud. If he was still alive.

****

Phantacea
Publications
proudly presents ...

Helios on the Moon

Jim McPherson

The third full-length entry in the
'Launch 1980'
Story Cycle

1st M<small>OON</small>: **His Stories**

========

October 21, 1968

On the third Sunday of October 1968, Loxus Abraham Ryne, the Mesopo-tamia-born, Dutch-Iraryan patriarch of the Illuminated Faith of Xuthros Hor, was on the Greek Island of Scorpios attending what some billed as the wedding of the decade. The Great Man's then Number One, O'Ryan James Maxwell, approached him with the latest news.

"No sign of the Zerosses, Abe, but Dem's Dim has come through again. Are-mar's hot on Heliopolis's heathen ass. How do you want it?"

"Well done, Max. Make that incinerated."

========

Big Max was a close friend of the now missing Angelo and Megaera Zeros. He'd worked with their equally missing eldest son Demonites for years in AMER-ICA (*'The Alliance of Man for the Extermination of Resisting International Crim-inal Associations'*) and for more than a decade before that. He was so tight to the Zerosses in particular that he happily acted as best man at the wedding of their youngest, Oriani, to the patriarch the year before.

Dem's Dim, Demonites' putative bastard, was Dmetri Diomad. His presumed mother was the then four years' late, still lamented Roxanne nee Heliopolis Kin-esis – the mother, when she was not quite sixteen, of Romaine Kinesis. In 1968 Diomad was only fifteen himself. Nevertheless, on behalf of the Ryne-funded, as well as Ryne-named, AMERICA, he'd been spying on the relatively recently re-vitalized Black Rose of Anarchy for almost three years.

Despite his close ties to the Zeross-Kinesis-Heliopolis clans – the *'Malan-thean Minoans'* or, equally often, the *'Etocretan Extremists'* of this day and dec-ade – Maxwell had absolutely no use for Kadmon Heliopolis and his cronies, the so-called Trigon Spartae. He quite rightly regarded the then twenty-eight year old son of Agenor Heliopolis (Hot Rox's much older brother) and Argiope nee Zeross (Angie's youngest sister), both of whom had died during the war, as ideological threats to worldwide prosperity, not to mention comparative stability.

In Max's view, Kadmon was much more than just the daring, but essentially unstable, leader of the modern day Black Rose. He was an undeclared – and until now unsanctioned – supranormal. The Great Man had left him alone for so many years simply because he seemed to have no extraordinary, as in meta-functional, abilities. As far as Max was concerned that's what made him so dangerous.

Kadmon did everything too damn well.

========

Acting on young Diomad's transmitted intelligence, one of AMERICA's best operatives, James Aremar, himself only twenty-five in 1968, tracked Heliopolis – El Draco as Kad had, not-so-jokingly been known as in his childhood – to the Island of Santorini in the Aegean Sea. With five companions, his so-called Spartae or Dragon's Teeth, the Greek revolutionary escaped in a high speedboat. Aremar was in immediate pursuit.

Hours later, off the shore of Trigon, the usually uninhabited, triple-peaked islet that had been the Zeross family homestead for most of the century, Aremar blew the boat out of the water. Heliopolis and his five Spartae weren't done yet, though. Showing off their remarkable strength and fitness, they swam to shore before Aremar could overtake them.

Fearing what traps the self-proclaimed anarchists may have laid for them on Trigon, Aremar ordered a softening air strike. It was a prudent step. Never take chances with a madman and his whiz-kid-followers on their home turf. This was all especially true of Trigon, which old-timers like his superior, Big Max Maxwell, once tried to convince him had actually, um, gone astray from the surface of the Aegean Sea during the Second World War years of barely a quarter century earlier.

Another twenty-five year old, Mik Starrus, piloted one of the planes that hit Trigon. It was his bomb that struck an outcropping of Gypsium on Mount Telepassa, the islet's third and smallest peak. The whole landform shook visibly then vanished. POOF! Gone – Trigon, Heliopolis, the Spartae! No blaze of glory, no volcanic eruption, marked its passage. It just wasn't there any more.

Trembling in terror, his hair going white almost on the spot, Aremar swore all on his boat, everyone who had seen the impossible happen, to secrecy.

He simply reported to Maxwell that their mission was accomplished.

========

"Jim got him, Abe," Big Max duly told the patriarch later that day on Scorpios. "Heliopolis is history."

In a minor burst of prescience, Ryne said he devoutly hoped not.

========

A few days later, during a particularly painful debriefing – call it a grilling, for that was what it amounted to, over very hot coals – Aremar, Starrus and the rest of those who had seen the incredible event finally told Maxwell and Ryne the truth. There was no longer any point in trying to hide the facts. Anyone with a month old map of the region could see for themselves.

The pistol-packing Great Man tried to put the best possible spin on it. "There were no bodies found on Salvation Island either," he nervously reminded his Number One, referring to the nuclear annihilation of Ryne's nephew, Jesus Mandam, in 1953.

"That's because everyone but Blind Sundown and Raven's Head was obliterated," snarled Maxwell.

"No bodies found on Damnation either, Max, but the Crimefighters are no more back than the Conqueror or The Rache's supras."

"But both Salvation and Damnation are still there, Abe. Trigon isn't. That's the point!"

"Maybe it sank. Island's do that, you know?"

"Most islands don't have Gypsium on them."

========

The invariably striated, like a human brain, ever-glowing rock was very hard to locate. It sort of appeared and disappeared, as if it had a will of its own – which of course some believed it did. Not for nothing was the miraculous substance sometimes called Godstuff. Even more furthermore, not for nothing was it as often, or perhaps even more often, called Brainrock.

Although pockets of it were found in the environs of Sedona Arizona, the Yucatan Peninsula and, perhaps surprisingly, around the Palestinian Dead Sea, Gypsium was generally dug out of the ground in the vicinity of volcanoes or, more commonly, around meteorite craters and cometary blast sites.

(To the Western World's abiding gall, the largest known deposit of Gyps was in Soviet Siberia, in and around the site of 1908's Tunguska *'event'*. This fluke of happenstance more so than planetary geology gave the Soviet Union a huge advantage in the Supra Wars of the late Forties, very early Fifties, when Sedon St Synne and the otherwise anonymous Gypsium Genius known as the King Conqueror secretly made their base in the Ukraine.)

It was also found on two other dinky, tri-peaked islets: Easter Island, in the Southern Pacific, far off the west coast of Chile, and much smaller Centauri Island, off the coast of Maui in the Hawaiian Archipelago. Additionally, one of the least advertised discoveries made by Neil Armstrong and his NASA buddies, when they physically went on the Moon the next year, was that Gypsium Godstuff was prevalent there.

That wasn't the reason why the United Nations of Earth Ship Liberty, with its multinational crew of well over a hundred men, was orbiting the planetoid today, over a dozen years after Aegean Trigon disappeared, never to be seen again. But it probably had something to do with it.

There were, sure as shit, aliens down there (from the Liberty's perspective). Had to be, if only because someone was bombarding the Whole Earth with thought-altering mind beams and who else but aliens could do something like that? Had – and this was only one of all too many theories 1980-currently being bandied about in the corridors of tremendous political and financial power – they come hither to mine it only to subsequently decide to stay around and conquer Planet Earth just because it was so pretty?

It was a question that needed asking, and answering. Which was why the Liberty would not be shooting first — at least not for a few minutes after arrival overtop.

========

Sunday, November 30, 1980

Some one hundred and seventy thousand light years earlier, Weirstar ex-
ploded. It wiped out the entire planetary system of Weir, possibly the first and,
according to descendants of its survivors, greatest civilization in cosmic history.
Its cause was artificial but the nearly insane Entity who instigated the star's
destruction had taken care to move the most progressive society in all of Weir's
worlds to a planet in a relatively nearby star system. That planet became what to
this day its inhabitants still occasionally call New Weir.

There, synchronous with the scheduled launching the Cosmic Express from
aforesaid Centauri Island, another astronomer – this one black-skinned, as were
all male, self-proclaimed 'Utopians' of Weir – was being called to task in the
Courtroom of the Visionary. Also like every other Utopian, regardless of whether
they were black-as-night males or white-as-light females, he didn't have a given
name, just a designation.

Completely unimaginatively, his was Mr Astronomer.

========

Throughout the cosmos, courtrooms were much the same as they were on the Earth. The judge sat on a raised dais behind his or hers bench, used a gavel and pronounced sentence. Secretarial staff sat in front of the judge's bench. Prosecutors, defenders, appellants, advocates, adversaries, all were arrayed facing the judge.

This being a courtroom of a visionary there was no jury nor any audience, save those invited. Above and behind the judge's dais was another platform, inset into the wall. Traditionally three empty chairs more so than thrones were placed upon it. They were for the three deities of New Weir, the Trigregos Sisters: Devaura, Sapiendev, and Demeter. Immortal and ageless, the Sisters rarely appeared, but the empty chairs remained as a symbol of those who truly ruled New Weir.

The judge was the nominal Visionary. Black-skinned and tattooed with the symbols of his office – in his case the letter, or chromosome, 'Y' – he would sit blindfolded as he listened to the person or persons making their case or cases. He would take in their arguments with both ears, whereupon he would open both eyes, the horns of the Y, and peer into the future, the shaft of the Y.

As with any prognosticator he would see any number of potential futures. His task wasn't to see *'the future'* as such; that even Utopians acknowledged wasn't possible. Rather, he was expected to *'judge'* the best possible future and thereafter pass sentence on ways appropriate to attain it. His ruling was made public and almost invariably heeded. At least it was until unforeseen circumstances changed such that it must *'needs be'* changed as well, sometimes by the same visionary, sometimes by other ones.

By a vagary of Utopian genetics, other than the pigmentation caused by their gender, all visionaries looked the same – just as all astronomers looked the same, just as all geneticists looked the same, and so on. Privately, every person was unique, with his or her own individual appearance and personality. Publicly, though, one could tell what anyone was bred to be just by looking at them.

Rebel or radical types seldom existed. Under New Weir's system they would have been detected while still in their development tanks and simply discontinued. Once born, though, life was both sacrosanct and very long by human standards. Talk to a Utopian and they would say theirs was the ideal society, which was why they deemed themselves Utopians. Capital punishment for example – indeed punishment in any form – had no place, never had, in either Old Weir or New Weir.

Of course, since New Weir had been around for millennia of millennia, almost no one used such terms as old or new on a regular basis anymore. Weir was just Weir. The Recurring Entity who founded it made one law and one law only: *'There shall be no law!'* As if, given such a solitary commandment, there could be any other way, consensus was how the vast planetary confederation of Weir was governed.

The role of the visionaries therefore was central, albeit not crucial, to the workings of Weir. Events could change and, with them, their visions of the best possible future for Utopian Kind. That it had thrived for thousands upon thousands of thousand years – that in all likelihood it would continue to thrive endlessly – was evidence that the most fabulous visionary of all time had been that selfsame Entity.

Illuminaries of Weir knew the Entity had a name, two of them. They and everyone else also there were two of them: a her-story and a his-story, as it were. No one paid much attention to Illuminaries any more, though. Very few of them were born and none were deliberately bred. Who cared about the past in a society dedicated to the future?

The present was just Nature's way of carrying on.

========

The judge's gavel was a pipe. He screwed off the top of the mallet, inserted a raw fibre called 'haoma' or 'soma', removed the nib at the end of its handle, struck a match, and lit the stuff. He puffed it into smoking cinder and inhaled deeply. Held it for a long while, mentally focusing himself for the task ahead, then exhaled profoundly.

With the courtroom thereby filled with the smell of interesting incense, he adjusted the blindfold covering his two eyes and summoned the appellant.

"Step to the bench, Mr Astronomer!"

========

The judge took another toke off his gavel. Relying on his ears only, he heard the heavy-set scientist shuffle to his allotted place in the courtroom.

"I am here, visionary."

"You have a petition to present."

"I have."

The astronomer was in his caste-mould. Overweight, with his genitals sucked into his physical mass and therefore out of sight, he would have been naked if there was such a thing on Weir. His black-skinned body was tattooed with comets, novas, nebulae, galaxies and other phenomena common to those in his trade. A planetary ring orbited around his head at eye level.

Officially he was just another scientocrat, one whose specialty just happened to be the stars. That he was one of the upper echelon in his field was the only reason he was dignified by the appellation of *'astronomer'*. Otherwise the visionary would have addressed him as scientocrat. Privately he would have his own name or names – but that was his business. Publicly, the astronomer was everybody's business.

"State your case and state it succinctly," the visionary dully yet duly recited his token rote. "Complications and contradictions, I shall perceive. Once you are finished, I shall gaze into the future. As myriad and as many, as many possible *'Ys'*, as I can foresee. I shall then render my decision, which is in no way binding and entirely subject to events yet to happen. Proceed."

The astronomer sized up the visionary, not that there was much to size up. This one looked much like any of his breed: blindfold, Y-tattoos (Y = Wise), steam pouring out of the top of his head like a sputtering volcano. If he had been a woman, the astronomer wouldn't have approached things any differently.

(Female Utopians were white-skinned. As a consequence their tattoos were black or shades thereof. Given that sex, as opposed to sexual category, was a private affair; given also that, next door to forever, the only embryos allowed to develop were those spawned by artificial, masturbatory techniques; gender bias had virtually never featured in the Utopia of New Weir.

"I believe I have discovered a link between our universe and another one."

"These galactic gateways are called wormholes." Visionaries had a tendency to make statements rather than ask questions. They also had a tendency to interrupt, for reasons of clarity.

"A wormhole between our universe and another one," the astronomer corrected himself obligingly. He spoke confidently, sure that the visionary would share in his personal vision.

"There are wormholes and there are wormholes. Just as there are universes and there are universes: macroverse and microverses. Ours may be a microverse to another macroverse and vice versa. It is as if the entire cosmos is a series of eggshells, one within the other. You've cracked one shell and found a way to another. This I understand. But you must be more specific, astronomer. I require exhaustive information."

The astronomer let out a foul-smelling fart. This was a typical reaction to a visionary and traditionally considered appropriate. Its odour mingled with that of the visionary's smoke. Those in the invitation-only audience, most of whom were scientocrats or members of the media, inhaled deeply. This would be a good session.

Suddenly there was an audible gasp. Someone pointed to the platform above the visionary. Three indistinct yet obviously female forms appeared in the chairs. The Trigregos Sisters had deigned to manifest themselves. This session wasn't just going to be good; it was about to become unforgettable.

In an ironic sense, the astronomer couldn't have been happier. He respected the ways of Weir but, like many Utopians, wasn't a big fan of the triplet goddesses. *'There shall be no law'*, the Entity had declared. Then why should there be deities to lord or lady over those at least nominally beneath them?

"To be more precise, I have discovered a wormhole to a specific planetary system. It is in the same microverse where, I have also discovered, the remnants of the devic race settled some seven thousand of its years ago." The excitement already filtering through the spectators became voluble. The visionary slammed his mallet on its pad so hard that the soma dislodged. He had to bring the gavel down on the still-burning wad two or three times just to extinguish it.

Silence returned to the courtroom even quicker. As a result the visionary felt no need to lecture the audience on proper decorum. He well-understood what his fellow Utopians were feeling. Already in his mind hundreds of possible Ys were roiling around. This would be the most difficult vision of his career.

"You have my attention, astronomer. Pray continue."

"How do I know this? Very simple. According to ancient documents, devils – Shining Ones, Great Gods, like the three now sitting above you, and their third generational Master Deva offspring – give off a distinctive, easily detectable energy signal: a signature, if you will. According to my readings, the third planet of this system is the only one inhabited."

"Devas like to be worshipped."

"Just so. It has a number of continental land masses separated by two major oceans and a number of lesser ones. The northern part of one of these oceans positively glows with devic radiance. I believe it curtains a hidden continent, a land mass that is largely unknown to those on the rest of the planet."

"I shall do the speculating, astronomer."

"As you please. Very well then. Based on my best evidence I would say that it has been somehow separated from the greater world by said devic energy for upwards of between five to seven thousand cycles of its solitary sun. Were it less then I would further postulate, as opposed to venture, that the energy would be more widespread."

"Astronomers do not commonly examine ancient literature. Manifestly therefore you gleaned such arcane notions as devic radiance from consultation with an Illuminary."

"I have access to an Illuminary, that is true. The detecting devices I, um, rediscovered are also exceedingly ancient. "

"This wormhole of which you speak. You say you detected it. You did not make it."

Now it begins, thought the astronomer. These visionaries were insidiously insightful. "It was either there all along or just recently appeared. However, I could not access it without additional devices, these ones of my own invention."

"So," grunted the visionary, relighting his pipe, "It seems I must now refer to you as Mr Astronomer-Inventor."

"The technology pre-existed. I simply adapted it to my needs. Should you wish to address me as Astronomer-Adaptor, I shall not object."

The visionary digested this impertinence without objection. Rudeness was welcome in his courtroom. "Technology which only an Illuminary would recall, no doubt."

"As you say."

"You must not seek to hide details, astronomer-adaptor. I cannot read your mind but I can see through you. Obfuscation has no place in this courtroom."

"I apologize for my lack of clarity."

"Utopians do not apologize. The comparative proximity to devils seems to have clouded your mental acuity – just as the Ys I can already perceive are muddying mine. You have found a cosmic interface with a sun system that radiates devic energy from a specific area of its third planet. You seek my approval to go through it, which you have not done as yet. You have a reason for that."

"It is not exactly open yet. There is a spatial membrane in place between our universe and theirs. In symbolic terms it is of a consistency similar to cellophane. I have reached into it and, while it stretches, it shows no sign of weakening or breaking. Clearly more experiments are required."

"This still somewhat sealed opening is not large."

"Presently no larger than a small man or big boy."

"It sounds a rather unique phenomena. And you discovered, as opposed to made it, Mr Astronomer-Would-Be-Explorer."

"I was tinkering in my workroom at home, looked over my shoulder, and there it was."

"You are telling me there is a trans-space tube of some sort in your house."

Although visionaries never made notes there were those who privately speculated they born with supersized biological storage systems wired into their brains. This might seem an admirable quality but Old Weir had once been ruled by a Mother Machine, a master computer. The Male Entity, who helped create the first devil and therefore, at least indirectly, the three sisters who'd fully manifested themselves only moments earlier, did not believe in masters, machine or otherwise. (When it came right down to it, he was quite old-fashioned.)

It wouldn't be a stretch to suppose the sisters shared their co-creator's feelings in that regard. Indeed, today's Utopians went to extraordinary lengths to ensure its equivalencies of First Weir's Mother Machine ruled no one, except perhaps lesser machines they oversaw and more like regulated than controlled.

"In my basement, yes."

"I see. And this anomaly suddenly just appeared."

"Some weeks ago, yes."

"And you did not notify the Planetary Council immediately because you wished to study it further."

"I needed to stabilize it first. I have done that."

"No doubt with the judicious use of cellophane, a technical term for adhesive plastic. You wish to exploit this phenomena."

The astronomer judged it time for the speech he had prepared with his mate in anticipation of just such an opening. "You don't have to be an Illuminary to be aware of the sorry history of Old Weir. How our ancestors, blessed with lives longer than even ours are today, were obsessed with becoming immortal. How that obsession led them to create what we call mandroids and into whose artificial beings they funnelled their spirits, or consciousness, just before imminent death claimed their birth bodies.

"We are taught that these manmade monstrosities, as they proved them-selves to be, very nearly came to dominate the entire planetary system. We are further taught that, in those distant times, Utopians publicly had individual names, and that the Geneticist Cabalarkon was the name of antiquity's greatest hero."

"As well as ultimately, though perhaps through no fault of his own, its greatest villain."

"Ironically rather ultimately I would say."

"And I would agree, if only in the interests of precision."

"Most generous of you." Buttering up a visionary was considered poor tac-tics, so the astronomer made sure he sounded sarcastic enough not to offend anyone. "Cabalarkon was leading the rebellion of natural-born Utopians against their artificial oppressors when the Male Entity appeared in Weir System once again.

"The geneticist or biomage, as they referred to his sort then, went to the Entity for advice and got more than he bargained for. The Entity used one of Cabalarkon's own eyes to create a new being — a living weapon, a champion of individuality, a nearly-omnipotent god-thing by the name of Sedon."

"Who named himself Sedon."

"If you prefer. And for reasons unknown I might add."

"Not a matter of might, astronomer. You just did."

"So I did. The might belonged to Sedon, who promptly slew the Entity and shortly afterward adopted Cabalarkon as his father. He thereupon went to extra-ordinary extremes to guarantee that Cabalarkon potentially as he would – and Sedon, like his offspring and theirs, proved immortal, perhaps even unkillable, though that was never proven beyond a shadow of a doubt.."

"I will not quibble with the word promptly. Nor will I quibble with your assertion that it was the Moloch Sedon, as his descendants acclaimed him, who vanquished the mandroids and their Mother Machine and not the Recurring En-tity. We can't be absolutely certain of that either which way and my interest is not with the past."

"I haven't said any of that yet."

"Which is why you are an astronomer and I am a visionary. You were also going to say something trite to the effect that the devil Sedon proved worse than the devils Cabalarkon and his freedom fighting confreres knew as mandroids. I shall spare you the embarrassment of unnecessary wordiness. Continue."

"I'm not sure I should, given you're so very good at anticipating me. How-ever, as the risk of embarrassing myself, it's not at all surprising that Sedon went on to destroy First Weir's Mother Machine; not when you consider Cabalar-kon's crusade and the attitude towards authority of who created Sedon in the first place. What is surprising – though not anymore – is that many, many centuries later the apparently ever-undying Entity returned to Weir System."

"Undying I shall quibble with, astronomer. The Entity recurs, that is adjec-tive sufficient for our purposes."

That got the visionary not just an obligatory burp and simultaneous fart from the penitent but an eruption of gas as noisy as it was noisome from most of the invitees. Even though as a consequence two members of the audience had to be hauled gasping out of the courtroom by their neighbours, this delighted the blindfolded Utopian.

What the Three Great Goddesses, who were more gaseous, as in insubstantial, than solid, as in corporeal, thought went unrecorded; albeit mostly because they'd yet to say anything. It was a safe bet they weren't very happy with the male centric tone of the visionary Plus, they almost certainly knew what the astronomer was coming to next however — them!

He didn't disappoint.

"By then Sedon had created the six Great Gods, the Thrygragos Brothers and the Trigregos Sisters, and they had procreated thousands of spirit beings known as Master Devas or, to us, if not to them, lesser devils. Cabalarkon was still alive, a vampiric being, in some respects – howsoever ironically – a living mandroid, kept going by absorbing the essences of Utopians suffering from Imminent Death, the very disease he'd hoped to eliminate, for future generations of True Utopians, with the creation of Sedon.

"The Entity was merciless. He deliberately destroyed Weirstar, caused it to go supernova. With it went its entire planetary system, what we refer to as Old Weir. But in many respect it was to no avail. Sedon and the Thrygragos Brothers, together with a few hundred – perhaps as many as a few thousand, but no more – Master Devas, somehow managed to escape. How, we don't know but escape they did."

"Radioactively rendered infertile," inserted the visionary.

"So we're to understand.

"Prior to this though, the Entity had already moved our ancestors to New Weir."

"Along with Cabalarkon and the esteemed Sisters sitting above you, yes. Yes also, in the interests of brevity, more time passed. The Entity, as is his wont, weakened with age. Sedon eventually found his way to New Weirworld and, as was his wont, preyed on that weakness. He contrived to slay the Entity yet again then, in the Sedonshem, a vessel of his own conjuring, departed Weirworld for parts ever unknown."

"Carrying with him Cabalarkon, the Three Brothers, and every other still-extant devil but for the Sisters. Who remained behind and became our deities."

"Quite rightly too. However, while a vastly reduced agglomeration of devils got away cleanly, they were pursued by our very own Warriors of Weir."

"A million of them, the Trinondevs, on generational ships, set out in pursuit of the fleeing devils. Very few Warriors of Weir ever returned to New Weir and, tens of thousands of our years later, not even ancestral Illuminaries know what became of the Devil Sedon, Thrygragos, the rest of their devils or, for that matter, the rest of our Trinondevs and their asteroid-sized starships."

"Allow me to add: Until now."

"Allowed ... provisionally."

The astronomer took that hint, too. "My petition is this: I want to go through the gap in my basement. I want to finish the job the Recurring Entity and our heroic ancestors started. I want to eradicate devils once and for all time. I want to do this for all of us, for everyone who has ever lived and for everyone who will ever live. We brought evil into the cosmos; it needs be falls to us to abolish it."

"Singlehandedly."

"Of course not. I wish permission to access ancient technology. With it, I want to outfit an expeditionary force with the best weaponry we can muster. Suchlike, I assure you, pre-exists. It only awaits rediscovery. Illuminaries and the descendants of Trinondevs, ones either once returned or left behind, will join with me. This we can accomplish."

"You are aware the Entity proscribed weaponry; declared it redundant, its manufacture both pointless and wasteful."

"I beg you – hear me out!"

"There are no beggars in Weir."

"Implore you then."

"Like violence, that too is counter-productive. Weapons have no place in any Utopia. It is otherwise, we find we have need for them, then ours is no longer a utopia. Yet it is, a true Utopia; has been for multiple thousands of years and so it shall remain. We can, do, and must live in peace and conviviality with each other. Aggression has been bred out of our gene pool. It is a vile contagion."

"Surely only aggression to each other; not to devils."

"Our deities are the mothers of what you so suspiciously referred to as Master Devas."

"Suspiciously? That is the term used in our annals."

"Annals written by Illuminaries. I shall not repeat this again. It is not my task, the task of this court, to focus on the past."

"Yet we cannot dismiss it. Our deities turned on their father, their incestuous, usurious brothers, and their disloyal offspring. They joined the Entity in trying to destroy them. I was going to summon an Illuminary to testify to that fact but now there is no need. Ask the Sisters yourself, if you do not believe me."

"Belief is not at issue. Neither am I, nor this court, ignoring the past and consequently doomed to repeat it. To imply otherwise is absurd. It indicates foolhardiness."

"And there are no fools in Weir either."

"Antagonism is only an offshoot of aggression, astronomer. Invoking higher authority is an intolerable transgression on the dignity of this court. I have no need to rule on your petition. It is denied on impropriety. You shall dismantle your apparatuses forthwith and present yourself to the College of Astronomers. They shall determine whether your genes are worth preserving."

The astronomer panicked, tried to mollify the visionary. "I meant no disrespect. My emotions got the better of me. I appeal to you to reconsider."

"Emotions too have no place in this proceeding. You are akin to your petition. You are both dismissed."

The astronomer tried a last strategy. "As you wish, but first I choose to exercise the right to know your rationale."

"Which would be only proper had I used my Y-vision and thereby rendered a decision. Which I have not. Your suggestions are out of line. That is the end of this business."

The astronomer stood firm. "It is your responsibility to rule on my petition; not to dismiss it on purely technical grounds. I shall have you impeached."

Murmurs from the courtroom told him he'd struck a responsive chord. He accepted that he had been a fool to challenge the visionary in such a way but the visionary had been a bigger fool in seeking to dodge his duty. Duty, what Utopians called *'dharma'*, was the glue that held their age-old society together.

"Much better." The visionary leaned back and, beneath his blindfold, closed his eyes.

Inwardly, he examined a thousand-million possible futures. Most had such infinitesimal differences that simple prophets, low grade pre-cognates, high grade logicians, and potential visionaries still in training would mistake them for the same possible future. To his mind he had done with them easily and quickly but, for those in the courtroom, he remained silent for what seemed like an eternity. For the visionary it was an eternity – a multitude of them.

And there was no doubt about any of them.

"Very well, here is my decision." Was he smirking? "Your petition is denied. You shall dismantle your apparatuses forthwith and present yourself to the College of Astronomers, who will determine whether your genes are worth preserving. Before complying, however, you wish to know why."

Choking back his anger, the astronomer forced himself to respond in a calm voice. "I do."

"As is only proper. In the interests of freedom, this court shall have no secrets. To restate the elementary, we of Weir live in a Utopia. Duty binds us but we exist for the furtherance of knowledge. In all our existence – New Weir and Old Weir – we have learned more than any other sentient race in the multiverse.

"Still and yet, we remain basically ignorant. It is that ignorance that provides us with our primary rationale for continuing our own existence. Were we completely omniscient, we would have no reason for carrying on. A fundamental precept – the fundamental precept – is that we do not interfere in the progress of another world until we know all there is to know about that other world.

"Not paradoxically, however, there is no such thing as knowing everything there is to know about everything. This does not mean that we are stagnant. It does mean that we concentrate on furthering our own self-interest; which is, as I stated at the outset, the furtherance of knowledge. It is not for us to influence others.

"Sedon and his three sons may be the epitome of evil but his three daughters are our deities. They do not interfere with us; we do not interfere with them. What you are proposing is an aggressive act against a planetary system that has housed Sedon and his devils, by your own estimation, for something like seven thousand years.

"It could be that the inhabitants of the specific planet you have identified have formed a symbiotic relationship with devils. I cannot countenance changing that relationship. At the same time, an opportunity has presented itself and we must protect ourselves." He paused as if considering how best to phrase the balance of his judgement.

"Granted, we could use this wormhole and refine your apparatuses such that we could observe what the devils are doing these days. Observe, not invade, I say again. However, I examined that possibility and discounted it out of hand. In devils, at least in the Moloch Sedon and his three sons, we are talking about highly intelligent beings; more: highly powerful ones.

"I have seen that the inhabitants of this third planet, the dominant race thereupon it, are also highly intelligent — albeit primitive, virtually infantile beings. They are riven by senseless tribalism, petty squabbles between organized religions, faiths and creeds. Even the colour of their skin and, to somewhat lesser degrees, their gender and sexual orientation drives them apart, not together.

"I have seen them using Atomics on a daily basis to fuel their homes and industries. I have also seen them use Atomics against each other. I looked into the possibility of sending some of us through your wormhole, in order to educate them about Atomics and other suchlike doomsday material. I have also seen what they will, more often than not, do after that. Indeed, to repeat myself somewhat, we could provide them with a great deal of useful knowledge. But they are so volatile, they may corrupt that knowledge to use against us.

"That is one reason your apparatuses must be dismantled. There are many others. For example, there is the strong possibility that this wormhole of yours is not some kind of cosmic accident. I have seen that it may not just be a way for us to go in pursuit of devils. It may be the devils' preliminary way of going in search of us!

"The Sisters do not mate with anyone anymore because they can't possess any of us. They might be able to mate with their father or brothers or even their own offspring. They might even desire it. But after all this time, who can say devils are still infertile? Certainly not you, I, or even them, the three above me. Besides, the Utopia of Weir needs no more devils.

"Comes to that, the entire cosmos needs no more devils. That does not mean we should seek to destroy the few who may be left. We are scientists, not warriors. Just as the Utopia of Weir needs no more devils, we do not need any more Trinondevs. That breed has been expunged from our genetic makeup. At least, so we thought.

"Look into yourself, astronomer. Ask yourself all the questions you need to ask yourself and others but never forget that I do not ask anyone anything. I see what will happen in terms of the minutest of probabilities. What you are proposing is Trinondev-style action, pure and simple. Aggression, intervention – call it what you will – but there is no denying its inappropriateness. At the same time, there is no doubting your genius. Just, sadly, your integrity.

"That is why I leave the matter of your genes being impounded to the College of Astronomers. It will be for them to decide what becomes of your legacy because there is little question you've more than just a trace of Trinondev in you. Somehow it slipped through your development team's fingers or, if it didn't – and that too is a possibility – then you are no more an accident than this wormhole.

"That about sums everything up. My obligations to you and everyone else are thereby met. As always I will be forwarding a complete recording of these proceedings to the Planetary Council. As always, they will form their own conclusions; as will the media here present. I need not remind them of their duty. I trust that is satisfactory for there is no more."

"So be it," agreed the astronomer. "Do the Sisters have anything to add?"

"If they do, they shall not do so in this courtroom. You have heard my vision. This court is adjourned."

He rose and strode out of the room. The astronomer looked to the three chairs above the visionary's bench. They were empty.

Had it been a trick of the light or had they actually been there?

=========

"Wake up, History. Something's just happened!"

The ouzo had put him to sleep. He came to with a start. "What is it, Mnemosyne?"

"Two LAC Squads have been sent down from the Liberty."

"So deal with them. Do as you've been programmed."

"As I've programmed myself, you mean."

"Same thing. Just follow your instructions."

"When haven't I, Kadmon?"

"Yeah, right! The genie and her three wishes. Lifetime after fucking lifetime. You're stuck in a rut, milady. And it's not purely because you love rutting either."

"That's not fair. I live to serve you."

"Precisely – unlike any other machine, you do live."

"Whatever you say, my love. Yet, despite a hundred deaths, so do you. Who's that down to except me?"

"I'd say Gypsium Godstuff but there's no point. You no more understand it than I do you. Just let's get it right this time, Memory. Okay?"

"Oh, I fully intend to, Hel!"

****

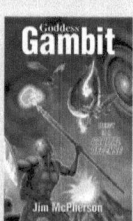

www.ingramcontent.com/pod-product-compliance
Lightning Source LLC
Chambersburg PA
CBHW030356030726
47497CB00002B/366